Advance Praise for *Bound to Love Her*

"A sexy, Legolas-type meets his match in Esri Rose's witty, fast-paced tale."—Colleen Gleason, author of the *Gardella Vampire Chronicles* series

"A delightful and sensual tale with a unique spin, *Bound to Love Her* has an endearingly practical New Age heroine who is suddenly thrown into a world where elves struggle to survive as their world is torn apart."—Marta Acosta, author of the award-winning *Casa Dracula* series

"A delightful fantasy sure to appeal to anyone who loves wit, mystery, and magic!"—Kathy Love, bestselling author of *Fangs for the Memories*

"Laugh-out-loud, girl-powered adventure!"—Stephanie Rowe, author of *Date Me, Baby, One More Time* (RITA nominee)

"WHY WOULD YOU *WANT* TO BE AN ELF?"

"Who *wouldn't* want to be an elf?" I waved my hands. "*Look* at you! You're gorgeous, you're magical, you can make paper mice and earrings!"

Galan touched my arm and smiled. "Humans have their good points, too, you know. You're warm, and funny, and generous. You may not be immortal, but you pack your lives with love and bravery and . . . silliness . . ."

"Elves aren't silly?" I asked, a little breathlessly.

He scanned my face and leaned forward. "Not usually. But sometimes we make exceptions."

Bound To Love Her

ESRI ROSE

ZEBRA BOOKS
Kensington Publishing Corp.
www.kensingtonbooks.com

This is dedicated to the ones I love.
Angel-man Joe and the 'rents, Roger and Toni.

Acknowledgments

Many thanks are due. To my agent at RLR Associates, Jennifer Unter, a/k/a "Tiger." Please buy my book so she can afford the castle she deserves. To my editor, Danielle Chiotti, who unerringly found my trouble spots. You improved the book 100%.

Squishy hugs to my endorsement blurbers—talented Kathy Love, witty Marta Acosta, and divine Noodlers Colleen Gleason and Stephanie Rowe—who said nice things about the book even before my editor got her hands on it. You all have to read it again. I'll send copies.

To all the wonderful folks at Kensington Publishing/ Zebra, like the excellent copy editor with the gray-and-white tabby that sheds on manuscripts.

Big smooches to all my noodly sisters in the Wet Noodle Posse. I'm not sure I'd be published without you. Vive la Pasta! Thanks to all my supportive friends, but especially Spacegirl Spiff Heather Doty (*first* to buy my book); Laura Hansen, who told me about Boulder's Tulip Fairy and Elf parade; Maria Mazzaferro, psychic twin to Madama Borotavia; Olde Crone Amy, Uncle Dennis and Neighbor Brad. Thanks to the Frank clan, for letting me join. Thanks to Debbie Kreuger (the inspiration for Lily) and the Crazy Horse bunch. Thanks to Tilly, the original Kitty Girl. You were a great cat.

To Georgia Jackson, secretary of the City of Boulder Parks and Recreation, for her help in exploring the process behind open-space sales. To Don Chapman, senior producer at Boulder Municipal Channel 8, for information on broadcasting city council meetings. Any departures from reality are either my mistakes or choices.

And finally, profound thanks to each and every

reader out there for partnering with writers to create worlds. We scribble the script, but you are the actors and the stage. Please visit me at http://ElvesAmongUs.com. As a reward for those who made it all the way to the end of the acknowledgments, my middle name actually *is* Firiel. Google *Firiel's song* for extra elfy goodness.

Chapter One

Things happen in the spring. New things, sexy things . . . odd things. In my case, all those things happened in one particular evening because I took my neighbor's dog for a walk.

A chill wind blew the tails of my long, black coat behind me as I walked to the house next door. Streetlights flickered to life over waving tree branches dotted with buds. I rang the bell and waited.

A small, elderly woman opened the door, accompanied by a huge, black Newfoundland. "Hello, Erin!"

"Hi, Mrs. Jamison. Would Thor like a walk?"

Mrs. Jamison looked down at her pet. "What do you say, Thor?" He grinned up at her, tail thrashing as his claws clicked restlessly on the wooden floor. "I think that's a *yes*." She handed me the leash that hung by the door. "I appreciate this so much, Erin."

"Hey, you're doing *me* a favor. I love to walk after dark, but I wouldn't do it alone." I took a deep breath. "The air is incredible tonight, isn't it?"

Mrs. Jamison peered at the waving trees, rubbing her knuckles as she did so. "We used to say this was the kind of night for ghoulies and ghosties and long-legged beasties."

"I'm not worried. When I hear a bump in the night, it's my cat jumping off the kitchen counter."

She chuckled. "Not a believer in the supernatural? I thought you worked at a New Age store."

"That's because I believe strongly in harp-oriented CDs and flower-fairy jewelry." I patted Thor. "We should be back within an hour."

Thor kept doubling back in excitement as we walked the few blocks to the trailhead. My hair blew across my eyes, and I pulled a silvery headscarf from my pocket and tied it over my head. I keep my hair short because that makes it curl, and I dye it mahogany because its natural color is mouse brown.

We left the road and stepped onto the dirt trail that enters the public wilderness. Thor gave me a pleading look, so I unclipped his leash and put it in my pocket. "Stay close, you savage. You're supposed to be protecting me," I yelled as he took off.

Pine trees swayed overhead, making sighing noises as I hiked upward along the ridge. Thor ranged in circles around me, crashing through the brush and flushing the occasional sleepy bird.

A few more minutes and we were at my favorite spot, a thirty-foot slab of red granite thrusting out of the ground at the top of the ridge, the first in a series of stones that snaked across the hill like the spine of some giant fossil. The remaining light showed a litter of broken beer bottles and empty cigarette packs scattered around the base of the first stone.

I called Thor to my side and pulled a plastic bag from the pouch on his collar. "Stay," I commanded. "I don't want you cutting your feet on that glass."

I squatted and picked up an empty condom wrapper with the very tips of my finger and thumb. "Ewww! I never used to find this kind of crap up here." My angry tone made Thor whine and look guilty.

I reached for a scrap of paper, but it whirled away as the wind strengthened, causing the trees to thrash and whisper overhead. Something plucked my headscarf off, and I jerked my head up to see the tip of a low branch toss it into the wind. The scarf flew across the rocks and disappeared in the darkness.

"Damn it!" That scarf had been last year's best thrift-shop find. I stuffed the bag of trash into my pocket and pulled out my keychain, with its small, squeeze-activated flashlight. The narrow beam of light blinked on, making the surrounding darkness that much blacker.

I held the ends of my hair out of my face with one hand and looked around for the scarf, trying not to notice the way the shadows seemed alive with half-glimpsed movement. There was a flash of something pale a short distance away, among a tumble of boulders.

The lichen-covered rocks were rough on my hands as I scrambled over them. "Too bad you're not a blood-hound, Thor." Taking his name as an excuse to be re-leased, Thor joined me, his eyes narrowed against the buffeting wind.

I stopped and moved the beam of the flashlight over the rocks, scanning for my scarf. The pale gleam was much larger now. I squinted and made out a man's crumpled shape on the ground. "Oh, my God!"

He was about four yards ahead of me, lying motionless

under the edge of a boulder. I hesitated. Maybe he was
hurt, maybe not. "I have my dog," I said loudly. "Thor,
speak!"

Thor's deep bark echoed off the rocks.

My fingers found the can of pepper spray on my keychain and slipped the safety off. "And I'm armed as
well, so you'd better not be faking."

There was no response. I picked my way through
fallen deadwood and rocks, keeping my eyes down to
avoid tripping. But when I reached the spot, there was
no man—nothing.

"Hello?" Had a bleached tree branch or some angle
in the rocks fooled my eyes? The wind rushed past my
ears, chilling them, and Thor leaned against my leg. I
shivered and bent down to pat him. "I swear I saw someone."

Then I straightened, shrieked, and dropped my flashlight. The man lay directly in front of me. How had I not
seen him?

Thor began to growl.

I scrambled backward, almost falling, only to realize that Thor wasn't growling at the man on the ground.
He stared off to my right, the massive ruff around his
neck rising as he snarled and barked. I scrabbled on the
ground for my keychain and found it under my foot, the
flashlight in pieces.

Thor's growls escalated into a series of ferocious
barks, and my mouth went sticky with fear. There were
mountain lions in these hills. I stepped toward the man
again. "Are you okay?"

His face turned slowly toward me, a pale oval in the
dark. Holding the pepper spray in my right hand, I
reached toward him. His outline seemed to waver for a

moment, as if he were about to disappear. Then I was touching him, and my senses clarified with a jolt. I shook his shoulder slightly. "Can you get up?"

He said nothing, but pushed himself up slightly before falling back again. I looked around anxiously. Thor was in a frenzy—lunging from side to side as he roared into the darkness. I gripped the man under one arm and he managed to stand. "We've got to get out of here."

The next few minutes were a nightmare of stumbling through the increasing darkness. The wind blew like a live thing, making me squint to avoid being blinded by blowing dirt. The man fell and stayed down once, as if he couldn't go on, but I tugged at his arm, willing him to move. "Come *on*," I shouted over the wind and the sound of Thor's barking. "It's not far now!"

When we reached the main path, Thor looked back with a final growl. "Good dog!" I said, and really meant it.

I pulled the man's arm more firmly around my shoulders, glad I was tall. He was probably a couple of inches over six feet. Luckily he was slender, although I felt muscles bunching around his waist where I gripped him.

The going was easier now, and the wind less violent. His long, fair hair drifted across my face, smelling like woods after a rain, and suddenly I was very aware of being so close to a stranger.

We crested the second, smaller ridge, and the lights of the city spread out before us. He straightened and took his arm from around me.

"Are you sure you're all right to stand on your own?" I asked.

He glanced behind us. "Apparently so, although I'm not sure why." His voice was beautiful—low and musical.

We followed the dirt trail to where it met the sidewalk

and the first street lamp. "Stop for a minute," I said, intending to check him for injuries. He turned toward me and my breath caught in my throat. He was quite simply the most beautiful man I had ever seen.

His face was angular and dramatic, with high cheek-bones and deep-set eyes. It was impossible to determine their color in this light, and equally impossible to check his pupils for signs of concussion.

He smiled, the wind blowing his hair across his lips. "Thanks for helping me."

"You're welcome." I reached down and scratched Thor's head, feeling shy. "What's your name?"

"Galan."

"I'm Erin. Do you need to go to the hospital?"

"No." He glanced back at the foothills again.

I thought he looked a little forlorn. I raised my voice over the wind. "Do you live near here? Do you need a ride?"

"I don't know." He shook his head. "I feel pretty shaky."

"So what happened to you?"

He put a hand to his temple. "It hurts my head to talk over this wind. Could we just walk for a little?"

"Sure. Sorry." We walked past a row of brick houses, leaves blowing down the street ahead of us. I stole glances at Galan.

His clothes were like something from the Renaissance Faire: a long-sleeved, loose shirt topped by a leather vest that was laced in front; pants that looked like suede and were tucked into cuffed boots.

A car drove by and he saw me looking at him, his long hair flashing silver in the headlights. I turned away, embarrassed to have been caught admiring the line of his long, muscular thigh in the close-fitting pants.

I walked on autopilot, and it wasn't long before we reached my house. I stopped at the end of the walk that led to my small front porch. "Wait here a sec." Holding Thor by the collar, I went to the front door. It was unlocked, so my housemate was home. I stuck my head inside and called, "Jed?"

"Yeah!" he shouted from the kitchen.

"I've got Thor," I yelled. "Can you shut Kitty Girl in my room?" I waited to hear his confirming shout before I let go of the dog and turned to Galan. He stood at the end of the walk, looking tired and pale.

"Do you want to come in for a minute?"

He nodded.

Thor galloped into the house ahead of us, his big feet sending area rugs skidding. "Thor! Calm down!"

Galan followed me into the small entryway. I took off my coat and hung it in the closet before leading the way into the wood-floored living room.

An enormous couch with faded green upholstery dominated the room and faced Jed's thirty-two-inch TV, which perched on a coffee table a little too small for it. The black-and-white Ansel Adams prints on the walls were mine.

I waved Galan to the couch. "Sit down and rest. I'll be right back." I went into the kitchen to find Jed.

He had his coat on and was pulling a six-pack of beer out of the refrigerator.

"Where are you going?" I asked.

He closed the fridge and hitched up his jeans, which rode dangerously low on his lean, muscled waist. "I've got a game tonight. Vampire role-play. Want to come?"

"No. Listen, you won't believe what just happened." I lowered my voice. "I found this guy on the ridge trail, pretty much unconscious. He might want a ride home, and I don't know anything about him."

Jed raised his eyebrows. "So if he does, you want me to go with you?"

"That would be great. I'll drop you at your game on the way back."

"Works for me. It'll be good to be off the bike. I must have done a dozen blueprint deliveries today, and those cardboard tubes are a bitch to carry."

"Thanks." I got a glass from the cupboard and filled it with spring water from the huge bottle we kept on the counter. "He hasn't told me what happened yet."

Jed put the beer back in the refrigerator. "Let's go see what the deal is."

Galan lay on the couch, his long legs crossed at the ankles. His eyes were closed when we entered the room, but they flicked open and fastened on me immediately, barely glancing at Jed. I couldn't help but feel flattered. Thor followed us in, claws clicking on the wood floor.

I pushed a battered hassock next to the couch and sat on it. "Galan, this is Jed. Jed, Galan."

Jed slid bonelessly into the overstuffed chair across from the couch. "Hey. How's it going?"

"Fine, thanks," Galan said.

I noticed that he had his arms wrapped across his chest. "Are you cold?" I asked. "Do you feel like you're in shock?"

"Shocked, perhaps. In shock, no."

"I brought you some water." I held out the glass.

He pushed himself upright and took it from me.

"So what happened to you?" I leaned forward, eager to hear his story.

Jed suddenly stood. "Is anyone else hungry? I think I need a snack."

I stared at him. "*No*, I'm not hungry. Don't you want to hear this?"

He waved a hand at me. "Yeah, yeah. I'll be back in a minute."

I watched in disbelief as he headed for the kitchen, then returned my attention to Galan. "Forget about him. I'm listening."

He handed me the empty glass. "It's a little difficult to explain. Someone attacked me."

"We should call the police." I rose to get the phone, but his hand caught mine. I froze, feeling the contact all the way to my stomach.

"I know who it was," he said quietly, "and the police won't be able to catch him."

He closed his eyes for a moment, and I noticed the color of his lashes and brows, a sort of tarnished silver. He let go of my hand, and I sat. "Who attacked you?" I asked.

"You might say it was a poacher."

"Like a hunter? This close to the city? What'd he do, bash you over the head with his gun?" Leaning forward, I took his face in my hands and angled it toward the light. "Let me check your eyes for signs of concussion."

Violet. His eyes were dark violet. I swallowed, feeling the warmth of his temples under my fingers. "Your pupils are exactly the same size. You don't feel an overwhelming need to sleep, do you?"

His lips curved at the corners. "Not at the moment."

Given that I had rescued him and was now taking care of him, I could probably tuck his hair behind his ear without it looking like a total come-on. It was a maternal thing.

My fingers pushed his hair back on one side. Like the rest of him, Galan's ear was beautiful. It was also extremely pointed at the top.

I jerked my hand back and laughed nervously. "Did you just get back from a Star Trek convention?"

He sighed. "No."

I looked again. It was definitely his natural ear. I was close enough to see that there was no latex involved anywhere. "Then all I can say is you've got one hell of a plastic surgeon."

He closed his eyes for a moment. "I'd love to lie to you, but you saved my life tonight and I need your help if I'm to keep on living. Erin, I'm not from your part of the world."

"Let me guess. You're from California."

"No, I'm from the woods where you found me. Until tonight, I owned that piece of land."

I spoke carefully. "That land is designated as public wilderness by the Parks Department. The city owns it."

"And it owned me, until a little while ago, when Fellseth broke my bond with it."

"Fellseth the poacher?"

"Fellseth the dark elf."

I scrambled to my feet. "Oh, I get it!" I said, surreptitiously patting my side to call Thor. "You're one of Jed's role-playing type people." Where *was* Jed, anyway?

"No, I'm not."

Thor came over and looked up at me. I plastered a grin on my face. "Then you're with the Society for

Creative Anachronism, and one of your buddies got carried away and conked you over the head with one of those big sticks."

Galan flushed, and his musical voice was irritated when he spoke. "I never thought I'd have to explain this to a human."

I couldn't help rolling my eyes. "Wow. You're deep into it, aren't you?"

He frowned. "Try to pay attention. I'm Galan of Longtail Rock. I've lost my land, my source of energy, and . . ."

I ran into the kitchen, leaving Galan still talking behind me. "C'mon, Jed. We're taking this guy to the hospital *right now*."

"Can I drive?"

"You bet." I grabbed my purse from the kitchen counter and handed him the keys. "Start the car. We'll be right there."

My Ford Focus was parked in the alley behind the house. Jed left through the door at the end of the kitchen, pulling it shut against the wind.

Back in the living room, Galan looked pale.

"Come on," I said, making my voice stern. "Time to go."

He didn't move. "If you would just listen for a minute."

I wasn't having any of it. "Come to the hospital and I'll listen. I think you're hurt worse than you look."

"That is certainly the case," he said grimly, and heaved himself off the couch.

Chapter Two

Boulder Community Hospital wasn't far. Once through the automatic doors, I took Galan to the main desk and watched as he filled out the paperwork. He signed his name as Galan Rock and put down a street address I had never heard of.

Trying to ignore how good he smelled, I pointed to the spaces he'd left blank. "You don't have a phone?"

"No."

"Or health insurance?"

"No."

"Ouch." I made a regretful face. "Well, I'm sorry about the money this is going to cost, but it's better than dying of an aneurysm in your sleep."

The three of us took seats in the waiting room, surrounded by the glare of white linoleum and the smell of antiseptic. There was only one other person there— a man holding his kneecap and grimacing in pain. A nurse took him away within minutes.

"Shouldn't have to wait too long," Jed said. "Boulder's not exactly the inner city." He hung his jean jacket on the back of his chair. "I'm gonna find a drinking fountain."

As soon as he left, Galan turned to me. "Please don't leave me." He took my hand, and his beautiful face was so woebegone that I let him. "I'm still not very strong. If I can't stay close to you, I'll die."

I pulled my hand free. "You're sweet. Psycho, but sweet. I feel like the lawnmower the baby ducks follow around."

A nurse approached, carrying a clipboard. "Mr. Rock? If you'll come this way, please."

Galan looked at the nurse with such naked panic that I took pity on him. "Would it be all right if I came, too?" I asked. "My friend is a little shook up."

"Of course." She led us to a large room and motioned Galan onto one of the high-tech beds, then twitched the curtain around it, leaving me outside.

I suppressed a stab of disappointment as she told him to disrobe. But I didn't want to get involved with him. Even if he was only temporarily delirious from a knock on the head, what kind of nutcase had his ears done to look like an elf?

I realized I was tired, and starving as well. "I'm going to get a candy bar. I'll be right back," I said to the room in general.

"Erin?" Galan's voice came through the curtain. "Please don't take too long."

"I won't." Sheesh. What a needy guy. Back in the lobby, I asked the receptionist for directions to the nearest vending machine.

It was quiet in the hall, save for the faint hum of the soda machine. I put my change in and pressed the button for a candy bar. When I tore open the wrapper, the smell of chocolate and caramel hit me like I hadn't eaten in weeks. Maybe it was hormonal. I finished it in three bites and bought two more, then wandered back to the waiting room, where Jed was immersed in *Outdoor* magazine.

"You want a candy bar?" I asked.

He held out his hand without looking up. "Thanks."

I dropped into the chair beside him and lowered my voice. "So what do you think about this guy? He told me he was an *elf*. He's even had his ears surgically pointed."

"Uh-huh."

I waved a hand in front of his face. "Hello? Reality speaking here. He *actually* thinks he's an elf. I'm not talking hit points and chaotic neutral."

Jed put the magazine down and looked around vaguely. "I need to go to the bathroom."

I whipped around at the sound of the nurse's cheerful voice. "Here's your friend," she said. "He checked out just fine."

Galan stood beside her, looking pale and shaky. A fine sheen of sweat shone on his forehead.

"What do you mean he's fine?" I said. "He looks worse than when I brought him in! You haven't had time to do a CAT scan or head x-rays . . ." I took a deep breath. "Have you seen his *ears*?"

She consulted her clipboard. "I looked in his ears. They were fine." She walked away.

I trotted after her, tugging on her sleeve. "What about money? Who's going to pay for this?"

"We'll bill him. Don't worry about it." She pulled her arm free and pushed open a door marked Staff Only.

"*Bill* him?" I yelled through the rapidly closing gap. "That's not even a real address!"

"Can we go now?" Galan asked from behind me.

I spun around and stared at him. He appeared marginally stronger, but that wasn't saying much. "I'd leave you here flat but you look like you're about to pass out. Do you have anyone to take care of you? Where do you really live?"

He didn't answer, just looked over my shoulder, a furrow of concentration between his brows.

I turned to see that Jed had rejoined us.

"He can stay in my room." Jed pulled on his jacket. "I'll sleep on the couch tonight."

"Am I missing something?" I waved my arms. "Do you know Galan from somewhere? Why would you be willing to let him have your bed?"

Jed shrugged. "Come on, let's go home."

As I watched him walk through the automatic doors and head into the parking lot, I was suddenly afraid to look at the man next to me. Jed, the nurse . . . People behaved very strangely around Galan.

I faced him, my skin crawling with nervousness. "You're doing something to them, aren't you?"

"I have a certain influence on humans. It's called glamour." He put his hand on my arm.

I jerked it loose and stepped away. "It's not working on me."

"I think that's because we're linked," he said, his beautiful face solemn.

I wanted to scream, but he went on.

"Fellseth was in the process of taking my land, and with it, my source of energy. With the bond to my land broken, I should have died. Instead, I somehow linked to you. Maybe it was your act of cleaning up the trash or just the timing. Whatever it was, you saved me, and now we're bonded."

I didn't believe him for a minute. He was either some kind of hypnotist or I was being set up. Whatever it was, I wanted it to stop. "Fine. I saved you. But why do you think you have to stay with me?" I took a step toward him, my eyes narrowed. "I want you to leave me alone."

His smile took obvious effort. "Nothing would make me happier, but you're all that's keeping me alive. I'm getting what little energy I have from you."

"That is the biggest load of—"

"*Luckily*, you're a very energetic person," he said, cutting me off. "But I'd eat that second candy bar if I were you."

I opened my clenched hand and stared at the dents my fingers had left in the wrapped chocolate. My hands shook slightly as I tore it open and took a bite. I really was ravenous.

Looking up, I noticed Galan's color had returned and he seemed steadier. "So how does this work? You have to stand next to me?" I looked into the parking lot and saw my car's headlights come on.

"I haven't determined the exact closeness required." His tone became urgent. "I know you don't want to believe me, and usually you wouldn't have to. I normally use glamour to move among humans undetected."

He stepped toward me, but I bit off another piece of candy and made a savage noise in my throat. His voice held a touch of desperation. "If you let me come back with you, I'm pretty sure I can prove I'm an elf."

I considered this. Then I walked back to the receptionist's desk. "Call the police. This man is crazy, and he's harassing me."

Her eyes grew wide with alarm and she picked up the

phone. Then she put it down again, and it was as if I had become invisible.

Galan stood beside me. "Please."

I marched out the hospital's automatic doors, heading for the parking lot. He followed. "I don't want to hurt you," I growled, "but if you lay a hand on me, I will remove it from your body."

"Erin, I don't have anyone else. You've got to believe me."

I glanced behind. He didn't look like a homicidal maniac. He looked like a man fighting terror, and losing.

I got in the car and closed the door. He didn't try to stop me. "Start the car, Jed."

Jed sat unmoving in the driver's seat, his gaze unfocused.

"Start the car, goddamn it!" I screamed. When he still didn't move, I got out of the car, ran to the driver's side, and opened the door. The lever to push the seat back was between Jed's shins. I grabbed it, shoved him back, and sat down right on his lap.

I thumbed the automatic locks and turned the key in the ignition. Jed didn't try to stop me. Through the window I saw Galan leaning against the car next to us. It wasn't a relaxed lean—more like the car was all that held him up.

I pushed Jed's feet out of the way with my own before carefully backing the car out of the space, bending sideways so I could see out the window.

When I cleared the line of parked cars, I pulled forward and drove toward the entrance to the street. I looked in the rearview mirror. Galan hadn't moved. Three cars passed while I waited to turn onto the road. I looked in my mirror one last time, to see Galan stagger away from the car he had been leaning against. Then he fell down.

Jed stirred under me. "What the hell are you doing?"

"Shit." I stared in the mirror. Galan wasn't moving.

"Erin, get off me!"

I put the car in Park and got out. "Stay there!" I yelled at Jed.

Galan lay sprawled on the asphalt, motionless. I bent down and took his wrist. At first there was nothing, then, without shifting my grip, I felt his pulse start up under my fingertips. "What are you? Some kind of alien?" I whispered.

His eyelids flickered and he shook his head weakly.

"You're an elf," I said.

He opened his eyes and nodded, looking at me.

"And you need to stay with me for the night." He nodded again, and I sighed. "Well, Jed hasn't been much help, but I still have Thor in the house." I changed my grip to pull him to his feet. "Let me ask you something. Assuming you're telling the truth and we really are linked, how would we go about unlinking us?"

He staggered against me. "I honestly don't know."

Chapter Three

I drove Jed to his friend's house. While he prattled on about his role-playing character as if he didn't have a man with pointy ears sitting behind him, I tried to imagine what I would do if Galan went berserk and tried to take control of the car.

After dropping Jed off, I drove home. Galan looked almost recovered on the walk up to the house. As soon as we got inside, I went straight to the kitchen and called Mrs. Jamison.

"It's Erin. I'm sorry to be out so long, but Thor ate a dead bird before I could stop him. I think I ought to keep him for the night in case he pukes." Mrs. Jamison had very expensive rugs.

"All right, dear," she said, relief evident in her voice. "I'll see you tomorrow."

I hung up the phone and turned to Galan. "Give me any trouble and Thor will take your head right off." My stomach growled, and I opened a cupboard. "If you need energy, why don't you just eat something?"

"Elves are immortal. Well, unless someone kills us.

But we can become mortal, and eating is one way to trigger that transformation. I'd rather not."

Thor trotted into the kitchen. I turned on the sink's tap and filled a mixing bowl for him. "Uh-huh, and what about water? You drank that with no problem."

"It was spring water. That doesn't seem to be an issue."

"You have an answer for everything, don't you?"

I grabbed a bag of corn chips from the counter and sat down at the wooden pedestal table. Thor lapped noisily from his bowl. "Your hypnosis thing doesn't work on dogs, does it?"

Galan pulled out the chair next to me and sat. "I can't glamour Thor, but I can communicate with him—and with other animals."

"Uh-huh. So what does he say?" I crunched a chip noisily.

Galan shrugged. "A dog is not a complicated creature. Basically, you take him on walks and he adores you. I could tell you what your cat has to say, if you want proof."

"Kitty Girl?" I stopped eating with a corn chip halfway to my mouth. My cat had been with me for six years. What kind of words would Galan put in her furry little mouth?

He pushed his chair back and stood. "Shall we?"

I followed him into the living room, trailed by Thor. Galan put his hand on the door to my room.

"Wait a minute." I looked at him suspiciously. "I can't let Thor in the bedroom with Kitty Girl. And I'm not going into the bedroom with you *without* Thor."

He sighed. "What if I go in there with Kitty Girl and you stay outside with the dog?"

"All right," I said reluctantly. "But don't take long. And don't look through any of my stuff."

"I have no interest in your *stuff*," Galan said, his hand still on the knob. "Is there anything particular you want me to ask her?"

"Surprise me." I wasn't about to give him anything to work with.

I took hold of Thor's collar and made him sit before nodding at Galan to go ahead. He opened the door enough to slip through, then shut it gently behind him.

"I can't believe I'm doing this," I muttered to Thor. He whined at me. I craned my head toward the door, listening for meowing, something, but it was silent. Thor huffed out a breath and slid onto all fours on the hardwood floor, head between his paws. I squatted beside him, my hand on his collar.

Galan came out a minute later. I let go of the dog and crossed my arms over my chest. "I didn't hear anything."

"It's mind to mind. She said she's been with you a long time."

Ooh-wee. "How long?"

"Cats don't think in years. She remembers that she was very sick, and you made her better."

This was creepy. I had gotten Kitty Girl through a newspaper ad, and she turned out to have parasitic diarrhea. A course of medication had cured it.

Galan put a hand on the side of his neck. He still looked tired. "She said you've recently changed her treats, and she liked the previous ones better. And she wondered if I would give her milk when you weren't looking, like the other man you brought home."

That sounded like Mike, my ex-boyfriend. I felt myself scowling. "Milk gives Kitty Girl the runs."

"She didn't realize that, but I'll tell her." He directed an intent look toward the closed door.

I heard a sharp, heartbroken meow and laughed in spite of myself. "Anything else?"

"She says the other man pushed her off your bed in his sleep, and she wants to know if I'll do the same thing." He grinned, half-moon dimples appearing on either side of his mouth.

"You can tell her *no*!" I said hotly. Thor rolled over and showed his belly.

Suddenly the reality of what was happening struck me. I backed away from Galan. "Elves do not exist," I whispered.

He stepped forward, lifting a hand as if to touch my arm. "Please don't be afraid. I know this is hard for you, but I promise, I don't mean you any harm."

"Except for sucking the energy out of me like a leech." I continued to back away, but he came closer. I could smell his hair again.

"You have enough energy to spare, trust me." He spread his hands in a pleading gesture. "All I'm asking is that you let me stay until I find a way to get rid of Fellseth. Then I'll get out of your life."

I ran my fingers into my hair and pulled. Which was more likely—that Galan was an elf, or that he was a regular guy who could control people and quiz cats?

"Erin . . ." He glanced at Thor, and the dog sat up and begged—a trick he had never managed before. "Please?" Thor cocked his head and whined.

I could feel my heart racing, but curiosity had edged out fear. "I can't believe I'm saying this, but I sort of believe you. You can stay for a while."

"I'm very grateful." He smiled. "Now, about sleeping

arrangements . . . I don't think Jed's bedroom is close enough that I can get energy from you."

I narrowed my eyes at him. "I'll move the couch so it's on the other side of my bedroom wall. That's as close as you're getting."

Once I'd turned the couch into a makeshift bed and Galan had settled in with Kitty Girl, I took Thor into my room and shut the door.

My jewelry-making workbench stood against the wall opposite my bed, its surface cluttered with tools, lengths of silver wire, and tiny containers of semi-precious beads. I felt an automatic pang of guilt at the sight. I needed to make more jewelry to sell at the shop.

With the help of a legacy from my aunt, I was in the process of buying the New Age store I worked at—the Celadon Rose. It was a big step at age twenty-seven, but I loved both the store *and* a challenge.

At least tomorrow was Sunday. Lily, the store's current owner as well as my best friend and mentor, would be holding down the fort. I would have the day free to deal with Galan.

I got ready for bed, feeling as though I would never sleep and doubting my own sanity. How could elves exist? Of course, people hadn't believed in electricity before they discovered it, or germs. Maybe there really was a first time for everything.

After Thor jumped on the bed for the third time, I let him stay. It took several hours and the warmth of his big furry body to finally put me to sleep. My last thought was to wonder if I'd be joining Tolkien reenactment groups and calling myself Firiel so guys with braided beards would hit on me.

Hunger woke me. I raised myself on one arm and looked at the alarm clock on my bedside table. "Six o'clock, and I'm *starving*." The bed creaked as I fell back onto the mattress. I had only gotten about four hours of sleep. If I could just drift off again . . .

A sudden clenching in my gut told me it was useless to try. Thor scrambled to his feet and tried to follow me into the bathroom. "Forget it," I grumbled. "You had all night to drink out of the toilet."

I stepped naked onto my scale and stared blearily down, hugging my chest in the early morning chill. The little blue numbers flickered and settled. "That can't be right." I stepped off and toed the reset button before getting back on. How could I weigh four pounds less than yesterday?

I ran my hands through my hair and imagined the cover of *The Weekly World*. LOSE TWENTY POUNDS WITH THE AMAZING ELF DIET!

My stomach growled louder, and I wandered back to the bedroom and rummaged in a drawer until I found a pair of plaid flannel pajamas. Once I was decently covered, I opened the bedroom door. "Come on, Thor. Time to go outside."

Galan was sitting on the couch next to a stack of neatly folded bedding, looking unnaturally gorgeous. I stared at him. He couldn't be an elf. *Could he?*

"Where's Jed?" I asked belligerently.

"Asleep. He had a late night."

"Where's Kitty Girl?" I held tight to the straining dog.

"I told her to make herself scarce." Galan gave me an amused look, from my bare feet to my tousled hair. "May I say you look particularly human this morning?"

"Can I stop you?" I made a face at him. "Just let Thor into the backyard, will you? It's through the kitchen."

He slid his hand next to mine under the dog's collar. As his scent washed over me, I had to stop myself from sniffing audibly.

I followed him through the kitchen and ran fresh water into Thor's bowl. Galan opened the back door and the dog streaked out, eager to explore the new space.

I opened the refrigerator, pushed Jed's beer aside, and found my Chinese leftovers from two nights before. "I feel like I could eat all day and not be full." The fried rice slid into the bowl in a solid lump. I put it into the microwave and looked around for something to snack on while it heated.

"Any requests," I asked Galan, "since I'm eating for two?"

One corner of his mouth lifted. "Whatever you usually have is fine."

I got a bowl of cereal and sat down to eat.

Kitty Girl wandered in from the living room and rubbed against Galan's legs. He took a can of cat food out of the fridge and scooped some onto a saucer, then showed me the mound of food. "Does she really get this much?"

I looked at Kitty Girl, who blinked innocently back at me. "Half that," I said.

While Kitty Girl and I ate, Galan found a receipt on the counter and brought it back to the kitchen table.

He folded it with his long, elegant fingers.

"What are you doing?"

He made a final crease and held up a lifelike paper mouse, complete with a twist of tail. Then he put it on the floor and blew gently. The mouse raced across the floor past Kitty Girl, who abandoned her food to chase it gleefully.

Galan stopped blowing and turned his attention to me, but the mouse continued to spin and dodge, finally darting out the kitchen door and into the living room, Kitty Girl following close behind.

"Magic . . ." I breathed, feeling as if the world were tilting around me.

"Air naturally wants to move. I just gave it a focus." He pushed his hair back, looking impossibly exotic even in bright daylight.

I stared at him a moment longer before I pushed my empty cereal bowl aside and got up to retrieve my food from the microwave. I wanted to know everything, but I couldn't help feeling shy in the presence of . . . well, a supernatural being.

"What are we going to do about this link thing?" I asked, sitting down and fluffing my rice. "I can't afford to eat this way for long. It's like owning a Saint Bernard who craves take-out."

"I understand. I thought we might do some research today."

"And where would we find that kind of information?"

"My parents."

My eyebrows raised to their fullest. "You have parents?"

Galan also raised his eyebrows, mockingly. "Did you think elves fruited on the underside of mushrooms and dropped off when they were ripe?"

"I don't know, maybe. Where do your parents live?"

"It's not as though they have a street address." His brow furrowed. "I don't know what you'd call it. I can show you how to get there."

"How long will it take us?"

"I'm not sure."

"Are we talking more than a day? A month? Are they in this hemisphere?"

"They're not *that* far. If I had to guess—"

"Please do."

He made a face at me. "Probably two hours."

I smiled at him. "See? That wasn't so hard. We'll go after lunch."

After putting the dishes in the washer, I put my coat on over my pajamas and shoved my feet into clogs. Then I whistled for Thor and clipped on his leash. "Come on," I said to Galan, who sat on the couch flipping through channels on the television. "Let's take Thor home. Mrs. Jamison will be up and she's sure to get a kick out of you."

When Mrs. Jamison came to the door, she took in my disheveled appearance and put a hand to her mouth. "Oh, dear. Did he keep you awake all night?"

"Hey, I just *met* him."

She looked confused. "I'm not sure . . ."

"Oh, you mean the dog!" Behind me, I heard Galan muffle a laugh. "No, Thor was fine. No puking."

Mrs. Jamison eyed Galan's clothes and dimpled. "And who is your friend? Are you an actor?"

"This is Galan," I answered. "He's an artist in, um, paper sculpture. Visiting. From out of town."

Galan took Mrs. Jamison's hand. "It's lovely to meet you."

She looked at him approvingly. "Would you like to come in for a minute?"

"We can't," I said quickly. "We're going somewhere after lunch, and I'm not even dressed."

Mrs. Jamison looked at her watch. "It's seven-thirty in the morning."

Galan gestured at my rumpled, pajama-clad self. "Well, it's never too soon to start."

I held my temper with an effort. "We have some errands to run first, Mrs. Jamison. I'll see you later."

When her door closed, I smacked Galan on the arm. "It's never too soon to start what?"

"You hit me!" he said, in mock reproof.

I stalked toward my house. "You're lucky I don't go on a diet. I suppose there's no such thing as a less-than-attractive elf."

"Of course not. But you're not unattractive."

"No?" I looked back at him.

"Just a little rumpled. You're actually very attractive, for a human."

"Please, my blushes."

Galan trotted ahead to open my front door for me. "Anyway, it's not beauty that makes elves go for humans."

My curiosity came flooding back. "Does that happen?" I took off my coat and tossed it over the back of the couch.

"Not often, but it does. Some elves are attracted to humans' exoticness, their unexpectedness."

I gave a hoot of laughter. "You think *we're* exotic? You, with your origami mice running around? That's funny." I headed for my bedroom. "We're going to the grocery store, but before that, I'm going to take a shower. It's either that or a second breakfast."

My shower finished, I slathered lotion on myself and stepped naked out of the bathroom.

Galan lay stretched out on my bed. I didn't have time to see his expression before I whipped back into the bathroom and slammed the door. "What are you doing out there?" I yelled, grabbing my green terrycloth robe off its hook and putting it on.

"Two walls between us was a little much," he said, when I opened the door again. "I was feeling weak." He put his hands behind his head and smiled at me. "I have to say, I feel better now."

I felt a twist of lust at his obvious appreciation. "Why don't you go back to the living room while I get dressed?"

He got up obediently, only to stop by my open closet and run his fingers over my mostly black clothes. "Is this your wardrobe or the inside of a chimney?"

"It makes it very easy to get dressed in the morning. Anyway, I can add as much color as I like with accessories. Go on, get out." I pushed the door shut behind him and huffed out a breath. "Honestly."

I *had* planned to wear a pair of black trousers and a tailored white shirt to meet Galan's parents, but now I wondered if I should dress up a little.

After much consideration, I chose a long-sleeved, fitted black dress with a scooped neck and flared skirt. Then I added a chain belt of silver links and red beads. Going back to the bathroom, I gelled my hair and slicked it into soft points before painting on some garnet-colored lip gloss. "There," I said, studying the results in the mirror. "Now I am *totally* overdressed."

But when I stepped into the living room, I had the satisfaction of seeing Galan's eyes widen. "Very beautiful," he said. "It only lacks one thing." He held out his open hand. Nestled in his palm were two earrings, shaped like a pair of tiny silver branches.

"Where did you get these?" I breathed, marveling at the delicate lines of veins in the leaves.

"I made them while you were in the shower. I hope you don't mind. Your workbench was right there, and I was bored."

"*Mind*? These are fabulous!" I ran to the hall mirror and put the earrings in, then turned my head back and forth. The tiny branches swung as if in a breeze, light glinting from them like sunshine dappling leaves.

"It took a bit of energy," he said, appearing behind me in the mirror. "Probably as much as a bowl of cornflakes."

"These are worth a week of sushi dinners," I said firmly. "Thank you so much!"

"Is the grocery store your only errand this morning?" He disappeared from the mirror.

I turned to find him lounging against the wall, looking as comfortable as a cat. I touched an earring. "I might stop by the shop and show these to Lily, just to make her crazy. I wonder what they would sell for?"

"I made those for you. Not to sell." His violet eyes seem to grow darker.

"I wasn't going to sell *these*. I just meant . . ."

"What?"

I waved my hands. "I don't know. What if you can't

get your land back? You might have to live like a regular person, with a regular job."

Galan pushed his hair back, and I felt a fresh shock at the sight of his pointed ears. "I can't live like this," he said. "Completely dependent on a stranger, separated from my home . . . Do you have any idea what it's like?"

At that moment, I believed everything he had told me, because I knew how I'd feel in that situation, and it was all there in his eyes. "I'm sorry. I guess I was only thinking of my own problems. Of course your situation is much worse."

He turned away, his hair hiding his face.

"Galan," I said. There was no response, so I put a hand on his arm. "I bet your parents will know what to do. And if not, I'll help you find a way to fix things. I promise." He finally looked at me, and I was touched by the hope in his eyes. Touched, and a little afraid.

I took Galan to my local health-food grocery store, where he appeared fascinated by the offerings. "This is beautiful," he said, admiring a pyramid of organic apples.

But when I tossed a box of instant Thai noodles into my cart, he snatched it back out. "This has very little food value."

"You sound like my mother."

"Let's go back to the place where they had all those vegetables. You pick out more of what you like, and I'll help you make it."

I decided to take him up on it. For all I knew, elves were magicians in the kitchen and I was in for a rare treat.

When I had picked out more produce, I found Galan

at the end of the fruit section, cradling a luminous orange persimmon in his hands. He put it in the cart so reverently, I didn't have the heart to tell him I didn't like persimmons. Maybe Jed would eat it.

Once in the car, I looked at my watch. "We can drop the food off at home before lunch." I pulled out of the parking lot and on to Broadway.

"I always forget how handy cars are," Galan said, watching traffic zip by in the opposite direction.

"So that's what makes elves hook up with humans—you've got no wheels. Speaking of which, how would you normally travel to see your parents?"

"I wouldn't. I haven't seen them since I left home."

"How long ago was that?"

"About two hundred and fifty years."

"What?" I gripped the wheel more tightly and tried to concentrate on the road. "I thought you were around my age."

"No, but we don't experience life the way you do. We spend some of our time in an energetic state, merged with our land."

"So in terms of human-type experience, you're what, a mere hundred twenty-five?"

He chuckled. "Something like that."

"Can you get energy from any land, or just wilderness?"

"Wilderness or something close to it."

I thought for a moment. "Colorado was pretty sparsely populated back then. Where do elf children set up house these days?"

"They don't. I don't know of any full-blooded elf children born in the last sixty years. There's barely enough undeveloped land for existing elves."

"Are you saying that your race is dying out?"

"In all likelihood."

I blinked rapidly to clear the tears welling in my eyes. "I don't see how you can stand to sit in this car with me. You must really hate us." Galan laughed softly, and I glanced at him in astonishment.

"Humans. So afraid of change." He leaned back, linking his hands behind the seat's headrest. "When a beaver builds a dam, whole valleys are flooded. A lot of life is lost. Oh, you'd call it insignificant life—bugs and plants—but life, just the same. They die, and other animals move in and increase."

"That's very philosophical of you." My voice was shaky as I pulled into my driveway and parked.

He rolled his head sideways so he could look at me. "Well, if it makes you feel any better, anytime there's a mudslide in Honduras or Mount Saint Helens blows its top, we reclaim some land. Your people die, and some of my people are saved."

I swiped a hand under my eyes and was rewarded with a smear of mascara on my fingers. I flipped the visor mirror down and grabbed a napkin from the glove box. "You said there hasn't been a *full-blooded* elf child born recently. What does that mean?"

"I told you elves sometimes get together with humans. Some of them believe that half-blood is better than none."

I stuffed the tissue in my purse and opened my car door. "So there are people who are *half elf* running around Boulder?"

"And quarter elf, and thirty-second elf." He got out, looking bemused. "Why does it matter?"

I took a bag of groceries from the trunk and handed

the other to him. "Because someone I know could be part elf, with whatever that entails!" I slammed the trunk. "What does it entail?"

"Not much. Good looks, certainly, and often increased artistic talent."

I put a hand to my chest as we walked to the front door. "Well, not to be immodest, but what if *I'm* part elf?"

"You're not."

"Maybe that's why you were able to link with me."

"Sorry."

"I *could* be!" I slammed the front door shut behind us.

"Nope. You're all human." He shook his head. "Why would you *want* to be an elf?"

"Who *wouldn't* want to be an elf?" I waved my hands. "*Look* at you! You're gorgeous, you're magical, you can make paper mice and earrings!" We were in the kitchen now, and I put my bag on the kitchen counter and draped my coat over the back of a chair.

He touched my arm and smiled. "Humans have their good points, too, you know. You're warm, and funny, and generous. You may not be immortal, but you pack your lives with love and bravery and . . . silliness . . ."

I was suddenly aware of the heat from his hand on my forearm, and the fact that Jed didn't seem to be home. "Elves aren't silly?" I asked, a little breathlessly.

Galan scanned my face and leaned forward. "Not usually. But sometimes we make exceptions." He put one hand at the side of my neck and slid the other around my waist.

His hair had fascinated me since I had first seen him, and I ran my fingers up the back of his neck. The silver strands were both thicker and silkier than I had imagined.

He cradled my face, tilting my head and stroking my temples with his fingertips. His mouth opened over mine, and when I didn't immediately follow suit, he moaned—a sexy, frustrated sound—and slid his tongue between my lips. Then he was kissing me fiercely, and I couldn't think, could only feel.

Something was filling the spaces between us, not only where we didn't touch, but in the infinitesimal distance that kept his lips from merging with mine. It felt as though an electrical web was forming between my body and his.

"Stop . . ." I drew back, frightened by the sensation. "What is that?"

"What's what?" He tried to kiss me again. "The energy you're giving me is incredible."

"Something feels weird!" I pushed against him, hard, and he let go.

"Erin, what is *wrong*?" He was so beautiful, he almost seemed to glow.

I was panting with fear. "That feeling! What was that feeling?"

"Lust?" He shook his head. "I just felt you giving me energy. Why don't we do it again and see?" He took a step toward me. "A couple of hours of sex, and I could have enough energy to take care of Fellseth once and for all."

"No!" I backed away from him, into the kitchen table. "Bad things happen to people who get it on with supernatural creatures! They go home to find that a hundred years have passed and everyone they know is dead."

"What are you talking about? You're already home."

"Or they're bound to servitude, or get obsessed and waste away to nothing. It's in all the fairy tales." He had stopped moving toward me, so I sat down in one of the kitchen chairs.

Galan pushed his hair back with a sigh. "Erin, I have had sex with human women before—*specifically* to get energy."

"You have?"

He leaned back against the counter and nodded. "Uh-huh."

"And what happened to them afterward?"

His forehead creased. "Nothing happened to them. We had sex and chatted, I pretended to eat breakfast the next morning, and then I left."

"So you don't actually *know* what happened to them afterward."

"I did see one of them later on, come to think of it. She was *fine*."

I studied his face, looking for signs that he was lying. "The problem is, I only have your word on that, and I really don't know you."

He gave a bark of laughter. "I just got through telling you how humans are driving elves to extinction, and *you* don't trust *me*."

"Maybe you're looking for revenge."

"All I'm looking for is a way to get back to my land." He pushed away from the counter and walked abruptly out of the kitchen.

I didn't follow him, but got up from my chair and slowly put the groceries away. When I was done, I picked up my coat and walked into the living room.

Galan was sitting on the couch, staring into space.

"I want to help you. I do. I just feel like I have to be careful."

He looked at me. "Fine."

His expression was so cold, I wasn't particularly reassured, but I put my coat on anyway. "Let's go see if your parents have any ideas." And if they trapped me underground for a thousand years, I would know I'd been right. The thought was not comforting.

When we were in the car, I asked, "How do we get to your parents' place? It would be good if I could follow some main roads."

He pointed. "Go that way for quite a while, in front of the foothills."

I put the car in gear. "All right. That sounds like Highway Ninety-three to Golden."

The road dipped and rose like a giant roller coaster. A green haze covered the fields to the right, but snow still lay on the north side of the scattered boulders and groves of trees. Beyond, the white-topped mountains loomed like the backdrop for a movie.

At first Galan sat stiffly, his arms crossed over his chest, but eventually he relaxed and looked out the window with interest.

When I judged that he was in a better mood, I spoke. "I'm sorry if I insulted you, but if you were in my place, wouldn't you be a little careful?"

He sighed. "I suppose. It was just frustrating."

I smiled. "Now you sound like any other guy."

"What I *meant* was that it's frustrating to know that you might have what I need to defeat Fellseth, only you won't give it to me."

"That's because I don't know what it'll do to me," I snapped. "Let's talk about something else. What are your folks like? Are they nice? Are they fun?"

He sat back. "Fun. That's not a word I usually associate with my parents."

"Well, you've been out of the nest for two hundred and fifty years. Maybe they've loosened up."

"My parents are good people, don't get me wrong." Galan tapped his fingers against the door. "But elves are in a serious situation, and we're usually, well . . ."

"Serious?"

"Exactly."

I looked at his profile. "How did they meet?"

"They had adjoining lands. In some ways, they were ahead of their time. Now that dark elves are around, most of us marry a neighbor, to strengthen the hold on both territories."

I took a deep breath and let it out. "I suppose you'd better tell me about dark elves."

Galan laced his fingers together. "When land is developed by humans, it releases a lot of stored energy. Trees are cut down, small animals die, waterways are sometimes diverted or closed off. Dark elves feed off that sudden release of destructive energy. To most elves, that would be unthinkable."

"So instead of getting a little energy all the time from their own land, a dark elf is like a snake that feeds big once in a while?"

"Very much like that. And it changes them."

I frowned. "So he wants destructive energy. Why not hang around construction sites? Why attack another elf personally?"

"For a couple of reasons. First, an elf that dies also gives up energy, and second, an elf that's alive is an elf doing everything he can to protect his land from developers."

I considered this. "It doesn't sound like he's gained anything from attacking you. He didn't manage to kill you, and your land is public open space—it can't be developed. Maybe Fellseth is trying to steal your land so he can bond with it and give up being a dark elf."

He shook his head. "Dark elves don't change."

I glanced sideways at him. "Are they more powerful? I mean, how could he . . . um . . ."

His smile was tight. "How could Fellseth kick me out? The pitiful truth is that I was depressed and neglecting my caretaking duties. It weakened my bond."

"What depressed you? Or is that too personal? I mean, the whole elf situation is pretty depressing, so maybe that was enough."

He looked out the window again. "I lost my mate."

I felt the tug of grief in my gut. If this was all fiction on Galan's part, he was better than Spielberg at tugging heartstrings. "I'm so sorry."

"It was some time ago, but I never quite got over it. Her land wasn't adjacent to mine. That was a mistake, I suppose."

So he married for love, and then his wife died. "How did she die?"

"Fellseth killed her." He nodded at my horrified expression. "It's been done before. Kill one of a couple separated by distance, then move in on the other one. Although he certainly took his time. Still, I should have been more careful. Somehow, I couldn't seem to care about anything after Timea died."

I shook my head angrily. "Galan, this whole thing is abominable! Don't you have any recourse? Isn't there some kind of court or law?"

He gave a bitter laugh. "The law of nature—the same

law that lets crows take magpie fledglings and cowbirds lay their eggs in warblers' nests." He gave me a sidelong glance. "You know, I will accept sex out of pity."

I shook my head in disbelief. "Let's see what your parents have to say."

"You mean if they told you go to bed with me, you would?" He put his hand on my thigh.

I lifted it off. "About unlinking us, and other ways you can get energy. You don't know for sure that sex would give you enough energy to defeat Fellseth, Galan."

"I'm willing to find out."

I looked at his mischievous face and smiled in spite of myself. I couldn't help liking him. Of course, he might just be an elf on the make and all this other stuff was a lie. After all, I hadn't ever *seen* Fellseth. I spotted a gas station and slowed down.

"Why are we stopping?"

"I thought I'd pick up some snacks for the road. You don't want me passing out from hunger behind the wheel."

An electronic ding welcomed us into the store. The young Hispanic woman behind the counter smiled flirtatiously at Galan with her luscious lips.

I found the snack-food aisle and picked out a variety of energy bars and a bag of pretzels while Galan examined a display of touristy key chains.

"Hey, they have El Dorado spring water," I said. "Do you want a bottle?"

He put down a miniature teddy bear dressed in a baseball jersey. "I don't need it, but it is kind of refreshing."

I joined him, my arms overflowing with food and

water. "Just out of curiosity," I said, lowering my voice, "do you ever go to the bathroom?"

"You're just full of prurient interests, aren't you?" He took the water bottles to lighten my load. "Maybe I pass my wastes back to you, have you ever thought of that?"

"Ew!"

"I'm kidding. Are there any of my other bodily functions you want to ask about while you're at it?"

"No thanks." We carried my purchases to the counter, and I took out my wallet while the clerk rang everything up. "It's just that I have a unique opportunity to find out about your people."

He picked up a bottle of water and unscrewed the cap. "I wouldn't bother if I were you. As soon as I get what I want, I'll make sure you don't remember me."

The clerk froze with an energy bar in her hand, her eyes wide. "Do you want me to call the police?" she whispered to me.

But I had already rounded on Galan. "You son of a bitch!" I yelled, giving him a shove. Water sloshed out of the bottle he held and darkened the front of his vest.

"Or maybe you just want to handle this yourself," the clerk said.

"It's a kindness, Erin," Galan said, brushing at the wet spots on the front of his clothes.

The clerk reached for the phone. "This guy is creeping me out."

"He's not talking about killing me," I fumed, turning back to her. "He's talking about a kind of hypnosis. What's the total?"

She gave me a doubtful look. "Thirteen eighty-seven."

I paid, then snatched up the bag and glared at Galan.

"Maybe I'll write down everything I know about you and mail it to my aunt in Tacoma. Then she can send it back to me. Ha! Let's see how you get around that!"

"I'd just hang around until you got it, then make you burn it or something."

The clerk shook her head. "Lady, you should get a restraining order."

By the time we reached the car, I was almost in tears. "How am I supposed to trust you when you talk like that?" I fumbled with my purse, trying to find my keys.

"You're happy to protect yourself. Can't you see I need to do the same thing? Humans can't keep secrets, Erin."

"I can keep a secret! You don't need to threaten me with some sort of lobotomy! Who would believe me, anyway?"

I got in the car and grappled with a bag of pretzels, finally ripping it open with my teeth. "You don't trust me, do you?" I asked, sniffling.

"Do you trust me?"

"Not *now*, obviously! But I was *trying* to!" I stuffed the pretzel bag next to the parking brake and pulled out of the parking lot, gravel spitting from beneath the tires. "Let's go find your parents. The sooner I get rid of you, the better."

I drove for about an hour without speaking—eating steadily, sniffling occasionally.

Finally Galan spoke. "That way," he said, pointing to a side road labeled Golden Gate Canyon State Park.

When we reached the park-service booth, I paid the fee and drove on until Galan pointed to one of the roads that led to a trailhead.

I followed the brown park-service signs and parked

the car in an empty lot. Past the tarmac, deep snow lay on the ground. On a sunny day, these woods would be a glittering paradise, but today the sky was overcast. Spruce and pine trees cast murky shadows on the smooth, unbroken surface. "Now what?" I asked.

He turned his head and looked out the back window. "We'll need to get out and walk a little."

"Wonderful."

"Just sit there a minute." He opened his door.

Icy air flowed into the car. I buttoned my coat as Galan went around to my door and opened it.

"I'll carry you," he said. "Come on."

Against the backdrop of snow and trees, his violet eyes and silvery hair suddenly looked alien, dangerous. "Why carry me? Afraid I'll run away?" I demanded.

His sigh was visible as a cloud of vapor. "This is deep snow. You don't have the shoes for it."

"Oh."

He turned around and crouched slightly. "Get on my back."

I balanced on the inside edge of the car's door frame and hiked my dress up a little so I could straddle his hips. When I was settled, he stood and lifted me a little higher, then closed the car door behind us.

I tried to hold myself slightly away from him, but the balance was all wrong. Finally I gave up and wrapped my arms around his shoulders. The heat from his body soaked into my legs where he gripped me, and his hair smelled like spring in the cold, sharp air. I rested my cheek on his shoulder and felt my anger cool. "Will your parents be glad to see you?"

He ducked to avoid a snow-laden branch. "I imagine they'll be shocked."

"Will you be glad to see them?" He was silent for so long, I thought he wasn't going to answer.

"I'd like to see my mother," he said finally.

"Do you send her flowers on Mother's Day?" I asked, and saw his cheek rise in a smile.

"She grows her own flowers."

The forest deepened. Galan didn't seem to tire, although he did stumble slightly when my coat sleeve caught on a branch. I put my head down and tried to feel comforted by the two energy bars in my coat pocket.

After what seemed like an hour of trudging through the snow, Galan stopped by a group of rocks in a small clearing. Standing by the largest, he took a deep breath and blew across the flat surface of the stone. Five inches of snow ran off like water from a duck's back. He backed up to it so I could sit on the edge, and I scooted onto the space he had cleared.

After taking a moment to stretch, he called in a loud, clear voice. "Anatelia! Trion!"

I stared hard in the direction he was looking, expecting to see forms materializing out of thin air. Instead, two people stepped out from behind a clump of trees.

Physically, they didn't look much older than Galan, but something in their faces suggested more experience, or simply more time. Their clothing was savage—animal pelts with the feet still on, feathers plaited into strands of grass that hung from their long, fair hair. But they were beautiful—so beautiful that I could only stare, enchanted.

"Galan!" The woman hurried toward him, but stopped when she caught sight of me. "She has you trapped!" She picked up a tree branch buried in the snow and hurled it toward my perch on the rock.

"Mother, no!" Galan lunged sideways and caught the hunk of wood against his chest, grunting with effort. "We were linked by accident. She's keeping me alive!"

Anatelia came forward, raking my cowering figure with her angry gaze. "What has happened here?" she hissed. "Why are you bound to this human?" Closer, she was even more beautiful, but also more frightening, as if barely civilized. Galan's father joined them, his long, smooth face as impassive as a mask.

"Fellseth, a dark elf, separated me from my land." Galan looked at the ground. "I was careless."

Trion's voice was a low rumble. "Why are you here?"

It wasn't clear if he meant *Why are you alive?* or *Why are you bothering us?* Either way, he didn't seem like a very warm person.

As Galan explained what had happened, Anatelia stopped casting hateful glances at me and began to look thoughtful. Finally she addressed me directly. "Why are you with my son?"

"Because . . . I want to help him?" I stammered. I got a grip on myself. "Yes. That's why. Fellseth can't be allowed to keep doing this."

"Hmmm." Anatelia narrowed her eyes and regarded Galan. "Have you been intimate with this woman?"

He looked uncomfortable. "Not really. She's afraid of me, for some reason."

"That's because I don't know what happens to humans who have sex with elves," I said.

Galan's father laughed. "They think themselves fortunate."

Anatelia frowned at him. "We live with the land. We don't make bonds where no bonds should be." She gripped Galan's forearm briefly. "I'm glad you are still alive, but I don't know how to help you."

Trion shook his head at her questioning look. "Nor do I."

"One thing I can tell you," Anatelia went on. "Humans destroy elves; they do not help them. When she claims that, she is lying."

Wind swept through the clearing, and I shut my eyes against the swirling snow. When I opened them, Galan's parents were gone. "Well, that was a nice visit," I said in disbelief. "Aside from the parts where your mom tried to kill me and called me a liar."

"I told you, elves aren't like humans," he said irritably.

"*You* are. I've known engineering students who were less human than you."

He positioned himself in front of the rock so I could clamber onto his back. "Elves influence humans, but humans also influence elves. My land is very close to the city; theirs is not."

As he carried me back to the car, I pictured a young Galan running through the woods, draped in furs and with that sharp, animal look I had seen on his parents' faces. The thought made me shiver, and I wrapped my arms more tightly around him. "I guess you were raised with a certain amount of paranoia toward humans."

He nodded. "Does that mean you forgive me for threatening to make you forget?"

"Maybe. Does that mean you're not going to do it?"

"Probably."

I pinched his arm.

He sighed gustily. "All right, I won't. It may not be an issue. You may be stuck with me and wish you *could* forget."

* * *

The drive back was mostly silent, but it felt more comfortable. I munched on my snacks, thinking about loneliness and snow, while Galan rested his head against the seat, his eyes closed.

I broke the silence when we reached the edge of Boulder. "I want to stop by the store on the way home."

He rolled his head to look at me. "You want to buy *more* food?"

"Not the grocery store. The Celadon Rose, where I work. We sell New Age books. Maybe we can find information on breaking energetic bonds. Or maybe Lily will know something."

"Who is Lily?"

"The shop's owner, at least for now. I'm buying the store."

"*You're* buying a New Age store? The woman who thought elves weren't real?"

"It's not *at all* the same thing. Anyway, we sell art and gifts, too."

I crumpled the empty pretzel bag and tossed it in the back seat. "Lily is my best friend. Maybe she can help."

"Best friend or not, don't count on introducing me as your elf friend. With a little glamour, she won't even know I'm here."

"Fine with me," I said, taking the last energy bar out of my pocket.

I parked in one of the two reserved spaces at the back of the Celadon Rose and opened the back door with my key.

Lily's voice came from the front. "Friend or foe?"

"It's me," I called. I tugged on Galan, who kept pausing to look at the merchandise. "C'mon."

He picked up a small statue of Morgan le Fey. "I think I've met this woman."

Lily appeared around the end of the aisle. "Did you come to restock the jewelry? That could have waited till Tuesday, you know." She looked directly at Galan and smiled. "Hello."

Galan froze with the statue in his hand, as if he'd been caught shoplifting.

My eyes flickered from one to the other. "Hello, yourself," I said to Lily.

She gave me a puzzled smile. "Who's your friend?"

Galan put the statue down and smiled winningly. "I'm Galan, a new friend of Erin's. Oh, look at those wind chimes!" He moved past Lily, then pointed to the back of her head and mouthed, "Part elf!" at me.

"New boyfriend?" Lily mouthed simultaneously, giving me a surreptitious thumbs-up.

"All righty then," I said, dazed by the exchange. "Lily, do we have books on elves?"

"I think we have something in mythology."

We followed her past a display of fountains to the first aisle in the book section, where she pulled a book with a beautifully colored cover off the shelf. "*Elven Magic and Lore.*"

"Thanks." I handed it to Galan. "We'll just look at this for a moment."

She raised her brows at me, but went back to the front of the store.

Galan flipped through the pages. "Lies, wishful thinking, *more* lies . . ." He snapped the book shut.

"Wait a minute . . . I want to see it."

He handed the book to me.

I looked through the first chapter. "Okay, I see what you mean." For one thing, Galan wasn't five inches tall. I reshelved the book and went to the front of the store. "That wasn't exactly what we were looking for," I told Lily. "How about something on energy or energetic links?"

"You're going to have to be a little more specific, kiddo." She led the way to another section and ran her finger down the spines. "These are all about energy. There's bodywork, Wicca, Kundalini, Tantric sex . . ."

Galan had joined us. "That last one sounds interesting." He plucked the book off the shelf.

"We'll just browse for a little," I said. "Thanks."

"Okay." Lily headed back to the front of the store, muttering "Yow!" as she passed me.

Galan flipped through the pages of the Tantric-sex book, pausing at a color photograph. "How limber are you?"

I tugged at the book. "Put that back."

He reached down with his free hand and pulled on the side of my leg. "Because if you could just lift . . ."

I giggled. His hand tickled, and he was leering at me comically.

Lily came back around the corner, holding a magazine. "I found this . . ." She stopped when she saw us.

Galan relinquished the book and my leg simultaneously, causing me to totter backward. "I don't think you should make that kind of suggestion at this stage of our relationship," he said, and walked into the next aisle.

Lily hustled up to me. "That is quite possibly the

most gorgeous man I have ever seen. Are you dating him?"

"No. Galan is, um, a friend of Jed's. You know, that whole role-playing, Ren Faire gang?"

She grinned. "Well, *huzzah!*"

I put the Tantric book back on the shelf. "Did you find something?"

She handed me the magazine. "*Blue Egg* put out a whole issue on energy work." She looked at me curiously. "Why the sudden interest?"

"Galan is designing a new role-playing game," I said, inventing as I went. "He wants to come up with some different ideas for characters' abilities."

Lily winked. "I'd say he already has plenty of ideas." The door chime sounded. "Customer."

"How did you like the store?" I asked Galan on the drive home.

"It's nice."

"Did you see the fountain display? I put the rock facing on the shelves. It took me a whole weekend. And the lighting under the crystal balls? I did that. I don't think you saw my jewelry display, though. I made a big, twisted-wire tree, and decorated it with silk leaves. Not that my jewelry is anything close to what you do." I realized I was babbling and stopped.

"I did notice your jewelry display. It was very pretty." He smiled at me. "You have good reason to be proud of the place."

I felt my face grow a little warm. "I guess I'm just excited about the prospect of it being all mine, you know?"

"I do know." His expression was sad.

I looked for a way to change the subject. "Is Lily really part elf?"

He took a deep breath and sat up a little, as if sensing my attempt to lighten the mood. "Yep. She saw right through my invisibility glamour."

"I've never noticed that her ears are particularly pointed."

"It's like blue eyes. You have to have it from both sides."

I furrowed my brow. "Why do you know so much about humans?"

"We have to, because you affect us so much. Young elves are taught to read and speak the local language, but mostly we learn from decades of listening and observing." He chuckled. "I do make the occasional mistake."

"Yeah?"

"I was at this woman's home, and she asked me to grate some cheese in the food processor. I almost put it in the toaster before she caught me."

"Just how many human women *have* you had sex with?" I realized I was clutching the steering wheel.

"I don't know. It gets a little blurry over the decades. But none of them slept for a thousand years afterward, I can promise you. They might have napped a little, of course."

We were home. I pulled into the driveway and turned off the car, but didn't unbuckle my seat belt. "You know, elves are supposed to be magical, elusive creatures, not playahs." I looked over at him.

He gazed back, his violet eyes dark. "If you must know, I've been with five human women." One corner of his mouth lifted, almost sheepishly. "I had an elf mate for a while, you know."

"Okay, so five women in two hundred and fifty years is not exactly promiscuous."

Once inside the house, I tossed my keys on the table in the entryway. "Anyone home?" When no one answered, I led the way to the kitchen. "What about pregnancy? What about diseases? Tell me, do elves wear condoms?"

"This one did. That was almost thirty years ago. I have to say, she was a little ahead of her time."

"And since then?" I opened the fridge and stared inside.

"Since then, I've walked through town, gone to your library, and snuck into some movies, but I haven't been with a human."

"What if you're carrying syphilis from some turn-of-the-century fling?" I closed the fridge door. Everything in there required cooking.

Galan raised his eyebrows at me. "I'm pretty sure becoming incorporeal gets rid of germs. And I haven't made any babies. Elves have control over that." He reached into the fruit bowl. "If you're hungry, eat something fresh."

I looked at the apple he held out and laughed nervously. "I bet symbolism comes naturally to the storybook races."

He replaced the apple in the bowl, then put his hands on my upper arms. "Erin, I know this is a strange and difficult situation."

"Well, it's not easy for you, either," I said, staring at his chest.

"And you've been very understanding."

"I've tried."

"So I just want to say thank you," he said, pulling me gently into a hug.

I closed my eyes and savored his smell, feeling the soft brush of his hair across my forehead and letting my own arms mold to the strong curve of his back as he bent over me.

His hands began making slow stroking motions. I felt as though I were a cat, with a static charge building up on my skin. Suddenly my stomach gave a loud growl.

I pulled back and looked at him from under my lashes. "You can thank me by making dinner."

I watched Galan chop onions with a chef's knife. "I thought elves couldn't touch iron. Or is that fairies?"

He slid the onions into a bowl and started on the peppers. "Sometimes you call us elves and sometimes fairies. That particular myth is pretty weird, considering we merge with land that contains ore and metallic rock. Someone must have killed an elf by winging a horseshoe at his head and decided iron was the trick."

I dumped the onions and peppers into a wok where tofu was already frying in hot oil and spices. The vegetables snapped and steamed as I stirred them with a wooden spoon. "Does this smell good to you?"

"It just smells."

As I piled the stir-fry on top of rice, I heard the front door open and close. Jed came into the kitchen a moment later.

"You remember Galan," I said. "Or maybe you don't. Anyway, it looks like he's going to be staying here for a while." I waited to see Jed's reaction to hosting a Renaissance-garbed Adonis with platinum hair.

"That's cool." He reached into the fridge and retrieved a six-pack of beer.

"Do you want some dinner?" I asked. "Tofu-veggie stir-fry."

"Uh, no thanks. I'm going over to a friend's. I just stopped off to pick up some stuff." He headed in the direction of his room, then passed the kitchen entrance a minute later, carrying the beer and an overloaded loose-leaf binder. "See you guys," he called. "I'll probably be home late." The door closed behind him.

I blew on a forkful of food. "He's probably playing an elf in some game tonight. You should have given him tips."

Galan put the lid on the wok. "Where's that magazine Lily gave you?"

"Over there, on the counter." I pointed with the fork.

He sat down and flipped to the table of contents. "There's nothing in here about breaking links. *However* . . ." He stabbed the page with one triumphant finger. "*Generating Energy through Sex* is at the top of the list."

"Uh-huh. What else?"

"Well, if you overlook the obvious, apparently music also works. Drumming, chanting, dancing. Then certain types of yoga, meditation . . ."

"Meditation?" I lowered my fork.

He looked up. "You meditate?"

"I've been doing Zen meditation for about a year, but it seems like releasing energy, not raising it."

"Let's see what they say." He found the page and read for a moment. "They don't specifically mention Zen, but there's an exercise right here!"

"We'll try it after I eat." I took another bite.

Galan rolled the magazine into a tube and tapped it restlessly on the table. "Do you always eat this slowly?"

I gave him a fake smile. "We'll try it after I eat and have some time to digest."

While I ate two helpings of stir-fry, Galan read the magazine, his forehead resting on his fist. Occasionally he pushed his hair behind his ears, and I marveled at their slender points.

This was the first time I had been able to study him to my heart's content. I made good use of it, letting my gaze linger on his thick, tarnished-silver eyelashes, the smooth curve of his cheek, and the firm bow of his lips, slightly parted as he read.

I wanted him. That was not the issue.

Could I trust that he was telling the truth? When you came right down to it, it was a leap of faith every time a woman kissed a man. You hoped he wasn't a serial killer, or married, or someone who thought it was funny to pick up his dog by the tail.

Of course, I usually considered a possible future with the men I kissed. Galan had made it clear he just wanted to get gone. And then there was the fact that he was an elf. Once you believed that, where did you stop? If he told me sex with him would give me eternal life, would I believe that? What if he told me he loved me?

I got up abruptly and put my empty bowl in the dishwasher, then came back and tapped the magazine. "Where's this exercise?"

He found it for me. Apparently earth energy was supposed to come up through the base of the spine like water through a tree's roots, then flow out into the sky.

I studied the illustration. "What are you hoping for from this?"

"Normally, I seem to take just enough energy from you to keep me going. I'm hoping that this will generate a big flow, and I can siphon some off."

"We'll do it in my bedroom. I'm used to meditating there, and if Jed comes back for any reason, he won't interrupt us. Give me a minute to change into some comfy clothes."

I went into my bedroom and changed into a pair of flannel pants and a loose-fitting cotton top. "Come on in," I said, opening the door.

Galan brought the magazine with him. Then he sat on the bed and began taking his boots off.

"What are you doing?" I asked, unnerved.

"We're going to be sitting on the floor, right?" He slipped off his vest. "I want to be comfortable, too."

"Oh." I pulled my round meditation pillow from under the bed and sat on it, legs crossed, spine straight. Then I huffed out a breath, my shoulders slumping. "How does it say to start?"

Galan sat on the floor and folded the magazine to the page with the illustration. "First of all, you're supposed to be relaxed. You seem a little tense to me."

"I'm not used to doing this with an audience, especially one that's desperate for me to perform." While I took the magazine and scanned it again, Galan scooted behind me and rubbed my shoulders. I tried to feel relaxed instead of turned on, but couldn't quite manage it. "Sorry. That's not helping."

"Funny. I thought I felt something," he said mildly.

I gave the article a last look, then put the magazine on the floor and closed my eyes. As usual, I had to fidget a bit, but finally I relaxed and called up my memory of the illustration. The first chakra was like a ball of red light surrounding my tailbone. I breathed deeply, and heard Galan do the same, synchronizing his breath to mine.

The second chakra was orange, low in the belly, and the third was yellow, at the level of my solar plexus. I took a moment to focus on each one, glowing like jewels along my spine. What was next?

"The heart. It's green, like new leaves in spring," Galan said quietly.

"Thanks," I whispered, entranced by the feeling of communion with him. I pictured the heart chakra, glowing like a cool light in my chest. "And then?" I asked softly.

"Your throat. Blue, like the summer sky."

I heard him shift, then his legs moved to the outside of mine and his chest pressed against my back.

When I reached the violet chakra at the crown of my head, it felt as if the top of my skull opened to let out the tremendous flow of energy along my back. I lifted my arms like branches, palms to the sky.

Galan was warm against me. I felt the soft kiss he pressed to the back of my neck, but it all seemed to come from a great distance, as did the sound of knocking on the front door.

"Ignore it," he said quietly, and brought his arms up to cup the backs of my hands in his.

The knocking stopped, but a minute later Galan scrambled to his feet. I opened my eyes, confused and off balance.

A strange man leaned against the door frame of my bedroom. "I thought you'd be dead," he said to Galan. He bent to one side, peering past Galan so he could look at me. "And now I see why you're not."

I looked up into his strikingly handsome face. *Why*

would anyone think Galan was dead? "Fellseth," I whispered.

He smiled, his mouth sensual and a little mocking. "The one and only." His silvery hair and high cheekbones marked him as an elf, but his eyes were dark green instead of violet. The lines in his face were deeper, too, as though he were marked by some strong emotion. Cruelty? Suffering? "What a sweet little mortal you are. Although I have to say, I liked you better in the black you wore the first time we met." His own clothes were midnight blue, but instead of a vest, he wore a jacket with long tails like a swallow's wings. Two slender braids hung by his temples, allowing his pointed ears to show plainly.

"We've never met," I said.

"We met the night you brought Galan out of the woods. You just didn't see me." He strolled to my bed and sat down.

Galan moved to stay between us. "Get out of here."

"Why should I? We can both go where we please. Well, within limits, in your case." Fellseth ran his hand over a throw pillow covered in red silk, then propped it against the headboard and leaned back to swing his legs onto the bed. "I don't bear you any personal grudge, you know."

"Don't listen to anything he says, Erin," Galan said. "He's trying to trick you."

"You're so tediously dramatic." Fellseth's voice was weary. Addressing me, he said, "I'm sure you think you're doing good, but it's like finding a baby bird and trying to keep it alive. There's a lot of suffering and confusion, and the damn thing always dies anyway. Survival of the fittest—didn't one of your people coin that term?"

I felt dizzy, almost queasy. "You stole his land," I managed.

"He wasn't pulling his weight, and the land was suffering." Fellseth's tone was matter-of-fact. "Trust me, if the land had really *wanted* him, I wouldn't have been able to break his bond."

"But you're going to have it destroyed or something, and then take all the energy at once," I insisted. Galan moved closer to me. I rested one hand on the back of his calf and felt steadier.

Fellseth gave a disbelieving laugh. "Is that what he told you?" He stood up and put the red pillow back where he had found it.

"Why are you here?" I asked.

He looked at me approvingly. "I like a human who gets right to the point. I'm here because you know about elves. This regrettable pairing has put my people at risk. It's nothing personal, but Galan needs to be cut loose and you need to forget all about us."

I reached up and took Galan's hand. His fingers gripped mine as I pulled myself up to stand beside him. "His parents didn't seem concerned that I knew about elves." My voice grew stronger. "They didn't say anything about survival of the fittest."

Fellseth's pleasant demeanor vanished as if switched off. "Apparently I'm wasting my time," he said, and lunged.

Galan met the attack with one forearm raised across his face, his other hand still holding mine. There was a sound like a giant spark of static, and I screamed as my body jerked uncontrollably. When my vision cleared,

Fellseth held Galan's forearm with both hands. The air where they touched was hazy, as if with heat.

Galan spoke, his voice low and comforting. "This is your home, Erin. Look around—you've shaped this place. It belongs to you."

I clung to his hand and looked around wildly, at the dresser I had painted myself, a photo of my parents above it. My workbench, with all my tools. A group of framed cards hanging above my bed. "My home," I said, and felt a little stronger.

Galan walked toward the bedroom door, pushing Fellseth ahead of him, and I followed, still gripping his hand.

The dark elf's face contorted with effort and fury. "He's using you," he growled, looking through slitted eyes at me. "He doesn't care about you."

"Maybe I care about him." We were in the living room now, and I saw the couch that had been my first garage-sale bargain, a pair of Jed's shoes in a corner of the room, an area rug rumpled from Kitty Girl's attack. "Get out of my house!" I shouted, and ran to open the front door.

"This isn't over," Fellseth gasped as Galan pushed him toward the threshold. "He'll leave you without a backward glance!"

"Get out *now*!" I screamed, and Galan threw Fellseth away from him. The air seemed to collapse and then Galan slammed the door and we were inside the house, alone.

My strength seemed to desert me. I sank slowly to the floor and gulped out words between sobs. "Will he come back? What's to keep him from coming back?"

Galan knelt and wrapped his arms around my shoulders.

"We hurt him. He'll have to recover." He rocked me back and forth. "Shh. He's gone now."

"My home," I sobbed brokenly. "He was here, in my home . . ."

He led me to the couch. "I know, but he's gone. You were too strong for him."

"*We* were too strong." I sagged against the cushions. "What would I have done if you weren't here?"

"You wouldn't have had to deal with him at all." He ran his hands down my arms. "This is my fault."

I sat up straighter. "Don't get stupid on me. I didn't save you so you could be all noble and sacrifice yourself."

He gave a surprised laugh. "You're amazing."

"I'm mad as hell is what I am." I pushed my hair away from my face and was surprised to find it sweaty. "I can't believe that son of a bitch showed up at my door. He has to be stopped." Suddenly my stomach cramped and I bent over.

Galan was already sprinting toward the kitchen. "Chips?" he called out.

"No. Protein." I dragged myself off the couch and staggered after him. "Look in the fridge door and see if there's an egg or two with a pencil mark on the top." I sank into a kitchen chair and rested my head on the table.

In a minute, I heard the clink of china and pulled the saucer with two hard-boiled eggs toward me. Galan watched me crack and peel the first one. By the time I finished it, he had the second egg ready.

I pushed the plate away when I was done. "Do you think he'll come back?"

He sighed. "I don't know. He wasn't able to defeat me here, with you, so maybe not."

"What about outside the house? We can't stay here forever."

"I know." He took my hand and smiled. "Are you sure you don't want me to be stupid?"

"Yes." I shivered and squinted up at him. "I don't feel good."

He put his palm against mine and frowned. "You *don't* feel good. Didn't the eggs help?"

"I don't know." I groaned, feeling shaky and cold.

"Maybe you should lie down."

He helped me to my bedroom. When I reached the bed, I picked up the red pillow Fellseth had fondled and dropped it on the floor, then flopped down to drag the covers over me.

Galan brought me some water from the bathroom.

I took the glass in shaking hands and gulped the contents, spilling some. "I don't understand why you seem okay but I feel like crap."

"I take enough energy from you to stay alive. In this case, that was a lot." He lifted the covers and climbed in beside me.

"What are you doing?" I was shivering now.

He put his arms on either side of me and cradled my face, his shoulders blocking the light. "Saving you."

He lowered his mouth to mine. My teeth were chattering, but his lips were warm. I closed my eyes, too weak to protest even if I had wanted to. It seemed as though the light was flickering in the room.

"Stay with me, Erin." His lips roamed over my face, and he moved to lie on top of me, more comforting than the comforter.

"You just want to stay alive," I muttered.

"You're right, there. For some reason, life seems more worthwhile lately."

My teeth stopped chattering. Galan opened his mouth over mine and deepened the kiss. I felt the electrical sensation again, but instead of fizzing on the surface of my skin, it seemed to pass directly from Galan's body to mine, as welcome as air to a drowning man.

I was warm and pleasantly aroused when he pulled away.

"You need to sleep." He pressed one more kiss to my lips, butterfly soft, and got up.

I would have argued, but I was fading fast.

The bedroom light clicked off. Outside the dark square of the window, tree branches fidgeted in a breeze—or was something else making them move? "You're sleeping with me tonight," I managed to say. "I'm not giving Fellseth a chance to catch us apart."

"You won't get any argument from me." He climbed back into bed, wearing only his close-fitting pants. As he pulled the covers back over us, moonlight shone on the curves and planes of his arms, as perfect as one of Michelangelo's sculptures.

I inched my arm across the bed until my hand encountered his.

He held it and rubbed his thumb across the back of my knuckles.

"Did you mean it when you said you cared about me?" I thought I heard him whisper, but sleep overwhelmed me then, and I couldn't answer.

I woke in the dim light of early morning and squinted at the clock on my nightstand. It was a little after six.

Galan lay on his back, fair hair spilling over the pillow, his lips parted slightly.

Watching his still form, I was suddenly afraid he was dead. What if his fight with Fellseth had injured him and he hadn't told me?

I switched my attention to the covers resting on his chest. Were they moving? It was hard to tell with a down comforter. Propping myself on one arm, I leaned closer, trying to hear him breathe. From six inches away, I could see slight shadows under his eyes. Was that normal? I stared harder.

Galan opened his eyes and jerked violently at the sight of my face hovering above his.

"Sorry!" I said, retreating to my side of the bed. "I was trying to see if you were dead."

He rubbed both hands over his face. "Well, I'm not." He turned on his side and looked at me blearily. "Do I look that bad?"

"No. I was being stupid."

"You're not stupid." He moved his hand to touch mine where it lay on the sheet. "How are you feeling this morning?"

"Tired, but much better."

"Then I suppose I should get up and make you something to eat." He threw back the covers.

"Or . . ." I put a hand on the smooth skin of his back before he could get up. "We could kiss some more."

He lay down again and smiled at me. "We certainly could, although I'm pretty sure you *do* have to eat, at some point."

"But we should experiment a little, don't you think? Just to find out?"

He didn't say anything, just slid an arm under me and

pulled me to his broad, bare chest. This was no careful kiss to save a weakened woman, but I felt infused with life, nonetheless.

The tingle started at our joined mouths, but I was expecting it. This time I relaxed and felt the sensation knit our bodies together in a dizzying rush. "Wow," I gasped, my head falling back against his arm. "I still don't know what that is, but it feels *great*."

He nuzzled my neck, opening his mouth and gliding his tongue over the skin. "It's our bond. I recognize that, even though it feels different than the link I had with my land."

"I hope so. I'd hate to think you get a hard-on for dirt."

He chuckled, then turned my face to his and reclaimed my mouth.

I had slept in my clothes, and it wasn't long before I sat up to pull off my shirt.

Galan gave my lacy pink bra an appreciative look and ran his hand over the back strap.

"It's in the front, actually," I said.

"What a good idea." He slipped the catch with one hand.

I had barely managed to shrug it off my shoulders before he was on top of me, sucking in a breath as our bodies met, skin to skin. He looked down at me, his eyes dark. "Does this mean you're not afraid of falling asleep for a thousand years?"

"Not anymore." The truth was, fighting Fellseth together had made me trust Galan in a way nothing else had—not to mention seeing for myself that he had told the truth about having a mortal enemy. But I didn't think he'd appreciate hearing that.

He stroked my cheek with a finger. "And do you care for me?"

Why did he want to know, if he was just going to leave? I might give him my body, but I wasn't going to hand him my heart so he could tie it up with a bow and give it back. "Not that way," I lied. "But with so much at stake, it's stupid for me not to . . . What I mean is, if it would help you get rid of Fellseth, because he *is* so terrible . . ."

He cut me off with a kiss so scorching, my eyes rolled back in their sockets.

I wondered fleetingly if there was anything different about the way elves did it, but from the warm, hard feel of him pressed against my leg, I guessed not. My eyes had closed at the touch of his lips, but now I opened them, determined to remember his face as he made love to me.

It wasn't easy. I wanted to give in, not think. My eyelids fluttered as his tongue slid between my lips, now teasing, now urging. I arched my back and he moaned in response—a beautiful, animal sound.

I opened my eyes and looked into his, the color of spring pansies. "You're so beautiful," I whispered, raising a hand and stroking his cheek.

"So are you." He turned his head and kissed my fingers one by one. "And sweet, and brave, and kind . . ."

Then why is he so eager to get away? The thought of life without Galan gave me an almost physical pain. Could I be thrilled by a mortal man again, or would this extraordinary creature leave me unable to love anyone else? I tried to push these thoughts from my mind as he cupped my breast with one warm hand, stroking it delicately before lowering his mouth. My eyes welled up, and I closed them.

"Erin?"

"Yes?" I answered, my throat tight.

"Sweetheart, what's wrong?"

"Nothing," I gulped, and felt tears break free and run into my ears.

He rolled to one side and pulled me tight against him. "We don't have to do anything that's going to hurt you."

"You weren't hurting me. It felt great," I sniffled.

"And that's why you're crying? Erin, I don't want to make you unhappy."

My grief was suddenly swamped by a great wave of resentment. "What's a little human unhappiness if it gets you back to your land? That's the whole point, isn't it? Nothing's *changed*." Pressing my forehead against his chest so I wouldn't have to see him, I cried in earnest.

Galan rested his chin against the top of my head and stroked my back. "Maybe I've changed. I thought we could approach this lightheartedly. I see now that I was wrong."

He continued to pet me and make soothing sounds while I choked out my tears. His kindness only made me cry harder.

My sobs eventually turned into sniffles. I put one arm over my face before turning toward the nightstand, so he wouldn't see my red eyes and runny nose. "I'm sorry I'm such an idiot," I said, pulling tissues from the box on the nightstand with angry little jerks.

"You're not an idiot."

"What do we do now?" My voice was muffled by the wad of tissue pressed to my eyes and nose.

"Let me make you a nice breakfast, and then we can

try that energy-raising meditation again. What do you say?" he asked.

I pressed the heels of my hands to my eyes. "All right."

When he had left the room, I blew my nose hard before going into the bathroom. I splashed my face with cold water until I thought my teeth would chatter, then studied my dripping reflection in the mirror. There was a thin line between beautifully tragic and unattractively swollen. I hoped I hadn't crossed it.

Inevitably, hunger pulled me into the kitchen, where I could already smell cooking. At least my grocery bill would go down once he was gone. *I wouldn't mind paying it if I could sit across from him every morning.*

He had dressed, and was pushing something around in my nonstick pan.

"What are you making?" I asked, sitting at the table.

"Fried egg on toast, topped with whatever kind of cheese you had in the refrigerator."

"Provolone."

"That's a beautiful name."

I watched him cook. "Galan, why didn't Fellseth just hypnotize me into running away so he could deal with you himself?"

He slid the sandwich onto a plate. "Elves can't glamour other elves. That privilege must extend to you while we're linked."

I wolfed down the sandwich and followed it with a handful of peanuts for good measure. "All right. Let's see if we can raise some energy."

We went back into the bedroom, where I sat on the floor in preparation for the chakra meditation. To my surprise, Galan took a seat on the bed.

"Why don't you get behind me, like before?" I asked.

"I thought it might be better if I didn't touch you."

I blew out a breath. "I can handle it, and anyway, you probably need to for this to work."

He sat down and scooted behind me. I allowed myself to savor the feeling before getting the energy flowing. Galan's body shadowed mine as my arms lifted, and I breathed deeply, as if to pull the sense of communion into every cell in my body.

Finally he whispered, "That's enough. I don't want to wear you out."

He moved away, and I dropped my arms. The sensations faded, leaving me feeling regrettably normal. "How did it work?" I turned to look at him and couldn't stop my mouth from dropping open.

Galan's skin was almost luminous. There were no shadows under his eyes now, and his hair had a sheen I had never seen before. "Not quite at peak energy, but pretty good," he said.

I tried to look happy. "Great. I suppose you'll go looking for Fellseth now?"

"I think it's worth the risk. If I'm lucky, he's still be recovering from yesterday." He sat on the bed to put his boots on.

"So this might be good-bye?"

He had tied his bootlaces, but he remained bent over, fussing with the knot. "It might be. Although I don't know if killing Fellseth will break our bond."

Hope winged into my heart like a dove that would crap on my head. I'd be better off if I never saw Galan again, but I couldn't help grasping at the possibility. "You're saying you might not automatically rebond to your land?"

"It's possible."

"So you might still need energy from me. In that case . . ." I found my purse and dug out a handful of change. "Do you know how to use a pay phone?"

"I've watched people use them. It shouldn't be a problem."

I scribbled my home and cell-phone numbers on a piece of paper and gave them to him. "If you need me, for energy or anything else, call the first number. If I don't answer, leave a message and try the other number, okay?"

"Okay." He tucked the paper in his vest pocket with the change.

I found my key chain and unclipped the pepper spray. "And take this, too."

He took it from me. "What is it?"

"Pepper spray. Don't push that!"

He took his finger carefully off the button.

"If you spray that in Fellseth's face, it'll burn his eyes."

Galan looked at the little can with awe. "Will they catch on fire?"

"No, I mean it'll sting his eyes so he won't be able to see anything, at least for a little." I smiled at his expression. "Sorry to disappoint you."

As I followed him to the front door, I wondered if he would kiss me before leaving.

"I guess I'll borrow Thor, just in case Fellseth shows up here."

Galan started to shake his head, but stopped midshake. "I was going to say he wouldn't bother you on your own, but Fellseth doesn't play by the rules."

"Plus, correct me if I'm wrong, but all he has to do is drop a big rock on my head and you're history, right?"

Galan took the pepper spray out of his pocket and gave it back to me. "I think you should keep this." He opened the door and stepped outside, then turned, his hand on the door frame. "In case this is good-bye, I want you to know that . . . I'll never forget you."

"Thanks." I pressed the edge of my hand against my mouth, willing myself not to cry. "Try not to die."

"I'll do my best." He ducked his head toward me and I put my cheek up, awkwardly, uncertain as to his intention. He pressed a kiss on my temple, then folded me into his arms.

I pressed my face against his chest and heard the dub-dub of his heart. We weren't so different. "Good-bye." I turned and went quickly into the house, before I made a fool of myself.

I paced the living room for a while, holding the pepper can like a talisman and expecting any moment to feel my bond with Galan dissolve as Fellseth killed him. Eventually I calmed down enough to take a shower, standing under the hot water until it ran cool.

I put my terrycloth robe on and was on my way to the closet when a sparkle on the dresser's surface caught my eye—the earrings Galan had given me.

I wiped new tears away and took the earrings to my workbench, snapping the work light on before I pulled the magnifying glass over on its gooseneck.

"Amazing," I sniffed, angling the tiny branches under the light. There was no way I could duplicate Galan's skill, but work was the best way to get over grief. I pulled a tray of semiprecious stone beads toward me and picked up my pliers.

* * *

After an hour and a half, I was finally satisfied with a single spray of twisted leaves. Clusters of amethyst beads hung from it like grapes. It wasn't small enough to be an earring, but it would work as a pendant. I arched my back, working the kinks out of my spine, and realized I was still in my robe. It was unnerving not to be hungry. I pulled on jeans and a sweatshirt, and went to the kitchen for a glass of water. On the way back to my room, I paused outside Jed's closed door, thinking maybe he could help take my mind off Galan. I put my ear to the door, listening for the sound of music or snores, but heard nothing. He must have gone to work while I was in the shower.

I stood in the middle of my silent living room, feeling tears threaten and wishing they would go away. I had barely known Galan, after all. So what if he was an elf? An elf wasn't . . . There were better things . . . Unfortunately, I couldn't think of anything more wonderful than elves in general, and Galan in particular.

I had to get out of the house. I decided to take my jewelry prototype into the Celadon Rose and see what Lily thought of it. I might look through some self-help books while I was there. *Women Who Want Elves They Can't Have*, for starters.

Lily looked up from checking inventory. "Didn't I tell you not to come in till Tuesday? You're supposed to be out having fun."

"Fun. Right." I put the little grapevine on the counter. "What do you think of this?"

She picked it up and angled it, watching the clusters of beads dangle. "Nice. How long did it take?"

"This version, maybe half an hour, but I should be able to cut that down to twenty minutes. Three an hour."

She poked the beads with the end of her finger. "Cost of materials?"

"Two bucks, max."

"Doable." She took a silver chain from a display board mounted on the wall and strung the grapevine pendant on it. "I'll wear it today and see what people think."

We both waved as one of our regular customers came in. After the woman disappeared down one of the aisles, Lily said, "So tell me about this yummy guy you brought in. Any possibilities there?"

I puffed out my cheeks and expelled a breath. "If only, but no."

"Why not? He seemed to like you."

I wanted so badly to confide in my best friend, but I couldn't tell Lily the truth. "It did seem as though he liked me, but it turns out he's determined to move. To Spain."

"You could visit him."

"And he's joining a monastery."

She grimaced. "Maybe you can convince him not to."

"I don't think so. His spirituality is really important to him. I couldn't ask him to give that up."

"That's very noble of you."

I put my elbows on the counter and covered my face. "I don't *want* to be noble. I want *him*, and I want *him* to want *me*."

Lily patted my back. "Oh, honey, I'm sorry. How long have you known him?"

I rubbed my hands down my face. "Oh, about a day and a half. I know that's silly."

"Sometimes that's all it takes," she said, her face serious. "It was like that for me and Jim. *Boom*. We were in love."

"Well, I don't know about *love*." I sighed. "I just think he's really sexy, and funny, and sweet, and I want to be with him all the time . . ." I trailed off.

She shook her head. "Definitely not love, then."

My cell phone rang, and I dug it out of my purse. "Hello."

"Erin?" Galan said.

"Oh, my God, are you okay? Did you get rid of Fellseth?"

"I couldn't find him, but I'm fine. Could you come to the Boulder Public Library? I need to see you."

Chapter Four

Sun poured through the soaring, mountain-shaped dome of glass that topped the large foyer of the Boulder Public Library. Galan had said he was in Reference, on the second floor. I ran up the huge spiral stairway two steps at a time. Galan wanted to see me! No, he had said he *needed* to see me, which was even better. Wasn't it? As I reached the landing, I felt a tug inside me, followed by a strong desire to eat. We were still bonded.

"Erin!" Galan waved at me from the Internet terminals.

I made myself walk to meet him instead of running like a kid. The way my face lit up when he called my name was bad enough.

"I have some good news." He put his hands on my shoulders.

My heart began to pound. He was going to tell me that he didn't care about Fellseth or his land, only me.

Galan tipped his head toward a woman standing at the terminal beside him. "This is Kutara. She might be able to help me find Fellseth."

The woman gave her mouse a final click and turned

her attention to us. My heart went from pounding to sinking as I took stock of her.

Close-fitting pants and a tunic in shades of gray hugged her slender curves. Under her long black hair, she had a heart-shaped face and large, almond-shaped eyes. I looked closer—*violet* eyes. "Is this your sister?" I asked Galan hopefully.

"I don't have any siblings. Kutara, this is Erin."

Kutara didn't smile, nor did she offer her hand. "So this is the human," she said, in the same tone someone else might say, *I see we have to call the septic-tank company.*

I lifted my chin. "That's right. The human who saved Galan. The human who's keeping him alive. That human."

She sighed and turned back to the computer. "I suppose we have to use whatever we can, these days."

I turned to Galan, outraged.

He gave me an apologetic look. "Kutara's land isn't threatened by Fellseth at the moment, but her two closest neighbors were both attacked. She's helping them while trying to figure out if Fellseth has a pattern that might show where he'll attack next."

"That's a good idea," I said reluctantly.

She turned to me, her expression bitter. "Tell me, do you *rent* or *own*?"

"Humans have no idea we're hurting you. Maybe if elves didn't skulk around, we'd be able to work something out," I shot back.

"We tried that. It didn't work. Nothing works when it comes to you people." She turned to Galan and pointed to the monitor. "Is there a way to take this picture with me?"

I answered her, still seething. "These terminals aren't hooked up to a printer. Send me the link and I'll print it out."

She didn't look at me. "What is she talking about?"

I put a hand on her arm and pushed her firmly aside. "Excuse me." The screen showed a topographical map. It took only seconds to e-mail the link to my own account. My smugness evaporated as I realized she would now be coming to my house for the printout.

Kutara managed to crowd me without actually touching me. "There are some others I want, if you will move."

I stood firm. "Just tell me how to get there and I'll e-mail them."

"I watched you do it." She put her shoulder against mine and applied pressure.

"I can do it faster." I pushed back.

We engaged in a brief, silent struggle, which ended when I suddenly stepped back. Kutara lurched sideways and wound up at the next terminal over, where she picked up the mouse as if nothing had happened.

"I'll just wait for you downstairs, shall I?" I smiled brightly at Galan's dazed expression.

Once downstairs, I plopped onto the edge of the library's fountain and stared at the coins shining on the bottom. "Haughty bitch."

I rummaged through my purse for some change. "I hope Kutara fails spectacularly and they never find Fellseth." The penny I threw hit the water with a soft plop, and I immediately felt terrible—not that I believed in this kind of thing.

I looked at the change in my hand. There were no more pennies. Sighing, I picked out a dime. "I hope Kutara finds Fellseth, they get rid of him, and Galan gets his land back." It was all I could do not to burst into tears while saying the last part, and I threw the coin with more force than was absolutely necessary. Of course I wanted Fellseth to stop hurting elves, but why did Galan have to leave if I could give him what he needed? A few minutes later, Galan and Kutara descended the stairs.

"Do you need something to eat?" Galan asked me.

"I'll eat at home. Kutara, why don't you come over? I'll print those maps for you." I would show Galan who was the better woman.

"Fine," she said.

Galan linked his arm through mine as we walked through the automatic doors. I squeezed it, grateful for his show of support.

When we reached my car, Kutara looked at it suspiciously. "I suppose I will ride with you this time, since I don't know where you live."

"How else would you get there?" I asked.

"We normally travel incorporeally." Galan opened the back door and got in. "I can't do it right now, since I'm not linked to the land."

"Traveling is not necessary or desirable anyway," Kutara said. "An elf's place is on her property." She sat in the front seat and looked at the car door as if expecting it to close on its own. After a moment she reached over and pulled it shut. "With Fellseth on the loose, the less I'm at home, the more I am at risk."

"I appreciate what you're doing for Galan and the other elves," I said.

"Why do you care?"

Galan shifted, and I heard his foot kick the back of Kutara's seat.

She cleared her throat. "I mean, that's very kind of you."

* * *

Kitty Girl came running up as we approached the house. "I'm sorry!" I scooped up the piteously meowing cat. "I know I've been neglecting you. Did Jed let you out?"

"Does she expect the animal to answer her?" Kutara asked Galan.

I put Kitty Girl down to unlock the door. She wound around my ankles before heading toward Kutara, who stepped back with a look of distaste on her features.

"You don't like cats?" I asked.

"They are unnatural animals."

I clamped my lips shut and led the way inside.

"I have never been inside a house before," Kutara said. "It smells odd."

"That would be me," Jed said, grinning at us over the back of the couch, where he was watching TV. "How's it goin'?"

Kutara frowned, and Jed abruptly turned and focused on the TV again.

I realized she had put the whammy on him. "You didn't need to do that. He wouldn't have known you were an elf unless you told him."

Kutara walked around the front of the couch and stared at Jed, who remained remarkably oblivious considering she was blocking his view of the set. "Is this your mate?" she asked me.

"*House*mate. My parents own this house. He rents a room here."

"You are keeping him from buying property." She nodded. "Good. Don't let him leave."

I rolled my eyes at Galan. "Come on, Kutara. I'll print those maps for you. I'm sure you have places to go." *And people to irritate.*

Galan went into the kitchen. Maybe he would make me something to eat. I could feel him pulling energy from me, and there was no way I could meditate with Kutara around.

Once she and I were in my room, I sat at my desk and accessed my e-mail. "What are you going to do with topographical maps?"

"I am looking for a pattern in the way Fellseth attacks."

I turned the printer on. "Where did he come from? I mean, did anyone know him before he became a dark elf?"

Kutara sat cross-legged on the floor. "Dark elves always come from a distance. As warped as they are, they apparently draw the line at attacking their neighbors." She looked around the room. "As for anyone knowing him—when Fellseth first came to this area, he approached me as a potential mate, but I rejected him."

"Fellseth was in love with you?"

She shrugged. "I doubt he is capable of love. He was seeking an energy source, and I am bonded to a large area. If I had known what a scourge he would become, perhaps I would have accepted him."

I watched as the printer pushed out the first map. "That's very noble, but what would have kept him from killing you?"

"Nothing, although it would have been unnecessary."

"Galan thinks that living off destructive energy changes dark elves."

"Galan spent too much time philosophizing and traveling and not enough caring for his land." She took the map I handed her. "Who knows what dark elves think?"

I tried to keep my tone pleasant. "You might have to figure that out if you want to beat them."

She stood, still looking at the map in her hand. "I understand you helped fight off Fellseth. You and Galan are bonded, in some way."

"That's right."

She gazed down at me. "And you think that you understand him, because of it."

I lifted my chin. "It's hard enough for any two people to understand each other. We're trying."

"I imagine it *is* difficult for any two humans to understand each other, but it is impossible for a human to understand an elf." She cut off my protest. "You help Galan because he is beautiful. Throughout history, that has been our best weapon against you, and we have learned to use it."

I shoved back my chair and stood, my toes almost touching hers. "Is the idea of me helping Galan so repellent that you want me to *stop*?"

"Would you?"

"No! Not for you or anyone else." I tried taking a deep breath, but it didn't calm me much. "You know, it could have been you in those woods that night, and I'd have done the same thing. I still would." I snatched up the rest of the printouts and thrust them at her. "Not all humans are out to get you. Maybe you should start taking that into account."

I strode out of the room and past Jed, the thought of food pulling me like a magnet. When I reached the kitchen, Galan was putting a plate with a sandwich on the table.

"Thank you, thank you, thank you," I said, grabbing it. "I was about to chew one of my fingers off."

"Where's Kutara? Has she left?"

I glanced back at the living room and swallowed. "Probably spray painting my room with antihuman propaganda." Kitty Girl jumped up on the chair next to me. "And what's with her crack about my cat being unnatural? Does she have something against litter-box training?"

"Against domesticated animals in general," Galan said, keeping his voice low. "Be glad you don't have a cow."

"Oh, I already did."

"Shh." He glanced meaningfully behind me.

Kutara came in. "I took the liberty of acquiring some more information from your machine." She glanced at Kitty Girl and grasped the chair's back as if to tip her off. Galan quickly scooped up my cat and cuddled her.

"She'd probably like some treats," I told him. "The bag is in the cupboard by her bowl if you want to give her a couple."

Kutara watched Galan feed Kitty Girl with a look of extreme distaste on her gorgeous face. Then she spread the printed maps on the table's surface. "I have determined a possible pattern for Fellseth's targets."

"Already?" Galan took a seat and gave Kutara his attention.

"It is generally accepted that dark elves are able to operate for quite some time on the destructive energy they absorb," she said. "But they would still have to keep up a tremendous pace of attack or risk becoming too drained to defeat their next victim."

"I don't understand," I interrupted. "Fellseth has Galan's land—why not stay there and call it home?"

"If Fellseth stops moving and becomes easy to find,

he faces reprisal, either from Galan or from family or friends of other victims. Do you have something to write with?"

I got a pencil from one of the kitchen drawers and watched as Kutara began outlining irregular areas on the topographic map. "How did you learn how to read these things?" I asked her. "And work the Internet, for that matter?"

"I observed. And when necessary, I asked." She pointed to each of the outlined areas in turn. "Do you notice anything?"

Galan shook his head. "I'm sorry, but I've never seen this kind of map. It doesn't make a lot of sense to me."

I pointed to a squiggly blue line that zigzagged between most of the marked areas. "That's a river or creek, right?"

"Correct." Kutara put the pencil down and sat back. "I believe Fellseth is following water."

"Why would he do that?" I asked.

"Water is the one source of energy that does not belong to a particular area. It is full of life but moves all the time. I believe that dark elves use that energy as they travel, to keep their advantage over elves who would otherwise be able to defeat them."

I studied the map. "Not all of these areas are along a creek."

"There are springs on the other lands," Kutara said.

Galan frowned thoughtfully. "There's nothing but a seasonal ditch on my land, and it's not running yet."

"There were other factors in your case," Kutara said. "As there have been in others."

I looked at the areas she had circled. "Can you tell where he's going to hit next?"

"Not from maps alone. His trail doesn't move in a straight line, but skips about."

"I guess he's too smart to make it obvious."

"That may not be the only reason," Galan put in. "From what I've heard, he mostly attacks elves with lands that are under development or that come under development shortly after he defeats them."

"The first makes sense," I said, "but how could Fellseth know ahead of time which land is going to be developed? Unless . . ." I put a hand to my mouth as the most likely answer hit me.

Kutara nodded. "In all likelihood, Fellseth is influencing humans to develop certain areas, so he can harvest the released energy." She stood. "I have to go."

Galan remained seated, but I trailed after Kutara as she walked briskly through the living room. "What are you going to do?" I asked. "What can *I* do?"

She turned and faced me at the front door. "There is nothing you can do."

"What if I get an idea?" I took hold of her arm to keep her from leaving. "How can I contact you?"

Kutara looked at my hand on her sleeve and her lips curved for the first time. "I am at the library fairly often, trying to learn what Fellseth already knows. If you feel you must talk to me, you can find me there." She twitched her sleeve from my grasp and left.

I watched through the window as she strolled behind a tree in the neighbor's yard and failed to emerge on the other side. "Sheesh!" I said, turning away.

On the couch, Jed blinked and looked at his watch. "Man! When did it get to be so late?" He scrambled to his feet and headed for the bathroom.

I went back to the kitchen to find Galan cleaning up. "You don't have to do that."

"I know."

I wanted to throw my arms around him and tell him I was glad he was back, but that was pretty pointless since he was only going to leave again. Instead, I took a sponge and wiped down the counter. "I don't know what to make of Kutara. On the one hand, she seems to be this amazing leader, and on the other, she's a major pain in the ass."

"I don't think the two things are exclusive," he said, closing the dishwasher.

"You said she was helping some elves who were under attack. What's she doing, and why isn't she doing anything for you?" I asked, forgetting that the sooner Galan got help, the sooner he could leave.

"The elves Kutara is helping are neighbors of hers— two males that she's taken as mates. Kutara is one of the most powerful elves in the area. She's bonded to a very large property, although most of it is covered with rocks."

"Somehow, that explains so much." I clasped my hands on top of my head. "I guess that's why no one's stuck a condo complex on her spread yet. I bet Fellseth would love to have her out of the picture. Did she tell you that he once asked to be her mate?"

Galan raised his eyebrows. "As a matter of fact, she didn't."

"Gosh. I guess that was girl talk, and I didn't pick up on it through the hail of insults." I sat at the table and stared into space while Galan pulled up a chair. "Do you think it's impossible for elves and humans to ever understand each other?"

"I don't know." He smiled. "Judging from Lily's elf heritage, at least two of them have tried."

I picked up the napkin holder Lily had given me. It was shaped like a monkey. "What do we do now? Should I meditate for you, so you can go out and look for Fellseth again?"

"Kutara advised me to stay here for a while."

I put the napkin holder down with a thump. "You're kidding me."

He shrugged slightly. "She wants to team up to fight Fellseth, and she wants to me to conserve my energy until we know where to find him."

I crossed my arms on the table and rested my chin on them. "So I'm your little battery charger until she snaps her fingers?"

He made a regretful face. "I'm sorry about Kutara. She's very antihuman."

"Yeah, I got that. She basically told me that you were using me, although presumably that's okay since I'm not fit to lick your elven boots."

"She's wrong."

I lifted my head. "About which part?"

He folded his hands on the table and looked at them. "I'd like to say both, but unfortunately, I am using you. I wish it didn't have to be that way."

I sighed. "Use me or die . . . it's kind of tough choice." I pushed back my chair. "I think I'll make some jewelry for the shop."

"I could help."

"I thought you were against selling your jewelry, or something."

He got up and pushed his chair under the table. "Just the earrings I made for you. That's different."

I felt a stab of joy, but tried to keep my face from showing it. "Oh. Well, in that case, let's get started. Bring that chair with you." I led the way to my bedroom and clicked on the light over my workbench while Galan arranged the extra chair.

"I only have one pair of wire cutters right now." I handed my spare pair of needle-nosed pliers to him. "These sort of have cutters built in."

"That's all right. I don't need them." He picked up an eight-inch piece of sterling-silver wire and held it between his thumb and forefinger at the halfway point. Then he put half of the wire down. Somehow, it had cleaved between his fingertips.

I picked up the piece he had discarded and examined it beneath the magnifier. The end was rounded—not cut, not melted looking, but softly finished, as if it had been filed smooth. "How do you *do* that?"

He laughed softly, his long fingers stroking the wire into curves. "I just do."

"Can all elves work with metal?"

"Some work with metal, some with stone or wood. I understand Kutara is quite the ice sculptor."

"So you're all artists."

"Yes."

I watched him work, fascinated. Sometimes his fingers touched the metal in precise places, sometimes he simply closed his fingers over a piece and it emerged a different shape. The design, whatever it was, was less than two inches square, but still he worked, making smaller and smaller modifications. This was the most relaxed I had seen him. His hair fell forward, revealing the tip of one ear and the strong line of his neck.

As he worked, he talked, his tone a little absent-minded. "Originally, we worked the land for our own aesthetic pleasure—arranging branches and flowers, stones and leaves. But over time, we looked for more of a challenge. Maybe contact with humans made us more ambitious. Here."

He placed a small pendant in my hand. It was a songbird, a chickadee perhaps, in flight. I could almost swear the tail angled a little as I held it, as if it were making use of an imaginary air current.

"This is amazing." I held it by its loop, mesmerized.

Galan took a small piece of wire and positioned it below the pendant. When he removed his fingers, the bird had tiny feet. I laughed in delight.

"I think it needs a perch," he said, and moved my hand until the bird hung just above the rim of the magnifier. He stroked his fingers down mine. The bird's feet grasped the magnifier's plastic rim while its head cocked toward me.

"Oh!" I gasped, taking my hand away. The tiny bird remained perched.

He chuckled. "I love showing off for you."

I wrenched my gaze away from the enchanting pendant. Galan's face was close to mine, his lips curved in a tender smile.

"You're so easy to please." He dipped his head and kissed my lips softly, chastely. "So easy to be with." He kissed me again, lingering this time.

Just plain easy, I thought. Our chairs clattered together as we pushed them back, still kissing. His hair fell on either side of my face like shimmering water. If this was what drowning felt like, I was all for it.

Moments later, he pulled back, resting his forehead against mine. "We shouldn't do this."

I put my hand to his cheek. "Look, I know I was very emotional last time, but maybe I *can* be lighthearted about this."

He turned his face and pressed his lips against my palm. "It's not you I'm worried about."

It took me a second to realize what he had said. "You mean . . . You mean you have feelings for me?"

Galan took my hands in his and studied our interlaced fingers. "You rescued me when I was dying, took me in when most people would have run the other way, helped me fight off Fellseth, then offered me your body so I could be free." Finally he looked at me, his eyes dark with emotion. "Of course I have feelings for you."

I made an incoherent noise of joy and scrambled onto his lap, wrapping my arms around him.

He held me tightly, his face buried in my neck. "Unfortunately, it doesn't mean we'll be able to stay together."

"Can we worry about the details later?" The joy of knowing he cared for me made future problems seem trivial.

"Later being when we're even more attached to each other?" he asked, his breath warm on my skin.

"Yes, that later."

He hooked his hands under my legs and stood, lifting me. "I want you too much to argue. I just hope you'll forgive me."

I buried my hands in his hair as he carried me to the bed, his mouth slanted over mine. He sat me on the edge of the mattress and we undressed between kisses, laughing breathlessly when our clothes tangled and caught because of our haste.

I ran my hands over his shoulders, feeling our bond

hum beneath my fingertips, a steady current that magnified each sensation.

When we were both naked, I squirmed backward onto the bed. He followed, long legs straddling me—and then came the delirious shock as we lay, skin to skin, the full length of our bodies making contact for the first time.

"Oh," I whispered, eyelids fluttering shut. My head swam and my limbs trembled, overwhelmed.

Galan's mouth found mine, wet and sleek. "I need to be inside you." His knee nudged mine apart.

I opened my eyes. "Yes."

He entered me, and my lassitude vanished. This was how animals mated, and we fought to possess each other, crying out and clasping hold as if the other tried to escape instead of surging even closer.

Our climax threatened to steal my breath as I arched, rigid and gasping, Galan's open mouth sliding across my sweat-slicked skin.

We lay together, exhausted, my head on Galan's shoulder. I lifted a heavy hand to stroke his chest and stomach, smiling as I did so. "No elf babies, right?" I asked, although it was a little late.

"No elf babies." His face was wistful. "Just a bond that is stronger than ever."

I snuggled closer. "I fail to see how that's a problem."

He brought my hand to his lips and kissed the knuckles. "And what if you get tired of me?"

I twisted my head so I could see him. "What do you mean? We're bonded."

"Which means I get my energy from you. It doesn't guarantee compatibility."

I was flabbergasted. "How can it not, when it feels like that?"

"It just doesn't. Six months from now, you might decide you can't stand the sight of me. Then what would I do?"

I nestled closer. "I think that's highly unlikely."

"Even though we've only known each other a few days?" His voice rumbled under my ear, but the words were not reassuring.

"Once you get your land back from Fellseth, you won't feel so dependent on me," I pointed out.

"*If* I get my land back and can rebond to it, then you and I won't be bonded. You might not feel the same way about me when the sex isn't quite the same."

I raised myself on one elbow and studied his face. Our lovemaking had given him a glow of health I had never seen before, but his expression was tense. "Are you *trying* to make difficulties?"

"I'm pointing out the difficulties that exist. An elf's bond with his land isn't like a day job, Erin. I'd be spending long periods of time incorporeal, merged with the earth. Then there's the fact that I won't age. How are you going to explain that to our friends? Your family?"

"I don't know. Maybe you have an addiction to plastic surgery." But I couldn't stop the worries that crowded around me. What *would* I tell my family? And would Galan still want me when I was sixty-four? Tears pricked my eyes. "Maybe there are some problems, but there must be ways around them."

"I wish there were." He slid out from under me and

stood, as smooth and beautiful as marble, and apparently just as cold.

I sat up. "So you're saying . . . what? You don't want to even try? Then why the hell did we just do what we did?"

"I said you'd have to forgive me." He found his pants on the floor and pulled them on. "Everything about you pulls me like a magnet, Erin, but it's like wanting someone made of fire. I can't seem to stop myself from touching you, even though I know the burn is coming." He pulled his shirt over his head and picked up his boots.

"You're not going somewhere, are you? We need to talk about this!"

"We could talk forever and not solve anything. I'm going to the library." He walked out of the bedroom, carrying his boots.

I ran to the bathroom and grabbed my robe, pulling it on as I went into the living room. "You know, you are really pissing me off."

"I can't help that." He didn't look up from where he sat on the couch, pulling on his second boot. "I'm going to find Kutara at the library, to see if I can speed up the search for Fellseth."

"And what happens when you run out of energy? Kutara told you to stay here for that very reason!"

"Boulder Creek runs past the library. Maybe the energy from that will be enough. I'll last for a while, thanks to you." He strode to the door, turning back for only a moment to say, "I'm sorry."

"You're a coward!" I yelled after him.

"Maybe someday, you'll thank me for it," he said, just before the door closed.

Chapter Five

It wasn't my day to work at the Celadon Rose, so I stayed home, alternating between rage and misery. The knowledge that Galan hadn't been able to keep away from me wasn't much comfort now that he had actually managed it.

There were no easy solutions to the difficulties he had brought up; it seemed a matter of bullheaded determination rather than anything else. But what was the point of my being determined if he wasn't?

The wind picked up. I went outside to make sure the trash cans were securely strapped to their posts and looked up to see dense, gray-black clouds blanketing the sky.

I was making nachos for lunch when the microwave clock gave a long beep and reset. Thunder cracked an instant later, followed by the sound of torrential rain.

I went to the front door and huddled under the roof overhang while spray dampened my face and arms. "Here, kitty, kitty, kitty!" I waited and called a few more times, but there was no sign of Kitty Girl. She was hiding under a car or someone's porch, and would come in, bedraggled and accusing, when the rain let up.

The storm made it so dark that I turned on the kitchen light to eat my lunch. Hunched over my plate, I crunched corn chips and read a magazine to keep my mind off Galan. When I reached "Can This Marriage Be Saved?" I burst into tears and shoved it away from me. "You think *you've* got problems."

The rain continued. At least Galan shouldn't have any energy problems. The creek would be frothing at its banks by now.

After lunch, I called my parents and heard all about Aunt Jean's cruise to Alaska.

"You're awfully quiet, honey," my mother said.

"Yeah, well. There's not much going on."

I cleaned out my closet, dropping tears onto jeans that no longer fit and blouses that were great deals but didn't suit me.

I made three necklaces for the store, all in shades of black.

I checked for Kitty Girl periodically, but she stayed out, apparently waiting for the rain to stop. Maybe I would install a pet door after all, even though raccoons routinely got in through my neighbor's dog door and trashed his kitchen.

Finally I parked myself on the couch and turned on the television. Jed hadn't come home, either. I often told him I didn't mind picking him up if the weather made bike riding unpleasant, but he usually just stayed with whatever friend he was visiting.

Someone pounded on the door.

I turned my head and stared at it as the pounding

continued. Jed had a key. Galan wouldn't bang like that.
Would Fellseth?

I got the pepper spray out of my purse and walked
quietly to the solid wooden door. In addition to a cat
flap, I would add a peephole to my list of things to install. The pounding was really getting on my nerves, and
my gut felt uneasy. "Who is it?" I said loudly.

"Open this door!" a woman's voice yelled.

"Who is it?"

"Kutara!"

I flipped the deadbolt and Galan staggered inside,
drenched to the skin, his eyes almost closed.

Kutara remained on the walk, rain running down her
face. "Take him," she snapped, pulling a strand of hair
out of her mouth. Then she walked onto my front lawn
and melted into the soggy ground with a shimmer.

I turned to find Galan hunched and shaking, a puddle
of water forming beneath him on the wood floor. I put
my hands on his arms, afraid he might fall. Despite his
shivering, heat poured off him. "Are you sick?"

"I guess it's not good to take water energy when the
creek is too high," he muttered.

I imagined Boulder Creek, turbulent and brown with
dirt, runoff from streets, chemicals from lawns, maybe
even a few dead animals. "Didn't anyone ever tell you
not to stick your finger in an electrical socket?"

He squinted at me blearily. "Wh-what?"

"Come on." I grasped the soaked fabric of his sleeve
and towed him into the bedroom. "Wet clothes off."

He was barely able to move. I sat him in my desk
chair and peeled off his clothes, then threw them in the
tub. "In the bed." I put my shoulder under his arm to
support him as he walked and was reminded of the first

time we had met. I hadn't known he was an elf then. It seemed like there was always something I didn't know, when it came to Galan.

He didn't seem to be taking energy from me at the moment, but I shut my bedroom door and got into bed with him, in case it would help. We lay facing each other, his knees trembling against mine.

His wet hair, the color of tarnished silver, clung to his scalp, leaving his ear exposed. The pointed tip was pink with fever.

I pulled the comforter close around his neck. "You shouldn't have left."

"I shouldn't have come back. It'll just make it harder next time."

"I'm not going to run after you, Galan. Maybe you're right and it is impossible for a human and elf to be together, or maybe it could be done with a lot of hard work, but I can't do it if you won't even try."

"Regardless of anything else, I don't think I could be dependent on a human." He closed his eyes. "I'm afraid I'd resent you."

"You'd rather be dependent on a patch of ground? Did your land fight to keep you?"

"It doesn't work that way."

"Or maybe you'd rather be dependent on Kutara?"

"Erin—"

"Everyone depends on someone, Galan. *Everyone.* Don't think you can be the exception."

As I showered the next morning, I wondered if the steam was from the water or me. I was angry that Galan had made love to me and then taken that love away, I was angry he had left without talking about things, and I was extraordinarily angry he had endangered his health with his stupid idea that he should do without my energy.

I put on my bathrobe, then went into the bedroom and nudged the sleeping lump that was Galan. "Get up. You're going to do some work for me at the store."

He pulled an arm away from his face and looked up at me. "I am?"

"Are you staying at my house? Am I eating to keep you alive?"

"Yes."

"And we're not a couple, so you'll have to earn your keep."

"We weren't a couple when you first agreed to help me," he said.

"I'm older and wiser now, so get dressed and let's get moving. Bring whatever you need to make jewelry."

"What time will Lily be here?" Galan asked as I unlocked the door to the Celadon Rose.

"She won't. Only one of us works on Tuesdays, since it's not that busy." I flipped on the store's lights. "I think we'll set you up in the office, so people can't look over your shoulder."

Galan set a paper bag on the counter. I picked it up and looked inside. "Did you bring everything you need?" I pulled out something wrapped in waxed paper. "What's this?"

"A sandwich. I thought you might get hungry. I made it while you were drying your hair."

"Thanks," I said, past the lump in my throat. He

didn't want me to make sacrifices for him, but he still looked out for me.

The morning passed uneventfully, and my anger cooled into a sense of resignation, tinged with hope. He might be an elf, but Galan was all man when it came to avoiding messy emotional scenes. If he was counting on me to drive him away with nagging and recriminations, he was mistaken. I had said my piece. The next step was up to him.

He was certainly doing his best to be useful. Working quickly, Galan turned out an assortment of pendants with workmanship so fine, I set the price at sixty dollars and still sold three in the first hour.

When it was time for lunch, I unwrapped the sandwich Galan had made for me, which turned out to be stir-fried tofu and veggies between two pieces of bread. Relationships weren't the only thing he was sketchy on.

He came and sat beside me while I ate. "If you're selling my necklaces through the shop, how are you making any money off them?"

"You sold them to me for thirty bucks apiece."

"I did?"

"Don't worry about it. I'll make a receipt on the computer, and Lily will give me money."

An hour or so later, I was unpacking new books when Galan emerged from the little office.

"I'm out of silver," he said.

"Already? How many pairs of earrings have you made?"

"Eighteen." He pointed to the box in front of me. "Do you need help unpacking those?"

"I'm almost done." I tapped the cover of the art book I was holding, which featured a picture of a river. "I've been thinking about what Kutara said—that Fellseth is using water energy."

He nodded. "It's a reasonable theory."

"So what if all the elves coordinated to somehow use up that energy so Fellseth couldn't? Then someone could take him out." I wondered what he would think about my helpful suggestion to get his land back. Let him wonder.

Galan's expression was unreadable. "Even assuming that would work, where would we put the extra energy?"

I took another book out of the box. "I can see where you might not want to do jumping jacks, but couldn't you put it into the land? So Boulder gets greener this year, or the trees grow a couple of extra inches—so what?"

"I suppose. Another problem is getting elves to cooperate at all."

"Why wouldn't they?"

"We're not used to it." He ticked off points, one finger at a time. "We spend a lot of time in an incorporeal state. We're fairly isolated. We really only get together when we want a mate." He dropped his hands. "Elves are basically territorial, like any wild creature."

I checked off the last book title on the invoice. "If magpies and jays can cooperate to mob a cat, surely elves can get together long enough to take care of Fellseth. Kutara's working with other elves, isn't she?"

"Just two, and that's only because they would have died otherwise."

"Hey, whatever it takes for her to get a date. And she's working with three elves, counting you." I stuffed bubble wrap back into the empty box and led the way back to the front counter, looking through the store as I did so. "There are no customers right now. What do you say I charge you up with a quick meditation? You can go to the library and ask Kutara what she thinks of the idea."

"All right."

With Galan gone to the library, my brave façade wilted a little, and more than one customer asked if I was feeling okay.

At the end of the day, I closed the store and walked to the bus stop one block down. The Celadon Rose was perfectly positioned on the route, so I didn't usually bother with my car. A bus pulled up a moment later.

I flashed my pass, then found a seat, checking for gum on the upholstery before sitting down. I had just put my wallet away when someone sat beside me. I zipped my purse closed and looked up into Fellseth's face.

"I really must commend you on the good you're doing in the elf community," he said. "It's a shame how little they appreciate it."

For a frantic moment, I wondered whether I should ask someone for help. *And what would I say? There's an elf talking to me—make him stop?* I opened the zipper on my purse again, intending to get out the pepper spray.

Fellseth put his hand over mine. "Whatever you're looking for, it isn't necessary."

I turned sideways in my seat, away from him. "I'll decide what's necessary."

Fellseth rested his arm along the back of my seat. I could smell his scent—darker than Galan's, with a musky undertone that was at once attractive and frightening.

I got my pepper spray out and turned back to him, ready to squirt at the slightest provocation.

He studied me. "You know, it's not uncommon for an elf to strike up a relationship with a human for the purpose of getting energy. When there's a drought on and the hikers are trampling the wildflowers, there's nothing like a little mortal dalliance to get you over the hump, so to speak."

"You're not telling me anything I don't know." I edged forward in my seat to get away from the warmth of his arm against my shoulders.

"And yet you persist in trying to help someone who is simply taking advantage of you. How is Galan any different from me?"

I gave him a level stare. "He's not trying to kill anyone, for one thing."

Fellseth smiled at me, his expression regretful. "I'd prefer not to be the bad guy, trust me. In fact, I'm here to propose an easy solution to the whole situation. I'll give Galan his land back if you'll agree to bond with me."

I gave a bark of disbelieving laughter. "Yeah, right!"

He tilted his head. "I hate to see you chasing after that boy. If you have a thing for elves, I'm more than happy to oblige." He reached out and brushed a gentle finger against the tips of my hair. "You're quite adorable."

Kutara's words came back to me. *If I had known what a scourge he would become, perhaps I would have accepted him.* I was not that noble.

"We could call a truce," Fellseth went on. "Give me a

chance, and I'll leave everyone alone." He gave a half smile, and I was struck anew at how dangerously handsome he was. "I wasn't always this way, you know."

"You just started hanging out with the wrong crowd," I said.

He laughed. "Well, now that you mention it, I learned most of my tricks from your people." His expression turned serious. "Spend a little time with me this evening. There's a beautiful restaurant up the canyon. We could have dinner together."

"You mean Flagstaff House? I thought elves didn't eat."

"We don't." His eyes crinkled with humor. "But we're very good at ordering."

I debated the facts. Fellseth was asking to talk with me in a public place. That was probably safer than if he followed me home. I could lead him to the library, but what if Kutara wasn't there? If Galan and I weren't strong enough to defeat him, he might kill Galan once and for all. Finally, there was the chance I could learn something helpful.

"All right. I'm willing to talk to you," I said carefully.

"That was a very generous decision, Erin. I appreciate your giving me another chance." He gave a little sigh and settled back in his seat. "Not everyone would."

I nodded, hoping those people weren't smarter.

We had to transfer once to take another bus up Canyon Boulevard to the restaurant. Fellseth made only the occasional polite comment, as if we were strangers who happened to be traveling together.

I had never been to Flagstaff House. Located on a

bluff in the foothills, it was known for its fabulous views and equally fabulous prices.

Either no one noticed Fellseth's elf garb, or he was glamouring them not to. I wondered how many people he could control at a time.

"Two for dinner," he murmured to the hostess, after I had checked my coat. She nodded and led us to a table by the huge windows. Muted conversation and the clink of silverware filled the vast room.

I sat down in the chair Fellseth pulled out for me, next to a window that looked out on the lights of Boulder below. The place was full, and I wondered if we were getting someone else's reservation. "Do you take all your dates here?"

He shook his head. "I'm afraid it's usually a business dinner with some developer from California. This is the best place in town for closing deals."

He was being *awfully* honest with me. Was it possible he was serious about giving up his dark-elf ways?

A server came by with water and menus. When we were alone again, I took a sip of my water. "Why did you become a dark elf?"

"What a quaint term." Fellseth leaned back in his chair, his green eyes intense beyond the flickering candle on our table. "Elves don't just wither up like the Wicked Witch of the East, you know. When your people broke ground for luxury homes on my land, I knew it was going to be a long, drawn-out death."

He smiled slightly. "I was only about three hundred at the time. That seemed very young to die. So when all that destructive energy poured out, I filled up and left."

"To do what?"

He shrugged slightly. "I thought I might be able to

share land with a mate, or maybe find a wetlands reclamation project with no elf in residence yet—something
to put me back in a state of grace. But there were no
wetlands to be had." Fellseth picked up his empty wine-
glass and toyed with it, his eyes downcast. "And once
you're tarred with the *dark elf* brush, no one wants you."

"So what did you do?" I pressed.

He looked up. "I made a career of rating construction
sites like good restaurants, and eventually it got to be a
habit." His tone became wistful. "Humans are so much
more compassionate than elves. You recognize alco-
holism as a disease, don't you? I never hear humans say,
that John, he's a dark drinker."

I tried to keep my tone neutral. "We're not as compassionate if an alcoholic starts killing people."

Fellseth put a hand on the table, "I don't—" The
waiter approached, and he sat back. "Go ahead and
order," he told me. "I understand that you have a time
limit."

I glanced quickly at the menu, wondering just how
much he knew about my bond with Galan. "I'll have the
vegetable terrine."

The server offered me some bread and left us alone
again.

"I don't make a habit of killing my fellow elves,"
Fellseth said. There were little lines of tension around
his mouth.

"So it's just the occasional treat."

He heaved an exasperated sigh. "Put yourself in my
boots. There I was, an outcast from my own people, and
I ran across Galan, who was neglecting a perfectly good
piece of land."

"He was depressed because *you* murdered his wife!"

"I didn't *murder* her!" he said, biting out the words. "I did what I always do when I run across some poor elf who has decided to give in when his or her land goes. I hurried the process along and put her out of her misery!"

I stared at him, aghast. "Did you ask if that was what she wanted?"

"As a matter of fact, I did. I also offered to show her how to live my way. She refused to talk to me, so I took that as a no."

"If you really wanted to help, why didn't you make the developers leave her alone, instead of speeding up the bulldozers?"

He shook his head. "It's easy to influence humans toward something they want—not so easy to get them to stop."

"You could have *tried*."

"There was no point."

"You could have asked for help."

"From whom?"

"From other elves!"

He half stood, jostling the table and causing the glasses to chime. "Other elves won't talk to me!"

I looked around, wide-eyed, but no one was paying any attention to us.

Fellseth sat down, looking more anguished than angry. "This is the first conversation I've had in fifty years that hasn't involved real estate, and we're going to spend it shouting at each other."

I realized his hands were shaking. "I'm sorry," I said, and couldn't believe the words had left my mouth.

"That's okay." He took a gulp of water. "At least I don't have to lie to you. It's a refreshing change."

I sat for a moment in silence, hating that I felt sorry

for him and not able to stop myself. I had wanted to get information from him. Now was as good a time as any. "Assuming I was willing to bond with you, how would I go about detaching myself from Galan?"

"You mean you don't know?"

I leaned forward. "Tell me how you would do it."

Fellseth studied me for a moment. "The bond will break when you want it to, Erin. When you want it more than anything. That's why I was able to take Galan's land. Because I wanted it *that much*, and he didn't."

I twisted my napkin in my lap while he continued.

"The irony is, all the elves in existence could survive just fine off the energy coming from land development. It's going to happen anyway. Humans can't be denied. You could think of dark elves as a kind of evolutionary offshoot. In the end, we'll be the only ones left."

The server appeared with my meal, making a small bustle as he rearranged plates and topped off my water. "Would you like some more bread?" he asked, ignoring Fellseth completely and reminding me of the power the elf had.

I looked across the table and whispered, "Make him go away."

The server turned and left without another word. Fellseth looked at me inquiringly.

"I don't think I can eat," I said. "This has all been too much."

"I understand." He reached inside his midnight-blue coat.

I watched as he counted out some bills and put them on the table. "You're going to pay? I figured you'd just . . ." I waved a hand vaguely.

"Would you have been satisfied with that?" He smiled

sadly. "It's not nice to stick your date with the check. I've been paid for my consulting services on occasion." He angled his head to check the watch on my wrist. "I believe the next bus isn't due for another hour. Would you like cab fare?"

"I've got it." I studied him curiously. "Are you living on Galan's land?"

"It's not so much where I live as how I live. Alone." He stood. "I hope you'll consider my proposal, Erin. If you're determined to save someone, I'm an excellent candidate."

He came around the table, and I sat very still as he leaned down and kissed my cheek, his silvery braids falling forward. "I'll be in touch," he said, and left.

When the server returned, I had him pack up the food. Then I got my coat and called a cab.

It felt surreal to come in the same door through which Galan and I had ejected Fellseth. I closed it quietly behind me and hung up my coat.

Galan and Kutara were on the couch, their heads bent in conversation. "Where's Jed?" I asked. "Not locked in a closet somewhere, I hope."

Galan got up and came to meet me. "Jed was already out when we got here. Where have you been?"

"I was waylaid by Fellseth."

"Are you all right?" He examined me anxiously, then pulled me into a tight hug. "Did he hurt you?"

"He bought me dinner," I said, my face muffled against his shoulder.

He pulled away so quickly, I had to fight to keep my balance. "What?"

Kutara came over. Her hair hung lank on either side of her pale face, and there were lines across her forehead, as though she had aged thirty years since I had last seen her.

"Are you all right?" I asked, alarmed by her appearance.

"I may have overestimated the number of people my land can support," she said calmly. "It doesn't concern you."

"Of course it concerns me—you're starving!" I took her arm and led her back to the couch. "Let me help."

"Kutara will be all right for the next five minutes," Galan said. He seemed to be swinging between anger and anxiety. "What happened with Fellseth?"

I plopped down on the couch. "It was bizarre. He showed up on the bus ride home, said he *liked* me, and offered to give you back your land if I would bond with him."

"He's lying," Galan spat.

"I'm not sure." I shook my head slowly. "From his perspective, he did what he did out of desperation and was then declared Public Enemy Number One, with no second chance. I think he'd like to reform, but since he's ostracized he doesn't have a choice. It was kind of sad."

"You saw him attack me!" Galan said.

I raised my eyebrows at him. "Kind of like how your mother attacked me? I'm not saying I'm ready to absolutely believe him, but maybe being outcast in this way would cause anyone to lose their humanity." I glanced at Kutara. "Elfmanity. Whatever."

Kutara looked thoughtful. "We call it *nassa*. I suppose there might be something in what you say."

Galan shook his head. "I don't believe this."

"You are relatively young, Galan," Kutara said. "There was a time when we would have given Fellseth a second chance. But with our way of life under attack from all sides, dark elves are seen as the ultimate betrayers, impossible to forgive."

I kicked my shoes off and stretched. "I guess I don't fully understand. Humans are pretty much the source of all your problems, but you're still willing to talk to me, and both Galan and Fellseth said that elves occasionally . . . fraternize with humans."

"But dark elves are aware of their actions, whereas humans are ignorant," Kutara said. "You have no comprehension, no understanding, no—"

"All right, all right, I get it."

Galan had been pacing, but now he stopped. "Dark elves willingly live off dark energy. It's as if a family member were dying and you decided to benefit from it."

I shrugged. "Quite frankly, that happens all the time with humans. Grandma's dying of cancer, and someone takes care of her in exchange for the house."

Kutara looked at Galan and shook her head. "No comprehension."

Galan sat next to me. "Let me put it a different way. Think of the spirit of the land as a suffocating child. Dark elves suck out its last breath."

I grimaced. "I can see there isn't going to be an easy solution to this. But before we go any further, let me try to do something for Kutara. Because honestly, you look like hell."

"*Do* something for me? What is she talking about?" Kutara asked Galan.

I stood up and made waving motions in front of her

face. "Hello? I'm right here. Come on, into the bedroom with you."

Kutara's eyebrows shot up. "Is this the fraternizing you were talking about?"

Fifteen minutes later, Kutara took her hands away from my shoulders. "I had no idea this was possible."

I took one last deep breath before opening my eyes. I was both relieved and annoyed to see Kutara restored to her usual stunning self. "How do you feel?"

"Much better. You have my gratitude."

Galan had been sitting on the bed. He stood and offered his hand to help me off the floor. "How do *you* feel? That's twice in one day."

"I'm fine." My stomach growled as I remembered my leftover dinner, still in its bag on the hall table. "Let's go in the kitchen. We can talk while I eat."

Once seated at the table, I noticed that Kutara looked away while I ate, as if I were messily blowing my nose instead of noshing on leftovers.

Galan scowled at my food. "Where did he take you?"

"Canyon House. Boulder's most expensive restaurant. He actually paid with real cash, too. I couldn't believe it."

Kutara risked a quick glance at me. "But you didn't eat there?"

"I couldn't. Frankly, it's a little nerve-racking to have the enemy suddenly turn all sincere and vulnerable."

Galan appeared to be grinding his teeth. "What exactly did he say about returning my land?"

I put my fork down. "First of all, you should know that according to Fellseth, he spoke to your wife and offered to show her how to live his way. Did she ever mention that to you?"

Galan looked at his hands, which were clenched together on the tabletop. "No, but she stopped talking at all toward the end."

I wanted *so much* to comfort him, but not if I would later be accused of leading him into temptation. "Fellseth also said that I could break my bond with you if I really wanted to."

He raised his head. "Do you think that's true?"

Now I was the one who looked away. "So far, there's no reason to think any differently."

Kutara broke the silence. "Galan told me of your idea to use up the water energy."

"What do you think?"

She shook her head. "Frankly, I think it would be easier to coordinate a hunting party, track Fellseth down, and overpower him."

"So why hasn't that happened?"

"I said it would be easier, not easy. With Fellseth on the loose, everyone is afraid to leave home—afraid to spend energy on anything other than essentials, and thus put themselves at risk."

"But *you're* doing all those things," I pointed out.

"I am convinced that the only way to solve the problem is by becoming . . . What is the word again, Galan?"

"Proactive."

I put my hand over my mouth to hide a smile.

Kutara went on. "The difficulty has always been in locating a dark elf efficiently. But this new development may help in gaining other elves' cooperation."

"What new development?" I asked.

"Fellseth wants you. You have effectively become bait."

I looked from one elf to the other. "Wait a minute. I'm not sure that's the way to do things."

"You promised you'd help me defeat him," Galan said.

"That was before he fed me a nice dinner." I frowned at Kutara. "I don't care for the idea of trapping someone who might want to reform while you guys wait outside with pitchforks and flaming torches." I turned to Galan. "What if I bonded with him, just to give him energy, and he gave your land back? Then everybody's problems would be solved, right?"

He looked unhappy, but said nothing.

Kutara's dry voice broke the silence. "We have no reason to believe that Fellseth will keep his word, but we do have an opportunity to deal with him once and for all—an opportunity that may never come again."

"You weren't there," I protested. "He said a lot of things he didn't have to. What was his purpose in meeting me if he wasn't sincere?"

Kutara stood. "If his purpose was to keep you from cooperating with us, he may have already succeeded." She put a hand up to forestall my response. "I have no hold on you, Erin. You have already done more than I expected. All I ask is that you consider this situation carefully before making any decisions."

"I'm doing that, trust me."

"I have to return to the library now. Galan, I will speak to you later."

After she left, I went to the refrigerator for something to drink.

Galan's voice came from behind me. "Fellseth's offer . . . You're not actually considering it, are you?"

I didn't turn around. Instead, I opened a carton of soy milk and poured some into a glass. "If we knew for sure that he would give back your land, wouldn't you want me to?"

There was a long pause. "I don't think I could stand it," he said quietly.

I picked up my glass and headed toward the living room. "*How sweet*. But since you're not going to stay, *someone* might as well have that energy."

He followed me. "I never said I would stay, Erin."

I set my glass on the end table and flopped onto the sofa. "No. You just tell me I'm amazing, and you care about me, and then you walk out the door."

He sat next to me. "Do we have to have all this anger?"

I got up and sat in the chair opposite the couch. "You can decide not to discuss the possibility of being together, but you *don't* get to decide how I feel, Galan."

He stared across the distance that separated us. "I don't have any experience with this, you know. Not that I've ever felt this way about a human before, but if a woman got attached to me, I could always make her forget with a little glamour."

"It's unfortunate for both of us that that doesn't work on me." I went into my bedroom and shut the door.

Chapter Six

When Galan and I arrived at the Celadon Rose the next morning, Lily met us at the door. "Where did you get those astonishing pendants?" she asked.

"Galan made them. If it's all right with you, I thought he could hang out here today and make some more, maybe take some special requests."

She gave his back a jaunty pat. "Wonderful! We'll put you in the tarot reader's booth, since she's not here today."

After making sure Galan had everything he needed, Lily came back to the front of the store, where I was sniffing perfume samples.

"Is he still moving to Spain?" she asked.

"Oh, yeah. *Asshole.*"

She made a sympathetic face. "I guess you're not trying to get him to stay anymore."

I put Amber Dreams to my nose and inhaled before answering. "It's up to him now."

* * *

Galan came behind the counter and handed me a fist-ful of earrings. "Nine more pairs. Do you think something with tiny acorns would sell?"

"Anything you make will sell. Let me find some backing cards and you can hook them on for me." I rummaged through the stuff on the shelves below the register.

He sighed. "It's tiring, being careful not to let the customers notice anything strange."

I found the box of earring cards and handed them to him. "Work from home tomorrow, if you want."

He frowned and took the box. "Maybe."

A woman approached the register. She was beautiful, with a mane of dark hair over fine features and doelike eyes.

Galan stepped to one side and muttered, "I'm not here."

She put a book on the counter without even glancing at him.

"Did you find everything you needed?" I asked.

"I'm looking for a deck of tarot cards with pictures of elves, but I don't see it in the store. Do you have a catalog I could look through?"

"Sure." I found the U.S. Games catalog and handed it to her. "If you find what you're looking for, we'll be happy to order it and save you the shipping." I glanced at Galan, who was putting earrings onto cards. "So you're interested in elves, huh?"

"Yes." She tapped the book. "This tells you how to attract elf energy to your home."

"Try eating five big meals a day."

"Ha, ha," Galan said, tossing a filled card down.

She looked at me uncertainly. "Pardon me?"

"Sorry," I said. "I'm getting over an eating disorder, and that's one of my affirmations. What does the book say?"

"Well, apparently elves love the sound of bells, so wind chimes are a good idea, although I'm a light sleeper, so I might have to take them down at night. And you're supposed to make everything really pretty, with lots of color and sparkly things."

Galan looked up. "Oh, honestly."

I took his wrist and hauled him in front of me. "Speak up. She can't hear you."

The woman drew back as he allowed her to see him. "I didn't see you there!"

"He was rearranging the bottom shelf," I said. "But you're very lucky. This is Galan Stone . . ."

"Rock."

"Galan Rock, and he has a Ph.D. in, um, folklore. His thesis was all about elves. Wasn't it, Galan?"

She smiled at him. "Have you published anything?"

"Not yet, but I might have to." He pushed the offending book aside with his fingertips. "While it's certainly true that elves love beautiful things, the rest of it is nonsense."

"But the author said . . ."

Galan shook his head. "Take this bell business. Elves are creatures of nature. The sounds they most appreciate are things like flowing water, wind in the trees, and birdsong."

She pursed her mouth thoughtfully. "I guess I could get one of those nature-sounds recordings."

"*Or* you could plant some trees for birds to nest in. How much land do you have?"

"About three acres. We've got some horse property a little north of Boulder."

Galan looked thoughtful. "Three acres has definite potential." He put both hands on the counter. "Okay, here's what you do. First, get rid of the horses. Second, plant as many trees as you can—all native varieties. And third, let the place go completely wild and stay off it as much as possible."

The woman's eyebrows almost met her hairline. "Are you serious?"

"If you want elves, that's what it takes."

"I don't think my husband would go for that." She edged toward the door. "At the most, I think he was up for a little redecorating."

"Elf habitat isn't something you throw together in a weekend," Galan said.

"You know, I think my parking meter might be running out." She made her escape.

I put the tarot-card catalog away. "I'll thank you not to scare away my customers."

"I'm sorry, but did you hear the stuff she was saying?"

"I was more interested in what you said. Would that actually work?"

"In time, yes."

"So I could conceivably buy a piece of land, let it go wild, and you could bond with it?"

He stared at me. "Why would you do that?"

"Oh, I don't know. Maybe to save your life?"

He shook his head, clearly astonished. "Since I was a child I've been told, *Take what you want from humans, because they take everything from us.* And now you're offering to buy me land? It seems impossible."

I lifted my chin. "Everything is theoretically impossible, until someone does it."

Now that I had come up with the idea of buying land for Galan, I was determined to go ahead with it. Maybe I couldn't change the way elves thought about *all* humans, but I could damn well change the way they thought about this one.

I sat on the couch with *Homes and Land of Boulder County* in my lap, slowly turning the pages. "I can get a bigger loan. I'll rework the numbers and put less of a down payment on the store." A listing caught my eye, and I pointed to it. "Here's one. Fifteen acres, mature woods, log cabin." I squinted at the tiny picture. "It looks pretty wild. Do you think there could be an elf already living on it?"

"I guess we'd have to check," Galan said, without looking up. He had my jewelry supplies out and was lounging against the far arm of the couch as he worked on something, his feet almost in my lap.

I folded the corner of the page to mark it. "Here's another. Twenty acres, borders national forest, builder will finish to your specifications. I'll just specify that he tear it down and cart it off."

"Mmm-hmm."

His indifference was not part of my plan, and I smacked him on the leg with the magazine. "Don't you want to be involved in this? You can make jewelry any time."

He made a final tweak to his project and sat up. "I wanted to do this now. It's for you." He put it in my hand.

I looked down at the perfect representation of Galan's profile, done in a single strand of silver wire.

"It's to remember me by. It's not enough, of course," he said. "I don't think anything is enough. We—elves, I mean—have gotten used to thinking of ourselves as doomed. Maybe that's why I didn't beat Fellseth. I'd become used to the idea of giving up. And then you came along and . . ." He laughed, the sound catching in his throat. "I didn't realize how much things could change, just because one woman *would not give up*."

The pendant blurred as I stared at it, and a tear fell onto the profile's cheek.

"So I want to thank you," Galan went on.

I swallowed hard. "You're welcome."

"I also want to say how sorry I am. I know I behaved badly, and you're angry at me." He hesitated. "But I wish I'd let you show me earlier that things don't have to be impossible."

I closed my fingers over the pendant. "It might not be too late to try. If you want."

He put his arms around me. "I do want."

"Good morning."

The sight of Galan's face on the pillow next to mine made me smile. "Good morning."

He pulled me to him and we wrapped our arms around each other. I had thought that caring and being cared for would be restful, but with so much at stake, I felt curiously vulnerable.

I inhaled his scent, wishing this moment could last forever. "Still happy about your decision?"

"Absolutely." He pulled his head back and kissed me.

I scanned his face, inches from mine. "You know I don't have a master plan for solving all our problems, right?"

"You disappoint me. I thought maybe it came to you during the night."

I giggled, relieved that we could joke like this. "Only one thing came to me during the night, but it came *a lot*. I'm not even a little hungry." My arm was falling asleep, so I rolled onto my back.

"Is there a plan for the day?" Galan ran one warm hand over my stomach before cupping first one breast, then the other.

"Sure." I closed my eyes. "I thought I'd call in sick, order a bunch of Thai food, and spend the day in bed with you."

"Really?"

The eagerness in his voice made me laugh. "That's what I'd like to do, but no. This afternoon, you and I will look at property. In the meantime, there's a bunch of fountains coming in this morning and they need to be assembled, priced, and shelved. I wouldn't be a nice person if I left it all to Lily."

"Should I come to the store this morning? I don't think you need more jewelry, but I can help with other things."

I clambered on top of him. "Yes, you should come to the store. I'll tell Lily I threw out my back having gymnastic sex, and you felt so bad about it that you're going to help me lift all those stone fountain bases."

He chuckled and rubbed against me. "What are you really going to tell her?"

"What I just said." I rolled off him and headed toward

the bathroom. "Never underestimate the frankness of girl talk."

Galan scrambled out of bed and followed. "Speaking of gymnastics, let me show you my back bend." He caught up and gave my butt a little spank. "Can we take a shower together?"

Lily was already at the store when we arrived. "We sold *five* of the sixty-dollar pendants yesterday," she said. Then she held up her clasped hands to Galan, pleading. "They'll let you make jewelry at the monastery, won't they? It'd bring in more money than cheese, or whatever they make in Spain."

"Um . . ." Galan looked to me for help.

I chuckled. "You'll get your pendants. He's going to help me put up the new fountains this morning. My back is bothering me a little because . . ."

Galan's face froze. "Erin, I need to . . ." He pointed down an aisle. "I'll just . . ."

"You go do that." I pulled his face down and kissed him before he trotted off.

Lily watched his departing figure a moment before turning back to me. "No more monastery?"

"He'd have a hard time keeping his vows."

"Did you say your back was bothering you?"

"Maybe a little."

She smirked. "Better lay off the gymnastic sex."

We went home for lunch, and I looked at the real-estate listings I'd circled. Three out of the five potential property listings were with the same agency. I called

Lily and made sure I could take the afternoon off, then called the real-estate office and made an appointment.

After hanging up, I went to my workbench, where Galan was drawing something in my jewelry sketchbook. "We're seeing the realtor at three." I looked over his shoulder. A series of playful line-drawn rabbits tumbled across the page—leaping, grooming, yawning. "Did you do all this while I was on the phone?"

He shook his head. "I got the idea last night and worked on it some while you were asleep. I thought it might make a nice bracelet."

I shook my head at the inadequacy of his description. "Sweetheart, this is stunning. We're going to need a bigger venue for you than the Rose. A Web site, at the very least."

He pulled the pad back and shaded the toes on a curved paw. "So what are we doing before land hunting? I'd hate for you to faint with hunger in front of the realtor."

I edged into his lap. "You're right, that would be terrible. Do you have any thoughts on how we might raise some energy?"

He put his pencil down and picked me up. "Let me show you my notes on the subject. I left them on the bed."

After raising enough energy to light a small city, Galan and I strolled through the Boulder Library's reference section in search of Kutara. We found her standing in front of one of the Internet terminals, mouse in hand.

"What are you two doing here?" she asked.

I took in her weary posture and the circles under her eyes. "I wanted to know if anyone had seen Fellseth. And I thought you might need a boost."

"There is no news on Fellseth."

I waited, but it was clear she couldn't bring herself to ask for help. "Come on. Why don't we find a private place in the stacks so I can recharge you? Just so the trip isn't wasted."

"I'll hold your place at this terminal," Galan offered.

Kutara shrugged. "If you insist."

I led the way through the quiet, book-scented library, glancing down the aisles of metal shelves. On my left was a row of glassed-in study rooms, but there were students inside each one. "Looks like they're all filled."

"This will do." Kutara stopped outside a room occupied by a young man who was obviously sleeping, his head resting on the table. She opened the door and walked over to him. "Out."

He gathered his belongings and departed, bleary-eyed.

"I've always wanted to do that," I said, grabbing a book at random and joining her.

She closed the door behind us. With the book open on the desk, I pulled the room's two chairs together and positioned Kutara in the one nearest the door. "Look like you're reading," I said, taking a seat and linking arms with her.

As I meditated, I seemed to sense not only the energy coming up from the earth, but also the current leading to Kutara. When I finished, I opened my eyes and examined her. "It's gratifying to see you recover—like watching a plant perk up from watering."

Kutara ran a hand through her hair, which was shiny

again. "I have never been compared to vegetation before." She started to rise.

I put a hand on her arm. "I want to tell you something."

"What?"

I hesitated. "If I see Fellseth, I'm going to tell him that I won't bond with him, but that Galan doesn't need his land back."

Kutara's face hardened. "I see. So Galan is to become your mortal husband and the elf community is diminished yet again."

"That's not it at all," I said, my temper flaring. "I'm going to buy a piece of land and give it to Galan, so he won't have to be dependent on anyone again."

At that moment, it was worth taking out a whopping loan just to see the expression on Kutara's face.

"I'm astonished," she said finally.

"I can tell." I knew I was smirking, but I couldn't help it. "So you see, no one needs to lynch anyone else. With some diplomatic overtures from the elf community, maybe Fellseth can be brought back into the fold and everyone can be happy."

"Perhaps. Assuming that's what he wants."

"I think it is. He seemed really lonely."

"Hmm." Kutara continued to stare at me.

"Well." I began to feel uncomfortable under her scrutiny. "I guess I'll let you get back to work." I stood and edged toward the door.

Kutara cleared her throat. "I didn't think humans could be like you."

I turned, one hand on the doorknob. "Is that a compliment?"

"I suppose. Although—"

I held up a hand. "Kutara?"

"Yes?"

"Don't spoil it."

She shifted restlessly. "Very well."

On the way home, the light turned red at Broadway and Canyon. I glanced out the window at the cluster of municipal buildings to my left. A man in a suit was strolling up the walk past the main office. A man with long, silvery hair. I stared. *Fellseth?*

He disappeared around the corner, just as the driver behind me tapped his horn. I made a left and turned into the parking lot.

"Where are we going?" Galan asked.

If I told him, would he insist that we get Kutara and then come back and kill Fellseth? I had not signed on for the killing part, but Galan seemed to take it for granted. "I just remembered, I need to pick up some forms at the city building. Real-estate stuff. You can stay here. It'll just take a second."

I trotted down the winding sidewalk and entered the building, then went straight through the lobby and out a side door.

The man with the silvery hair sat on a bench against the wall.

I walked toward him, trying to peer and look casual at the same time. "It *is* you!" I said, when I could see his face.

Fellseth smiled, looking delighted to see me. "Erin! How are you?" Close up, his charcoal suit looked very expensive.

"What are you doing here?" I gestured to his clothes. "Dressed like that."

He gave a wry smile. "Sometimes I play with the idea of becoming mortal. A few night classes, some glamoured business references, and then a bite of falafel to trigger the change. I hear Mediterranean food is very good. Would you like to sit?"

I sat on the other end of the bench. "Are you really thinking of becoming human?"

He stared out at the park. "I've seen a lot of misery— caused some of it. Being an elf is a depressing proposition these days." He turned and looked at me, a crease between his winged brows. "Have you considered my proposal?"

I took a deep breath. "I did, but I can't bond with you."

He sighed and looked away again. "I was afraid that would be your decision."

"But . . ." I put my hand on his jacketed arm for a moment, and he met my gaze. "I'm buying some property for Galan, which means he won't need his old land anymore." I tilted my head and gave him a significant look before going on. "You have the chance to rejoin the elf community. I've been talking to Kutara about it."

He chuckled. "You never fail to delight me. What does the indomitable Kutara say?"

"I think she's open to the idea, if you make it clear that's what you want. She's not so bad, once you get to know her. Kind of like you."

Fellseth reached out, as though to touch my hand. He stopped and cleared his throat instead. "Erin, I want to thank you. I've experienced more compassion from you and your kind than I have from my own people. At this point, I feel more human than elf."

"Well, don't let that stop you from making peace. It's important to heal those old wounds."

"I agree." His expression was serious. "And even more important to belong somewhere."

"Absolutely." I stood. "I have to go now."

He moved toward me, tentatively, and I accepted his hug, feeling awkward. "I'm grateful to have met you, Erin," he murmured, before releasing me.

"I really hope things work out for you."

"I'll do my best."

I felt hopeful as I went back to the car. If my diplomacy worked, this duel-to-the-death nonsense could stop, and Galan and I could focus on more important things.

I got in the car.

Galan looked up from the real-estate magazine we had brought with us. "Did they not have the forms?"

I wanted to get him away from here in case Fellseth rounded the corner and Galan decided to fight. "I'm going to download the forms from home."

I waited until we were home to tell Galan about my encounter with Fellseth.

"You did what?" He stood by my jewelry workbench, vibrating with anger.

Obviously, he didn't share my hopeful mood. "You should be happy!" I said. "Now that you don't need your land back, he can stop being a dark elf."

"He could have stopped being a dark elf before!"

"Except that everyone was after him." I reached for

Galan, but he moved away and began to pace. I chewed on my lip a moment. "I know your experience with him has been horrible, but he hasn't had an easy time, either. He only became a dark elf because it was that or die. I really think he wants to reform."

He swung around. "He killed my wife, Erin. He tried to kill me. Even if he promised never to hurt another person, it wouldn't mean anything. He's a liar and a murderer." He sat down abruptly in my workbench chair, his back toward me. "And you left me in the car while you went and talked to him." He shook his head.

I touched his shoulder. "I did it for you. Now there's no reason for him to come after you."

He stared forward, saying nothing.

"I'm sorry, Galan." I squatted on the floor beside his chair and looked up at his closed face. "I'm sorry and I won't ever talk to him again, I promise."

He rubbed his forehead. "I guess that'll have to be good enough. I mean, what choice do I have?"

I put my hand on his thigh. "Galan, I am *so* sorry. It seemed like the thing to do, but if I had it to do again, I wouldn't go near him, I swear."

He reached down and pulled me onto his lap.

I held him tightly, my face buried in his neck. "Thank you."

"Let's just forget him," he muttered. "If we're lucky, you're right, and we'll never hear from Fellseth again."

The offices of Land-Max weren't far. I pulled into a parking spot and unfastened my seat belt. "Since you don't have an official identity, it'll be just me on the paperwork. That's something the realtor is likely to ask about."

We reached the lobby, and Galan opened the door for me. "We'll have to deal with my unofficial status, eventually. I'd hate to be the cause of an audit."

I lowered my voice. "There must be people on the Internet that you can contact for that sort of thing. I think you get some dead guy's ID."

"Or I could just glamour the proper authorities to set me up."

I kept forgetting about the whole glamour thing, since it didn't work on me. "Or you could do that."

Two young women with headset telephones sat at the curved reception desk. I waited until one of them disconnected and looked up. "Hi, I'm Erin Chandler. I have an appointment with Barbara Findleman to see some properties."

She smiled. "I'll tell Barbara you're here, Ms. Chandler."

I nodded and went to join Galan. He was scanning the pictures of properties posted on the curved lobby wall.

"There will be periods of time when I have to become incorporeal," he whispered. "You'll be alone then."

I gave him a confident smile. "I'll just think of them as business trips. It's no big deal."

A woman approached us. "Ms. Chandler?" Barbara Findleman was around forty-five, with short, prematurely white hair. She wore a chic black pantsuit and a businesslike smile.

"Call me Erin. And this is my boyfriend, Galan. He'll be living with me."

"Call me Barbara, please. It's nice to meet you both. Let's go back to my office."

We followed her down the hall and through a door, which she closed behind us.

"Have a seat," she said, waving at two upholstered chairs in front of a desk awash in paperwork.

I glanced around at the Realtor-of-the-Year awards and vacation pictures covering the walls of the office.

Barbara sat down and pushed a coffee cup aside before handing me a sheet of paper. "If you could fill out this form, it'll give me a rough idea of what you can afford."

When I was done, Barbara entered the numbers in her computer and studied the result. "Well, I don't think you're going to be in Boulder County proper, unless you're looking for a one-bedroom condo." She looked at me over the top of her glasses.

"Actually, I was thinking of buying land. Maybe . . . two acres?" I looked at Galan, who nodded.

She tapped her keyboard a few times. "You won't be able to afford that in Boulder. How does Berthoud sound?"

It sounded like I'd have to commute for sex. "Berthoud's a little far. I knew the market was tight, but I guess I didn't realize it was this tight."

She nodded. "Boulder's growth restrictions keep it that way. However, the city listened to a proposal today to sell some public wilderness to a developer. Of course, those homes will be completely out of your price range, but it may loosen the market a little." She clicked her mouse and the printer whirred to life.

I sat bolt upright. "What public wilderness? Where?"

"That strip that runs behind the therapy center." Barbara scanned the property listings on her computer screen, tapping away at her keyboard.

Galan's land. I looked at him. He was slumped in his chair, eyes closed, an expression of pain on his face.

"I thought open space was protected against that kind of thing," I said. "Are you *sure* that's the land they're talking about?"

Barbara picked up a printout and studied it. "I guess there's a piece of private land for sale in the mountains, still in Boulder County. The plan is to sell the land down here and designate the bigger piece a park of some sort. There'll be a public hearing first, but I guess the strip down here is pretty compromised. Erosion, et cetera. Some developer will pay big bucks to build upscale homes right next to the foothills, and the city will be able to buy something really pristine. I imagine it'll go through. I hear the consultant who's working on it is very persuasive."

I thought of Fellseth in his suit, sitting beside the city buildings. "I'll bet he is," I said grimly.

Barbara looked up at me, apparently sensing something was wrong. "I don't have an opinion on it either way. You can easily argue both sides. But it's certainly causing a stir in my line of work." She looked at Galan. "Are you okay?"

He wasn't even bothering to glamour her. I put my hand on his shoulder. "He had some food poisoning yesterday. I thought he felt better, but maybe not." I turned to Barbara. "I think we need to go. I'm sorry."

"That's okay. Feel better." She got up and followed us out. "Listen, I have your number. I'll call you and we'll set up another appointment."

"Sure."

Galan allowed me to tow him out of the office. It

wasn't until we were sitting in the car that he said, "I have to see Kutara."

"We'll go there now." I swung the car in a tight arc toward the parking lot's exit. "I can't believe this."

"I can."

"Galan, I—"

"No." He shook his head. "I can't talk about it right now."

We found Kutara with three other elves in one of the small study rooms. Galan told them about the latest development, his voice low and strained.

When he had finished, Kutara drummed her fingers on the table before speaking. "I've been watching the public-hearing listings on the city's Web site. Presumably they'll announce the date for this soon. Fellseth will attend, in order to glamour as many people as possible." She looked around at the other elves. "And we will be there as well, to counteract him."

And maybe to kill him, I thought. "I am so sorry," I said, my voice catching.

"Why?" Kutara looked at me curiously. "You haven't actively aided Fellseth and you've been very helpful to us."

But I knew I was really apologizing to Galan, for listening to Fellseth, *trusting* him, for even a moment.

He hadn't looked directly at me since the real-estate office. Instead, he sat with the other elves and stared at the table.

"Is there anything I can do to help?" I asked the room at large. If only he would look at me.

"Not at the moment," Kutara said. "We'll let you know."

"Galan," I said quietly, looking at his downturned face, "Can I talk to you outside for a minute?"

He followed me outside, his eyes shuttered.

I closed the door of the study room, so the other elves wouldn't hear us. "I never gave him any information that would have helped him. You have to believe that."

"All right." But he still didn't look at me.

I grabbed his hands and shook them. "*Now* is when we need to stick together the most. I know this is a shock, but can you try not to shut me out?"

"It's hard." His voice was hoarse. "That land was part of me, and he's going to kill it."

"We won't let that happen," I said firmly.

"Who is we?" He was looking at me now, and it wasn't comfortable. "I told you Fellseth couldn't be trusted, and you trusted him! We had the chance to get rid of him once and for all, but you had a secret chat instead!"

"I just gave him a chance, because it was possible that he could change."

He shook his head slowly, as if he couldn't believe what I was saying. "Not in this case, Erin. Fellseth isn't a nice guy who's just misunderstood. He isn't a little dark—he's black to the core."

"I understand that now."

"Do you? I worry that you can't understand elf things without being an elf."

"Oh, no, you don't." I was angry myself now. "That's like saying I can't understand you because I'm not a guy. If that kind of understanding were necessary for a relationship, none of us would be here."

"Our relationship is not my top priority at the moment." He pulled his hands out of my grasp. "I have to get back to the meeting. This is an elf issue, and it's going to take elves to solve it."

"Except that you're going to need my energy. Don't put yourself in danger just because you're mad at me, Galan."

"I'll call you if I need you. In the meantime, Boulder Creek isn't flooded anymore. I'll take a page out of Fellseth's book and get my energy there."

I felt the strap of my purse dig into my fingers as I gripped it. "I'll go talk to the bank about that loan, just in case."

He didn't respond—just went inside the study room and closed the door.

I walked through the periodicals section with my head held high, but the magazines blurred as tears welled in my eyes. Galan was right. I hadn't understood Fellseth at all, and it was only luck that had kept me from doing actual damage.

Our relationship is not my top priority at the moment. Until now, I had felt like the one with all the expertise. Now it was Galan's turn to know what needed to be done, and I felt both helpless and foolish. Lives hung in the balance, and all I could think about was whether I got to keep my boyfriend?

I reached the bottom of the staircase and began to run—past the check-out counters, past the children's section with its hobby horse and fish tanks.

Once in the parking lot I tripped over the parking median and landed on one knee. "Ow," I whimpered. "Ow." I sat on the concrete curb, covered my head with my forearms, and abandoned myself to tears.

The sun was significantly lower when I raised my head. I stood and wiped my face with my hands. Looking around, I spotted my car two rows over. I would go home and clean up, and tomorrow I would visit my loan officer. It was the only thing I knew to do.

My hands were shaking, but I managed to unlock the car and fasten my seat belt. I was about to turn the key when my stomach growled, sending a wave of fresh grief washing over me as I remembered Galan's words about the creek. "He doesn't need me," I sobbed, raking my hands through my hair. "And now he won't want me."

Tears ran down my face as I backed out of the parking spot and headed, not toward the bank, but to Lily's.

Chapter Seven

I lay on the bed in Lily's guest room. "I was stupid, and now it's all ruined!" I gasped into a damp wad of tissue.

Lily came back from the bathroom with a washcloth soaked in cold water. "I know, honey," she murmured. Jim, her husband, had taken one look at my face and fled the house. "You have to calm down."

"You don't know!" I wailed. "No one knows!"

She pressed me back against the pillows and put the cloth over my eyes, then sat on the edge of the bed and stroked my hair. "Is Galan going to Spain after all?"

I moved my head fretfully. "No."

"Well, that's good, isn't it?"

"No!" I pressed the heels of my hands into the cloth where it covered my eyes. "You don't understand."

"Then *tell* me," she said.

I dragged the cloth down my face and looked at her. She regarded me steadily. "You can tell me."

I heaved a deep sigh. "Galan's not going to Spain. He was never going to Spain. He's an elf."

* * *

"You can't say a word to anyone. Promise me," I urged, after I had told Lily everything. We were both lying on the guest bed now. Damp tissues littered the flowered spread.

She shook her head in wonder. "Who'd believe me?"

"That's what *I* said. But you believe me, don't you?"

"Actually, I do." She scrunched the feather pillow tighter under her head and turned to study me. "Mostly because it's you, but also because Galan kept making jewelry the day he worked in the shop, even though he forgot the wire cutters on my desk. And you say I'm part elf?"

"Apparently. That's why Galan couldn't be invisible to you the time you first met." I started to sniffle again at the memory of Galan in the store.

Lily patted my thigh. "Everything could still work out, honey. Galan and the others can still get rid of the bad elf, and Galan can come running back to you, flushed with triumph."

"I don't know if they can defeat Fellseth. He's been doing this for decades, and he's so *slick*." I clenched my fists. "I really believed he wasn't bad. I *wanted* to believe him, so Galan would have to stay with me, and I'm sure Galan knows that. But if you love someone, you should have their best interests at heart, right? Even if it means you might lose them?"

Lily gave a humorless laugh. "That's what they say. Then there's real life, where you just want someone, no matter what."

"Oh God, yes." I closed my eyes over the tears that threatened to spill. "I can't bear the thought of being without him."

"Telling him that will go a long way toward having

him forgive you. Not that I think there's much to forgive."
She slid off the bed. "Come on, let's go eat something. It's
way past dinner."

"I'm not hungry." I turned my face into the pillow.

She patted my shoulder. "I'll make you a sandwich
and leave it in the fridge, in case you want it later. You
can stay as long as you like."

I heard her footsteps on the carpet. "Thank you," I
said, waving a limp hand in her general direction. The
door closed softly.

It was dark when I woke up. After fumbling with the
small lamp on the nightstand, I took my cell phone out
of my purse so I could check the time. Two o'clock in
the morning. There were no missed calls or messages.

My face felt hot. I went into the small bathroom,
popped a paper cup out of the dispenser, and drank three
cupfuls of water in quick succession.

I could go home. Somehow, the thought of being
there without Galan seemed more than I could bear. Besides, driving home might wake me up enough to think,
and thinking was the last thing I wanted to do. Still in
my clothes, I went back to bed and crawled under the
covers, escaping into sleep once more.

"Erin. Come on, wake up."

"No."

Lily persisted. "Weren't you going to see your banker
today?"

I rolled over, keeping one arm draped across my face.
"What?"

She tugged the covers down a little. "Did you sleep in your clothes?"

I sat up and slumped against the headboard, blinking in the morning light. "I don't have an appointment with my banker. I was just going to show up and see my loan officer. But I'm not even sure Galan would accept land from me now." I stared blearily around. "What time is it? Do you want me to go to work?"

Lily snorted. "I don't think you could provide our trademark nurturing vibe." Holding out a juice glass of something pale and thick, she said, "Drink this. It's a protein shake."

I took the glass and sipped at it listlessly.

"Drink," Lily said threateningly.

"Okay, okay." I gulped the rest down.

"That's better." Lily took the glass and gave me an encouraging look. "Now, did Galan say anything like, *I hate you, and I never want to see you again*?"

I shook my head.

"I didn't think so. He probably needs some time to cool off, but I think he'll be back. So I want you to go home, maybe take a bath, and go see your loan officer, just in case. Then, if you feel up to it, you can come to the Rose. Okay?"

I looked at her hopefully. "Do you really think he'll come back?"

"I do. Keep telling yourself that, and practice the heartfelt speech of passionate love you're going to give him when he does. Stuff like that never hurts."

I threw my arms around Lily and hugged her. "You're the best friend in the world."

"You may be right." Lily gave me an extra squeeze

before pulling back. "Now go home so my husband can come out of hiding."

When I reached the front door to my house, Kitty Girl shot out of the bushes and meowed frantically. I picked her up and buried my face in her soft fur. "You still love me, don't you, angel?" I murmured. "Even though I'm a bad mommy."

Inside, I caught sight of myself in the hall mirror— red eyes set in puffy bags, hair sticking out at all angles, and pale, pale skin.

"He's coming back," I said to the mirror. "Lily says so." My reflection didn't look convinced.

The front door opened right beside me, making me jump.

"Hey!" Jed came in and shed his messenger bag. "Where have you been? I was kind of worried about you last night."

My heartbeat returned to normal. "Oh, um . . . Galan and I stayed out late and crashed at a friend's." I looked at my reflection again and decided to take a bath.

I was closing the bedroom door behind me when Kitty Girl shot through the narrowing gap.

"Do you want to keep me company?" I looked around, hoping to see some sign of Galan, maybe a note, but there was nothing.

I ran a bath as hot as I could stand and sank into the tub with a little whimper. Kitty Girl jumped on the tile surround and stared pointedly at me. I closed my eyes to avoid her laser stare. "I don't want to bother with bubbles."

Silence, and then a little warbling meow.

"Oh, all right." I dumped some sudsing bath oil into the water and swished it around vigorously before lying back again. The only sound was the faint snap of bubbles as Kitty Girl batted at the resulting foam.

He's going to come back. I made a mantra of it while I soaked.

But when evening came and there was still no sign of Galan, my mantra sounded more like *He's never coming back.* I had already gone to the bank and successfully reconfigured my loan. Now I decided to go to the library, to see if there had been any point.

A beautiful hippie kid grinned at me as I walked through the foyer. I managed a weak smile in return, but once I reached the Reference section, my spirits sank. There wasn't an elf to be seen—not by the Internet terminals, not in the study rooms.

I canvassed the entire second floor twice, feeling more panicky by the second. What if they weren't meeting here anymore? What if Galan had decided to leave town and look for some other human to give him energy? Would he even say good-bye?

Walking down the stairs, I was so emotionally exhausted that I stumbled and would have slipped if someone coming up the stairs hadn't reached out and steadied me.

"Erin?"

I looked into Kutara's face. "Is Galan with you?"

"No." Her features gave nothing away.

"Did he spend the night with you?" I felt my face flush. "It's just that I'm worried about him."

She walked up the stairs, leaving me to follow.

"There is no running water on my land. I believe he spent last night here."

I hated to beg, but I didn't see any choice. "Do you know where he is now?"

"After spending the night near the creek, he felt well enough to do some reconnaissance for me." Kutara went to the nearest Internet terminal. The woman using it promptly gathered her things and walked off.

I chewed my lip while Kutara brought up the Web browser. Was that all she was going to tell me? "Is there any way I can help?" I asked. "Can you tell me what's going to happen?"

"I could, but it might not be the wisest thing, for either us or for you."

"I wouldn't tell Fellseth!"

She turned and studied me. "I know you wouldn't mean to, but I have learned at some cost never to underestimate Fellseth. When I know the date of the public hearing, I'll let you know. You can help protest the sale of the land, if you like."

"Okay. Thanks. Listen . . ."

She watched while I searched for the right words.

"When you see Galan, would you tell him . . ." My voice broke a little. "Would you tell him I miss him?"

Something like compassion softened her coldly beautiful features. "Certainly."

When I walked in the door of the Celadon Rose the next day, Lily took one look at me and pulled me into the little office behind the counter. "No offense, kiddo, but your face is not an advertisement for our self-help section."

I dragged the desk chair out. "I thought I could sit in here and answer the phone, maybe get a head start on quarterly sales tax. I don't think I can stand to be at home."

"Hmmm." She opened a file drawer. "I was just going to call in the essential-oils order, but you can do it."

I settled myself at the desk with a sigh.

She pulled out a catalog and handed it to me. "You know, now that you've told me all this, I'll be seeing elves everywhere. Some guy came in earlier and I really wondered if he was one of your fey friends."

I dialed the vendor's number. "How come?"

"He had that same fair hair and drop-dead-gorgeous looks. And these little braids."

The phone clattered as I hung up abruptly. "In front of his ears?"

Lily nodded. "I thought it was kind of odd, considering he was wearing a suit. He looked a little surprised when I asked if he needed anything."

I dropped my head in my hands. "No. Not here!"

"What's wrong?" Lily squatted beside me.

"That was Fellseth!" I hissed. "He was surprised because he couldn't glamour you." I raised my head, then pasted a smile on my face as I noticed someone standing at the counter. "We have a customer."

Lily rang up seven kinds of incense and a sage bundle. "Don't set anything on fire," she joked to the departing customer. When the door closed, she darted back into the office. "That was *Fellseth*?"

"It had to be. Maybe he came to see if he could get information out of me." I chewed on my fingertip. "He doesn't know I'm on to him yet. What should I say if I run into him again?"

"Tell him you just came from the gun shop and you're on your way home for a little target practice."

The rest of the day passed without incident. At six o'clock, Lily handed me my jacket. "Go home. You look exhausted. And don't talk to any strange elves."

"I won't." I put my jacket on and got my purse. "Did he seem creepy to you?"

"No." Lily frowned. "That's what's so creepy. Now go home. And be careful."

Another day, and still no word from Galan. Driving home, I realized I needed a few things at the small grocery store in my neighborhood.

When I got there, the parking lot was crowded with dinner-hour shoppers. I took out my cell phone and called the house. Jed answered after the third ring.

"Hey. Did anyone call?" I asked.

"Nope. What's up?"

"Nothing. I just wondered. Do you need anything at the grocery store while I'm here?" I tugged a cart loose from the logjam outside and pushed it through the automatic doors.

"I could use a couple of jars of peanut butter," he said. "And none of that health-food crap with two inches of oil on top."

"You just stir it back in, Jed."

"That's too much like work."

"All right. I'll see you."

I must have thought that food would make me feel better, because I had enough groceries for a month by the time I checked out and headed toward my car.

I looped the plastic bags over my arms. Halfway

through the parking lot, one of them started to pinch, and I stopped to redistribute the weight.

"Can I help you with those?"

I almost gasped at the sound of Fellseth's voice. "Um, no. That's okay, I've got it." I picked up my pace slightly.

"I know you don't have any reason to want to see me, but I've missed talking to you." We reached my car. "Here, let me hold those while you get your car keys." He took two of the bags.

I unlocked the door, glancing surreptitiously around the parking lot. There were a lot of people around. Could he glamour all of them to stand by while he forced me into the car? I put my bags in the backseat.

"The city is considering selling my newly acquired land," he said, handing me another bag. "There's a public hearing on Monday."

I paused in the act of taking the groceries from him, not sure I had heard him correctly. "What?"

He smiled. "Ironic, isn't it? Apparently they've been eyeing that particular plot for years. It's just my luck that I stole property about to be put on the block."

"What are you going to do?" I knew I was doing a good job of seeming surprised. In truth, I was flabbergasted. Could he be telling the truth?

"I'll be at the hearing, trying to influence the city into leaving it alone. I wondered if you might come. They're allowing commentary from concerned citizens." He leaned into the car and deposited the last bag on the seat, then ducked back out, his lips curved slightly. "Or is it too much to hope that you might be concerned about me?"

"I'll definitely be there." That much was true, at least.

"I appreciate that," Fellseth said. "I'm headed over to

the city buildings right now, to see if there's anyone I can talk to. I know I shouldn't ask, but could I catch a ride as far as your house? It would be an easy walk from there."

Little alarm bells went off in my head. "I would, but I'm cooking dinner for a sick friend tonight and I'm already late." I slid into the driver's seat. "I'm really sorry, Fellseth."

"I understand completely. I'll see you at the hearing." He shut the car door for me and waved through the window.

I turned the key with unsteady fingers. As I drove away, I looked in the rearview mirror at his departing figure. "And what the hell is an elf doing at the *grocery store*?" I muttered. Not only that, but it was Saturday evening. Municipal offices were closed.

When I arrived home, I piled the bags on the kitchen counter and yelled, "Anybody home?"

The distinctive squeak of Jed's door sounded, and he came in a moment later. "Yo."

I handed him the grocery receipt. "You can figure out what you owe me."

"Cool." He dug through the bags and pulled out the peanut-butter jars, then turned one so he could read the label. "Made with real diglycerides—just like Mom's."

"Did anyone drop by or call for me while I was out?" I asked. *Preferably Galan and not Fellseth.*

"Nope. It's just been me and the cat. I let her out the back door a few minutes ago, so you can unpack the kitty kibble without any begging." He put some frozen vegetables away for me. "You want to watch a video tonight? Mike loaned me a couple."

It was tempting to stay home and veg out, but I knew

I needed to tell Kutara about Fellseth. "Maybe tomorrow. I've already got plans for this evening."

He slumped against the counter. "You're never home anymore."

"Did we get married when I wasn't looking?" I put the last of the food away and shut the cupboard with a bang. "You're usually out with your role-playing buddies anyway."

"James came down with mono, and tonight's game was canceled." He trailed behind me into the living room.

"Sorry. Another time." I pulled my long, black coat out of the closet and traded it for the light jacket I had been wearing. The sky had clouded over and it was getting cold. "I'll see you later. If Galan comes by, tell him to call me on my cell."

The car was still warm inside, but I turned up the heat anyway. I was pretty sure the library was open until nine o'clock some days, but was it tonight?

As I turned the corner at the end of the block, I passed a man with long, silvery hair walking along the sidewalk. I slowed, prepared to turn around if it was Galan. Then I realized that whoever it was wore a suit. I pushed down on the accelerator and my car shot up the hill. If Fellseth really was following me, Galan and Kutara were the only ones who could help.

The glassy bulk of the darkened library loomed over me like the set piece in a horror movie, obviously closed. "Shit." I turned my coat collar up and pulled a knit cap out of my pocket.

I decided to make a circuit around the building.

Galan might be spending the night inside the library. Maybe he or one of the other elves would see me through the windows.

To my left, Boulder Creek rushed alongside the concrete bike and pedestrian path—a favorite place for would-be rapists to hang out. It wasn't exactly safe to wander this area at night, but the thought of an ordinary mugger seemed positively tame compared to Fellseth.

I took a firm grip on my can of pepper spray and started with the side of the library that ran along the street. Most of the windows were on the second floor, so I moved back and cupped my hands around my mouth. "Hulloooo!" I called.

On the sidewalk, a couple waiting for the bus exchanged a look before turning away.

I made it around two sides and paused under the glassed-in walkway that spanned the creek. It connected the current library building to the original, which had been remodeled into a space for art shows and movies when the new addition was built. Across the water, the old building was lit up like a Christmas tree.

A dark figure came down the creek path toward me.

I pushed away from the wall and sprinted down the creek path, sucking cold air into my lungs.

"Hey! You got any change?" he called out.

"Sorry!" I responded automatically, pounding across a nearby footbridge toward the lighted building.

A poster-board sign on an easel stood outside the front door. I read it while my breathing slowed. NO ARCHITECTURAL ANDROGYNY—A STUDY OF PRONOUNCED GENDER IN BUILDING STYLES.

I pulled off my knit cap and went inside. A harpist played in a corner of the lobby while beyond her, people holding small plates and glasses of punch wandered past freestanding walls plastered with black-and-white photos.

I made a beeline for the refreshment table. I still hadn't eaten dinner. A little snack would calm me down before I walked back to the car. After that, I wasn't sure what to do.

The woman at the table poured punch into my glass and gave me a polite smile. "Are you familiar with Guy's work?"

"Um, no. I just kind of stumbled onto this show."

"It's quite fascinating. Guy's master's thesis at Naropa was on the power politics of window placement. He's on the library board now, and helped interview the architect for this extension." She pointed to a vigorous-looking man in his mid-forties, speaking to a small cluster of people. He had a beard, and wore wire-rimmed glasses and a corduroy jacket. "That's Guy over there, if you have any questions."

"Thanks." I took my glass and wandered toward the photos in an effort to look like I wasn't just mooching refreshments.

All the pictures featured buildings—cathedrals, office blocks, monuments, mansions, government buildings—there didn't seem to be any particular theme. Little cards were pinned under the photos, dense with text. I was too busy trying to balance my cookies and punch to read them.

A burst of laughter made me look up. Guy was holding court directly in front of me.

"And you understand, these are just things that have been *constructed*," he said. "Then there are the cathedral plans drawn up by Cardinal Bonivetti in the sixteenth century. The plans show one dome after another, with a row of *huge* freestanding columns in front, *thrusting* up between them. You should have *seen* the shape of the capitals. Well, I'm not surprised it was never built. I practically had to go lie down."

I looked at the photo closest to me, of a church with a large dome in the center. The words "erect" and "rounded" seemed to occur quite frequently in the text of the accompanying card. I wondered if Guy's formative sexual experiences had somehow involved masonry.

"Erin?"

I turned in a hurry and recognized the hippie kid who had smiled at me in the library. Now I had the chance to notice his blue, tilted eyes and black hair, as glossy as Kutara's. It was a good bet his ears were pointed under the black knit cap he wore. "If there's a secret handshake, I haven't learned it yet," I said.

He laughed. "That's okay. I'm Lenny."

What kind of elf name was that? I balanced my cookie plate on top of my cup and shook his hand. "Do you know where Kutara is?"

"Come on."

I followed as Lenny walked casually through the photo exhibit and past the auditorium. We entered an area that was obviously dedicated to administrative offices. He made a left down a hallway and knocked on the third door. It opened, and I quickly scanned the five or so elves assembled there. Galan wasn't one of them.

Lenny closed the door behind us. All the elves wore human clothes. Kutara sat at a desk in front of a computer monitor, wearing a rose-colored sweater set and looking like Hollywood's version of a Junior League member. She swiveled her chair to face us. "Erin! How did you find us?"

"I didn't." I threaded my way through the bystanders. "I looked for you at the library, then came over here by chance. Lenny found me." I gestured around me. "What is all this?"

"Nighttime headquarters. One of us was attacked."

"By Fellseth? Who was it?" Immediately my thoughts went to Galan. "Is he okay?"

"I'm fine," Lenny said.

"I'm glad. But why did Fellseth go after you?"

Kutara answered. "Lenny was assigned to watch you, and to make it fairly obvious that he was watching. That kept Fellseth occupied while I set up a network that was not so obvious, in order to monitor Fellseth's movements."

I tapped my chest. "*I* can tell you about his movements, at least for this evening. He came up to me outside the grocery store and asked for a ride. What I'd like to know is how he knew I'd be there. Could he be working with some other dark elf?"

Kutara thought for a moment. "To our knowledge, dark elves do not cooperate with each other. But Fellseth is extremely familiar with the human community. It's possible that he hired a private detective to track your movements."

"Oh, great." I sank onto the edge of the desk. "And get this—he brought up the hearing on Monday, and asked if I'd come and help protest the sale of Galan's land, which he fully admitted he stole."

Kutara's eyes narrowed. "What did you say?"

"That I'd be there." I spread my hands. "Basically, I pretended I didn't know anything but what he's told me.

I don't know if he bought it or not. To top it all off, I lied and said I wasn't going home, but I'm pretty sure I saw him headed for my house as I came over here."

Kutara stared into space, her graceful fingers tapping the arm of her chair. "I wish I knew his primary target— you or Galan."

"Where is Galan?" I asked, trying to sound casual and failing.

"Doing some work for me." Her fingers continued to tap.

"Did you pass on my message?"

"Yes."

"Did he say anything?" Whatever she said, I would not cry. All the elves were watching us.

Kutara's fingers stilled. "Don't you have some distant relatives you could visit? That would take at least one variable out of the equation."

I swallowed hard. Had Galan said nothing? Or had he said something terrible about me, and Kutara was saving my feelings? Did she even understand feelings? "I don't want to leave town. Someone might need me." I hoped it was true. "Any other ideas?"

"Be hard to find. Is it possible for you to stay with someone locally for a few days?"

"I guess could stay with Lily," I said, slumping. "Kutara, I know you're worried about Fellseth getting information out of me, but don't you think I should be a little more prepared? At this point, he could tell me something that would help you and I wouldn't know it."

To my surprise, Kutara leaned forward and took both my hands. "Erin, I've come to trust you in a way I never believed possible with a human. I'm asking you to trust me now."

I gripped her hands. "All right."

"Thank you." Kutara released me and sat back in her chair. "I can tell you that things are progressing. As far as we know, Fellseth is not bonded to Galan's land or any other, so he can't become incorporeal. And living with humans for so long may have dulled some of his instincts."

"So it's just a matter of tracking him down with enough elf power to overcome him?"

"Something like that. But I want to warn you—don't try to handle Fellseth yourself, even with the help of other humans. We're the only ones who can deal with him now. If you see him, just get away. We'll keep watch over you whenever possible, but it would better if you left town."

I shook my head. "And what if one of you needs more energy? Speaking of which, do you want me to meditate for you?" I looked more closely at her. "Although I have to say, you're looking pretty perky."

She smiled faintly. "Desperate times call for desperate measures. I am getting all the energy I need from another human."

I was mildly shocked. "Are you saying what I think you're saying?"

Kutara had already turned back to her computer screen. "Let's just say I've developed an interest in architecture."

I stood on the porch of Lily's house, light from the open door spilling onto me. "Can I stay the night? You can tell Jim I promise not to cry."

"Of course." She led the way inside. "What's going on?"

I dropped my voice. "Fellseth may be after me. Kutara has some of her people shadowing me, or I wouldn't risk coming here. Are you still sure you want me to stay?"

Lily took my coat from me and hung it in the hall closet. "Come on in."

Lily's husband waved as we walked through the living room, where he was watching TV. "Hey, Erin." He was a big man, with short brown hair and a large collection of flannel shirts. A computer programmer, he smiled more than he talked.

"Hey, Jim."

"Do you want something to drink?" Lily asked, leading the way to the kitchen.

"Just some water." I sat in one of the kitchen chairs and crossed my arms on the table. On the wall, a clock shaped like a black cat swung its tail back and forth.

"Have you heard from Galan?"

"No." I rested my chin on my arms and closed my eyes. "I don't think he wants to have anything to do with me."

"Oh, come on." Lily put two glasses of water on the table and pulled out a chair. "It's been what, two days? Give him some time."

"He'll have plenty of time. I'm not supposed to go home until after Monday. I guess I'll see him at the hearing." I laughed bitterly. "That won't be *too* awkward, seeing both him and Fellseth at the same time." I sat up and drank some water. "I think I'll go to a motel tomorrow. I just couldn't face trying to find one tonight."

"I don't suppose it would do any good to call the police if Fellseth came near you again."

I shook my head. "As soon as he got close enough to put a whammy on the cops, they'd handcuff *me*."

"I didn't tell Jim about all this, just so you know," Lily said.

"I don't blame you." I drained the water glass and put it down with a thunk. "Lily . . . in case I should disappear, find Kutara." I waved away her expression of alarm. "Just in case. She hangs out at the Internet terminals on the second floor of the library. Luckily, she won't be able to glamour you."

Lily made a noise of resignation. "What does she look like?"

"Gorgeous, with long, black hair and violet eyes. Looks at you like you're a bug." I smiled to myself. "Well, until she gets to know you. Then she looks at you like you're an interesting, possibly useful bug."

The next morning, I lay in bed staring at the unfamiliar ceiling and wondering if I should go back to sleep. The store didn't open till ten on Sunday. Someone tapped on my door. "I'm awake. Come on in."

Lily came in. "I went over and put a CLOSED FOR INVENTORY sign on the Rose's door, just in case Fellseth looks for you there." She sat on the edge of the bed. "I thought we could spend the morning putting files in order for the sale, then go to Denver, maybe hit the Natural History Museum."

"You are a lifesaver," I said. "I was just trying to think of ways to kill time without going to any of the usual places. Let me clean up and I'll be right out."

"I know you're a health nut, but do you eat cereal?" Lily got up and opened the door.

"I'll eat whatever you put in front of me. I'm in no position to be picky."

"Captain Crackle it is. With chocolate milk." She laughed at my horrified expression. "I'm joking. I think I have some muesli somewhere."

Two hours later, I pushed a stack of manila file folders across the breakfast table. "Here's this batch. Are there any more?"

"That's the last of them." Lily riffled through the folders and shook her head. "It's no wonder you cracked and took to making up stories about elf lovers. It's not natural to be so organized."

I laughed. "When I was a kid, I used to group the M & M's candies by color before eating them."

"That is so wrong." She lifted her head and yelled in the direction of the living room. "Jim! Do you want to go to the Natural History Museum with us?"

I heard a faint noise in response. "What does that mean?" I asked.

"It means yes, but we have to go to his favorite Thai place for lunch."

"Astonishing. How long have you two been together?"

"Long enough not to need consonants."

I managed to relax during the course of the day. The three of us ate lunch in Denver, then went to the museum and finished the day with an IMAX movie.

Lily drove home. As we entered Boulder, I looked in the backseat. Jim was asleep, his handsome face open-mouthed.

"Do you think it would be safe to stop by my house and get some clothes?" I asked quietly.

Lily looked over her shoulder to change lanes. "Sure. Jim is with us, after all."

"That doesn't count for much. After all, what do you think the chances are that both you and Jim are part elf?"

Lily thought for a moment. "How about you crouch down in the car and I'll go in for the clothes?"

"Okay. My underwear and socks are in the top dresser drawer. Grab some of those and whatever looks good from the closet and get out. And maybe you should put it all in a grocery bag so it's not obvious what you're carrying. There are some bags on top of the refrigerator."

Lily gave me a wry look. "Since you're micromanaging, what should I tell your housemate if I run into him?"

"If you see Jed, tell him I broke my leg and I'm at the hospital. Be rude if you have to, but don't stay longer than three or four minutes, okay?" We were at the end of my block now. I got out my house key to give her, then slid off the seat and wedged myself uncomfortably into the floor space.

I stayed down as she got out and locked the car doors behind her. In the backseat, Jim made a little grunting noise and slept on. I wondered what I would tell him if he woke up. Something about playing a trick on one of my housemates, maybe.

I looked at my watch, wishing I had thought to do that as soon as Lily got out of the car. How long since she'd been gone? Two minutes? Three? I kept my head resolutely down on my knees, trying to be as invisible as possible. "Come *on*, Lily," I muttered, then breathed a sigh of relief as I heard footsteps outside the car.

I raised my head. Fellseth stood outside the driver's side window, looking down at me. My mind kicked into high gear. *Maybe I could still bluff him.* I held a silencing finger to my lips, then pointed at the house and grinned.

Fellseth laughed, the sound coming through the car windows. There was movement in the backseat, and then Jim leaned forward and unlocked my door.

I shrieked and struggled upright from my cramped position, fumbling with the car's door handle. I had just managed to push it open when I felt a hand on my shoulder. Lunging forward, I half fell onto the sidewalk, then scrambled to my feet and began running toward the front door of the house, screaming "Lily!" at the top of my lungs.

I was halfway down the walk when someone tackled me from behind. The breath left my lungs in a huff as I hit the front lawn.

I lay there a moment, making feeble gasping noises. My lungs filled just before a hand covered my mouth. Twisting my head, I managed to get my captor's finger between my teeth, but stopped myself from biting down just in time. It was Jim who had tackled me—Jim who held me captive.

Fellseth stood over us, an expression of concern on his beautiful features. "Erin, calm down!" He put his hands out pleadingly. "I don't want to hurt you."

Jim got up and hauled me to my feet.

Every word of self-defense advice I had ever received came back to me. *Never let them take you to a second place.*

The front door to the house opened, and Fellseth

turned to look. I kicked my foot up and felt it connect with a satisfying thump.

Fellseth grabbed his crotch and crumpled to the ground.

Jim let go of me and looked from Fellseth's writhing body to Lily, who was charging down the walk with a frying pan in her hand. "What in the hell?"

"Get in the car!" I screamed at both of them.

Lily hesitated. "I left your clothes in the house."

"Get in the car *now*! As soon as he recovers, he'll have control of Jim again!" I grabbed Jim's hand and pulled him behind me.

Lily ran to her side of the car. I looked at the pan she still clutched, wishing I had the nerve to cave Fellseth's head in but knowing I didn't.

"What's going on?" Jim asked. "What just happened?"

Lily pushed him into the backseat and shut the door. "I'll tell you later," she gasped, throwing herself in the front and jamming the keys into the ignition. The car tore away from the curb, tires squealing as she accidentally popped the clutch.

I looked back. Fellseth was still down.

Jim took his cell phone out. "I'm calling 911."

I snatched it from him. He looked at me, outraged. "You don't want to do that, trust me," I said. "Trying to explain this might get you locked up. Think *X-Files*."

"Lily . . ." he began.

"She's right, honey," Lily said firmly. "I'll tell you all about it, but not right now."

Behind us, I saw Fellseth get to his feet before we turned the corner. "It's not safe for me to stay with you now," I said. "I'll get my car and leave."

"What if he shows up at our house?" Lily looked at me in the rearview mirror, her eyes wide and frightened. "Do you know if he has a car?"

"I have no idea." I looked at my watch. "I think the library closes at six today. After you drop me at my car, go there and try to find Kutara. Ask her what to do. If Fellseth does manage to track you down, tell him I left town and didn't say where I was going."

"*Are* you leaving town?"

"Yes," I lied. "But I'm not going to my parents'. He might find me there." I slumped in my seat and thought of options while Lily tried to explain to her husband that he had just had his mind taken over by an elf.

"So I'm not going crazy?" Jim asked anxiously. "It seemed like the best idea in the world to go after Erin, and then I kind of woke up and realized there was no good reason for it." He put his hand on my shoulder. "I'm really sorry."

"You couldn't help yourself." I turned and gave him a tight smile. "Just be glad I realized it was you before I bit your finger off at the first knuckle. Hand me my coat, will you?"

My car was parked on the street in front of Lily and Jim's house. "Go see Kutara *now*," I told Lily. "Boulder Public Library. Second floor, at the Internet terminals. Long dark hair, violet eyes, gorgeous. Go." I slammed the door and they accelerated down the street.

I got in my own car and threw my purse and coat into the passenger seat. How could I make Fellseth think I had left town? There was a bus terminal with a Park & Ride on Baseline Road. I could leave my car in the garage and take a cab to a hotel. If Fellseth did find my car, he would think I had taken a bus to the airport.

Since it was Sunday, the multilevel parking garage was almost empty. I drove to the second floor and pulled into a space near the stairs, then ran in a low crouch to the front of the building, so I could keep watch on the street below.

After calling information and the cab company on my cell, I realized that I had spent the last of my cash on lunch. I found an ATM and withdrew the three-hundred-dollar maximum, then sat in a corner behind a potted fig to wait for the taxi. A long ten minutes later, I saw the yellow cab approaching.

The driver got out. He was young, with short, dread-locked hair sticking out in all directions.

I trotted over to him as soon as he entered the lobby. "I'm kind of hiding from someone," I said tensely. "So I'm going to duck down in the backseat. Keep an eye out for anyone following us, especially a really good-looking man with silvery hair and little braids in front of his ears." I stopped him as we reached the front door. "Are you okay with this?"

"Yeah, man. I'm cool." He shoved his hands in the pockets of his jeans and leaned toward me as we walked. "Is it drugs?" he whispered.

"No." I pushed open the door and followed him to the cab, keeping his body between me and the street. "It's . . . a subpoena. Take me to the Saint Julien hotel at Ninth and Canyon."

He opened the door for me and got in himself. "If it's a subpoena, shouldn't you be *leaving* town?"

"I did leave town. Now I'm here." I lay down on the backseat and pulled my coat over me. "Take your time, and don't talk to me unless you think someone's following us."

He started the car. "Can I sing along to the radio?"

"Yeah, I guess."

"I'm just checking."

I walked quickly into the hotel lobby and approached the reservation desk.

"I'd like a room for two nights."

The reservationist tapped the touch screen of her monitor. "That'll be $514.75," she said, sliding a form and a pen across the counter.

I gulped and took out my wallet. "Let's just make it one night, then."

Tap, tap. "Your new total is $253.13."

I handed her the money.

"May I see an ID?" she asked.

"I paid with cash. What do you need ID for?"

"I'm sorry, but that's hotel policy."

I snapped my wallet shut so my driver's license wouldn't show. "My ID was stolen. I don't get a replacement for another week. Sorry."

"Do you have a credit card?"

"If I had a credit card, I would have paid with that," I said pointedly. We stared at each other for a long moment.

She broke first. "Here's your keycard, ma'am," she said, handing it to me with a tiny sigh. "Checkout is at noon. Have a pleasant stay."

I took the card. "I'll do my best."

* * *

My room had a view of the Flatirons, but I pulled the curtains anyway, then tossed my coat and purse on one bed and sat down gingerly on the other. My left shoulder and hip felt bruised from where Jim had tackled me.

I looked around the beautifully antiseptic room, feeling very alone. "I wish Fellseth had never been born," I groaned, and was struck by the irony of the statement. If Fellseth had never been born, I would never have met Galan.

"All right, but why can't Fellseth go away *now*?" I asked the room in general. The Boulder phone book was in the top drawer of the desk. I looked up the Boulder Public Library and followed the automated menu.

"Reference, may I help you?" a friendly voice asked.

"I hope so." I let all the exhaustion I felt come through in my voice. "I need to get hold of my aunt. We've had a family emergency and I think she's doing research at your computer terminals. Her name is Kutara. Could you see if she's there and bring her to the phone?"

"Certainly."

I paged through the hotel directory while I waited, looking for the room-service menu. When I ran across a listing of executive services, I paused. The hotel featured a twenty-four-hour business center.

Kutara's dry voice came down the line. "Which niece is this?"

"It's Erin. Did Lily and Jim find you?"

"My long-lost cousins? Yes. I seem to be awash in relatives today. Give me your number and I'll call you back. I want to discuss this family emergency a little more privately."

I gave Kutara my hotel and room numbers, then sat down and looked at the directory more closely while I waited. When the phone rang, I snatched it up. "Where are you now?"

"Still in the library, but not for long," Kutara said, her voice echoing strangely. "I'm glad to see my cell phone gets reception even in the ladies' restroom."

"You have a cell phone?" Somehow that didn't seem very elflike.

"With enough time and a convenient attitude toward theft, much can be accomplished. You may as well have the number." She rattled it off and I wrote it down on the hotel notepad.

"What did you tell Lily and Jim?"

"I told them not to worry. Fellseth doesn't have any reason to hurt them. As long as they're not with you, they won't be in his way."

"So now I'm a danger to my friends. Wonderful."

"Where is your hotel?" Kutara asked.

"Ninth and Canyon—just a couple blocks from the city buildings. If I had a window on the right side, I could probably also see the library from here. I don't suppose you want to tell me what your plans are?"

"You suppose correctly. One thing I can say is that we will be on the move from now on, so if you need to reach us, call this number—but only if it's an emergency."

"Are you doing anything to publicize the hearing tomorrow?"

"I considered it, but our resources in time and expertise don't stretch to that."

"Mine do, and there's a business center here in the

hotel. If I make up a bunch of flyers in the next few hours, could you send someone to pick them up? You could give them out to every hiker and dog walker on that trail tomorrow morning."

"Too bad you're not an elf," Kutara said. "You'd make an excellent assistant."

I was suddenly extremely glad I wasn't an elf.

"Someone will be over in about two hours. Will that work?" she asked.

"Yeah. Send them up to my room."

"You want seventy-five of these on Radioactive Pumpkin paper, right?" the woman at the business center asked.

"That's right." As the neon orange paper shot out of the copier, I heard my stomach growl.

Once I was back in my room, I ordered a grilled-cheese sandwich and a salad from room service.

The sound of knocking woke me sometime later. I got up, heart pounding, and peered through the peephole, relieved to see a young man with a tray and not an angry dark elf. I paid him, then turned on the television and retired to bed with the food. Room service still made me feel luxurious, even if I was a temporary refugee.

I had finished dinner and was channel surfing when someone knocked on the door. I tiptoed to the door and peered through the peephole, then stubbed my finger trying to unlock the deadbolt. "Galan!"

He wore a navy windbreaker over jeans and a T-shirt, and his silvery hair spilled out the back of a black baseball cap in a shimmering ponytail. They were ordinary clothes, but he looked amazing to me. I had only a moment to notice all this before he had scooped me into his arms and was kissing me.

We stumbled inside my room, still kissing, and he pushed the door shut with a couple of distracted kicks. Finally we paused for breath.

"I've been going crazy with worry," Galan said. "Kutara said she might as well send me to pick up the flyers, since I wasn't good for anything else. Are you all right?"

"I'm fine now that you're here." I studied his face. There were blue circles under his eyes, and shadows hollowed his cheeks. "You look tired," I said, leading him to the bed.

He lay down and sighed wearily. "I don't want to say anything against Kutara, but the words *slave driver* occasionally come to mind. I've been doing a lot of work on very little reserves."

The television was still on. I turned it off and nestled beneath his arm. "Do you forgive me? Are we all right?"

"Of course I forgive you." He took a moment to kiss me. "It was a shock, finding out about my land—that's all."

I shook my head, still astonished. "I was so sure that developing open space wasn't possible, but I wasn't taking the glamour thing into account. It's amazing that elves don't rule the world, frankly."

He sighed. "It's a problem of manpower, which is also why Fellseth got so close to you." He stroked my upper arm. "Tell me what happened."

Describing Fellseth's attack was almost more unpleasant than the actual experience. At the time, I had been fueled by adrenaline—acting rather than thinking. With Galan's worried face opposite me, I realized for the first time how much danger I had been in.

Galan's expression was grim when I finished. "I wish we had a better understanding of his motives."

"Do you think he planned to use me as bait?"

He squinted in thought. "Possibly. He might have thought Kutara wouldn't help a human and I would show up by myself—an easier target. There are only a handful of us against him, you realize. We outnumber him, but not hugely. And while we have to worry about communication and getting together, he has no one to worry about but himself. He can move much quicker."

I chewed on my lip. "With only a few of you against him, it would make a big difference if he got rid of even one of you."

He nodded. "But he might have attacked you for less strategic reasons. You're the one who saved me, and then you helped me fight him. It could be that he wants you just so he can make you pay."

I pressed myself against Galan, disturbed by the thought of such twisted motives. Fellseth had called me adorable and petted me. Was that simply foreplay to catching and hurting me? Psychopaths were the stuff of nightmares and horror movies. I had never thought I would encounter one.

"I need you," I said suddenly, tugging at the shoulder of Galan's windbreaker. "Now."

We undressed as quickly as possible. When he pushed me onto the bed, I wrapped myself around him as though we'd been apart for months instead of days. Before this separation, I had gotten somewhat used to the sensation of our bond. Now it sizzled between us, erotic yet alien.

Galan placed his hands on either side of my face as

he slid inside me. "I'm not going to wait to say this. I love you."

"I love you, too," I gasped, moving with him. Tears leaked from the corners of my eyes. I had expected to feel secure when hearing Galan say those words for the first time, but now the circumstances hinted at loss, and I was afraid.

The beeping of the hotel's clock radio made me flail at the red-lit numbers on the bedside table. Galan had asked me to set an alarm for eleven P.M. I felt him stir, and his open mouth found mine in the dark. I pressed myself against him, suddenly overwhelmed by a need to be close. "I wish this were all over."

"So do I," he said, cradling the back of my head with one hand.

I turned on the bedside lamp. "What happens after Fellseth is caught?"

"I don't know." He pulled me back to lie with my head on his chest. "Kutara has brought elves together in a way that's never been done before. If Fellseth isn't killed outright, she's made arrangements for a court, to decide what should be done with him. After this is over, she may travel to other communities who need help with dark elves. It's possible she may ask me to go as well."

"And would you?"

He kissed my forehead. "I don't know. It's been a kind of awakening, for all of us. The idea that we can do something instead of just surrendering. Working together like humans do. I wish the circumstances were different, but it's been rewarding." He sighed. "I should go."

"When will I see you again?" I sat up and watched him dress.

"I'm not sure. Everything is up in the air until we catch Fellseth."

"What should I do in the meantime?"

He pulled on tennis shoes, fastening the Velcro strips a little uncertainly. "If it were up to me, I'd keep watch over you, but Kutara has a plan that requires every one of us. The one thing we're sure of is that he'll be at the hearing, which is at three o'clock." He straightened and gripped my upper arms. "It would be best if you could stay here until the hearing starts. Then go somewhere random and far away."

"How far?"

"South Dakota. We're pretty sure he's never been there."

I gave a huff of surprise, but fear made me acquiesce. "Okay."

He stood and wound his hair around his head, then jammed the cap over it.

I got up, still naked, and hugged him. "Be careful."

He leaned down to kiss me, stroking my back down to my bottom and up again. "You, too. With any luck, this will be over tomorrow and we'll get back to normal."

He donned a pair of orange-tinted sunglasses. "Whatever that is."

After Galan had pulled the door shut behind him, I turned the deadbolt, then burrowed under the covers, searching for his warmth in the sheets. I was reaching out to turn off the light when I heard a knock. I got up and peered through the peephole before opening the door and letting him in again.

"Forgot the flyers," he said.

Chapter Eight

After a full eight hours' sleep, my natural optimism had reasserted itself. Yes, Fellseth had attacked me, but I had fended him off and gotten away. My bruises barely ached, Kutara had a plan, and most importantly, Galan loved me. He had made that quite clear last night.

With any luck, Fellseth would be out of the picture by this afternoon. I made a vow not to let overconfidence make me careless, then called room service and ordered an enormous brunch to hold me until a late dinner.

After eating and showering, I decided to stay in the room until someone kicked me out. I ironed my clothes, then turned on the TV.

I was immersed in a soap opera when a woman's accented voice called, "Maid service!" and the door opened.

"This is amazing," I said, waving at the TV. "Jack and Sally were trying to get together when I was in college, and they still haven't managed it."

The maid, a squat Hispanic woman in a white uniform, glanced at the TV screen. "They did, but Sally had another man's baby and Jack left her for her twin sister. Now she's trying to get him back." She gave me a pointed look. "Checkout is at noon. If you want to stay longer, you have to pay for another night."

"Couldn't you clean around me?" I smiled ingratiatingly. "I'm really into this show."

"Sorry."

"How 'bout if I help you clean, then leave afterward?"

"No."

"What if I gave you a twenty to let me stay?"

"Someone's checking in at three o'clock." She disappeared into the bathroom and came out with the dirty towels. "Why don't you just find a cheaper hotel?"

"Because I don't want to leave the building." I took a deep breath. "Somewhere out there, a man is trying to kidnap me."

This statement did not have the desired effect. "So call the police," she said, dumping the dirty towels into her cart.

"They can't help me. It's a long story."

"So is Jack and Sally's, and I don't have time to listen to that, either." She turned off the TV, then put her hands on her hips. "Go sit in the business center. If anyone hassles you, say you're waiting for somebody."

I got up. "That's a good idea. I appreciate it."

The maid tilted her head. "Really? I don't see no tip."

I went to the business center, lighter in spirit and also by five dollars. I should have thought of going there myself, since I needed to research a route to South Dakota and someplace to stay once I got there. It might also be a good idea to rent a car, in case Fellseth walked into a police station and glamoured someone into keeping an eye out for my license plate.

At a little before three o'clock, I was gathering my printed maps and various hotel and car confirmations when my cell phone rang. I hesitated on seeing the unfamiliar number, but answered anyway.

"This is a call from the Boulder County Correctional Facility," an automated voice intoned. "You will be charged one dollar and seventy-five cents to accept. Press One to accept."

"What on earth?" I pressed One, then got up and went into the hall.

"Erin? It's Jed. Where have you been?"

I ignored his question. "You're in *jail*? What happened?"

"I was fixing myself a sandwich when I saw this guy outside the house, kind of looking around, right?"

"What guy? What did he look like?"

"Good-looking in a pretty kind of way. Blond hair, with little braids in front. Anyway, he starts messing with the windows, so I call 911, and the cops came on the double."

"Good," I said with relief.

"No, *not* good!" Jed's voice rose. "I went outside when the cops came, and somehow they got the idea that this *other* guy made the call, and they hauled *my* ass away for breaking and entering!"

"You're kidding! You live there—didn't you show them some ID or something?"

"I didn't have my wallet on me, and they wouldn't let me go back in the house to get it. Plus, this other dude was wearing a suit, and I just look like me."

I put my hand to my forehead and closed my eyes. "I don't believe this."

"Listen, you've got to come to the jail. They're saying it's going to cost two hundred and fifty bucks to bail me out unless you come down, show them you live there and vouch for me. Then I'm off the hook."

"Jed, this really isn't a good time. Couldn't someone else get your wallet and bring it over?"

He dropped his voice. "I never got around to updating the address on my driver's license, okay? Erin, they put me in a holding cell, and the dudes I'm with are *not nice*. I really need to get out of here."

I thought for a moment. The city council meeting would start in a few minutes, so it was time for me to leave here anyway. And if I left Jed in jail, who would feed Kitty Girl?

"All right." I was jittering one leg in my eagerness to get gone. "I assume it's that big place with all the razor wire, out on Airport Road?"

"That's the one." He sounded relieved. "I really appreciate this."

"That's okay. I'll be there soon, okay? Bye." I thought for a moment. The rental-car office was close to the Park & Ride. The quickest thing would be to take a cab to the jail, pick up Jed, then go to the Park & Ride. He could drive my car home, dropping me off at the rental place on the way.

I scrolled up the cell phone's list of numbers until I found the one belonging to the cab company.

"Boulder Cab."

I didn't want to explain to yet another driver why I was crouching in the back of his cab, so I said, "Hi. I got a ride in one of your cabs yesterday, and I wondered if I could get the same driver. He was young, wearing a bowling shirt and jeans, and he had dreadlocked hair."

"You the gal on the lam?"

I closed my eyes. "That's me. Could you send him to the Saint Julien? Tell him to come in the lobby and get me. I don't want to wait outside."

"Will do. He'll be there in about fifteen minutes."

After hanging up, I decided to get some sort of disguise, just in case Fellseth wasn't at the council meeting, or had someone looking for me. The hotel's gift shop sold a headscarf printed with columbines, Colorado's state flower. That would do.

I went into the public restroom on the ground floor and tied the scarf around my head, covering as much of my hair as possible and tucking my bangs in for good measure.

When I was satisfied, I put on my sunglasses and examined the effect in the mirror. It was very Jackie O.

When the cab driver arrived, I sidled out from behind a potted palm and gave him a furtive wave.

He grinned at me, his hands in his pockets. "This just gets better and better. How about if you hunch over, and I'll pretend you're an old lady and I'm helping you out?"

"Sure. Why not." I pulled the scarf forward around my face and let him take my arm.

"This probably isn't necessary," I whispered as we shuffled along. "There's no one out here but the valet-parking guy."

"Might be a disguise," he whispered back.

"I don't think so. He looks about nineteen."

My driver nodded wisely. "All the narcs look young these days, so they can go undercover in high schools."

"I told you, it isn't drugs."

After we were in the cab, I leaned forward. "We're going to the Boulder County Jail."

"You gonna turn yourself in?"

"*No.*" I hunched in my seat, trying to look aged. "I'm bailing out a friend, sort of." The driver shook his head. "What?" I demanded.

"I'm just amazed, that's all. You look so straight."

"Thanks. It opens up a lot of career opportunities."

I sat up a little as we drove down Valmont and out of central Boulder. The jail was near a small airport. It seemed both cruel and ironic that prisoners saw small planes flying in and out all day, going places they couldn't.

We had driven perhaps a third of the way up the winding road to the jail when I saw a figure walking on the dry grass verge. "Stop! I think that's him."

The taxi pulled over and I threw open the door. "Jed!"

"Hey! Where's your car, and what's with the getup?" He gestured at my scarf and sunglasses.

"I'll tell you later. Get in."

"Where to now?" asked the driver.

"The Park and Ride on Baseline." I turned to Jed. "They let you go?"

"Yeah. When that guy with the hair first showed up, I couldn't find the portable, so I called 911 from my cell phone. Somebody finally got the bright idea to check the record and they found my phone number, which is billed to the house. The whole thing was just screwy."

"Definitely." I thought for a moment. "I have a favor to ask. That guy who was poking around the house is kind of dangerous."

"Holy shit! Have you called the police?" He frowned. "Although I really can't recommend that."

"The police can't do anything about it. But I left my car in the garage at the bus station on Baseline, and I wonder if you'd be willing to drive it home for me. Leave it there, then take Kitty Girl and stay with someone for a few days."

"Where are you going to be?" he asked.

"I can't tell you. If I'm lucky, I'll be back right away. I'll call you when I am."

"Man, this is some serious shit." He shook his head. "Is there anything else I can do?"

"No." I gave him a quick hug. "You're a good friend, Jed."

The digital tones of the Star Wars theme filled the car. Jed pulled out his cell phone and answered it. "No, I haven't picked up the beer—I've been in *jail*. Seriously, you won't believe the shit that's been happening. Not right now. I've got to go over to the bus station and pick up Erin's car at the Park and Ride. Not too long— it's over on Baseline. Hey, how do you feel about cats?" He paused. "All right, later."

"Who was that?" I asked, wishing he hadn't said anything about me.

"One of my gaming buddies." He leaned back against the seat and punched up a number on his phone. "One good thing came out of being in the lockup. I think I got some ideas for new characters." He dialed another number on his phone. "Hey, Sean? Do you still have that pit bull, or did your girlfriend take it when she left?"

While Jed tried to find a place to stay, I sat back and planned what I would grab from home.

I was still thinking when the cab driver pulled up to the front of the Park & Ride.

The cabbie handed me the change while Jed got out of the cab. "Tell me I didn't just aid and abet a jail break."

"You didn't." I passed him a hefty tip.

"Now that you've got your man, are you out of the woods?" he asked.

I adjusted the headscarf around my face. "He's not my man. And no, I'm not out yet."

"Sorry to hear that." He grinned at me. "You sure you don't want to tell me what's really going on? I'd love to know."

"It's all about elves and real estate."

He shook his head sadly. As I slid out of the cab, he called to Jed through the window. "Get your friend to take her medication, man."

I hustled Jed through the empty lobby of the Park & Ride and opened the door to the stairwell, taking a moment to look inside before starting up the stairs.

We were almost at the second level when the sound of a door opening below us echoed off the concrete walls. I looked back at Jed and mouthed, "Come on!"

"What? I'm coming," he said, continuing at the same deliberate pace.

I heard footsteps on the stairs as I reached the landing. The door to level two and my car was a mere five feet away. I reached back and pulled on Jed's arm. "Come *on*!" I whispered.

The footsteps from below grew closer. Jed's other hand came up and closed around my forearm.

"Is that you, Erin?" Fellseth's voice drifted up the stairwell, eerily calm. He came into view a moment later. "I thought I might find you here."

I twisted my arm in Jed's grip. "Let go!"

He stood there, expressionless.

Fellseth leaned against the wall of the landing below, looking elegant and controlled in his charcoal suit. "He's quite strong, isn't he? That was a bonus."

I changed tactics and tried to come down the stairs toward Fellseth, but Jed was like an anchor attached to my arm.

"You won't catch me that way again," Fellseth said, moving back a few steps. "I can still feel that kick when I run."

I gave a shriek of rage and turned on Jed, kicking his legs, but he wrapped his arms around me and bore me to the cement floor, pinning me with his weight.

Behind me, I felt Fellseth kneel across my calves. I screamed louder, filling the stairwell with a cacophony of sound. Something closed around one ankle and then the other. Fellseth had manacled my legs.

"And now the wrists, I think," he said. "Jed, if you could turn her over."

Jed rolled me over. As his arm neared my face, I bit it, hoping the pain would break Fellseth's glamour on him. I ground my teeth together through his jacket, feeling sick as I did so. He didn't seem to notice.

"Trust me, that's not having any effect," Fellseth said, as he handcuffed my wrists. "If it makes you feel any better, it's a bit of work to glamour him. I think he really cares for you."

I let my head fall back and gasped.

"I have to say, those role-playing games are a hoot. I didn't even have to change my name, although I did make them see me as a pimply eighteen-year-old."

"That was you on the phone!"

"And me who put Jed in jail. Time to stop talking

now." Fellseth took a generous cotton handkerchief out of one pocket and wadded it up.

"Put this in her mouth, please," he instructed Jed. "I don't want to lose any fingers."

I kept my tongue forward, but otherwise lay still as Jed stuffed the fabric in my mouth. There didn't seem much point in struggling at the moment, and I wanted to save my strength. I looked pleadingly at my house-mate, hoping to break the spell, but he worked like a robot.

Fellseth took a small roll of duct tape out of his pocket and tore off a four-inch length, obviously with the intention of putting it across my mouth. Fear of suffocation closed over me like a wave. I thrashed and whimpered, breathing heavily through the handkerchief that filled my mouth.

"Sinus trouble?" Fellseth asked. I nodded violently, and he applied the tape diagonally across my mouth, leaving the corners free. He picked up my purse from where it had fallen, then peered out the door. "Let's go, Jed."

They picked me up, one on each end. I thrashed about, but there was no one to see. Within minutes they had deposited me in the trunk of a late-model Acura parked next to my car. Jed kept hold of my legs while Fellseth held my handcuffed wrists still.

I lay on a folded blanket, which cushioned me somewhat. The trunk smelled of burnt metal. I tilted my head down and was just able to see a steel loop welded to the inside of the car.

Fellseth took two climbing carabiners out of his pocket and handed one to Jed. Then he clipped my wrist chain to the loop while Jed hooked my ankles to something out of sight.

The amount of preparation that had gone into this operation scared me more than anything.

"I never needed a car before this," Fellseth said conversationally. "You're turning into an expensive project, but I fully expect you to be worth it." He leaned over, as if to kiss my forehead, but something in my eyes must have warned him.

"I suppose I won't risk a broken nose," he said, drawing back. "Honestly, you make it so difficult to be nice." He shut the trunk, plunging me into darkness.

Soon the motion of the car suggested we were in traffic. I wondered if I could lift my head and bang my forehead against the inside of the trunk lid. Maybe the noise would attract the attention of a nearby car. A brief and painful experiment convinced me that I would have to concuss myself to make even a tiny thump that could be heard from the outside.

Claustrophobia overwhelmed me then, and the conviction that I was going to suffocate. I spent the rest of the ride trying to relax and calm my breathing. Even so, I felt a little light-headed when the car finally stopped and the trunk opened.

I kept my eyes shut, feigning unconsciousness. *If I could just get Fellseth to let down his guard . . .*

Gentle fingers explored the lump on my forehead. "My brave, stupid girl," Fellseth said. It was all I could do to keep from opening my eyes and glaring at him.

Someone unclipped my hands and feet from the trunk. "Take her shoulders," Fellseth said.

I felt myself lifted into the air and heard the crunch of gravel under the men's feet. I also heard something that might be a nearby creek, and the soughing of wind through trees, accompanied by the crisp smell of evergreens.

It occurred to me that knowing my location would be a good thing. I opened my eyes just in time to see the front of a stylish, cedar-sided house as Jed and Fellseth carried me over the threshold.

We passed through an expensive-looking living room and a kitchen. The counters were notably lacking in appliances. I turned my head back and forth, trying to see something through a window, but they were all covered by miniblinds or curtains.

My feet dipped suddenly, and I realized they were taking me down stairs. If Fellseth fell and was knocked unconscious, I could have Jed unlock me. I waited a moment, then kicked my feet out as hard as I could.

There was a clatter as Fellseth stumbled and dropped me. My legs hit the edge of a step with a painful jar. Above me, I saw Jed's face looked confused for just a moment before it took on its shuttered look again.

"That was a very good effort, my dear," Fellseth said from below me. His voice was tight, as if he were in pain. "I can see I'll have to use the handrail." He picked my feet up and tucked them under one arm. I bucked and kicked, but we made it to the bottom of the stairs without a second fall.

Our destination was a comfortable-looking basement den, complete with overstuffed couch, wet bar, and TV. A metal-framed desk chair was incongruously bolted to one wall. Jed held me in it while Fellseth connected my handcuffed wrists to a chain looped through one of the arms, and my manacled ankles to the central post of the base.

When I was fastened to his satisfaction, he carefully untaped my mouth and had Jed remove the gag.

Standing well away from me, Fellseth rubbed one hip gingerly. "What a lot of work you are."

I glared at him. "Aren't you going to say, *No one can hear you scream*?"

"I should think that was obvious, since you're no longer gagged, but if it pleases you, I'll be happy to say it."

"Don't bother," I snapped.

"All right." He walked over to the couch and sat down heavily. Jed went and stood in front of the room's closed door. There was silence for a moment.

"What is it you want?" I asked, wishing my voice was less shaky. "Maybe we can come to a solution that will work for both of us."

Fellseth leaned forward and rested his elbows on his knees. Steepling his hands, he regarded me over them. "I see we're already to the bargaining stage. Unfortunately, you'll just have to trust that I have your best interests at heart."

He put two fingers in front of his lips and smiled behind them. "Don't you have any questions? Outraged remarks? Threats of vengeance?"

I glared at him. If I didn't say anything, maybe he would fill in the blanks. He did seem to love the sound of his own voice.

"No?" He waited a moment, then stood. "All right. I'll just go up and supervise while Jed makes you some dinner."

"Wait!" I yelled.

He turned.

"I need to go to the bathroom." I managed to look sheepish.

"Ah. Fortunately, you won't be a prisoner for long, so

we won't have to deal with any arrangements that will embarrass us both or leave me with broken bones."

"What are you talking about?"

He sighed. "Just hold it."

When Jed opened the door, I screamed, "Fire!" as loudly as I could.

Fellseth shook his head wearily and pulled the door shut behind him.

Chapter Nine

I tried a variety of ways to get loose while I was alone, failing miserably and managing to bruise, cut, and chafe myself in the process. Finally I gave up and leaned my head against the wall behind me.

What did Fellseth want? The answer could be so many things. He might want me dead, or Galan dead, or both of us plus every other elf in the universe dead. Maybe he wanted to mate me with Jed and create a race of human slaves. Who knew? Closing my eyes, I resisted the urge to cry.

At least he didn't seem inclined to hurt me. But what did he mean by saying I wouldn't be a prisoner for long? As I contemplated the possibilities, a single tear trickled down my cheek.

The door opened, and a savory smell preceded the arrival of my captors. Jed came in, carrying a large plate with a bowl and a sliced grilled-cheese sandwich.

"I understand from Jed that this is one of your favorite childhood dishes," Fellseth said. He carried a small tray table, which he set up next to my lap.

Jed arranged the dishes on the tray. The bowl contained tomato soup.

"Why are you being so nice to me?" I asked, my voice low. "Is this some kind of hostage brainwashing thing? Because if it is, it won't work. I took psychology in college."

"I'm being nice because I have the utmost respect and affection for you. I always have."

I jerked violently on my chains, knocking against the table and causing soup to slosh out of the bowl. "Is *this* respect?"

At a nod from Fellseth, Jed tidied the dishes, then tore the sandwich into bite-sized pieces.

"The handcuffs are an unfortunate necessity," Fellseth said. "You'll understand later. Or rather, you won't, because you won't remember it."

"Why, because I'll be dead?"

"No." Fellseth got up and began to pace the room. "Because you'll be mine. We're going to be married."

I gave a bark of laughter. "Married?" My voice became mocking. "That's your great plan? To marry me? Is that supposed to flush Galan out so you can get his land? Because I can tell you right now—"

"I don't give a damn about Galan's land!" Fellseth snapped. "Or Galan himself, except that he keeps getting in the way. It's *you* I've wanted, ever since the day I saw you raising energy for Galan."

"He would have beaten you without me," I shot back, my chin up.

He came and leaned down in front of me. "No, Erin. He wouldn't. Do you have any idea what you are?"

"Yes!" I screamed in his face. "I'm the woman who won't be helping you!"

"You *will* help me," he said. "You'll be my own personal power source, with no choice in the matter. For a while now, I've wanted to team up with other dark elves. Now I'll be able to offer them something." He smiled. "As for the marriage part, I think a wife makes a businessman look so much more trustworthy."

I lunged to the limit of my chains, goaded beyond reason. The small table fell over, food and dishes making a mess on the carpeted floor.

"I can see you're not in the mood to eat right now," he said heavily. "Come on, Jed."

I shrieked in frustrated rage.

Fellseth looked back. "Try to calm down. It hurts me to see you injure yourself."

As soon as he was gone, I looked wildly around the room, searching for the remotest chance of escape. I knew now what Fellseth was talking about when he said I wouldn't have any choice. There was only one way he could hope to glamour me—by killing Galan and breaking my bond with him. Then I would be a zombie like Jed, but for the rest of my life.

"Think, Erin. *Think.*" I looked at the grilled-cheese sandwich on the floor. If I could somehow get to it, could I make my wrists oily enough to slip them out of the handcuffs? A quick wriggle told me that my wrists were already too swollen, even if I could somehow get hold of the sandwich.

I twisted in the chair, examining all the connections. I had seen that the chair was bolted to the wall right through its back. A padlocked chain looped through one of the arms and my handcuff chain. Another chain connected my cuffed ankles to the wheeled base.

Holding on to one of the chair's arms with both

hands, I managed to push my butt off the seat and ease over the chair's arm. Hunched and hobbled, I shuffled around until I faced the wall.

The chair's heavy back was flush with the wall, so there was no chance of digging out the drywall around the bolts. Maybe they didn't go into a stud? Even if they did, it might be possible to shear them off with repeated pressure from the side.

Balancing carefully, I gripped the chair's arm and gave it a sharp push. It didn't budge. The chains allowed me to move maybe six inches away from the chair, if I hunched even more. I shuffled as far as I could to one side and swung my hip against the chair's arm.

My feet slipped out from under me and I fell sideways. "Goddamn it!" Blood ran freely down my forearm from a cut on one wrist. It wouldn't help Galan for me to be in the hospital. Or would it?

If I were hurt badly, would it break Fellseth's concentration enough to free Jed? If I had to be taken to the hospital, surely there would be too many people for Fellseth to glamour all at once?

I was shaking now, but I managed to stand again. The chair would break or I would. Either way, I might be able to keep Fellseth from killing Galan. Taking careful aim, I gave the chair another sideways blow with my hip. This time I didn't fall.

I hit it again, and now there was definitely some play between the bolt and the chair back. Panting with exertion and excitement, I took aim again, only to hear footsteps coming down the basement stairs.

By the time Fellseth came through the door, Jed trailing behind him, I was seated, my lacerated wrist tucked against my lap. I didn't want them to know I was hurt—not yet.

"What was all that noise?" Fellseth asked, looking around.

"Am I keeping the neighbors awake?" I said nastily. "Maybe you should call the cops."

Fellseth gave Jed a little push. Jed came forward and began examining my bonds. When he came to my injured wrist, he paused.

"It's not important, Jed," I muttered, scowling at his blank face. "I'm still fastened up."

"Is everything still secure?" Fellseth asked.

"Yes," Jed said. I gave a small sigh of relief. "But she's bleeding," he continued.

"It's nothing." I managed to sound bored.

Fellseth came over. "Show me." Jed turned my wrist over. The cut oozed blood, and Fellseth shook his head at the sight. "I'll be happy when Galan is dead."

"What is *wrong* with you?" I shouted. "Don't you know that sooner or later, someone is going to kill *you*, because you're such a horrible person?"

"No one's managed it yet." Fellseth walked to the wet bar and reached under the counter. "Here," he said, producing a roll of duct tape and handing it to Jed. "We're going to have to figure out some way to keep her still."

"I promise to do what you want if you leave Galan alone," I babbled, as Jed approached with the tape. "I'll meditate for you and be nice all the time, if you'll just stop hurting people."

Fellseth laughed. "And then you'll push me in front of a bus. My way is better. You'll be very happy, I promise."

Jed unrolled the end of the tape and tried to wind it around my arms, but I dodged it as much as the chains would allow. The tape stuck to itself, and Jed paused uncertainly.

"That's the problem with servants who can't think for themselves," Fellseth grumbled. "The least little complication stymies them."

He took the tape from Jed. "You hold her and I'll wrap." Jed pulled my wrists together and held them against one of the chair's arms.

"Ow, ow, ow! The cuffs are cutting me!" I stopped struggling and let my head fall back.

"Hold her forearms instead," Fellseth instructed. "And get her wrists and the cuffs out past the chair arm." He stood at arm's length as he began wrapping, but moved closer as he became more immersed in the task.

I stayed still, barely breathing, until Fellseth leaned forward to tear the roll free, and then I struck out with my forehead. He jerked away, but my brow bone caught him on the mouth.

Fellseth raised a cautious finger to his lips and brought it away bloody. He turned to Jed. "Is this the part where I call her a spitfire?" Jed stared back impassively, and Fellseth rolled his eyes before turning to me. "You used to like me, you know."

"I never liked you. I just felt sorry for you."

He didn't bother to reply, but had Jed finish up my arms and then directed him to help tape my legs to the chair leg.

I decided to talk to Jed while he worked. Maybe I could get through to him, or at least make it more of an effort for Fellseth to keep him docile. But did it really matter if I tired Fellseth? He had said he would "have

Galan killed." That sounded as though he wouldn't be doing it himself.

"Hey, Jed, remember when we took that road trip to Las Vegas and sang karaoke with the Elvis impersonator? That was so much fun." I laughed lightly.

There was a flash of something in Jed's eyes, but it disappeared almost instantly.

"Stop it, Erin, or I'll gag you again," Fellseth said severely. He continued to wind tape around my legs while Jed held them still.

I caught Jed's eye and dimpled at him. "You know, I've always had a crush on you. I was thinking of coming to your bedroom one night to seduce you." This time I felt his grip loosen momentarily.

"I did warn you." Fellseth stood and tore off a length of tape. I turned my head back and forth, evading him. "Hold her head," he instructed.

Jed's fingers kept slipping in my hair, but eventually Fellseth managed to tape the lower part of my face. I began banging my head against the wall behind me.

Fellseth's cell phone rang, punctuating my thuds. "Oh, for fuck's sake," he growled, pulling a length of tape off his fingers and throwing it to the ground. He pulled the phone out of his jacket pocket and checked the number before answering. "This is Seth."

I stopped banging and screamed behind the tape. Fellseth covered his other ear with one hand as he spoke into the phone. "I *told* you what to do. Follow him out after the hearing and do the job." He turned slightly away from me. "What do you mean, he's not there?"

I stopped screaming and listened.

"Hold on, let me look." Fellseth grabbed a remote off

the bar and switched on the TV, then flicked through the channels until he found what he wanted.

I turned my head so I could see. Apparently Boulder City Council meetings were broadcast live on a local cable channel. The screen showed a large, horseshoe-shaped desk with each of the council members seated behind a small microphone. I listened as a council member droned on about zoning regulations.

"Come on, come on . . ." Fellseth grated. The camera cut to the auditorium and panned slowly across the audience. A nondescript man in a jacket and glasses leaned against the back wall, holding a cell phone to his ear. Gooseflesh broke out on my arms. *This must be the man hired to kill Galan.*

The camera continued to pan while the speaker pointed out additional staff members in the front row of the audience. I glanced at Fellseth. His fingers turned white as he gripped the cell phone.

The camera completed its sweep of the audience, showing the auditorium in its entirety. The tape across my mouth pulled tight as I grinned under it. Galan wasn't at the City Council meeting, waiting to be assassinated by some hired killer. Lenny wasn't there. And perhaps most telling of all, Kutara wasn't there. I chuckled behind the tape that covered my mouth, breath coming out of my nostrils in little huffs.

Fellseth snarled a word in a language I didn't understand and spoke into the cell phone. "Stay where you are, in case he shows up. I'll contact you later." He snapped the phone shut and shoved it in a pocket before grabbing Jed by the arm and hauling him out of the room.

They were back in moments, each with a kitchen knife. I felt a moment of terror, but they used the knives to cut through the duct tape that held my arms and legs to the chair.

When they finished cutting through the tape, Fellseth took a key ring out of his pocket and handed it to Jed, who unlocked the padlock on the chain that held my wrists to the chair. With a glance at me, Fellseth took the knives they had used to cut me free and put them somewhere behind the wet bar.

While he was doing that, Jed bent to unlock the padlock near my feet. Seeing my chance, I leaned forward and swung my joined fists as hard as I could, hitting him solidly on the temple. He crumpled to the floor without a word.

Fellseth whipped around. I leaned over and yanked on the loose chain by my feet, intending to use it as a weapon, but it tangled in the chair's legs. Before I could pull it free, Fellseth crossed the room and grabbed the chain linking my wrist cuffs, jerking me to my feet. The pain in my wrists made me gasp.

"Nice try."

I changed tactics and went limp, dropping to the floor. He didn't say a word, just dragged me rapidly toward the stairs. I fumbled for the cuff's chain with my fingers, trying to keep the metal from biting into my cut wrists.

He was hideously strong. As he dragged my prone body up the stairs, I lifted my feet and tried to jam them under the handrail, but he pulled hard and my shoes skidded uselessly across the wall.

He had gotten me into the kitchen when I heard a car pull onto the gravel drive outside. I screamed. The tape across my mouth muffled the sound, but I made up for it by swinging my feet from side to side, banging them against the cupboards as Fellseth towed me across the floor.

We reached the living room and he headed toward a sliding glass door in the rear wall. I glimpsed a deck outside, and past that, the glint of something that might be water in the woods beyond.

A sudden noise at the front of the house made Fellseth drop me with a thud and turn, just as the front door burst open. Galan plunged through, followed closely by Kutara, Lenny, and three other elves.

I flattened myself on the floor as Fellseth flung his hand up and fired a crackling burst of energy at the pursuing elves. It arced across the room like red lightning, headed for Galan and Kutara. They each raised one arm and the burst bounced aside, crawling across the metal base of a floor lamp before it dissipated. From behind them, an answering blue burst lanced across the room toward Fellseth.

I pushed myself across the floor on my back, away from Fellseth. As I squirmed past the sliding glass door, more energy hit it, and I felt the hair on my arms rise as blue sparks crackled down the metal frame.

I had moved past the glass doors when Galan fired a blast that made Fellseth stumble backward.

Fellseth returned fire, then slid the door open and leapt through.

The pursuing elves poured through the door like a pack of hounds and were lost to view within moments. I lay back and listened, but couldn't hear anything over my own panting breaths. Elves were apparently silent when they hunted.

It occurred to me that Fellseth might circle back to the front of the house to reclaim me. I put my back to the wall and pushed myself upright, then hobbled out of the living room and down a hall. When I came to a bedroom, I went in and slumped onto the floor in the space between the bed and the closet.

Tape still covered the lower half of my face. I raised my hands and worked it loose, one painful piece at a time. I was down to the last two strips when I heard Galan's voice.

"Erin! Erin, where are you?"

I gave up on the tape and banged my hands against the closet door beside me. Galan was by my side in a moment, lifting me to sit on the edge of the bed.

"Oh, sweetheart," he murmured, examining my bloodied wrists. Placing his fingers over the keyhole on the first cuff, he concentrated a moment. I heard the latch click open.

Kutara came in and stood beside him. As he bent to work on the second cuff, she reached over and pulled the tape off my mouth with a quick jerk.

"Aaaah!" I wailed, putting my free hand up to my burning skin.

"Trust me, it's better to do it fast." She flicked the tape onto the floor.

"Like you would know!" I yelled at her.

She shrugged and left.

Galan tossed the handcuffs away and gathered me gently into his arms. "I was so afraid," he whispered in my ear.

I buried my smarting face in his neck and allowed myself to cry a little as he rocked me back and forth. "How did you find me?"

He knelt to unlock the cuffs around my ankles. "Kutara managed to find out where Fellseth lived not long after I left you this morning. I took up watch on the road to his house. When I saw him drive toward home with Jed in the car, I called Kutara. She rounded up the troops and here we all are."

"What took you so long?" I pulled down my socks and examined the red marks on my skin.

"Logistics. Transportation." Galan sat on the bed and put his arms around me again. "I'm so grateful you're safe."

I leaned my forehead against his. "Did you catch him?"

He sighed. "No. Lenny is out there reading the trail right now. Everyone else is with him."

"Oh, God," I groaned. "So this still isn't over."

"Not quite, but at least you're okay. That's the important thing." He raised a hand and caressed the side of my face.

I sat up, determined to tell him everything. "I wasn't the one in danger! Well, not of being killed, anyway. He just wanted to make me a slave, and he hired some hit man to go after you."

"Wait until Kutara can hear it, too," he said. "She'll need to know."

We returned to the living room and found Kutara settling a groggy-looking Jed onto the leather couch.

"Oh, man," he groaned, catching sight of me. "Did you *really* kick me in the head?"

I hesitated. As much as I hated to see Jed hypnotized anymore, how in the world were we going to explain everything? I looked at the two elves for help.

Apparently Kutara felt Jed had been glamoured enough. "Drugs," she said briskly. "You were under the influence of powerful drugs."

My mouth dropped open. It was a brilliant lie.

Jed seemed skeptical. "What about the fight? I made it as far as the kitchen, but there was all this crazy electricity shooting around." He waved his arms. "Pow! Zzzt!"

Kutara nodded sagely. "Psychotropic side effects."

"Who are you, anyway?" Jed asked.

"Federal Agent Kutara."

He squinted up at her. "Where's your badge?"

"Federal *undercover* Agent Kutara. My team has been on the trail of these psychotropic drug people for six months. You should be fine in a day or so."

Jed rubbed his temple, wincing as he did so. "So it wasn't electricity? What were you really fighting with?"

Kutara sighed. "Guns. Regular guns."

Jed looked at her pocketless skirt and blouse, plus the tiny purse she carried. "Where's your gun now?"

Kutara frowned. "As an undercover agent, naturally I don't keep my weapon where it's obvious. Now, if you'll excuse me . . ."

She started to turn away, but Jed caught hold of her sleeve. "Wait a minute. If there was shooting, shouldn't stuff be broken?" He looked blearily around the living room. "There should be bullet holes or something."

"You can't see the bullet holes?" Kutara stared down at him, a pitying expression on her face. "Your recovery is clearly going to take longer than we thought."

Jed looked as though he might cry. "Oh, *man!*"

"Now if you'll excuse me." She went outside to join the other elves, who were visible through the glass doors.

While Kutara talked with her troops, I checked Jed's

injuries, and Galan searched the cabinets for first-aid supplies to treat my cuts.

"I couldn't find even a Band-Aid," he said, joining me in the kitchen. "I'm afraid we'll have to tend to you a little later."

I had already rinsed my wrists and dried them gingerly with paper towels. "Do you think it's safe to take certain people home?" I tipped my head subtly toward Jed. "And if so, how are we getting there?"

"I'll ask." He went into the back yard, leaving the sliding glass doors open. I heard Kutara giving instructions and spare phone batteries to the elves. Then she and Galan spoke for several minutes, their voices too low to hear.

Galan and Kutara came back inside, while the others disappeared into the woods behind the house.

"Aren't the others coming?" I asked.

Kutara shook her head. "One will watch the house. The rest have other destinations. You're coming with Galan and me." She headed for the front door.

"Come on, Jed," I said, patting his shoulder. "Looks like the government is giving us a ride."

He stood, then leaned close so he could whisper in my ear. "Can I ride up front with Agent Kutara?"

"I think that's a fine idea."

Kutara led us outside to a battered beige hatchback with a bumper sticker that read, "Architects have the largest erections."

Jed's brow furrowed. "That's your *car*?"

"Good, isn't it?" Kutara opened the driver's side door. "You wouldn't believe what's under the hood."

"Can I see?" he asked eagerly.

"No."

Once seated in the back with Galan, I whispered, "Does this car belong to that guy from the library, the one with the photo exhibit?"

"You mean Guy? That guy?"

"Whatever. The one with the building fetish."

"That's the one."

As Kutara backed carefully out of the drive, I rested my head on Galan's shoulder. "Should we be letting her drive?"

"Guy's been giving her lessons. She's a very quick learner."

"I see that. First the Internet, then cell phones, now driving. Let's hope she never takes it into her head to run for mayor."

"I think she's shooting for something else," Galan murmured. "I saw her looking at the FBI online recruitment page the other day."

I snuggled closer to Galan, ignoring my various bruises. In the front seat, Jed chattered away to Kutara, receiving monosyllabic answers in reply. "Did all of you ride up in this thing?" I asked Galan.

"I volunteered to ride in the hatchback part, and you have no idea how uncomfortable it was."

"Oh, I might." I looked out the window as the dirt road we were on joined a paved, two-lane highway. "I can't believe I was right off Boulder Canyon. I must have driven up this road a thousand times."

"Where are we going?" Jed asked.

Instead of answering, Kutara waved a vague hand in his direction. Jed's head dropped, his chin coming to rest on his chest.

I reached alongside the door and reclined the passenger seat so he wouldn't get a stiff neck.

"He'll need to sleep a fair amount after being under Fellseth's control," Kutara said. "Now, what happened up there?"

I told both elves what had taken place. When I finished, Kutara said, "We'll go to Guy's house. We should be safe there until we hear more from Lenny."

"What about the hearing? Do you need to go back to it?"

Kutara shook her head. "It turns out that this is the first of several. We still have time to save Galan's land."

"Good." I slumped against the seat back. "Do you have any idea where Fellseth went?"

"Not yet, but we'll find him."

Chapter Ten

Guy's house was in Martin Acres, a subdivision on the south end of Boulder. The house looked as though it had originally been a seventies-era split-level, but it had been heavily modified and now resembled one of Frank Lloyd Wright's designs.

After pulling into the driveway, Kutara rested a hand on Jed's shoulder.

He raised his head. "Where are we? Is this where I get debriefed?"

"You've already been debriefed. Don't you remember?"

He blinked at her. "I thought that was a dream. It didn't seem like you were dressed for debriefing."

Kutara gave him a stern look. "I'm afraid you're still having blackouts from the drugs. Later I'll give you something that will help." She opened her car door. "Come on. This is the safe house."

"I sure hope so," I muttered, getting out of the car and following Kutara inside.

On the upper level, Guy's living room was a marvel of blond wood, dark blue upholstery, and steel accents.

Black-and-white photos of buildings covered the walls. I clasped my hands behind my back to hide my wrists.

Guy was in the eat-in kitchen, setting the table. He came over and kissed Kutara on the cheek. "Darling! I would have cooked more if I'd known we were having company."

"They can order pizza," she said. "I'm sorry I didn't phone ahead. These are my friends. Their house was robbed and vandalized this afternoon, and I was hoping you might be able to put them up for the night."

Guy's expression changed to deep concern. "That's awful! Of course you can stay."

"We really appreciate this," I began, but Kutara cut me off.

"They're a little too traumatized to feel social right now," she said, herding Jed toward the stairs. "I'll go down to the guest room and get them settled."

Once in the lower level, she took us to a pretty room with a double bed and a folding foam love seat, which she quickly converted into a twin bed for Jed.

"I guess it really is a safe house if even your host doesn't know what's going on," Jed remarked. "Or was that some kind of code you were using?"

"Very clever, Jed. It *was* code," Kutara said. "So it's better if you don't try to talk to him. You never know what you might be saying."

She patted the unfolded love seat. "Could you come here a moment? I'd like to run a quick test to see how you're recovering."

Jed sat down. Kutara looked in his face and his eyes promptly closed. She caught his shoulders and lowered him to a horizontal position, then put her hands on either side of his head, her expression intent.

"Is there something wrong with him?" I asked, going over to watch. Galan joined me.

"His head is a little bruised inside," Kutara said, closing her eyes and moving her hands gently over Jed's temples. "That must have been some kick."

"I didn't kick him in the head," I said, a little defensively.

Galan took my hand. "I didn't think you would."

"I hit him with my fists," I admitted.

"Well, that is *completely* different," Kutara said.

I made a face behind her back. "I'm going to find a restroom. I'll be back in a minute."

When I returned, Kutara was sitting on the double bed, talking to Galan.

"Is Jed all right?" I asked.

"He'll be fine now. We'll leave him to sleep," she said.

"Kutara is a healer," Galan said, sounding prouder than I would have liked.

"I gathered that." I sat down on his other side, as close as possible. "Is that common among elves?"

"Not very," Kutara said. "And it was only recently that I discovered the capability. It was something I read on the Internet that allowed me to develop the skill. Bruises and burns are easiest. I don't believe I could fix a broken bone yet." She got up and stood in front of me. "Let's tend to your injuries, Erin."

"It would take too long to work on everything." I held out my wrists. "These are the worst."

I held very still as Kutara moved her fingers from one area to another. My skin tingled slightly as she worked, but at first it didn't seem as though anything else was happening. Then I looked back at one of the first cuts she had touched. The area was knitted together with pink flesh, as though several days had already passed.

"That's amazing," I breathed. "Does it take a lot of energy? Do you need me to meditate for you afterward?"

"It does take a fair amount of energy, but I'm getting plenty these days."

I cleared my throat. "Um, speaking of Guy, did you use any glamour when you asked him if we could stay? And does he know what you are?"

"No to both questions. He would have asked you to stay without any prompting from me. He's a very generous person."

I couldn't have stopped my next words for a million dollars. "Kind of ironic that you're seeing an architect. Tell me, has he built anything lately? Maybe a nice block of condos up in the mountains?"

Kutara gave me a bland look. "He is primarily a scholar, but I'm thinking of encouraging him to run for city office. He seems to prefer renovation and remodeling to unchecked expansion."

"Very wise," Galan said smoothly.

Now that the pain in my wrists was gone, some of my other aches became more noticeable. I ignored them. God forbid Kutara should think I was a wimp. "When will we know about Fellseth?" I asked.

"When I hear something, I'll let you know. It's too soon to interrupt Lenny's concentration by calling him." Kutara pointed to a pine desk in the corner of the room. "Phone book and phone—for ordering pizza. The phone number for this house is on the handset. They can get the address from that."

"Will we see you before tomorrow?" Galan asked.

"I'll bring your pizza down when it comes. We'll talk then." She left the room, closing the door behind her.

"Alone at last," Galan said, putting his arms around me.

I glanced over at the unconscious Jed and laughed. "Sort of."

Galan leaned down and pulled me close, but when he kissed me, I felt his lips curve against mine in a smile.

I pulled back. "Is something funny?"

"Your face is a little sticky from the tape, and it's still kind of red." He put his hands on either side of my face and examined me. "You've also got a pink mark on your eyebrow."

"I head-butted Fellseth. Busted his lip," I said proudly. "And I've got a bruise on the back of my leg from when I kicked him going down the stairs, and he dropped me." Disengaging myself, I leaned over Jed and rolled up his sleeve. "I forgot to tell Kutara about this."

Galan looked at the angry mark and frowned. "Did Fellseth *burn* Jed?"

"Um, no. I bit him."

He backed away from me. "Do I dare take you to bed?"

I took a step toward him. "I dare you not to."

"I'm sure you wouldn't *want* to hurt me," he said, holding up his hands in mock defense, "but you might do it absentmindedly, as a sort of habit."

I laughed. "To be honest, right now all I want to do is order pizza and take a nap, so you're safe."

"Oh." He looked disappointed. "I was willing to take a little risk."

* * *

I don't know how long I napped. I woke up slightly when I felt Galan leave the bed. I woke up fully when the smell of pizza permeated the room.

Kutara set the pizza box on the room's small desk and flipped up the lid.

"Have you heard anything?" Galan asked.

"I'm going to call Lenny now. It's been long enough." She sat on the bed and opened her cell phone.

In addition to pizza, Kutara had brought paper plates, napkins, and some juice boxes. I pulled out the desk chair and helped myself to food.

Jed slept on, but he murmured something and smacked his lips.

Kutara had been on the phone for a few minutes when her voice rose. I looked up, cheese hanging down my chin.

"Then spread out more," she said. "Follow it upstream as well as down. There must be a trace somewhere." She hung up, frowning.

Galan sat on the bed, looking grim. "He's still on the loose?"

Kutara let out a frustrated breath. "He could just as easily be dead." In response to my questioning look, she said, "Fellseth left a very clear trail, which led to the edge of the creek and then stopped. We checked the land. He hasn't merged with it, so where is he?" She got up and began to pace.

I licked sauce off my lip. "Could he have merged with the creek and got away?"

Galan shook his head slightly.

"Of course, I don't know much about elves," I said.

"At this point, your guess is as good as ours. To our knowledge, no elf has ever merged with a body of water. But we don't *know* it's impossible. I just wouldn't try it unless I had a death wish."

"So if Fellseth did try it, he's probably dead?" I asked.

"Probably. Maybe." Kutara stopped pacing and fiddled with her phone. "Lenny and I checked for traces of his energy in the stream. There was nothing."

"But water moves. Wouldn't any trace have been washed away?" I asked, eager for Fellseth to be gone.

Galan looked thoughtful. "We hit him pretty hard before he left the house. Maybe he was so weak he didn't leave a trace."

"Another possibility." Kutara sighed. "I would be happier with proof."

I closed the pizza box, my appetite suddenly gone. "So we don't know anything. It might be safe for Jed and me to go home, and it might not. Fellseth might have dissolved into fish food, or he could be waiting outside the door."

"Succinctly put." Kutara went to the door, her usually erect spine a little bowed. "We'll spend the night here. I may know more by morning. If not . . ." She shrugged.

"Someone needs to let Kitty Girl in the house and make sure she has plenty of food and water," I remembered.

Kutara sighed. "We'll see to that as well." She paused on her way out the door. "Galan, I realize you want to spend time with Erin, but I would appreciate your input after she is asleep. I'll be in the living room." She gestured toward Jed, who stirred. "Speaking of feeding animals, could someone give that creature some pizza?"

* * *

Fellseth was choking me. I tried to pull his hands away from my throat, but my fingers fumbled ineffectually, bending like rubber.

Across the room, a flight of stairs led down. I saw Galan running up them, coming to save me, but then my viewpoint skewed and I realized the stairs were crumbling, or getting longer, or breaking loose and tipping him off. He would never reach me.

I woke, breathing hard and unable to move for a few seconds. Galan wasn't in the bed. In the dim light from the window well, I found the door and crept upstairs until I could hear Galan and Kutara talking, their voices low.

"The important thing is to keep Erin safe," Galan said.

"I agree, but how?" Kutara sounded worried. "Till now, Fellseth was simply a dark elf—a relatively known quantity. If he has succeeded in merging with water—"

"It's not possible," Galan insisted.

"It shouldn't be possible for your bond with Erin to exist, and yet it does. Who knows what is possible anymore?"

I crept back to bed. The uncertainty in Kutara's voice scared me more than anything. I burrowed under the covers and rolled into a ball, unable to get warm.

When I woke again it was morning, and Galan was beside me in the bed. I rolled toward him.

He pulled me close and settled my head on his chest. "How did you sleep?"

"I had a nightmare."

His arm tightened around me. "Why didn't you tell me?"

"I am telling you. You weren't in the bed when I had it." I tilted my head so I could look at him. "Did you and Kutara come up with a plan?"

His expression went from tender to serious. "As much of a plan as we could, considering the circumstances."

I waited a moment. "Well, what is it?"

"Let's go upstairs." He gave me a smacking kiss on the forehead. "Guy has gone to some meeting, and we have the house to ourselves. You can eat while we tell you."

We got up and dressed. Jed was still asleep, his stubbled face peaceful as I tiptoed past.

Kutara sat at a small table in the kitchen, staring into space and tapping her fingers on the glass tabletop. "Good. You're up. There is some fruit on the counter."

"That is *not* gonna be enough."

She found me some cereal and I poured a heaping bowlful. "Any more news?" I asked, sitting down at the table.

"Nothing useful."

"So what's the plan?"

Galan rubbed his chin in a nervous gesture. "We don't think it's safe to go home until we know more. In fact, we still think it would be a good idea to leave town—Jed, too."

I swallowed, scratchy cereal traveling painfully down my throat. "For how long? And what about the store? Lily and I still have a closing date."

"The Celadon Rose is closed. Lily and Jim are gone," Kutara said flatly.

"Gone? What do you mean, *gone*?"

Galan put a reassuring hand on my shoulder. "There's a sign on the shop's door saying that Lily is dealing with a family emergency and will return soon."

"What if Fellseth has them? We've got to find out!"

"He doesn't," Kutara said. "I had her number on my phone, so I called. They are fine, and have not seen Fellseth." She retrieved her purse from the counter. "As for you and Jed, I did worry about the financial cost of traveling. Luckily, that is not a problem." She took a folded piece of paper from her purse and handed it to me.

"What's this?"

"One of Fellseth's bank statements."

I unfolded it and sucked in a breath at the balance. I didn't know how Fellseth made his money, but he was very good at it.

"You'll be fully reimbursed for any expenses relating to your travel." Kutara took the statement back and snapped her purse closed. "I understand Cancun is a pleasant destination this time of year."

I looked at Galan. "South Dakota isn't far enough away anymore?"

"Wouldn't you rather go to Cancun?"

I could tell he was trying to be reassuring, so I did my best to look on the bright side. An all-expenses-paid trip to Mexico. Galan wearing swim trunks and holding my hand as we strolled along a beach. "Do elves tan?" I asked him.

"Um, just you and Jed are leaving. I'm staying here."

"Are you crazy? *You're* the one Fellseth wants to kill!"

"Only so he could acquire you," Kutara said calmly. "Lenny is putting all of his energies into finding Fellseth. I need Galan here to help with other things."

"And how long is this situation going to last?" I managed to ask.

"I'm not sure yet. I think one-way tickets would be best."

I pushed back my chair. "Galan, can I talk to you in private?"

I walked through the house to a room that was obviously Guy's home office. Blueprints covered an oak desk, and books on architecture filled two floor-to-ceiling bookshelves. I perched on the edge of the desk and clasped my hands to still their trembling.

Galan came in and shut the door.

"I don't like this. We don't know if Fellseth is dead or still after us. We don't know *anything*."

Galan took my hands and held them. "I'm sure Kutara will figure out what to do."

"Will she? For all we know, Fellseth has taken over her body and is just biding his time before he comes after us with an axe!"

Galan shook his head, one corner of his mouth turned up. "Erin . . ."

"No, I'm serious!" My voice rose. "Kutara said it herself—we don't *know* what's impossible. There aren't any rules, or logic . . . How can you stand to live like this?"

He pulled me upright and wrapped his arms around me. "I can stand it because I have you."

Tears welled up in my eyes.

"I love you." He bent his head and kissed me softly.

"I love you, too," I said, but the words didn't make me feel magically better. Or maybe magic itself had betrayed me—magic in the hands of Fellseth, who might or might not be alive.

* * *

When Galan and I returned to the kitchen, Lenny was seated next to Kutara at the table.

"Well?" Kutara asked me.

I slumped into a chair. "Sunny Mexico, here I come."

"Good. Lenny has brought your purse and your passport."

I took them from his outstretched hands. Had anyone ever doubted I would take this trip? "I know my purse was at Fellseth's, but how did you get my passport?"

Lenny grinned. "It was filed under *P* in your desk at home. I let your cat in, by the way."

"Thank you. She'll still need big bowls of food and water, okay?" I turned to Kutara. "I don't have any clothes and neither does Jed."

"The stores in Cancun take credit cards and U.S. currency." She pointed to my purse. "I've given you some cash. We'll pay off your charge account from here."

"What about Jed?"

"There should be enough for both of you, within reason."

I sat, feeling numb, while the bustle of preparations washed over me. Lenny made hotel reservations and bought plane tickets using Guy's computer and Internet connection, while Kutara called for a car to pick us up.

Finally she went down and woke Jed. After bringing him to the kitchen, she pushed an apple into his hand. "Eat this and listen very closely. There are some loose ends to tie up in this case. In the meantime, you and Erin will go to Cancun at our expense. Don't tell anyone the real reason you are there. Act like brother and sister. Do you understand?"

Jed nodded vigorously, his mouth full of apple, his eyes shining with excitement.

Kutara went on. "I can't guarantee that your current job will remain secure while you're gone, but I can tell your employer that you've been in an accident. That may help when you return."

Jed waved a hand. "I can get another job if I have to."

Lenny stood at the window, keeping watch. He let the curtain drop and turned. "Time to go."

Outside, a long limousine idled at the curb, its windows tinted black. The elves bundled us in quickly, but only Galan got into the car with us. Kutara and Lenny went back to the house, looking around them in all directions.

Jed threw himself against the leather upholstery and breathed in the luxurious smell. "Score!"

"Uh-huh." I rummaged in the limo's various drawers and cabinets until I found a pair of headphones, then plugged them into a jack in the console and handed them to Jed. "Would you mind if Galan and I had a private conversation?"

"*No problema.* That's Spanish for *go right ahead.*" He put the headphones on and fiddled with the controls.

I turned to Galan. "This is all happening so fast. We didn't even get to . . . *you know* . . . have a real goodbye."

Galan glanced at Jed, whose eyes were closed as he nodded to something that thumped. "I suppose he might not notice."

"I'm serious," I said, gripping his hand. "What if something happens and we never see each other again?"

He kissed me. "Erin, stop. You're going to go to Mexico and have a nice time while we find out what happened to Fellseth. Then you'll come back."

I rested my head on his chest and listened to his heartbeat a moment before speaking. "I've never been afraid for my life before. Not to mention your life, and Jed's. Also Lily's and Jim's."

"Things got worse than we expected, I know." He kissed the top of my head.

"This must be what it feels like to be married to a police officer." I turned my face into Galan's chest, wanting to block out the world.

We stayed like that for a while. When I saw trees passing by the limo's windows, I sat up, feeling panicky. "This is too early for DIA! Where is he taking us?"

"It's okay," Galan said. "We're not going to Denver International Airport. Kutara thought it would be better to fly out of Rocky Mountain Metro Airport. We're booking you on a charter plane to Utah, and you'll fly to Cancun from there."

"Oh." I saw Jed watching me with concern, his headphones still on. I must have looked like I was freaking out.

Galan reached into his vest and pulled out a piece of paper. "This has all of our cell-phone numbers. Kutara asked that you not call unless Fellseth shows up on your doorstep."

I must not have looked happy at the idea, because he hurried on. "I opened a new e-mail account for you." He tapped the paper. "This has our e-mail addresses. We'll keep in touch every day, all right?"

"All right." I put the papers in my purse.

The limo pulled up to the side of the terminal, and we got out. As we walked inside, Galan leaned over and whispered, "I'll pay for your tickets with cash, and then I'll glamour security to delete your records. Fellseth won't be able to track you."

Rocky Mountain Metro was a corporate airport. Jed and I showed our driver's licenses and walked through the metal detector, I showed the contents of my purse, and we were free to go to gate A-2, where a fiftysomething pilot waited for us. He wore khaki pants and a windbreaker, and introduced himself as Captain Bradshaw.

Jed looked him up and down. "They don't make you wear a uniform?"

Captain Bradshaw's smile creased his weathered face. "I own the plane, so this is the uniform."

Jed nodded, grinning. "Right on!"

Galan handed our pilot a stack of twenties. "There's a little extra there."

Captain Bradshaw didn't raise an eyebrow—just counted the money rapidly and stowed it in an inner pocket of his jacket. "Thanks. You two ready to go?"

Galan motioned for Jed to follow him. "Erin will be there in a minute."

Bradshaw ushered Jed toward a door. "C'mon, kid. I'll show you the cockpit."

"Can I steer the plane a little?" Jed asked.

"You got a pilot's license?"

"No."

"Then I don't think so."

Galan turned me to face him. "I have to get back. Come on, kiss me."

I kissed Galan with all the love and fear that I felt, standing on tiptoe to press against him and pull his head down. He wrapped his arms around me, lifting me slightly.

"I don't want to go," I murmured against his mouth, when his arms loosened around me.

He kissed each corner of my lips, then pressed his face against my neck and breathed deeply. "I wish you didn't have to, but it's safest." He straightened and pushed my hair back on one side, his face luminous after our kiss. "Fellseth wants you. With you out of the picture, he's bound to come sniffing around us, trying to find out where you've gone. And then we'll get him."

"Bring me back as soon as you can, okay?" I grabbed his arm as he pulled back.

"Absolutely. Now go on."

I walked toward the door, resisting the urge to run back to Galan as he stood, tall and broad shouldered, with one hand raised.

Captain Bradshaw stood at the bottom of the stairs that led to the plane. "Watch your step."

I gripped the railing with one hand and pressed the other to my stomach. "I don't suppose you have any food on board, do you?"

"Sure do."

I ducked through the doorway and saw a built-in seating area with a small refrigerator. "I can't tell you how happy that makes me."

"As soon as we get airborne and level, you can help yourself."

I took the plush seat next to Jed's and belted myself in. Captain Bradshaw opened communications with the tower, and the plane started with a roar.

I looked out the window and felt tears threaten as the terminal building disappeared behind the plane's wing.

Jed patted my arm sympathetically. "Did you know Galan was in the Bureau when you met him?"

"Woo hoo!" Jed hooted, some six hours later. "We're in Mexico!"

We were in a taxi, headed for our hotel. The tropical

heat was intense, even in April. Humidity frizzed my hair and swelled my sinuses.

Jed already looked every inch the tourist, since he wore T-shirts year-round. As for me, I thought I might expire as the sun beat through the cab windows on my long-sleeved black shirt.

I stared out the window. Between the two lanes of the road, the median was decorated with one long hedgerow, clipped in a continuous, undulating wave. Every bush in the city had been clipped into the shape of waves, birds, even a chair.

"Can you believe this?" Jed asked.

"No," I grunted. "I can't."

I doubted he even heard me as our cab stopped to let a bevy of women in sarongs stroll by.

The light changed, and Jed turned back to me. "Do you think the Bureau will get upset if I buy some drinks with their money?"

I shook my head. We had a wad of money that would choke a burro. "Agent Kutara told me they wouldn't quibble with our expenses." The more time he spent playing, the less I would have to dodge his questions.

"Sweet!" He leaned out the window and waved at more passing beauties. "Hey, there!"

"I suggest the first thing you do is get some more clothes," I said.

The beauties waved back.

"And some condoms," I added.

Chapter Eleven

"What do you think of this one?" Jed held a Hawaiian-style shirt up to his chest. It featured a border of hot-pink palm trees around the hem.

"It's you." I felt a trickle of sweat run down my arm as I listlessly examined the hotel gift shop's beachwear selection. They had everything I could possibly want as long as I wanted something in neon pink, neon green, neon purple, or neon turquoise, occasionally accented by swaths of gold paint.

The only black swimsuit I could find featured heavily structured bra cups and a skirt obviously designed to hide large quantities of cellulite. I put it back on the sale rack and chose a white sundress with a fish pattern in neon green and purple, plus a matching pair of sandals.

I took the clothes up to the cashier. "*Dónde están los . . .*" Oh crap. "Toothbrush and toothpaste?" I asked helplessly.

She pointed behind me. "Third shelf down."

After shopping, Jed and I took the elevator to the third floor, where we had rooms next door to each other. "I'm going to take a shower and maybe a nap," I said, pausing outside my door. "You don't need to wait for me if you want to go out. We can leave each other messages on our room phones."

He grinned at me. "Glad I'm single. *Hasta luego*, baby."

I unlocked my door and went in. The suite was beautiful, with polished granite floors, a small desk in white wicker, and a table and chairs cozily arranged in front of the glass doors to the balcony.

I dumped my purchases on the floral bedspread and stripped off my clothes, then went into the marble-faced bathroom and showered. As the water spattered around me, I looked down at the bruises on my legs—souvenirs of my struggle with Fellseth. Maybe I wouldn't bother buying a bathing suit.

I toweled myself dry and sat naked on the bed to order a meal from room service. When I had hung up, I sighed and reached for the bag from the hotel's boutique. The sundress had the stiff feel of new clothing. I put it on and went to stand in front of the mirrored closet doors. The white dress made my skin look pale, and one of the printed fish was unfortunately placed over my left breast, its mouth open as if to nibble.

"Hello," I said to my reflection. "I'm Erin Chandler, and I have no idea what happened to my life."

I fell asleep after eating my meal, but awoke suddenly from a dream where Jed was cutting himself with a knife, oblivious to the pain. In the dim evening light, a lone mosquito bounced off the ceiling.

"Jed is safe now," I said aloud, making it sound like fact. "He's probably out there having hot sex with some sunburned tourist, all on Fellseth's dollar. Fellseth, who is dead. Unless he's not."

Sheer curtains covered the glass doors to the balcony. I stepped outside, into the sweetly scented humidity. Couples strolled on the sand below, laughing and talking. A Michael Jackson song played on the speakers in the open-air bar, overlaying the deep, continuous sound of the sea. Beyond the hotel lights lay the huge void of the ocean, with only the breaking surf visible as white lines curving across the sand.

Was Fellseth dead? It seemed impossible that someone who had loomed so large in my life could no longer be a threat. If only I had seen a body, something. I went back inside. *Closure*. That's what I didn't have. Instead, I had a beautiful room in a foreign country, with Jed for company instead of Galan.

I woke the next morning at six-thirty and scratched a bite on my arm. The lone mosquito perched on the ceiling above me, looking fatter. I rolled over and picked up a tourist magazine from the bedside table, then clambered to my feet on the mattress. Holding my breath, I took careful aim and whacked the ceiling with all my might.

I lowered the brochure and peered up at the textured plaster. It was unmarked. I scanned the room, swaying slightly on the bedsprings, then thought to check the brochure I still held. Sure enough, the former mosquito was now a black smear on the photographic rump of a beachwear model. "Bleah." I tossed it aside.

There was no way Jed would be awake this early, so I took my time getting ready, making sure to slather myself with sunscreen. When I had dressed, I went downstairs and ate breakfast at the hotel restaurant, which was almost deserted.

What was happening in Boulder? I was dying to check my e-mail, so I went to reception after breakfast and waited while the pretty woman behind the counter finished a phone call. "*Hola, señorita,*" she greeted me, after hanging up the phone. "Can I help you?"

"Does the hotel have an Internet terminal for guests?"

"We have Internet service if you have a laptop."

I shook my head. "I don't."

"Then you might try one of the Internet cafés in town," she said. "You can take a cab, but there is also a regular bus service that runs down the main road. Just two U.S. dollars, if you don't have Mexican currency."

"Great. *Gracias.*"

I caught the bus, and was the only obvious tourist on it at that hour. The rest of the passengers appeared to be locals on their way to work or shopping. I sat in the hard plastic seat and smiled at a solemn little girl with dark eyes, sitting on her mother's lap. The smell of diesel and salt water blew warmly through the windows.

Finding my destination was easy. I simply repeated, "Internet café?" to everyone I met, starting with the bus driver.

The Café Digital, when I reached it, was populated by young men who were apparently on their way back to their hotels after a rough night. I claimed a terminal next to one yawning specimen and took out the piece of paper Galan had given me. My new account name was "BeachBabe1369." There was one message from Galan, sent late the previous night.

Hello, sweetheart. Kutara called the hotel to see if you had checked in, so I know you arrived safely. I wish I could be with you.

The search for signs of Fellseth has progressed as far south as Littleton, with Lenny contacting elves all along the way. That alone is worth noting, because it's never happened before. While it's very exciting to see Kutara's network take shape, it's also distressing as we hear for the first time the things that have taken place in other areas.

I felt a swell of panic at his words. What other areas? How far had Fellseth traveled? How many dark elves were out there, anyway?

Because of my relative familiarity with humans, I'm helping Kutara as she goes through Fellseth's documents. There is still no trace of him, but at least I know you're safe. I'll write more when I have time.

I hit Reply and began to type.

I hate being here without you. I want to wake up with you in the morning—touch your face, smell your hair, make love to you and feel you inside me. I wish more than anything that this were all over.

I'm so sorry to hear about the other elves, but I'm not surprised to hear that Kutara's plan is going full steam ahead. That woman has more balls than a stable full of Clydesdales.

Realizing that I had drifted somewhat from the standard love-letter format, I dragged myself back on track.

I hope you find out what happened soon. I hope Fellseth is really, truly dead. Take care of yourself, because if anything happened to you, I don't know what I'd do. All my love, Erin.

After hitting Send, I logged out of that account and accessed my regular one, where I was relieved to find a message from Lily.

Hey, kiddo. Hope you're safe. Jim and I decided we would run away and live to fight another day, so we're visiting his parents for a week. We're fine, but I consider saving our lives from a supernatural psychopath still counts as a "family emergency." Sorry to shut down the store as we start the busy season, but that can't be helped. We'll make it up later.

Send me an e-mail or call my cell phone, but let me know you're all right. It's driving me crazy not knowing. I've got to go now. Apparently there's leftover cobbler, and Jim's mom will be hurt if I miss watching Oprah with her. Take care of yourself, Lily.

Swallowing my guilt as best I could, I sent Lily an upbeat message and a profuse apology for the shop's closure. Maybe Kutara could see her way to reimbursing her from Fellseth's funds.

I logged back into the other account, in case Galan had already responded.

There was a new message, but not from Galan.

You should be aware that both G and I are reading your messages as soon as we get them, in case you require help. G and I are working at F's house, so G brought your animal here and is caring for it. Thank you for the horse-related compliment. Kutara.

I went back to the hotel and found Jed in the lobby, chatting to a redhead with a wide grin and a sprinkling of freckles across her peeling nose.

"Hey, Erin!" Jed waved me over. "This is Cheryl. We're going on a pirate cruise. Come with us."

"I don't have a swimsuit," I said, visions of being a third wheel dancing in my head.

"So go get one," he said. "You've got time."

Cheryl nodded. "Matt went back up to get his snorkeling gear." Her voice held an appealing Midwest twang. "I'm here with my brother, too!"

I squirmed in indecision. "I need snorkel stuff?"

Cheryl waved a hand dismissively. "The tour provides it. He just likes to bring his own."

Jed poked me in the arm. "C'mon. Don't stay in your room and mope."

Cheryl looked at me. "Why would you mope?"

"My boyfriend couldn't come," I said, by way of explanation. "And I wouldn't mope."

"Prove it." Jed grinned. "Come with us."

I made a whirlwind tour of the gift shop and managed to find a hat, bathing suit, sarong, and snorkel gear in less than fifteen minutes, plus a tote bag to put it all in.

Cheryl's brother was there by the time I got back. Matt's hair was chestnut instead of red, and there were no freckles—just six feet or so of buff, friendly male. "Hey," he said, smiling.

"Hey." I busied myself with organizing my purchases.

The bus for the tour came shortly afterward. Jed sat next to Cheryl.

Matt took the seat next to me. "Have you ever snorkeled before?"

I shook my head. "Is it hard?"

"Nah. It's easier than swimming. You just have to make sure your mask fits. Can I see what you got?"

I took the mask out of my tote bag and handed it to him.

"First, we need to get rid of this." He peeled off the price sticker. "Don't want the fish to know you're new."

"There won't be any sharks, will there?" I asked.

"Nope. The most dangerous thing down there will be your fellow snorkelers. Watch out for their feet. They love to kick." He looped the band around the front of the mask, out of the way. "Let's see how this fits your face. Push your hair back. That's good." He placed the mask against my face. "Now close your mouth and breathe in slowly through your nose."

I did. He took his hand away, but the mask stayed on. "Perfect!" he said.

The bus bounced over a rough patch in the road, and the mask fell in my lap. I laughed.

"Number one rule in snorkeling," Matt said. "Watch out for potholes."

The snorkeling was great, thanks to Matt's tutorial. Now we were on the return trip, and the crew was dosing the passengers with tequila and taking pictures, which were available for an extra charge.

"*Hola, hola, hola*! Can everyone say *hola*?" yelled one of the brown-skinned young men in pirate costumes.

"*Hola,*" I muttered.

A flushed woman shrieked with laughter as she squeezed the firm rump of the crewmember posing with her. He obligingly put his plastic saber under her throat and leered as the camera clicked.

Matt came to stand beside me. "It's quiet on the upper deck."

"Show me the way." I followed him up the metal stairs, holding tightly to the handrail as the boat cut through the waves.

The wind swept away the sounds of hilarity downstairs. I leaned on the railing that surrounded the small deck and let the salty air blow my hair back. "I must have looked like the proverbial wet blanket down there."

He chuckled. "Perhaps slightly damp. I'm not much of a drinker, either. The snorkeling was good, though, wasn't it? I'm glad you got to see a damselfish."

"They were so pretty!" My sarong clung to my wet bathing suit and flapped against my legs. I wrapped my arms around my shoulders, feeling sticky with salt and chilly from the wind.

Matt stepped a little closer. "You cold?" His still-damp hair curled in dark tendrils around his face.

I felt a twinge of desire, and with it, a moment of panic. "I have a boyfriend," I blurted.

He chuckled. "Good for you. It's just that there are more dry towels downstairs, if you want one."

"Sorry. I'm sorry," I babbled. "You were just being nice, and I'm just . . . an idiot."

"No, I actually *was* coming on to you, so you're not an idiot."

I gave a gasping laugh as my teeth started to chatter. "A dry towel would be great."

I hugged myself while he went down the stairs. He was back in moments with two enormous towels. I took one from him and wrapped it around my hips while he draped the other around my shoulders.

"Thanks," I said, pulling it around me. "That helps a lot."

"Do you want to go back downstairs? I promise to respect the boyfriend boundary, although . . ." He glanced down at my ankles, barely visible beneath the bottom of the towel, and still bruised from Fellseth's manacles. "I couldn't help noticing that you look a little beat up. Is that why your brother is here instead of your boyfriend?" He raised his eyebrows questioningly.

I broke into peals of laughter.

Matt looked relieved. "So you're not a battered woman?"

"I *am* a little battered, but not by Galan."

At his expression of renewed concern, I suddenly felt the need to talk. "It's like this," I said, pulling the towel more tightly around my shoulders. "My boyfriend, Galan, is in law enforcement. And somebody he was after attacked me to get to him."

Matt's expression darkened. "Bastard."

"And then this criminal disappeared, so Galan sent me here secretly. Even Jed doesn't know the whole story," I added, "so I'd appreciate it if you didn't talk to *anyone* about it."

He still looked angry. "How long have you and Galan been together? I mean, is this sort of thing common?"

"I don't know." I realized I had been trying not to ask myself that very question. "We've only been together a little while, and then all this terrible stuff started happening. I really love him, but some of my friends got dragged into the situation." I began to cry. "And I hate being afraid."

He put his arms around me then.

I stood, wrapped in his kindness and warmth, and thought, *Don't be normal and nice. I don't want to think about that kind of life, and how I might be giving it up.*

"I think you should get some counseling," he said, resting his chin against the top of my head. "You've been through a really tough time."

I straightened and rubbed the towel across my eyes and nose. "Sorry to dump on you."

"I'm not complaining. I just think a professional would be more help."

"Oh, I don't know." I stepped away and gave him a watery smile. "You're pretty good. But I will talk to someone," I added, thinking of Lily and the shelves of self-help books at the Celadon Rose. "I'll figure it out."

The boat pulled up to the dock, but Matt looked reluctant to go downstairs. "Your Galan, is he a really good guy? I mean, is he—"

"Worth it?" I finished for him, and nodded. "It's not a question of that. More a question of what I can handle." I gave a little shiver.

He rubbed his hand across my towel-covered back, warming it. "I guess we should go downstairs."

Down on the main deck, the rest of the passengers were gathering their things, in some cases a little unsteadily. Jed had his arm around Cheryl's waist.

We got on the bus, and Matt and I talked about ordinary

things, comforting things, as I did my best to ignore the hollow feeling that was growing inside me.

The next morning, I sat naked on the bed and studied the bruises on my legs. As I trailed my fingers over a particularly purple mark, I remembered the way my skin felt as it knit under Kutara's touch. A pale streak emerged slowly through the bruise, like light at the edge of a storm front.

"What the hell?" I touched another spot experimentally, but nothing happened. I took a deep breath and touched it again, concentrating on the tingling I remembered. When I lifted my finger, the bruising beneath was gone. "Wow," I whispered.

I spent the next fifteen minutes clearing my legs of the worst marks. I was tired and hungry afterward, as though I had just taken a long hike.

Had Kutara's earlier work on my cuts somehow taught my body to heal itself? Could anyone do what I had just done, if they only knew how? Considering *I* didn't know how I'd done it, that seemed unlikely.

The alternative was that my bond with Galan was somehow changing me. The question was, would all the changes be good ones?

I wrapped my arms around my legs and stared past my balcony to the sea, turquoise and silent on the other side of the glass doors. Would I have to stop eating food? Would I be able to glamour people? Or would my ears just become pointed, making everyone think I was a freak?

I reached up and felt my ears. They were still reassuringly rounded. It was time to get out of my room and see if I could find some answers to my questions.

* * *

Downstairs, I ran into Matt at the display of tour brochures.

"You're everywhere," I said, walking up to him.

"Your brother took my traveling companion. So much for sisterly love."

"And you're so shy, you can't find anyone to play with." I gave him a mock sympathetic look.

He laughed. "This may damage my reputation, but I really did come for the snorkeling." He waved a brochure at me. "Or we could swim with the dolphins."

"Maybe. Right now, I'm going to the Internet café."

"Great idea. Can I come with you?"

"Sure."

I chose a terminal next to the wall, a little distance from Matt. My regular e-mail account had a message from my parents. Thank God they were okay. Lily had also left a message.

> Glad to hear the bogeyman didn't get you! Any word from Galan as to when it might be safe to go back? Jim is in no hurry to leave, but you and I are due to close on the store in four days. Let me know what's happening with that. Love, Lily.

There was only one new message in the other account, and it was from Galan.

"Hello, sweetheart," it began. My eyes immediately prickled with tears. I could *hear* him saying the words.

I can't believe you've been away only two days.
It seems much longer. But I have good news. You
can come home tomorrow!

Had they caught Fellseth? I read on.

Lenny and his team have finished an exhaustive
search without finding a trace of Fellseth. I'm convinced that he tried to escape in the creek and
was unable to maintain his form. Kutara is looking
up flight times for you right now, and will call
tonight at around eight for your approval.

She wanted my approval? That was different.

I can't wait to see you again. Being away from
you like this has made things very clear for me.

I leaned back in my chair and stared at the message.
Unfortunately, things seemed far from clear to me. I
went back to Lily's message and hit Reply.

I'm getting the all clear from the pointy-eared
gang. Looks like Fellseth died in his escape attempt.
They're shipping me home tomorrow. If you can't
extricate yourself from Jim's family that fast, maybe
it would be better to stay for a while. I'll open the
shop and check with the bank to make sure everything is progressing. See you soon. Love, Erin.

I sent the message and went back to answer Galan's
email.

Something really freaky happened—I was able to heal my bruises by touching them, the way Kutara did with my cuts. What does that *mean*? As for Fellseth, are you *sure* he's dead? Of course I want to come home, but not if it's not safe. I wish we knew more.

I sat in front of the screen, tapping the Check Mail button, but no response came through. Were they on a shopping spree with their newfound wealth, or had Fellseth suddenly leaped out from behind a door? The idea of living with an elf, once so attractive, now seemed as alluring as living in the Middle East.

I gathered up my things and touched Matt's shoulder on my way to the checkout desk. "There's an open-air restaurant right across the street. I'll be over there."

I took another sip of icy margarita and gazed around the courtyard where Matt and I sat. Trees shaded our little table, and pots of pink geraniums competed with bougainvillea and exotic lilies for the most color.

"Any news?" he asked.

I put my glass down. "Apparently there's no more bad guy."

He paused with a bottle of Dos Equis midway to his mouth. "That's great, right?"

"Sure." I watched a weathered man with a large iguana wander through the crowded tables, putting the lizard on tourist's heads and taking pictures for tips.

"Erin? You don't seem too excited."

I shrugged. "There are plenty more bad guys where he came from."

He frowned. "What are you going to do? You have to go home eventually."

I rested my chin on my fist. "Do I? Maybe I'll stay here, drinking margaritas and chatting with unattached men. That sounds like a fine lifestyle to me."

Back in my room, I kicked off my shoes and lay on the bed with my hands behind my head, scanning the ceiling for mosquitoes. There weren't any. "Oh, sure," I said. "Maybe you're not there, but then again, maybe you're just hiding."

I was so tired of being afraid. I closed my eyes and tried to feel trust, certainty—even relief. Instead, as I lay on the bed, the white sundress rumpled around me, I realized I was angry.

The phone shrilled. I rolled over and fumbled the receiver off the hook. "Hello?" I croaked.

"Erin? Are you sick?" Kutara's voice came down the line, crisp and inquisitive.

"No." I cleared my throat. "I guess I fell asleep."

"What is this about healing your own bruises?"

"Exactly what I said—I ran my finger across them and they disappeared."

Silence. Then, "Could it have been dirt?"

"Yeah, Kutara. Fellseth rubbed dirt on me, but I was looking the other way and didn't notice. I think I know bruises. Have you ever heard of a human being able to do that?"

"Never, but I have not made it my business to research humans."

"Do humans change, when they're bound to elves? What else do I have to look forward to?"

"I have no idea."

"Is Galan there?"

"No. He is working."

I heaved a sigh.

"I have your itinerary," Kutara said. "Your flight leaves tomorrow afternoon, just after three. Write this down."

"Hold on." I went to the desk and pulled a piece of paper toward me. "Go ahead."

Kutara recited the flight information. "You're arriving at Denver International this time. Galan will be picking you up."

"Kutara—"

"Do you have luggage?"

"Just carry-on. *Kutara . . .*" There was an expectant silence. "Do *you* believe Fellseth is dead?"

There was a pause before she answered. "There's no reason to believe otherwise. Do you want to stay in Mexico longer? It's just that your pet seems to be pining. By that I mean your cat, although Galan also seems to miss you excessively."

I smiled momentarily. "That's nice to hear. But I still want to know what you really, *really* believe."

Kutara's voice didn't change. "I think there is a chance that Fellseth is alive. If he is, he may have decided to move on to someplace less prepared for him. Or he might wait, who knows how long, until he feels our defenses are down."

That was the last thing I wanted to hear. I closed my eyes. "What would you do, if you were me?"

"I would come home. It was overconfident of Fellseth to capture you first and then try to kill Galan.

If he did try again, I don't think you would be his first target."

"Galan would be."

"Yes."

"Then why didn't you send *him* to Mexico? Why me?" I asked, feeling fear grip my heart all over again. Only now it was fear for Galan.

Kutara sounded sad. "Even though my people are threatened, there are still many elves. You, however, are unique. With your energy available to him, Fellseth would have an advantage that would be hard to overcome."

"You make it sound like I'm the ultimate weapon. Boulder is littered with people who meditate!"

"That's true, as I have learned over the last few days. But none of them were of any use to us."

"Have you been doing *experiments*?"

"I posed as an author doing research. The people at the Naropa Institute were very helpful." Kutara's voice dropped slightly. "Something in you *changed* when you bonded to Galan, but we may be able to keep you out of the hands of dark elves in the future, if the idea I have works."

"What idea?"

"We'll talk about it when you get back. I'll fax the e-ticket itineraries for you and Jed to the hotel's front desk. I'm looking forward to seeing you again, Erin." She disconnected.

I stared at the receiver. "You are?"

Jed, Cheryl, and Matt decided to take another snorkeling trip in the morning. They all asked me to come, but I decided to stay in my room and give some serious thought to what a long-term relationship with Galan might entail.

Sitting at the desk in my room, I scribbled notes on a piece of hotel stationery while I thought. *Galan will not grow old. I will.* I'd be the one with the plastic-surgery addiction, *unless . . .* If I were changing somehow, would I stay younger longer? What if I was already immortal? I shivered. The idea had appeal, but it was just so . . . *bizarre.*

What will I tell friends and family? I would have to tell my parents, but they could be trusted to keep our secret, although they might not be happy about it.

Regular customers at the store would probably notice if I didn't get older, or if I got older but Galan didn't. We could try not to let them see us together, but they might run into us at the grocery store. Maybe Galan could glamour them to not notice, or maybe I . . .

"This is stupid." I wadded up the paper and threw it across the room. No one asked regular couples to map out every detail of their futures. *What if I develop schizophrenia? What if your legs fall off and you can't work?* Anything could happen to anyone. There were no guarantees.

Anyway, we had time to see how things went. It wasn't like we'd signed a contract in blood. Except that we sort of had.

I became aware of the sound of the ocean, as steady as a pulse. Our bond was like a contract we had accidentally signed, affecting me in ways I didn't understand and tying Galan to me whether he wanted it or not.

Fellseth had tried to kill Galan because of our bond. Was he still trying? Would others?

Chapter Twelve

I told Jed I'd meet him in the lobby at twelve-thirty. When I rolled my new suitcase off the elevator, Jed and Cheryl were already saying their good-byes.

Cheryl rubbed her freckled nose against Jed's. "Thanks for coming to Mexico," she murmured, then kissed him quickly.

Jed took a piece of paper out of his pocket and pressed it into her hand. "At least e-mail me."

Cheryl pouted adorably. "That long-distance stuff never works, you know that." She kissed him again, longer this time. "Just remember what a nice time we had. Okay, Tiger? I gotta go."

Jed watched her walk away, an expression of longing on his face. "Jesus Christ, those Nebraska girls are heartbreakers."

I patted him on the shoulder. "It probably wouldn't have worked out. Was she even a gamer?"

"I don't know," he said glumly. "I never asked."

Matt crossed the lobby toward us. "I glad I didn't miss saying good-bye."

"Dude, it's been real." Jed held out his hand, but Matt

had already passed him and wrapped his arms around me in a hug.

"Urmph," I said. My suitcase fell over as the handle slipped out of my hand.

Jed looked on with interest.

Matt let go of me and held out a piece of paper. "Here's my e-mail address. Promise you'll e-mail so I know you're all right."

"I'll be fine."

"*Promise*. Otherwise I'll worry."

His attention was both sweet and exasperating. "Matt, you barely know me."

He grinned. "That's not because I didn't try."

I couldn't help smiling. "All right, I'll e-mail you. Once."

"And let me know if you ever come to Nebraska. Or if you break up with that cop."

"Federal agent," Jed volunteered.

Matt's face lost its humor. "Seriously? Erin, make sure you e-mail me, okay?"

"I said I would. But don't worry. Everything's under control." I gave him a bright smile.

I bought a fat historical romance at the airport, determined not to think about anything on the trip home. Sometime later, I folded the page's corner and stretched. In the seat next to me, Jed slept, looking tan and rested.

I envied the book's heroine, Lady Isabel. At least when Laird Roderick killed an archenemy, she knew that enemy was good and dead. The head on a pike pretty much proved it.

By the time the plane taxied into the DIA terminal, I

had a stiff neck from reading and my butt had fallen asleep on one side. I put the book away.

Jed woke up and wiped the corner of his mouth. "Back to the salt mines, huh?" he said, leaning forward to look out the window.

Guilt descended on me like a black cloud. "I hope you still have your job."

"I e-mailed. They said it was no big deal." He stretched his arms above his head. "We can both go back to work and forget this whole thing ever happened." He frowned. "Those were some wacko drugs, though. I hope I don't get flashbacks."

I thought about the possibility of Fellseth's return. "I hope so, too."

Galan was waiting for us at the terminal, holding a bouquet of daylilies. I felt two kinds of hunger as he picked me up in a hug, people streaming around us on both sides. I closed my eyes and relished the smell of him, made new again by absence. He put me down, and I gazed up at him, trying to let my face show all my love and not my anxiety.

"You look a little tired," he said, handing me the flowers while he took my bag. "Beautiful, but tired."

"It was hard, being away. I missed you." Would I miss him any less, if I was the one choosing to separate?

"Where's Agent Kutara?" Jed asked as we walked toward the doors to the parking garage.

"She had to work." Galan winked at me as he said it. Had he just learned to wink or was it just the first time I had seen him do it? The smallest detail seemed precious.

The cold air of the parking garage chilled me when we stepped outside. "Let me get my coat out of my suitcase."

"We had a little cold snap while you were gone." Galan zipped the bag for me as I put my coat on. "Kitty Girl would ask to go out and then look at me like the weather was my fault."

"She does that." I marveled at how normal our conversation sounded from the outside. *I might be that normal again.*

On the drive home, Galan signaled every lane change and generally behaved like a cautious new driver while I sat in the passenger seat and listened to him answer Jed's questions with lies. The outskirts of Denver looked bleak and brown after the lush green of Mexico, and new snow powdered the mountains.

When we reached the house, Kitty Girl ran out from beneath a bush, meowing frantically as I came up the walk. I scooped her up and whispered into her soft fur. "I know, baby, but hopefully it's all over now, and you and I can get back to normal."

The familiar smell of the house welcomed me. Jed went off to his room to send e-mails, and I sat down on the couch as if my legs would no longer support me.

Galan sat next to me and took my hand. "I thought I might take you out to dinner."

I looked around at the familiar furnishings. "We fought with Fellseth, in this very room. Remember?"

He kissed my temple gently, and I could hear the worry in his voice as he said, "Let's make some new memories."

I turned my face and fell into his kiss, my body welcoming him without question even as my mind chattered with uncertainty. When he finally pulled away, I followed him, seeking his mouth.

"That's more like the Erin I know," he chuckled, kissing my nose. "Shall we go out to dinner?"

"I'm not hungry," I lied, feeling my hunger grow the longer he was with me. But I was tired of strangers and public places. "What if we got some food and drove up Left-Hand Canyon? We could park and look at the stars."

"I'm not sure that's the best idea," he said carefully.

"Why?" The anger I had tamped down flashed to life. "Because it's not safe?" I pushed myself off the couch. Galan wasn't to blame, but that didn't keep me from being mad as hell that our lives felt threatened and uncertain.

He remained seated, his expression wary. "We have to be cautious for a while. We don't have much of a choice."

"Don't we? Fellseth said I could break my bond with you if I wanted it more than anything else. That would take at least one person off his to-do list. You." I could *feel* our bond at that moment, stretched taut and suddenly fragile between us, even as Galan's face paled with hurt.

"Erin, don't." He stood and reached for me, but I stepped back. "Please. It won't solve anything. Come and talk to Kutara."

"Kutara says that if Fellseth is still alive, he'll try to kill you first. I couldn't stand that, Galan." I stumbled past him and knelt on the couch, crossing my arms on the back and hiding my face as I sobbed. "I couldn't." I felt his weight settle next to me. His hand touched my shoulder, tentatively, and I turned and pressed my face against his chest.

"Sweetheart." He wrapped his arms around me and stroked my hair again and again. "I know it's hard. Don't you think I know?"

I could barely talk through my tears. "Then we should break our bond and you should go away. I'm just putting you in danger!"

Galan rocked me back and forth. "I don't care. I don't want to be without you. I don't think I can anymore."

After I had cried myself out, Galan fixed dinner for me and insisted that I eat it. Then he drove me to Guy's house to meet with Kutara.

We stood on the stoop, Galan's warm hand holding mine, as he pressed the doorbell.

"Kutara has been doing a lot of research on really old elf customs," he said. "She may have found some way of setting up a barrier to dark elves."

The door opened, and Kutara stood there. "Guy is at an architectural conference, so we have the house to ourselves." She ushered us into the living room. "Erin, would you like something to drink? A soda, perhaps?"

"Water, no ice," I said automatically, then stared at her back as she went toward the kitchen. Turning to Galan, I asked, "What's with the hostess bit?"

"Guy had a dinner party for some of his city council friends the other night." He pulled me down next to him on the love seat. "I think she anticipates a fair amount of that kind of thing, so she's working on her technique."

Kutara came back with a glass and a coaster and put them on the low table. "Did you enjoy Mexico?" she asked, sitting in a chair across from us.

"Not really." I was on my guard. Kutara wasn't going to wheedle me into changing my mind.

"I assumed from the size of the hotel bar bill that you had at least tried to relax."

"Bar bill? Oh, that was Jed and probably twelve of his closest new friends. Sorry about that."

Kutara shrugged. "It's not a problem. I was just hoping you enjoyed some sense of safety while you were there."

"I don't feel safe anymore. I don't know if I ever will again." I picked up my glass and drank in the ensuing silence.

"So much for small talk," Kutara said dryly. "How are the two of you getting along?"

I sighed. "I thought we were through chatting."

"We are," Kutara said. "My question is quite pertinent to tonight's discussion."

"We're fine," Galan said, before I could respond.

"I'm glad to hear it. Presumably neither of you would have any objections to getting married, then."

We both gaped at her. I recovered first. "What are you talking about?"

"Nuptials. Wedded bliss. The merging of two into one." Kutara's voice was matter-of-fact. "I understand it's so popular among your people that you sometimes do it two and three times, but I'm talking about something more permanent."

I waved a hand wildly. "How is marriage going to help anything?"

"I think I know." Galan's face was grave. "You're talking about *penansel*, aren't you?"

Kutara nodded.

"Did you say *pencil*?" I looked from one to the other. "And please don't go all elf-mysterious on me."

Galan took my hand. "In this case, it can't be helped. I know very little about it, but penansel is a marriage ritual that hasn't been performed in, what, over a thousand years?" He looked at Kutara questioningly.

"Twelve hundred and four years, from what I was able to find." She turned her attention to me. "Penansel was fairly common among European elves when there was plenty of land and elves married exclusively for love. Very romantic times."

"But what *is* it?"

Galan answered. "It's a ritual that binds an elf couple beyond death. And elves died fairly frequently in that violent age, so it took a lot of conviction."

"Binds them how? I still don't understand."

Kutara leaned forward. "Let's say an elf couple bonds, in the standard way. If they decide to separate or if one of them dies, the bond dissolves, leaving the remaining elf free to bond with someone else."

Galan nodded. "But when a couple undergoes penansel, the bond exists forever."

I shook my head in disbelief. "So you're suggesting that we do this and then, even if you die, my bond with you will continue."

Kutara sat back with a satisfied look. "And Fellseth won't be able to glamour you. Ever."

I huffed out a breath. "That is the *worst* idea I have ever heard. First of all, I'm not an elf, so it probably wouldn't work. And let's say it did work. If Fellseth *is* dead, then Galan would be bonded to someone he'd likely outlive. He'd be loveless after I was gone, and for a long time. That's not fair to him."

Kutara looked thoughtful. "Before we go on, I have a question for Galan. Are you willing to go through penansel with Erin?"

He looked from his hands to me, and the love I saw

in his face broke my heart. "Yes," he said. "I want to be with her for as long as she'll have me, and I'll do anything to keep her safe."

Kutara nodded and turned to me. "Then you should have no objection to trying."

"Except that we wouldn't know if it worked until Galan *died*, and Fellseth will still have a reason to kill him if we're bonded!"

Her face hardened, and she stood. "You have to understand that if a dark elf gains control of you, more people than Galan will be at risk."

I shook my head. "Haven't you ever thought that if we break our bond, all my weird abilities—to heal myself, to raise energy for elves—might just disappear?"

"And what if a dark elf finds a way to bond with you, and your abilities come back stronger than ever?"

I shot to my feet and came around the coffee table toward her. "So now elves are like the Mafia? Once you get involved, you can never get out? What if I don't want anything to do with elves anymore? *Any* elves— not just dark ones!"

Kutara didn't back down an inch. Instead, she leaned toward me. "If it weren't for humans, there wouldn't *be* any dark elves!"

"Stop it!" Galan stood, towering over both of us. "You're both looking for someone to blame, and Fellseth isn't here." He expelled a breath and sat. "Maybe he isn't anywhere."

My shoulders slumped. "I hope that's the case, but my decision still stands."

"I think I should take Erin home now," Galan said, looking down at me. Kutara started to say something, but he shook his head. "Leave it, Kutara. It's up to her."

* * *

I watched Galan's profile as he drove under the streetlights toward my house. "Do you hate me?"

"I thought I made it pretty clear that I don't."

My fingers rubbed at a scuff on the handle of my purse. "Are you angry with me?"

"Because you're afraid of getting hurt?" He glanced sideways. "Some. I'm afraid of getting hurt, too, but I love you more than I'm afraid."

I looked out the side window, my throat tight. "Maybe it would be different if it were just about you and me, Galan, but I'm also thinking of Jed, and Lily and Jim. And what if a dark elf tracked down my parents?"

"What if Kutara is right, and breaking our bond doesn't get rid of your abilities? Then you'll be even more vulnerable to dark elves."

"That seems so unlikely. I never showed any special abilities until I met you." I leaned my head against the glass. "Do we have to decide this moment? Can't I have a little time to think?"

He pulled up in front of my house. "Do you even want me to stay the night?"

He had once made love to me because he wasn't strong enough to refuse. Now it was my turn. "Yes. That is, if you want to."

There were no lights on in the house. "Jed must be catching up with friends." I unlocked the front door and fumbled for the light switch, feeling panicky in the darkness.

Once the light was on, Galan stood behind me and put his hands on my shoulders. "I haven't said it, but

I'm sorry." He rested the side of his face against mine. "I wish you'd never had to go through this."

I turned and wrapped my arms around him. "It might sound like I regret meeting you, but don't ever think that."

"If it makes you feel any better, Kutara still has people watching your house, the store—any place she thinks Fellseth might show up."

"That does make me feel better." I let go of him and hung up my coat. "I'll get ready for bed."

When I came out of the bathroom, Galan was already in bed, his silver hair spilling across the pillow. He flipped the covers back for me.

I felt tears threaten at the sight of his beautiful body, so familiar and dear. Regardless of whether it was sensible, could I bear to leave him?

We made love slowly, softly, our bond humming like a quiet song of contentment in an uncertain world. My tears spilled over with my climax, and Galan's mouth, pressed against mine as he came, tasted of salt.

I crossed my arms behind his neck, holding him against me. "I wish with all my heart that I didn't have to leave you."

"Then don't," he whispered, his voice catching.

But when I woke the next morning, he was gone.

I didn't know if Galan agreed that we had to part, or if he was just leaving it up to me. Whatever the case, I would take the little breathing space his absence offered. Apparently I didn't want our bond broken more than anything yet, because I couldn't bring myself to try.

The cash register was still turned on when I arrived at the Celadon Rose—mute evidence of Lily's hurried departure. I opened the drawer and noted the bills that were there. At least we hadn't been burgled.

I went through the start-of-day procedures on autopilot: checking voice mail, topping up the fountains, turning on the essential-oil vaporizer. The last thing I did was remove the sheet of paper taped to the inside of the glass door. CELADON ROSE TEMPORARILY CLOSED DUE TO FAMILY EMERGENCY, Lily had written. WE'LL BE OPEN AGAIN SOON. UNTIL THEN, BREATHE DEEP— DON'T PANIC!

I took a deep breath.

My first customer wasn't a regular. I smiled and chatted over the New Age music, taking refuge in my people skills as I doled out advice. "I personally believe depression is fifty percent nutrition and fifty percent mental habits."

I sent the customer home with a book on affirmations and another on the evils of sugar, then raided the drawer in the office where Lily and I kept the emergency chocolate.

The phone rang. I swallowed my bite of York Peppermint Pattie, coughing a little as the sugary goo ran down my throat. "Celadon Rose," I croaked into the receiver.

"Erin? Is that you? It's Geraldine Krupper."

"Oh, hi, Geraldine!" Geraldine was one of our regulars—a kind but bossy woman who treated us like erring daughters. I wiped my mouth with my hand, then wiped my hand on a stray piece of packing paper. "What can I do for you?"

"I was just checking to see if you were open. I came over yesterday and saw the sign. Is everything okay?"

"Everything's fine, thank you. Lily should be back

any time, and then she can tell you about it." I had already rehearsed this statement for clients.

"What about you? I worried so when I saw that you weren't there, either."

Unfortunately, my rehearsal hadn't progressed this far. "Oh. Um . . ." Squeezing my eyes closed, I smacked my free hand on my forehead. "Well, she and I took turns driving. To Nebraska. That's where her folks live. The ones with the emergency."

"I thought that was where Jim's family lived. Didn't he go with her?"

I blew out a breath. "He had a work emergency. Couldn't leave."

"Oh." Geraldine sounded unconvinced. "Well, I hope everything is all right. Are you still having an open house the day after tomorrow, to celebrate taking over the store?"

I almost groaned. Throwing a party was surely the cruelest self-torture, but it was Saturday, and we were due to close the sale on Monday. The party supplies and arrangements had been taken care of ages ago, and Lily had left a message that she would be here in plenty of time. "That's right. Big open house Monday evening."

"Then I'll see you both there," Geraldine said. It sounded like an order.

"All right. Thank you." I put down the receiver. Someday, it would be possible to care about these things again. Wouldn't it?

I was eating a sandwich in a rare moment between customers when I heard someone come in the back door. I tiptoed to the front door and opened it halfway, ready to flee. "Who's there?" I yelled toward the rear of the store.

"Me!" Lily called. There was a thump and a clatter. "Ow! Who left this vacuum right in the middle of the floor?" She emerged into the shop, rubbing her shin. "Oh that's right, it was me."

I walked to meet her, one hand over my heart. "You scared the crap out of me! I didn't expect you here today." I hugged her so hard, she gave a little gasp.

"It's good to see you, too." She took her purse into the office and came out with the inventory list. "Still feeling a little goosey? The bad guy's all gone."

"Mostly gone," I muttered, leaning on the counter.

"What?"

"Probably gone."

"What are you talking about?" She prodded me in the shoulder. "They killed him, didn't they? Erin?"

I took a deep breath. "He tried to escape by becoming incorporeal in a creek, which no elf has ever tried. They can't find a trace of him, so it probably didn't work and he's dead. Most likely."

Lily tossed the list on the counter. "Most likely?"

"Almost certainly. And Geraldine Krupper called to find out why we were gone and I told her that I helped you drive to Nebraska to see your parents, because Jim had to work," I continued quickly.

"Wait a minute," Lily said, momentarily distracted. "Geraldine knows my parents don't live in Nebraska. Did you say anything about why we went there?"

"I didn't get that far."

"And Fellseth may not be dead?" Lily scowled. "Should I go back to Nebraska and my parents that don't live there?"

"You could, but it would probably be a waste of time. There's no reason whatsoever to believe that he's still alive. Anyway, Kutara says that even if he *were* alive, he wouldn't mess with trying to kidnap me first. He'd try to kill Galan before that, which is why I'm going to break my bond with him and never see him again." I burst into tears.

"Oh, honey." Lily put her arms around me and squeezed. "I'm so sorry."

"It's the only way to keep him safe. To keep all of us safe." I rested my head on her shoulder.

She patted my back. "Maybe you should tell me the whole story."

It took me the rest of the afternoon to tell Lily everything that had happened since I'd last seen her.

When I wound down, she said, "It sounds to me like you're making the right decision. And after all, you've only known Galan about two weeks, right?"

Was that possible? He felt as much a part of me as my skin. "Yeah."

She hesitated. "I don't want to sound self-centered, but you haven't changed your mind about buying the Rose, have you?"

I shook my head. "I'm buying it. What else would I do with myself?"

"Work is probably the best thing for you." She smiled. And the next two days are going to be a lot of work. Now let's close up."

That evening, I sat on the floor of my bedroom, gathering the last financial records necessary for the store closing. Kitty Girl napped on the bed, whiskers twitching occasionally.

I slid a final bank statement into the folder. "That's that." I tossed it on the floor beyond the semicircle of my mess, then heaved a sigh as the papers inside kept going and slid under the bed.

I got on my knees and retrieved them from between a box of old photos and some dusty slippers that were slightly too small for me. What was that scrap of white, farther back?

Kitty Girl made an enquiring meow and landed on the floor next to me as I withdrew from under the bed. I sat back on my heels and looked at the scrap in my hand. It was the paper mouse Galan had made.

Missing him was like a physical pain.

I put the mouse on the floor and blew at it shakily. It lifted slightly, showing a dust-covered edge, then fell back. Kitty Girl gazed at it a moment, then wandered out of the room.

I wiped tears from my cheeks. "This is really hard."

The next day, Sunday, I worked like there was no such thing as rest, cleaning the Rose and preparing the decorations so they could be put up quickly.

When Lily caught me emptying the fountains so I could wipe the bottoms, she pulled the sponge out of my hand. "Erin, go home."

"I can do more. I still have three Cokes left."

"I poured them down the sink. Now go."

I ate my dinner on the couch with Jed, watching him

laugh at the appropriate places in the sitcoms. He didn't seem scarred by his experience, but then again, Jed thought most of what had happened was a drug-induced hallucination.

He turned to look at me. "Isn't that your phone?"

"What?"

"Your cell phone."

I ran into my bedroom and scrabbled through my purse for the phone. "Hello?"

"It's Kutara."

I had a moment of heart-stopping fear. "Is Galan all right?"

"He's fine. In fact, I may have a piece of good news. Galan had the idea of checking news items and police reports to see if there have been any strange events."

I sat on the bed and pressed my ear against the phone to hear her better. There was some excitement at elf headquarters, to judge by the ambient noise. "Strange events. You mean like weird hitchhikers or stolen cars?"

"Exactly. We found an online item about a Kansas housewife who looked out her window and saw a naked, wet man stealing clothes off the clothesline. She described him as having long, gray hair and said he looked ill. The incident appeared in the local police blotter."

"When did it say this happened?"

"Yesterday evening. We spotted it this morning."

"Have you tried calling the woman?"

"There's no answer, so I'm flying out there. I'm calling you from the airport."

I realized that the voices I had taken for other elves were actually airline announcements. "You're not going alone, are you?"

"I will be met by a contingent of eight elves. That should be more than enough to handle Fellseth, if it is him."

"How did you find other elves?"

"They had formed something called a Yahoo Group. Have you heard of it?"

My jaw actually dropped. "I have heard something about that, yes." The thought of elves who were even more organized than Boulder elves was mind-boggling.

"It looks as though my flight is boarding, but I thought you should know."

"Thank you, Kutara. That was very kind of you."

"Was it?" She sounded pleased. "I'll call you again if we kill Fellseth."

"You do that."

I disconnected and stood, the phone in my hand. Then I shut my bedroom door and dialed Galan's cell number.

He picked up after two rings. "Erin?"

"Hi." For a moment, I couldn't think of anything else to say. "Kutara called from the airport."

"Did she tell you that we may be able to find Fellseth?"

"I can hardly believe it." I went over to the window and looked out, noticing for the first time that the apple tree by the side of the house was in bloom.

"How are you?" he asked.

"Okay. Not exactly happy." I wandered over to my desk and saw the rabbit bracelet he had sketched. "Miserable, actually."

"Should I not have left?"

"No, I'm grateful to you for that."

There was a small silence.

"If you knew without question that Fellseth were

dead . . ." Galan hesitated. "Would it make a difference to you and me?"

I sat in the desk chair and ran my finger over the leaping rabbit. "I honestly don't know."

"But you wouldn't say it's impossible."

I smiled. "I would never say that. Will you call me when you hear something?"

"You'll be the first."

I found that I didn't want to hang up yet. "Tomorrow is the day I buy the Celadon Rose." Should I invite him to the open house? No. I hadn't made my decision yet, and seeing him again would make it harder.

"That's great news, Erin. It's a wonderful store. I know it'll make you happy."

"Thanks." I'd give up the store in a heartbeat if I could have a life with Galan. I put a hand up and pinched my nose, so I wouldn't start to cry again. "I changed my loan. I still want to buy you some land."

"I'm not in any hurry. Let's wait and see what happens."

Chapter Thirteen

I spent the next morning organizing my materials for the closing. When it was time to leave for the lawyer's office, I stepped out of the house in black jeans and a dark green sweater and immediately realized I was dressed too warmly.

Kitty Girl threw herself down on the sun-warmed concrete and rolled luxuriantly.

I stooped to pet her, but she suddenly flipped over and streaked into the back yard.

"Hello, Erin!" Mrs. Jamison came down the sidewalk, towed by Thor. "How are you today, dear? *Sit*, Thor."

"I'm okay," I fondled the dog's massive head. "I'm sorry I haven't walked this monster recently. I've been out of town."

"That's quite all right. Now that the weather is warmer, it's good for me to get out and work the arthritis out of my knees. Did you go on a little holiday with that artist fellow?" She gave a wink so quick it was almost invisible.

"Unfortunately, no. Are you coming to the open house at the store tonight? I'm on my way to the lawyer's office to close the sale, and we'll be celebrating tonight. I'd love it if you could come. Seven o'clock."

"I'll bring some of my gingerbread." She changed Thor's leash from one hand to the other as he circled around her feet. "Someone's getting impatient. I'd better get going."

"Thanks, Mrs. Jamison. Let me know if you want a ride." I went into the house to exchange my sweater for a T-shirt.

I arrived at the lawyer's office a little early, but Lily was already in the waiting room. She took her attaché case from the chair beside her and put it on the floor so I could sit.

"Did you have to kick anyone out of the store?" I asked.

"A couple of high-school kids, but they weren't going to buy anything anyway. I hung a back-after-lunch sign on the door and here I am. Ready to be the boss?"

I clutched my file folder full of papers. "I think so. As long as you work part-time until I get my feet under me, I should be fine."

"I might work part-time indefinitely. It'll be more fun when I don't have all those ownership headaches." She put a hand up to her mouth. "Did I say headaches? I meant incredibly rewarding challenges."

A tubby man in an impeccable suit came into the lobby. "Ms. Chandler? Ms. Savchuk? I'm ready for you."

We emerged an hour later. I suspected I had the slightly stunned look of someone who had handed over an enormous check, and Lily definitely had the satisfied expression of someone who had received it.

She clapped me on the back. "What do you say we pick up some celebratory doughnuts on the way to the store? I'll buy."

"You can afford it. But you know I don't eat doughnuts."

"All right. Chocolate-chip muffins, then."

"Those might be *marginally* healthier," I said. "How about some fruit?"

"Oh, forget it," Lily said. "I'm buying doughnuts. Get your own damn food."

Chapter Fourteen

I saw the Celadon Rose through different eyes when we walked in. The store was mine now, from the impeccably dusted stock to the slightly peeling veneer at the bottom of the counter. I should probably have that fixed.

Lily opened the drawer that held our stock of paper napkins. "One of us should call King Soopers and double-check on the platters."

"I can do that. What time is it? I forgot my watch this morning."

"Twelve-fifty. Shall I go ahead and open up?"

"Sure. It's not like the customers haven't seen us eat before." I picked up the bunch of grapes I had bought and headed for the bathroom to rinse them.

When I came out, Lily was standing at the door, signing for an enormous bouquet of blush-colored roses.

She sent me flowers for my birthday every year, so I had expected something like this. "You are so sweet! Thank you!" I put the grapes down and gave her a hug.

She set the bouquet on the counter and adjusted a flower. "It is sweet, but the ones I ordered aren't here yet. Maybe these are from your parents."

I opened the card and read it. "You already have a Celadon Rose, so these are pink. All my love, Galan." I smiled mistily.

Lily turned and stared at me. "Wait a minute . . . Are you two back together?"

I tucked the card into my purse. "No, but Kutara is in Kansas with a posse of elves, following a lead on Fellseth. If he is still alive, I don't think he'll get away this time."

"That's great news! I mean, it would be better if they had found his corpse, but this is a start." She pointed out the front window at a brown UPS truck that was parking at the curb. "Hey, look! Your first delivery as new owner."

"Maybe it's the wind chimes. I was hoping we'd get them today."

The deliveryman pushed open the door, dressed in classic polyester from his brown shorts to his billed cap. I was disappointed to see he carried only a padded envelope. *Not wind chimes, then.*

I pushed the flowers and food to one side of the counter so I would have a place to sign for the delivery. "Hey, there," I greeted him.

"Hello, Erin," he said cheerfully, and pulled a gun out of the envelope.

I stood, shocked and frozen, as Fellseth tossed the envelope on the floor and pushed his cap off. His hair spilled out limply, damply—no longer silver, but gray. His skin was puffy and had an unnatural sheen, as if it were waterlogged.

The words of the Kansas housewife came back to me. *He looked ill.* Fellseth didn't look ill, he looked drowned.

He reached behind without looking and locked the deadbolt. Then he waved the gun at Lily. "Get out from behind that counter and stand with Erin." She scrambled to comply, and he smiled. "I don't know why I resisted firearms for so long. They really are quite effective."

"What do you want?" I asked, putting my arm around Lily.

"I have always admired the way you get to the point," he said. "I want Galan, and you're going to get him for me."

"No."

"All right. Then I'm going to shoot your friend and anyone else who comes in the store today." His thumb adjusted something on the gun, which made a nasty clicking noise.

"Why bother with Galan? I'll go with you." Why had I not broken our bond when I had the chance?

He narrowed his eyes. "You'll come with me, but not until I kill him. I would have done it already, but I can't seem to find him. So if Mohammed can't find the mountain, Erin will call the mountain on his cell phone."

"He doesn't have a cell phone, and I don't know where he is," I said.

Fellseth raised the gun and took a step forward, his face contorted in anger. "Don't lie!"

I shrank back and felt Lily cringe.

Keeping the gun pointed at us, Fellseth backed up to the counter and dumped our purses out one-handed. He picked up my phone first and brought it to eye level. "All of Kutara's little slaves have cell phones," he muttered, working his way through the LCD menu. "It's the only way they could have rescued you so quickly. Ah!"

His eyes lit up. "Galan Cell. An organized mind is a beautiful thing."

He walked over and put the gun to Lily's head, then shoved the phone at me. "Call him and tell him to come here."

I started to push the button.

"Not yet!" Fellseth barked, causing Lily to gasp. "You're going to hold the phone so I can hear it, too. If you try to warn him, or if you let him come with anyone else, I will shoot . . ." He paused and nudged Lily's head with the gun. "What's your name, dear?"

"L . . . Lily . . ."

"I will shoot Lily."

"If you shoot her, Galan will hear it and know not to come," I said, my voice shaking.

"Oh, he'll still come. But it will be messier all around, and your friend will be dead." He smiled at me, the flesh around his mouth swollen and white. "I *will* get what I want. It's your job to decide how many people are killed in the process."

"There are elves watching the store," I said. "You got in, but if you shoot anyone, they'll hear it and come."

He tilted his head. "I suppose that's possible. If that happens, I'll kill Lily, Galan, and anyone else I can. It's your choice, Erin. How many deaths do you want to be responsible for?"

"I wouldn't be responsible!" I yelled. "You would!"

Fellseth gripped Lily's hair with his free hand and pulled her head against the gun while he stared at me. "One more outburst like that, Erin, and I'll shoot her ear off as a friendly warning. Now call him."

I pushed the Send button and held the phone to my ear, my hand sweating. Fellseth pressed his temple against mine so he could hear. I could *feel* the damp coming off him, along with a sickly sweet odor.

The phone rang. Maybe Galan wouldn't answer.

"Hello?"

I shut my eyes at the sound of his voice. "Hi."

"Erin?" When I was silent, he said, "Is something wrong?"

Fellseth stepped away from me and pushed the gun into Lily's mouth with a rattle of metal on teeth. Her eyes rolled up, showing the whites.

"I got your flowers," I said, my voice trembling.

Fellseth glared at me. "Get him here," he mouthed.

"But, um—the open house is in a few hours," I said shakily. "And we . . . we just had a pipe burst in the bathroom." I closed my eyes to block out the sight of tears running down Lily's face. "The plumber is on his way, but we need to move a lot of stock so it doesn't get wet. I wouldn't ask, but it's kind of an *emergency*." Fellseth pressed against me again so he could hear, and I swallowed a sob.

"I'm glad you called," Galan said cheerfully. "I'll be right over."

"Galan, I . . ." But he had hung up.

Fellseth gave a grunt of triumph and snatched the phone out of my hand. "Isn't he *nice*?" he sneered, pulling the gun out of Lily's mouth. She sagged, and he jerked her upright. "Don't be rude, Erin. Get your friend something to sit on. Carefully, of course, and without doing anything that might make me shoot her."

I went behind the counter and got a stool, feeling my heart pound and sweat gather on my upper lip. Galan was on his way. Fellseth would shoot him, and maybe

Lily, too. There had to be something I could do. I brought the stool over.

He had the gun to Lily's temple again. "Where's the best place to fire from?" he mused, looking around the store. "I know. Put that stool at the end of the counter, against the wall. Lily and I will stay back there, and you can stand up front, so he sees you first." He chuckled. "And last, of course."

I did as he directed. How long would it take Galan to come? Eight minutes? Ten? I watched Fellseth arrange Lily to his satisfaction.

"Now go over there," he ordered me.

I went to stand in front of the door.

Lily took a deep, gasping breath. "What if a customer comes in?"

Fellseth furrowed his brow in thought. "Do you have a Closed sign?"

"No," I said. "We just turn off the lights."

"Make a sign. CLOSED FOR THE MORNING—WATER DAMAGE. And let me see it before you tape it to the door."

As I got out paper and a marker, I tried to think of a way to work a message into the sign. My hand hovered over the page.

"Just write what I said," Fellseth barked. "It doesn't take a lot of thought."

I wrote the message, a new idea forming in my mind. Fellseth had said that I could break my bond with Galan if I wanted to more than anything. If I did, could I convince Fellseth that he didn't need to kill Galan? Or would Galan feel it break and know something was wrong? Was it worth the risk to Lily to warn him? Was there any guarantee that Fellseth wouldn't shoot Lily anyway?

I finished the sign and showed it to Fellseth.

"Fine," he said, waving me toward the door with his free hand. "Tape it to the door, without making any funny head or hand movements."

I taped up the sign.

"Now, get back about ten feet. Another foot. A little more toward me. That's good."

Once Fellseth had positioned me, he didn't seem interested in further conversation. I watched him rest the gun on Lily's shoulder and sight along it, toward the door.

I concentrated. *I want to break our bond. I want it more than anything. I have to save Galan.* Nothing seemed to be changing. I couldn't even feel the bond, as I had the one other time I'd considered breaking it.

Someone parked a car across the street. I tensed, my brain a black haze of fear and despair. A woman and two children got out and disappeared down the street.

This was no good. My legs were shaking and sweat ran down the side of my neck. I glanced at Fellseth. He grinned at me around the gun.

I have to relax. If I can relax, maybe I can access the bond. I closed my eyes.

"Open, please," Fellseth said. "I don't want you standing there looking tragic."

I opened my eyes. An internal voice was chanting phrases of failure and desperation: *He's going to kill Galan. There's nothing you can do.*

I silenced those thoughts. *I am grounded.* The meditation I learned with Galan welled up in my mind. Maybe it would help me to concentrate.

I focused on the base of my spine. *Red is for survival*

and foundation. Galan feels like my foundation, my home. He worked here in the store with me.

Orange is for passion. I moved my attention to low in my belly. *I love him so much. I need him, too. All I want is for us to be okay.* The first stirrings of energy came up through the soles of my feet, but still I couldn't feel the bond.

Fellseth whispered something to Lily and chuckled. My concentration faltered slightly, but I went on.

Yellow is for the intellect. I thought of Galan's talent, and rabbits frolicking across a page. The flow strengthened, traveling up my legs.

Green is for the heart. I remembered the first time I had seen Galan's face, beautiful and strange under the streetlight. He had wanted to bond to me forever, even when I pushed him away. My throat tightened.

Blue is for the throat, and my ability to communicate. I would love him forever, and I wanted to be able to tell him.

Indigo, the third eye, for vision and intuition. I could *almost* sense the bond. There was only one more to go.

And violet is for the universe, and my connection to everything in it. The fine hairs on my arms stood up, and something moved in my vision.

Galan stood outside the front door, reaching for the handle.

Our bond flashed between us like an invisible line of flame. Galan opened the door as if in slow motion. I turned and saw Fellseth's finger tighten on the trigger. "No!" I screamed, and raised a hand toward the dark elf.

There was no crackling bolt of electricity—just a disturbance in the air that flowed from my palm like a lightning-fast ripple on a lake. I saw Fellseth's eyes widen just before it reached him, and then he exploded outward in a cloud of silver motes. I watched as the cloud expanded and disappeared, like sparks burning out.

The gun slid down Lily's arm and clattered to the floor. She stared at me, open-mouthed, then slumped against the wall with a sob.

The last thing I saw before my vision went dark was Galan, standing ashen faced in the doorway.

Someone was holding my hand. I opened my eyes to see Galan looking down at me. He smiled, squeezing my fingers. "It's good to have you back."

I reached up and ran my fingers through the silky curtain of his hair. "It's good to be back."

We were still in the store. Beyond Galan, Lily looked down, her face still tear streaked.

Galan helped me off the floor.

I leaned against the counter and blinked to clear my vision. "What happened?"

Galan looked at Lily. "We were hoping you could tell us." He went to the end of the counter and picked Fellseth's gun off the floor.

I rubbed my face. "Well, I was going to break my bond with you . . ."

"What? *Why?*" he demanded.

"So Fellseth wouldn't have to kill you, and also to warn you that something was happening."

Lily stared at me. "But Fellseth said he'd kill me if you warned Galan."

I sighed. "Did he seem like the kind of person who wouldn't kill you anyway?"

"Well, when you put it like that, no." She waved at the empty stool. "But what happened to him?"

Galan ran his hands over the wall behind the counter. "He's laminated all over your store."

"Eeeeeew!" Lily and I both said.

"It's just an energy signature. It won't require a sponge. But there's no question now that he's dead."

"And you killed him," Lily said. "How?"

I furrowed my brow. "Like I said, I was trying to break my bond with Galan, but I was so terrified I couldn't concentrate. So I meditated to calm down, and automatically did the energy-raising meditation I learned with Galan."

I looked at him. "I had just finished when you came to the door, and I could almost *see* our bond at that moment." I shook my head in wonder. "All I did was put my hand up."

"Chi." Lily nodded firmly at Galan's perplexed expression. "She must have had quite a chi flow going, and when she raised her hand it all went toward Fellseth, with her intention behind it. The top martial-arts masters use chi to break boards by simply putting their hands against them." Lily raised her own hand to illustrate. "No chop, just energy."

"In all fairness," I said, "Fellseth looked pretty bad. Maybe that's why he used a gun. It probably didn't take much to finish him off. How long was I out?"

Galan pulled me close with both hands at my waist. "For the worst twenty minutes of my life. I think I should take you home."

"I can't go home. There's too much to do!" I stood on tiptoes and kissed him. "I'm spending the rest of my life with you, and we're having a party to celebrate!"

He cradled my face, joy dawning on his own. "Do you mean that?"

"When you came in that door, I knew that I wanted to be with you more than anything. No amount of dark elves will change that."

He wrapped his arms around me, and his chuckle rumbled beneath my ear. "If dark elves know what's good for them, they'll stay away from you."

Chapter Fifteen

Galan called Kutara and gave her the news, then stayed on to help with the open house—hanging silk flower garlands mixed with twinkle lights, and running errands. A real delivery person delivered the wind chimes I had hoped for, and we hung them throughout the store.

When it was done, the three of us stood by the front door and surveyed the results.

"This is the best it's ever looked," Lily said, "and I don't own it anymore." She pretended to sniff back tears.

I laughed and looked at my watch. "We got done in time to close for an hour and get some dinner." I laced my fingers through Galan's hand and smiled at him. "A lot of that was due to you."

He smiled back. "I enjoyed it."

Lily squeezed past us to get her purse out of the office. "What do you think, should we get a Nick and Willy's pizza?"

"Sure." I turned to follow her.

Galan tugged on my arm. "Um, could you and I maybe stay here?"

"What for?"

"Just because."

I blinked. "Okay."

"Have fun, kids." Lily grinned at us and left.

Galan turned the deadbolt on the front door and switched off the main light fixtures. Overhead, the flower garlands glowed and sparkled with tiny lights. "Stay here. I'll be right back."

I watched as he disappeared down an aisle toward the back entrance. My car was parked out there. When he returned, his arms overflowed with sheets, blankets, and pillows.

I laughed in surprise. "When did you make a raid on my linen closet?"

"When I was out getting more lights. I also packed you a sandwich." He led me down an aisle that couldn't be seen from outside the shop, then knelt and layered the bedding on the floor.

I giggled. "And is eating what you have in mind?"

He pulled me down to lie beside him. "I have been doing some research." He began to unbutton my blouse. "I found two tales of human-elf penansel. They might just be legend, but one of the stories talked about a human who was able to heal wounds after her elf marriage. I think our bond may already be stronger than we know."

I ran my fingers through his hair, letting the silvery strands cascade down and stroking the pointed tip of one ear with my finger. "Even so, that would be a very big step to take."

He brushed my shirt aside and pressed a kiss on the

curve of my left breast, over my heart. "The other tale said that the human lived for much, much longer than normal." He raised his head, and his violet eyes were dark and calm. "How can I pass up the chance at more time together, loving you the way I do?"

I pulled him to me, holding him tightly. This was more than I asked. Maybe more than he should give. "But when I'm *gone* . . . Forever is a long time."

"These are uncertain times for elves." I felt his lips curve against my neck. "But you I'm sure about."

We undressed each other tenderly. In between kisses, Galan stroked his hands over every inch of my skin, until I felt liquid with pleasure.

He moved away. I whimpered a little at the loss, even as I saw him pull his vest out of the tangle of our clothing and take something from the pocket.

"I made something for you, trusting that we would be together," he murmured, returning to lie on top of me. He covered my mouth with his own and slid a hand under my head to cradle me even closer, making me moan at the urgency of his kiss.

When I wrapped my legs around his and lifted my hips in invitation, he slid inside me. I felt the heat and length of him, and a dissolving between us, until I could feel his pleasure as well as my own. The intensity of our union made my mind whirl, and my ragged breathing turned to gasps as I felt our climax approach.

Galan took my left hand from the back of his neck and held it above my head with his right. "*Ech torash lannan,*" he murmured, moving deeper, faster. "*Sil fass, non tiem.*"

An unseen current swept the store, causing the wind chimes to ring softly. I threw my head back and cried out as my body arched into release. Galan's shuddering matched my own, and I felt him slide something onto my ring finger as we strained together.

Our trembling subsided slowly. He collapsed on top of me, heavy and warm, and dearer to me than I thought possible. When I was able to move, I lifted my hand to see what he had given me.

The light from the decorations was dim, but I didn't need it to see the cool band of white gold that glowed on my finger. It was shaped like a wreath of leaves. A pale green stone decorated the center, carved in the shape of a rose.

"Those words you said, what did they mean?" I whispered.

Galan raised himself and took my hand, folding it in his so the ring pressed between us. "From my body to yours, one heart, forever."

Epilogue

The Celadon Rose's open house was a smash success. Kutara had even managed to fly back in time to attend.

As the crowd milled through the aisles, I saw Geraldine Krupper advancing on me, holding a piece of Mrs. Jamison's gingerbread.

"I must say, Erin, I have never seen you look so well. The drive to Nebraska must have been good for you, even if I can't get a straight answer from Lily as to what the emergency was."

I dropped my voice and leaned close to Geraldine's snowy hair. "Actually, Lily and I were working so hard that we drove to Las Vegas for a break, but she didn't want me to tell anyone."

"Oh, for heaven's sake," Geraldine tutted. "You Boulder types are prudish about such silly things."

"You are absolutely right. Excuse me, I have to check on the food." It took me a while to find my elderly neighbor in the crowd. "Mrs. Jamison! I saw your gingerbread, so I knew you were here."

"I should have made two batches. All these people!" Mrs. Jamison pointed to where Galan stood, tall and handsome, surrounded by a group of admiring females. "I see your fellow over there. You might have to be careful someone else doesn't snatch him up."

"I'm not worried." I smiled and held out my left hand to show Mrs. Jamison my ring.

"Oh, isn't that *beautiful*." Mrs. Jamison squeezed my hand in her fragile one. "You know, I thought there was something different about you. You look better than I've ever seen you. It's like you're lit from within."

"I think it's happiness," I whispered, and kissed her cheek.

"Hey, store owner!" Lily waved at me from the refreshment table. "We've run out of napkins. Could you get some paper towels?"

I excused myself and went to the bathroom at the back of the store. The paper towels were stored in a cupboard over the sink. I was reaching up to get them when I heard Kutara's voice through the open door.

I came out, the towels in my hand. *Oh, no.* She was being talked at by the woman who was interested in attracting elf energy to her home.

"I was in here to buy a book," the woman said, "and that man over there said he had a Ph.D. in elves or something. So I asked him how to attract them, and he fed me the biggest line of you-know-what."

Kutara made a dismissive noise and looked away.

"I know! Can you believe it? Something about getting rid of my horses and letting the weeds grow. Anyway, none of it made sense to me. What do you think elves would want?"

"Since you ask." Kutara raised an elegant fist and flicked up her index finger. "First, a companion with a vigorous sexual drive."

The woman took a small step backward.

"Second, a private base of operations with a loyal staff."

"I . . ." the woman squeaked.

"And last but certainly not least . . ." Kutara raised a third finger and leaned toward her trembling listener. "A really high-speed Internet connection."

I put my hand over my mouth to cover a grin and saw Galan smiling at me from across the crowd.

The world was full of new things, odd things, and wonderfully sexy things. As far as I could tell, anything was possible.

Romantic Suspense from
Lisa Jackson

See How She Dies
0-8217-7605-3 $6.99US/$9.99CAN

The Morning After
0-8217-7295-3 $6.99US/$9.99CAN

The Night Before
0-8217-6936-7 $6.99US/$9.99CAN

Cold Blooded
0-8217-6934-0 $6.99US/$9.99CAN

Hot Blooded
0-8217-6841-7 $6.99US/$8.99CAN

If She Only Knew
0-8217-6708-9 $6.50US/$8.50CAN

Unspoken
0-8217-6402-0 $6.50US/$8.50CAN

Twice Kissed
0-8217-6038-6 $5.99US/$6.99CAN

Whispers
0-8217-7603-7 $6.99US/$9.99CAN

Wishes
0-8217-6309-1 $5.99US/$6.99CAN

Deep Freeze
0-8217-7296-1 $7.99US/$10.99CAN

Final Scream
0-8217-7712-2 $7.99US/$10.99CAN

Fatal Burn
0-8217-7577-4 $7.99US/$10.99CAN

Shiver
0-8217-7578-2 $7.99US/$10.99CAN

Available Wherever Books Are Sold!
Visit our website at www.kensingtonbooks.com

The wise man has long ears, big eyes, and a short tongue.
Proverb

September 9, '78

your Susan
with love xxx

The Social Philosophers

Community and Conflict in Western Thought

The
Social
Philosophers

Community and Conflict
in Western Thought

ROBERT NISBET

THOMAS Y. CROWELL COMPANY

NEW YORK   ESTABLISHED 1834

Library of Congress Cataloging in Publication Data
Nisbet, Robert A.
    The social philosophers: community and conflict in Western
thought.
    Includes bibliographical references.
    1. Political science—History. 2. Sociology—
History.   I.   Title.
JA81.N.57   301'.01   72–83132
ISBN 0–690–74406–4   ISBN 0–690–74405–6 (pbk)

To Caroline

*Text design by Angela Foote. "The Ball Puzzle" on the
cover and at the chapter openings is by sculptor Charles
O. Perry of Rome. The cover and chapter openings
were designed by 20/20 Inc., photography by Jacques
Hutzler.*

Manufactured in the United States of America

1 2 3 4 5 6 7 8 9 10

Preface

A few words on the general nature of this book will perhaps be of use to both students and general readers. I regard the book as falling in the area bounded by what is commonly called intellectual history on the one hand and social history on the other. The title properly suggests that the larger part of the book is concerned with the philosophers and the systems of ideas that form the mainstream of Western social philosophy and provide indispensable background to any full understanding of the contemporary social sciences. No single trend in recent years has been more vivid in the social sciences than the reawakening of interest in the sources and channels of the ideas, perspectives, and values that lie beneath the varied theories and methodologies of the social sciences.

But as I look over what I have written, the book seems to me to be almost equally a social history of western Europe since the time of the Greeks. It has never been possible for me to think of ideas except in their relation to institutions, processes, and events. I would have found it very difficult, if not impossible, to have presented the history of the fundamental ideas of Western social thought apart from the nature and crises of the fundamental institutions in Western social history. Hence the attention I have given in each chapter to the sociological elements of the type of institution—or as I choose to call it, *community*—that is under consideration. Apart from the social history of militarism, politics, religion, revolution, ecology, and pluralism, however abbreviated such history must be for purposes of a single volume, I could not have made the ideas discussed seem other than disembodied. Hence, too, the considerable amount of attention, often necessarily at the expense of detailed treatment of certain philosophers and their ideas, to key events and processes, to conflicts and crises in the social history of the West, reaching all the way from the fragmentation of kinship society in ancient Greece and Rome through the rise of Christianity, the first ecological communes, the national state with its fateful centralization of power, the rise of modern revolution and war, down to the great military-revolutionary states of twentieth-century Russia and China.

That this book is selective in its treatment goes without saying—or apology. How could it be otherwise? If there are ideas and events the reader expects to find and doesn't, I can only offer him in counterpoise those in the book which he perhaps had not expected to find.

Although the structure of the book, its division by themes or topics instead of conventional periods of Western history, is discussed at some length in the Introduction, let me say here, by way of prefatory emphasis, that I have long distrusted the conventional narrative method as the means of trying to bring history, either intellectual or social, alive. The truth is, history—in the objective sense of all that has happened in the past—falls into no pattern or structure in and of itself. To suppose that the narrative, unilinear, storylike, first-this-and-then-and-then pattern of historical writing so commonly found *is* history is to suppose nonsense. I do not suggest that there is any method or structure we can provide that will be a faithful representation of subject. Modern historians are only just beginning to be aware of the profound issues regarding the relation between investigator and subject matter that physicists have been aware of ever since the seminal works of Bohr and Heisenberg. I mention this in passing only to reassure those readers who may think at first sight that my topical approach to Western history in this book is a wanton violation of what used to be called the "seamless web of history."

If the flavor of the classroom is occasionally to be found in the book—the pedagogue's inevitable references backward and forward to subject matter—I apologize to those it annoys. From experience I know there are others for whom it will be helpful in trying to keep on course in waters that are notoriously difficult of passage. Suffice it to say the book took shape in, and is bound to have retained the imprint of, classes taught for many years at first Berkeley, then Riverside, in the University of California. I acknowledge with pleasure the generous and stimulating atmosphere of that great university. Parts of the chapters on the revolutionary and plural communities were used in my William Allan Neilson Lectures at Smith College in the fall of 1971. To President Thomas Mendenhall and his colleagues I offer sincere thanks for the privilege of membership in their distinguished academic community. I would like also to express thanks to several editors of Thomas Y. Crowell Company for their help: to Thomas Simpson for suggesting the book in the first place, to James F. Bergin and Herman Makler for valued suggestions and counsel, and to Virginia N. Brinkley for careful editing of the final manuscript that became at times near-collaboration. Finally, this book is dedicated to my wife. There is no other way of suggesting the measure of her participation in it.

R.N.

Contents

The
Social
Philosophers

Community and Conflict
in Western Thought

Introduction

The history of Western social philosophy is, basically, the history of men's ideas and ideals of community. That fact is the essential theme of this book. By *community* I refer to much more than what is denoted by mere local community. I use the word throughout the book in its oldest and lasting sense of relationships among individuals that are characterized by a high degree of personal intimacy, of social cohesion or moral commitment, and of continuity in time. The basis of community may be kinship, religion, political power, revolution, or race. It may be, in fact, any of a large number of activities, beliefs, or functions. All that is essential is that the basis be of sufficient appeal and of sufficient durability to enlist numbers of human beings, to arouse loyalties, and to stimulate an over-riding sense of distinctive identity.

Closely related to the idea of community, forming its negative back-drop, as it were, is the idea of anticommunity. There are many ways in which this idea can be expressed, given vivid manifestation, and all of them are current in our own time. There is the fear of the social void, of alienation, of estrangement from others, even from one's own self, of loss

1

of identity, of great open spaces of impersonality and rejection. Throughout the history of social thought, indeed throughout human history, the power of the idea of community has lain in large degree in fear or apprehension of the opposite of community. Man, Balzac wrote, has a horror of aloneness—not physical aloneness: no one fears that, in ordinary degree at least. Mental, spiritual, emotional, social aloneness is, however, very different. And it is the fear, above all other fears in the human condition, of that kind of human aloneness that generates cravings for community— for the sense of relatedness to others as persons that transcends all momentary isolations, separations, and other trials of life, endowing one with the sense of identity that can never come from germ plasm or from internal consciousness by itself.

Our age is preoccupied by community. A host of evidences of this fact lies all around us. We see youth's search for community take the form of activities ranging from musical festivals all the way to communes remote from the centers of civilization. But the quest for community is found no less among other age groups in our society, among the middle-aged, the elderly. Scores of manifestations of this quest for community are to be seen: in political, ethnic, and economic groups, in increasingly communal types of living, in popular crusades often less notable for their varied objectives than for the prized intensity of fellowship to be found in pursuit of these objectives. So do the literature and philosophy of our time reflect this obsessing interest in community and its values. What else indeed is the by now widespread search for personal identity but one side of a coin that bears on its other side the search for community within which identity is alone reinforced?

Our age differs from other ages, however, only in the distinctive cultural character of this quest for community. The preoccupation with, the search for, community and the concern with anticommunity are to be seen, as I show, in all major ages of Western social philosophy. Ages may differ in type of community sought and in degree of fear of the social void. But there is quite literally no age since social philosophy began for the West in the writings of the ancient Greek philosophers—themselves deeply concerned with the loss of the kinship community that had been for countless millennia mankind's major, and even exclusive, form of community—when concern with community has not been present in social thought.

From Plato's lasting portrait of the political community, written amid scenes of perceived breakdown and of alienation, through Augustine's masterful detailing of religious community in his *City of God*, through the vital and influential works of Sir Thomas More, Hobbes, Locke, Althusius, Rousseau, and many others, down to Marx's brilliant vision of socialism, to Tocqueville's premonitions of mass society, and to Kropotkin's memorable essays on mutual aid and anarchism, the over-

arching quest of these social philosophers has been, I suggest, the quest
for community.

As the chapter headings alone indicate, the paths to community
which have been proffered for two and a half millennia in the West are
diverse. What is one man's community is, plainly enough, often another
man's anticommunity. There are those who have seen the light of community shining most clearly from kinship or from one or another of its
numerous social progeny: groups and associations that have consciously
modeled themselves on the family. Others, however, have seen community, the ideal community, in terms of politics. Still others have found
lasting community in religion, in revolution, even in war, or among those
supposedly natural, ecological types of interdependence that man shares
with the rest of the organic world.

I do not say that community and its properties are the sole subject of
the works of the major social philosophers since the Greeks. This would
be absurd. In these works we find innumerable treatments of other aspects
of society: status, authority, roles, values, change, stability, and so on.
What I do say, however, is that overwhelmingly the great social philosophers of the West, beginning with Plato and Aristotle and coming down
to the present, have made the search for legitimate community, for lasting
community, the principal object of their thought. Within this obsessive
quest, it seems to me, are to be found the ideas on authority, power, status,
among others, which are indubitably important elements in the history of
social philosophy. Seeing the larger society as filled with the traps and pit-
falls of egoism, avarice, naked force, chaos, and fear and, as the means of
escaping or forestalling these evils, to concern oneself with the nature of
the good community, the community within which man has the sense of
escape from the void combined with justice and personal fulfillment—
this, I suggest in this book, has been, and still remains, the major preoccupation of those we call the social philosophers in the West.

Western social philosophy, as we know it, begins with the fall of the
kinship community in ancient Athens. When Cleisthenes, one of the
authentic revolutionary geniuses of history, instigated his reforms in
509 B.C. leading to the annihilation of the tribes, phratries, and clans
under which the Athenians had lived for countless centuries, he not only
brought into being the city-state that was to be the context of Athenian
life and culture for the next century or two—a context that proved to be
one of the richest in all history for the efflorescence of knowledge and the
arts—but he also set in motion currents of thought that have never ceased
to be vital parts of the Western tradition, right down to our own day.

Out of the fall of the ancient kinship community in Athens emerged
three distinctive types of organization in the Mediterranean world, with
patterns of social thought to match: the military, the political state, and,

in due time, the religion we know as Christianity—a product of Judaea, of course, but hardly less, in theological terms, the product of Greek and Roman ideas, themes, and circumstances. As I show in the first three chapters, the rise of the military, political, and Christian communities, in both life and thought, is inseparable from issues posed by conflict between kinship values and the very different, even profoundly antithetical values associated with these new structures, each dependent in its origin and early development upon the fragmentation of tribe and clan and the dispersion of their members into a world in which for the first time in man's history the problem of community would become obsessive. This is not to say that all subsequent philosophical searches for community have been, at bottom, merely efforts to return to the security of kinship society. That would be too simple. It is, however, to emphasize that the distinctive quests for community which form Western social philosophy very clearly have their beginning in the collapse of kinship.

If we ask what was the primal cause of the fall of kinship in the West, the answer must be war. By the same token, war and the special community created by war are the real point of departure for the rise of Western social philosophy. It was the continuing and accelerating pressure of war on ancient Athens that resulted in the momentous reforms of Cleisthenes, which achieved as their very first effect the great improvement of Athenian military, and then economic and cultural, activities. Dislike war and its effects as we will, the fact remains that, apart from the continued press of war in the West for some twenty-five centuries, it would be impossible to account for a very great deal of what we call Western civilization. And, as I suggest in some detail in the first chapter, from ancient Athens to modern Europe, war has been the continuing object of philosophical concern in Western society. We dare not underestimate the military form of community.

Likewise have politics and the political community been obsessive concerns of philosophy in the West. Very probably the political community, as reflected in writings beginning with Plato and continuing without interruption to our age, is the single most powerful form of Western community—certainly since the waning of the Middle Ages— and, clearly, the form that has been most attractive in modern times to non-Western peoples struggling to cope with Western imperialism, to shake off Western domination, and to create societies as autonomous and self-sustaining as those of an England, an America, a Germany, or a Russia. Between the military and political communities, as I show, there is very close affinity. A great deal of the centralized power and the collectivization that we find in the Western political state is the product of the transference to civil society of conceptions born of war. And the conflict with kinship society has been as intense in the history of the state as in that of the military. It was on the ruins of Athenian kinship that the first genuine political order rose in the West, and the struggle between kinship and the state has been relentless ever since.

The third of the major Western forms of community, religion—specifically the universal religion that is Christianity—must also be seen, in its origin and continuing early development, in the light of the same kind of conflict with kinship society. The rise of the universal type of religion—Buddhism, Confucianism, Islam, Christianity—is invariably associated with historical periods of sustained war and intense social conflict. Only within such circumstances, on the evidence, does it become possible for prophets of a universal deity to detach individuals from their traditional, largely kinship, structures of belief and weld them into new communities based upon a faith that transcends all local and ethnic ties.

Christianity is a striking illustration of what happens, or of what is involved, in the rise of all universal religions. Christianity began, as we know, as no more than a tiny Jewish sect in ancient Judaea. It claimed as its deity, however, one of universal scope, available to all who would forsake old gods and idols and render worship to the one true God. In potentiality, then, the religion of Christ was universal from the outset. What was required, however, to convert potentiality into actuality was a surrounding society in the grip of war, fragmentation of old and cherished kinship ties, and deep moral and social conflicts. It was in such a society that Paul transformed Christianity from sect into universal church. From the beginning, Christianity was in conflict with traditional kinship values in Roman society, as it was to be shortly afterward with the Roman state and with still other sectors of Roman society. And from the time of Paul down to our own age, the history of Christianity has been one of almost incessant conflict between religious values and those to be found in other spheres of society.

In sum, if community, or the quest for community, is the essence of Western social philosophy, conflict is, and has been from the very beginning, the indispensable context. We commonly think of conflict as disintegrative in effect. Only a moment's thought, however, is required to remind us that it is in circumstances of conflict with external forces that almost every social group achieves its highest unity. Precisely the same is true of the history of social thought in the West. Prophets of the military community have from the beginning been in conflict with prophets of the political and the religious communities. From Cleisthenes, Plato, and Augustine, this conflict has been written deeply into the pages of Western social philosophy.

Military, political, and religious values have predominated in the Western search for community, but we must not be blind to other types. Of the several which also have had their due share of philosophical concern in the West during the past two millennia, I have chosen three:

revolutionary, ecological, and pluralist. No one of these can be said to compete seriously in terms of amount of attention received or effect of sheer philosophical devotion, with the military, political, and religious communities. Even so, as I believe I show in the last three chapters, Western social thought would be a great deal poorer apart from those such as the Jacobins and the followers of Marx and Engels in the revolutionary tradition and Benedict, Thomas More, and Peter Kropotkin in the ecological tradition, and those from Aristotle to Burke and Tocqueville who have represented the pluralist tradition.

The idea of revolution, as it has been known in the West—and increasingly in other parts of the world—since the French Revolution, scarcely existed in the ancient world, though of course there were revolts, civil wars, and coups d'état from time to time. Nor did it exist in medieval times, though, as I suggest, a prototype of it can be found in those millennialist-terrorist groups, activated almost entirely by visions of the Second Coming, that began to erupt on the European landscape from about the fifteenth century on. Likewise, we find the revolutionary community foreshadowed to a degree in what has come to be called social banditry, a form of combined criminality and revolt that began to take form among peasant sectors of society in western Europe. The legend of Robin Hood epitomizes and romanticizes this form of prerevolutionary community for most of us. But the revolutionary community itself actually comes into being with the Jacobins in France, foreshadowed, to be sure, by the English Puritans under Cromwell the century before. From the Jacobins' manifestos and laws, and from the dedicated, not to say fanatical, zeal with which they prosecuted the first total revolution (in aim at least) in Western history, comes the beacon light that since the nineteenth century has illumined those writings like Marx's, Sorel's, Lenin's, and Fanon's that are so widely read today, and the spark that has ignited vast areas of Asia and Africa and Oceania as well as of the West. In every sense, as I try to show, revolution is just as intense and militant and allegiance-begetting a raison d'être of community as any other known to Western man.

I have used the term *ecological* to describe another vital tradition of communal thought in the West, especially since the early Middle Ages. The word refers clearly and specifically not only to those interdependences that exist between organic and inorganic life, or among plants and animals, or between man and the physical world, but to any and all forms of interdependence that are *natural*, or believed to be natural—in contrast to the artificial, and especially to the artificial that is regarded as corrupt and degenerative. From the time when Saint Benedict of Nursia wrote and promulgated his immensely influential little book *The Rule*, through Sir Thomas More's *Utopia*, down to the writings of such nineteenth- and twentieth-century protagonists of the ecological community as Proudhon and Kropotkin, this type of community, stressing nature, simplicity, and the natural bond between man and the rest of the organic and physical world, has been one of the most brilliant—but also neglected —traditions of Western social philosophy. I have not hesitated to give prominence to this tradition of community. The present valiant efforts to restore the ecological community once again to a signal place in our highly technological, politicized, bureaucratized society are enough to ensure the relevance of this part of my book.

Last among the types of community I have dealt with in this book is the plural community. It is the fate of pluralism that at no time in the history of Western philosophy has it ever seriously rivaled other forms of community in general appeal. The basic reason is not far to seek. As against the claims of unity, those of diversity and plurality must often seem an invitation to disorder, even anarchy. And the quest for the One is very old and sacred in the history of religion and philosophy alike. It is not easy, in short, to make the values of pluralism, diversity, localism, and the dispersion of power compete successfully with those of the philosophies of Plato, Augustine, Rousseau, and Marx. And yet from Aristotle through Althusius, Burke, and Tocqueville down to Max Weber in our own century, the attraction of the plural community, of *communitas communitatum*, has been a strongly persistent feature of Western culture. Living as we do in a world grown increasingly more centralized and collectivized, with the roots of localism and cultural diversity seemingly cut by the forces of modernity, it is possible to see in the plural community man's last best hope.

One final point: the structure of this book. It could well be asked why I have organized the materials in this fashion. Why not in strict chronological order, as is most commonly done, with all the ancient materials together, and with those of the medieval, early modern, modern, and recent ages similarly brought together in their respective chapters? Admittedly, this is the arrangement with which we are most familiar, the way most histories of ideas are written. I do not say the chronological, unilinear framework is wrong: it can serve excellent purposes. But it is not infallible, and it is, at bottom, as arbitrary as the divisions of time it is made to serve. Worst of all, it tends to conceal or to distort persistent patterns of ideas which are very real and which cannot really be fitted to the Procrustean bed of unilinear narrative. The plural community, for example, is a pattern of thought as old as Aristotle, as recent as Weber or Jacques Ellul. In one form or other, it has never really been absent from Western thought. But the same is true of the religious and political and military communities or patterns, and also, though in less degree, of the ecological and revolutionary.

I would argue that there is more in common between Aristotle's and Burke's philosophies of community, separated though they are by more than two thousand years, than there is between Plato's and Aristotle's, separated by only a few years but by a veritable universe of moral and social values. There is more in common between the thought of a Robespierre in Jacobin France and a Fanon in our own age, each pledged to absolute terror in the service of absolute virtue, separated though they are by a century and a half, than there is between, say, Robespierre and Burke, contemporaries and neighbors, as it were, but a million light-years apart in their view of man's proper relation to society. How like in spirit and aim are Plato, Hobbes, and Rousseau in their rendering of the political community, despite the stretches of time which separate them. So, too, with the other patterns of ideas I have treated in this book. To break up these patterns—these communities, as I call them—would surely serve no good purpose. The unity conferred by chronological division is often a spurious unity.

I do not deny that unilinear, narrative, chronological history has its legitimate purposes. Indeed I have more or less followed this type of organization within the treatment of each form of community considered; to do otherwise would be antic and absurd. But for the same reasons that social historians are increasingly finding such presentations of history unsuitable, so, I believe, must intellectual historians concerned with ideas, their contexts and relationships. What the French call *histoire événementielle*—to be identified less by its common focus on politics or its narrative rhetoric than by its unswerving view that earlier events, acts and ideas beget later events, acts, and ideas, quite as butterflies beget butterflies, to use Sir Isaiah Berlin's delightful phrasing—may be useful in recovery and representation of political or diplomatic history. But this form of historical presentation leaves much to be desired in economic, social, and intellectual realms.

In the same way that we are able to discern classes of events, changes, and conditions in economic and social history—classes without whose existence genuine comparative history would be impossible—we are also able, I suggest, to discern classes of ideas for the purposes of intellectual history, comparative or other. Such classes would seem at least as real, though consisting of ideas, theories, and assumptions, as the classes of data employed by the economic or social historian. What in this book I have called communities are basically classes of ideas, which may be seen to form the intellectual landscape of Europe just as classes of institutions and groups may be seen to form the social landscape.

We must not, to be sure, in the process of discerning patterns of ideas, neglect the vital contexts in which the major representations of these patterns have made their crucial appearances. To the best of my ability, within the space limits of this book, I have not. I have tried in every significant instance to show that what the ruins of the Greek city-state were to Plato, what the disintegration of the Roman Empire was to Augustine, what the moribundity of *l'ancien régime* was to Rousseau, and what the perceived imminent collapse of European capitalism was to Marx, some analogous context of crisis or challenge has been for the other major thinkers considered in this book. Certainly the task is a vital one; for, as I have indicated, ideas do not beget ideas genealogically in time. The major ideas are invariably stirred into being by crises, by the perception of conflicting values, institutions, and modes of community. That Hobbes was profoundly well read in Greek, especially Platonic, thought is a matter of importance, of course; but of greater importance from the historian's point of view is the seventeenth-century English revolutionary setting that stimulated Hobbes to bring his learning and his imagination to bear upon the problem of the political community. We should not possess Burke's greatest work had it not been for the French Revolution and his powerful reaction to it, though all of the really vital ideas in his *Reflections on the Revolution in France* may be found in his lesser writings. So it has been with all of the major social philosophers. Without the perceptions of deep crisis that recur in western European history, there would be very little indeed of what we call social philosophy.

If western European civilization seems the richest in the profusion and diversity of its ideas of community and society, it is because, as I have sought to show in the early chapters, that civilization, for a number of reasons, all geographical and historical, is richest also in number of crises perceived. From the time of the fall of the kinship system in ancient Athens under the Cleisthenean revolution, Western society has been little other than a succession of perceived crises, each with its notable result in social philosophy—or, as I prefer to say, in the philosophy of community. Conflict, crisis, community: these are fundamental aspects of the Western intellectual tradition.

1 The Military Community

War and Western Values

Although it may seem strange to deal with war and militarism in a book on social philosophy, the history of Western society, and particularly the history of Western ideas and values, requires this. In every age since Western philosophy as we know it came into existence in ancient Greece, major thinkers have occupied themselves either directly with war and the distinctive military community that war brings into existence or else with the pressing issues generated by war: issues of authority, hierarchy, and organization, as well as of change, disorganization, and reconstruction.

Whether we like it or not, the evidence is clear that for close to three thousand years, down to this very moment, Western civilization has been the single most war-ridden, war-dominated, and militaristic civilization in all human history. This is not to say that war and militarism are the essence of Western culture, nor to argue that our basic ideals, our systems of morality, art, and literature, and our culture in general have all been predicated upon or suffused by military values. Such a statement would be mindless calumny. Much of what has been engendered by Western thought and morality, far from being governed by basically military

11

values, has been in the forefront of efforts throughout the world to abolish war once and for all.

But this said, it is still true that there have been more wars in Western civilization during the past three thousand years, more preparations for war, more armies, more battles, a greater toll of human life as the direct result of war, more physical devastation in consequence of war, and more governments established or toppled by means of war than in any other civilization in recorded history. Add to this the almost continuous impact of war making upon other institutions of society, especially the state and the economy.[1] The priority of the political state in Western society, and the profound tendency toward politicization of life that has been a recurrent phenomenon in the West, especially during the last three centuries, come from one overall fact alone: the persisting influence of war and its values. For, as we shall have frequent occasion to note in this book, there is a close and lasting affinity between war and the state.

From a geographical and historical point of view, there is nothing mysterious about the incidence, intensity, and overall effects of war in the West. For many thousands of years, western Europe—which is no more than a small promontory of the great Eurasian continent—has been subject to an almost constant inflow of diverse peoples. Easy access, at first by land, then by sea, has assured this, given the strong incentives provided by soil and climate, especially in the Mediterranean region. Such population movements could hardly have occurred in a setting as relatively small as western Europe without leading to frequent contacts of peoples. Such contacts carried with them possibilities not only for the clash of cultures, making for high rates of change, but for the clash of arms. War became very early a nearly constant part of life in this whole area, as such epic tales as those found in the Old Testament and in the *Iliad* remind us. It is no more possible to separate the diverse ways of human thought from the incidence of war than it is politics, economics, technology, and religion. So enduring and vital a function as war inevitably became from earliest times in western Europe was bound to have created from the beginning a powerful set of values, a powerful community of function and purpose.

Western social philosophy begins in circumstances of war. It was war, above anything else, that dictated the revolutionary reforms of Cleisthenes in Athens in 509 B.C., reforms which brought into existence the polis—and also, for the first time, an army and navy capable of defeating even the great and mighty Persia. And it was again in circumstances of

---

[1] See Quincy Wright, A Study of War, 2 vols. (Chicago: University of Chicago Press, 1942), especially chaps. 7 and 8. And as Wright emphasizes (p. 248), the clear tendency during the past four centuries has been for war to become more, not less, dominating in Western life.

war—but this time the humiliating defeat of Athens by Sparta during the latter part of the fifth century B.C.—that the greatest of all Western philosophers, Plato, wrote his *Republic,* which was suffused with not merely political but military values. Roman law, the greatest single contribution of Rome to the West, came into existence largely on the basis of institutionalization of the military *imperium* for Roman society as a whole. And when we come to the modern world that arose from the ruins of medieval society, we find scarcely a major philosopher not concerned in some degree—that is, if he deals at all with political and social matters—with the role of war and the values of war in their relation to society and to social change. Machiavelli, Hobbes, Rousseau, the leaders of the French Revolution, Marx, Engels, and Lenin: these are only a few of the major philosophers in the West for whom war making was a matter of profound interest and on whose thinking about such matters as sovereignty, nationalism, and revolution the model of military action and military command exercised some degree of influence. We shall come back to all of these minds in later sections of this chapter.

Why has war exerted this deep and lasting effect upon so much of Western thought and action? The answer does not lie, surely, in the carnage and devastation of war, those aspects of the military that are commonly considered repugnant. It lies, one cannot help thinking, in some of the moral values associated with war. After all, valor, heroism, courage, and sacrifice are admired by us all, and it is in time of war that these qualities are likely to be vividly manifest. War can also offer release from the boredom and monotony that so often dominate our ordinary existences. Most especially was this the case during the long ages leading up to the present. For large numbers of young men, going off to war was the only respectable means of breaking away from the routine authority of family and village and the relentless monotony of work on farms or in factories.

There is, however, another and, I believe, more compelling factor in the appeal of war to a great many Western people, lay citizens as well as philosophers and statesmen. This is the lure of the kind of community that can be created by war. We shall see later in this chapter the profound linkage that has taken place in our century between war and revolution, with huge military forces, as in Maoist China, acting as the primary agent of revolutionary change. From the very beginning in the West, there has been revolutionary potential in war. War has been associated with some of the most momentous changes in the history of Western society. Not until the nineteenth century, in the aftermath of the French Revolution, was this affinity between war and revolution seen clearly by philosophers—Marx and Engels foremost among them. Nevertheless, it has been there from the beginning. In war, through war, and from war comes, in short, the possibility of breaking up a society grown intolerable and also the possibility of achieving a new form of society that offers greater rewards. There have been many cultures, and long periods in the history of every culture, in which war was the only means of breaking the cake of custom and effecting the release of individuality, however briefly.

Beyond this, however, the fateful attraction of war has lain in the mobilization of energies, the focusing of actions into a single purpose, and the solidarity that is almost always created by the threat of a foreign enemy. The integrating effects of conflict that the sociologist Georg Simmel stressed in his writings on the subject in the early part of the present century have surely been evident to military chieftains and commanders from earliest times. And from such integrating effects can and very often has come especially in the mass-based societies of the twentieth century, the sense—or illusion, as the case may be—of community.

Such community begins, of course, in the military organization itself, primitive or modern. Under the spur of danger ahead, of dangers and hardships faced communally in the past, of the fruits of victory won in common effort, and of the moral exhilaration that comes from achieving objectives in concert, the feeling of community can be very intense indeed. One need only ask any soldier who has ever experienced the growing together of individuals in squad or platoon, the submergence of egoistic identity in the identity of the larger group, when life itself is dependent upon this process. The many sociological and psychological studies of combat in World War II, and of the varying reactions of soldiers to combat, all attested to a truth that has surely been known from earliest times: the individual soldier fights in, finds psychological reinforcement in, the communal spirit of mutual aid that develops to a far higher degree from membership in a military unit than from anything arising out of the alleged purposes of a particular war. This was just as true, as we learned, among American and Allied troops in the early 1940s during the "popular" war against nazism and fascism as it has proved to be in the extremely unpopular war America has conducted in Vietnam. Military community, for whatever larger purpose, is a very intense and evocative form of community. This was no less true among Nazi soldiers, as postwar studies revealed, than among those who fought against nazism; and it has been equally true from the very beginning of the history of warfare.

But the sense of community inspired by war can go well beyond the military organization itself. What we know to have been the bond between the Roman masses and the conquering legions, with a Julius Caesar or Tiberius at their head, between the French people and Napoleon, with his revolution-spreading armies in nineteenth-century Europe, has been no less evident in recent times. We may hate war and its carnage and its devastation of culture and landscape, but no one who studies World War I and World War II can be oblivious to the deep sense of moral unity, of collective purpose, and, with these, of national community that came over the civil populations of the warring powers. In America alone, who can forget, if he was then alive and aware of what was going on, the sudden termination, once the Japanese bombing of Pearl Harbor took place, of discord, division, and internal strife, products of a decade of depression and of bitterly antagonistic attitudes regarding such matters as isolationism and intervention with respect to Europe? One knew then what the English philosopher L. P. Jacks had had in mind when he wrote in the 1920s of "the spiritual peace that war can bring." At a stroke, dissension and belligerence within the nation were put aside, to be replaced by the kind of unity and communal purpose that not even the hardships of the depression had been able to induce in the American people. We may say that the sense of community induced by war is an evil sense, or even a bogus sense, but the fact remains that during World War II many millions of Americans knew for the first time in their lives of the community-making properties of collective crusade.

It would be absurd to suppose that matters were any different in earlier times. Granted that democracy has brought with it "democratic" wars—that is, wars fought for popular and moralistic ends rather than the earlier ends of dynastic rivalry, religious dispute, or territorial aggrandizement—yet everything we know about these wars makes abundantly clear the healing properties of foreign war when applied to internal strife, the sort of civil conflict described in the Shakespearean lines ending "Cry 'Havoc,' and let slip the dogs of war. . . ." Surely this insight has not been lost upon military commanders and political rulers for as long in history as there have been states and armies.

We must not overlook, either, the signal economic and social reforms that can be accomplished or at least facilitated during time of war. The masses of ancient Rome learned that they were more likely to receive liberal grain doles and other benefits when Rome was engaged in a difficult war, needing troops and sacrifices to be made at home, than in times of peace. And in our own day—during the Civil War, World War I, and World War II—we have seen reforms take place ranging from leaps forward in public education to mass welfare benefits and civil rights for minorities, all as the consequence of the government's desire for maximum solidarity at home in order to give impetus to the troops abroad. It is not, though, simply a matter of benefits. There are also opportunities for sacrifice, of whatever degree. To give up luxuries or ordinary opportunities for profit and reward, to know the feeling, however mild, of doing without, of forgoing privilege—all of this, quite as much as the achievement of mass reforms, conduces to the feeling of community. For community is never a vital or lasting thing unless it involves common sacrifice and hardship on occasion as well as common enjoyment of rewards.

If war were uniformly and unmitigatedly a thing of ugliness and hardship, brutality and carnage, it would surely be more easily ended once and for all than would appear to be likely. Hateful though the idea may be to most of us, war can bring—on the evidence has brought— things the West has cherished: liberty, democracy, socialism, social welfare, civil rights, technological and scientific progress, and, perhaps above all else, the feeling, however temporary, of membership in a collective, communal crusade. When, at the beginning of the century, William James wrote his essay "The Moral Equivalent of War," in which he declared the importance of society's finding some form of crusade or purpose, short of armed strife, that could emphasize the attractive aspects of war—courage, self-sacrifice, heroism, pomp, and the feeling of victory—he knew exactly what the historic attraction of war has been despite its manifestly lethal essence.

The Elements of the Military Community

My aim here is—and similarly will be in each of the other chapters at the appropriate point—to identify in advance the crucial social and psychological elements of the type of community under consideration. Whether in the history of society or the history of social thought, we find in each distinguishable form of community—military, political, religious, and so on—elements of thought, feeling and behavior which vary widely from one form to another. Over and over we find these elements emphasized, dissected, and analyzed by the protagonists of each major type of community in Western thought. Thus, different as is the legislation—or, rather, its underlying philosophy—of Cleisthenes from the ideas of Machiavelli, Clausewitz, Marx, and Lenin in their respective treatments of the military and war, there are certain persisting elements that give a common identity to them. The same is true, as we shall see, in each of the other types of community in Western thought.

Violence

The first and most obvious element of the military community is its consecration to violence. This is true whether we are dealing with the primitive war band, the militia, or the modern army. The ascription of legitimacy to violence and the grounding of association in the ethos of violence is the single most distinctive characteristic of the military and also the philosophy that has given it support in the West. It may be granted that there is probably no form of organization totally without at least a moderate degree of violence. Even kinship knows the violence of the vendetta, not to mention the use of force for disciplinary purposes. But violence is not the purpose of kinship, or of any other form of social organization save the military and the revolutionary communities. War and revolution have in common this consecration to violence, this acceptance of the legitimacy of violence in the pursuit of given ends. War, we are justified in saying, is the heroic mode of violence, though, as we shall see, revolutionary violence has produced its own pantheon of heroes. Violence, then, or rather willingness to engage in violence—in killing, wounding, and devastation—is, obviously, the first element of the military community.

Youth

The second essential element of the military community is youth, that is, the physical and mental qualities ordinarily associated with youth. I have in mind especially the vital qualities of physical strength, endurance, speed, quickness and agility, adaptability, and, above all, capacity for effective aggressiveness. Such qualities, obviously, are more likely to be found in young males than old ones, and it is the concentration of these qualities in military groups, together with the monopoly of force, that has made the military so often feared by leaders of civil society. This fear indeed goes back to the beginnings of human society in kinship, with its altogether different purposes and values.

When combat becomes necessary, victory clearly lies with the side capable of most quickly and effectively mobilizing the attributes of strength, endurance, valor, and aggressiveness. Above all, there must be the sheer capacity to survive in adverse circumstances. Such qualities and attributes, as is evident enough, belong to youth rather than to the elders of the tribe, whose eminence is more properly fitted to social, moral, and religious matters and is unquestioned only in the more leisurely matters of tribal life. Supremacy in war—at least the kind of war waged by physical prowess with its weapons of spear, bow, or knife—was likely to be found among those individuals who also showed a clear-cut supremacy in sport. This is exactly why such great philosophers as Plato among the ancient Greeks and Ernst Cassirer in our own century have found so vital an affinity between sport and war and why the latter even declared sport to be the source of that form of organization that was the primitive state. But I am inclined to think the direct needs of war—of protection from other tribes—were anterior to those of sport.

Individualism

The third element basic to the military community is individualism. This may seem surprising to many readers. Individualism, in what we are inclined to regard as the mechanized, regimented forces of war, serving under the despotic command of the military leader? Nonetheless, individualism is a quality of mind fundamental to the military

organization, most especially the primitive kind, in which resourcefulness of mind, more often found in youthful imagination than in elderly
caution, is itself a vital expression of individualism. And war, with its
demands for quick, youthful resourcefulness, must therefore very probably be accounted the first context in history of the efflorescence of individualism. What Émile Durkheim has written on this matter is illuminating and authoritative:

> Rather than dating the effacement of the individual from
> the institution of a despotic authority, we must, on the contrary,
> see in this institution the first step toward individualism. Chiefs
> are, in fact, the first personalities who emerge from the social
> mass. Their exceptional situation, putting them beyond the level
> of others, gives them a distinct physiognomy and accordingly
> confers individuality upon them. In dominating society they are
> no longer forced to follow all its movements. . . . A source of
> initiative is thus opened which had not existed before. There is,
> hereafter, someone who can produce new things and even, in
> certain measure, deny collective usages. Equilibrium has been
> broken.[2]

The individuality possessed by the war chief, who under the imper-
atives of war dangers can flout tradition and collective usage generally,
is possessed in substantial degree as well by the warriors under the chief,
who by their respective skills and judgments in battle must also challenge, as it were, that age-based, purely traditional form of authority
nourished by kinship. For many millennia in man's history, the military
camp was, with the possible exception of the hunting party, the only
possible refuge from the conventionalities and authorities that must
surely have seemed oppressive from time to time to the young and
vigorous, the brilliant and imaginative, in the tight social system of
the tribe or clan.

But there was still another sense in which the war band was individualistic in a way the kinship community could not be. The latter
tends to be cellular and concentric in character. Not the individual,
but the small group—the household—was the irreducible unit of kinship culture. Between the authority of the household and its members
no outside authority could extend itself, not even that of the clan or
tribe. Very different, however, was the war band. It was composed not
of irreducible groups, each capable of withstanding the authority of the
chief, but of individuals, arranged in whatever units were valuable to the
tactics of war but individuals nonetheless, subject while in the war band

---

[2] Émile Durkheim, *The Division of Labor in Society,* trans. George Simpson (New
York: Free Press, 1947), p. 195.

to the warrior chief's authority alone. In sum, the war band could not help but have an individualizing effect upon the minds and personalities of those males who served in it, for however brief a time.

Centralization

The fourth distinctive characteristic of the military society, separating it sharply in nature from the kinship community, has already been implied in the paragraph above, but it must be made explicit and given emphasis. I refer to the centralization of military command. As indicated above, the power of the warrior chief extended directly to each and every warrior in the military band. There were no intermediate structures, like household and clan, that could properly claim autonomous control of individual members. Whereas in kinship society authority arose from tradition, with the power of the elders no more in fact than their power of interpreting tradition, the authority of the warrior chief was prescriptive, centralized in him and his lieutenants, and applied directly, without qualification, to each and every individual in the war band.

Competition

Next must be mentioned the inherent competitiveness within the war band. One criterion alone prevailed: effectiveness in battle. Those who proved themselves the ablest rose to the top; those who were inferior remained at the bottom or else were removed through death, injury, or expulsion from the war band. The kinship community was anything but competitive. All positions of seniority and esteem in the tribe were reached, and could be reached, only through the noncompetitive principles of age, birth, and family line. Age and tradition were the overwhelming values of kinship society. One did not compete to become patriarch or matriarch—any more than one competed to become the oldest son in matters of property inheritance. One acceded to each of these, as one did to one's sex or age—if not by physical processes, then by those of tradition and binding authority. But competition was structurally built into the war band, an ingrained attribute of the war band internally as conflict between war bands was externally. The spirit of competitiveness we find today—as well as in other ages long past—in commerce, in politics, and in sports had its origin, beyond any question, in the community of combat.

Contract

Closely related to competition is another attribute that must be ascribed in its primordial form to the war band: the idea of contract. No such relation existed between father and son, mother and daughter, or anywhere else in the tribal community. Not contract but status—inherited or ascribed—was dominant. But between the warrior chief and his soldiers existed a tie that can best be thought of, I think, as contractual. In return for his successful leadership, others promised obedience to his command. Even more fundamentally, however, contract sprang from the transitory character of the military tie. It was good only for so long as emergency dictated. Throughout history a great deal of warfare had a militia nature. One volunteers, one enters into a contract, as it were, for the duration—no longer. It is understood by everyone that when the needs of armed warfare disappear, so do the members of the militia. The idea of permanent standing armies is far from common in the history of society. In the ancient world, the Roman Empire brought the idea to highest fulfillment through its paid, long-serving legions. Not until about the sixteenth century did the idea return in western Europe of standing armies for whom war was a profession. Contract was the very essence of the feudal military tie throughout the Middle Ages.

Secularism

I should also mention secularism here, for want of a better word, as an original and vital element of the war band. Those serving were, for the period of service at least, freed of their obligations to the sacred traditions, to the gods, to the whole moral thrust of their kinship community. I do not mean that those engaged in war were oblivious to the favor of the gods, or of luck. Far from it. But propitiation of gods was the responsibility of those at home, for whom the war band fought, and apart from that passing prayer or talismanic word that every soldier has always, when facing the possibility of death or injury on the battlefield, been prone to utter, there was little of this in the military camp. Nor was the military life itself likely to promote the virtues fundamental to the kinship community—which, after all, was founded not on the ways of war but of peace, the giving, rather than the taking, of life. Even beyond what is ordinarily denoted by secularism, there was the degree of moral freedom, of license even, that has everywhere and at all times gone with the military life. When dealing with the enemy, one was freed from commandments regarding the sanctity of human life, one's neighbor, and women and children, as well as those regarding property and sexual probity. Stealing, killing, and raping took on, in battle with the enemy and their families, the cast of if not actually morality, at least amorality.

Discipline

Next, I stress the element of discipline in the war band. This was to the military community what traditional authority was to the kinship community. I referred above to the importance of the element of centralization of power in the military organization. Such centralization was indeed the source of the very structure of command. It was also the source of that distinctive mode of human relationship we term discipline. Among modern sociologists Max Weber has given greatest stress to the importance of discipline as a factor in not merely military but political development. Changes in patterns of discipline, as Weber emphasized, have had more to do with the sociology of war than have changes in the technology of war.

The content of military discipline, as Weber puts the matter,

> is nothing but the methodically trained and exact execution of the received order, in which all personal criticism is unconditionally suspended and the actor is unswerving and exclusively set for carrying out the command. In addition, this conduct under orders is uniform. Its quality as the communal act of a *mass* organization conditions the specific effects of such uniformity.[3]

In the discipline exerted through centralized command in the war band lay the first, and by all odds the greatest, of the challenges to which the authority immemorially resident in the kinship community has been subjected periodically in history. From military discipline, not from kinship authority, later sprang the all-important concept of sovereignty, which is, as we shall see in some detail in the next chapter, the central element of the political community.

There is still another major result of military discipline in history to give strength to Weber's declaration that "the discipline of the army gives birth to all discipline." This is the large-scale economic organization, the great workshop or factory, the same kind of discipline that we see highlighted in the military. As Weber notes, from the pharaonic workshops in ancient Egypt through the Roman plantations, the mines of the Middle Ages, and the slave-worked plantations of colonial times down to the modern factory, military discipline has been, in Weber's phrase, "the ideal model."

Communism

The final element I want to stress in the military community, also one that may be seen from the primitive war band down to the great rationalized, bureaucratized armies of our century, is communism. Here again we shall follow Weber's useful leadership in the matter:

---

[3] Max Weber, "The Meaning of Discipline," in *From Max Weber: Essays in Sociology*, trans, and ed. H. H. Gerth and C. Wright Mills (New York: Oxford University Press, 1958), p. 253.

The primeval way of creating trained troops—ever ready to strike, and allowing themselves to be disciplined—was *warrior-communism*. . . . It may take the form of the bachelor house as a kind of barracks or casino of the professional warriors; in this form it is spread over the largest part of the earth. Or, it may follow the pattern of the communist community of the Ligurian pirates, or of the Spartan syssitia organized according to the "picnic" principle; or it may follow Caliph Omar's organization, or the religious knight orders of the Middle Ages.[4]

Whatever the type, whether primitive, ancient, or medieval, equality of reward was stressed. In the war band, indeed, lay the earliest expression of the maxim—later to be made the ideal of Marxian communism—"From each according to his abilities; to each according to his needs." Here again, its members could not have failed to sense the vivid contrast between the primitive war band, with its rude equality, and the kinship community at home, where everything was stratified by age and custom. Gradually, of course, there sprang up in the war community, too, a differentiation of status, with privilege attaching to higher ranks. But these ranks, we must remember, were competitively achieved, and, more important, the ethic of communism remained a strong one in the face of either privations and sufferings in the field or the booty that rewarded success.

More to the point in this chapter, though, is the persistence through time of the ideal of communism in military contexts, to be seen in the elite corps of warriors from primitive times through the knighthood of the Middle Ages down to the kind of military communism that the Nazis sought to instill in their special bodies of young picked troops.

Under warrior communism, as Weber emphasizes, the life of the warrior is a counterpart to the monastic communism to be found in many religious circles. In the one form as in the other, we find a stress on the separateness of the community from the rest of society, on a distinctive purity of relationship, through the community's own means of socialization, that transcends all other ties, blood included, and that even takes priority over the family.

Dissociation from the family, as well as from all private economic interest, is, as Weber tells us, crucial to the most intense of military communities, primitive and modern alike. Celibacy can become an ideal as often in the cult of war as in that of worship. Precisely as indulgence in sexual relations can be deemed both corrupting and distracting to purity of worship, so it can be regarded as corrupting and distracting to purity of preparation for combat.

But celibacy is perhaps less common in the history of the military

4 Ibid., p. 258.

community than is the ideal of sexual communism. That community is the immediate source, almost certainly, of the sexual communism that we shall find Plato insisting upon for his guardian class. Here, with the same exclusion of the family or kinship principle on the ground of its psychological and social distraction of allegiance to the war community, sexual desires of the members are given fulfillment through legitimated alternatives, communal and eugenic.

The important thing, however, is the ethic of communism—whether concerning celibacy, sexual indulgence, or possession of property. And we should be hard pressed to account for the origin of the ideal of communism in Western history apart from its first appearance in those primordial war bands composed of individuals for whom rude equality in all matters in the field must have been welcome contrast at times to the predictable inequality of the kinship community and its ranks established by age and tradition.

War and the Fall of Kinship

So much for the constitutive elements of the military community. We cannot appreciate their historical importance, however, until we have seen these elements in conflict with those of other types of organization in the history of human society. Of all such conflicts the earliest, most fundamental, and even today very probably the most universal is that between the military and kinship. It is in circumstances of the general collapse of kinship structure, through the impact of war and its demands, that the territorial state is most likely to make its appearance. For of all forms of human society, the state, as will be emphasized in a number of contexts in this book, is the most ideally suited to the waging of war.

The oldest of all forms of human community is, of course, kinship. For how many tens, even hundreds, of thousands of years mankind has been organized in units springing from kinship—such as household, clan, tribe, and confederations of tribes—we do not know. All we know is that wherever mankind first comes to our historical attention, in whatever area of the earth's surface, we find kinship organization either sovereign or else only just losing its sovereignty to some other form of social organization, usually military or political.

There are, of course, many types of kinship society—as many, surely, as there are types of political society today. But in the same way that all types of political society rest upon *territory*, that is, segments of territory marked by jealously guarded boundaries, all types of kinship society rest ultimately upon the fact of *generation*—upon either consanguineal descent or the relatedness conferred through adoption or marriage that entitles one to the benefits of blood relationship. In political society one identifies himself primarily in terms of residence on a given piece of territory—as a Greek, Roman, Frenchman, or American. In kinship society, of whatever type, one identifies himself by particularizing his personal or blood relationships. Clan, kindred, tribe—all of these, like the household, are personal relationships, flowing from the personal descent, rather than territorial. Quite evidently, one of the greatest of all changes in the history of human society—and one that has taken place many times in many places in the history of mankind—is the change from a condition characterized by the predominance of personal-kinship ties to one characterized by the predominance of territorial ties. And fundamental to this momentous change has been the conflict of kinship society with the military community. Only when the needs of war and the requirements of almost constant military service make kinship structure in a social order obsolete does the territorial tie tend to become victorious over the personal relationships of kinship society.

It would be hard to find any sharper contrast among social relationships than that existing between kinship society and the military community, built around the needs of war. Where the military community tends to be individualistic, kinship society is cellular—existing, in terms not of aggregates of discrete individuals, but of cell-like groups, with the household or perhaps the clan the most fundamental. Where the military community is built around the principle of command and the direct relation of the warrior chief to his men, kinship society is built around the principle of intermediation. The sanctity of each group in the kinship society is guarded; responsibility is communal, with the individual buffered, so to speak, by the structure of the family, kindred, or clan. Where competition is the very essence of the war band, with individual vying with individual in combat for the laurels that are awarded valor and bravery, status—ascribed status—is crucial in kinship society. Moreover the prestige of youth in the military group hardly holds in time of peace in the kinship structure. There age and experience and the wisdom presumably coming with age count for more. Finally, tradition, rather than the kind of discipline emanating from command, tends to flourish in all societies where the family principle is dominant.

Where crisis, especially the crisis of war, never rears its head, there is no reason why kinship society cannot be adequate to human needs indefinitely. And it is precisely in those parts of the world where peoples have been able to remain isolated from one another over very long periods of time, as in certain of the Pacific islands, in remote parts of Africa and Asia, and, until the coming of the European, in most parts of the Americas, that kinship structure has lasted the longest. For, as the evidence shows clearly enough, kinship organization is qualified to deal with most of life's eventualities—economic, religious, cultural, and other. But where kinship organization fails—fails by very virtue of its embedded principles of tradition, age-based hierarchy, cellular intermediation of authority, and reliance upon the ties of blood rather than those of pragmatic efficiency—is in circumstances of war. As Edward Jenks has written:

A society which discourages individual competition, which only acts indirectly upon the bulk of its members, which refuses to recruit its ranks with new blood, contains within itself the seeds of decay. However admirable as a peace organization, it is no fighting machine. Where . . . there is practically boundless territory, in which weaker communities can maintain themselves without interference by more powerful rivals, the Clan system may last indefinitely. But, so soon as pressure begins to operate, its weakness becomes apparent. . . . The disasters of the Clan give rise to the war chief with his band of followers, chosen exclusively for their devotion and military ability. After all, in fighting, the chief thing is to fight well.[5]

The kinship community is invariably defeated by the military community when the two come in confrontation. No more important generalization is to be found about the history of mankind. To state the matter differently: the principles of tradition, of age-based wisdom and hierarchy, of the concentric structure of household, clan, and tribe, and of intermediation cannot possibly hold out against invading principles such as those we have seen to be basic in the military community. Tradition is no more a match for centralized command and discipline than units composed of blood kinsmen are a match for units composed of those chosen for pragmatic efficiency in war.

But a view of history as the one-sided confrontation of kinship and military is too simple. For what we see over and over in history is the adaptation of kinship under the stress of emergency to a more militarized type of organization. We shall come momentarily to three of these adaptations which have had profound consequences to the West and to the history of social philosophy. Let us look first at a very telling example in our own day of what I have been describing: the relation of Western powers to the Vietnamese people, most particularly the people of North Vietnam. When the French colonized this part of Southeast Asia a century or so ago, they had not the slightest difficulty in laying political claim to any of the territory or in exacting acquiescent obedience from the natives to their command. A relative handful of French military forces proved sufficient to the task. And, as we know, for several decades French rule of Indochina was virtually unchallenged. The reason for the ease of this conquest is not far to seek. The peoples of Indochina knew no other organization than that of kinship—or of the tiny village based

---

[5] Edward Jenks, *Law and Politics in the Middle Ages* (New York: Henry Holt and Company, 1898), pp. 306–7. See also Jenks's more generalized *State and the Nation* (New York: E. P. Dutton, 1919). No scholar, not even Sir Henry Maine or Sir Paul Vinogradov, has shed more light on the historic conflict between war and kinship than has Edward Jenks.

largely upon kinship or a form of religion in which kinship figured prominently. A single company of French soldiers was capable of holding hundreds, even thousands of square miles. From what possible source could opposition come—effective opposition?

But during the decades of French suzerainty, more and more of the Indochinese themselves learned military organization as well as strategy and tactics, particularly those of guerrilla warfare. And the time came, just after World War II, when the French, troops and all, were driven from the area by an aroused—and militarized—force of Vietnamese. No longer was the situation one of an ineffectual kinship society against an external military community, but now one of military against military.

And in the 1960s, when the fateful American decision was made to send American troops into Vietnam to fight the North Vietnamese, what began as only a few thousand military advisers became within two or three years a vast invading army numbering more than a half million, with huge bombing missions carrying on raids into the north day after day, week after week, month after month. The finest strategy that our Defense Department could muster was brought to bear, and hundreds of billions of dollars were spent, but to little avail. The record, as requires no emphasis here, is one of substantial failure of the American military forces. Had America sent troops into the same kind of Vietnam that the French soldiers had found a century earlier, no more than a few thousand lightly armed Americans would have been necessary. It was, however, a radically different Vietnam they found—one that had become militarized, one that had effected that most powerful of unions, the union of war and revolution, and one that proved invincible, as we know, in the decade of the 1960s.

The kind of experience undergone during the last century by the people of Vietnam has taken place literally thousands of times in human history, on both small scale and large, on every continent. Not that the issues have been as crucial in every instance, or the forces as large. But the defeat of kinship society has repeatedly set in motion within that very society the operations necessary to military effectiveness. And the first of these operations is, of course, the creation of the military community— war band, militia, guerrilla group, legion, army, whatever it may be called.

It is possible, I believe, to see the kinship community and the military community as the two most fundamental archetypes of all the associations and structures that have come to constitute human society. From kinship and its embedded norms have come such groups as castes, village communities, guilds, churches, monasteries, and a host of other types of organizations concerned with religion, hierarchy, tradition, crafts, learning, and the like. I do not mean these groupings have emerged developmentally from kinship, only that universally they have founded themselves for the most part on the norms of kinship, many of them even making heavy use of kinship nomenclature, like the terms *brother, sister, father,* and *mother.*

From the military community has come, foremost, the territorial, sovereign, centralized political state. We shall have much more to say about this in the next chapter. But there have been other organizations, too, that have taken the discipline, the centralized command, the rationalized regimentation, and the barracks collectivism of the military as models. Among them are the kinds of factories that replaced the guilds in postmedieval Europe, the workhouses, prisons, and asylums that began to spring up in increasing numbers, and even the publicly operated schools. So, too, have certain religious and ethnic groups, in the interests of militant action, occasionally adopted military principles of organization and action. And finally, as we shall emphasize in some detail later, much of the most successful revolutionary strategy in modern times has been based upon principles that are military in foundation.

None of this is to suggest that kinship and military are the only fundamental models in the history of social organization. Plainly, there are others. But, without any question, the kinship and the military communities are the oldest in man's history and, even today, among the most universal types of association. It would be strange indeed if each had not become the source or model of other powerful and distinctive types of organization in social history.

Although conflict between military and kinship is universal and timeless so far as underlying principles are involved, to be found wherever war and its demands intrude upon the kinship setting, there have been certain periods in history when this conflict becomes overt and dominant, with profound consequences for both social organization and social thought. No major area in the world is without record of such overt conflicts, whether in the distant past or in more recent times. Here, of course, our concern is solely with western Europe, and we shall examine three such periods of conflict, each of them the context of momentous changes and significant eruptions of social and political ideas.

The first is to be found in ancient Greece in the seventh and sixth centuries B.C., culminating first in the momentous Cleisthenean reforms of 509 B.C. and then in the rise of the Athenian city-state, the famous Greek polis, which was to become in the century that followed the setting of one of the greatest periods of cultural flowering in the entire history of the West. In a very real sense, Western social thought begins with the issues which were created for intellectual contemplation by the impact of war upon the age-old kinship community of the Athenians in this period.

The second period we shall consider is in Rome primarily in the first century B.C., a period of almost incessant civil war following a century or more of foreign wars of steadily widening scope and deepening intensity. Out of these foreign and civil wars emerged the Roman Empire, and with it a system of law and of legal philosophy that was to have lasting effect upon the subsequent history of western Europe. As with Athens earlier, the militarization of Roman society, the impact of war and the principles of military organization upon what had been a predominantly kinship-structured society, proved fruitful in generating issues that were to become basic in social and political thought.

The third period is our own, that of modern western Europe, commencing in the postmedieval era when the requirements of warfare became once again imperative, when the technology of war underwent striking change, and when the traditional medieval structure of war making, based largely upon the knighthood, proved obsolete. This is the period of the rise of the modern, national, increasingly large-scale army and, with this, the beginning not only of successive impacts of the military on society but also of a succession of philosophical works on warfare and military organization, unbroken since the sixteenth century, that is, for good or ill, among the major strands of Western social thought in modern times.

War and the Greek Polis: Cleisthenes

When Greek society first comes into our ken, it is organized almost entirely in kinship terms. At the bottom of the social system lay the household, the center of religious, economic, cultural, and social existence. It, not the individual, was the irreducible unit of the social order. Generally the household comprised several generations and lateral degrees of kinship, as well as any slaves, servants, or retainers the household may have contained, depending upon its wealth, and all property. Next highest was the gens, a union of those households most directly descended from some common and fairly recent ancestor, whose name and lasting prestige gave identity to the gens. Beyond this was the phratry, an organization that had become rather tenuous well before the time of Cleisthenes, concerned chiefly with kinship-religious rites and essentially a kind of larger, more inclusive gens. Above these three kinship entities was the tribe, which, like the others, derived its name and being from some very distant eponymous ancestor. In Athens there were four such tribes, given a substantial degree of unity by long coresidence. Each of the tribes was broken down into three phratries, thirty gentes, and a much larger number of household groups.

It is not necessary here to go into the details of this Athenian kinship community. It is enough to say that nothing else existed—no political state, as we would define the state today or as the Athenians themselves would define it after the Cleisthenean revolution. To become a member of Athenian society in any degree whatever, it was necessary first to be a member of one or other of the tribes, phratries, and gentes which were the units of social existence. Descent was traced through the male line alone: Greek society was patriarchal, patrilineal, and patrilocal, which is to say that authority was vested in the father or male elder alone, that family name and genealogy were traced solely through the male side, and that residence in a household was invariably in that derived from the male line of descent.

Property was not an individual but a collective right. There was the property of household, of gens, of phratry, and of tribe. The head of the household was its custodian or trustee. Property could not be alienated from the kinship line and was not regarded as being either created by or endowed in the individual. What was earned or produced was deemed the family's. Authority was kinship authority. At the top was the authority of the tribe, limited, however, to those matters that involved the tribe as a whole. Great as this authority was, it did not, could not, penetrate the concentric authorities of phratry, gens, and household, each of which was regarded as sovereign within its own legitimate province. Religion was, at bottom, for a very long period little more than consecration of those beings who had been signal figures at one time or other in the life of the kinship community. The foundation of religion was the hearth, which symbolized the unity and perpetuity of the family line. Marriage, far from being a means of creating a new family or household group—that is, of uniting two separate individuals into a new family— was instead a simple rite of adoption whereby the girl was brought into her betrothed's family not merely as wife to him but as daughter of the household into which she was marrying.

Over the whole structure of Athenian kinship society—as over any fully developed form of kinship society—towered the obsessive belief that only authority embedded in kinship is legitimate authority. No control over individuals was held legitimate except insofar as it was mediated by family. Criminal law in our sense of the term was virtually lacking. The only offenses that were deemed crimes, that is, offenses against the entire community, were treason, sorcery, and murder by stealth. All else fell in the category of what we would today call torts: private offenses of individual against individual, with justice a matter of negotiation among the families involved. Even the powerful council of tribal elders was reluctant ever to step into ordinary matters of theft, robbery, arson, assault, injury, or killing. For, after all, each tribal elder was himself patriarch of a family line, accustomed to seeing family matters dealt with within the family or by negotiation among families.

The sense of family, of family descent, and of the good or evil that could be perpetuated in a given family line was a powerful one among the Greeks. A good man was, virtually by definition, a man of good family. An evil man was held to have acquired his evil from some cankering strain in his family heredity. One's sole lasting, forever-ineradicable identity came from his kinship line. Those, such as immigrants to Athens, who had not been assimilated by adoption of one kind or other into one of the great family complexes—clan or tribe—were, in a sense, proletarians: individuals in but not of Athenian society. Religion, property, law, education, economy, all the signal aspects of society were rooted in kinship.

Had Athens managed somehow to remain aloof from the results of its own penetration, through commerce, exploration, and war, of other parts of the world, there is no reason to suppose its kinship structure would not have held together in the sixth century B.C. as it had for all the numberless centuries of Greek existence before. But the strains and tensions were becoming all too apparent by the beginning of the sixth century B.C. Nothing in kinship society, given the cardinal elements of role, status, and membership that go with this type of society, could long be adequate to the demands that were now being made upon it, especially by the unending needs of war. As we have seen, whatever else kinship society may be good for, it is not an effective machine for war. It lacks the centralized command that can break through intermediate units of clan and household to individuals, the unity of organization that successful war societies require, and the overall sense of collective solidarity undistracted by the presence of internal groups such as households and clans, each sovereign within its own sphere, that forms the needed background of effective fighting forces.

In the sixth century B.C. we see the full results of the preceding centuries of war and the mobility of thought and belief that went with war. The strains upon the Athenian kinship system proved during this century impossible to contain any longer. On the one hand, it is a century marked by the spread of the rationalism associated with the rise of physical philosophy in such places as Ionia; but on the other hand, it is also one filled with war and the impact of war upon the traditional society of Athenians and other Greeks as well, the Spartans included. In Athens during this century we witness a succession of efforts to reform, to alter, or to patch up the kinship structure, to preserve it so far as possible, but also to adapt it to the needs of the military and to offset the rising pressure of disaffected groups at home, those on whom the economic consequences of war had been severe.

Early in the sixth century B.C., the great reformer Solon had attempted to deal with Athenian problems through the creation of horizontal "classes" that cut across the ancient ties of kinship, with their autonomous tribes, phratries, clans, and households. Military service would thenceforth be made an obligation of the class one belonged to, with foot soldiers coming from one of the classes, horsemen from another, and so forth. Solon also, in the interests of economic peace at home, canceled all debts in Athenian society. But, despite these not insignificant actions, Solon was able to effect no lasting improvement of the situation. Within a decade or two, Athens was plunged once again into the kind of internal disorganization, civil conflict, and fundamental military ineffectuality that had plagued this city-state for so long. Clearly, what Athens required, so far as the needs of war and domestic solidarity were concerned, was a reconstruction far more basic than Solon's—which, after all, had not touched the underlying kinship structure of society.

This was left for Cleisthenes, one of the most brilliant reformers—revolutionists, we should say—in Western history. It is unfortunate that we know so little about this remarkable mind, its roots, its ways of detailed working, and its effective contexts. Suffice it to say that through whatever means, through whatever techniques of persuasion and force, Cleisthenes effected one of the most sweeping changes of a social system known to history. Indeed, we shall find nothing quite like it until we come to the French Revolution at the end of the eighteenth century. It was in 509 B.C. so far as we can tell, that the Cleisthenean revolution took place. We can deal only with its major aspects in the space at our disposal.

Like all great revolutionary reconstructions, Cleisthenes' was the work of nihilism on the one hand, and of powerful affirmation on the other. His first act was to declare the four ancient Athenian tribes dissolved forever. They and their centuries-old accumulation of symbols, purposes, allegiances, and divisions, based upon common descent, or belief in common descent, through all time, were now a nullity, destroyed by Cleisthenes at a stroke. Inevitably the destruction of the ancient kinship tribes carried with it destructive implications for the other kinship structures of Athens, even though none of these was formally abolished. The whole vast, penetrating *culture* of kinship, including morality and social and psychological incentives, was, at a single blow, rendered illegitimate in the strict sense of the word.

But Cleisthenes was too shrewd a revolutionary strategist to leave a vacuum, a social void, in Athens. The affirmative aspect of the revolution must be seen in two far-reaching steps that were taken immediately upon dissolution of the ancient kinship groups. First, Cleisthenes created ten new organizations, which in keeping with traditional nomenclature he called "tribes" but which were in no sense related to kinship or common descent. All the freemen of Athens, however brief their residence there, whatever their social and economic position, whatever their origins, were made members of one or other of these ten tribes. And, in a stroke of military genius, Cleisthenes caused each of these ten tribes to be given the name of some remote military hero. One's tribal identity in Athens became henceforth a matter not of kinship procreation, nor of any kinship rite or process whatever, but of the symbolism and the rites of war. In this fashion, in short, was Athens militarized in that most basic of ways: through the processes of symbolism and conferred identity.

The second main step was no less fundamental; indeed it was possibly more so, given the ingenious manner in which Cleisthenes fused it with the first step. This involved the establishment in Athens of a hundred small townships or counties called *demes*, all equal in size, each a territorial rather than a personal unity, with distinct boundaries like those existing today among our townships, counties, and precincts. Henceforth all Athenians would belong not merely to one or other of the ten military tribes but also to one or other of the hundred territorial demes.

The final element of genius in the Cleisthenean reconstruction lay in the relation of the demes to the tribes. Ten demes were declared the units of a single tribe, but instead of allowing these ten to be contiguous, thus forming a territorial aggregate that might in time become the center of a distractive, even potentially insurrectionary group in Athens, Cleisthenes saw to it that the ten demes belonging to each tribe were scattered throughout Athens, hence with no possibility of forming any kind of alliance based upon mere contiguity. This principle—an earlier variant of the famous Roman principle of *divide et impera*, "divide and rule"— was, in a sense, the very heart of the Cleisthenean revolution.

Henceforth the deme or township became the essential unit of residence, rights, duties, voting, and public office in Athens. All free Athenians were not merely permitted but obliged to vote and, when elected, to hold public office—either in the deme itself at the local level or in one or other of the elected councils, rising from the deme governments, which governed the whole of Athens. But the deme was something else, too, deriving directly from the motivation of the Cleisthenean reforms: the unit of military conscription. For all able-bodied Athenian males, irrespective of age and excepting only the physical infirm, were made constantly subject to military conscription. It is the first clear instance in Western history of the military draft. And, it must be stressed, along with the military-sprung reorganization of Athenian society, with the suddenly created reservoir of soldiers no longer hindered by the conflicting authorities of household, clan, and tribe, went some fundamental reforms, too, in the character of military strategy and tactics. For Cleisthenes was himself a skilled military commander, well schooled in both the technology and the technique of war.

What we see, therefore, taking place with revolutionary suddenness and sweep is a total transformation of a social system. Instead of the traditional, kinship-based pluralism of Athenian authority, there is now a monolithic unity that arises from a governmental system reaching directly down to the individual citizen. Instead of a system of law based upon immemorial tradition, its interpretation subject to the elders of kinship society and always slow and uncertain, we have now a system of Athenian law that is prescriptive, that is made, rather than merely interpreted out of tradition, and that is deemed binding upon all Athenians irrespective of kinship lineage. We see, too, a growing communality of all Athenians, one that did not and could not exist so long as the sense of community rose primarily from the fact of generation, through tribe or clan. And finally, there is in the new Athens a manifest individualism, sprung from the fact that henceforth the individual, not the kinship group, was the irreducible and unalterable unit of the Athenian military-political system.

How effective, how powerful the new system was is evidenced by the sweeping and notable victory the Athenians achieved over the feared and aggressive Persians early in the fifth century B.C. This victory, one of the most famous in the ancient world, represents the real taking-off point of the new city-state, the polis. It is well to be clear on the profoundly military character of the new Athens. This new society was not, to be sure, nearly so military in character as was that of the neighboring city-state of Sparta, whose totalitarian type of militarism was destined at the end of the fifth century B.C. to defeat Athens—resoundingly, humiliatingly, and with fateful consequences for Western religion and social thought. For all the cultural progress and economic prosperity that existed in Athens for nearly a century—a period marked by one of the world's greatest eruptions of individual creativity, as seen in the matchless works of the great dramatists and architects, sculptors and philosophers, statesmen and generals of the period—nevertheless, there is no mistaking the military emphasis of the Athenian state. Often, indeed, great generals and great artists were one and the same person, as in the case of Sophocles. And often, too, the motivations of art, ritual, drama, and even philosophy and historiography were military motivations.

Equally to the point, however, is the ascendancy during this brilliant age of social and psychological qualities for the most part lacking in Athenian society before the fifth century B.C. I refer to such qualities as individualism, the upthrust of youth in all areas of thought and life, competition—evident not only in economic and political life but even in the writing of dramas and the design of buildings, with the best receiving handsome prizes from the government—and, most dramatically perhaps, the new spirit of secularism in Athenian life. These qualities, as I have stressed above, have been associated with war and the military during most of mankind's history, not because anything in war as such is based absolutely upon these qualities, but because it is circumstances of war that have most often brought forth their existence, providing man the opportunity to break through the cake of custom, to become liberated from traditional authority. It would be impossible to account for the spirit of youth, individualism, and secularism so dominating Athenian life and culture during most of the fifth century apart from the great fissures in the traditional kinship morality and government that had been opened by war and then filled by values, incentives, and motivations Athenians had scarcely known before the Cleisthenean revolution.

Not that there were no tensions, contradictions of mind and morality, and social strains in Athens during this period. As we shall have occasion to note in detail in the next chapter when we examine the background of Plato's political thought, there were many of these strains and tensions throughout the fifth century; and they arose, one and all, from the same fundamental processes that we can now see to have been instrumental in forming the golden age of Athens. For, as is well known, individualism, competition, mobility, and secularism continuing long enough in a people can awaken sensations of rootlessness and estrangement, of being cut off from either belief or membership. It would appear that the world's great cultural ages, such as the fifth century B.C. in Athens and the Elizabethan Age in modern England, represent a kind of halfway point between very strong tradition and an apparent lack of tradition, between ascendancy of community, strongly rooted in kinship, and an individualism that bursts the bonds of community, and between a strong spirit of the sacred, of consecration to dogma and ritual, and a virtual repudiation of the sacred, with secularism rampant.

It is easy to see Athens during most of the fifth century B.C at this halfway point. Commencing with glorious military victory against the hated Persians, the century went on to be marked by liberation of individuality, especially youth, from the age-old dominance of kinship; by emancipation of belief from strict conformity to the worship of the traditional gods, by exposure to new ideas and values introduced by people who flocked to Athens eager to take advantage of the relative freedoms of the polis; and by the wealth brought in by Athenian merchants and their ships. It was the century of great soldiers, victorious generals and sea captains, and conquests abroad. It was the century that produced perhaps the most beautiful temples ever known to man, the greatest tragedies of world literature by Aeschylus, Sophocles, and Euripides, such comedies as those of Aristophanes, philosophy at the level of the incomparable Socrates, poetry, architecture, song, painting, oration, and sculpture—in an intensity of creativity and a volume of production such as the world had not known before and rarely if ever since. Throughout, as I say, the themes of war and the fruits of war, not to mention the psychology of war in all its diverse details, were dominant in Athens. Seldom, not even in Rome or Elizabethan England, has the material and intellectual prosperity of war, and the special community fashioned by war, been more notable than in the Athens created by Cleisthenes and brought to greatness by Pericles.

Behind it all, however, lay a progressive attenuation of the kinship community and of the deepest roots of belief. The military community could support for a while the kind of greatness achieved by fifth-century Athens, but not forever. If war, in its confrontation with oppressive kinship tradition, can create psychological and social motivations, it can also destroy these selfsame motivations. We shall come back to Athens in this somber light in the next chapter.

The Augustan Revolution: 27 B.C.

We turn now to another historically important instance of the fateful conflict between the kinship and the military orders. This one is set in Rome, some five hundred years after the Cleisthenean revolution in Athens. Its consequences proved no less significant in their way than those that followed the age of Cleisthenes in Greece. Although in its entire history Rome never produced an age of philosophy and the arts to compare even remotely with that of fifth-century Athens, we cannot deny Rome its creation, starting during the final years of the first century B.C., of what is still undoubtedly the most remarkable political and legal structure in the history of human society: the Roman Empire. For good and ill alike, this empire extended over a very large part of the then known world. What is today western Europe, as well as parts of eastern Europe, northern Africa, and the Middle East all the way to India, fell under Roman governance during the high point of the empire. And such was the extent of its commerce that Roman trade reached all the way to China. Until the twentieth century the Roman Empire remained the largest, most centralized, bureaucratized system of political society ever known. The British Empire of the eighteenth and nineteenth centuries rivaled it in size, perhaps, and the totalitarian states of the twentieth century in degree of centralized unity. But taking all elements combined there is still nothing in the world that may be said to rival the Roman Empire at its height.

It, too, was the work of war and revolutionary reform. It must be considered to be as much the result of the powerful reforms initiated by Augustus at the end of the first century B.C. as the early Athenian polis was the result of Cleisthenean reforms. And these reforms, as we shall see, were instigated no less clearly in behalf of war and war-making effectiveness and were no less destructive of a predominantly kinship society than were those of Cleisthenes.

It is not necessary to go into any detail regarding the structure of Roman kinship society down to about the end of the second century B.C. In all important functional and structural respects it was hardly different from that of pre-Cleisthenean Athens. It will be useful, however, to describe in some detail the momentous Roman kinship doctrine known as the *patria potestas*. No more famous kinship term has ever existed.

To understand the meaning and significance of the *patria potestas* in early Roman society, we must see this society as composed of corporate households, each united under its house father, or, as the Romans called this patriarchal figure, a *pater familias*. To the Romans the word *pater* did not signify, as the word *father* does to us, the mere fact of procreation, of generation: above all else it connoted authority and protection. Likewise the concept of the *patria potestas* connoted more than merely power or authority—though this was fundamental: it was rooted also in a tissue of obligations and responsibilities. The *patria potestas* was authority, yes, but it was also the responsibility of the house father for the lives not only of those related directly through kinship but also of all others who had, as servants or slaves, any relation at all to the household. The *patria potestas* stood for the legal, social, and religious unity of the family and for its continuity in time.

The family, not the individual, was the irreducible unit of tradition and law in the Roman Republic down until the time of the Augustan reforms, which I shall come to in a moment. Until very late in the history of the republic, the family was made to bear responsibility for most individual offenses, and it was the prime agency of retribution for injuries suffered by one of its members. Something akin to a highly stabilized, fully accepted blood feud existed under the *patria potestas*. That is, if a member of a family suffered assault, injury, trespass, or death at the hands of a member of another family, the problem was dealt with directly by the two families concerned. There was no higher authority proceeding from the surrounding society, as there is today in our form of political society and as there was to be later in Roman society, that could legitimately enter the negotiations. Settlement or restitution came from the family to whom the guilty individual belonged. The reason for this was that guilt was a collective concept: the family, not the individual, was held responsible in law, and whatever punishment or compensation emerged went directly to the family whose member had been injured or killed. Most of the matters that are dealt with in fully developed political society by the state and its tribunals were handled by the early Romans privately, much as are matters of conflict between two sovereign states today. Offenses such as murder, assault, arson, trespass, and injury were held by the Romans to be private offenses, to be privately negotiated, and not, as we today regard them, crimes against the state itself.

There were, to be sure, offenses considered to be crimes against the entire community; these included treason and certain heinous acts against the gods. But even here, although the force of the entire community was brought into action, the family, not the individual who actually committed the offense, was the subject of this force. It was the family that was duly pronounced guilty for the offense of its member, and the family remained guilty in the eyes of the community until it exercised punishment deemed appropriate to the offense. Even in capital offenses, such as treason or murder by stealth, the larger community, or its agency, did not inflict the death penalty; this was done by the guilty individual's family. Only thus could be removed the strain of guilt that had been visited upon the entire family by the dereliction of its member.

The important point about the *patria potestas* is that it stood for the autonomy of the family in which this authority was lodged. Officers of the commonwealth, consuls and other magistrates, could not and did not cross the threshold of the authority embedded in the Roman family.

They assumed no power to interfere in the affairs of the family. The head of the family, the *pater familias,* was its sole representative in the commonwealth; he alone had legal identity in the tribunals of the larger community. If a wrong was done by or to any member of his family, he and not they must answer for it or demand proper compensation.

The *patria potestas* also carried with it profound religious significance. The head of the family was not merely father, judge, and protector; he was also priest. The traditional religion of Rome was scarcely more than an extended spiritualization of the high points of family life: birth, marriage, and death. Nothing violated the religious, any more than the legal, autonomy of the family. The father was the supreme priest of the private gods of the family and its hearth, the Lares and the Penates. No child was ever born into a family; he had to be accepted, following birth, through the religious authority of the house father. Marriage was a rite of induction of the new female; she might be her husband's mate, but in a larger and much more important sense she was a new daughter in the larger family. Death rites were no more than the ceremonies involved in speeding the deceased from living to dead—but not less important— status in the family and its partnership of the dead, the living, and the unborn.

Finally, property and wealth were attributes of the *patria potestas.* At no time during the Roman Republic, which is to say down to the latter part of the first century B.C., could a son under the authority of his father (and he remained under this authority irrespective of his own age until his father died) legally own his own property or, for that matter, retain income personally earned except by explicit consent of his father. There were also strict limits placed upon property owned by a family; it could not easily be alienated from a given family line. Tradition and law joined in enforcing the corporate, collective sense of property upon the Roman mind. Individual rights of use and abuse of property were simply not recognized.

So much for the nature and scope of the *patria potestas.* Before the last years of the first century B.C. it was the single most important legal concept in Roman society, the rock on which all other concepts rested. The kinship community was autonomous within the larger commonwealth, and within this community the authority of the *pater familias* was absolute. Both the authority of the house father and the autonomy of the family were perfectly epitomized by the concept of the *patria potestas.*

What we must now do is show how this vital concept became dislodged from Roman jurisprudence in fact—although the fiction remained for a long time—and how the autonomy of the family was destroyed. For this dislodgment and destruction resulted not only in the republic's becoming the centralized, bureaucratized empire but in the enunciation of a series of legal principles that was to contain the future Western doctrine of political sovereignty and the view of society as composed of, not concentric and autonomous communities, but a mass of legally and socially separated individuals.

Once again we are in the presence of conditions created largely by war: by the demanding and exhausting sequence of wars that engaged Rome ever more during the two centuries leading up to the end of the republic and the rise of the empire. We need not go into the details of these wars. It will do simply to note that military considerations, military values, and military objectives became paramount in Rome. Foreign wars were paralleled by civil wars within Rome itself during the first century B.C. The authority of the general over his troops—the *imperium,* as this military authority was called by the Romans—began to be as fixed a part of the society as the father's authority over his family. The *imperium* was from earliest times the only authority in Rome that in effect suspended the *patria potestas* in matters concerning members of the militia. The reason is obvious: it is not possible to remain under the authority of one's house father and, at the same time, be under the authority of one's military commander. So long as wars were infrequent and the number of persons involved small, the conflict between *imperium* and *patria potestas* took small toll of Roman tradition and of the kinship community. But as more and more men found themselves under the military *imperium* for ever-longer periods of time in the field, the strain that was placed upon the authority of kinship began to reach the breaking point.

This breaking point was reached effectively in the first century B.C. It was then that Octavian, the man whose military skill had triumphed over all other generals in Rome, became the supreme political figure of Rome. A disorganized, conflict-ridden, nearly anarchic society had no alternative but to accept rule by the one man who, seemingly, could promise it peace and order. The general Octavian, grandson of a sister of Julius Caesar and an adopted member of the Julian gens, became Rome's first emperor in 27 B.C., later taking the name Augustus. His full title was *Imperator Caesar divi filius Augustus.* His initial authority was as commander in chief of the Roman legions, and then ruler over the public affairs of the Romans. Like Cleisthenes several centuries earlier, Augustus left no texts or philosophical essays to posterity, but also like Cleisthenes, he has a secure place, nevertheless, in the history of social thought. For it was within the context of his bold political acts, beginning almost immediately from his accession to virtual dictatorship, that the most fundamental principles of subsequent Roman law were forged.

There was first his centralization of political power in Rome. No longer would Rome be, in terms of structure of authority, a decentralized, cellular society as it had been for centuries. Precisely as he, with his own rule, supplanted the substantive authority of the traditional Senate—the body of "conscript fathers"—so did he, through centralization of power, dislodge all other social bodies lying intermediate between the individual and the government. By declaring legitimate governmental authority to be vested in the emperor alone, he laid the basis for the doctrine of the sovereignty of the political state, the cornerstone of those Roman legal texts that were to culminate several centuries later in the code books of Justinian. And, as we shall have occasion to note well in the chapter on the political community, the preserved texts of Roman law were to have great influence in shaping the idea of political power that flourished in the seventeenth and eighteenth centuries in western Europe. From Roman law more than from any other single source came the fateful notion that the sovereign is by nature above the law, is indeed the maker of law, and is supreme over all that is merely customary and traditional.

Second, and closely related to the Augustan idea of centralized political power, is the potent idea of legal individualism. A century of social disintegration and turmoil preceding Augustus facilitated its development, but the theoretical essence of legal individualism lay in the conception of society as an aggregate of discrete individuals, possessed of rights and duties as legal individuals, rather than as a community of lesser communities. The implication for the Roman kinship system is obvious; we need only think back on the impact of legal individualism in Athens under the Cleisthenean revolution. If the individual is the proper and only recognized unit of law, the corporate family cannot be. In the same way that the idea of political centralization takes authority away from intermediate groups, so the idea of legal individualism diminishes the juridical identity of these groups.

The view was to arise, shortly after the Augustan regime, that all communities and groups other than the political state itself have only a fictive identity, an artificial identity that is conferred on them by the state alone and that remains in existence only through concession by the state. The concepts of fiction and of concession as applied to intermediate groups like the gens and the corporate household could be applied, and were applied by the Roman government itself after Augustus, to all forms of social life, including guilds and churches. It is clear enough what extraordinary possibilities of social change, and also of direct power, lay in these concepts of fiction and concession. Anything that could not be plainly deduced from the nature of the individual or that did not emanate directly from the state had a very precarious existence indeed in the social order.

Now let us go to the heart of the matter so far as Augustus was concerned: the ancient and still powerful *patria potestas*, symbol of the autonomy of the kinship community and its absolute authority over its own membership that had been ascendant for so many centuries in Roman history. We turn to the famous Julian Laws of 18 B.C., the professed object of which was the cleaning up of sexual immorality, including adultery and pornography, so rife in Rome at that time, and also the restoration of marriage to what Augustus declared its proper dignity.

We need not question his motive in this matter; the austerity of his personal life—unchallenged by even his enemies—is sufficient proof of his intent.

But what we are obliged to concentrate on is the fact that, regardless of motives and conditions, these laws, decreed by Augustus with the aid of a compliant Senate, represent the first significant invasion of kinship authority in the recorded history of Rome. Never before had any public figure, any consul or magistrate, dared to intervene in the life of the family or gens. As we saw above, public power stopped at the threshold of the family. Only the traditional *patria potestas*, the authority vested in the house father, could legitimately concern itself with matters of personal, including sexual, morality. Now, at a single stroke, the public power, represented by Augustus, arrogated to itself this traditional right to control individual conduct.

It is interesting to note that so far as we can glean the facts from contemporary writings, the first object of Augustan punishment was his own daughter—who, from accounts in Suetonius and other writers, very probably deserved whatever happened to her, even by the loose standards of the day. She was punished by exile from Rome to an island in the Mediterranean. There was political genius in this act, if indeed it was the first implementation of the new laws, for while Augustus made clear that he was acting as political ruler, the action was that of a father exercising his traditional authority over a delinquent child. The example, in short, had a kind of lulling influence upon the public imagination, more concerned with the subject and the act than with underlying legal rationalization.

Equally important in the limitation of the *patria potestas* was the succession of decrees affecting the character of marriage. The ostensible aim was to encourage marriage and the procreation of children (birth rates were declining, in substantial measure as a result of the century of disorganization, and the number of young men had been reduced by fatalities in the wars) . And no conservative Roman elder could take issue with that intent, for marriage and procreation had always been regarded as among the very highest goals of Roman life. But the more perceptive and thoughtful must have been aware, nevertheless, of the political intrusion into a realm that had always been bounded by kinship lines alone. For good or ill, this political reform of marriage represented still another depredation on the traditional *patria potestas*.

Also political and profoundly invasive of the kinship authority was the assignment of marriage rights to classes. Augustus sought to ban intermarriage between patricians and those of the lower classes, including the recently emancipated slaves known as freedmen. He was not apparently very successful, though; and no doubt many a traditionalist patrician in Rome tended to applaud the motive even while recognizing the act as an invasion of the *patria potestas*.

Next to be noted are the intrusions into Roman property rights and responsibilities. These too, as we have seen, were vested solely in the kinship structure. Property was communal within kinship, not a right of the individual, no matter what his age. Augustus changed that within a very short time after his decrees on immorality and on marriage. The first exception was for war veterans—those men, of whatever age, who had served as legionaries in the foreign wars. These individuals were permitted to keep for their own all that they had acquired in booty or pay as soldiers. The prospective implications of this were assuredly not lost at the time on those men still serving in the legions of Rome. Later the same rights of individual ownership of property and income would be extended to civil servants, and in time to all individuals, leaving the corporate economic solidarity of the family largely a memory.

Finally, there was the impact of Augustan decree upon the religious character of the *patria potestas*. The family, as we observed, was a deeply religious entity—made so by the daily ritualization of the family's being through veneration of the Lares and Penates—symbols of the hearth and of family unity and continuity in time. Nothing in the whole idea of kinship autonomy was more sacred than its religious character. And nothing was more private than religious rites within the family. Before Augustus no public authority would have dared to intrude in any way or degree on this religious privacy. But in 12 B.C. Augustus took the title of *pontifex maximus*, an act that united the political and religious life of the realm for public purposes by giving him supremacy in the public worship of the Romans in their temples. The next step, not long in coming, was identification of his being with the private worship within Roman households. We learn that images of Augustus began to appear within family domiciles, to be placed by his more adoring or sycophantic followers alongside the sacred Lares and Penates. Thus Augustus saw to it that the political monopoly he desired for the new *imperium* was associated with religious values. It was not long before emperor worship became very common in the Roman Empire, Augustus himself being declared an immortal god by a fawning Senate at the time of his death.

Relationships between the individual and the state became ever more direct after Augustus's death in A.D. 14. The central state, having broken through the ancient *patria potestas* in matters of social and moral offenses, property, income, and religion, faced few more obstacles in its advance toward an increasingly absolute power over individuals. By the second century A.D., Roman life was as nearly totalitarian as any political existence can be. The state was utterly supreme in all respects. Bureaucracy had become immense in size and almost limitlessly penetrating into economic, social, and religious life. Quite literally no aspect of Roman private life was left; all was, in one degree or another, a function of the political state.

At the bottom of the entire structure was the army. For centuries the emperors of Rome served essentially at the will of the military. From the time that Augustus took office, first as *princeps*, then as emperor, there was no question about the ascendancy of the military community. And thereafter the succession of emperors, beginning with Tiberius, was governed entirely by an individual emperor's popularity with the military. For a period of time the system worked—at least by military, political, and administrative criteria. By the third century, however, the constantly augmenting centralization and bureaucratization of Roman political life were beginning to suffer reverses. A time came when it proved impossible to govern areas as distant as England, Spain, and the Near East from Rome, given the degree of bureaucratic detail with which such government was conducted. Gradually the borders of the Roman Empire contracted, the Germanic host on the outside constantly advancing. Other difficulties of economic and epidemiological nature arose. There were periods when emperors succeeded one another with lightning rapidity, the army executing as the army gave. From the late fourth century on, the disintegration of the once proud Roman Empire proceeded quickly. It can be said to have been vanquished, not alone by the rising might of external enemies—Goths, Visigoths, Franks, Lombards, Vandals, and others—but by the fatal consequences of centralization of power, which could not help but breed a kind of administrative apoplexy, and a progressively anemic condition in the population at large, resulting from loss of traditional centers of function and authority, the *patria potestas* being but one, though the oldest.

There are two final points to be made here, both related to the decline of the *patria potestas* and the enhancement of the military *imperium* in Rome. The first is the growth of that vast, powerful, and exceedingly influential intellectual force we call Roman law and, with it, the corps of political intellectuals—lawyers, magistrates, and others—who interpreted the law and made it coterminous with the Roman Empire. Few forces in Western history have proved more powerful, even fifteen hundred years later when the modern national state was coming into existence, than the set of principles to be found in Roman law regarding the nature of power. We shall come back to this body of law and to its interpretative corps of intellectuals in the next chapter; we cannot fully understand the political community in the West otherwise.

The second point to be noted in connection with the decline of the *patria potestas*, with its atomization of the traditional social and economic unity, under the successive penetrations of the centralized power of the *imperium*, is the rise of the Roman masses. I use this word in its contemporary sense of large aggregates of people in a society largely devoid of social ties possessed of any great meaning, cohesion, and durability. The Roman Empire contained the first great proletariat in history, product alike of Rome's size, urbanization, centralization of political power, and social dissolution.

In the long run, Rome disappeared under the weight of masses it was never really able to assimilate into a functioning society—despite the purely political and military successes it achieved for at least the next two centuries after the Augustan revolution. But Rome did not disappear without leaving behind a dual heritage of social elements that were between them to shape western Europe for the next fifteen hundred years. One of these elements was Christianity. It would be hard to imagine a more fertile ground for religion, especially the kind of religion that the followers of Christ proffered—one based as solidly upon the reality of tight, cohesive social community in this world as upon the promise of eternal community of the saved in the next. We shall come back to this conversion of the Roman masses to Christianity in the chapter on the religious community.

The second of the two social elements was to be found in what A. J. Toynbee has well called Rome's external proletariat: the Germanic people. It was their wandering westward from central Asia (in part as the consequence of the building of the Great Wall of China, which had made impossible any thought of migration eastward) that eventually brought them into lands along the Danube and the Rhine rivers which the Romans desired to keep under their own control for military purposes. The militarization that, as we have seen, destroyed the kinship system of Rome, with *imperium* replacing *patria potestas,* was the immediate product of Rome's efforts to repel the Germans, to drive them as far back from Roman borders as was possible. As everyone knows, in the process Rome became a military-based empire, with outposts reaching England in the north and with a long line of forts and other military emplacements along both the Danube and the Rhine. Eventually, however, the Germanic peoples triumphed. To what degree their triumph was due to their own numbers, fortitude, mobility, and military skill, or to the progressive deterioration of first the society, then the state, and finally the army of Rome need not concern us here.

The important fact is that by the sixth century vast areas of western Europe that had once been Roman in government were now inhabited by the Angles, Saxons, Burgundians, Goths, Visigoths, Lombards, and many other individual peoples which in aggregate were the Germans. It is to them and to their fundamental institutions that we turn now for the third great crisis of kinship: the conflict of kinship and military in medieval history. It is in many ways the most significant of the three crises, for we are living even today in structures of power and under military-political influences which had their origins in the early Middle Ages in the conflict between kinship and the military.

The Rise of Western Feudalism

Two very different and at first extremely unequal sets of institutions were to be found among the Germans who invaded and in time took over most of the western Roman Empire. On the one hand were kinship institutions, different only in name and occasionally in emphasis from the kinds of kinship institutions we have seen to mark the early histories of both Greece and Rome. Tribal, clan, kindred, and household allegiances were as dominant among the Germans when they first come under our historical observation as ever these allegiances were before Cleisthenes in Greece or before the Augustan revolution in Rome. Property, law, religion, mutual aid, culture—to the extent that it existed—all were rooted in kinship and its highly decentralized, pluralized, localistic norms. The identities of the individual German peoples were jealously guarded. To be an Angle or Saxon or Visigoth, for instance, was to belong to an ethnic strain that was envisaged as no more than an enlarged tribe, though in fact each such people contained a number of distinct tribes, each of which was in turn broken down into lesser kinship groups. Tacitus, who may or may not have actually gone north and visited the Germanic peoples in the first century as the basis of his notable little book on the Germans and their customs, found much to admire in their kinship customs, their sense of mutual dependence, their hardihood, and their moral uprightness—qualities which he used to hold the glass up, so to speak, to his own Romans, by this time showing the signs of corruption that was eventually to destroy Rome.

In any event, the Germanic invasion of the Roman Empire meant the replacement in huge areas of western Europe of Roman imperial, military-political institutions by kinship structures and values. Admittedly, as is usually the case in these matters, the Germans assimilated something from the Romans in the process—for example, elements of Latin that, when mixed over the centuries with their own tongues, were to result ultimately in the languages, and with them the several national cultures, of medieval and modern Europe. But for present purposes the central point to be kept in mind is that with Germanic replacement of Roman influence in the West, we are once again in the presence, for several centuries, of a society based largely on kinship. Largely, but not wholly! And here lies the basis of that same crisis, that same fundamental kind of conflict between kinship and military, that we have seen taking place in earlier centuries; first among Greeks, resolved by the Cleisthenean reforms in Athens in the sixth century B.C., then among Romans, resolved by the Augustan reforms in Rome in the first century B.C.

For among all the Germanic peoples, side by side with the authority of kinship manifest in the traditions grown out of family, clan, and tribe, was to be found the authority of the military chieftain manifest in the war band, the community formed by the needs of combat. Conflict with the Romans had brought this military community into great prominence. How could it have been otherwise, given the rising frequency of military engagements between Germans and the legions of Rome? And while the eventual defeat of the Romans and their falling back to the city of Rome itself was due substantially to internal weaknesses and to the sheer pressure of the numbers of Germans who moved into once-Roman areas with their tribes, families, and communal modes of agriculture, nevertheless we can hardly be blind to the military skill of the Germanic war bands, the militias under chiefs who had learned much in the way of military skill and technique from the Roman legions. The *comitatus*, the bond between the military chief and his dedicated young warriors, was to become among the Germans, just as a similar bond had become centuries earlier among Greeks and then Romans, a powerful threat to the sanctity of kinship authority, a formidable basis of change within the larger structure of Germanic society in the West. War, as we have seen, breeds a form of community, of felt loyalties and devotions, fully the equal—when war is continuous and insistent enough—of anything to be found in kinship.

We can omit the details of the struggle between kinship and military, between clan elder and warrior chief.[6] Naturally this conflict varied with time and place. There were areas of the once-Roman West which by virtue of fortunate geographic isolation succeeded in retaining their kinship basis for many centuries, with the impact of war minimal and the internal powers of war chief intermittent and negligible. There were other areas, however—especially those that were subject to the terrifying invasions of the Norsemen during the early Middle Ages—where the processes of militarization assumed command, where warrior replaced kinship elder early and permanently as the ultimate authority. It was precisely in these areas that there came into existence what was much later in European history to be called feudalism.

The essence of feudalism was the personal tie of protection and service, military at the core, which can be seen proliferating throughout western Europe from about the ninth century on. In its way, feudalism was as personal a relationship as kinship; and as Marc Bloch, among other historians of the Middle Ages, has emphasized, we are justified in seeing feudalism, in the strict personal sense of the word, as a substitute for kinship. "The relationships of personal dependence had made their entry into history as a sort of substitute for, or complement to, the solidarity of the family, which had ceased to be fully effective." Just as the primary duty of the kinsman was mutual aid, protection, and vengeance where called for, so the primary duty of each vassal to his liege lord was one of service mixed with the protection which the vassal in turn received from his superior. "The obligation was equally binding on the lord in his relation to his vassal and on the vassal in his relation to the lord."[7]

Different as the military relation and the kinship tie are in nature and origin, one cannot but be struck by the degree to which the feudal-military tie in the Middle Ages took on social and psychological characteristics of kinship. What else was the manor, the primary economic unit

---

[6] See Jenks, *Law and Politics in the Middle Ages*, especially chaps. 3, 4, and 8.

[7] Marc Bloch, *Feudal Society*, trans. L. A. Manyon, 2 vols. (Chicago: University of Chicago Press, Phoenix Books, 1964), 1: 224, 225.

of the feudal system, but an enlarged family, with the lord of the manor considered in all important respects a patriarch? The fateful conflict I have just described between kinship and military, between the authority of the clan elder and that of the war chief, was won, as we know, by the latter. But the price of this victory was, in a sense, the assimilation of many kinship elements in the feudal system during the succeeding centuries.

Nevertheless, the triumph and ascendancy of the military class were complete; and while neither the military class nor the nobility that eventually sprang from it in the Middle Ages was ever to attain the degree of political power over the social order that governments of the national states would acquire after the breakup of the medieval order—there was too much localism, decentralization, and pluralism in the Middle Ages for any one class or interest to win that kind of power—we are obliged nonetheless to respect the military as one of the most powerful classes in Western history. The true origin of the Western system of social classes that has come, with significant changes, down to the twentieth century, the source of the immensely influential Western aristocracy, lies in the military class that everywhere in the West sprang into prominence by the tenth century. From this original military class and from the nobility to which it gave rise come most of the martial values, as well as many other kinds, that have maintained the affinity between war and Western society we have already seen to lie deep in Greek and Roman history.

As Marc Bloch has stressed, military values were foremost in the medieval social hierarchy:

> If the possession of manors was the mark of a genuinely noble status and, along with treasure in money or jewels, the only form of wealth which seemed compatible with high rank, this was due in the first place to the authority over other men which it implied. (Could there ever be a surer basis of prestige than to be able to say: "It is my will"?) But another reason was that the very vocation of the noble prevented him from engaging in any direct economic activity. He was committed body and soul to his particular function—that of the warrior. This fact, which is of fundamental importance, explains the role of the military vassals in the formation of medieval aristocracy.[8]

Let us turn now to some of the distinctive attributes of this military class, the knighthood. Its technology was simple: sword, dagger, lance, armor, shield, and above all, of course, the horse. The very word *knight* means "mounted soldier." There were foot soldiers in medieval Europe, but they were regarded with contempt, especially on the Continent, and

---

8 Ibid., 2: 289.

even after the French knights at Crécy were decimated by English infantry with their longbows, the prestige of the mounted knight remained for a long time undiminished. We should not be under any illusions about the life of the knight in combat. It could be, and generally was, a rough one, characterized by intense hardship, deprivation, and constant danger. Chivalry, which we shall consider shortly, had its due obligations in the forms of fighting fair, but nothing can diminish the appalling brutality of combat that was inseparable from the mode of warfare itself.

Hence came the requirement of physical strength and durability in the knight. In medieval works of imagination, as Bloch observes, the good knight is commonly referred to as being "big-boned," "large of limb," "well-proportioned," his body pitted with scars. He was known, too. for his mighty appetites—gastronomic and also sexual. But, as Bloch goes on to point out, physical strength alone was not sufficient for a knight. He had to have also courage in high degree and, with this, a downright love of danger and combat. It is difficult for modern man, accustomed to a very different kind of life and of war, to conceive the reserves of strength and courage the medieval knight was obliged to draw on constantly.

But if there was danger, there was also relief from routine.

> Accustomed to danger, the knight found in war yet another attraction: it offered a remedy for boredom. For these men whose culture long remained rudimentary and who—apart from a few great barons and their counsellors—were seldom occupied by very heavy administrative cares, everyday life easily slipped into a grey monotony. Thus was born an appetite for diversions which, when one's native soil failed to afford the means to gratify it, sought satisfaction in distant lands.[9]

Hence comes the well-attested knightly disposition to be mobile, to seek distant, novel rewards and conquests, to search for opportunities to protect and salvage as well as engage in combat. It is no wonder that hundreds of legends and tales began to accumulate around the medieval knights' journeys—the kind of literature that in retrospect, in the seventeenth century, Cervantes was to satirize.

One would be hard put to find a better example than the medieval knighthood for display of the qualities I described early in this chapter as the constitutive elements of the military community. Not to Caesar's legions, nor to contemporary guerrilla forces, does the knightly community of the Middle Ages have to take second place when it comes to such traits as youthful vigor, discipline, individualism, and the like.

The significance of the knighthood and of chivalry—the word we use to describe the whole complex of norms, incentives, and codes that formed

[9] Ibid., p. 295.

the framework of the knightly community—was well known in medieval times. Indeed, on the basis of what we know to have been the popularity of tales and legends in which knights figured prominently, we may judge that these had the same appeal to medieval man that tales and legends of cowboys and Indian fighters have for modern man. No doubt the same combination of fact and idealization is to be found in each.

There were the innumerable chansons de geste, the most famous of which undoubtedly is the *Chanson de Roland* with its epic account of the two great knights Roland and Oliver, pledged in eternal friendship and devotion, serving Charlemagne to the death, according to the legend, in battle with the Saracens. The heroism of these two knights was to play a large role in the poetry and song of not merely the Middle Ages but early modern centuries as well. In any event, the chansons de geste, irrespective of the knights and battles they celebrate, are among our sources of knowledge.

More important, however, so far as historical understanding is concerned, are the chronicles by men like Jean Froissart and the philosophical works of Bernard of Clairvaux and John of Salisbury. These, which come as close to being treatises in social analysis as any we are likely to find in the medieval period, give us excellent insight into the knighthood and its relation to society. Nor can we overlook the postmedieval Castiglione, whose celebrated book on the ideal courtier tells us so much about the knightly class from which came the European aristocratic life style, and, most especially, Machiavelli, whose *On the Art of War*, published in 1521, not only signalized the advent of new strategies of war making in the context of modern political aims but also sounded the death knell of the medieval, knightly mode of war that Machiavelli much admired but knew had become obsolete. And finally but not least, there is that classic among treatments of the knighthood, albeit in satirical form, *Don Quixote*—the Man of La Mancha—by Cervantes, published during the first years of the seventeenth century, long after the European knighthood had ceased to flourish in fact but at a time when legends of the knighthood were to be found everywhere, many of them, as Cervantes knew well, hopelessly romanticized. In short, there is no dearth of literature on the medieval knight, and we have no difficulty in discerning the essential characteristics of the knighthood and of its code, chivalry.[10]

The medieval knight is as good example as any to be found of the medieval passion for organizing all activities in guild form. Basically the knighthood was no more than a guild of warriors, just as the university of that day was a guild of scholars—just as, indeed, almost every social,

[10] The best single scholarly work on this subject remains Sidney Painter, *French Chivalry: Chivalric Ideas and Practices in Mediaeval France* (Baltimore: Johns Hopkins Press, 1940). With it in hand, one has no difficulty in avoiding either the romanticizations or the depreciations which abound and in fixing upon the crucial elements of the subject. I have drawn substantially from Professor Painter's book in this section.

economic, political, and cultural pursuit was to be found in the context of a guild placing highest value upon mutual aid and solidarity in time of trouble and seeking with every means to discourage the kind of competition from within that was later to spring up in the Western economy and polity. Precisely as there were apprentices, journeymen, and masters in such guilds as those of the silversmiths, fullers, apothecaries, scholars, and stonemasons, so there were in the guild we call the knighthood—there known, respectively, as pages, squires, and knights. And just as the practice of any craft was held to require long training at the feet of masters within the craft guild, so the art of war required training from boyhood on, with each knight theoretically attended by at least one page and one squire in his preparation for and participation in battle.

Ideally in the Middle Ages, war was regarded as the privilege only of those trained for it, in short, only of those who belonged to the guild, who had already demonstrated fitness for both the rigors and the etiquette of war. This last is important: probably at no other time in history has the function of war making been surrounded by so many ritual obligations, so many canons of right and wrong, so many strictly social and even religious requirements. Hence arose the innumerable sagas and legends throughout the Middle Ages of knights known as well as for their trust, gentleness, courtesy, and protection of the weak as for their valor in battle; hence the fascination with the legends of King Arthur and those like Roland and Oliver who fought, or were believed to have fought, under Charlemagne in defense of the West against the Moslems; hence the "best-seller" status of the thirteenth-century *Roman de la Rose*, its subject chivalry and romance; and hence the featuring in Chaucer's *Canterbury Tales* of the knight as one of the most notable of the types the author admired. Let us concede the elements of idealization and legend in much of all this. What is important, basically, is the symbolic appeal of chivalry to whole populations who believed—often wrongly, alas—in the infallible moral perfection and military valor of the knight. The bravery and, at the same time, gentleness of a Richard the Lionhearted, or of a Saladin among the Moslems, were the stuff of countless fireside tales in the Middle Ages as well as of much written chronicle and poetry. And however exaggerated many of these tales were, there is no question but that, by the criteria of the increasingly large-scale mass-oriented, passion- or ideology-ridden, and unlimited wars of modern times, the mode of war in the Middle Ages was quite remarkable in the restraints and limits imposed upon it both by its technology—armor, lance, sword, and little else—and its guildlike social character. And if peasants were generally considered too base for the practice of war, this was, obviously enough, their protection!

Organized around the function of combat, the guild of knights in due time took on several other functions, a few of which, though strictly ancillary, long survived the military community in which they arose, as customs in Western culture at large. One of these was the ritualized courtesy or *civility* with which one knight was enjoined to deal with another, even when they were enemies who would shortly engage each other in battle. Few activities in the Middle Ages were as highly formalized as the manner of making war among knights—and, of course, the tournaments and joustings in which knights were obliged to be almost perpetually engaged. Closely related was the custom or idea of *honor*. Only the knighthood and the nobility could claim honor, which was the most important single thing in a knight's or noble's life. To have one's honor stained, or challenged in any way, was a matter of enormous importance to the knighthood. To break one's word was tantamount to being expelled from the community, to be made an outcast and the prey of others. The dishonored knight was regarded much as in modern nations we regard the convicted traitor.

A third such function of the knighthood was *romanticism*. I refer specifically to sexual romanticism, that between the sexes. In Western culture romanticism arises directly from the medieval knighthood and its increasingly ritualized adoration and idealization of the female. The emergence, in the early Middle Ages, of the Virgin Mary to her present position in the symbolism of the church was an adjunct of a more general romanticism, that which involved the knighthood's ceremonial devotion to women.

Despite common supposition, romantic devotion of male to female is rather recent in history, and confined largely to Western society and to those parts of the world where Western culture has been diffused. In the human race, the characteristic relationship between the two sexes has at all times been strictly functional, with the female serving as necessary means to procreation and to that more general division of labor by which mankind both works and meets ordinary survival needs. I am not suggesting that women have not been objects of respect at other times in history. They assuredly were in ancient Greece and Rome, and we know them to have been in other, non-Western, civilizations. Respected for mind, character, learning, and creative imagination, women were above all respected as matrons; and household mothers and grandmothers could assume immense influence and power in even the most masculine-oriented of kinship societies.

But romanticism as we in the West have known it since about the eleventh century is quite different. It is not respect so much as adoration and idealization that are involved. Not, let us emphasize quickly, of one's wife: we have it on the best of authority that wife beating was far from uncommon among knights as among others. Where romance entered was through extramarital or nonmarital love and devotion of knight to lady. The legend of Tristram and Iseult, with its overtones of illicit love and mutual adoration, perfectly expresses the reality of at least a knightly break with the religious injunctions against sexual love outside the confines of marriage. What was in time to become burlesqued as knight's search for fair damsel needing to be saved from ruthless oppressor was based on the incontestable fact that many a knight did not let marriage restrain him from finding a paramour or concubine who may or may not have been married herself.

The vivid strain of romanticism in Western literature, as also in many other spheres of Western culture, which Denis de Rougemont has so brilliantly dissected in his *Love in the Western World*, had its actual beginnings in a military community that regarded itself as above all ordinary custom and restraint. The idea that love is a matter of feeling alone and that where such feeling exists it must be honored by response, irrespective of tradition and law, spread from knightly love into a score of spheres in Western culture, including war itself. Feudal war was limited by a host of conventions and ecclesiastical dictates and by its own technology. As Denis de Rougemont emphasizes, a great deal of modern, increasingly unlimited, unrestricted and ideological war is a development of the very romanticism that first arose in the knighthood with respect only to the limits and restraints of marriage.

There was also a profound strain of *religiosity* in the knighthood. As with all other elements of this community, this could easily be exploited, more honored in the breach than the observance. But a great deal of the complicated ritualism of the knights, the long training from their beginning as pages through the rank of squire, up to the finished rank of knight, sprang directly from the close ties with Christianity that the knighthood formed during the Crusades. Going to war with the Moslem to save Christianity could not help but establish a two-way relation between a grateful church and a rewarded body of knights, hence the common practice of giving religious sanction and identity to many an order of the knighthood.

So, too, with a good many other attributes of the knighthood: civility and courtesy, for instance. The medieval idea of noblesse oblige —that nobility *obliges*, that high status can only manifest itself by an elaboration of certain civilities and generosities not found in the population at large—early took root in the knighthood. And long after the military utility of this body disappeared for all time, the elaborate ritualism of ceremony, heavily stylized relations with others, dedication to service, and protection of the young and the helpless, above all women and priests —all of these qualities, hardly to be seen in the peasantry or merchant class, continued in Europe to be the infallible attributes of the aristocrat and the gentleman.

But behind all of these religious, sexual, and ritualistic attributes of the community lay, for some centuries, the hard fact of the community's prime reason for being: the making of war. The knighthood was, for the period of its eminence, *the* military arm of society. Limited though its technology seems to us today, it nevertheless required long and dedicated training. As early as the tenth century such training, which could sometimes extend over at least ten years, was replete with those religious, cultural, and purely social characteristics that were to identify every knight throughout his life.

The community sense was bound to be a powerful one from the outset. As is the case with so many communities, the knighthood educated its members into the sense of superiority over the rest of society: superiority of its function to the ways of mere peace and superiority of its membership to all other members of society. The qualities I have already referred to in this chapter as constituting the military community—youth, individualism, mobility, secularism, discipline under command, communism in material possessions—could all be found in one or another degree in the feudal knighthood.

The community or guild was open to all freeborn youths who chose, or whose parents chose, the arduous and dangerous life of the knight. They began this life as boys quite literally apprenticed to masters—who were the knights. They were obliged to go wherever their knightly masters went, to learn from the ground up all aspects of the calling: not only the strictly military but also the complex codes of morality and religion and social decorum that went with the knighthood. They would come to know even as boys ten and twelve years of age the actualities of the battlefield: its glories and occasional booty, and also its deaths and injuries, its hardships, brutalities, and cruelties. Usually, by the time an apprentice was twenty years old he was regarded as fit for his profession of arms and inducted into it with elaborate ceremony. Thenceforth he was assessed everywhere by the canons of the community. Any flouting of these could be, as noted above, a very serious matter for him.

If it was a life of often-zestful escape from the boredom and routine of ordinary civil, especially peasant, life, it was just as often a life of extraordinary danger, of incessant discipline and perfecting in the arts of war, and, rising above all else, of being on constant call to one's liege lord. Feudal society was a tissue of personal obligations, and none of these exceeded in stringency those which the knight owed his lord. The luster that service, as a value, was to acquire in the European aristocracy—in almost every branch of royalty, for that matter—sprang in the first instance from the absoluteness of the vow of service each knight was obliged to give his lord.

Ideally, service—never cash or other material reward—was the tie that bound knights to one another as well as to their superiors. From the time a knight began his training as a page boy, through his middle years of training as a squire, and then for the rest of his active life as a master of his craft, service, devotion, and fealty were of the very essence. True, in accordance with the communitarian philosophy we have noted as one of the prime elements of the military community at all times everywhere, the medieval knight could expect booty and other forms of reward for his service. Division of spoils was theoretically equal. And when the knight became too old for battle, or rendered infirm by injury, he could generally expect to be looked after when necessary by the lord he had served in a warrior role. In short, there existed among knights, as among others in the Middle Ages bound by guild ties, an unmistakable ethic of mutual aid.

So much for the feudal military community. Small, limited, and confined though it was, by comparison with either Roman or modern European military forces, nothing can detract from its having, by the earliest period of the Middle Ages, achieved dominance over the kinship community brought by the Germanic peoples into the areas of Europe once governed by Rome. Slowly at first, then with increasing speed and effectiveness, the power of the military chieftain succeeded that of house father or clan elder as the center of gravity in the West. Once again, in short, the crisis posed by confrontation of kinship and military had been resolved in favor of the military, as it always has been.

True, the military community of the Middle Ages, the guild of knights bound by service and mutual aid, did not last very long. As we shall see momentarily, the knighthood was early attacked by forces from within which heralded a good deal of what we commonly think of as Western nationalism, political centralization, and capitalism. But while the knighthood itself was short-lived, the class that arose on the basis of the feudal-military force—that is, the nobility, the aristocracy—was not. Down until World War I, it is fair to say, the war-sprung European aristocracy exerted immense influence upon society in all its reaches, not least in the sphere of moral values that helped make virtues originating in war supreme over all others in the West.

Western Warfare: *Gemeinschaft* to *Gesellschaft*

It would be possible to write the history of postmedieval western Europe in terms of what happened to the feudal military community and then to the whole military sector of Western society. Capitalism, nationalism, the territorialization of power as well as its centralization, large-scale organization, mass society, technology; all of these make their first appearance in the modern West in circumstances strongly characterized by war and the military. This fact has received far less attention from historians than it deserves. Much that is said to have been caused by capitalism, nationalism, the middle class, and technology might better be thought of in terms of the pressures of war and of a rapidly expanding military force in modern Europe.

During the past six centuries there has been an almost constant increase in the scope, magnitude, and intensity of war in the West. The one possible exception is the nineteenth century, though this is true only to the degree that we concentrate attention upon the continent of western Europe. Certainly the West in the larger sense, which includes the United States with its bloody and devastating Civil War along with the numberless small wars in various parts of the world resulting from Western expansion, was anything but free of war in the nineteenth century, despite the myth, common in that century as today, that as the result of the growth of trade and the enlargement of world communication generally, both war and the military were rapidly becoming obsolete. In fact, irrespective of the actual toll of nineteenth-century war in terms of life and property, the power and extent of the military were increasing steadily. And, as everyone knows, the twentieth century—the century of democracy, of the spread of politics and affluence among the masses, of science and technology, and of education to a degree never before dreamed of in man's history—has proved to be the most war-ravaged and, as military budgets in Western and non-Western countries alike make clear, the most militarized century in all history.

To fail to see the impact of war on the political, economic, cultural, and intellectual history of the modern West is to leave out of consideration what is very probably the most fruitful single causal factor in what Max Weber referred to as the rationalization of Western social life. For it is in the military sphere that we can see the process of rationalization occurring earlier in postmedieval Europe. Well before the Middle Ages had come to an end, the feudal military community showed distinct signs of succumbing to the lure not merely of technology in the form of gunpowder but also of the wage system with its sharp division into categories of "owners" and "workers" and, not least, of a nationalization or territorialization of war making that was in signal contrast to the small communal militia system forming the military core of feudalism. Most of the qualities that Weber emphasized as marking the transition of Western society from the feudal-traditional-patriarchial system dominant during the Middle Ages to the modern system resting upon bureaucracy in nearly all spheres made their first appearance in the context of war.

The typology of *Gemeinschaft* and *Gesellschaft* that Ferdinand Tönnies gave to modern sociology (the former term, in general sociological usage, referring to social relationships of whatever function characterized by relative smallness, cohesion, long duration, and emotional intensity; the latter, conversely, to large-scale, impersonal relationships, dependent upon a higher degree of formality) is particularly applicable to the history of Western warfare since the Middle Ages. What else but *Gemeinschaft* was medieval warfare, with its dependence upon small communal, largely patriarchal military units, along with ritual, tradition, and a sense of both continuity and cohesion in time that made the guild of knights almost indistinguishable, as we have seen, from other guilds of that age? Medieval war was limited war: limited by its simple technology, by its inability to take command of other vital areas of society such as the church—not to mention the new free towns, which were everywhere burgeoning, and the merchant and trade guilds—and, finally, by a conception of war that confined it for the most part to small, privileged elites. That the period of the Middle Ages was in many respects a violent one does not, cannot, offset the fact that, by comparison with ancient Greece and Rome as well as with the centuries since about 1400 in the West, its war making was simple, stylized, and limited almost to the point of primitivism.

But *Gemeinschaft* in war is succeeded everywhere in the West by *Gesellschaft*; that is, by increasing use of the wage system (even the economic-oriented Karl Marx wrote that the wage system in the strict sense began in the modern West with the military), by ever-larger social units of war—national armies instead of feudal militias, by a constantly improved technology along with a constantly improved system of military accounting in matters of supplies and weapons, and, finally, by all the attributes of secularism, impersonality, and contractualism that were later to be found in almost all parts of Western society. In short, as such social and economic historians as Edward Jenks, Werner Sombart, and Max Weber have seen very clearly, the passage of Western warfare, beginning in the late Middle Ages, from a traditional *Gemeinschaft* character to a *Gesellschaft* one is scarcely less than a preview of a similar passage to be observed in economy, polity, and many other areas of society.

We are chiefly concerned in this book, however, with the history of social thought, and this, in the context of what I have just described, will be the subject of the rest of this chapter. The institutional transition from *Gemeinschaft* to *Gesellschaft* in warfare is paralleled by what the history of thought reveals. The disappearance of the feudal, *Gemeinschaft* type of war, based as we have seen on close communities of warriors bound by service, and the rise in the late Middle Ages of the new type of warfare based increasingly on the wage system—that is, upon mercenaries, as such soldiers were called—presented a great many problems of not merely a military but also a political and social kind.

Machiavelli, Renaissance mind par excellence, is the first major figure in Western thought after the disappearance of feudal warfare to deal seriously and systematically with the problem. As we shall see, Machiavelli had nothing but distrust for mercenaries, and his plea for the use of citizen-soldiers has to be recognized as an imaginative and far-seeing effort to revive within the context of the emerging political state something of the tie of service he admired in the now obsolete feudal militia system. What gives greater importance, however, to Machiavelli's treatment of war is his keen sense of the necessary union between politics and war. It is this that stamps him the first major political thinker of the modern era as well as a military philosopher and strategist of major stature.

The disappearance of the limited, local, technologically simple, feudal type of warfare in Europe and the rise of a new type based upon ever-more-lethal technology and ever-larger armies led to rising concern with war's devastation. This concern we shall see is most evident in the writings of the Dutch jurist Hugo Grotius. Largely from his works—though there were other jurists no less interested in the matter than Grotius—came the whole of what we today think of as the international military conventions which seek to restrain troops as far as possible in their relations with civilian populations and with prisoners, and in other ways to limit war.

The next vital stage in the development of Western military philosophy is what can best be called the totalization of war; that is, the conception of war as involving not simply technical military forces but whole nations, labor forces, industrial armies, even the whole of culture with its educational system, its art, and its literature. Here we have moved utterly from the feudal concept of limited war. In the writing of Clausewitz, himself profiting from what he had been able to observe in the Napoleonic wars, we see war become total: a matter of the total resources of one nation pitted against the total resources of another.

Finally, we shall deal with what I regard as the most distinctive feature of twentieth-century war, its union with revolution. Although this fateful union is scarcely to be seen in fact prior to our century, it is presaged, as we shall see, in the works of Marx and Engels. In these works and especially the works of Marx's greatest disciple, Lenin, author of the Russian Revolution, we see the final extension of the military philosophy through total war to permanent revolution.

Machiavelli and the Art of War

Everyone knows that the Italian Renaissance is one of the great ages of art in the history of mankind. Not so many know, however, that this age is notable also for its literary, philosophical, and tactical interest in war. During this age, as Jacob Burckhardt has pointed out in his classic study *The Civilization of the Renaissance in Italy*, we witness the appearance of "war as a work of art." In using that phrase Burckhardt is not suggesting, of course, that war became a more beautiful thing in its essential aspects —only that to a degree hardly known before, war became the preoccupation of gifted minds who saw it in basically the same terms in which they saw everything else around them, as being subject to the inventive and artistic mind. In many instances the same men who were writing drama, poetry, and song, or who were painting and sculpturing, were also writing on and frequently advising on the strategy and tactics of war.

This keen interest in war must be regarded as one of the consequences of the decline of the whole feudal system in Europe and of the limited type of militialike warfare that went with it. In the Middle Ages war was, as we have seen, the sport of a small class or guild, the knighthood. Now, however, by the fifteenth century in Italy, warfare was more and more the work of mercenary soldiers and officers. Bands of these frequently were hired on a contractual basis by city-states and princi-palities. Having everything to gain by participation in war, the mer-cenaries saw to it, or so Machiavelli among many others of the Renaissance believed, that there was a sufficiency of wars, with their opportunities for loot and pillage. Burckhardt tells us that Italy

> was the first country to adopt the system of mercenary troops, which demanded a wholly different organization; and the early introduction of firearms did its part in making war a democratic pursuit not only because the strongest castles were unable to withstand a bombardment, but because the skill of the engineer, of the gun-founder, and of the artillerist—men belonging to another class than the nobility—was now of the first importance in a campaign.[11]

Among the several contributions of the Italian humanists during this period was a literary dedication to war making that at times became nothing less than glorification of war. For the humanists saw in the new structure of war the means of liberating the individual, his talents and strengths, from the whole ecclesiastical and feudal system they hated with such fervor. As Burckhardt has so notably emphasized, the essence of the Italian Renaissance was the growth of the modern conception of individuality; and this involved separation of the individual, so far as was possible, from those corporate and communal structures within which individuality tended to be confined during the Middle Ages. The humanists celebrated qualities of individual assertion, boldness of man-ner, achievement of fame and renown, and, above all, release of mind and imagination from traditional obligations to knighthood as well as to guild, monastery, church, and manor.

No wonder, then, that war itself became a means of lustrous indi-vidual achievement, whether directly or through perfection of the philos-ophy and art of war. It is a matter of record that Leonardo da Vinci was as proud of his technological and strategic contributions to the art of war as he was of his painting or sculpture. And even had he not been so, there was the matter of his livelihood to be considered. The political rulers of the Italian Renaissance, and also of other countries in fifteenth- and sixteenth-century Europe, were willing to pay handsomely for inven-tions and strategies which aided them in time of war. Many, therefore, were the treatises written during this age on war, its strategy and tactics

[11] Jacob Burckhardt, *The Civilization of the Renaissance in Italy*, 2 vols. (New York: Harper & Row, Torchbooks, 1958), 1: 115–16. Burckhardt's famous study was originally published in 1860 and remains even today the best-known, most widely read work on the period.

and its implements of destruction. These ranged all the way from largely literary works, modeled upon such Greek and Roman writers of antiquity as Xenophon and Caesar, often written with the sole purpose of flattering some prince from whom the author expected patronage, to the very serious and deeply thought out *Art of War* by Machiavelli, published in 1521. Machiavelli's book opens with the following passage:

> In the past, Lorenzo, many have held and now still hold this opinion: that no two things are more out of harmony with one another or differ more from one another than civilian life and military life. Because of this we often see one who plans to excel in the soldier's calling at once not merely changing his dress, but also in habits, manners, voice, and presence departing widely from every civilian custom, because he does not believe that civilian dress can be worn by one who strives to be active and ready for any and every violent deed. . . .[12]

It is the fundamental purpose of Machiavelli's treatise to demonstrate that such a conception of war and the military is false in itself and, more important, destined to make a truly just and strong political order impossible of fulfillment. Machiavelli had himself served as minister of defense in his beloved Florence. He was every inch the Renaissance man in that he was not merely philosopher, poet, and artist but also statesman, as skilled in practical matters of statecraft and war as he was in matters of thought and style. He had become convinced that rulers' use of mercenaries for their military needs was wasteful and inefficient in military terms and also destructive of the true concept of citizenship. The disrepute into which war had fallen after the knighthood, with its consecration to service and mutual aid, had passed its zenith is to be explained, Machiavelli thinks, by the increasing role of the mercenary soldier. Good men no longer engage, as they once did, in combat.

> Because he will never be reckoned a good man who carries on an occupation in which, if he is to endeavor at all times to get income from it, he must be rapacious, fraudulent, violent, and must have many qualities which of necessity make him not good; nor can men who practice it as a profession, the big as well as the little, be of any other sort, because this profession does not support them in time of peace. Hence they are obliged either to hope that there will be no peace, or to become so rich in time of war that in peace they can support themselves. And neither one of these two expectations is to be found in a good man, because from

12 *The Art of War* in *Machiavelli: The Chief Works and Others*, trans. Allan H. Gilbert, 3 vols. (Durham: Duke University Press, 1964), 2: 566.

the desire to support themselves at all times come the robberies, the deeds of violence, the murderous acts that such soldiers commit as much against their friends as against their enemies; and from not wishing peace come the deceits that the generals practice against those by whom they are employed, in order that a war may last; and if peace does come, it often happens that the generals, being deprived of their stipends and of their living, lawlessly set up their ensigns as soldiers of fortune and without any mercy plunder a region.[13]

Nor is this all, Machiavelli argues. It is only too easy for the professional general to become a civil tyrant, just as, first, Gaius Marius, then Sulla and a whole succession of Roman generals culminating in Octavian so profoundly transformed the ancient Roman Republic. In Machiavelli's words, these men were brave generals but they were not good men. Hence the state must be based upon citizen-soldiers, whose stake in war will be only their stake in the country they belong to and love.

A well-ordered city will then decree that this practice of warfare shall be used in times of peace for exercise and in times of war for necessity and glory, and will allow the public alone to practice it as a profession, as did Rome. Any citizen who in such an activity has another purpose is not a good citizen, and any city that conducts itself otherwise is not well governed.[14]

Reading Machiavelli's work carefully, we cannot help but be struck by his underlying interest in the nature of the political order, its laws and customs, its capacity of stimulating the patriotism of its citizens. There is a great deal in *The Art of War* about technical details—methods of organizing troops, leading them, and selecting them from the citizenry, and the varieties of weaponry available in attack and defense—but despite the sheer volume of these details it is clear that the overriding purpose of the book is to argue the necessity of the citizen army, of dispensing once and for all with mercenary soldiers and officers, and of making war seem once again to members of the state as just a pursuit—when the war itself is just—as any of the civil activities in which they engage. Like Plato, two thousand years earlier, Machiavelli saw the indissoluble tie that exists between the man who loves his country and the man who fights for it as he does his family and friends. War had had this function in the Greek polis, in the Roman Republic, and, in a way, among the feudal militia, the knights, even though it fought not for country but for personal, feudal ties. Wherever hired soldiers come into the picture,

[13] Ibid., pp. 573–74.   [14] Ibid., p. 576.

Machiavelli thinks, with the consequent end of citizen-soldiers, there is every reason to prophesy loss of freedom in the state and, in due time, loss of civil and political strength. Thus it is vitally necessary to make the soldier a citizen, the citizen a soldier.

This is, I think, Machiavelli's greatest single contribution—for better or worse in the light of subsequent Western history—to modern thought: the firm uniting of the military to the political and the vivid sense that within the political order the military machine must be rooted, not in an obsolete guild of knights, not in mere mercenaries who will fight to the limit of their wages and no more, but rather in a conscript army that will reflect the full manhood of the political order. For Machiavelli, viewing the small city-states of his own day such as Florence, the political order was not large. It does not matter. By the time the full implication of Machiavelli's book on the art of war had been grasped in the West (his book continued to be studied by experts in politics, including Thomas Jefferson in the United States, down into the nineteenth century), the political order had become as large as the modern nation-state. And what Machiavelli wrote about the necessity of intimate fusion of military and political bonds in the larger social order was no less applicable when armies became mass armies, as they did in France during the Revolution at the end of the eighteenth century, than when a conscript militia of eleven thousand troops could be regarded as sufficient.

In *The Prince* we find the sentence "There cannot be good laws where there are not good arms, and where there are good arms there must be good laws." This, it is not far-fetched to say, became the governing maxim of Machiavelli's life, both as philosopher and as skilled public administrator and diplomat. To see that there cannot be a good army apart from a reinforcing state, or a strong state without a reinforcing army that would be drawn, not just from nobles looking for diversion, not from obsolete knights, not from mercenaries seeking quick booty or pay, but instead from *citizens*, conscript citizens: this was Machiavelli's great contribution. From his perception of the necessary union of military and political values, it was really a short and easy step to that later eighteenth-century perception of the necessary union of military values with those of economy, spiritual life, culture, education—that is, of the nation as a whole.

It was Machiavelli's genius to see, amid the humiliation and devastation of his beloved Italy, the virtual sport of French armies, that no hope was left of a city's or people's protecting itself through any remnant of the once noble feudal art of war. If we bear in mind that, for all the social and technological obsolescence of the feudal military community, there remained nonetheless dozens of reminders of the esteem in which the knighthood and chivalry were still held, we can understand the sense of urgency, of crisis, that lies behind not only his first great work, *The Art of War*, but all of his subsequent writings as well. It is hard not to believe that even his *Discourses*, which were reflections on the greatness of the Roman Republic and the early Roman Empire and are filled with ruminations on the vital link between the military and the political community, had its impetus beyond anything else in Machiavelli's desire to show the basic elements of the Roman military system.

I am not suggesting that Machiavelli was the militarist pure and simple. He was anything but that. He was, as much as Leonardo or any other luminary of the time, a Renaissance man—which is to say a lover of fine art, dress, food, and beautiful women, as well as science, history, literature, and politics. And as I noted above, even Leonardo (and he was far from alone in this) took enormous pride in his complicated military inventions for war. But, I repeat, if any one contribution from Machiavelli rises above all others, it is his clear and unwavering perception that the feudal community of combat was hopelessly obsolete, that mercenaries were dangerous, and that the community of war must be widened to become coterminous with the citizenry of the city-state, every healthy and vigorous free citizen being eligible on a conscripted basis, *and as a patriotic duty,* for war service whenever political security demanded it.

Machiavelli has sometimes been criticized for seeming indifference to the uses of artillery, which for a century had been employed fairly extensively in Europe. The criticism is not, however, a just one. There is a long chapter on the subject in *The Art of War,* which shows to the full the author's awareness of the massed fire power that could come from the lines of large guns. It is simply that Machiavelli was more interested in the infantry; and he was, of course, right in this. For, as I have already stressed, it was the infantry whose sheer mass had done the most to destroy the knighthood and make feudal type of war forever obsolete in the West; it was the infantry, as Machiavelli correctly foresaw, that would be the key to all military successes in future ages; and it was the infantry that was composed in largest number of citizens, Machiavelli's ideal type of infantry, thus making this branch of the service more crucial to the republic than any other. Even so, for all his devotion to the idea of infantry and cavalry, Machiavelli was far from insensitive to what he called "the fury of the artillery" and the capacity of heavy guns to destroy in due time even the most formidable of emplacements and fortresses.

Some of Machiavelli's maxims or aphorisms are worth quoting for their applicability today as well as in the past:

> What helps your enemy hurts you, and what helps you hurts your enemy.

> Never lead your soldiers to battle if you have not first made yourself sure of their courage and established that they are without fear and in order. Never make a trial of them except when you see that they expect to win.

> No plan is better than one hidden from the enemy until you have carried it out.

Nature brings forth few valiant men; effort and training make plenty of them.

Discipline does more in war than enthusiasm.

Get advice on the things you ought to do from many; what you then decide to do, discuss with few.

Men, steel, money, and bread are the sinews of war; but of these four the most necessary are the first two, because men and steel find money and bread, but bread and money do not find men and steel.

Train your soldiers to despise dainty food and costly dress.[15]

Suitably altered, these aphorisms set forth by Machiavelli in his *Art of War* are very much like his political aphorisms in *The Prince*. And in fact, politics was for Machiavelli as much an extension of military practice as the latter was, in different circumstances, an extension of politics. This was, indeed, the major contribution of the Italian Renaissance to statecraft: to see war and politics as two sides of the same coin.

Machiavelli has been criticized repeatedly for the vein of cynicism to be seen, or at least easily imagined to be present, in his writings. It would be better, however, to say that, like a good many of his immediate predecessors and contemporaries, Machiavelli was simply subjecting politics, war, and morality to the same dispassionate gaze that many an artist was giving his oils or marble.

He has also been criticized for seeming indifference to the role of money, of credit, of finance generally, in the political order, in both war and peace. There is no doubt that Machiavelli retained much of the aversion to matters of business and finance that had characterized the upper-class mind since the rise of the knighthood and feudal nobility. And from Machiavelli through Bodin, Hobbes, and Rousseau and down to contemporary exponents of the political community, there has generally been a strong hostility to the commercial classes and their pursuits. Throughout history indeed, right down to the beginning of America's fully military involvement in Vietnam, the origins of war and of the war mentality have lain, less in commercial pursuits, than in those of political and military intellectuals, those whose primary interest is in power rather than money for its own sake. Machiavelli was such an intellectual. He is indeed the very archetype of the modern political-military intellectual. His distaste for commerce sprang not from aloofness to money—obviously indispensable to war making, as one of the aphorisms quoted above recognizes clearly enough—but rather to those who deal professionally in money and credit, those in business for its own sake, a class that Machia-

---

[15] Ibid., pp. 718–20 passim.

velli strongly detested, as have all political-military intellectuals in history.

What we see, thus, in Machiavelli—not only in *The Art of War* but also in *The Prince,* the *Discourses,* and, often maliciously, in his poems and dramas—is contempt and distrust for all classes and sectors of a political population in which the values of citizenship are not deeply ingrained. Machiavelli is not the first in modern Western thought to have the idea of political virtue, nor the first to be aware of the stratagems and devices rulers must employ if political virtue in a country is to be maintained, but his brilliance as a stylist and resourcefulness as a thinker make him the most significant of the early moderns in this respect. It was his ill fate early to be tagged a mere manipulator of men, a broker in power, or worse, a political cynic; and the result was that although a great many later European political philosophers clearly drew from Machiavelli in inspiration and content, not many, if any, were willing to declare this dependence. He became the object of almost universal dislike for his writings.

Today, however, from the detachment of greater distance in time, we are able to see that while Machiavelli was assuredly not above advising rulers in techniques of power and of rule, not above a certain cynicism toward men's professed morality, not above a pragmatic philosophy of "divide and rule," there is nevertheless to be found in him, underlying all else, a preoccupation with the problem of order that had been left by the breakup of medieval social organization. If it was the military consequences of this breakup that first engaged his attention, very probably as the result of his one-time political post as minister of defense for Florence, he cannot be declared to have been oblivious to the wider aspects of the problem. There are more than a few reflections of this wider concern in *The Art of War,* as the aphorisms quoted above might suggest. And in his better-known works, the *Discourses,* the *History of Florence,* above all in the still widely read *Prince,* we can see these wider aspects—political, social, psychological—very clearly indeed. For all the fame of these works, however, it is Machiavelli's approach to the problem of war that most vividly sets him off from his contemporaries, in his realization that in the European world to come only mastery of the techniques of war would lead to mastery of the techniques of power in society. Cleisthenes and Augustus had known this, as we have seen, in the ancient Mediterranean world. Above anyone else it was Machiavelli who taught the lesson to the modern world—and in the context of basically analogous circumstances.

Grotius and the Limitation of War

Now we must turn briefly to a very different aspect of the problem created in western Europe by the disappearance of the localized, limited, and decentralized character of war known in the Middle Ages. Precisely as the political map of Europe became one of increasingly large national units—France, England, and Spain, instead of the multitude of smaller principalities and fiefdoms that had flourished in the medieval age—so the military scene became one of ever-larger armies and ever-more-devastating patterns of warfare. Machiavelli's writing had signalized the transformation of feudal and then mercenary war, limited by its nature in scope and impact, to war that was declared inseparable from the very essence of the political tie. As the political tie became stronger in Europe, relative to the ties of local community, religion, and family, and as the unities containing the political tie—that is, the national states—became larger in size, it was inevitable that the relation between war and society would become quantitatively as well as qualitatively very different from what the feudal period had known.

Adding to the problem created by the expansion of war was the momentous Protestant Reformation in the sixteenth century. It is one of the many tragedies of modern history that the same century in which war became, once and for all, national war, no longer the sport or occupation of small institutionalized groups but instead the very serious business of governments and subject populations, was the century, too, in which Christendom became passionately and lastingly divided between Catholic and Protestant. Religion, one of the most intense of all human allegiances and, correspondingly, the cause of one of the bitterest of all forms of human conflict, became inextricably involved in the political affairs of Europe. For the first time in history, Christian became relentlessly and bitterly opposed to Christian. Nations all of a sudden ceased to be merely political structures; they became, before the sixteenth century had ended, religious entities as well, either Catholic or Protestant. Religious wars in all their well-known ferocity broke upon the European scene. Had these been, as they would have been in feudal times, of chiefly local intensity, as disparate and diffuse as the feudal system itself, their impact upon society would have been less. Coming, however, as they did when the fundamental units of war were the new large national states and when the instruments of war were the new ever-enlarging standing armies of the European political order, the impact of religious war had to be devastating. We see this impact in the sixteenth and seventeenth centuries in Germany, France, the Low Countries, and England. The results were to be registered in extremes of military brutality, atrocity, and savagery not previously known in the West, at least since the invasions of the Norsemen in the very early Middle Ages. The religious element meant the carrying of war beyond combatants to civilian populations; for if the purpose of a war was extermination of Protestant heretic or Papist, as the case might be, it was not enough to limit killing to soldiers alone; war must be the means of extinguishing evil wherever it could be found, among women and children as well as combatants.

The sixteenth century marks the first appearance of unlimited warfare in western Europe—unlimited in every sense of the word, including moral. As we shall see in the next section, unlimited war reappeared in the eighteenth century, at the time of the French Revolution, and then, too, the context was, if not religious, possessed of a degree of political and ideological intensity that came very close to being religious. Likewise in the twentieth century we have known unlimited war; and here, as in the religious wars of the sixteenth and seventeenth centuries and in the French revolutionary wars, the ideological-moral element has been profound. When the enemy is more than a military opponent, when he becomes the vessel of evil, of heresy, of boundless wickedness, it is inevitable that ordinary limits upon war making will dissolve and war will be carried by every possible means to all parts of the enemy's culture and society.

Such had become the case in western Europe by the end of the sixteenth century. Montaigne, in his notable *Essays,* bore witness to the boundless hatreds and cruelties toward one another that Europeans had become capable of in the latter part of that century. Montaigne made frequent references to these and also to the contrasts between the far more humane types of war he found from his reading to be waged among the so-called savages, the primitive peoples of the earth, and the religious and national ferocities of his own day—from which he had deliberately removed himself to his country estate in order to read and, to our lasting edification, to write the famous *Essays.*

Nor was Montaigne alone in his sense of horror at the new unlimited mode of warfare that was sweeping Europe. The Spaniard Balthazar Ayala, the German Conrad Brunus, and the Italian Alberico Gentili, all jurists and philosophers, saw that unless war was somehow brought within limits, European culture would be in for atrocities and devastations beyond anything ever known in the world. War itself, they were wise enough to realize, could not be banished. There had always been wars; there would always be wars, given the centrality of conflict in human affairs and the endless, diverse opportunities for such conflict to become physical. What was desired, they thought, was no utopian proposal for the abolition of war—after all, there were just wars, they believed—but, rather, the control and limitation of war, confining it to actual combatants rather than allowing it to spread its devastation to civilian populations, the relatively humane treatment of prisoners of war instead of the fearful tortures and prolonged executions to which they were everywhere being subjected as the religious wars spread.

The greatest, certainly most influential, of all seventeenth-century philosophers who concerned themselves with these problems was the Dutchman Hugo Grotius. Born in 1583, he became at the age of twelve the pupil of one of the most famous of all scholars, Joseph Scaliger, who directed his study; and well before Grotius was twenty he had already made a European reputation as a scholar and philosopher of law. Like so many of that period, he entered politics, and it is from his experiences in that arena, which were bound to bring him into contact with the realities of war and of the military mind, that his classic work, *The Rights of War and Peace*, was given to the world. Begun in 1623, published in 1625, it is without question the greatest of all works in the sphere of international law, which was brought into existence by the fall of feudal Europe and the rise of the great modern nation-states.

Unable to find a clear basis for the kind of religious limitation of war that had once existed in a religiously unified Europe, Grotius turned, as so many philosophers in all fields were doing in that age, to the principles of natural law: the law that was—or so it was then widely believed—anterior to all purely positive or political laws, even to all customs and traditions. Others in Grotius's day were using the principles of natural law to find warrant for the political state, Hobbes foremost among them, as we shall see in the next chapter. What preoccupied Grotius, however, was not the natural law of persons within a state but the natural law of states within the larger international order—or, rather, lack of order, as the incessant struggles of that age indicated.

Grotius begins with the concept of natural right, which is, he writes, the "dictate of right reason, showing the moral turpitude, or moral necessity, of any act from its agreement or disagreement with a rational nature, and consequently that such an act is either forbidden or commanded by God, the author of nature." [16] His next step is to ascertain through reason and through search of the classics, especially Greek and Roman, whether war can ever be just and therefore in accord with right reason. His answer, like that of the other jurists mentioned above, is that just and right wars do exist, wars of defense against those seeking to destroy or capture a people.

> After examining the sources of right, the first and most general question that occurs, is whether any war is just, or if it is ever lawful to make war. . . . So far from any thing in the principles of nature being repugnant to war, every part of them indeed rather favours it. For the preservation of our lives and persons, which is the end of war, and the possession or acquirement of things necessary and useful to life is most suitable to those principles of nature, and to use force, if necessary, for those occasions, is no way dissonant to the principles of nature, since all animals are endowed with natural strength, sufficient to assist and defend themselves.[17]

[16] Hugo Grotius, *The Rights of War and Peace*, trans. A. G. Campbell (London: M. Walter Dunne, Universal Classics Library, 1901), bk. 1, chap. 1, sect. 10.
[17] Ibid., chap 2, sect. 1.

Grotius follows this observation with a detailed listing of authorities ranging from ancient Greek and Roman philosophers through the early Christian fathers in support of his proposition. But, as did all the seventeenth-century philosophers concerned with every aspect of reality, Grotius offers the law of nature, capable of being deduced, he and others believed, through right use of individual reason, as the crowning warrant for just warfare and also for necessary limits upon war.

What follows in Grotius's work is at once a treatise in natural law and the geography, politics, and sociology of war and an exhaustive look into the practices and ideas of war to be found everywhere. His book, in short, is no mere exercise in the ideal or desirable, but a learned historical examination of modes and methods of war and also limitations upon war, that is, taboos and other proscriptions upon certain intensities, corruptions, or barbarizations of war. Grotius deals with such topics as obligations, titles, and jurisdictions among individuals and with respect to property; oaths, contracts, and treaties; and damages and war claims. He considers the proper rights of embassies, the infliction of punishment on the captured enemy, and the slain enemy's right to proper burial. Likewise, he deals directly with the peculiar kind of ferocity and savagery that the religious wars of his age had brought with them: such things as the calculated devastation of crops and fields, the poisoning of wells, the burning and torturing of prisoners of war in the name of religious purity, and the notorious breaches of faith by both Protestant and Catholic nations in matters of treaties and other accords.

In all these and other respects we find the gentle and humane Grotius on the side of moderation, limits, and moral justice. War, though necessary at times, must, he argues, be kept within strict military confines, never extended to neutral nations, or above all to civilian populations—noncombatant males, women and children. Prisoners have their rights, as do, even more surely, the populations over which a victorious military force exerts rule. And always Grotius sees the sole purpose of war—of just or legitimate war—to be peace: the achievement in the earliest possible time, with the minimum of killing and destruction, of the peace that is, for him, the very purpose of human life. Over and over Grotius sounds this theme.

It is in these terms that Grotius seeks, too, the avoidance of the kind of issue between nations that takes on moral or religious overtones, knowing well the ease with which such issues can lead to abandonment of all limits on war. Thus does Grotius argue the military as well as moral advantage of holding depredations upon the enemy to an absolute minimum; for, as he tells us, memory of these can generate revenge that might easily wipe out original gain or victory. War should never be allowed to reach the point where all nonmilitary communications between opposing forces are ruled out. There should be neither unconditional war nor unconditional surrender to conclude a war. All things,

Grotius believes, must be considered finite except the power, wisdom, and love of God.

While Grotius believed natural law to be the root of his propositions and proposals, as did nearly all philosophers of his day, we cannot miss the fact that what his proposals add up to is an effort to restore the limited kind of war that had once existed under the code of chivalry.

And it has to be conceded that by the end of Grotius's century something approximating a limited form of warfare among the nations of Europe had been achieved. With the waning of religious and national hatreds, the consolidation of a more or less stable family of Western nations, and the full and frank acceptance of the system of professional troops fighting under an increasingly ritualized form of troop movement and in limited numbers (if only because of the extreme cost to monarchs of their paid professional armies and the heavy expenses of artillery and uniforms), there was a marked cessation of the kind of ferocity that had appalled such minds as Montaigne and Grotius a century earlier. Dynastic wars, by their nature, are not as likely to arouse savagery in soldiers, much less in the population at large, as religious wars and those fought for moralistic principles: hence the "limited wars" of eighteenth-century western Europe. Once again something approximating a code of warfare came into being, one that for the most part spared civilians and did not lead to wanton spoliation of the landscape. To this extent at least, the lost community of combat of the Middle Ages, with all its restrictions and limitations on waging war, had been regained; in the almost geometrically ordered ranks of the professional soldier of the eighteenth century, making war a profession, not a means of seeking to achieve a political-moral millennium.

The French Revolution and Total War: Clausewitz

With the eruption and spread of the French Revolution at the end of the eighteenth century, war takes on the mass, total form it has had ever since in western Europe. We shall have much to say about this revolution in the chapters that follow. No more significant event, assessed in terms of influence upon thought and culture, has ever occurred in the West. Although the actual institutional structure of France was little changed during the brief span of years in which revolutionary governments held sway, the fundamental principles of the Revolution were to have immense effect upon not only France but the rest of the West, even non-Western parts of the world, during the century following its outbreak in 1789.

The Revolution declared legitimate government to lie only in the people as a whole, and traditional intermediate structures of authority such as aristocracy, church, monastery, guild, and even patriarchal family to be null and void so far as having any kind of power over individuals.

Revolutionary social reality lay in France one and indivisible and in government representative of the whole people considered as a unified mass. We shall confine ourselves to this statement of the principles actuating the new France: it will suffice to give background to the conception of the military and of war that held sway in France not only during the Revolution proper and during the Napoleonic period in which it culminated but, with rarest and briefest exceptions, during the nearly two centuries since the outbreak of the Revolution in France. And what began in France only with respect to the new mode of war and military organization soon spread to other countries in one degree or another, not least to Prussia and other parts of Germany in the nineteenth century. In fact, as we shall shortly note, it was a German, Karl von Clausewitz, whose military theory was based directly upon what he had observed during the revolutionary and Napoleonic wars, who most strongly affected the subsequent envisagement of war in western Europe. Marx and Engels, too, as we shall note in the final section of this chapter, were likewise deeply influenced by what they could draw from their studies of the relation between the French Revolution and the new mode and role of war in Western society.

We have seen how, beginning with Machiavelli, the feudal concept of limited war based on the elite knighthood, and also the equally limited conception of war involving the use of small bands of mercenary soldiers was succeeded by a conception in which war making was declared a vital aspect of citizenship. We have also seen the effect upon war of the Reformation—the replacement of merely local and territorial aims by deeply, passionately held religious objectives which gave Europe a foretaste of total war—and the effort of philosophers like Gentili and Grotius to create, through international law, effective limits upon the ferocity of war and its wanton extension to whole populations, including women and children and property of every kind. For a short time, during most of the eighteenth century, it might have seemed to any observer of the matter that the objectives of Gentili and Grotius had been fulfilled; for there is no doubt that, with rare exceptions, the wars of the eighteenth century were of a relatively limited type, confined almost wholly to battles between small armies of professionals conducting themselves in accord with classic principles of strategy. There was little if any of the ideological fury that characterized the religious wars of the sixteenth and seventeenth centuries.

But now, with the outbreak of the Revolution in France and the rise of the new secular ideology of democracy, whose followers were so often religious in the intensity of their belief, advancing it indeed with the kind of fanatic determination of Protestant and Catholic alike in the Reformation, a very different age of war and military philosophy dawned for western Europe. This age, stretching down through two twentieth-century world wars, is with us still.

The Revolution in France expanded Machiavelli's idea of the citizen army in the small city-state he knew in Italy to the massed national army based upon the democratically sacred principle of universal military conscription—of property, wealth, service, and, above all, human life. Never again after the French Revolution would the art of war be thought of in terms of small professional armies serving limited political or economic objectives. Thenceforth both the art of war and the science of military strategy would be concerned with mass armies of citizens drawn, in theory at least, in accord with the principle of strict equality.

The idea of modern total war was born in the famous decree of the National Convention, August 23, 1793, declaring that a *levée en masse* was made necessary by the efforts of foreign powers to interrupt and destroy the Revolution in France. The following sentences have a very contemporary ring indeed:

> *Article I.* From this moment until that in which our enemies shall have been driven from the territory of the Republic, all Frenchmen are permanently requisitioned for service in the armies.
>
> Young men will go forth to battle; married men will forge weapons and transport munitions; women will make tents and clothings, and serve in hospitals; children will make lint from old linen; and old men will be brought to the public squares to arouse the courage of the soldiers, while preaching the unity of the Republic and hatred against kings.[18]

Within scarcely more than a year this decree had French armies in the battlefields of Europe, crushing opposing European armies with ridiculous ease for years, bringing to the fore as military leader Napoleon Bonaparte, one of the greatest military geniuses of all time, and with him a dozen or more scarcely less able generals, all of whom had risen from the ranks of private soldiers. More important, with this mass army, the first in human history, went the vivid banner of the Revolution, displaying its ideals of *liberté, égalité,* and *fraternité* for all the world to see. The immense influence of the French Revolution, to be seen across the Atlantic in Latin America as well as the United States and in due course eastward all the way to India and China, would never have been possible had it not been for its armies carrying its message wherever they went. And it is well known that the almost fantastic success of French citizen armies against the competently trained and prepared professional armies of the European monarchies came in very large part from the reckless courage and boundless intensity of men who

---

18 Quoted in Crane Brinton, Gordon A. Craig, and Felix Gilbert, "Jomini," in *Makers of Modern Strategy,* ed. Edward Mead Earle, with Gordon A. Craig and Felix Gilbert (Princeton: Princeton University Press, 1941), p. 77.

were fighting, not for obscure dynastic ambitions of kings or for mere wages, but instead for the spiritually energizing ideals of freedom and democracy in a world that seemed ripe for the transmission and development of these ideals.

Napoleon's armies were to be defeated in time, as we know, though only after a display of strength that was to remake the whole European continent. What the French had invented in the way of mass strategy and military tactics could be emulated by other nations, like England whose manufactures were superior. The army of the single nation of France, for all its revolutionary intensity, could not hope to be a match forever for the other national armies assembled against it. The important fact here, though, is not defeat of France but the insemination in European polity everywhere of the theory of mass warfare, to be fought by citizen armies, and to be expressed not only in strategy and tactics but in a philosophy that recognized no social, cultural, or human limits to warfare.

It is to the momentous work *On War* by Karl von Clausewitz that we are obliged to turn for the first great expression of this new philosophy and science of warfare. Clausewitz did not live to see publication of the book, much less the profound influence it was to have over the world during the several decades immediately following. But response to lectures and articles he presented before his death was sufficient to show that from his vision of war would spring a very different conception of it than any known before. The general view of Clausewitz's ideas on war as falling in the narrow sphere of military thought is absurd. The very nature of his doctrines on war lifts them immediately to the rank of political and social theory. Like the doctrines or not, they have been as vital as any of those contemporary philosophers such as Adam Smith, Jeremy Bentham, and Karl Marx, in remaking the structure of European society in the nineteenth century.

The reason for this lies in the concept of total war. Clausewitz was himself an officer in the Prussian army that opposed and eventually helped defeat the Napoleonic armies. But from the beginning, we are allowed to infer, Clausewitz knew that success lay solely with armies that practiced most efficiently the principles introduced by the French under Napoleon, following the *levée en masse* of 1793. What the Prussian Clausewitz learned from Napoleon and the military strategy of the French revolutionary army he adapted after the Napoleonic wars to his lectures and writings, and eventually to his masterpiece, *On War*. It is important for many reasons to understand the essence of this book, which is social and political as well as military. It is without doubt the single most influential book written in modern times on war and its relation to national policy. Quite apart from the numerous military schools and the endless numbers of officers in Europe, America, and other parts of the world that the book has influenced, we can find direct evidences of its effects on the minds of such revolutionists as Engels, Trotsky, and Mao Tse-tung.

War, declared Clausewitz, must be understood in terms of its relation to society as a whole. It must also be understood in relation to the individual will, compounded of not only intellectual but emotional and instinctual drives. There is a profoundly romantic quality in Clausewitz's celebration both of the mass and the individual, a romanticism heightened by his contempt for all the seventeenth- and eighteenth-century theories of war that had been based upon relatively small professional armies, in which strategy and tactics were exercises in geometrically designed, classic maneuvers. The true reality of war, he believed, with the memory of Napoleon's great victories still fresh in his mind, lies in the people and in vast popular armies. As for the older limited form of war, Clausewitz wrote:

> And on this field where the conduct of War spins out the time with a number of small flourishes, with skirmishes at outposts, half in earnest, half in jest, with long dispositions which end in nothing, with positions and marches, which afterwards are designated as skilful only because their infinitesimal causes are lost, and common sense can make nothing of them, here on this very field many theorists find the real Art of War to exist; in these feints, parades, half and quarter thrusts of former Wars, they find the aim of all theory, the supremacy of mind over matter. . . .[19]

Bear in mind that what Clausewitz is pouring his contempt on is a form of warfare which was the most limited in scope, the most specialized, and the most restricted in its operation on civil populations that Europe had known since the small feudal knighthoods of the Middle Ages. It was Clausewitz's genius to recognize that the same tendencies which were generating political states based on the masses, with the powers and functions of governments extending increasingly to aspects of social life and the individual mind that even the most absolute of monarchies had never touched, were also generating forms of war to match, in which the mass, rather than the specialized professional military group, would dominate and within which there would be a maximum of free play for individual ability, skill, luck, and cunning to rise to the top. The lessons taught by the French revolutionary armies and by Napoleon and his marshals were, in short, not lost upon the mind of this brilliant Prussian theorist of war in its relation to society. No philosopher in western Europe had a keener appreciation than did Clausewitz of the profound

---

[19] Karl von Clausewitz, *On War*, trans. J. J. Graham, rev. ed., 3 vols. (London: Routledge & Kegan Paul, 1949), 1: 229.

changes that had taken place in society, and thereby in war, since the Middle Ages.

> The great and small monarchies of the Middle Ages carried on their Wars with feudal levies. Everything was then restricted to a short period of time; whatever could not be done in that time was held to be impracticable. The feudal force itself was raised through an organization of vassaldom; the bond which held it together was partly legal obligation, partly a voluntary contract. The armament and tactics were based on the right of might, on single combat, and therefore little suited to large bodies. In fact, at no period has the union of States been so weak and the individual citizen so independent. All this influenced the character of the Wars at that period in the most distinct manner.[20]

As feudal ties waned, however, and modern states became organized around the principle of absolute monarchy, and as economies in Europe became increasingly money oriented, the nature of war and of armies changed.

> In this manner, in proportion as the Government separated itself from the people, and regarded itself as the State, War became more exclusively a business of the Government, which it carried on by means of the money in its coffers and the idle vagabonds it could pick up in its own and neighbouring countries. The consequence of this was that the means which the Government could command had tolerably well-defined limits, which could be mutually estimated, both as to their extent and duration; this robbed War of its most dangerous feature: namely, the effort toward the extreme, and the hidden series of possibilities connected therewith.[21]

Given these circumstances, war became more and more of a game in which "Time and Chance shuffled the cards" and in which the controlling features of victory and defeat in Europe bore only the slightest relation to the actual political and economic strength of the nations involved. But all of this was changed with the onset of the French Revolution. As the nature of French society changed, so did the nature of the military in France and, hence, of war in Europe.

> War had suddenly become an affair of the people, and that of a people numbering thirty millions, every one of whom re-

---

[20] Ibid. 3: 91–92.   [21] Ibid., p. 96.

garded himself as a citizen of the State. . . . Henceforward, the means available—the efforts which might be called forth—had no longer any definite limits. . . .[22]

The relation between politics and war had become closer, Clausewitz thought, as the result of revolutionary-democratic changes first in France and then in other areas of Europe. Nation and army are but two sides of the same coin. Wherever there is politics in the modern state, there lies the beginning of war, even if in fact armed war does not emanate from politics at that particular time.

> The war of a community—of whole Nations and particularly of civilized Nations—always starts from a political condition, and is called forth by a political motive. It is therefore a political act. . . . Now, if we reflect that War has its root in a political object, then naturally this original motive which called it into existence should also continue the first and highest consideration in its conduct. Still, the political object is no despotic lawgiver on that account; it must accommodate itself to the nature of the means, and though changes in these means may involve modification in the political objective, the latter always retains a prior right to consideration. Policy, therefore, is interwoven with the whole action of war, and must exercise a continuous influence upon it, as far as the nature of the forces liberated by it will permit.[23]

Then follows what is undoubtedly the single most widely quoted sentence in Clausewitz's entire work: "We see, therefore, that War is not merely a political act, but also a real political instrument, a continuation of political commerce, a carrying out of the same by other means." [24]

The inseparability of war and politics, of the military and the political state, in modern times, is the central thesis of Clausewitz's book. He recognizes clearly the reciprocal relation between modern war and the social composition of a given people, and also the relation between the kind of war that will be fought and the psychological state of the peoples beforehand:

> The greater and more powerful the motives of a War, the more it affects the whole existence of a people. The more violent the excitement which precedes the War, by so much the nearer will the War approach to its abstract form, so much the more will it be directed to the destruction of the enemy, so much the nearer will military and political ends coincide. . . .[25]

22 Ibid., p. 100.   23 Ibid., 1: 22.   24 Ibid., p. 23.   25 Ibid.

At the time Clausewitz wrote those words, there were still military philosophers and strategists, as well as philosophers in other spheres of thought, who believed that the effect of modern democracy might well be to lessen the intensity of war and restrict its scope. Clausewitz has proved on the whole, however, the better prophet. He regarded war, in some form, as an eternal part of the human condition. More to the present point, he thought the nature of war and the nature of society at any given point in history were closely linked. Seeing the democratization of society in Europe, the consequence of the French Revolution and its currents, and the democratization of war—the creation of armies of the people, first in France, then in other parts of Europe, the opening up of the military as a means of the individual's advancement through the ranks, and the shifting of war from specialized, limited feudal or dynastic aims to those of entire nations—Clausewitz did not doubt that war would of necessity become ever more total in its relation to both life and death. Most of *On War* is concerned with technical matters of strategy and tactics, but the careful reader will find in it a philosophy as much of society as of war alone.

Nor was Clausewitz the only one to perceive the profoundly changed character of war in the nineteenth century. There were others, among them Alexis de Tocqueville and Hippolyte Taine, who echoed the sentiments of Clausewitz's *On War*, with its message of the relation between war and society.

Tocqueville, in his monumental study of modern democracy, concerned with the impact of revolutionary-democratic values on all aspects of modern civilization, thought that while the spread of the the middle class would have the effect of lessening popular desire for war at any given time, it would have the additional effect of deepening and widening the character of war once it burst upon a democratically constituted people.

> War, after it has destroyed all modes of speculation, becomes itself the great and sole speculation, to which all the ardent and ambitious desires that equality engenders are exclusively directed. Hence it is that the selfsame democratic nations that are so reluctant to engage in hostilities sometimes perform prodigious achievements when once they have taken the field.[26]

Moreover, Tocqueville observed, it is the unhappy nature of democracy's armies to seek war to a degree that was not true either in feudal times or in the era of the absolute monarchies. Then war offered individuals no particular advancement to be gained in social position; they

---

[26] Alexis de Tocqueville, *Democracy in America*, trans. Phillips Bradley, 2 vols. (New York: Alfred A. Knopf, 1944), 2: 277.

already had positions as high as they could properly and reasonably aspire to, which success in war did not materially affect. However, Tocqueville tells us, the position of democratic armies and their leaders is very different:

> In democratic armies the desire for advancement is almost universal: it is ardent, tenacious, perpetual; it is strengthened by all other desires and extinguished only with life itself. But it is easy to see that, of all armies in the world, those in which advancement must be slowest in time of peace are the armies of democratic countries. . . . All the ambitious spirits of a democratic army are consequently desirous of war, because war makes vacancies and warrants the violation of that law of seniority which is the sole privilege natural to a democracy.[27]

Tocqueville also observes that in democratic armies it is the lower-ranking, especially noncommissioned, officers whose desire for war is likely to be greatest, for promotions come rarely in time of peace. In wartime, however—and also, Tocqueville notes, during revolutionary periods—opportunities for advancement multiply. Such officers

> are therefore bent on war, on war always at any cost; but if war be denied them, then they desire revolutions, to suspend the authority of the established regulations and to enable them, aided by the general confusion and political passions of the time, to get rid of their superior officers and to take their places. Nor is it impossible for them to bring about such a crisis because their common origin and habits give them much influence over the soldiers, however different may be their passions and desires.[28]

There is, finally and most profundly, Tocqueville's awareness of the linkage between the centralization of command that is native to the military and the centralization of government to which, through erosion of intermediate and local institutions, democracy tends always to advance. An affinity thus develops between certain types of democratic leaders, especially those of much personal vigor and ambition, and military leaders:

> All men of military genius are fond of centralization, which increases their strength; and all men of centralizing genius are fond of war, which compels nations to combine all their powers in the hands of the government. Thus the democratic tendency that leads men unceasingly to multiply the privileges of the state

[27] Ibid., p. 266.   [28] Ibid., p. 274.

and to circumscribe the rights of private persons is much more rapid and constant among those democratic nations that are exposed by their position to great and frequent wars than among all others.[29]

Clausewitz, no believer in democracy, would have understood and agreed with Tocqueville's words. So did that mordant analyst of modernity in Europe, Hippolyte Taine. His extraordinary study of the French Revolution and the modern age of politics that followed may have its due share of prejudices, but these are not likely to seem as irrational in our age as they did when Taine's several volumes on the subject were first published in the last quarter of the nineteenth century. At the time, Taine, strongly influenced by Tocqueville and also by certain political reactionaries of his time, seemed willfully blind to the capacities of democracy and technological progress—in which liberals and democrats of the day so ardently believed—to end for all time militarism and chronic war. As the following passage suggests, however, Taine would not be regarded today as so blind to reality:

> One war after another and the institution becomes worse and worse; like a contagion, it has spread from State to State; at the present time, it has overspread the whole of continental Europe and here it reigns along with its natural companion which always precedes or follows it, its twin-brother, universal suffrage, each more or less conspicuously "trotted out" and dragging the other along, more or less incomplete and disguised, both being the blind and formidable leaders or regulators of future history: one thrusting a ballot into the hands of every adult, and the other putting a soldier's knapsack on every adult's back: with what promises of massacre and bankruptcy for the twentieth century, with what exasperation of international rancor and distrust, with what waste of human labor, through perversion of productive discoveries, through what perfection of destructive appliances. . . . It is sufficient for us to place the two military systems face to face, that of former times and that of today: formerly, in Europe, a few soldiers, some hundreds of thousands; today, in Europe, eighteen millions of actual or eventual soldiers. . . .
>
> Such is the terminal fruit of the new regime; military duty is here the counterpart, and as it were, the ransom of political right; the modern citizen may balance one with the other like two weights in the scale. On the one side, he may place his prerogative as sovereign, that is to say, in point of fact, the faculty

[29] Ibid., p. 300.

> every four years of giving one vote among ten thousand for the
> election or non-election of one deputy among six hundred and
> fifty; on the other side, he may place his positive, active service,
> three, four, five years of barrack life and of passive obedience. . . .
> He will probably end by discovering that the two sides of the
> scales do not balance and that a right so hollow is poor compensa-
> tion for so heavy a burden.[30]

One does not have to share all of Taine's dislike of the modern centralized, national-democratic state to see in the foregoing words more
than a few grains of hard truth. Here, too, Clausewitz, first philosopher of
popular, total war would have been in agreement. Precisely as total government brings with it total war, so does total war bring with it total
government.

War and Communism: From Marx to Mao Tse-tung

The affinity between war and revolution has been very close in the
twentieth century. For the two largest and most powerful communist
states, Soviet Russia and the People's Republic of China, war was the
crucial context of realization of revolutionary aspiration. And as is evident enough, the symbolism, the strategy, the theme of war—whether
against internal "enemies of the people" or enemies abroad—has been,
and remains, inseparable from the political governments of these nations.

There is nothing remarkable in this. As we saw early in this chapter,
following Max Weber's insight in the matter, the ethic of communism has
always been deeply embedded in the military community. Communism
of life, of danger, of relationship, as well as of booty and possession, has
always been, as Weber emphasizes, a vital element of the military,
whether in the original form of war band or in the great modern mass
armies and their peculiar form of "military socialism."

It was, however, in the nineteenth century that the relation between
militarism and communism as a social-revolutionary philosophy became
an intimate one. And why not? If social reconstruction could seem to
more and more transparently military minds an indispensable means of
welding disparate parts of a population into a military community on a
national scale, why could the matter not be seen in reverse? Why could
not the ingrained elements of the military community—its innate centralization of command, its discipline, its abolition of all moral considerations that might in any way retard victory, and its spirit of combined
militancy and communism—be utilized to bring about, or to aid in bring-

---

30 Hippolyte A. Taine, *The Modern Regime*, trans. John Durand, 2 vols. (New
York: Peter Smith, 1931), 1: 230–32. Taine's work was first published in France as
part of his six-volume *Origins of Contemporary France* (1876–93).

ing about, the social revolution? Rarely in the nineteenth century was the question asked as baldly as this, but it is implicit in the writings of an ever-widening sector of the revolutionary left in the nineteenth century, and particularly in the sector that included Karl Marx and Friedrich Engels.

That both Marx and Engels were, throughout their adult lives, keen observers and reporters of military actions, of wars in various phases of history and in different parts of the world, is a matter of abundant record. The correspondence of each man is filled with references to military tactics and strategy, which reveal minds keenly alive to the changing technology of war and to the significance of changes in military organization like those invoked by Napoleon, to be seen in both the American Civil War and the Franco-Prussian War. Each man wrote journalistic articles, for such newspapers as the *Neue Rheinische Zeitung* and the *New York Tribune* among others, in which the insights of the reporter were clearly fused with the historical knowledge of the careful student of military history. One could fill a fair-sized book with the pieces written directly on war or with sections on warfare and the military drawn from larger works such as *Anti-Dühring: Herr Eugen Dühring's Revolution in Science* and *The Class Struggles in France*. All of this is well known and a matter of no novelty or special significance here.

What is less well known, and of infinitely greater importance, is the close relation Marx and Engels saw between war and revolution, between their techniques and between their whole psychology. There is a straight line reaching back from the twentieth-century militarized communism of Stalin and of Mao, and also from the revolutionary guerrilla warfare of this century in so many parts of the world, to the ideas and writings of Marx and Engels. Consider the following passage of theirs:

> Now, insurrection is an art quite as much as war or any other, and subject to certain rules of proceeding, which, when neglected, will produce the ruin of the party neglecting them. . . . Firstly, never play with insurrection unless you are fully prepared to face the consequences of your play. Insurrection is a calculus with very indefinite magnitudes, the value of which may change every day; the forces opposed to you have all the advantage of organization, discipline, and habitual authority; unless you bring strong odds against them you are defeated and ruined. Secondly, the insurrectionary career once entered upon, act with the greatest determination, and on the offensive. The defensive is the death of every armed rising; it is lost before it measures itself with its enemies. Surprise your antagonists while their forces are scattering, prepare new successes, however small, but daily; keep up the moral ascendancy which the first successful rising has given you; rally those vacillating elements to your side which always

> follow the strongest impulse, and which always look out for the
> safer side; force your enemies to a retreat before they can collect
> their strength against you; in the words of Danton, the greatest
> master of revolutionary policy yet known, *de l'audace, de l'au-
> dace, encore de l'audace!*

Those words might easily come from texts and tracts on revolutionary
guerrilla warfare by Mao Tse-tung, Lin Piao, Ho Chi Minh, or Che
Guevara in our own century. They were in fact written under the name
of Karl Marx in the *New York Tribune*, September 18, 1852.[31] From an
early date in their closely related lives, Marx and Engels were keenly interested in guerrilla warfare as it appeared in various parts of the world,
and, given their already-well-formed revolutionary aspirations for the
working classes, it can easily be inferred that their interest in such warfare
was, from the beginning, an aspect of a larger interest in the mechanisms
of revolution. Among other lessons both men drew from the failures of
the several revolutions of 1848 in Europe, and the resulting counter-
measures taken by established governments, was the lesson of military
preparedness by revolutionaries.

Marx's admiring words on the Paris Commune of 1871, which
followed the initial, abortive military operations of the French government against Prussia, show a mind that, twenty years later, was no less
fascinated by the military arts that must underlie revolutionary success:

> . . . If you look at the last chapter of my *Eighteenth Bru-
> maire* you will find that I say that the next attempt of the French
> revolution will be no longer, as before, to transfer the bureau-
> cratic-military machine from one hand to another, but to smash
> it, and that is essential for every real people's revolution on the
> Continent. And this is what our heroic party comrades in Paris
> are attempting. What elasticity, what historical initiative, what
> a capacity for sacrifice in these Parisians! After six months of
> hunger and ruin, caused rather by internal treachery than by the
> external enemy, they rise, beneath the Prussian bayonets, as if
> there had never been a war between France and Germany and
> the enemy were not at the gates of Paris. History has no like
> example of like greatness. If they are defeated, only their "good
> nature" will be to blame. They should have marched at once
> on Versailles, after first Vinoy and then the reactionary section
> of the Paris National Guard would themselves have retreated.
> The right moment was lost because of conscientious scruples.[32]

31 They are to be found also in Friedrich Engels, *Germany: Revolution and Coun-
ter-Revolution,* quoted in *Guerrilla Warfare and Marxism,* ed. William J. Pomeroy
(New York: International Publishers, 1968), p. 53.
32 Pomeroy, op. cit., pp. 61–62.

In many ways, however, Marx's and Engels's concern with the history of military tactics, particularly guerrilla tactics, is of less importance in their social philosophy of warfare and the military than their recognition of the vital relation between successful warfare and the nature of the society involved in such warfare. In the Marxian philosophy of history there is a fundamental emphasis on the interdependence of all social, economic, and technological elements in any given historical age. Marx and Engels argued that patterns of warfare, no less than patterns of political power or of the arts or of religion, depend upon technological and economic factors. Engels has this point clearly in mind in the following passage:

> . . . Nothing is more dependent on economic pre-conditions than precisely the army and the navy. Their armaments, composition, organization, tactics and strategy depend above all on the stage reached at the time in production and communications. It is not the "free creations of the mind" of generals of genius that have revolutionized war, but the invention of better weapons and changes in human material, the soldiers; at the very most, the part played by generals of genius is limited to adapting methods of fighting to the new weapons and combatants.[33]

The passage is to be found in Engels's *Anti-Dühring*, a work concerned with the social aspects of technology and science in history and of the relation throughout human development between thought and action of any kind, on the one hand, and the social conditions provided by stage of development, on the other. Following the passage just cited, Engels treats us to a brief evolutionary account of war in Europe, noting the impact of gunpowder in the fourteenth century and its revolutionizing of Western military technology; the rise of the foot soldiers, or infantry, and the effect of this profound change upon the feudal system of military organization; and the decisive significance of varied formations of infantry in battle. He deals also with the military aspects of the American War of Independence and the French Revolution and with the whole political significance of Napoleon's massed citizenry backing up his massed battalions in the field:

> The revolutionary system of arming the whole people was soon restricted to compulsory conscription (with substitution for the rich, of payment of money) and in this form it was adopted by most of the large states on the Continent. Only Prussia attempted, through the *Landwehr* system, to draw to a still

---

[33] Friedrich Engels, *Anti-Dühring: Herr Eugen Dühring's Revolution in Science*, quoted in Pomeroy, op. cit., p. 63.

greater extent on the defensive power of the people. After the rifled muzzle-loader, which had been improved between 1830 and 1860 and made suitable for use in war, had played a brief role, Prussia was also the first state to equip its whole infantry with the most up-to-date weapons, the rifled breech-loader. Its successes in 1866 were due to these two factors.[34]

Engels was a particularly devoted and keenly perceptive student of military strategy and tactics. His newspaper dispatches about the war in Hungary, conjoined with its attempted revolution, reveal a mind of subtlety and skill. He was especially interested in the Crimean War, and was disappointed when he failed to obtain the post of military correspondent there with the London *Daily News*.

Both Marx and Engels saw immediately the great strategic and tactical significance of the American Civil War when it broke out in 1860. Both men were well acquainted with the principles of total war, of massed military action, that had been set forth by Clausewitz and others following the French Revolution and the Napoleonic wars. Both Marx and Engels were among those Europeans who perceived that whatever else the Civil War in America bespoke, it was bound to become the first major example of the kind of war about which Clausewitz had written in general and abstract terms. They saw this significance before many professional military students in the war colleges of Europe. Whereas the renowned German general Moltke is said to have declared that he did not care to witness or study "movements of armed mobs," referring to the titanic battle between North and South, both Marx and Engels from the outset recognized that this war contributed as profoundly to the whole science of mass warfare as to the history of capitalism. In the Preface to the first edition of *Capital* (1867), Marx wrote, "As in the eighteenth century the American War of Independence sounded the tocsin for the European middle class, so in the nineteenth century the American Civil War sounded it for the European working class." We can see in that passage alone the implications for the proletarian struggle that Marx found in mastery of military power.

Of the two thinkers, Marx seems to have had slightly superior foresight on the outcome of the Civil War. Engels's sympathy lay, of course, with the North, if only because a Northern victory would mean capitalism ascendant and hence, by the logic of the Marxian theory of history, nearer to its ultimate and inevitable collapse and to the emergent rise of socialism. But as early as 1861 he wrote of the Confederates' greater will to fight, their superior command of strategy and tactics, and the high probability, he feared, of a Southern victory. Marx, however, from the outset took the view that apparent technical military superiority

---

[34] Ibid., p. 66.

alone could be delusory, that victory would lie with the side best able to mobilize factory and field as well as troops; clearly, this was much more likely for the North than for the South. And, of course, Marx's view in the matter proved correct.

We do not, however, acquire a correct sense of the real relation of Marx and Engels to the military community and the fusion they effected between it and the revolutionary community by considering merely their interest in ordinary strategy and tactics. The major difference between Marxism and other nineteenth-century theories of socialism or communism was Marx's emphasis upon what he termed "scientific" socialism, in contrast to the "utopian" socialism he so detested. And for Marx and Engels, scientific socialism consisted, first, in relating socialist aspirations to what they regarded as the inexorable course of historical development and, second, in conceiving socialist achievement in terms of the means actually at hand—means that had indeed been created by capitalism and the national state, as Marx and Engels saw the matter. From the time when they wrote their *Communist Manifesto*, Marx and Engels made it evident that they would have nothing to do with those utopian socialists who, in rejecting capitalism, chose to reject also the works of capitalism, including militarism and all other degrees of force and violence.

Toward the end of the *Manifesto*, Marx and Engels summarize the steps that must be taken to consolidate the gains of the revolutionary proletariat once it has managed to overthrow the capitalist government. The first step, they write, is "to raise the proletariat to the position of ruling class, to win the battle of democracy." Clearly the military image of revolution is ascendant here. It is even more obviously so in the steps that are to follow, all clearly specified:

Confiscation of the property of all emigrants and rebels.

Centralization of credit in the hands of the state, by means of a national bank with state capital and an exclusive monopoly.

Centralization of the means of communication and transport in the hands of the state.

Equal liability of all to labor. Establishment of industrial armies, especially for agriculture.

I am not suggesting that these are the only steps indicated by Marx and Engels for the inauguration of a revolutionary-socialist regime. Nor am I suggesting that Marx and Engels were in fact militarists rather than revolutionary socialists. They were precisely what they declared themselves to be: self-appointed spokesmen for the working class, or, rather, the revolutionary proletariat, in its struggle against the rulers of the capitalist system. But Marx and Engels, more than any other declared socialists of their day, saw in the military, and in the means of centralized command and of unified force to be found only in the military, the surest means to the defeat of capitalism and the establishment of socialism. And they were nearly alone in the nineteenth century in seeing the affinity between the military and the revolutionary communities. We shall come later in this book to the latter community and the powerful roles played in it by Marx and Engels. It suffices here to place them, as they must be placed, in the military as well as the revolutionary community.

For the effects of the Marxian envisagement of the military and its strategic involvement in society went, as they have continued to until the present, far beyond anything that could be confined to socialism as such. What Sigmund Neumann wrote thirty years ago, in part analytically, in larger part prophetically, is superbly pertinent here:

> It is not too much to state at the outset that the writings of Marx and Engels gain in significance and perspective while the twentieth century's pattern and problems of warfare become clear and fully developed. *Marx and Engels can be rightly called the fathers of modern total war.* What has long been recognized in the history of political organization and internal politics, namely that the "totalitarian" party had its inception in the socialist movement, may be applied also to the field of military affairs. The proud discovery of Dr. Blau, a National Socialist strategist, that modern warfare is of a fourfold nature—diplomatic, economic, psychological, and only as a last resort military—was common knowledge to Marx and Engels. They were fully aware that military campaigns could be lost long before the first bullet was shot, that they would in fact be decided beforehand on the preliminary battlefronts of economic and psychological warfare. They certainly recognized that the many-fronted war was one and undivided and thus could be won or lost on the international battle line as well as by a nation's civil strife or within each citizen's faltering soul. *War and revolution—unmistakably established as twin movements in our time—were at that early period seen in their fundamental and continuous interrelationship by these keen strategists of the world revolution.*[35]

Professor Neumann is not suggesting that Marx and Engels had a fully developed view of the strategic relation between war and revolution, between the military community and the revolutionary community. That

---

[35] Sigmund Neumann, "Engels and Marx: Military Concepts of the Social Revolution." in Earle, op. cit., p. 156. Italics added.

is to be found only in the twentieth century, beginning, as we shall see, with the writings of Lenin, before the Bolshevik Revolution in 1917. What Marx and Engels did contribute, however, was a clear view of the relation between war and revolution each considered as a form of violence, as a mode of attack upon some established structure, and of the interchangeability of military and revolutionary techniques. And there was, finally, as Neumann points out, the Marxian conception of history and of society, in which all social, political, economic, and intellectual elements are seen in dialectical relation.

There were a good many militarist and nationalist minds in the nineteenth century fully prepared to pay the price of moderately revolutionary reconstruction of the social order in order to accomplish their objectives of a militarized nationalism; Friedrich Jahn and Richard Wagner in Germany and the leaders of the Action Française in France were among them. What we see in Marx and Engels is the beginning of the line of socialist revolutionaries who thought war and militarization not too high a price to pay for the socialist revolution, for an eventual classless society.

There is no reason at all to believe that Marx would have dissented from these words that Engels wrote after Marx's death:

> Contrary to appearance, compulsory military service surpasses the general franchise as a democratic agency. The real strength of German social democracy does not rest in the number of its voters but in its soldiers. A voter one becomes at twenty-five; a soldier at twenty; and it is youth above all from which the party recruits its followers. By 1900, the army, once the most Prussian, the most reactionary element of the country, will be socialist in its majority as inescapably as fate.[36]

To see the military community, especially the youthful elements in the rank and file and among the officers, as a potentially revolutionary force in society, willing to lend its aspirations and techniques to the overthrow of political and economic society, called for a good deal of vision in the nineteenth century. But there is no reason to doubt that this was precisely the vision of the matter that appealed to Marx and Engels. Those already in the army were used to the centralization of command, the austerity of life, the discipline, the overall communality of experience, and, perhaps above all, recognition of the importance of quick and decisive actions, even at the cost of bloodshed, that the revolution would demand of its supporters. Such awareness, such habitude of mind, was lacking among the vast majority of workers, not to mention other elements in civil society. For this reason there took

---

[36] Quoted in Neumann, op. cit., p. 169.

root in the minds of Marx and Engels, as did so many other aspects of the French Revolution, the powerful example provided by the Jacobins when, in the interest of protecting the Revolution from foreign attack, they adopted the far-reaching concept of the nation in arms and placed banners bearing the Revolution's key words, *liberté*, *égalité* and *fraternité*, in the soldiers' hands. Thus Clausewitz's famous theory of total war was widened by Marx and Engels to include war that would contain total revolution. No great feat of imagination was required to see in the disciplined, dedicated, fearless, and austere soldier who has been trained for battle involving foreign objectives the very image of the disciplined, dedicated, fearless, and austere revolutionary soldier, whose training is easily converted toward, not foreign, but domestic objectives.

This view became an increasingly popular one among European socialists—at least those who were Marxian, and they were preponderant. In France the socialist Jaurès wrote a book, *The New Army*, filled with the exciting vision of every man a soldier, the nation a total militia, which would democratize war and also instill military virtues in civil society. And as the revolutionary movement widened and intensified, especially in Russia, after the death of first Marx and then Engels, more and more revolutionaries saw the indispensable advantages of military centralization and discipline. What Lenin wrote in 1906 on the matter is evidence enough of this:

> It is not guerrilla actions which disorganize the movement but the weakness of a party which is incapable of taking such actions *under its control*. . . . What we have said about disorganization also applies to demoralization. It is not guerrilla warfare which demoralizes, but *unorganized,* irregular, non-party guerrilla acts. . . . A Marxist bases himself on the class struggle, and not social peace. In certain periods of acute economic and political crisis the class struggle ripens into a direct civil war, i.e., into an armed struggle between two sections of the people. In such periods a Marxist is *obliged* to take the stand of civil war. Any moral condemnation of civil war would be absolutely impermissible from the standpoint of Marxism.[37]

By 1916 Lenin had reached the point in his thinking that not only civil wars but also national wars could be good in themselves. Throughout the nineteenth and early twentieth centuries, there were substantial numbers of anarchists, socialists, and social reformers who were pacifist in commitment, who regarded *all* war as evil. Marx and Engels never counted themselves among these; neither did Lenin, as the following passage shows us. Lenin is addressing himself to the published statement

---

[37] Quoted in Pomeroy, op. cit., p. 90.

in 1916 by a leading group of European Marxists, among them Rosa Luxemburg, Karl Liebknecht, and Franz Mehring, that national wars are invariably wrong in that they play into the hands of imperialists and reactionaries:

> The fallacy in this argument is obvious. That all dividing lines, both in nature and society, are conventional and dynamic, and that *every* phenomenon might, under certain conditions, be transformed into its opposite, is, of course, a basic proposition of Marxist dialectics. A national war *might* be transformed into an imperialist war, *and vice versa. . . .*
>
> . . . But the mistake is very harmful also from the standpoint of practical politics, for it gives rise to the absurd propaganda of "disarmament," since it is alleged that there can be no wars except reactionary wars. . . . National wars *against* the imperialist powers are not only possible and probable; they are inevitable, *progressive,* and *revolutionary; though,* of course, to be *successful,* they require either the concerted effort of huge numbers of people in the oppressed countries (hundreds of millions in our example of India and China), or a *particularly* favorable conjuncture of international conditions. . . .[38]

The relevance of this passage from Lenin to twentieth-century revolutionary movements—especially in eastern Europe, Asia, Africa, and elsewhere—is apparent at first reading. To turn away from all wars, national wars included, as was the wish of pacifists, among whom were many socialists and social reformers, seemed to Lenin an act of blindness so far as the ends of revolution were concerned. Accept the fact of national war, most especially the kind that involves liberation of a colonial people from its imperialist government abroad, and then seek to convert the violence of war into the necessary violence of revolution: this was Lenin's message. And it became, as we know, the message of other twentieth-century revolutionary leaders.

Almost immediately after the successful overthrow of the government of Russia by the Bolsheviks in 1917, work commenced leading to the combined militarization of the Russian people and the socialization of the Russian army—or what was left of it after its disastrous defeat by the Central Powers in World War I. It is Lenin's closest associate, Leon Trotsky, himself a lifelong revolutionary, who is properly regarded as the father of the Red Army. Trotsky did not hesitate to declare the building of a powerful army as almost the number-one priority of the revolution. This came in large part, of course, as reaction to efforts of England, France, and the United States, through their own use of military force,

---

[38] Ibid. Quoted in Pomeroy, op. cit., pp. 107–8.

to put down the Bolsheviks and return political authority to the previous government or place it in the hands of other, less revolutionary, elements in Russia. But Trotsky's motive in building a powerful Red Army was more complex than that alone. He also saw the very process of militarization as a means of bringing many disparate, potentially subversive or counterrevolutionary elements in Russia into a disciplined unity that could serve as the instrument of Russian policy with respect to international communism.

It was Trotsky, though with Lenin's at-first-reluctant approval, who seized upon the idea of allowing both troops and officers of the czarist army to become members of the new Red Army. A very substantial number of czarist officers became the military leaders of the new army in Russia, providing not only strategic and tactical leadership in the field or in camp but all-important leadership in the education and training of new recruits as well. Half the czarist army—the largest ever known in Europe, for all its demonstrated ineffectuality—had been totally illiterate. The work of schooling, of teaching reading and writing on a mass basis, really began in Soviet Russia with troops, and then with workers and peasants. For how can either military or revolutionary policy be implemented by those unable to read and write? The ease with which czarist army officers transferred allegiance and skill to the new Red Army taught a good many military powers in Europe, and in other parts of the world, a lesson in the interchangeability of the military, as well as in the natural affinity of military and revolutionary life styles, including motivations.

It was also Trotsky's inspiration to attach to each major military unit of the Red Army a political commissar, who, without interfering in actual military matters, would make sure of, first, the military leaders' continuing loyalty to the new government and, second, the constant development among the troops of a revolutionary spirit—directed, of course, abroad, not in Russia itself.

Also in line with not only Lenin's and Trotsky's but also Marx's and Engels's views of the nature of revolution was the use of military symbolism in Russia on a constantly widening scale. It is difficult for revolutionary ardor to remain intense after a successful coup d'etat; and it is equally difficult for discipline to remain great. It was realized very early in Soviet Russia that the work of militarizing society, through incessant exposure of the people to military symbols—constant use of the words *attack, war, enemy, victory,* and others like them—could not help but generate all-important processes of unification. Workers in the factories and the fields were called industrial soldiers, fully in keeping with the *Communist Manifesto*'s reference to "establishment of industrial armies." Working from the sound psychological insight that solidarity is greatest when an external enemy is perceived, the Soviet government did not relax in its determination to make the entire rest of the world —incipient communist-revolutionary movements excepted—seem an armed camp of enemies hostile to the Russian people and especially to the soldiers of the Red Army. This army, especially after Stalin's triumph and his ensuing total militarization of Russia—which was no more, actually, than the fruition of the hated Trotsky's design—was incessantly referred to as the vanguard of the revolution.

More recently, we have seen the unification of the military and the revolutionary communities in China under Mao Tse-tung and his lieutenants. Mao began as a revolutionary, became a soldier and general in the communist forces which fought the nationalist Chinese and the Japanese armies alike during the latter part of World War II, and went on, as we know, to become the supreme military and political leader of mainland China, the People's Republic of China. The dream we have seen to lie in the writings of Marx and Engels, in Jaurès's *New Army*, and, perhaps, above all, in Trotsky's vision of the socializing mission of the Russian Red Army, has been in large measure fulfilled in Mao's China. From the 1930s, when Mao led his communist followers on the Long March to northwestern China, instilling the principles of revolutionary militarism wherever he could, down to the present moment or at least until very recently, not only has the army been the most visible symbol of the revolution but revolution has been the major objective of the army. It would be hard to find a government anywhere in history which used the symbols, incentives, and disciplines of the military more widely and concertedly than that of China during the past two decades. Whether in industry, government, education, agriculture, or any other major sector of Chinese society, from the highest level of authority down to the smallest village council, the role of the military has been ubiquitous and for the most part decisive.

Cleisthenes and Mao

Ironically, this chapter ends precisely on the note on which it began: the confrontation between kinship and military, followed by the militarization, with revolutionary result, of an entire people. Different as China is and has been from ancient Athens, we are obliged to recognize that both societies in their traditional forms were organized entirely around kinship. In traditional China as in the Athens before Cleisthenes, household, clan, kindred, and village were the dominant loyalties. Custom, tradition, and the authority of the elders reigned in both countries alike. Both may be seen to have had their time of troubles—for Athens during the sixth century B.C., for China during the nineteenth and early twentieth centuries—when the problem of vulnerability to foreign invasions became acute, when leader after leader proved unable to resolve the political and economic tensions that had resulted from exploitation or to organize the people into a new and effective unity. Both may be seen to have undergone a radical reorganization, largely under the leadership of a single man, which effectively destroyed the traditional kinship society and its ancient symbols and authorities, setting up in that society's place a new one organized overwhelmingly in terms of military values and disciplines with the inevitable consequence of liberation from older roles, statuses, and authorities. In China, as in post-Cleisthenean Athens, we have seen erupting—oftentimes destructively, to be sure—the values of youth, social and cultural competition, secularism, mobility, communality, and individualism, values which were born of war and the military.

It is much too soon, of course, to do more than speculate on whether China during the next century will know a period of cultural efflorescence comparable to that of Periclean Athens, or for that matter, to any one of several such periods in China itself in its earlier centuries. Looking today at the often bleak, regimented, strongly authoritarian surface of China, one would find it hard to be very optimistic. In any event, exact parallels are never to be found in history. As there are similarities, so are there great differences between China and ancient Athens. But all this notwithstanding, there has been in this century a change on the vast scale of China strikingly like that which inaugurated a whole new civilization in ancient Greece. Now, as then, we see the momentous substitution of a social system resting upon military-territorial principles for a very old one resting upon the personal ties of kinship. And the principles of organization conceived by Cleisthenes twenty-five hundred years ago which became the basis of a totally new civilization in the Greek world have, in the twentieth century, reached the non-Western worlds of Asia and Africa, with consequences that must surely in the long run be cataclysmic for the West. The end result of the loss of kinship and the militarization of Greek society was the military empire of Alexander the Great and the implantation in Western society of a militarism from which it has never recovered. It is perhaps the supreme irony that that militarism reached Asia, particularly China, in the twentieth century.

2 The Political Community

Conflict and Politics

From war and the military community we pass directly to politics and the political community. The transition is a natural one, for both historically and sociologically there is the closest relation between war and the state. There is no known historical instance of a political state not founded in circumstances of war, not rooted in the distinctive disciplines of war. The state is indeed hardly more than the institutionalization of the war-making apparatus; its earliest function everywhere is exclusively military; its earliest rulers, generals and war lords. Only much later begins the work of transferring to the political arm functions previously resident in other institutions; family, religion, and voluntary association of one kind or another. Only later too, when philosophy becomes one of the creations of the human mind, begins the work of seeking other than military justifications for the institution of the state. It is then, as in the fateful age of Plato, whose own political writing forms the real beginning of this chapter, that we find thinkers dealing

93

with the state as justice, as law, as reason, as community, and so on. But it is clear, nevertheless, that the historical beginnings of the state lie in war, in violence, and in a short time the monopoly of force. As Max Weber has correctly pointed out in his *Politics as a Vocation,* "Ultimately, one can define the modern state sociologically only in terms of the specific *means* peculiar to it, as to every political association, namely, the use of physical force." [1]

> The origin of the State, or political society, is to be found in the development of the art of warfare. It may be very sad that this should be so; but it is unquestionably true. Historically speaking, there is not the slightest difficulty in proving that all political communities of the modern type owe their existence to successful warfare. As a natural consequence, they are forced to be organized on military principles. . . .[2]

Likewise, the comparative historian Teggart stresses the relation between, on the one hand, war and conflict and, on the other, the emergence of the military king who assumes control over territory and supersedes traditional, personal, chiefly kinship relations. Everywhere, Teggart shows us, the rise of the institution of the state has accompanied conditions of war or threat of war and the emergence of more and more individuals from the ancient protective ties of clan and kindred.

> The crucial point to be observed here is that kinship and territorial organization represent simply the institutionalization of a situation which arose out of the opportunity for personal self-assertion created by the breakup of primitive organizations. . . . Thus throughout the past we are presented with the anomaly of men fighting to maintain the institutionalized vestiges of the self-assertion of aggressive individuals on occasions of long-past upheavals." [3]

Granted, however, that the political community originates in war, that it may be seen, indeed, as in the beginning no more than a kind of consolidation of military conquest or occupation, and that throughout history war has been, in Randolph Bourne's phrase, the health of the

---

[1] Edward Jenks, whom we have already seen on the historical character of the confrontation between kinship and military organization, also stresses the vital relation between the state and war.

[2] Edward Jenks, *A Short History of Politics* (London: J. M. Dent, 1900), p. 73. See also Jenks, *Law and Politics in the Middle Ages* (New York: Henry Holt and Company, 1898), and *The State and the Nation* (New York: E. P. Dutton, 1919), for detailed elaborations of this point.

[3] Frederick J. Teggart, *The Processes of History* (New Haven: Yale University Press, 1918), p. 89.

state, the infallible means of maximizing its powers and functions, nevertheless a long and distinguished line of social philosophers has sought to explain and justify the state in terms other than of war and force. Of all forms taken by the Western quest for community, in philosophy and life, that of the political state has been unquestionably foremost. So incessant and widespread, so inclusive and penetrating, have been analyses of the state ever since Plato, writing amid the ruins of the polis that had begun in the Cleisthenean revolution, that for a long time we have tended to regard the political and social categories as synonymous, overlooking in the process other and equally compelling forms of community in Western man's consciousness.

Man in the West has been fascinated by the state: its properties, powers, functions, and potentialities for good. This has been especially true in ages of endemic social and moral conflict. In this respect the state has competed strongly with the religious community, also intensified during ages of conflict and dislocation. The major periods of development of Western political thought have unfailingly been characterized by widely perceived rootlessness, instability, dislocation, and conflict in the social and economic sphere. This is true of the period in which political thought begins, the age of Plato. It is equally true of the period when the Roman lawyers, after Plato and Aristotle the greatest political intellectuals in the ancient world, developed their remarkable legal philosophy of power in imperial form. And it is just as true of the later period when first Hobbes, tormented by the English Civil War, and then Rousseau, obsessed by the conflict he perceived everywhere in surrounding society, wrote their lastingly influential treatises on the political community. Between social conflict—or perceptions of it, at any rate—and the political community there is a close, even symbiotic, relation in the history of social thought.

There have been a great many Western writers since Plato who deserve the title political philosopher, whose contributions to the political community and its elements have been notable. We shall, however, limit our attention to the very greatest of these, as must necessarily be the case throughout this book. Let us turn now to the elements of the political community as these may be disengaged from the great body of philosophy that has been evoked by this form of community.

The Elements of the Political Community

Monopoly of Force

"Every state is founded on force," Trotsky is said to have declared. He was entirely correct. There is no known instance of a political state's ever having come into existence except on the basis of claimed power resting upon force—military force. The intellectual energies of philosophers have been devoted ever since Plato to proving that the essence of the state is something other than force—justice, freedom, equality, as the case may be—but the irrefutable fact remains: the political state differs from all other types of social institution in that its basis is power, or rather, the monopoly of power. And this institutional quality of the state passes over into the philosophy of the political community. No matter where we look in the history of this idea system, from the Greeks to the present age, we invariably find an insistence on the authority of the state as absolute, illimitable, and imprescriptible with respect to all persons and all relationships in the given area covered by the political community. Force exists, to be sure, in all spheres of society, family and church included. But it is the essence of the political community that, above the level of the most moderate form of physical chastisement, the only *legitimate* force in society is claimed for the state. It alone, declares a long line of Western philosophers as well as spokesmen for the institutional state, can take life, imprison, exile, fine, expropriate, or otherwise use force upon individuals. That is, it alone can do these things legitimately.

Sovereignty

This difficult-to-define concept springs directly from the monopoly of force we have just seen to belong to the political community. Historically it is no more than the transference to the whole of the population of the commander's military power over his troops, though one should not dismiss the subtleties of moral and legal rationalization that have accompanied this transference. The claimed directness of power over individual citizens that we saw in Athens following the Cleisthenean reforms is an instance of the rise of sovereignty in the West. So, four centuries later in Rome, following the civil wars and the triumph of the military *imperium* over the ancient *patria potestas*, was the claim of absolute rule in the person of the emperor. The essence of sovereignty is its assertion of rule or government that extends directly to the individual, cutting through the intervening authorities of kinship, religion, and guild.

To be sure, this directness of rule, this individualization of authority, does not arise immediately in any area. Much of the substance of an area's political history is taken up with the efforts, at first often futile, of its political rulers to unseat, to destroy, the claims of such traditional authorities as kinship or religion. Families, churches, and other groups will seek, for as long as they can hope to get it, some mode of autonomy, some status of enclave, that restricts the state's authority over individuals. What is today called "conscientious objection" in matters of political law is no more than a final, individualized remnant of the autonomy, the independence from the power of the state that for a long time was claimed by the collective unities of kinship, religion, guild, and other forms of corporate association. In the Middle Ages, in fact, a "liberty," technically speaking, was simply the autonomy a given group or association retained within the centralized power of the rising monarchical state. From the very beginning, the profound importance of the philosophy of the political community has been its assertion of, its insistence upon, the sovereignty of the state over every other form of association in society—that is, within the territory covered by the state.

Territorialization

The idea of the territorial sovereignty of the state brings us to the third crucial element of the political community. Unlike such forms of relationship as kinship or religion, that of the political community or state is inseparable from a given piece of territory over which the right to govern exists, along with the monopoly of force that underlies sovereignty. As we saw earlier, the militarization of Athenian society brought about by the Cleisthenean reforms carried with it certain inescapable consequences of a territorial kind. For the first time, rights, privileges, and duties incumbent upon individuals sprang not primarily from the personal kinship ties of tribe, clan, and family, but from the fact of coresidence within the new city-state of Attica.

Much of the conflict that is everywhere inseparable from political history rises from the effort of rulers to territorialize the groups and associations that contain human beings, that is, to make the boundaries of these groups and associations coterminous with the political boundaries of the state itself. In modern times we call this process nationalization, but its essence is really territorialization.

The first and most formidable opposition to this territorialization of identity comes, of course, from kinship; for the essence of kinship, as we have seen, is personal—a relation of interdependence deriving from the fact of common generation, not common territory. This great conflict between kinship and state is to be seen everywhere, even in the very latest new states in Africa and Oceania, where tribal ties are old and not easily relinquished.

Almost equally formidable, however, is the conflict between religion and the state, also rooted in the state's effort to make a matter of territorial identity out of what religion believes to be irretrievably personal. Here, as we shall see in greater detail in the next chapter, is where the rise of the *universal* religions greatly aided the development of the political state in the ancient world. These religions, which offset the influence of family, clan, village, and regional deities by emphasizing worship of some remote, universal, transhuman deity, aided profoundly in the work of clearing away those fixed loyalties to clan and household that for so long impeded the development of the political state, with its insistence upon sovereign power and its right to extend this power directly to individuals. It is a fair, easily documented surmise that had not the universal religions come into existence in the ancient world, in Asia as well as Europe, about when they did, with their emphasis on a universal, remote, and super-natural being whose subject was the whole of mankind, the territorializa-tion and politicization of social and economic relationships would have been far more difficult.

Prescriptive Law

Not for a long time in the actual history of individual states does a clear notion of prescriptive law appear. The claims of tradition and custom and of folkways and mores of kinship, locality, and religion are too great. Moreover, the attention of leaders of the early states is so largely directed toward military matters that little can be spared for internal direction and prescription of behavior. But the same force that lies in military command lies also, at least potentially, in prescriptive law: in the power to make law, to declare law, and to decide which among existing traditions shall be enforced or sanctioned as law. For a long time, as I say, the history of any given political state reveals very little of this kind of law. Internal matters are still left largely to the traditional unities of kinship, locality, and religion. When the state does enter internal matters, it is usually in a kind of judicial role. Thus, in the history of England—the first of the gen-uine states to arise in modern Europe—the earliest function of Parliament was not legislative but judicial. But by the reign of Henry VIII, the pre-scriptive, legislative role of both king and Parliament was clear-cut. Grad-ually, as the state acquires stability, it claims the same monopoly of *law* —that is, as distinct from mere tradition or custom, from the inner orders of other associations such as family, clan, village community, or church —that it claims of *force*.

Bureaucracy

Also slow in coming into recognizable being is bureaucracy. At first there is hardly more bureaucracy in the state than that constituted by the king's personal servants and retainers. In Weber's sense of the word, it is not so much bureaucracy as it is a retinue of followers and supporters, serving in return not for fixed income but for booty received in war, largesse at home, and protection of one kind or other. But in all states known in history, the more formalized bureaucracy of paid, regularized political technicians shortly comes into being, no matter how primitive by modern standards. Bureaucracy has not, of course, been historically confined to the political state alone any more than it is in our own day; there are religious and economic bureaucracies. But it is in the political state that the idea of bureaucracy makes its first appearance—rivaled in age and extent only by the bureaucracies that began to appear in the universal religions, with their fixed, paid priesthoods.

Citizenship

The citizen in the state compares with the soldier in the military community. Each is conceived in theoretical abstraction, if not actual isolation, from all his other roles in society. As we have noted above, one of the most momentous aspects of the Cleisthenean reforms in ancient Attica was the emergence of a clear idea of citizenship. The individual had direct membership and identity in the newly formed city-state in his own right, rather than through the traditional mediating structures of household, clan, and tribe. One became, and still today becomes, a citizen of a state by meeting specifications set by the state; these might require being born to a citizen or being naturalized—that is, political adoption, through formal rites. But the revolutionary essence of the state, in its impact upon other forms of association, lay in its concentration upon, first, *subjects* —that is, all individuals conceived primarily as subject to the king's authority, irrespective of other affiliations or memberships—and, second, *citizens*—that is, individuals conceived as subjects of the whole political community of which they are themselves the cardinal elements. We can see the advancement of the idea of the political community and the actuality of the state in history precisely through the spread of the idea of citizenship, a form of membership the status of which in the state or political community is like the kinsman's in the family, or the communicant's in religion.

Positive Rights

The notion that the state can create or give legitimacy to "rights" of individuals is a corollary of the prior notion of prescriptive law. If the state alone can make law, or give sanction to law, it follows that no individual or group rights exist save those expressly sanctioned by the political state. But, plainly, this notion cannot help but be the center of controversy, of passionate commitment and antagonism, which must result in a great deal of instability in the histories of states. Prepolitical associations such as kinship, military, and religious did not offer rights, only duties. The idea of rights, that is, of individual and associational immunities from state power, came out of the state's struggle with competing internal forms of association such as kinship and religion. To be free to follow one's kinship, religious, or other duties is to be free to follow one's commitments of conscience, as we would see the matter today. Inevitably, upon the rise of a competing agency, the power of the state and its military, in an area, there will be conflicts: conflicts between decrees or laws of the state and those selfsame commitments to family, religion, or other nonpolitical authority.

Such conflicts are the stuff of political history and the reason why political history is inseparable from the impact of political power upon the more ancient forms of social organization in an area. These conflicts may be regularized over a period of time by the state's concession of people's right to believe in this or that religion, to marry, to baptize, to bury their dead as their kinship traditions enjoin, to hold property that belongs to individual, family, church, or business enterprise, and so on. Substantively, the state is creating nothing. It is, for reasons of civil polity, only recognizing what has long been in existence. But such recognitions are the bases of what we call political or civil rights in the political community. Men will commonly appeal to anterior practices, to earlier beliefs and activities, and declare these sacred under religious or ethnic or "natural" law. Sometimes the political state will recognize these, declare them legitimate, and "institute" them as rights—that is, as practices within the law and subject to the protection of the law.

But we would miss much of the revolutionary essence of the state in Western history if we did not see that the political state can in fact create rights for segments of the population that have never had them, either substantively or within legal definition. I have reference to women and children under patriarchalism, to ethnic minorities under ethnic majorities, to workers in business enterprises, and so on. When the state declares that children, women, Catholics, Jews, blacks, or others who may have long endured some form of subjection henceforth are entitled to a particular mode of existence, to justice, to recognition as individuals in their own right, to liberty of mind and conduct, and to freedom from oppressive authority in other spheres of society, then it may assuredly be said that the state, despite, or rather because of, its base in sheer power, can become the creator of rights and freedoms for individuals in the larger order. It is indeed this very capacity for creating new freedoms and rights for populations that has made the Western political state the inherently revolutionary form of organization it has been from the time of the Cleisthenean reforms.

On the other hand, it would be folly to overlook the capacity of the state for becoming a power in human lives so great as to be total, so encompassing in its demands, so monolithic in its structure of functions, authorities, and allegiances as to exterminate all other social functions, authorities, and allegiances. The total state, as we must now see in our consideration of Plato, the first and greatest of Western apostles of the political community, is bred, as possibility at least, in the very nature of the political community.

The Crisis of the Polis

Plato lived, thought, and wrote during the waning years of what is without question the greatest single age of Western cultural history, the so-called Golden Age of Athens in the fifth century B.C. We have already dealt briefly with the immediate background of this age, the momentous Cleisthenean reforms at the end of the preceding century through which there occurred at one and the same time the rise of the political state and the emergence of the individual, the former notable for the appearance of the first genuine political democracy in the ancient world, the latter made forever memorable by the extraordinary outburst of creativity in many areas of expression.

It is, however, the invariable fate of the great ages in history to decline almost as quickly as they come into existence. Athens was no exception, and by the time Plato had reached his young manhood Athens was showing unmistakable signs of a decadence in culture, a visible waning of creative power, and a social conflict that threatened the very existence of the polis. In short, Plato must be seen, for all his own individual creative greatness, as a mind shaped by the torments of perceived social disintegration and breakdown. There is no other way of understanding the specific thrust of his *Republic*.

The greatness of Athens had begun, following the Cleisthenean reforms, with her defeat of the Persians, very early in the fifth century B.C. This victory, made possible only by the strengthening and unifying of Athens through Cleisthenes' military as well as political genius, was the prelude to a military ascendancy during the fifth century without which there could have been no such vast influx of wealth through commerce as occurred. But the old adage "Those who live by the sword die by the sword" was abundantly exemplified by Athenian fortunes. The neighboring city-state of Sparta, totalitarian in the intensity of its own militarization, jealous of Athens, covetous of Athenian wealth, status, and power, brought Athens to humiliating defeat in 404 B.C., after twenty-seven years of war between the two states and their respective allies. One could make a strong case for the defeat of Athens as the single most momentous one, in terms of intellectual consequences, in Western history. It was more than simple military defeat: it marked the ending of the one democracy that had ever existed in the ancient world, with an accompanying degradation of moral ethos and the beginnings of a radical change in type of thought and culture. There is abundant testimony to the effect of the shock, the traumatic derangement, of Athenian life, politics, culture, and thought in consequence of defeat by the hated Spartans, who had built an entire culture around military values alone. To all of this Plato responded as he could hardly have helped responding, given the sensitivity of his mind.

But there was more involved in Athenian disintegration than military defeat alone. We cannot help but be struck by the rise and spread of a form of social and moral conflict in a real sense bred into the Athenian polity by the nature of the revolution—the Cleisthenean reforms—that had brought this polity into existence. The major social consequence of the Cleisthenean reconstruction was the release of the individual from the traditional and constricting ties of kinship. With the political destruction of ancient tribalism and the establishment of a purely territorial polity, one based upon the individual's residence in one or another of the demes that were the central units of the state, the triumph of the individual was assured. Citizenship, with its multifold participation in state decisions through voting and incessant meetings, was the political mark of this individuality; the magnificent efflorescence of the arts and philosophy was the cultural mark of this same individuality. Athens had become known by 475 B.C. as the freest city in the world, and also the city that rewarded its artists and philosophers most richly, through applause and following as well as through money paid out directly by the state as prizes for great dramas, poems, sculpture, and architecture. From all over the Mediterranean world came artists and thinkers to participate in Athenian life.

But individualism and freedom in such proportions as these inevitably carry with them major conflicts of great intensity, however sublimated these conflicts may at first be. Social change is always a form of crisis in the lives of individuals, as they feel accustomed roles, statuses, and memberships being altered, with estrangement and anomie the common result. For all their zest and exuberance, the unchallengeable greatness of their cultural works, the immense pride they took in their magnificent city and its intellectual works, for many Athenians there were bound to be tensions, often agonizing ones. After all, Athenian society had been for countless centuries indistinguishable from kinship organization. Tribes, clans, and households were of supreme importance politically and also socially and psychologically. Now, with the rise of the new polis following Cleisthenes, the political importance of these kinship entities was destroyed—*but not their social, psychological, and spiritual importance.* And this fact underlies a very great deal in the thematic content of both art and philosophy as well as in the personal, day-to-day life of fifth-century Athens, so commonly are disorganization and conflict, to a degree at least, the reverse side of the coin that bears on its face the marks of intellectual creativity. Great ages are never tranquil ages.

From a study of the philosophy, the literature, and other works of Athens during the first age of the new polis, in scores of ways we can see how the two distinct orders, the kinship and the political, both continued to exert powerful influence upon the minds of citizens. It was not easy to obliterate the immense effect of family, of kinship ties and values, on matters of belief, religious worship, education, and culture.

Let us consider, for example, the concepts of responsibility and guilt. For countless ages both of these were matters for kinship valuation. Not the individual but the family, even the clan and whole tribe, bore the guilt and also the responsibility for offenses committed by that individual. The notion of individual guilt and responsibility was unknown, except within the strict confines of the household itself. The idea of the stain of guilt for a major offense persisting in a single family line for generations was well known and deeply believed in among all the Greeks, and many earlier and later peoples as well. What mattered profoundly, in the deepest recesses of the Athenian mind, was *kinship* guilt, dishonor, treason, or betrayal, as the case might be, not *individual* guilt, with its overtones of immunity for other persons related to the individual.

The Cleisthenean revolution set into operation forces which were to change this conception of guilt and responsibility, making each, in due time, a subject of purely individual concern. Crime was legally defined by the new political order as offense against the state committed by the individual alone, not his family or tribe. But for a long time, despite the law and its novel associations of individualism, the Athenians were obsessed by the thought of guilt inhering in a kinship line. We see this idea resplendent, at the level of genius, in some of the great tragedies of Aeschylus, Sophocles, and Euripides, written during the half century and more that followed Cleisthenes. At the heart of a number of these majestic works was the age-old problem of guilt and responsibility, of retribution and nemesis, of expiation and redemption, all subjects that had been, however inarticulate by the standards of the great fifth century B.C., of concern to men ever since the dawn of conscience in man.

Likewise, we see the conflict between kinship and polity in other forms of art and philosophy. In painting, sculpture, poetry, and comedy as well as tragedy during the first fifty years that followed the Cleisthenean revolution, we can see kinship principles and political principles struggling with one another for ascendance. Out of the first came the long-persistent communal, sacred, and traditional character of Greek art, with striking representation of the kinds of themes and perspectives that reached far back in time. If, as all historians of Greek art and culture have stressed, the essence of the art of this period is profoundly sacred, it is also—and the two qualities are indissolubly linked—corporate or communal. Both aspects, the sacred and the corporate, can be seen rooted deeply in the persistence of kinship and tribal themes in the Athenian mind. The great and agonizing conflicts of mind and conscience that we see in the plays of Aeschylus, Sophocles, and Euripides mirror perfectly what must have been equally agonizing conflicts in the mind of many an Athenian: between duty to family, name, and kinship identity, on the one hand, and to the state, on the other. Looking at the sequence of these plays through the fifth century, we can see easily enough how the largely sacred and communal emphasis of the earliest of the dramatists, Aeschylus, becomes rather muted and transfigured in Sophocles, who grants the individual a somewhat greater moral and also aesthetic importance than did Aeschylus, and then nearly erodes away entirely in the works of Euripides, for whom the individual and individual will, at the expense of kinship and sacred tradition, takes on a degree of emphasis hardly possible a generation or two earlier.

We see not only in the art but in the moral and social philosophy of the century this conflict between kinship norms and those of the new political order. The Sophists were, in all probability, the first philosophers in the West to make the conflict between tradition and law the basis of speculations that went often deeply into the nature of morality. They were on the whole critical of tradition, assessing Athenian traditions in light of what they had learned from their travels abroad to be the very different customs of other peoples. The inherent rationalism of the new political order founded by Cleisthenes appealed to the Sophists, but in time they became as critical of this as they were of the ancient codes and structures of kinship. "What is right?" This probing question of the Sophists is, in a sense, the very cornerstone of moral philosophy as a discipline in the West. "Is there to be discovered, through reason, a form of social life that is natural to man, in contrast to those forms he merely inherits through tradition and cultural insularity?" This somewhat more subtle but equally powerful question may be said to be the Sophists' foundation for social philosophy and the social sciences. "What law is truly legitimate?" From that question, clearly, proceeds the whole of what we know as political philosophy.

If the Sophists were the first philosophers, the greatest before Plato was Socrates. He was apparently deeply admired by Athenian youth; but his lectures, dialogues, and random observations in the agora and adjacent areas must have appealed as well to all of rationalist, reformist, or revolutionary frame of mind. Everything must be questioned; nothing is so sacred that it can be made immune to doubt and skepticism. How else are we to reach the truth? Thus asked the incomparable Socrates. He was only giving expression, as we can see easily enough, to the individualism, secularism, and emphasis upon positive change that had been the very foundations of Athens during the decades after Cleisthenes; but he was giving these principles an eloquence and personal power that must have had whole troops of philosophical and revolutionary minds in his wake.

And this, as all the world knows, proved to be in time Socrates' undoing. For all the appeal his doctrines may have had to minds of a certain type, these same doctrines could not have helped but alarm minds of a very different type: those of conservatives and traditionalists, who saw in Socratic discourses the causes of a political turmoil and a disintegration of the social fabric that were becoming, by the final quarter of the century, all too evident. The result was the enforced death of Socrates, brought about by those who thought by muting his single voice to arrest the processes that were so profoundly affecting the solidarity of the Athenian political order.

Such, however, was not to be. The same forces of individualization which early in the fifth century had led to the creative release of human energies in all spheres, which had modified but not destroyed traditional symbols and themes, and which had brought into existence a new form of community, the polis, were now, in rising intensity, leading to very different results. Whereas the first effects of the acids of individualism and secularism upon the social fabric had been tonic, the prolonged effects were to be seen not in creative release but in alienation, not in new solidarity but disorganization, not in new modes of art and life but in anomie.[4] There seems to be no doubt that the great cultural ages of history are always the products of delicate equilibrium between tradition and revolt, between the sense of community and the sense of individuality. Such an equilibrium had existed in Athens for close to three-quarters of a century, leading, as we have noted, to one of the greatest of all ages of creative achievement. But now this equilibrium had been destroyed. A very different Athens was the result.

In purely institutional terms, the transformation of Athens may be seen in the sudden rise of increasingly despotic regimes, of governments based upon force but with roots in the political masses. A turning to political power was the Athenian response to the rising crisis in the social order and to the social and psychological problems created by the sense of estrangement from old solidarities, with nothing new and viable to take their place. Some degree of social anarchy is always the prelude to the rise of systems of political and military power, of what the Greeks called tyranny. In a short time this combination of social anarchy and a turning to power would produce in Greece the military empire of the Macedonians, begun by Philip and continued by his son, Alexander, which was to subordinate not only Athens but virtually all the rest of the Mediterranean world, stretching indeed as far east as Persia and India, to the most effective system of bureaucratized and militarized political power the world had ever seen or would see again until the appearance of the Roman Empire three centuries later.

Plato and the Emergence of the Political Community

The intellectual effects of Athenian disorganization and alienation at the end of the fifth century B.C. were, however, infinitely greater than the insti-

---

[4] The best detailed account of this change in the nature of Athens is to be found in Gustave Glotz. *The Greek City and Its Institutions* (New York: Alfred A. Knopf, 1951). Above all other students, Glotz stresses the conflict in Athens between traditional-kinship values and those of the emerging military-political order.

tutional changes just mentioned, for they included the first and still greatest of all portraits of the absolute political community. I refer to Plato's *Republic*, the book that, above all others, has had the effect of making the ideal of politics, of political power, of the political bond, of the political community, the most distinctive and most influential of all types of community to be found in Western philosophy. The intellectual line from Plato to both the democratic and totalitarian states of the twentieth century is a clear and direct one. Whatever the signal differences between the two types of modern state, what they have in common is the ascendancy of the political bond over all others in society; of the political role over all roles of kinship, religion, occupation, and place; of the political intellectual over all other intellectuals; of political authority over all competing social and cultural authorities; and, finally, the proffer of the political state as the chief protection of man from the uncertainties, deprivations, and miseries of this world. And to Plato more than any other philosopher or intellectual is due this ascendancy of politics. His influence upon all subsequent Western political philosophers and intellectuals has been constant and penetrating.

So, for that matter, has it been on all philosophers. It has been said that Western philosophy is little more than a series of commentaries on Plato's fundamental ideas. Whether in the realm of philosophy as such, in theology, in the history of mathematics and the physical sciences—at least down into the early Renaissance—or what we today call the social sciences, Plato's influence has been formidable and persistent. In large part this comes from the fact that in so many areas of understanding we have found ourselves looking at the world and man through spectacles fashioned in the first instance by Plato. Changing the metaphor, there is, as John Dewey once stated, Platonic tissue to be found in the minds of each of us in the West.

From Plato above any other thinker derives the concept of "the chain of being" which, with its implicit placing of every being in a continuous hierarchy of existence, was to exert such a powerful influence upon both Christian and secular thought in western Europe. The first clear statement of social developmentalism is to be found in the third book of his *Laws*. Although the basic idea of growth and development in time comes from the earlier Heraclitus, and although there are foreshadowings of the idea of cultural stages in cyclical succession in Hesiod, it is not until we come to Plato that we are given a full and more or less systematic theory of the slow, gradual, and continuous evolution of man's institutions from the primitive to the advanced.

Nor should we overlook his momentous distinction between appearance and reality. The former is presented to us by our senses and ordinary experience; the latter by reason alone. What we perceive, Plato argued, is but the shifting, evanescent, and transitory world of the merely apparent. Reality can be found only by use of pure reason, by the rational mind cutting through layers of the transitory and ephemeral until it has reached the ultimate constituent elements, structures, and processes. It is within the larger context of this distinction between appearance and reality that Plato gives us his famous doctrine of ideas—or, as we are entitled to call them, ideal-types. For every being or entity in the universe, Plato declared, there is a perfect prototype or form. In the *Timaeus*, he tells us that in the actual, sensory world there are only corrupt and hence imperfect representations of these ideal-types. One can see instantly the revolutionary as well as merely philosophical implications of such a doctrine.

And finally, still as background for Plato's philosophy of the political community, there is his notable distinction between nature and convention, a distinction which he acquired from both the Sophists and his own revered teacher Socrates, but which he developed far beyond anything earlier presented. "Nature" (or *physis*, as the Greeks called it) refers to the condition that may be found in either an organism or institution after all the strictly artificial and conventionalized attributes have been stripped from it by one's mind. "Convention" (or *nomos*) is, by contrast, that which is accidental or superficial, the chance result of time or place or culture. To go to the "nature of things" is the prime responsibility, Plato argued, of the philosopher.

For Plato the political community, which is our sole concern in this chapter, could be illuminated by each of the distinctions and perspectives I have just described. In the chain of being the political community ranks highest in this world among all communities; it is the result of a long process of development; it is man's associative *reality*, in contrast to the merely spurious and superficially attractive; and, finally, it is in its perfect condition the mode of community most natural to man.

Born about 427 B.C., in Athens, Plato was, we know, in the thick of political affairs from boyhood onward. He tells us, in a letter written not very long before he died in about 347 B.C., that he had high hopes as a young man of being able to accomplish good things in the government of his own city-state after its disastrous defeat by Sparta. But it was not to be. Plato tells us how a revolution occurred in Athens, leading to arbitrary rule of the city by a group of some fifty-one men; how he at first thought, despite its tyrannical nature, this new government "would lead the city from an unjust life . . . to habits of justice"; how in a short time "these men made the former government look like an age of gold"; and, finally, how they came to execute Plato's adored teacher and friend, Socrates, on the false ground of his having subverted public morality.

> The result was that I, who had at first been full of eagerness for a public career, as I gazed upon the whirlpool of public life and saw the incessant movement of shifting currents, at last felt dizzy, and, while I did not cease to consider means of improving this particular situation and indeed of reforming the whole con-

stitution, yet, in regard to action, I kept waiting for favourable moments, and finally saw clearly in regard to all states now existing that without exception their system of government is bad. Their constitutions are almost beyond redemption except through some miraculous plan accompanied by good luck. Hence I was forced to say in praise of the correct philosophy that it affords a vantage-point from which we can discern in all cases what is just for communities and individuals; and that accordingly the human race will not see better days until either the stock of those who rightly and genuinely follow philosophy acquire political authority, or else the class who have political control be led by some dispensation of providence to become real philosophers.[5]

Here, we are justified in saying, is the origin of the political community in the West. Observe in the passage just quoted the perception of radical disorder, which Plato compares to a "whirlpool," to "shifting currents," that leave him "dizzy." And observe also the response: the declaration of the necessity to begin all over again. All existing governments are bad, Plato tells us, are indeed "beyond redemption." We must therefore deal radically with a radical problem: that is, construct, through pure philosophy, the ideal community. This combination of perceptions of social disorder and philosophical perspectives of the ideal political community which would save man from chaos and anarchy, we shall see again in almost identical form in the writings of Hobbes and of Rousseau—each, like Plato, an architect of the political community.

It is this quality that we find in common between visions of the political community and visions of the religious community. Whether in the political filiation of Plato to Hobbes to Rousseau or the religious filiation of Augustine to Luther to Newman, what we have in each instance is an overpowering perception of the world as conflict ridden, disorganized, tending toward the anarchic, and needing, therefore, the sovereign anodyne of community.

I do not mean to suggest that in either instance the response is necessarily nonrational, much less antirational. No more relentlessly rational mind ever existed than Plato's—or, for that matter Hobbes's or Rousseau's. Reason serves for all three architects of the political community as something not merely vital to knowledge and the good life but also a thing of beauty. Precisely because the world around Plato seemed ugly, in its disorder and its failure to reflect some single theme, he abandoned it, as his letter tells us, and turned instead to philosophy, to founding a school where he could teach as well as study and write, and above all,

---

[5] Plato, *Epistle 7*, in *Thirteen Epistles of Plato*, trans. L. A. Post (Oxford: Clarendon Press, 1925), pp. 64–65.

as is clear from everything we have that he wrote, to the world of pure reason.

What Sir Karl Popper has written is wonderfully pertinent here:

> Nowhere do we find this estheticism more strongly expressed than in Plato. Plato was an artist; and like many of the best artists, he tried to visualize a model, the divine original of his work, and to copy it faithfully. . . . What Plato describes as dialectics is, in the main, the intellectual intuition of the world of pure beauty. His trained philosophers are men who "have seen the truth of what is beautiful and just, and good", and can bring it down from heaven to earth. Politics, to Plato, is an art—not in the metaphorical sense in which we may speak about the art of treating men, or the art of getting things done, but in a more literal sense of the word. It is an art of composition, like music, painting, or architecture. The Platonic politician composes cities, for beauty's sake.[6]

Plato is the quintessential rationalist in that he finds the good, the beautiful, and the just all contained in the true—in what can be deduced or distilled from experience by pure reason. Thus the vision he gives us of the political community in the *Republic,* as well as in the *Statesman* and the *Laws,* is founded not only in rationalist currents of thought but also in currents of aestheticism and moralism. This was to be no less true of Hobbes and Rousseau, as we shall see. For all three, the political community is not only true but also good and beautiful.

But we must not forget that the vision of the political community, like that of the religious community, is born in perceptions of anticommunity, of a world overwhelmingly characterized by strife, dissension, and uncertainty. The single greatest objective of Plato's entire life, of all the myriad aspects of his philosophy, was to find a secure and timeless form of reality, which would not be dependent upon the winds of doctrine and the shifting tides of fashion. His famous theory of ideas is no more than this: a bold effort to show that behind the mercurial world of the senses there is a world of reality accessible to reason alone, a world composed of the timeless real instead of the transitory apparent that is the sole yield of the senses. This is indeed the quality that philosophical rationalism has in common with religious mysticism, and that has made the essence of each the search for the absolute.

It is thus as philosophical rationalist that Plato must be understood in his magnificent *Republic,* the true source of the entire tradition of political mysticism—there is no other phrase for it—that links his day with our own. What Plato saw around him in Attica, as well as in other parts of the

---

[6] Karl Popper, *The Open Society and Its Enemies,* 2 vols. (London: Routledge & Kegan Paul, 1945), 1: 145.

Greek world that he had visited, was a scene of intellectual and moral and social disorder. Social fragmentation was matched by individual alienation. The bases of the old society were gone, or else eroding away; internal strife—what Thucydides had called *stasis*—was endemic; the individual was left ever more precariously exposed to the conflict of allegiances and to moral uncertainty.

All of this Plato defined as the inevitable response of men when caprice and transitory experience govern instead of reason and true knowledge. Hence his determination to find, through reason alone, the outlines of the kind of community that would be in harmony with the needs and aspirations of men, that would reflect a timeless truth, and that would be attainable wherever there were men of rationality and goodness. And this, above all else, is what the *Republic* is about. It has been called a vision of many things: of justice, of true education, of beauty of proportion, of moral greatness, and so on. It may be—it is, in fact—all of these. But the *Republic* is essentially an image of the kind of community that can be had from following the design of the city-state to its full and logical conclusion.

Plato loved the city-state, the political order that had been created by Cleisthenes, that had lifted its citizens, as had no other form of political society known to man, to heights of bravery in war and of cultural creativity in peace. But its original design had become tarnished by use and wont; its virtues had become suffocated by the avarice of the marketplace; its unity had become lost in a multitude of groups and associations each claiming special privilege; its pristine ideals had become corrupted by poets and philosophers more interested in their audience than in the welfare of the state; and its moral supremacy had become dissipated in the special concerns of those whose only interest was capturing the government. And this, it seems to me, is how we may best interpret Plato's political philosophy, most especially that of the *Republic*, which was throughout the ancient world, and has remained ever since, the single most vital expression of the political community.

Many interpretations of Plato have seen in this book, and others related to it, no more than a reactionary desire to forsake the city and to advocate return to some prepolitical, largely imaginary Golden Age of tribalistic order. Nothing could be further from the truth. Plato's book is not reactionary—not in the literal sense nor in any connotation that implies unyielding conservatism.

His political philosophy is a blend of rigorous social nihilism and political affirmation. The nihilism springs from his desire to cleanse from the political state all the influences he saw as erosive and destructive of political unity: such as money, unrestricted freedom in the arts, factionalism, loose and licentious individualism, wanton immorality, and the various other influences, social and moral, which had made political unity impossible by the end of the fifth century B.C.

Had Plato been merely nostalgic for the dim past of Athens, as Sir Karl Popper and others have suggested, he would surely have given us a picture of something approximating the kinship society that had in fact existed, and that Plato so brilliantly described in his evolutionary account of primitive society in the third book of the *Laws*. But Plato gave us no such picture. What we have instead is the picture of a society in which kinship is virtually abolished and in which the social and juridical features of kinship society, such as decentralization, concentric circles of membership, gerontocracy, tradition, and the like, are utterly absent. The spirit of revolutionary nihilism in Plato extended, in short, even to the structure of the family.

Likewise it extended to the kind of free, largely unregulated capitalism that existed in Athens in Plato's time. There is no room for capitalism or for any other system of unchecked private property in his political community. This does not necessarily mean that Plato was a socialist or communist, much less a fascist. These words are modern coinages and cannot easily be applied to ideas and structures of Plato's day. It is sufficient to observe that Plato opposed private property on precisely the ground that he opposed all other manifestations of traditional society around him: he thought they would, one and all, militate against the kind of spiritual unity necessary to the political community.

Particularly does Plato's social nihilism envelop individualism. The Sophists, whom Plato abhorred more the older and more experienced in matters of statecraft he became, were preaching a gospel of secular individualism that was bound shortly to become anarchic in quality. It is in stringent opposition to the Sophists and their doctrines that Plato declares all individualism to be evil and therefore to have no place in his political community.

This does not mean that Plato hates the individual or desires to see the individual repressed by the state: far from it. Whatever may be our view of the political community he proposes, however exterminative of individuality we may believe it to be in fact, we are obliged to honor Plato's motive. And this motive is, clearly, to emancipate the individual from the torments and stresses of the faction ridden, rootless, and anomic society of the time, and to give the individual precisely the haven, the moral fortress, that Plato believed man's nature to require. No more inspired words in behalf of the individual, his needs, his emotions, his mind, are to be found in Western literature than in Plato's *Republic*. But it is the very essence of Plato's method to place this individual in the liberating and also reinforcing contexts of the political community.

This, I suggest, is the great objective of Plato, as it was to be of Hobbes and, especially, Rousseau many centuries later. I have called his philosophy a blend of social nihilism and political affirmation. So, as we shall see, are the philosophies of Hobbes and Rousseau. And the affirmation in each instance is the state conceived as being, not force, not repression, but justice, freedom, and tranquillity for the individual. The mission of the political community is for Plato no more and no less than the means whereby all the native powers and excellences of the individual are brought to fruition.

It is this emphasis upon the natural harmony of state and individual that accounts for the *Republic*'s long treatment of the nature of man: his feelings, mind, and needs, especially his ineradicable need of others in proper communal context in order for the best that is in him to be brought out. Rousseau was to declare the *Republic* the greatest book ever written on education, nor is there anything strange in the fact that Rousseau himself was fascinated by the close relation between education and the good state or that Rousseau pronounced Plato to be the major influence on his own mind. Almost without exception the admirers of the political community have historically taken education very seriously. For in their writings education appears as no more than the means whereby the natural proclivities of man become harmonized with the requirements of social order and of individuals' secure membership in that order.

We are, when all is said and done, obliged to say that Plato allows no genuine freedom of thought and utterance to exist in his ideal community. That is, such freedom may be permitted up to the point where the ends and structural necessities of the community become threatened, but no further. There is room for tolerance in Plato's vision, but only to the extent that such tolerance does not become the means of sapping the foundations of justice—which is for Plato no more than the harmonious articulation of all individual parts into a rational and aesthetic whole.

Such articulation of parts is exactly how Plato defines justice, as Rousseau will define freedom in contrast to anarchy. Justice is for Plato the sign of health in both individual organism and political community. Justice and its attributes may be easily inferred from the following passage in the *Republic*:

> But in reality justice was such as we were describing, being concerned however, not with the outward man, but with the inward, which is the true self and concernment of man: for the just man does not permit the several elements within him to interfere with one another, or any of them to do the work of others,—he sets in order his own inner life, and is his own master and his own law, and at peace with himself; and when he has bound together the three principles within him, which may be compared to the higher, lower, and middle notes of the scale, and the intermediate intervals—when he has bound all these together, and is no longer many, but has become one entirely temperate and perfectly adjusted nature, then he proceeds to act, if he has to act, whether in

a matter of property, or in the treatment of the body, or in some affair of politics or private business; always thinking and calling that which preserves and co-operates with this harmonious condition, just and good action, and the knowledge which presides over it, wisdom, and that which at any time impairs this condition, he will call unjust action, and the opinion which presides over it ignorance.[7]

In this passage are to be found all the essential elements of Plato's idea of the political community, which, like the idea of anything in Platonic philosophy, must be seen as the necessary point of departure for our assessment of the real and the lasting. Harmony is the essential theme; but we could as well say that community is, for that is how Plato sees the individual human being: as an organic community of parts and elements, given unity by mind. So, too, with the state: it is also a community of parts and elements, given unity by the spirit of justice; otherwise it is force and repression alone.

Thus we have in the *Republic* the long and fascinating treatment of division of labor, with the several economic and social functions arranged not merely in hierarchic order, proceeding from the most menial at the bottom to the highest, lodged in the guardian class as we shall see in a moment, at the top, but also in communal order, that is, in an organic interdependence that makes each function vital and good no matter how low in the scale of intelligence or training it may fall. Division of labor, with its necessary web of specializations, is the social and economic structure of the political community.

Thus, too, we have in the *Republic* the long and detailed account of education, to which I have already referred briefly. What is the function of education? Overwhelmingly—totally, indeed—social: that is, the system and the goals of education must reflect the political community, and the overriding objective of the political community is to train individuals to be proper members of the community. How, Plato asks more or less rhetorically, do we get artisans, soldiers, and others necessary to the health of the community except by training individuals specifically for the purpose required? It is no different, then, with citizenship. Citizens are to the body politic what cells are to the natural body. But there can be no citizens unless they are educated to be such; and the task of education is, first and last, so to prepare men's minds that there will always be harmony among them, a harmony that is itself but another word for justice—and goodness and freedom.

Curriculum, plainly, must be incessantly guarded, for if there is in what men study a preponderance of the bad, the conflict ridden, and the

---

[7] Plato, *Republic*, trans. Benjamin Jowett, bk. IV, 443–44.

irrelevant, then there cannot possibly be good citizens, any more than there could be good plumbers, carpenters, or musicians if the course of training for each were not tied straight to the objective. From the necessity to guard curriculum, therefore, springs the vital necessity of controlling, of setting standards, for the life of the mind generally—for culture, including music, art, and philosophy as well as the practical arts. To train citizens requires unflagging zeal in protecting the community from ideas and values which are alien to its essence. Such education must begin, as the following passage suggests, in infancy, "for the beginning is the most important part of any work, especially in the case of a young and tender thing":

> Then the first thing will be to establish a censorship of the writers of fiction, and let the censors receive any tale of fiction which is good, and reject the bad; and we will desire mothers and nurses to tell their children the authorised ones only. Let them fashion the mind with such tales, even more fondly than they mould the body with their hands; but most of those which are now in use must be discarded.[8]

How far Plato was willing to carry the matter may be easily inferred from what follows the final words of the passage just quoted. When asked who, specifically, should be discarded, he replied: Homer and Hesiod. On what ground? Because lies are to be found in each, lies that if believed—as writings from minds so revered by the Greeks would certainly be—and allowed to be taught, or even read casually, would militate against the virtues that must underlie the good political community. Repression of thought must be total and unyielding, then, if the political community is to be achieved and made secure.

How far his zeal for the political community had carried Plato by the time he was well under way with the *Republic* is evident enough from the above lines. But control of thought and idea and literature was only a small part of the matter. It is the *total* community that Plato seeks: the good community, yes, and also the just community. But by Platonic standards none of this—not goodness, not justice, not community itself —can be achieved apart from bringing all lives, all ends, all values, and all means into total articulation with one another. We have seen anticommunity to lie for Plato in the anarchic individualism, factionalism, stasis, that he found in the Athens around him, all of which he considered to be consequences of the incomplete achievement of the idea of the political community. Hence came the need, if the healing, securing political community was to be brought into existence, for total control

8 Ibid., bk. II, 377.

of actions, total supervision of mental and moral lives, total articulation of functions. Otherwise, Plato tells us, disease will arise just as quickly in the body politic as it appears in the human body when one function or process is at odds with another.

It is in the celebrated guardian class that we may see Plato's ideal both of citizenship and community best represented. The guardians are those, selected at birth on eugenic grounds for the arduous and demanding discipline of education in statecraft, who are, so to speak, the very exemplars of what Plato means by citizenship. That their own function within the division of labor in the political community is to guide and govern is of less importance than that they are the embodiments, the avatars, of citizenship in its highest expression. What Plato demands of his guardians in the political community may safely be taken as his supreme vision of all that is required in the total political community.

There must be, first of all, *asceticism*: willingness to forgo the creature comforts to which the pleasure-seeking but basically miserable members of the Athenian commercial and business classes turned for refuge. But there must be willingness, too, to abjure the ordinary comforts of family life, neighborhood, and idle companionship. Above all, there must be willingness to forgo money and property, except as these, or rather the material goods they command, are required for bodily health.

Second, there must be absolute *communism*. Only when the needs of the community take precedence over those of the individual can the just community be brought into being. Personal possessions, personal loyalties, personal attachments, none of these can do other than militate against communality, the mystic feeling of oneness demanded by political justice. Hence arises Plato's prescription of communal property, communal dwelling places, communal pursuits, even—and especially—communal sex and child rearing. Plato's was not the first nor the last prescription of sexual communism, but it has proved to be the most influential of any written in the whole history of Western thought. No emotions or entanglements, he thought, are more likely to breed discord and jealousy in the community than those springing from sex and rearing one's own children. Hence permanent unions of the two sexes are banned; men will cohabit with women as fancy may decree—provided, of course, that the women are themselves eugenically equal to the men with whom they lie—and the children issuing from these unions will be brought up in the communal quarters supplied by the state for this purpose. The family, in short, will be as absent from the political community of the guardians as will any other form of social attachment, whether guild, club, business enterprise, or fellowship. Sexual, economic, and social communism is but the necessary groundwork for development of that mystic sense of unity that, above all other ends, the political community is designed by Plato to achieve.

Third, and following from the above, the political community must be *monolithic* in structure. If several forms of authority and function are to be permitted, how can that necessary articulation of function and will so indispensable to justice be attained? All such internal authorities would very shortly become no different from the plethora of factions and divisive loyalties that Plato so detested in the Athens of his time. Apart from a single unified, monolithic power structure that reaches all individuals, there cannot be community. It is not possible to read Plato on the monolithic character of his political community without seeing the immense appeal the values of *militarism* had for him. He admired the military severity of Sparta, the city-state that had dealt Athens such an ignominious defeat in the Peloponnesian War; and even though he deplored Sparta's lack of devotion to learning, the absence there of culture as he defined it, he could yet see the importance of seizing on the military model of Sparta, adapting it as necessary, embellishing it in various ways, and making certain that in the education of the young the ideals of courage and boldness and aggressiveness in battle would always be highlighted. For Plato the military community would be the political community at war, as the political community could be seen as no more than the military community —embellished and ornamented, of course—at peace.[9]

There is, finally, the quality I have mentioned several times, which is as fundamental to the political community as to the religious: *mysticism.* As we have noted, no more powerfully, relentlessly rational thinker has ever lived than Plato. But for him reason is undergirded by a kind of faith that is indistinguishable from religion. Not until Augustine, whom we shall consider in the next chapter, do we encounter in Western history a mind that equals Plato's in its combination of brilliant rationalism and inexhaustible faith in a truth that lies beyond the reach of rationality.

It is the mystical quality of Plato's political thought that has made him endlessly fascinating ever since to all those who, whether in scholar's study or in the battlegrounds of power, have drawn from the *Republic* a conviction not only of the superiority of the political community to all other forms of community but also of the possibility of attaining such community through the wedding of absolute faith and absolute reason. It is this mysticism that allows Plato to see the political community as at once a refuge from the torments of individualism in society and a medium for the development of a higher form of individuality; as absolute in its authority over its members but at the same time capable—alone capable —of endowing man with the highest of all forms of freedom; as man's emancipation from politics in the sense of strife and division but at the same time his achievement of a final oneness with others through the political bond alone.

---

9 All of the qualities fundamental to the military community—discipline, centralization, communism (sexual and economic), and so on—are to be found in the *Republic.*

It is no wonder that of all books in the West that have been dedicated to the political mind and to political redemption, Plato's *Republic* should even today stand the highest. Plato brought to the political community not merely the rigorous intellect of the rationalist but also the arts of the poet and the faith of the true believer. The *Republic*, as well as all his other writing on social, moral, and political issues, had its origin in the profound social conflicts of Athens at the end of the fifth century B.C., between class and class, group and group, individual and individual. Clearly, these left a deep impress upon Plato's mind and conscience. He was, not the first, but the greatest of those who, recoiling from dissension and conflict in the social sphere, have found surcease in the political state: the state, however, magnified and intensified to the absolute political community. Such was the power of his portrait of the political community that it has remained for some twenty-five hundred years the major inspiration of all other portraits of this form of community.

The Rise of the Political Intellectual

Plato was not merely the first of the great philosophers of the political community; he was also the first in what has proved to be a long line of political intellectuals in the West. By political intellectual I mean, not statesman, ruler, bureaucrat or politician, each of whom is a practitioner of power, but, rather, the type of mind, equipped with knowledge, insight, and devotion, that prefers to sit, as it were, at the right hand of power. The political intellectual may or may not be a philosopher or scholar in the strict sense of those words; he may not even write in any systematic way. But wherever we find him, he is the keen student of political power, its properties, uses, and functions, and never loath to give freely of advice to rulers in the management of power.

Plato was not merely a philosopher; he was also, during a considerable period of his life, adviser and consultant to rulers in the Mediterranean world. He was, in short, as fascinated by the spectacle of political power in action as by its philosophical character. We may properly assume that far more political intellectuals, in the sense in which I use that phrase here, than philosophers sprang from Plato's teachings. Indeed, to this very moment, political intellectuals have continued to be nurtured and given a sense of direction by their reading of Plato's teachings in the *Republic* and other works, not least the *Statesman*, which is something of a practical compendium of advice to rulers.

Several times in the subsequent history of the West, the center of the stage has been occupied by elites of political intellectuals, alike in their dedication to the political state as the highest form of organization, to power, and to the uses of political power against other, competing forms of social organization in a given society. This was certainly true during the age of Alexander that followed Plato's death. There is no question of the popularity of this type of thinker with Alexander the Great, whose vast expanse of conquered territory and imperial government to be managed inevitably made him willing to use all the good political counsel he could get.[10] The Roman Empire was virtually built, administratively and legally, by the kind of political intellectual I have in mind. We shall look more intently at the elite of Roman lawyers in a moment; they are, after Plato, the real founders of the Western tradition of political intellectuals.

In the Middle Ages, largely on the basis of the renewed study of the principles of Roman law in the universities, a class of intellectuals sprang up and penetrated all parts of the European feudal polity, serving as advisers to feudal princes, barons, and lesser lords and also to the many popes and bishops of the huge, far-flung, but nevertheless centralized Christian church. To this class of medieval political intellectuals, bred for the most part in the principles of the philosophy of law created by the Romans during the period of the empire, never lacking in appreciation of the Platonic political community, goes a large share of the responsibility for effecting the changes in government, economy, church, and military through which the medieval system was finally destroyed—with nationalism, capitalism, and a divided Christianity the result.

Nor can we overlook the famous humanists of the Italian Renaissance. It used to be thought that these individuals were chiefly important for their recovery of Greek scholarship and literature specifically and of classical learning generally. Today we know that assertions of this kind for the humanists were vastly exaggerated, as was their claim to be called the founders of modern science and philosophy. The humanists were first and foremost rhetoricians, of course, but their most enduring significance lies in their role as political intellectuals: constant advisers to rulers, financiers, even churchmen on occasion—to all, in other words, who wielded power. Machiavelli, whom we have already considered in his character of military philosopher, was himself a humanist, and his *Prince* is a prime example of the kind of political advice that humanists had been giving in Italy for more than a century.

Likewise, the philosophes of eighteenth-century France were primarily political intellectuals. Some were historians, some philosophers, after a manner of speaking, some encyclopedists and essayists. The greatest of them, in terms of long-term effect upon the West, was Rousseau, himself a devoted student of Plato and author of a portrait of the political com-

---

[10] Let it be emphasized here that among Alexander's teachers was Aristotle, himself in the beginning a student of Plato. But Aristotle's momentous revolt against the unified, collectivized, absolute Platonic political community and his never-ending subsequent influence on the pluralist tradition in the West properly place him in the final chapter of this book, along with Althusius, Burke, and Tocqueville.

munity that must be regarded as second only to Plato's *Republic* in sheer devotion to the political community as well as in far-ranging influence. We shall have more to say about both the philosophes and Rousseau later in this chapter. For the moment I am concerned only with identifying them as members of a group, stretching through some twenty-five hundred years of Western history right down to this moment, that had its beginning in Plato's age, and that has been consistently through the ages preoccupied by the nature, the properties, and the uses of power.

The influence of the political intellectual has perhaps been more widespread in the twentieth century than ever before. Quite apart from Western society, in which political intellectuals are among the dominating elites of our day, there is not one of the new non-Western nations that has not been almost literally the product of political intellectuals, themselves overwhelmingly products of their university educations in Europe and America. Apart from the political strategies, goals, and calculatedly political techniques (and often military ones as well) employed by this class who sit on the right hand of power, not one of the new nations in our century could ever have emerged from its traditional, largely kinship, village, pretechnological past.

Now let us go back to the origins of the political intellectual in the West. We find these, as I have said, in the Greece of Plato. It was not in Greece, however, not even Alexandrian Greece, that this class first rose to full power and influence, but in Rome, especially the Rome that followed Augustus's military triumph and his acquisition of supreme authority, first as *princeps* and then as emperor. I refer to the immensely influential corps of lawyers, the real founders of the texts and codes of law that have been known ever since as Roman law, still the essential core of modern legal systems in many parts of the world, including the European continent and large parts of Latin America.

That the Roman lawyers during the Empire were, and undoubtedly remain, the greatest *legal* elite ever known is not, however, my central point here, but their role as the profoundest *political* philosophers that Rome was ever to produce. Commonly, when reference is made to Roman political thought, we think of those such as Cicero and Seneca who wrote speeches and essays on one or another aspect of what they had observed or read in politics. But both Cicero and Seneca were barely second-rate minds, never at any point in the same sphere of excellence occupied by Plato and Aristotle in the ancient world or Hobbes, Rousseau, and many others in the modern. Rome's real political philosophers—and in cumulative influence over a period of centuries the equal of any known to us —were the masters of law and polity we know as the Roman lawyers.

Strictly speaking, Roman law goes back, of course, all the way to the earliest days of the Roman Republic, to the celebrated Twelve Tables of legend that mark the beginnings of Rome's legal system. But the true essence of what has come to be known in all subsequent Western history as Roman law does not really antedate the age in which Augustus transferred the military *imperium* from the realm of the military to the structure of civil society and, as we have already seen, in so doing laid the foundations of the Roman Empire in the first century. This was the age, as we have observed, during which the kinship-based *patria potestas* was in effect destroyed once and for all in Roman society, transmuted into what shortly became no different from the family relationship in our own overwhelmingly state-dominated twentieth-century society. It was the age in which the central, military-sprung power of the emperor succeeded the more pluralistic, decentralized power of the traditional Roman Republic. It was the age in which individualism—a result of the atomization of the corporate family—became ascendant in Roman culture, economy, and social life. It was the age of Rome's greatest technical accomplishments in all spheres of life, as well as of achievements in literature and the other arts.

It was also the age, as I have noted, of the efflorescence of classical Roman law—political, business, and administrative law, public and private law—and it is simply impossible to account for the special character of the Roman Empire from the first century on apart from the specific contributions of that growing class of intellectuals whose primary business was the management of power as its consequences spread in traditional Roman society. One can write the basic history of the Roman Empire in terms of the impact upon society of the principles of centralization, collectivization, and at the same time individualization which flowed from the ever-growing body of Roman law, as conceived, applied, commented upon, and codified by the legal experts of the time, the political intellectuals.

Conventional history has made us think of the government of the Roman Empire—until the modern British Empire the greatest and most far-flung machinery of administration known to mankind—as the work of its line of emperors, beginning with Augustus, continuing through Tiberius, Caligula, Nero, and all the others down until the final days of this originally awesome structure of power. But a great deal of the emperors' time was spent in matters of war, shoring up the military, and the usual intrigue which is inseparable from politics. It is to the personalities of those lawyer-intellectuals such as Papinian, Gaius, Ulpian, and Paul that we might better look for the true wisdom and ingenuity of which the Roman political system was built.

These individuals not only advised and, on occasion, directly administered; they also taught others, sometimes by lectures or written texts on the nature and practice of legal administration, but more often through performance as example to apprentices in the craft. These latter, many of whom outdid their teachers in skill and acumen, carried the principles of

Roman law, and the political strategies it contained, to all parts of the Western world. Dedicated as they were to the vision of political society that, in all its philosophical magnitude, they found in Plato and his numberless successors, these political intellectuals did more than any other single group in Western history to popularize, systematize, and codify the essential legal principles of the political community.

Written codifications of Roman law began to appear by the end of the third century, and by the sixth century there must have been a vast number of texts and codes available, oftentimes conflicting in character because of the diverse areas and different times in which they had been published. It was in the sixth century that the emperor Justinian, who resided in the eastern part of the empire—where the largest number of intellectuals and scholars of every type was then to be found, so much of the western empire being already in the hands of the Germanic invaders —caused the most famous of all codifications of Roman law to be brought into being: the so-called *Corpus Juris Civilis* or, more popularly, the Justinian Code. In fact, as is well known, it was not Justinian personally but one of his chief intellectual advisers in political and legal matters, Tribonian, who actually conceived the idea of this famous code of laws, without question the greatest single work in politics as well as law of the ancient world after those of Plato and Aristotle. Rarely if ever in human history has any document or set of documents proved to have the wideranging, insistently penetrating, and enduring effect upon society of the Justinian Code. As it was copied and recopied, glossed and annotated, this code was for a long time during the Middle Ages almost the only curriculum in the universities for their faculties of law. The great lawyers and law teachers of the Middle Ages and much of the modern era were, essentially, spokesmen of the Justinian Code. When Calvin came to write his momentous *Institutes*, which had so much to do with making the Reformation the force it was, he virtually modeled his religious work on the spirit and structure of the codified Roman law he so admired. It was largely in terms of problems and issues regarding power that were first presented in Roman law that modern political theory can be seen to originate. And when Napoleon, having conquered much of the European world, decided the time was ripe for a codification of French law, his legal intellectuals followed closely the Roman code. Thus, through the Napoleonic Code, the underlying principles of Roman law were extended to even wider sections of the world, all those areas which were to come under French colonialism in the nineteenth and early twentieth centuries.

Now let us turn, though briefly, to the central, constitutive principles of Roman law as these may be seen to affect the larger social order. We must bear in mind that these principles came into being, for the most part, when the Roman Republic was being systematically replaced by the centralized structure of the Augustinian *imperium*, when the militarization and developing politicization of Rome were creating a form of society characterized by centralized administration, individualized society, and the progressive disappearance of all forms of social relationship that were products of tradition alone. It is impossible to understand the fundamental political principles of Roman law, in short, except in terms of the kind of society Augustus created in the first century. And it is basically only in that type of society, or in the systematic efforts of individuals to achieve that type of society, that these same political principles of Roman law have subsequently become ascendant.

The first and most seminal principle of Roman law is that of the *sovereignty*—Latin *majestas*—of the political order over all other groups, associations, and interests in society. Such sovereignty carries with it the state's monopoly of legitimate force. Such force, as we have seen, is military in foundation. From this insistence upon the sovereignty of the political authority over all other authorities, including kinship and religion, comes, of course, that centralization we have seen to be paramount in the political community.

The second principle, flowing directly from the Roman stress upon sovereignty and centralization of power, is the famous doctrine of *concession*, according to which, in brief, no other authority or form of association properly exists in society except insofar as it is conceded the right to existence by the political sovereign. The obvious effect of the doctrine of concession is to make precarious the existence of all associations intermediate between individual and state, dependent upon political authorization.

The third principle is the doctrine of *contract*, found primarily in economic and civil sections of Roman law. In one sense this word applies in Roman law to the very foundations of the political order, for reference is made to an aboriginal compact among human beings by which the state was deemed to have been founded in the first place. The idea of contract in this sense was to become especially powerful in the political theory of the seventeenth and eighteenth centuries, though it had existed in the Middle Ages. But in the fullest sense of Roman law, the doctrine of contract applied to the interpersonal relations of citizens. The doctrine says, in effect, that no relation is legal, to be given countenance and protection by the sovereign, unless it be founded upon an express, volitional contract. At a stroke, under this concept, all relationships of purely hereditary, ascriptive, and traditional character, all conventions, customs, and mores, are declared to be without binding effect except insofar as they may be converted into contractual relations. The consequence of the Roman doctrine of contract was, in largest terms, to convert *Gemeinschaft* relationships into *Gesellschaft* relations. It is no wonder that Roman law is as much that of the capitalist-industrial form of society as it is of the political-military form. In the postmedieval period of European history, the ideas and principles of revived Roman law played a powerful role in the beginnings of modern capitalism.

According to the fourth principle, the only valid, recognized units of society are *individuals*—or, if we prefer, citizens. This follows both from the doctrine of centralized sovereignty and that of concession. For if the only legitimate authority is in the hands of the state, and if all other forms of association in society have, at best, only the precarious existence granted by the sovereign's will, the only genuine units left in the social system are individuals. There are also individualistic implications in the doctrine of contract, for contract always gives emphasis to the volitional, the contrived, the rational—in contrast to the communal properties of precontractual forms of association—and these are qualities with strong individualistic thrust.

These, then, are the essential *political* principles of the great system of Roman law. Their singling out for mention here cannot possibly do justice, of course, to the full sweep and complexity of Roman law.[11] But they make clear at a glance how revolutionary such principles can be when they are applied as the Romans applied them, first to their own society, after the devastating civil wars of the first century B.C., and then, on a widening scale, to other societies that came under Roman suzerainty.

Despite the great differences between the Roman Empire and the small political community that Plato had so lovingly described in his *Republic*, there is nonetheless a core of values common to the two societies: the idea of a unitary, centralized, collectivized structure, resting, at bottom, not on smaller groups and communities, but on legally discrete, socially "free" individuals. It is impossible to doubt that the Platonic vision of the political community was very well known indeed to the architects of Roman law. That vision had been brought to Rome by Greek rhetoricians after Rome's conquest of the entire Mediterranean world had extended the Pax Romana to the very land in which Plato had been born. What the Roman lawyers added to this vision was the vital set of perspectives and techniques whereby it could be vastly enlarged.

The Romanization of the Modern West: Machiavelli and Bodin

In one of his essays, the great legal historian F. W. Maitland writes: "At the end of the Middle Ages a great change in men's thoughts about groups of men was taking place, and the main agent in the transmutation was

---

[11] For present purposes, they are best to be seen in detail in Joseph Declareuil, *Rome the Lawgiver*, trans. E. H. Parker (New York: Alfred A. Knopf, 1927) ; and in James Muirhead, *Historical Introduction to the Private Law of Rome* (London: A. and C. Black, 1916).

Roman Law." [12] Maitland, who was only too aware of the political pressures of centralization and individualization in his own day, at the turn of the present century, goes on to refer to the "pulverizing" and "macadamizing" qualities of Roman law in their impact upon communities and other groups of medieval society. There is no need to repeat what has just been said about these qualities; as we have seen, they lead, at one and the same time, to centralization of power, individualization of traditional community, and conversion of *Gemeinschaft* into *Gesellschaft*.

With much intervening scholarship to draw from, we can go farther than Maitland and say that without the principles of Roman law and, even more important, the incessant activities of the political intellectuals whose thinking was formed in the medieval universities by the study of this law, very little of what the sociologist Max Weber has memorably called the rationalization of modern European society and culture would ever have taken place. I am not suggesting that there were not other powerful forces involved in late medieval and early modern European history, only that apart from the perspectives and values derived in the first instance from the study of Roman law, these forces might well have produced little more than sound and fury. Say all we will about the priority in human history of the material, the economic and the political, we can never ignore the role of ideas and ideals—as Marx well knew and stressed —and it is the very capacity of the human species to endow the material with ideas and ideals that often makes the latter seem positively primary in social change. Once Roman law and its envisagement of society became ascendant in the minds of Western scholars, intellectuals, and students, as it did in the thirteenth century, it could not help but become a distinguishable, major force of change.

We can put the matter differently: once the varied areas of Western society began, at different times and under different motivations, to resemble in however small degree the society in which the principles of Roman law had emerged, it was inevitable, given the presence in the universities of these principles, that Roman law would itself become a major force of change. There is something ironic, even tragic, in this; for while Roman law was one of the central elements of that most medieval of institutions, the university, its application to the society outside the walls of the university, in the long run provided the theory and the justification for the destruction of the medieval social order.

Medieval society was the very opposite of the kind in which Roman law had emerged. It was plural in its system of authority; its law came from diverse sources; and it was unconcerned, we might say, about differences between "law" and "custom" or "tradition," and as deeply local in

[12] W. Maitland, *Collected Papers*, 3 vols. (Cambridge: Cambridge University Press, 1911) , 3: 309.

allegiance as it was variegated. Kinship had almost as much sway as it had had in earliest Rome, during the period of the republic, and in earliest Athens, prior to the Cleisthenean reforms. Medieval society was a vast web of groups, communities, and associations, each claiming jurisdiction over the functions and activities of its members. The church was powerful; but so, after the twelfth century, were guild, profession, monastery, and manor It would be hard, finally, to think of two more unlike structures than feudalism, decentralized and localized in essence, and the kind of imperial Roman society that had given rise to the system of law we are here concerned with.

Nevertheless, Roman law was a favored part of the medieval university curriculum. And once the West was infused with the new political and economic life that followed the reopening of trade routes, the growth of a merchant class, the efflorescence of the arts, and the ever-increasing use of technology, intellectuals fresh from the universities where they had been trained in Roman law began to participate in activities and movements which had a great deal to do with the downfall of medievalism and the rise of modern capitalism and nationalism.

For kings and princes struggling against the rights and authorities of feudal groups in their realms, for popes such as Innocent III seeking a higher degree of centralization in the church, and for businessmen seeking an end to the limitations put upon them by guild or monastery, the centralizing, individualizing principles of Roman law could seem a very gift from heaven. For, as we have seen, it was one of the central principles of Roman law that no authority or right intermediate between individual and state could legitimately exist save by "concession" of the sovereign; and another of its central principles was that in the civil sphere all relationships were at best nonlegal, at worst illegal, which were not based upon explicit contract between willing and consenting parties. Few indeed were the relationships of ordinary medieval society that could demonstrate basis in contract, explicit or implicit, nearly all of them being products of unwritten, immemorial tradition; hence came the popularity of Roman-law intellectuals with those rulers and early capitalists seeking to expand their power and wealth.

There was another, distinctively medieval doctrine that conjoined with the Roman doctrine of concession in opposing the natural communalism and corporation of medieval society. This was the metaphysical doctrine known as *nominalism*. It is distinguished in the history of philosophy from what was called *realism*. The latter philosophy argued that wholes—including social wholes such as guild, community, church, and family—are real, that they have a reality in their wholeness that is distinct from the individuals opposing them. In a sense, realism, as here defined, was the heart of the whole medieval view of not merely society but the world at large. Collective entities were deemed to be real entities, their collectivity as much a part of reality as each of the individual units ostensibly composing them. Nominalism, on the other hand, declared that belief in the reality of wholes is without either metaphysical or logical foundation. There is no reality, argued the nominalists, save in the individual atoms that make up wholes. To refer to a university, a church, or a guild is to refer to a *name* that we give to corporate behavior of individuals. Reality, concluded the nominalists, consists only in individuals whose ties are at best ephemeral, at worst illusory.

It is easy to imagine the delight taken by radical medieval minds in the philosophy of nominalism, on the basis of which such mighty entities as the church, and each of its corporate units like monasteries, abbeys, and chapels, could be declared metaphysically nonexistent—nonexistent, that is, except insofar as their individual members had reality. The church declared itself to be no less real than any human person—to be, indeed, a person, a corporate person as entitled to recognition in and for itself as any individual person. But nominalism declared, in effect, that such belief in corporate reality was hardly more than superstition; and in so putting the matter—however subtly and carefully, in that day of extreme ecclesiastical power—nominalism was, by its very nature, an attack upon the church.

It is equally easy to see the affinity between the Roman-law doctrine of concession and the metaphysical doctrine of nominalism. They have utterly different histories and basic cores of meaning; but each was in its own way a powerful weapon against the corporatism, the deep sense of community, and the pluralism of the Middle Ages. For each argued that reality lies in individuals alone, not in wholes. There was, to be sure, one major political difference between the two doctrines: whereas nominalists insisted that even the state itself is without separate reality, Roman-law intellectuals were willing to endow the state with a degree of corporate reality they would grant to no other form of social unity in society. Suffice it here to say that political intellectuals were generally inclined to use nominalism as a valuable ally of the individual in all his relationships except those with the state.

By the end of the Middle Ages, largely through the spread of the universities and their students, the fundamental ideas of Roman law were to be found all over Europe: objects of ever-more-intense study and intellectual development but also, in widening degree, instruments of power and aggrandizement. Even England, once supposed to have been free of the impact of Roman law, showed, as modern research has made clear, the effects of its principles both in state and church. Centralization of political power, which took place earlier in England than on the Continent, largely as the result of the Norman conquest at the end of the eleventh century and the oath of direct allegiance William exacted from every freeman in England, could only have been helped by concepts that the rising class of monarchical advisers was able to extract from Roman-law texts in the universities.

Throughout Europe, as the Carlyles have written,

> the notion that the essential foundations of law reside in custom began to give way before the conception of law as the purposeful creation of a conscious legislative will at the same time the assumption that the customs of the community were the ultimate source of authority began to be challenged . . . by the statement that it was the prince who had the power to legislate and that it was he therefore who must be regarded as the source of law.[13]

And, all the while Roman-law principles were leading to the aggrandizement of the central political power, they were leading also to increasing emphasis upon the individual, more specifically, the individual will. As Roscoe Pound writes:

> In the Romanist system the chief role is played by the conception of a legal transaction, an act intended to create legal results to which the law carrying out the will of the actor gives the intended effect. The central idea in the developed Roman system is to secure and effectuate the will. All things are deduced from or referred to the will of the actor.[14]

Whatever may have been the rate of diffusion during the Middle Ages of these related ideas of centralization and individualization, it was as nothing compared with what we find in the Renaissance, beginning almost spectacularly in Italy, where the study of Roman law was most intense and its appeal most obvious to the rulers of the many small states into which Italy was divided, then spreading rapidly throughout the rest of Europe in that century and the one following. In these Italian city-states, as Burckhardt has told us in his great study of the Italian Renaissance, the vision of the political state as a work of art made its earliest appearance:

> In them for the first time we detect the modern political spirit of Europe, surrendered freely to its own instincts, often displaying the worst features of an unbridled egoism, outraging every right, and killing every germ of a healthier culture. But wherever this vicious tendency· is overcome or in any way compensated a

[13] Robert W. and Alexander J. Carlyle, *A History of Medieval Political Theory in the West*, 6 vols. (London: W. Blackwood and Sons, 1903–36), 5: 463–64.

[14] Roscoe Pound, *The Spirit of the Common Law* (Boston: Marshall Jones, 1921), p. 21.

new fact appears in history—the State as the outcome of reflection and calculation, the State as a work of art.[15]

We have seen, in the preceding chapter, how war also became, again in Burckhardt's words, "a work of art," its strategies and tactics ever more widely and remuneratively the subject of works by those who gave themselves as often to matters of military art as to political. There is nothing surprising in the fact that Machiavelli, at whose textbook on the art of warfare we have already looked, should have been equally devoted to the art of politics, as is displayed in detail in his *History of Florence* and *Discourses on the First Ten Books of Titus Livius,* both filled with evocations of Italy's great Roman past, and in succinct and memorable form in his noted *Prince,* which is little more than a handbook for the political ruler.

The recrudescence of Greek and Roman images and models that was in many ways the very heart of the Italian Renaissance, the primary devotion of most of the humanists of the age, carried with it, in short, military and political images and models as well as those drawn from sculpture, painting, and literature. The fifteenth-century Italian humanist was a rhetorician, a compiler of ancient texts, if we like, but he was also typically the political intellectual, serving whatever city-state or ruler was most willing to pay well for humanist advice in matters of state and war. In this respect the humanists were much like the intellectual class of Plato's day, the Sophists of ancient Greece, and also much like the train of intellectuals produced by Plato's example and ideas in the ancient Mediterranean world.

For many reasons the humanists detested the medieval groups around them—the church foremost but also the guilds, communes, monasteries, and other corporate associations in which medieval society abounded— and this animus is perhaps the largest single element the humanists had in common—apart, that is, from their consecration to Greek and Roman values, which, after all, was a major part of their war on medievalism. From their consecration to these ancient values the humanists drew, on the one hand, their passion for individuality in thought and behavior— manifest in bizarre and extreme modes of dress and speech, patterned on the Greeks and Romans—and, on the other hand, their passion, with the rarest exceptions, for despotism, for the kind of power that was unhindered by medieval custom or religious constraint.

Despotism, as we have already seen, fostered in the highest degree the individuality not only of the tyrant or *condottiere* himself, but also of the men whom he protected or used as his tools —the secretary, minister, poet, and companion. These people

[15] Jacob Burckhardt, *The Civilization of the Renaissance in Italy,* 2 vols. (New York: Harper & Row, Torchbooks, 1958), 1: 22.

were forced to know all the inward resources of their own nature, passing or permanent; and their enjoyment of life was enhanced and concentrated by the desire to obtain the greatest satisfaction from a possibly very brief period of power and influence.[16]

The works of the Italian humanists show little if any direct influence of Roman-law principles, substantially, no doubt, because of the fact that Roman law was so considerable a part of the curricula of the universities—organizations the humanists for the most part detested as much as they did other medieval entities. But there can be no question whatever of the substantive influence on the minds of the humanists of Roman principles of centralization of power, individualism, contractualism, and, far from least, hostility to intermediate social structures such as church, feudal manor, and guild. For the humanists, as for the direct exponents of Roman law, centralized power and individualism in cultural and social matters were but opposite sides of the same coin.

Machiavelli

Nowhere does this union of power and individualism show to better advantage than in the writings of Machiavelli. We have seen how essentially repugnant to him by virtue of its obsoleteness was the feudal art of limited war, and what emphasis he placed upon the tie between political ruler and a citizen militia. Machiavelli's more directly political ideas hardly depart in substance from this emphasis. There is little if any notion in his writings of the idea of the state, as we will find it to some extent in Bodin and, complete and encompassing, in Hobbes and Rousseau, but they show a very real and powerful conception of the supremacy of the political over the religious or social, and the vital necessity for centralization of political rule:

> "This we must take as a general rule: seldom or never is any republic or kingdom organized well from the beginning, or totally made over, without respect for its old laws, except when organized by one man. Still more, it is necessary that one man alone gives the method and that from his mind proceed all such organization. Therefore a prudent organizer of a republic and one whose intention is to advance not his own interests but the general good, not his own posterity but the common fatherland, ought to strive to have authority all to himself.[17]

[16] Ibid., p. 144.

[17] Niccolò Machiavelli, *Discourses on the First Ten Books of Titus Livius*, in *Machiavelli: The Chief Works and Others*, trans. Allan H. Gilbert, 3 vols. (Durham: Duke University Press, 1964), 1: 218.

As did all the humanists, Machiavelli disliked and distrusted the Christian church; not, primarily, for its doctrines, though he shows little evident love of these, but for its complex of social, economic, and cultural structures, all of which, he felt correctly, were barriers to the kind of political centralization and collectivization he prized. So, too, as a political intellectual, Machiavelli detested the nobility of his day, seeing, again correctly, in its affluence and social power a lasting barrier to the achievement of the political community with its necessary unity. Like Plato, and like the Roman lawyers both in ancient Rome and in later centuries, Machiavelli gave the political power supremacy over all others. If this meant a transgression of traditional rights and liberties, of customary morality, so much the worse for them.

The Prince, as I have said, is no more at bottom than a book of practical maxims for the aspiring political ruler. It is filled with pieces of advice and counsel and expressions of insight, occasionally profound, all of which are calculated to help the political ruler as *The Art of War*, Machiavelli's first major work, was calculated to help the military commander. Long before Clausewitz or Marx, as we observed in the preceding chapter, Machiavelli had a vivid conception of the affinity between war and politics—of the need, indeed, each has for the other. Just as the military commander must be ruthless when necessary, willing and ready to jettison all moral consideration, so, Machiavelli tells us, must the political ruler be ruthless, oblivious to all personal, social, and moral considerations which might in any way limit political power and abridge the unity of the political order. The ruler must be willing, when required by political considerations, to use cruelty, murder, and obliteration of family name and property. In his *Prince*, Machiavelli writes: "A prince therefore who desires to maintain himself must learn to be not always good, but to be so or not as necessity may require." Plato would have agreed with that, though doubtless, given his identification of the good and the political, not shared by Machiavelli, Plato would have found the good and the moral to be intrinsic to the pure political act. The emperor Augustus and the long succession of Roman lawyers would also have found Machiavelli's statement acceptable, at least in its implication that political law must be sovereign over moral tradition.

It is true that a fairly substantial number of Machiavelli's readers, in his own time and later, did not find his single-minded devotion to political power attractive. There are many references to him in the centuries following, few of them laudatory. The reason is clear and simple: Machiavelli never made the slightest pretense of reinforcing either traditional morality or any new morality stitched into the fabric of politics. Cynical though he may have seemed, he refused to give absolute power the garments of conventional morality. We may applaud his honesty in the matter, and agree that in that age marked by the decline and corruption of the old and the eruption of new forces of naked power—political, military, and economic—there was little warrant for serious effort to clothe power in morality. But the fact is that the rest of the history of the political community in Western thought amounts to precisely this: the moralization of power that was founded in the force born of war.

Bodin

How difficult it was for the modern theory of the political community to break free of medieval restraints and to attain anything like the unitary quality one finds in Plato or the Justinian Code is well illustrated by Jean Bodin's *De la République*, published in Paris in 1576. It is said to be the first work in the modern history of political thought that contains a clear statement of the idea of political sovereignty. "Majesty or sovereignty," he wrote in a classic definition, "is the most high, absolute, and perpetual power over the subjects and citizens of a commonwealth." [18] The definition is impeccable; we shall not find Hobbes, Rousseau, or any other later philosopher improving on it. But between the starkly stated definition and the actual nature of the political society Bodin prescribes lies a whole realm of medieval values—pluralist, localist, and decentralist—that try as he might, he could not dissociate himself from altogether. He had ceased to be medieval so far as his conception of legitimate authority is concerned, but he did not yet show the modern emphasis on the unitary nature of the state.

Philosopher and historian though Bodin was, he was also in every sense a political intellectual. He was a key member of a group of such intellectuals in Paris—composed of civil servants and businessmen as well as writers—that called itself the Politiques. It is erroneous to translate *politique* into "politician," for most of the members were little interested in what we today think of as politics. It is enough to say the word was designed to set themselves and their aspirations squarely behind the political state as the sovereign unit of society and, at the same time, to make clear that in their view the day of the church's ascendancy had long since come to an end.

Bodin lived during the fearful religious wars set off by the Reformation in France. He knew that once Christendom had been torn by deeply rooted doctrinal hatreds, there would no longer be any possibility of the Christian religion's supplying a base of necessary unity, stability, and order in Western society. The only possible base, Bodin and his fellow politiques thought, was the political nation, which would be given legal force by the recognized sovereignty of the political arm over all other

---

[18] Bodin's book was translated into English in 1606 by Richard Knolles as *Six Books of a Commonweale*, and published in London. References here are to that translation. The definition of sovereignty is on p. 84.

sectors of society. Here a few words on the idea of the nation are in order, for no more vital unit—whether for good or ill—has ever been spawned by Western society. If many of the problems of the contemporary world spring directly from nationalism, from the division of mankind into the military-political-cultural units called nations, then their origin goes back substantially to the age of Bodin.

Formerly, down until about the period of Bodin, the word *nation* (which comes from the Latin *natio*, originally "birth," from *nasci*, "to be born" referring to common parentage) was applied almost as a synonym of extended family, and covered any group that came from some common locality. Thus students in the medieval university arranged themselves into "nations," each of which reflected the common derivation of its members from some point in Europe. Sometimes, indeed, the word was applied in the subhuman organic kingdom to aggregates for which we should use the words *species* or *genus* in modern biology. And when the explorers of North America first came upon the Indians there, they used the word *nation* for their groupings as often as the word *tribe* was to be used later.

Prior to about the fifteenth century, there was no very clear notion in western European thought of an "England" or a "France," much less a "Germany" or a "Russia." Such territorial divisions did not matter to the European mind nearly so much as did divisions in terms of peoples—Franks, Teutons, Slavs, Normans, Saxons, and the like. But obviously these peoples all lived, more or less permanently, in their respective areas of the Continent; and from the sixteenth century on, these areas *conceived as belonging to, inseparable from, the ethnic strains which inhabit them* acquire a constantly enlarging meaning in political and social thought. Gradually the idea of an England or France—and these were the two first nations in the modern sense—became a luminous one. We can trace the subsequent history of western Europe in terms of the constantly increasing significance of the concept of the nation. In contrast, while in the ancient world territorialization had significance that was either very local, as in the case of the Greek city-state, or imperially vast, as in that of the great empires like Persia and Rome, it had no *national* connotations.

But the most fundamental aspect of modern Western history is that almost everything of importance—politics, reform, capitalism, democracy, even religion and science—has risen and assumed prominence within the national framework. What we have known is *national* monarchy, *national* democracy, *national* socialism, and even *national* religion. And, although the full burst of nationalism is not to appear until the French Revolution, which succeeded in uniting nationalism to almost everything culturally significant, we can see vivid instances of nationalism, and of the spreading sentiment known as national patriotism, by the sixteenth century. To a very large degree, the nation succeeded the universal church, just as in the course of time nationalism was to succeed religion itself. Nationalism has been well called the religion of the modern state.[19]

It would be absurd to suggest that in Bodin we find anything resembling the modern religion of nationalism; that really comes only after the French Revolution. But it is not absurd to see in Bodin the first systematic exponent of the nation conceived in political-territorial terms and as the proper substitute for the network of feudal and religious ties which had been coterminous with European government virtually since the downfall of the Roman Empire. Nationalism in any modern sense of the word did not exist much before the sixteenth century, and it is to Bodin that we are indebted (if that is the word) for its appearance as a significant concept in social thought. We have no difficulty in finding earlier advocates of absolute political power, among them Machiavelli and, earlier in England, Wycliffe. But there is little if any notion in these writers of the state, that is, a territorial aggregate given unity and thrust by the claimed supremacy of political government in that territory over the mass of persons contained within its boundaries. This is Bodin's signal contribution to the modern history of the political community. He is the first to provide systematic justification for sovereignty and for the nation-state.

What truly arouses our interest in Bodin, though, is not so much his theory of sovereignty but, rather, our perception in him of a mind in the toils of conflict: conflict between the values of medievalism, which he could not help loving in great part, and those of modernity, which he could not help regarding as necessary and foreordained. As I have said, Bodin had ceased to be medieval in his conception of the nature of legitimate power, but he had not become really modern.

Thus we find an affection in Bodin for that whole realm of intermediate society—guild, monastery, walled town, autonomous cultural association, university, and patriarchal family—that we have seen to be the social essence of the Middle Ages. There were others in Bodin's day, as well as earlier, with little affection for this realm; they would have gladly seen it exterminated, as Hobbes in the next century and Rousseau in the century after that were to prescribe in their political writings. Bodin writes: "To demand whether communities and colleges be necessary in a commonweale is as much as to demand whether that a commonweale can be maintained and unholden without love and amity, without which the world itself cannot long stand." [20]

He is indignant at those who declare "that all corporations and

---

[19] See the excellent discussions of the rise and significance of modern nationalism in Hans Kohn, *The Idea of Nationalism* (New York: Macmillan Co., 1951); and Boyd Shafer, *Nationalism: Myth and Reality* (New York: Harcourt, Brace and World, 1955).

[20] Bodin, op. cit., p. 379.

colleges are out of a commonweale to be excluded and banished; not knowing that a family and the very commonweale itself are nothing else but communities." [21] True, a profusion of such associations runs the risk of disorder, of the kind of internal dissension that as a politique, a devoted exponent of absolute political sovereignty, Bodin deplored. Nevertheless, the suppression of all such groups would be an act of tyranny. On this very point Bodin writes: "Whereby it appeareth, tyrants always to have hated the corporations and communities of the people, and by all means endeavoured to have them utterly extinguished." [22]

It is a further mark of the persistent medievalism in Bodin's writing that we find in it the last major effort to maintain the medieval solidarity of the household group in society. However willing Bodin was to see the absolute power of the king, of the national state, penetrate through the large number of medieval corporations and communities, he was not willing to see this power extend across the threshold of the family to the individual. Bodin was firmly convinced that the family, not the individual, should be the basic juridical unit of the political order. He denounced the theory that the children, the wife, and the dependents within a household should be brought into the full legal purview of the sovereign. Such individuals should be subject only to the house father, who alone should represent them. Bodin is even willing to propose the restoration of the *patria potestas* to the point of absoluteness it had possessed in ancient Rome before the Augustan legal changes. "It is needful in a well-ordered commonwealth to restore unto parents the power of life and death over the children, which by the law of God and Nature is given them." [23]

It was not from Roman law that Bodin derived this view of the family —not, that is, from Roman law in the form and content of the great code books and institutes that had come into being after Augustus and that were, in Bodin's day, the staple of the universities' study of law. For, as we have seen, this absolute authority of the father had disappeared from Roman law by the late imperial age. It is, rather, to the *patria potestas* of the still earlier Roman Republic that Bodin is looking.

Precisely the same is true of his conception of the relation of property to the family. In his mind only the indissoluble union of family and property will preserve either in the social order. Property, he tells us, is not the right of the individual—as would be argued by theorists in the following centuries—but of the family. Property must not be alienated from the household through the assumed right of any individual, even the house father, to dispose of it in accord with his own wish. The family cannot maintain its social solidarity except on the base of economic unity; nor, Bodin points out, can property long remain a basis of freedom

---

[21] Ibid.   [22] Ibid., p. 384.   [23] Ibid., p. 23.

in the commonwealth if it once becomes detached from the kinship group.

What Bodin does not recognize, in his long and devoted testament to the kinship community, is the complete irreconcilability of his desires for the family, on the one hand, and for the political state on the other. He wants, at one and the same time, an absolute political sovereignty in the state—sovereignty that will be, in his words, "the most high, absolute and perpetual power *over the subjects and the citizens* in a commonwealth" (I have added the italics to indicate specifically those on whom the force of sovereignty would fall, thus showing where the irreconcilable conflict is to be found) —and also freedom for a very large number of "subjects," that is, the household's women, children, and dependents, from the sovereign authority of the state. For these individuals, he has told us, should be under the absolute power of the house father and thereby insulated from the sovereign authority of the state. What he gives to the political sovereign, he takes away, so to speak, through what he gives to the house father—and vice versa.

Such conflicts need not bother us, however. As I have noted above, Bodin is a transitional figure, in part still medieval, in part modern. The crisis of his own day, reflected by the religious wars that raged in France between Catholics and Protestants, called, he thought, for a new basis of order: the absolute state. That he also strove to preserve the solidarity of the kinship community is but testimony to the degree of compromise of which, to some extent, we are all capable.

Hobbes and *Leviathan*

By the time we reach the political writings of the Englishman Thomas Hobbes in the middle of the seventeenth century, all limitations on the political community drawn from the medieval tradition have vanished completely. In time, only seventy-five years separate Bodin's *Commonweale* from Hobbes's *Leviathan;* in philosophical content the two books are centuries apart. Gone utterly from Hobbes's mind are Bodin's troubled reflections on the place of intermediate religious and social groups in the political order; gone, too, is Bodin's affection for the patriarchal family and his conviction that the family, not the individual, should be the irreducible unit of political society.

We are obliged to go all the way back to Plato's *Republic* to find a single book as rigorous and complete as Hobbes's *Leviathan* in its presentation of the essential elements of the political community. They are all there: monopoly of force by the state; centralized sovereignty; supremacy of territorial-national values over those of either localism or internationalism; atomlike citizens; and, proceeding from the others, relentless hostility to all groups or allegiances intermediate between sovereign and citizen. It is not Roman law but natural law to which Hobbes appeals in his defense of the absolute political community. But natural law, as Hobbes and many of his contemporaries conceived it, is hardly more, so far as the seventeenth-century theory of society was concerned, than a transmutation of Roman law. As Ernest Barker has perceptively written, natural law in the seventeenth century may be the product of pure reason, but no one familiar with its central political elements will doubt its debt to the principles of Justinian Roman law. Precisely as Roman law had elevated state and individual as the crucial concepts of society and had repudiated all forms of association that could not be vindicated either by contract or by concession of the sovereign, so did the seventeenth-century doctrines of natural law. Apart from the immense influence of Roman-law intellectuals from the Middle Ages on, it is difficult to imagine that very much of the actual political theory of so-called natural law would ever have come into existence in the modern age.

There is little wonder that Hobbes's *Leviathan*, the first complete rendering of the absolute political community in the modern age, should appear in seventeenth-century England. The Tudors, particularly Henry VIII, had seen to it that England was the most centralized political government in Europe, the state with the fullest conception both of nationhood and of citizenship, and also the one social order in the entire West in which all competing allegiances—aristocracy, church, guild, monastery, university, and local community—had either been subjugated, destroyed, or welded firmly into the unified national scheme. How powerful the English government had become by the end of the reign of Henry VIII is suggested by A. F. Pollard's statement, in his biography of Wolsey, that "the whole sum of English parliamentary legislation for the whole Middle Ages is less in bulk than that of the single reign of Henry VIII." [24]

But while England had indeed become Europe's first genuine political nation, the first to subordinate or destroy medieval internal challenges to monarchical and parliamentary power, it would be false to infer from this any unanimity of English opinion regarding government. Henry VIII may have broken once and for all with the Roman church and forced the English church into a position permanently subordinate to the political government, but he did not thereby extinguish the convictions of those who believed in religious autonomy—nor did he of those in other areas of society. The earlier subordination of guild, university, and town, and the dissolution of the monasteries assuredly did not destroy or disperse historic loyalties to these structures. Tradition never dies easily, and despite the sheer power of the Tudors, followed by

[24] A. F. Pollard, *Wolsey* (London: Longmans, Green, 1928), p. 218.

the doctrine of the divine right of kings proclaimed under the first of the Stuarts, James I, who came to the throne in 1603, there remained in early-seventeenth century England a powerful body of opposition to political centralization.

Add to these considerations the constantly increasing conflict between king and Parliament and, above all, the Civil War, largely the consequence of Puritan hostility toward established church and state, with the beheading of Charles I and the interregnum of more than a decade while Cromwell's Commonwealth and Protectorate governed England, and it is plain that few ages in Western history have been more troubled and conflict ridden than the England in which Hobbes conceived and wrote his great *Leviathan*.

It has been said that the modern centralized Western state is an inverted pyramid, its apex resting on the first edition of Hobbes's *Leviathan*, published in 1651. There is much truth in this with regard to the theory of the modern state, for no one has been more instrumental in perfecting this theory than Hobbes. However unwilling many of Hobbs's successors may have been to accept all the implications of this theory of sovereignty, not one of them—not even Locke, much less Rousseau, Bentham, and Austin—has departed significantly from the fundamental perspectives of power to be found in the *Leviathan*. Hobbes was himself utterly ruthless in his attitude toward conflict or dissension of any sort. Not only his politics and his ethics but also his metaphysics make this plain. It could well have been Hobbes that Edmund Burke was thinking of when, more than a century later, he said that "nothing is harder than the heart of a metaphysician."

We have already seen the capacity of ages of bitter social and ideological conflict for producing works in which centralized power is exalted. The middle of the English seventeenth century is no exception. Add to this conflict, highlighted by the Puritan revolution, the genius of a philosopher like Hobbes, and the result is perhaps predictable. In his theory of the political community is to be seen the extermination of all possible social, religious, or cultural limits on the sovereign. As we have just seen, Bodin, though committed intellectually to the principle of sovereignty in the political arm of society, could not divest himself of the medieval values of corporateness of individual groups and of at least a *social* pluralism that could not easily be brought within the unitary claims of absolute political sovereignty. As we saw, Bodin stopped the power of the political sovereign at the door of the household, and he showed a disposition to allow the continued existence of the profusion of *collegia*—guilds, monasteries, universities, and other social groups—that lay intermediate between individual and state.

No such disposition governed Hobbes's mind. The only units Hobbes recognized as being metaphysically real are individuals. And the only forms of social relationship he was willing to accept are those that geometrically rigorous logic can establish as arising from the very nature of man, *individual* man, with his instincts and his reason. That history and convention can bring into existence social relationships which deserve legitimacy by very virtue of history and convention was a proposition utterly foreign to Hobbes's way of thinking.

For Hobbes the problem of order was a simple if completely unhistorical and unsociological one: How can individuals in a state of nature, where each is presumed to be politically, socially, culturally, and psychologically separate from every other and where a condition of war or conflict is the abiding one, ever achieve the condition of society, of order, peace, and tranquillity? As is apparent enough, the statement of this Hobbesean problem of order is possible only on the premise that at some point in the past there was actually a time when individuals lived in a condition of presocial strife and opposition. Using certain selected contemporaneous accounts of preliterate peoples in North America and elsewhere as his evidence, Hobbes even asserted that in his own day were to be found peoples living in this state of nature. Among such people, Hobbes tells us, there is no industry, no arts, "no society; and which is worst of all, continual fear, and danger of violent death; and the life of man, solitary, poor, nasty, brutish, and short."

That, for example, the Indians of North America did not in fact live the "nasty, brutish, and short" existence Hobbes described could no doubt have been discovered by Hobbes himself had he chosen to read more carefully the accounts set down by Jesuits, explorers, and other visitors to North America. As we know, there were political philosophers virtually contemporary with Hobbes who, on the basis of the same materials available to Hobbes, presented an altogether different picture of the so-called "state of nature"—a picture stressing a high degree of order and solidarity resting on kinship, tribe, even complex confederations of tribes, was stressed.

But even had Hobbes chanced or chosen to read these contemporary accounts of the actual preliterate life in the Americas and elsewhere, it is highly unlikely that they would have affected in the slightest his fundamental argument. This argument was, as I have noted, based upon the allegedly natural atomization of the state of nature and, within this, the allegedly solitary character of the individual, who lives in a condition characterized by incessant fear, war, and abject insecurity. Therefore Hobbes would have been unaffected by correct ethnological data regarding primitive people, since he would most likely have carried his presumptive state of nature back into some primordial age, real or imaginary, beyond the power of any empirical evidence to prove or disprove. For, as is clear enough, Hobbes is concerned with what he believes to be the *natural* character of the individual—his precultural, presocial, and prepolitical character. And Hobbes declares this character to be inherently and unmitigatedly bellicose.

His question, therefore, must be, How did men ever get from this awful state of nature to the social state? How did they liberate themselves from the endemic fear and insecurity of the natural condition, to find refuge in the settled, secure, order of society?

To anyone who reads Hobbes's *Leviathan*, it is clear that he is concerned with justifying and rationalizing the absolute political community, which is founded upon illimitable sovereignty and upon the boundless obedience of individual to sovereign. He nevertheless presents us with detailed and extended analysis of how man's *nature* was capable of at some point achieving this absolute political community—which for Hobbes, unlike Bodin, is society itself. This achievement was possible, Hobbes declares, through two basic principles in man's psychology: desire—that is, *instinct*—and *reason*. What Hobbes calls natural law is, so far as man is concerned, compounded of the operations of these two motive forces. The relationship Hobbes establishes between instinct and reason is anything but clear. It will suffice for our purpose here to say only that in time the individual's egoistic desire for his own greatest advantage—that is, his instinct for self-preservation—managed somehow to unite with the reason which is native to man and through which even in the presocial state he could presumably foresee the advantages in sovereignty and absolute political association; and that the momentous result was a "social contract," out of which came, once and for all, the absolute political community—Leviathan!

As we have seen above, Hobbes wrote at a time of severe internal crisis in England, when the followers of the Stuarts were locked in bloody civil war with the Cromwellian Puritans, when devastation beyond anything England had seen in centuries took place in certain areas, when looting, pillaging, burning, and robbing were daily occurrences in one place or another, and when the monarch himself, Charles I, was publicly beheaded. Of the effects of this scene upon Hobbes there can be no question. His sole and consuming objective became to find intellectual justification for a political order so absolute, so total in its power, that civil wars, insurrections, and crimes could not destroy the fabric of society, could not release the ugly elements of man's essential being that had once dominated the state of nature, when—as again now during the Civil War—there was only "continual fear and danger of violent death; and the life of man, solitary, poor, nasty, brutish, and short." [25]

It was the emergence of the political state, through the instrumentality of contract, out of the state of nature, that first brought upon

[25] All quotations from Hobbes are from the Oxford edition of the *Leviathan* (Oxford: Clarendon Press, 1909), a reprint of the first folio edition of 1651.

the earth any form of society whatsoever.[26] And it is the theoretical rein-forcement of this redemptive state that engages all of Hobbes's efforts throughout his *Leviathan*. He does not shrink from making the state's power absolute over man because, first, the contract made it absolute, and, second, apart from its absoluteness there could be no protective society and man would sink once again into the dismal condition of fear and brutishness that had characterized his beginnings.

Here, then, in his identification of the state with all association and culture, lies the foundation of the political edifice which Hobbes builds. Unlike Bodin, he does not recognize any prepolitical order of society based upon kinship, religion, and other associations within which the sociability of man is nourished. For Hobbes there is no middle ground between man as a helpless, isolated creature of fear and man as the citizen of the absolute state. And, unlike Bodin, Hobbes manifests little sym-pathy for the customs, traditions, and moralities that exist outside the framework of sovereign law. Law, writes Hobbes, is "to every Subject, those Rules which the Common-wealth hath Commanded him, by Word, Writing, or other sufficient Sign of the Will, to make use of, for the Dis-tinction of Right and Wrong." For the rigorous mind of Hobbes, law is not in any way dependent upon the social institutions of a people. Law is the command of the sovereign, nothing else. Among the diseases of the state, he declares, one of the greatest is the belief "that every private man is judge of Good and Evil actions." This was true in the fearful state of nature, "but otherwise it is manifest, that the measure of Good and Evill actions, is the Civill Law."

Nor is there any question in Hobbes's mind about the need to centralize all authority in the state. Division and multiplicity of authority can have no place in a stable order: "For what is it to divide the Power of the Common-wealth, but to Dissolve it, for Powers divided mutually de-stroy each other." He treats with contempt those writers who hold that since "there be three Soules in man; so there also . . . may be more Soules (that is, more Soveraigns) than one, in a Common-wealth." Authority in a society is unitary and indivisible, or else it is nothing, And, finally, Hobbes gives the death blow to that most cherished of all medieval legal doctrines, the doctrine that the political ruler is below the law. It is, he declares, "repugnant to the nature of the Common-wealth . . . that he that hath the Soveraign Power, is subject to the Civill Lawes." Bodin had stated the same principle, but his essentially medieval conception of a nonpolitical society had made it impossible for him to develop it fully. No such limitations are to be found in the *Leviathan*.

---

[26] This and the material that follows, to p. 145, is only slighty adapted from my book *The Quest for Community* (New York: Oxford University Press, 1953), pp. 129–40. Copyright 1953 by Oxford University Press, Inc. I am grateful for permission to use these paragraphs here.

Within the monolith of power that Hobbes creates in the state, there is little room left for associations and groups. Hobbes does not see in these the multifold sources of sociability and order that Bodin had found in them. For Hobbes they are breeding areas of dissension, of conflict with the requirements of the unitary state, not reinforcements of order and justice. He compares associations within the state, "which are as it were many lesser Common Wealths in the bowels of a greater," to "wormes in the entrayles of a naturall man." Economic monopolies of any kind he detests. In the body of the commonwealth these associations "breedeth there an inflammation, accompanied with a Fever, and painful stitches."

He is suspicious of the universities, for these teaching bodies, he declared, have ever tended toward the support of ideas and actions that are not in the best interests of the state's unity. All teaching establishments should give their first devotion to, and be instruments of, the commonwealth. Large associations founded upon mutual aid and protection, especially those in the upper classes, similarly arouse his distrust: "Leagues of subjects (because Leagues are commonly made for mutual defence), are in a Common wealth (which is no more than a League of all the Subjects together) for the most part unnecessary, and savour of unlawfull designs." Guilds, even those of beggars, not to mention the more powerful ones, are regarded by Hobbes as potential infringements upon the autonomy of the individual as well as upon the majesty of the sovereign. All such associations seek to represent their members in matters of protection and security; but in the state, correctly formed, the sovereign himself is the absolute and sufficient representative of his subjects. Therefore "no other can be representative of any part of them, but so forth as he shall give leave." And this leave is to be given sparingly, grudgingly.

The meager treatment of the family that Hobbes gives us is in marked contrast to the extensive discussion that Bodin had offered. For Bodin, one of the chief reasons for family solidarity was the protection of the right of property. But Hobbes specifically declares all property to derive in law from the permission of the sovereign. And the kind of parental authority that Bodin had claimed, together with the legal inviolability of the household, is for Hobbes unthinkable. The parent, Hobbes declares, "obligeth his Children and Servants as farre as the Law permitteth, though not further, because none of them are bound to obedience in those actions, which the Law hath forbidden to be done." But Hobbes is not content to place the family's authority under the strict regulation of the state. He must also do to the family what earlier legal theorists had done to ecclesiastical and economic corporations; that is, individualize it through the fiction of perpetual contract. In discussing the nature of "Dominion Paternall," he insists that it "is not so derived from the Generation, as if therefore the Parent had Dominion over his Child because he begat him; but from the Child's Consent, either expresse, or by other sufficient arguments declared." In short, contract is, in Hobbes's rigorous terms, the cement of even the family itself. Not from custom, nor from divine law itself, does the solidarity of the family proceed. It proceeds from, and can be justified by, voluntary agreement, either express or implied.

The conclusion is inescapable that for Hobbes the sole purpose of the family is that of procreation. He does not conceive it, as did Bodin, as the true source of man's moral nature, the model of all forms of association. In Hobbes's system of thought, everything proceeds from atomistic individuals, their instincts and reason, and from contractual agreements among them. There is no place for relationships of ascribed, historically given status.

But of all associations, it is the church that Hobbes fears the most. By reason of its tenacious hold upon men's spiritual allegiances, the church will always be a divisive force within the commonwealth unless it is made strictly subordinate to the political power. It is unthinkable that an autonomous spiritual authority should exist. To grant corporate freedom to the church would be to set up "Supremacy against the Soveraignty, Canons against Lawes, and a Ghostly Authority against the Civill." An autonomous church would mean nothing less than a divided sovereignty within the state; and this, as we have seen, is for Hobbes the most deadly of all diseases afflicting the body politic: "For seeing the Ghostly Power challengeth the Right to declare what is Sinne it challengeth by consequence to declare what is Law, (Sinne being nothing but the transgression of the Law)."

How far Hobbes considered himself a Christian is debatable. Whether he was, as many of his contemporaries bitterly accused him of being, an atheist, or whether he was at heart a believer and opposed only to the authoritarian aspects of institutional Christianity, is a matter we need not consider here. What is alone of importance in this connection is to mark the heavy blows Hobbes gave to the medieval idea of an autonomous church. The religious life of the people must always be governed by the head of the state. A church Hobbes defined as "a company of men professing Christian Religion, united in the person of one Soveraign; at whose command they ought to assemble, and without whose authority they ought not to assemble." From this it follows that any supposition or claim of a universal church is false:

> There is on Earth no such universal Church as all Christians are bound to obey; because there is no power on Earth, to which all other Common-wealths are subject. . . . There is therefore no other Government in this life, neither of State, nor Religion, but

Temporal; nor teaching of any doctrine, lawfull to any Subject, which the Governour both of the State, and of the Religion, forbiddeth to be taught: And that Governor must be one; or else there must needs follow Faction, and Civil war in the Commonwealth between the Church and State. . . .

Above all other religions it was Roman Catholicism that Hobbes most feared and hated; for it was this church, and most especially its militant Jesuits, that in his time provided the strongest challenge to the development of national Christianity. But Hobbes could be severe toward Protestants as well: he denounced "Factions for government of religion, as papists, protestants, etc., as being contrary to the peace and safety of the people, and a taking of the Sword out of the hand of the Soveraign." In truth Hobbes was agreeable to the existence of any religion, irrespective of its dogma, provided it placed itself unquestioningly under the state; and, conversely, he opposed any religion, Catholic or Protestant, that did not so place itself.

Despite the severity of Hobbes's attitude toward all associations, despite his centering of all authority in the state, it yet remains true that for him the power of the state is not an end in itself. Too many students of Hobbes have read him through the pages of his enemies, rather than through his own statements. Despite the rigorousness of his theory when compared with Bodin's, despite his powerful animus against autonomous associations and the limitations he puts upon religion and all other autonomous systems of morality, it is the individual whom Hobbes has in mind as the embodiment of virtue. Hobbes seeks not the extermination of individual rights, but their fulfillment, which can be accomplished only by removing social barriers in individual autonomy. In his eyes the greatest claim of the absolute state lies in its power to create an environment for the individual's pursuit of his natural ends. In this, Hobbes was one with Plato.

Too often the emphasis in the next century on the natural order and the natural rights of individuals has been described as a reaction to the seventeenth-century political system of Hobbes. Locke, Hobbes's successor and critic, is made the philosophical source of this later contemplation of nature, but actually, although by virtue of his later position with respect to Hobbes, Locke could give more explicit emphasis to individual rights, the fact remains that it was Hobbes's own brilliant sketching of the political environment of individualism that made the later system possible. In many senses Locke is a derivative thinker, whose master in all important respects was Hobbes.

However extreme the *Leviathan* may be, however savage its rejection of pluralism, localism, and sectionalism, what Hobbes always has in mind is the creation of an impersonal environment of law within which individuals may rationally pursue their proper interests. It is not the totalitarian state that Hobbes gives us, but the necessary political environment for the natural system of liberty, which was to become identified later with the Enlightenment in France and England. Later theorists such as Locke could give more space to the rights themselves, but Hobbes, with the spectacle of a still-potent residue of medievalism before his eyes, had to give the greater part of his attention to the political environment itself.

Nor can Hobbes be described simply as the voice of the "middle class." That his theory of the state was a powerful factor in bringing into existence the new entrepreneur and the new system of economic relationships is a good deal less an indication of his affection for the middle class than of his hatred for the economic groups that were hindrances both to the new middle class and to the attainment of a unified and impersonal political order. Hobbes could write bitterly about the representatives of the new economic order and condemn sharply their treatment of the poor. He was no more concerned with deliberately and consciously furthering their interests than he was with doing the same for the Protestants. What relates the political theory of Hobbes to both economic rationalism and Protestant individualism is the Hobbesean environment of impersonal law in which both could flourish. We may add also their common dislike of intermediate social and moral associations.

Only the invincible economic determinist would see in the pages of the *Leviathan*, with their brilliant and eloquent portrayal of the impersonal, absolute, imprescriptible state, a piece of ideology reflecting the alleged interests of the middle class. In light of Hobbes's plain distrust of the marketplace and his preference for the rural countryside, in light of his explicit condemnation of the political practices of the merchants and manufacturers of his day, whom he charged with the blame for the civil war, and his general hatred for their acquisitive and exploitative proclivities, and, above all, in light of the relentless political direction of his writings, it is difficult to understand interpretations that relegate his beliefs to the vague categories of economic determinism. If there is any element of reluctant praise in Hobbes for a class of men whose activities he despised, it is because he could see that this class, by reason of the very tenuousness of its internal social relationships and its lack of any sense of noblesse oblige, could never become, as the older aristocracy had been, a threat to the unity of the political state. Hobbes's early affection was for the aristocracy, but through the iron logic of his political thought he cast this affection aside. The landed aristocracy, with its large retinues and its rooted allegiances, must constitute a perennial threat to political unity; hence comes the notable shift in his thinking regarding such matters as honor. But it is nonsense to suppose that his affection for the landed aristocracy was transferred to a middle class. It went, ruthlessly and rigorously, to the state itself. It would be far more correct to say that Hobbes's appreciation of the middle class—reluctant as it was—derived from the logic of his politics than that his politics derived from a middle-class orientation of thinking.

What Plato did for the ancient city-state Hobbes did for the modern nation-state: gave it an ideal expression that made it triumphant over all competing types of social structure. Bodin, as we observed, was the first to see the nation-state as the key unit of the European polity as a whole: successor to church and to Holy Roman Empire, as well as to all other forms of organization. But Bodin could not get beyond a strictly monarchical view of the nation-state. He tended to place sovereignty in the monarchical government; and he could not free himself from certain medieval values. Hobbes, however, located absolute power, not in monarchy, not even in government as such, but in the legal framework of the state. In sum, the state became for Hobbes the legal-political community that is Leviathan: a community which does not permit within itself any lesser form of community that could conceivably challenge its unity, its indivisibility, and its absolute authority.

Rousseau and the General Will

The next, and basically final, step in the development of the modern philosophy of the political community is taken in eighteenth-century France. Rousseau is beyond any question the preeminent figure here. Not even Hobbes's brilliance of thought and writing puts Rousseau in the shade. Plato may be the essential architect of this vision of community, but no one has equaled Rousseau's role in making it the single most attractive vision for modern man. Rousseau is the very archetype of the political modern, the embodiment of what might be called the modernist revolt in politics. If he is rightly known as the major philosopher of democratic sovereignty, through his notable concept of the general will as the sole source of legitimate power in society, he must also be regarded as a part of the intellectual tradition in western Europe that was to culminate in the total state of the twentieth century. Whether Rousseau is best thought of as, at bottom, democratic or totalitarian in philosophy need not concern us. All that is important is to recognize his crucial translation of the idea of the absolute state as presented by Hobbes into a concept rooted in the mass of the people. It is fair to say that as many popular movements of revolt have emanated from Rousseau's revolutionary philosophy of the general will as from Marx's ideas of the revolutionary proletariat a century later.

The eighteenth century in France was the age of the Enlightenment, with the philosophes the self-declared spokesmen of reason against tradition, of secularism against religion, and of the single power of the political government against the varied authorities of the surrounding social order around them—authorities in most instances lineal products of the age of feudalism, which, although they had flourished centuries earlier, not even the power of the absolute monarchy during the seventeenth and eighteenth centuries had been able to destroy. What the philosophes detested above everything else in their society was the social and political power of the Christian church. To win its destruction they were, virtually without exception, willing to lend their talents to even the most absolute of European monarchs in the middle of the eighteenth century.

The philosophes, Rousseau among them, are members—in many respects the most brilliant members—of the line of Western political intellectuals that had begun, as we have seen, with the lawyers and legal philosophers of ancient Rome. While it is doubtful that any of the philosophes knew, or had any interest in, Roman law, there is no doubt whatever of the close affinity between their principles and those we have seen underlying Roman law. Such French intellectuals as Diderot, d'Alembert, Condorcet, d'Holbach, and Voltaire had the same basic devotion to centralization of power, individualization of social groups, conversion of status relationships to those of contract, and, not least, extermination of all intermediate groups which in any way militated against the individual's assimilation into the rational state that had, both in ancient Rome and again in the late Middle Ages and the Renaissance, formed the foundations of Roman law.

Of all the eighteenth-century French philosophes, Rousseau's work has proved to be the most fateful in both content and thrust. That he was rather widely distrusted in his own time, and rarely if ever given the respect he regarded as his due from fellow intellectuals and philosophers, does not offset the fact that by the beginning of the nineteenth century Rousseau was without question regarded as the foremost mind of the Enlightenment, at least in political matters. The revolutionary implications of his doctrine of the "general will" ensured him this estimation.

We learn from Rousseau's *Confessions* that both Hobbes and Plato had influenced him, but Plato most significantly. It is easy to believe that. As one reads Rousseau's *Social Contract* or any of his three earlier *Discourses*—on the arts and sciences, on social inequality, and on political economy, each vital to any understanding of the more famous *Social Contract*—it is plain that Plato and Rousseau have a great deal in common. Such, indeed, was Rousseau's devotion to the communal spirit of Plato's political philosophy that when he committed his own children to a foundling asylum, he tells us in the *Confessions*, he felt as though he were behaving as a true citizen and thought himself a worthy member of Plato's Republic. Like Plato, Rousseau was obsessed by intimations of corruption, disorganization, even of breakdown in the society around him in France. And, also like Plato, Rousseau saw the political community, absolute, indivisible, and omnipotent, as the only possible haven from the ills and torments of society.

Rousseau's first major political work was his *Discourse on the Arts and Sciences,* a long essay in which he sought to show that the arts and sciences have generally brought men unhappiness, and had their origins, not in true morality, but in human cupidity, egoism, ambition, and idle desire for status. In this essay we can see not only Rousseau's alienation from his society but also the passion for the simple and natural, the hatred for the complex and overdeveloped, that would later culminate in the picture of the ideal political community he gives us in the *Social Contract.*

If there is a single condition that Rousseau thought epitomized his age in France, it was hypocrisy. In his *Discourse on the Arts and Sciences,* written some twenty years before the *Social Contract* appeared, he declares:

> Sincere friendship, real esteem, and perfect confidence are banished among men. Jealousy, suspicion, fear, coldness, reserve, hate, and fraud lie constantly concealed under that uniform and deceitful veil of politeness; that boasted candor and urbanity for which we are indebted to the light and leading of this age.[27]

How do we account for the corruption of culture, the breakdown of human morality, and the alienation of man which Rousseau saw around him? His answer, given in one of the most brilliant works of the century and a forerunner to much nineteenth-century writing, is given in detail in his second discourse, *On the Origins of Inequality.* In a word, inequality is the source of both social instability and cultural decay. Originally, Rousseau tells us, mankind lived in a condition of natural simplicity, one in which human relationships were unforced and uncoercive, in which morality sprang from what is ingrained in us by nature. Mankind would have endured forever in this state of simplicity and relative equality, Rousseau tells us, had it not been for the discovery of agriculture and metals and the accompanying rise of ever-more-complicated relationships among individuals. Most important of all was the discovery of the idea of private property. From the time when a single man first laid claim to a portion of the earth, declaring "This is mine," and thus driving other men to like behavior, the world has been filled with strife, envy, jealousy, conflict, and exploitation. As culture became more and more complicated, social interdependences became more common. And in social interdependence, whether of kinship, guild,

---

[27] Jean Jacques Rousseau, *Discourse on the Arts and Sciences,* in *The Social Contract and Discourses,* trans. G. D. H. Cole (New York: E. P. Dutton, Everyman's Library, 1950), p. 149. All quotations from the *Social Contract* and the *Discourses* are from this edition.

religion, or extended family, there are always to be found the seeds of the kind of inequality from which our society today suffers.

Such, very briefly, is Rousseau's diagnosis of what he felt to be the ills of the society in which he lived. Only through our awareness of this diagnosis, to be found in his first two discourses, is it possible to understand the special character of the political community Rousseau describes in such passionate terms in his third discourse, that on political economy, and in his *Social Contract*. For, like Plato, Rousseau makes his primary objective the emancipation of the individual from the corruption and conflicts and uncertainties of society. And also like Plato, Rousseau sees the political community as the surest means of effecting this liberation.

That there is a strongly authoritarian, even totalitarian, character to Rousseau's political community admits of no doubt whatever. One would have to go back to Plato's *Republic*, or come down to the twentieth-century theory of the totalitarian state, to find the equal of the authoritarianism of Rousseau's general will.

But it would be unfair to Rousseau, as it would be to Plato, to accuse him of indifference to the plight of the individual and the individual's freedom in society. It was the individual's freedom that obsessed Rouseau above all else—*but freedom from society, not from the state*. It was society that drew Rousseau's harshest criticisms: society in the sense of the traditional institutions of church, guild, extended family, monastery, local community, economic enterprise, and school, and the whole apparatus of traditional bureaucratic government. Here, as I have indicated, Rousseau found nothing but hypocrisy and uncertainty. Here he found, too, a ceaseless form of conflict. "It is of the essence of society," Rousseau wrote in a letter to Mirabeau, "to breed incessant war among its members; and the only way of combating this war is to find a form of government that will set the law above them all."

Rousseau seeks to liberate the individual from the toils and traps of society and to provide a condition of equality approximating as nearly as possible the state of nature. "Each citizen would then be completely *independent* of all his fellow men, and absolutely *dependent* upon the state: which operation is always brought by the same means; *for it is only by the force of the state that the liberty of its members can be secured.*" [28] There is no other single statement in all Rousseau's writings which better serves as the theme of his political philosophy than this. In it is incorporated the essential argument of the two *Discourses* and of the *Social Contract*. His ideal is independence for the individual, but independence, it will be observed, not from the state but from fellow members of society.*

28 Jean Jacques Rousseau, *Social Contract*, p. 52. Italics added.

* The remainder of this section on Rousseau is a slightly modified version of "Rousseau and the Political Community" in my *Tradition and Revolt* (New York: Random House, Vintage Books, 1968), pp. 17–26.

The function of the state is made apparent by the same statement. Its mission is to effectuate the independence of the individual from society by securing the individual's dependence upon itself. The state is the means by which the individual can be freed of those restrictive tyrannies which compose society. It is the agency of emancipation which permits the individual to develop the latent germs of goodness heretofore frustrated by a hostile society. By entering into the pure state, Rousseau declares, "man's actions receive a moral character which was wanting to them before," and "from a stupid and limited animal he now for the first time becomes a reasoning being and a man." [29] The state is thus essential to man's potential being, and far from being a check upon his development, it is the sole means of that development. Through the power of the state, man is spared the strife and tyranny which arise out of his selfish and destructive passions. But in order to emerge from the dissensions of society, and to abide in the spiritual peace of the state, there must be "an absolute surrender of the individual, with all of his rights and all of his powers, to the community as a whole." [30]

Rousseau's emphasis upon the community has been too often interpreted in a sense that is foreign to his own aim. Commentators have occasionally written of his "community" as the revival of a concept which had disappeared with the Middle Ages. The mystic solidarity which Rousseau preaches is not, however, the solidarity of the community existing by custom and unwritten law. The social community, as it existed in the thought of Thomas Aquinas or, later, in the theory of Althusius, is a community of communities, an assemblage of morally integrated minor groups. The solidarity of this community arises out of the moral and social observances of the minor groups; its unity does not result from being permeated with sovereign law, extending from the top through all individual components of the structure. Rousseau's community, however, is a political one, which is indistinguishable from the state and which shares all the uniformitarian qualities of the state. It is in his mind a moral unity, but it is a unity conferred by the sovereign will of the state and directed by the political government. Thus he uses the familiar organic analogy to indicate the unitary structure of his political community. The same centralization of control which exists in the human body must dominate the structure of the community; unity is conferred by the brain, which in Rousseau's analogy represents the sovereign power. The general will is the analogue of the human mind, and as such must remain as unified and undiversified as the mind itself. The general will, as he is careful to indicate, is not synonymous with the "will of all." It is the will of the political organism, an entity with a life of its own quite apart from that of the individual members of which it is built.

---

[29] Rousseau, *Social Contract*, p. 19.   [30] Ibid., p. 14.

In its suprahuman reality, the general will is always right; and while the will of all may be often misled, the general will never deviates from the strictest rectitude. The general will is indivisible, inalienable, and illimitable. It demands the unqualified obedience of every individual in the community, and implies the obligation of each citizen to render to the state all that the state sees fit to demand. This preeminence of the state in the life of the individual is not, however, despotism; it is the necessary basis of true individual freedom. "In order that the social contract shall be no empty formula it tacitly implies that obligation which alone can give force to all the others; namely that anyone who refuses obedience to the general will is forced to it by the whole body. *This merely means that he is being compelled to be free.*" [31] In this last phrase is clearly revealed the relationship between individualism and authoritarianism in the thought of Rousseau. The same rationale, the same scheme of values, which leads him to restrict morality to life within the state compels him similarly to regard the state as the sphere of freedom. The individual lives a free life only within the frame of his complete surrender to the omnipotent state. The state is the liberator of the individual from the toils of society.

The totalitarian implications of Rousseau's thought do not arise merely out of the severity of his theory of sovereignty. The most common criticism of this theory—that it sets up an illimitable power—is applicable to all monistic theories of sovereignty. In any social theory where the sovereign state exists as a concept, there is at least implicit the idea of potentially unrestricted power. What gives uniqueness to Rousseau's doctrine is not so much its severity as its subtle but explicit identification with freedom. What has connoted bondage to the minds of most men is exalted as freedom by Rousseau. To regard the power structure of the state as only a device by which the individual is compelled to be free is a process of reasoning that sets Rousseau apart from the tradition of liberalism. The phraseology of liberalism in this case merely intensifies the authoritarianism which underlies it. What Rousseau calls freedom is at bottom no more than the freedom to do that which the state in its omniscience determines. Freedom for Rousseau is the synchronization of all social existence to the will of the state, the replacement of cultural diversity by a mechanical egalitarianism.

It is, however, in the bearing of Rousseau's general will upon traditional society that the full sweep of its totalitarian significance becomes manifest. It has been made clear that the object of Rousseau's dislike is society, and the special merit of the state lies in its power to emancipate the individual from traditional society. The relationship among individuals that forms the general will, and that is the true state, is obviously

---

31 Ibid., p. 18. Italics added.

an exceedingly delicate one. It must be unitary and indivisible for its nature fully to unfold. In short, it must be protected from the operations of extraneous channels of constraint. "For the same reason that sovereignty is inalienable, it is indivisible," he writes; "the Will is general or else it is nothing." [32] To achieve a pure sovereignty, one which will be untrammeled by social influences, one which will encompass the whole of man's personality, it is necessary that the traditional social loyalties be abrogated. A unified, *general* will is incompatible with the existence of minor associations; hence they must be banished.

> When the people, having been adequately informed, hold its deliberation, and the citizens have had no communication among themselves, the whole number of individual opinions will always result in the General Will, and the decision will always be just. But when factions arise, and partial associations are created at the expense of the great association, the will of each of these associations becomes general so far as its members are concerned, and particular in its relation to the state: it may then be said that it is no longer a number of votes equal to the number of men, but equal only to the number of associations. . . . It is therefore essential, if the General Will is to be able to express itself, that there should be no partial society within the state, and that each citizen should think only his own thoughts. [33]

The proscription of all forms of association except that which is identical with the whole being of the state: such is Rousseau's drastic proposal. This is not to be regarded as one of these hasty, ill-considered remarks for which Rousseau is famous. Nor is it true that his banishment of associations is out of harmony with the rest of his thought. We have seen that Rousseau's animus is against society, against those ties which make individuals dependent upon one another. We have seen, further, that his conception of sovereignty demands the attributes of unity and indivisibility; the general will is *general* or else it is nothing. Is it not then logical that the right of nonpolitical association should be sharply restricted? In his earlier *Discourse on Political Economy*, Rousseau had presented in almost the same words this analysis of the relation of associations to the state. There is to be no bond of loyalty, no social affiliation, no interdependence, save that which is embodied in the general will. This will, as we have seen, is meticulously distinguished by Rousseau from the mere "will of all." The latter is the collective opinion or judgment reached by the people in their ordinary

32 Ibid., p. 24.   33 Ibid., p. 27.

social roles; those of businessman, soldier, cleric, family member, and so on. This will is *not* the "voice of God"; it is *not* necessarily just, right, and equitable. But the general will is. What makes the general will, in Otto von Gierke's words, a process of permanent revolution is that by its very nature it must seek to dissolve away all of the social roles which, by their very existence, militate against both the individual's freedom and his capacity to enter into the absolute political community.

The genius of the idea of the general will lies in its masterful utilization of the ancient distinction between appearance and reality. We must, Rousseau is saying, beware of the *apparent* will of the people —the will that simple majority vote may make evident—for this is the will of the people still incompletely emancipated from the private authorities and the separate roles that are given them by history. The *real* will of the people is the will that lies latent in man and that requires as its condition man's liberation from these authorities and roles. *This* is the general will and is alone the "voice of God."

How, in practical operation, is the general will to be ascertained? Representation through parliamentary institutions is out of the question, for, as we are told, the general will cannot be represented. To seek to represent it is to distort it. Moreover, representative institutions are themselves a part of the hated legacy of the Middle Ages. Balloting will not do, for, as we have seen, it may yield only the spurious and deceptive "will of all." Rousseau's answer to his question is a fascinating one:

> But how, I shall be asked, can the General Will be known in cases in which it has not expressed itself? Must the whole nation be assembled together at every unforeseen event? Certainly not. It ought the less to be assembled, because it is by no means certain that its decision would be the expression of the General Will; besides, the method would be impracticable in a great people, and is hardly ever necessary where the government is well-intentioned: for the rulers well know that the General Will is always on the side which is most favourable to the public interest, that is to say, most equitable; so that it is needful only to act justly, to be certain of following the General Will.[34]

How can the ruler be certain of acting justly? He must be, above all things, virtuous. Only "the most sublime virtue," Rousseau writes, "can afford sufficient illumination for it"—that is, for the distinction between the real will and the apparent will. But what is virtue? And here we come back full circle to the general will:

[34] Jean Jacques Rousseau, *Discourse on Political Economy*, pp. 296–97.

If you would have the General Will accomplished, bring all the particular wills into conformity with it; in other words, as virtue is nothing more than this conformity of the particular wills, with the General Will, establish the reign of virtue.[35]

Was ever, in the whole history of political theory, a doctrine more beautifully tailored, more ingeniously complected, than the doctrine of the general will? In it lie, at one and the same time, ideas of widest range: liberation from social tyranny, emancipation from self and its egoistic demands, the achievement of a form of spiritual communion that had previously been reserved for heaven, the attainment of virtue, and withal a conception of power as absolute as it is sealing and providential. Others in history, from the Roman lawyers through the great Hobbes, had justified the power of the state in terms of order. Rousseau is the first to justify absolute power in the name of virtue, equality, and freedom. Power is more than power: it is refuge from the inequities and uncertainties of ordinary society.

In a host of ways the practical implications of the doctrine of the general will are made evident by Rousseau. I shall confine myself to but two of them: his treatment of religion and of the family. A socially independent church, like any form of nonpolitical loyalty, would constitute an interference with the functioning of the general will. It would represent a flaw in that spiritual unity which Rousseau prizes so highly in his political order. Yet it would not do to repress the religious propensities of man, for "it matters very much to the community that each citizen should have a religion. That will make him love his duty. . . ." [36] But, argues Rousseau, it is not enough that a nation should have a religion; the religion must be identified in the minds of the people with the values of national life, else it will create disunity and violate the general will. It is not enough that a religion should make good men; it must make good citizens. Religion has a responsibility toward civic or political ends before any others. It must reflect, above all, the essential unity of the state, and find its justification in the measures it takes to promote that unity.

In light of these criteria, Christianity must be rejected as the religion of the true state. "For Christianity, as a religion, is entirely spiritual, occupied solely with heavenly things; the country of the Christians is not of this world." [37] There are even greater objections to Christianity:

Christian charity does not readily allow a man to think hardly of his neighbors. . . Christianity preaches only servitude and dependence. Its spirit is so favourable to tyranny that it

[35] Ibid., p. 298.   [36] Rousseau, *Social Contract*, p. 138.   [37] Ibid., p. 136.

always profits by such a régime. True Christians are made to be slaves, and they know this and do not much mind: this short life counts for too little in their eyes.[38]

It cannot be overlooked that it is the essential humanity in the Christian faith that Rousseau despises. Its very virtues, he tells us, are its vices, for a society of Christians with all its perfections would be neither the strongest nor the most lasting. The very fact that it was perfect would rob it of its bond of union. The disregard of the Christian mind for secular law, for the values of the nation, would be the undoing of that unity which is indispensable to the true state. The spirit of subserviency which Christianity embodies would prevent any real flowering of the martial spirit. "Set over against Christians those generous peoples who were devoured by ardent love of glory and of their country; imagine your Christian republic face to face with Sparta or Rome; the pious Christians will be beaten, crushed, and destroyed before they know where they are." [39] The ancient Romans were possessed of military valor until Christianity was accepted, "but when the Cross had driven out the eagle, Roman valor wholly disappeared." [40] Christianity, then, because of its pacifism, its depreciation of the state, and its concentration upon men rather than citizens, must be replaced by another religion, one which will perfectly embody the measure of nationalist ardor necessary to the state.

A purely civil religion must be instituted whose articles of faith the sovereign should fix. "While it can compel no one to believe them, it can banish from the state whoever does not believe them . . . ; if anyone after publicly recognizing these dogmas behaves as if he does not believe them, let him be punished by death: he has committed the worst of all crimes, that of lying before the law." [41] Other faiths will be permitted to exist alongside the civil religion, providing there is nothing in their articles which is deemed by the sovereign to be inimical to the development of citizenship. "Tolerance should be given to all religions that tolerate others, so long as their dogmas contain nothing contrary to the duties of citizenship," [42] It will be remembered, however, that the criteria of good citizenship are far-reaching. Rousseau's prior criticism of Christianity on the ground of its intrinsic irreconcilability with good citizenship should serve as the grain of salt with which to take his protestations of tolerance. The articles of faith of the civil religion as fixed by the sovereign have as their fundamental objective the cementing of the social contract. We have already seen that the most basic values of

38 Ibid.   39 Ibid., p. 137.   40 Ibid., p. 138.
41 Ibid., p. 139.   42 Ibid., p. 140.

Christianity are not regarded as compatible with the state; we may perhaps speculate on the extent to which tolerance as a practical policy would be deemed commensurate with civil religion.

It is political religion which Rousseau extolls, one which in essence is indistinguishable from the law of the land. Like his forerunner Hobbes, Rousseau holds sin to be no more than a transgression of civil law, and in that fact lies the inspiriting aim of his civil religion. Respect for the sovereign, allegiance to the state alone, and subordination of all interests to the law of the realm: these are the primary attributes of the civil religion proposed by Rousseau. The symbol of *patrie* is uppermost; religion and patriotism will be but two aspects of the same thing. "If it is good," Rousseau wrote in his *Discourse on Political Economy,* "to know how to deal with men as they are, it is much better to make them what there is need that they should be. The most absolute authority is that which penetrates into a man's inmost being, and concerns itself no less with his will than with his actions." [43] So had declared the militants of the church in the Middle Ages; so would declare Dostoevski's Grand Inquisitor.

The family, too, must be radically altered, especially in its hold over the young. This follows inevitably from the demands of the general will and from the nature of virtue, which, as we have learned, is nothing more than conformity with the general will. To form citizens is not the work of a day, nor is it a responsibility than can be left idly to the influences of traditional society. The unitary state calls for a remodeling of human nature so that there will be no irritants to the body politic. According to Rousseau:

> He who possesses the courage to give a people institutions, must be ready to change human nature, to transform every individual, who by himself is a complete and separate whole, into a part of a greater whole from which this individual in a certain sense receives his life and character; to change the constitution of man in order to strengthen it, and to substitute for the corporeal and independent existence which we all have received from nature a merely partial and moral existence. In short, he must take from man his native individual powers and equip him with others foreign to his nature, which he cannot understand or use without the assistance of others. The more completely these natural powers are annihilated and destroyed and the greater and more enduring are the ones acquired, the more secure and the more perfect is also the constitution.[44]

43 Rousseau, *Discourse on Political Economy,* p. 297.

44 Rousseau, *Social Contract,* p. 38.

It is necessary to inculcate from infancy in the minds of the people the surpassing claim of the state to their loyalty. "If, for example," Rousseau writes, "the people were early accustomed to conceive their individuality only in its connection with the body of the state, and to be aware of their own existence merely as parts of that of the state, they might in time come to identify themselves in some degree with the greater whole. . . ." [45] The family should not be granted the all-important duty of education, for too great a responsibility hangs in the balance. The traditional educative function should be transferred from the family to the state, so that, as Rousseau states it, the "prejudices" of the father may not interfere with the development of citizens. However, the disintegration of this age-old basis of the family should in no wise create alarm:

> Should the public authority, in assuming the place of father and charging itself with this important function, acquire his rights in the discharge of his duties, he should have little cause to protest; for he would only be altering his title, and would have in common, under the name *citizen*, the same authority over his children, that he was exercising separately under the name of *father*, and would be no less obeyed when speaking in the name of the law than when he spoke in that of nature.[46]

Family relationship is transmuted subtly into political relationship; the molecule of the family is broken into the atoms of its individuals, who are coalesced afresh into the single unity of the state.

Just as the religious bond is transformed into a spiritualized patriotism, the family tie is in effect disintegrated, and its members reunified in the tissue of the state. Underlying this proposal to eradicate the social unity of the family is Rousseau's encompassing desire to replace the natural diversity of society with the rigorous egalitarianism of the general will:

> If the children are reared in common in the bosom of equality, if they are imbued with the laws of the state and the precepts of the General Will, if they are taught to respect these above all other things, if they are surrounded by examples and objects which perpetually remind them of the tender mother who nourishes them, of the love she bears them, of the inestimable benefits they receive from her, and of the return they owe her, we cannot doubt that they will learn to cherish one another mutually as brothers.[47]

[45] Rousseau, *Discourse on Political Economy*, p. 307.
[46] Ibid., p. 309.   [47] Ibid.

From Rousseau more than from anyone else in his time or since, has come the profound sense of the political state as community, as a haven from the torments, inequalities, and insecurities which he and many others have thought to be inseparable from the structure of modern society. Just as the medieval philosopher had seen the church as a fortress against the corruptions and tyrannies of outer society, so Rousseau and the line of political intellectuals descending from him have seen the political community as such a fortress. In his *Confessions* Rousseau tells us he had come to see that everything social and cultural was radically connected with politics and that no people would ever be other than what it was made by the nature of its government. As we noted above, Rousseau declared forcefully in his *Discourse on Political Economy* that while it is good to know how to deal with men as they are, it is "much better to make them what there is need that they should be." And his injunction, in the same discourse, to *establish the reign of virtue* was to ring through all succeeding decades, down to our own day, as the basic theme of all those committed to politics as the proper approach to human welfare and human community.

After Rousseau, the state would be regarded by a rising number of Western intellectuals and philosophers—and in our own century by many in non-Western parts of the world—as the most magnetic of all forms of association. To it would be referred for solution problems of not merely economic and social but even psychological and spiritual character. The ancient attractions of kinship, religion, guild, and local community paled in the nineteenth century before the increasingly luminous cast of the state, as interpreted by the successors of Rousseau. The French Revolution, coming hard on the heels of Rousseau's ideas, seemed afterward, to a constantly growing number of liberals and radicals throughout the nineteenth century, and well into the twentieth, to be fit embodiment of what these ideas had promised. We shall have more to say of this momentous revolution in the chapter on the revolutionary community. Suffice it here to say that the combination of social nihilism and political affirmation to be found alike in Rousseau and in the Revolution proved an irresistible combination for thinkers as different as Richard Wagner, Karl Marx, Jeremy Bentham, and many others down to the political intellectuals of our own time, all of them consecrated to the use of politics as the instrument of social reconstruction and to the political community as the bearer of man's best hope.

True, there were those in the nineteenth-century West, among them Tocqueville, Proudhon, and Max Weber, who looked with suspicion on the shape of the political community Rousseau had designed, who saw the political community as a means of man's liberation from the tyrannies and deprivations he perceived in the surrounding society; as the source of a degree of popular participation in government beyond anything known before in history, at least on so wide a scale; as the creator of rights, equalities, and liberties where none of these had existed before—as all of these, yes, but also as the seedbed of centralized bureaucracy that could stifle man's spirit and of collectivism that could destroy cultural diversity and even the roots of personality, to lead in time to the alienation of growing masses of individuals, a loss of the sense of self as well as of community. We shall come to these forebodings in the final chapter of this book. Here it is enough merely to note that those central elements of the political community first brought into prominence by Plato amid the ruins of the ancient Greek city-state attained a magnitude and thrust in nineteenth- and twentieth-century Europe beyond anything he or any other Greek could easily have imagined.

3 The Religious Community

Religion and Society

Third among Western man's most fundamental and universal forms of community is religion. There is no subject on which Western philosophers have written more profusely and intensely than on religion—or on the varied ideas which have sprung from the religious matrix. Kinship is the oldest of all forms of human community, but religion is without question the oldest source of human thought, taking that phrase in the large sense that includes the rudiments of art and magic as well as science and philosophy. There have been long periods of time when there was no culture—high culture, that is—except what emerged from the religious imagination.

Nor is it necessary to go back to the most ancient or primitive times for evidence of this. One need but think of the vast amount of thought and art in the West that has proceeded directly from religious minds or from those working in one capacity or another within ecclesiastical structures. The magnificent art of the Middle Ages, to be seen in cathedrals such as Chartres, in book illumination, in painting, in music, in drama, and in carvings or sculptures of exquisite design, would not exist at all had it not been for the inspiration of religion and the patronage of the church. And for nearly twelve hundred years, until approximately the eighteenth century, there was almost no serious writing that did not concern itself with questions tinged at least somewhat with religion. Modern Western philosophy is hardly more than a secularization of religion.

The relation between religion and society is, and has always been, very close. The deepest religious experiences are precisely those connected with birth, marriage, and death—the "crises of existence," as these are well called. We know of no religion that has not based itself in some degree upon man's social needs and aspirations. We may commonly think of religion as concerned with the supernatural, and it usually is; but the deepest roots of religion lie in this earth, in man's experience of the social and moral community that religion has everywhere provided in one shape or other. The successes of a given religion in proselyting and converting have been overwhelmingly correlated with the sense of community it may have been able to instill in the minds of the lonely, estranged, alienated, and socially or spiritually disinherited. As we shall see in a moment, Christianity's greatest appeal in the Roman Empire of its origin was to the masses, who had come to feel increasingly dislocated—*in* but not really *of* their state and society. A religion may or may not have a belief in heaven and hell, may or may not have gods in the ordinary sense, may or may not have rites, ceremonies, priests, and formal worship. But what religion always has is the sense of the sacred community. The great French sociologist Émile Durkheim did not err in finding in this sense the very origins of religion.

So close is the relation between religion and society that it is possible to trace the history of key social, economic, and political developments through the episodes of religious history. The heart of the Reformation was religious, expressed in terms of the changed view of man's relation to God, but between that change and changes of political and economic nature there was the closest of relationships. Max Weber has shown us how vitally connected in the seventeenth and eighteenth centuries were the Puritan belief in the sacredness of work and the rise of capitalism. And innumerable historians have shown us how the modern political state is rooted in the fragmentation of the single, ecumenical Christianity that had existed for more than a thousand years, only to be broken on the jagged rocks of political and economic ambition in sixteenth-century Europe. As religious ends have, for good or ill, dominated the political and military energies of men, so these energies have imposed themselves on the nature of religion—indeed on the very ways men have defined God and the spiritual.

It is sometimes said that political nationalism is contemporary man's substitute for religion in the ordinary sense. And it has to be admitted that during the past two centuries the political state has taken on many of the meanings that medieval man found in the church alone. In the political sphere we have our full share of allegiances, devotions, rituals, feast days, and commemorations of saints, just as medieval man knew these in the religious sphere alone. But the fact that nationalism—or the economic pursuit of wealth or any other secular aspect of life—has taken on religious overtones does not mean that religion as such has significantly declined, if indeed it has declined at all in any demonstrable sense. There was a time—in the eighteenth century and during periods of the nineteenth and twentieth centuries as well—when it seemed that religion was fast being made obsolete by science, technology, democracy, education, and other major elements of modernity. Religion, it was said by many rationalists, would in due time be relegated to the lumber room of history, there to join other outmoded beliefs. But there is not the slightest evidence of this. Religion remains, to this very moment, a powerful source of loyalty and also community in the modern world. Whatever may be the occasional signs of diminished faith in the old and traditional religions, they are more than offset by the attractions of new, often bizarre, forms of religious faith.

Our concern in this chapter is almost exclusively with Christianity. There is no help for this in a book concerned with the major themes of Western social philosophy. Since the end of the Roman Empire, the main currents of religious and social thought alike have been Christian, governed basically by distinctively Christian envisagements of man and God. Western social philosophy during the past fifteen hundred years has acquired its character to a great degree from struggles of the Christian community with the military, political, revolutionary, and other types of community. From the first century in Rome, when primitive, apostolic Christianity struggled for survival in the congeries of tiny, Christ-dedicated sects that were then the only manifestations of this religion, through successive ages in the writings of Augustine, Aquinas, Luther, Calvin, Newman, Kierkegaard, and many others, down to the contemporary works of Maritain, Niebuhr, and Ellul, the search for the Christian community has been a crucial element of Western history.

The Elements of the Religious Community

Charisma

The personal nature of religion is as strong as it is in kinship. It is epitomized in the word charisma, which Max Weber made fundamental to religion. As Weber pointed out, in all the great world religions there was in the beginning the charismatic individual—Moses, Buddha, Jesus,

Mohammed—who, as we know, communicated his charisma in diverse ways to followers, disciples, and communicants. All of these, through one or another type of worship or ritual, have believed themselves to be graced by the charisma of the founding figure. Granted that charisma may come in due time to be absorbed by things—crosses, altars, and food or drink; its origin, nevertheless, lies in the person of the founding figure, in the Moses or Jesus from whom alone, it is believed, can come the qualities celebrated in communal fashion. As we use the word charisma today, it may be attached to other than religious figures—to political leaders of special luster, for example—but this only suggests the degree of religious intensity we are prone on occasion to give nonreligious symbols and spheres of experience.

The Sacred

Second is the element of the sacred. As Émile Durkheim has lastingly stated the matter, basic to every religion, however simple or complex it may be in faith and in organization, is the contrast between the sacred and the profane. The sacred, it must be emphasized, does not mean necessarily good, pure, or holy. Devils, demons, and evil spirits are no less sacred in the religious sense than gods or saints. The sacred draws its nature from all the beings, things, and values deemed beyond the criteria of simple utility or ordinary pragmatic experience and believed to have a suprarational quality of either good or evil. A given religion may lack belief in a god or immortality or any other commonly identified attribute of religion, but no religion can be said to exist at all where there is no differentiation made between the sacred and the profane. Of all the distinctions or differentiations that man makes, none is as basic, Durkheim wrote, as the separation he makes between the sacred and the profane.

Dogma

A third, and closely related, element is dogma. We refer here to a proposition about the universe, society, or man's behavior that is held to be right or true irrespective of supporting means of proof or verification. To be sure, one may believe strongly in the *possibility* of proof or verification, given sufficient time and means, through rational or empirical modes of investigation. Few if any of us declare as dogma something antirational or nonrational. All of us are continually reminded of a certain dogma through the reinforcement it receives from experience or reflection. But it is the essence of dogma that it is held by its believers to be supreme in and for itself, beyond the ordinary tests of rationality or utility we are prone to insist upon for nondogmatic articles of belief.

"God is good"; "Killing is evil"; "Incest is wrong"; "Love of country is right"; "Human life is sacred": all of these are dogmas. Each *may* be justified or proved empirically or rationally; but the validity of each, and the power each may exert in our lives, is assumed without further necessity of demonstration every moment that we utter it or live by it. The theologian John Henry Cardinal Newman once declared, "Men will die for a dogma who will not even stir for a conclusion." Plainly, dogma —whether explicit or implicit—produces heights, and also depths, of human action that ordinary propositions could not be expected to produce. Men have sacrificed themselves and exhibited extraordinary courage, and have also killed, tortured, and devastated whole lands, for dogma. It is hard to imagine anyone becoming fanatical about, say, any of the multiplication tables or the formula that two parts hydrogen and one part oxygen yield water. But on the clear evidence of experience and history, men are fanatical about dogmas relating to God, morality, and even politics.

Dogma is a steel rod in one's belief system, on which can be fixed all manner of lesser beliefs, opinions, and views. No one can live without possession of dogma in some degree. What Tocqueville wrote is valuable here:

> In order that society should exist and, a fortiori, that a society should prosper, it is necessary that the minds of all the citizens should be rallied and held together by certain predominant ideas; and this cannot be the case unless each of them sometimes draws his opinions from the common source and consents to accept certain matters of belief already formed. If I now consider man in his isolated capacity, I find that dogmatic belief is not less indispensable to him in order to live alone than it is to enable him to cooperate with his fellows. If man were forced to demonstrate for himself all the truths of which he makes daily use, his task would never end.[1]

Religion is by no means the sole home of dogma: it also dwells in other realms of experience—political, economic, educational, and so on. It is the dogmatic status of certain beliefs that, more than anything else, leads to fixity and inertia in fields of thought, including science. But unlike other spheres, religion is indistinguishable from bodies of dogma. Dogma is its essence. And it is this fact that goes far to explain the powerful influence exerted by religion upon human culture from the beginning of civilization.

---

[1] Alexis de Tocqueville, *Democracy in America,* trans. Phillips Bradley, 2 vols. (New York: Alfred A. Knopf, 1945), 2: 8.

Rites

Fourth, religion is composed of rites, by which I mean ways of behavior that reflect either the sacred or the dogmatic through fixed and binding ceremony or ritualized observance. Baptism is a rite; so is that final ceremony known as the "last rites" administered to the dying; so is marriage. The great religious festival days—Easter, Christmas, All Saints' Day among the Christians, Passover among the Jews, the Sabbath among both, and so on—are no more than days in which certain mandatory rites, that is, ritually prescribed ways of behavior having some reference to dogma or to what is cherished as sacred, are duly observed. A rite, in short, is a way of behavior, individual or collective, just as a dogma is a way of belief. A rite becomes just as sacred as that element of belief it is designed to celebrate. The Christian Mass is a rite; and, like the wine and the wafer that are its crucial elements, it is considered just as sacred as the belief in transubstantiation which is, in theory at least, the sole reason for its existence.

It is the mark of a rite that it can become almost independent of belief. We do not know, can hardly guess, how many of those who go through the motions of a given rite actually believe in, or even consciously think about, its underlying idea or dogma. A great deal of culture has a certain ritualistic character. We often follow a certain folkway or participate in a certain ceremony, more or less automatically, rarely if ever stopping to reflect on why we do it.

The Cult

Fifth among the central elements of religion is what Durkheim and other students of religion have called the cult. We may think of it as a kind of social molecule: the smallest structure capable of containing the elements of the sacred, of rites, and of dogmas that we have just examined. It is, of course, the collective or communal aspect of the cult that is distinctive. Anyone who has ever "really practised a religion," Durkheim writes,

> knows very well that it is the cult which gives rise to those impressions of joy, of interior peace, of serenity, of enthusiasm, which are, for the believer, an experimental proof of his beliefs. The cult is not simply a system of signs by which the faith is outwardly translated; it is a collection of the means by which this is created and recreated periodically.[2]

[2] Émile Durkheim, *The Elementary Forms of Religious Life*, trans. Joseph Ward Swain (London: Allen & Unwin; New York: Macmillan Co., 1915), p. 417.

Every cult, as Durkheim goes on to point out, presents a double aspect: one negative, the other positive. The two aspects are inseparable, but they are distinguishable. The negative pertains to those activities within the cult designed to forbid certain activities which might be a transgression or violation of the sacred. Here we are in the realm of taboo; through the negative rites of the cult, the individual is freed from contamination or possible contamination emanating from the profane world. The positive aspect of the cult is, however, the more important, for here are to be found the symbols and rites through which, in the company of others, the individual maintains directly his relationship to his god. Here, in the positive aspect of the cult, we are dealing with human beings taking on, as it were, the substance of their god, and in the process finding sources of strength they would not otherwise have.

The cult in religion is cellular; it is also constitutive to society as a whole where an intimate relation exists between religion and the social order. Without the cult, religion—however individualistic it might seem at first glance, or, at the opposite extreme, however vast and bureaucratized, as in certain modern religions—could not last long. It is, as Durkheim stressed, not merely the structure within which religion originated in the first instance; it remains the crucial molecule of the social structure of religion, however large and impersonal that structure may be or seem.

These, then, are the central elements of the religious community, no matter what may be the specific modes of faith and doctrine accompanying them in any given religion. That they are as distinctive as are the elements of the military and political types of community is evident enough. It is, of course, the very distinctiveness in each of them that provides the substance of the oftentimes bitter conflicts among the three sets of elements, the three radically different types of community, to be found from earliest times in the West.

Christianity, War, and Politics

The relation between Christianity and social philosophy in the West is rooted in the circumstances of Christianity's origin in first-century Rome. The same currents we have already seen in connection with the politicization of Roman society by Augustus and the emergence of Roman law carried with them the crucial elements of Christianity's rise as one of the world's great universal religions. We are inclined to think of Christianity as an offshoot of Judaism. This is correct enough if we have reference solely to the life of Jesus, but it is inadequate in reference to the origin, development, and diffusion of Christianity conceived as a *universal* religion—that is, a religion open by creed to everyone, irrespective of kinship, ethnic, or geographical background. I shall have more to say momentarily about the nature of universal religions and about their almost invariable historical relation to special circumstances of war and politics. It will suffice here to say only that when we refer to the universal religions, we mean faiths such as Christianity, Buddhism, Confucianism, and Islam, in all of which the emphasis rests on a belief or set of beliefs available to everyone without regard to nationality, race, sex, or locality. Clearly, when such a religion takes hold and becomes a reigning influence in human belief, more than strictly doctrinal elements are involved. We are obliged to look also at the social and cultural conditions surrounding these doctrinal elements.

The rise and developing success of Christianity as a universal religion is incomprehensible apart from the breakdown in the Roman world of traditional forms of belief, most of which were rooted in ancient ties of kinship and locality. Gilbert Murray, in his notable study of the successive phases of Greek religion, *Five Stages of Greek Religion*, has dealt with Christianity as precisely a phase of Greek belief, set in post-Alexandrian social, cultural, and spiritual dislocation. This is incontestable, especially as it concerns the central theological elements of Christianity, overwhelmingly Greek in substance. But it must be remembered that the Greek world was wholly under the government of Rome at the time of Christianity's emergence and subsequent development. If we are to understand the institutional progress of Christianity during the first century, its extraordinary record of conversions, proselytizations, and establishment of religious communities everywhere in the Roman world, we must see this religion in the light of what it was able to displace in that world. And here, once again, we are in the presence of the ancient and powerful kinship group—battered, as we have already seen, by the forces of war and politicization in the Greco-Roman world, now battered by the gospel of Christ.

In the beginning in Rome—as in Greece and indeed everywhere in the world—religion was little more than a function of the kinship community and of its cornerstone, the *patria potestas*. We shall follow Fustel de Coulanges here in his classic account of the traditional, patriarchal, household religion of the Greeks and Romans, before its destruction by the forces of war, political centralization, and, finally, Christianity.

> In the house of every Greek and Roman was an altar; on this altar there had always to be a small quantity of ashes, and a few lighted coals. It was the sacred obligation of the master of every house to keep the fire up day and night. Woe betide the unfortunate house where it was extinguished. Every evening they covered the coals with ashes to prevent them from being entirely consumed. In the morning the first care was to revive this fire with a few twigs. The fire ceased to glow upon the altar only

when the entire family had perished; an extinguished hearth, an extinguished family, were synonymous expressions among the ancients.[3]

The sacred fire, Fustel de Coulanges tells us, was the very symbol of the unity and the continuity of the family. The flame represented the ancestors, those who had founded a given family line and whose spirits in the world of the departed would be in anguish and torment if the living did not render them respect through tending the eternal flame. But the flame also represented the unborn, those whose future lives would keep the family line intact, who would render devotion to those now living but soon to be departed, precisely as the present living rendered respect to those in the supernatural world. The kinship community, as we observed, has always been regarded, where it has been sovereign, as a partnership—to borrow here from Edmund Burke's great definition of human society—of the dead, the living, and the unborn.

The most fundamental elements of the kinship community were rites connected with birth, marriage, and death. To consider the first: no one in the ancient family system, or even in many family systems that exist now, was literally born into his family. The biological fact of birth made it all possible, of course; but until one was baptized, given formal entry into the family through rites that could be counted upon to appease the souls of the departed and that would confer upon him proper kinship identity, he was not, strictly speaking, really "born." The all-important ritual, coming usually about eleven days after biological birth, through which the child was accepted into the family, was the "birth" that counted. It was the family's right—exercised through its head, usually after consultation with other elders—to reject the infant, to put it to death as painlessly as possible, if it was not physically normal or if pressure on available food supply made any new mouth a threat to the community's well-being. Birth was thus the first of the crises of existence that had to be met through sacred means. The social identity given an infant through this ritual was the basis of that sanctity of human life within the community which has extended in diverse ways down to the present time.

Likewise marriage was a major element of the kinship community, and of the religious community embedded within it. In the ancient kinship system, such as that among Greeks, Romans, Persians, and many other peoples known to us, a marriage did not in itself necessarily establish a new family or even household. Marriage was not conceived as a contract uniting two distinct people, the one male, the other female.

[3] Numa Denis Fustel de Coulanges, *The Ancient City*, trans. Willard Small (Boston: Lee and Shepard, 1889), p. 29.

It was rather, like the birth rite, essentially a means whereby one person, the female, was "adopted" into a family to be the legitimate mate of a male in that family. Again we can turn to Fustel de Coulanges's words on the subject:

> Two families live side by side; but they have different gods. In one, a young daughter takes a part, from her infancy, in the religion of her father; she invokes his sacred fire; every day she offers it libations. She surrounds it with flowers and garlands on festal days. She asks its protection, and returns thanks for its favors. This paternal fire is her god. Let a young man of the neighboring family ask her in marriage, and something more is at stake than to pass from one house to the other. She must abandon the paternal fire, and henceforth invoke that of her husband. She must abandon her religion, practise other rites, and pronounce other prayers. . . .
>
> Marriage is therefore a grave step for the young girl, and not less grave for the husband; for this religion requires that one shall have been born near the sacred fire, in order to have the right to sacrifice at it. And yet he is now about to bring a stranger to this hearth; with her he will perform the mysterious ceremonies of his worship; he will reveal the rites and formulas which are the patrimony of his family. There is nothing more precious than this heritage; these gods, these rites, these hymns which he has received from his fathers, are what protect him in this life, and promise him riches, happiness, and virtue.[4]

Death was likewise an integral part of this religion. In many ways death rites were the most important of all observances, for it was only through the small amounts of food left on the hearth at night and libations offered that the souls of the departed members of the family were sustained in the afterworld. This was a cardinal element of belief in the traditional Roman family of earliest times.

> The worship of the dead in no way resembled the Christian worship of the saints. One of the first rules of this worship was that it could be offered by each family only to those deceased persons who belonged to it by blood. The law . . . forbade a stranger to approach a tomb. To touch a tomb with his foot, even by chance, was an impious act, after which the guilty one was expected to pacify the dead and purify himself. . . . The worship of the dead was nothing more than the worship of ancestors.

4 Ibid., p. 53.

Lucian, while ridiculing common beliefs, explains them clearly to us when he says the man who has died without leaving a son, receives no offerings, and is exposed to perpetual hunger.[5]

Far worse than hunger, though, for departed souls was the dread threat of loss of identity, of being cut off from ties with the living and those yet to be born. No fate was held to be worse than losing one's name and identity; and fear of this happening in the afterworld, together with the belief that only males could perform the rites necessary to preserve the identity and spiritual being of the departed, led to every family's absolute need for at least one son. If a son was not born naturally, adoption was the invariable expedient, and Roman tradition made no distinction whatever between the rights and privileges of natural and adopted sons.

It should not be thought that Roman religion down to the beginning of the age in which Christianity appeared was exclusively devoted to the Lares and Penates, to the family rites of birth, marriage, and death. There were cherished gods of the Roman people as a whole. As in Greece, some of the most beautiful temples were for the express purpose of honoring these gods of the larger community. Even in them, however, the spirit of exclusion was dominant; that is, they were Roman gods, whom no other people could worship. Just as Jahweh, on his first appearance in the Old Testament, is the god of the Hebrews and no other people, so with the gods of Rome, and, for that matter, of all the other peoples of whom we have record in an equivalent phase of religious history. The Roman community was only an enlarged family, and the same attitude prevailed toward the gods of the community at large as toward those of any given household. Religion was the very opposite of what we call universal religion.

Nevertheless, it was precisely in a Roman setting that one of the greatest of universal religions, Christianity, made its initial appearance and became within a very few centuries the greatest single structure of authority in the entire Western world. The success of Christianity, its development from the tiny Judaic sect that Jesus founded in a remote corner of the Roman Empire into what became increasingly the religion of the Roman masses, especially in the cities, and then the supreme and official religion of the Roman Empire; all of this is intimately connected with matters we have already touched upon in a different frame of reference. For, apart from the kind of disintegration of the Roman kinship community with which we have already dealt in the context of war and the military and the kind of political centralization of Rome that followed, with the inevitable devitalization of regional and local culture

5 Ibid., pp. 42–43.

and the creation of atomized masses, it would be very difficult to account, at least in scholarly terms, for the rise and success of Christianity.

The Rise of Universal Religion

It will be useful at this point to digress briefly in order to consider in more detail the origins and the distinctive characteristics of the universal religions, Christianity among them. As I have noted above with respect to Christianity, the essence of a universal religion has nothing to do with the number of its adherents or the number of places in the world where they may be found. Christianity would have been a universal religion had it failed to survive the Roman Empire. Buddhism in India, and then in nearly all of Asia, would have been a universal religion no matter how few its followers. So too with Confucianism, Taoism, Zoroastrianism, Pythagoreanism (never more than a small sect), and, finally, Islam. What gives identity to the universal religion is, as I have stressed, its openness to all individuals willing to accept its doctrines, willing to worship as it prescribes. It does not matter that one may be of alien race, religion, or family. All that matters is that he be willing to cast out alien gods and fully accept the tenets, prescriptions, and prohibitions of the new faith.

It is interesting to note that the universal religions first made their appearance on any significant scale of influence about the sixth century B.C. This is one of the more remarkable, and still largely unexplained, phenomena of comparative history. The magnitude as well as fascination of the problem is suggested instantly when we become aware of the sheer geographical spread of these simultaneous eruptions of religious universalism. In the same century we find Confucius and Lao-tze in China, Buddha and Mahavira in India, Zoroaster in Persia, Isaiah (that is, the so-called Second Isaiah) in Israel, and Pythagoras and Thales in the Greek world. Great as are the differences among these religious thinkers, and among the religions that bear the names of some of them, they are alike in their repudiation of kinship, race, or locality as the constituent principle of religious belief. In each of them, whether rooted primarily in ethics, as in Confucianism, or in the mystic doctrine of numbers, as in Pythagoreanism, or in the foretelling of the "suffering son," as in Isaiah, we are in the presence of a religion that is open to all who will but accept and believe in the set of doctrines that is its heart. When, a half millennium later, Christianity and, a full millennium later, Islam made their appearance in the world, they too, though in radically different ways, espoused the kind of universalism of belief and membership that first rose on the grand scale in the sixth century B.C.

Conflict among religions became inevitable with the rise of universal religions. Whereas the older, traditional, preuniversal religions were positively opposed to proselytism—given the indissoluble tie between religion and one's inherited status in family or people, and given also the spirit of exclusiveness that was therefore bound to prevail—the newer universal forms of religion made conflict with "false" or "alien" beliefs a matter of bounden duty for their proselytizers and missionaries.

But the relation between conflict and universal religion is more fundamental than anything that might be inferred from the foregoing remarks. For, without a prior condition of conflict of peoples, values, and allegiances—the kind of conflict that has also, as we have seen, led to the rise of military forces and of political organization—it is inconceivable that the universal religions would ever have arisen in the first place. Far more than coincidence is involved in the fact that the universal religions of the world have arisen in areas and during periods of intense military and political strife. From such strife and the various conflicts of values and allegiances involved came growing numbers of dislocated individuals and peoples, who were shaken in their relationship to old ethnic or kinship gods. A field was thus created that could not help but become ever more fertile ground for the rise of new and attractive forms of religious faith. Nothing is more difficult than to shake people free of religious beliefs in which they have found uninterrupted security. But when such security has been shattered or seriously threatened the work of conversion, of transferring religious membership and worship, is made much easier.

There is, however, another and possibly more fundamental relation between the rise of universal religions and the kind of conflict immemorially brought about by war and political organization. As Edward Jenks writes:

> Success in battle lies with big battalions; and, in order to get big battalions, it was necessary to weld together related but more or less independent tribes or clans. . . . But to achieve such a union, in the face of religious and social differences, must have been no easy task. As we have said, patriarchal society is easygoing, ill adapted to submit to the discipline and precautions necessary to successful military operations. Only a very powerful influence will bring about this result.[6]

Hence comes the value of a new religion that, transcending tribal and local jealousies, could at least create the possibility of a state of mind whereby a people's religious belief could be dislodged from family or racial status and made common, at least in theory, to all peoples.

[6] Edward Jenks, *The State and the Nation* (New York: E. P. Dutton, 1919), pp. 123–24.

I am not suggesting anything so absurd as the idea that the universal religions were founded by military leaders in quest of big battalions; nor am I suggesting that there is a natural affinity between the universal type of religion and the continued existence of large-scale warfare—though Christianity and Islam might both imply this, given their notable association during the past two millennia with extremely warlike peoples and settings. I am only making the point that a kind of natural identity of interest existed between political or military leaders, eager for their own reasons to weld unlike, highly particularized and localized communities into larger aggregates of state and empire, and the prophets of those religions, seeking, also for their own reasons, to weld these same communities into larger aggregates of common believers in a single god—the one, true God of all mankind, as each of the universal religions has proclaimed.

Inevitably, of course, the rise—and most especially the development and diffusion—of any universal religion carries with it some willingness on the part of its leaders to compromise now and then, to take over a people's ancient rites and beliefs and give them new significance, of course, as the means of encouraging conversion in large numbers. Every major universal religion is a composite of beliefs and rites which, in many instances, go back to earliest forms of religion. For example, no one familiar with Christian theology can do other than suppose the symbolism of family and kinship—manifest in the Christian's devotion to father, mother, and savior-son, Jesus, as well as in countless other uses of kinship nomenclature—to have been powerful in the minds of those early Christian missionaries seeking to lure Romans and others away from traditional household faith to become members of what they believed was the only true religion, that of Christ.

Christianity and Conflict

This brings us to the period in which Christianity, both as gospel and as social philosophy, took form, the age of the Caesars in imperial Rome. Conflict was the very essence of Christianity's relation to this age. In some degree, of course, conflict is involved in every form of religion, by the very nature of the fateful contrast between the sacred and the profane, between good and evil, between true gods and alien ones. But the conflict is on a much higher level and much more intense whenever a religion such as Christianity or Islam comes into existence; for, as just noted, one of its most sacred responsibilities, as reflected in the lives and actions of prophets and missionaries, is conscious and consecrated conflict with other religions as the means of liberating individuals from false beliefs and converting them to religious truth.

Among all the other social and psychological conflicts in first- and second-century Rome is the struggle between Christianity, first as a sect, then as a church, and those forms of traditional belief and membership that militated against Christian effort. We are accustomed to think of this conflict as largely one between Christians and the emperor, one of our favorite images of this conflict in legend being Christians thrown to the lions in the Colosseum. And we should never doubt that conflict between Christianity and the Roman state did indeed exist, often becoming very intense, with executions, tortures, and public spectacles of humiliation occasionally taking place. For Christians resisted service in Roman legions, even payment of taxes to the Roman government; often to the very end. They could seem, and often were in fact, subversive of Roman values. As late as the age of Diocletian, just prior to the time when Christianity became the official religion of Rome, there were executions of Christians in substantial numbers in one part of the empire or another. The elements of Christian theology that stress pacifism were anything but popular with Roman administrators and generals whose job it was to keep up Roman military strength.

Even so, we are obliged to look to still another type of conflict in order to explain a great deal that from at least the late first century on has been fundamental in Christian belief and practice. Here I refer to a conflict of values and allegiance at a level well below that of politics but in many ways far more intense and penetrating far more deeply into the psychological aspects of Christian proselytism, a conflict rarely thought of in the usual history of Christianity: that between Christianity and the Roman family. Let me begin by citing three very important passages from the New Testament Gospels:

> Do not think that I have come to bring peace on earth; I have not come to bring peace, but a sword. For I have come to set a man against his father, and a daughter against her mother, and a daughter-in-law against her mother-in-law; and a man's foes will be those of his own household. He who loves father or mother more than me is not worthy of me; and he who loves son or daughter more than me is not worthy of me; and he who does not take his cross and follow me is not worthy of me. He who finds his life will lose it, and he who loses his life for my sake will find it. [Matt. 10: 34–39.]

> And his mother and his brothers came; and standing outside they sent to him and called him. And a crowd was sitting about him; and they said to him, "Your mother and your brothers are outside, asking for you." And he replied, "Who are my mother and my brothers?" And looking around on those who sat about him he said, "Here are my mother and my brothers! Who-

ever does the will of God is my brother, and sister, and mother."
[Mark 3: 31–35.]

> Now great multitudes accompanied him; and he turned and
> said to them, "If any one comes to me and does not hate his own
> father and mother and wife and children and brothers and sisters,
> yes, and even his own life, he cannot be my disciple." [Luke 14:
> 25–26.]

The words, of course, are the words of Jesus to his followers. But
none of them could have been set down in writing prior to the middle
of the first century A.D., and in the cases of Mark and Luke quite possibly
nearer the end of the century than the middle. To what extent the words
were quite literally spoken by Jesus—in contrast to having received the
shading and glossing the words of great religious leaders commonly
receive from later interpreters whose responsibility it is to put these
words into lasting text—we cannot be absolutely sure. But it does not
matter, for whether the context is Roman Judaea during Jesus' lifetime
or some other part of the Roman Empire later, the practical import is the
same. Plainly, the words register sharp conflict between the religious
community and the values of kinship. Why, we must ask, did Jesus speak
as he did? Or, if we prefer, why was he made by later Gospel writers to
speak as he does in the passages? It is a question for the historian as well
as the theologian.

We begin our answer by calling attention to the profoundly communal character of Christianity from the very beginning. Such character,
to be sure, was not unique to Christianity at the time. As the Dead Sea
Scrolls have told us recently, there were other, earlier, communities of
belief and practice, complete indeed with many of the very articles of
faith that in due time were to become Christian. The notion of communal separation from the ills and corruptions of the larger society was
far from uncommon in the urban world of the Middle East during the
century or two leading up to the birth of Christianity.

Nevertheless, it is a fact that Christianity seems to have been from its
beginning profoundly oriented toward a communal character. There was,
of course, no unified church in the beginning. For a full century at least,
Christianity was no more than a congeries of cults or sects pursuing more
or less common rites, holding more or less common beliefs, centering
around the idea of Christ: his nativity, crucifixion, and resurrection. Not
until the assembly of Christians in the city of Rome, themselves reflecting
the priority of Rome in all other parts of the known world, assumed a
kind of headship over other Christians, with the leader of this assembly
becoming first among all Christian leaders in the Roman Empire, could
anything resembling a unified church be said to have existed.

It was, however, almost certainly the intensely communal character of each of these manifestations of Christianity that was chiefly responsible for the astonishing spread of this new religion in an empire and at a time when new religions were rife. On this point Gilbert Murray has written: "When I try to realize it [Christianity] as a sort of semi-secret society for mutual help with a mystical religious basis, resting first on the proletariats of Antioch, then spreading by instinctive sympathy to similar classes in Rome and the West . . . the various historical puzzles begin to fall into place." [7]

This, then, is the first point to keep in mind if we are to understand the conflict between Christianity and the family that is so vividly etched for us in the passages from the Gospels quoted above. Christianity was no mere pattern of belief spread among multitudes of people. It took form as primitive community: community in the hard sense of small groups of persons who often lived together, who sometimes pooled their property, and whose bounden responsibility it was to look out for one another in this world.

The second point to be clear on is the kind of people Christianity spread among in its amazing record of conversions during the first century, and the kind of society in which they lived. This society was deeply disorganized by the impact of war, depression, and the uprooting of membership in ancient structures. In the first chapter, specifically in our consideration of the Roman *patria potestas* in the age of Augustus, we saw something of this, and there is no need to repeat in any detail. It is important, though, to stress the fact that ages of perceived disorganization and dislocation are almost invariably rich in efforts to achieve forms of community through religious, as well as political and social, channels. Rome during the first century A.D. was fertile soil indeed for the proliferation of religious cults which could offer their communicants not merely hope of a better world after this life but also some kind of communal release from alienation and insecurity in this life. Christianity, most especially in its primitive first-century form, was almost ideally equipped to respond to such alienation and insecurity; for its message, its "good news," was precisely that of communal refuge.

Third, we must not overlook the fact that, disorganized as Roman society must have seemed to all those constituting what the historian A. J. Toynbee has in our own day so well called the "internal proletariat," there was yet one structure at least which continued to command a great deal of allegiance. This was the historic and still powerful family, organized on the basis of the *patria protestas*. Enfeebled though the family was, relatively speaking, by currents of change, it could yet be,

[7] Gilbert Murray, *Five Stages of Greek Religion*, 3d ed. (Boston: Beacon Press, 1951), p. 185.

and must very often have seemed to Christian preachers of the Gospel and other evangels, a formidable barrier to acceptance of Christianity's tenets. For, as we have already seen, the Roman family was itself a religious organization, centering around the Lares and Penates, spirits of hearth and ancestors. Christianity, like all evangelizing religions, addressed its message to individuals—men, women, even children. And so long as the family remained an intact structure, just so long did its very structure act to mediate, even to interfere with, the proselytizing efforts of the missionaries of Christ.

The strategy from the Christian point of view was thus a vital and almost obvious one: to denigrate so far as possible the historic and still deeply rooted kinship tie and to offer the community of Christ as itself the only real and true form of kinship. Thus we have, in the passages I chose from the New Testament (and there are others besides these which make the same point), the stress placed by Jesus on the insubstantiality and unreality of the kinship relation, even and especially his own relation to mother, father, brothers, and sisters; and thus, too, his transcending emphasis at one and the same time on the family character of Christianity.

"He who loves father or mother more than me is not worthy of me. . . ." "Whoever does the will of God is my brother, and sister, and mother." "My mother and my brothers are those who hear the word of God and do it." In such stark pronouncements we are permitted to sense very clearly indeed the kind of conflict of loyalty involved in Christianity's efforts to win adherents from the ranks of those in the Roman world who were still tightly bound to family. Christianity, as we know, addressed a great deal of its message to women. There is some ground in fact for regarding this religion, during the first century in any event, as involved in a kind of women's liberation: from the powerful patriarchal and masculine orientation of the traditional family. To succeed in disengaging women from their family ties—single women in high probability, for there is little if any evidence to suggest that Christian missionaries strove to interfere directly with marriage ties—it was necessary at one and the same time to denigrate the family and to proffer Christianity as itself a family—the highest of all types of family.

It is interesting, and in further documentation of the point I have just been making, that the word the Christians came to use widely for all non-Christians, for all who resisted the blandishments of Christian evangelism, was *pagan*. Now the Latin word *paganus* meant "rural dweller" or "countryman," in contrast to one who lived in the city or town. Why should such a word have become converted in time to mean one who resists the tenets of Christianity? The answer lies clearly in the fact that it was among rural inhabitants—invariably more conservative, as we know, than urbanites in acceptance of new and exotic values—that the Christian evangels had their greatest difficulties in winning converts. In rural areas the family ties and local religions were so strong and created such tenacious loyalties, that the collective term for the inhabitants of such areas, *pagans*, became in time the term for all nonbelievers.

Nor did conflict between kinship and the Christian community terminate with either official acceptance of Christianity as the religion of Rome in the late third century or the general disappearance of Roman imperial polity after the fifth century in many areas of Europe. In fact, we can see a major revival of such conflict during the period known today as the Dark Ages. For this was the period during which the Germanic tribes settled over all western Europe, with their own customs frequently supplanting those of the Romans and almost always proving to be in contrast and conflict. And the Germanic peoples were as thoroughly constituted in kinship terms as the Greeks and Romans had been a thousand years earlier, when they, too, had lived overwhelmingly in tribes, clans, and households. The conflict between Roman—Christian Roman for the most part, of course—and Teuton was to be seen in scores of ways; cultural, moral, and social. Not least among these conflicts was that between the kinship norms of the Teutons and the sacraments and dogmas of the Christians.

One illustration will suffice for this conflict. Marriage among the Germanic peoples was what it had once been among the Romans: a purely private transaction between two families through which one person, the young woman, became quite literally a member of a new family, that of her spouse. And the evidence indicates that the Germanic people, everywhere in western Europe during the centuries immediately following the fall of Rome, were exceedingly jealous of the preservation of this private, purely familial character of marriage. But within official Christianity, marriage had become one of the sacraments. It is, declared Christian writ, God alone who effects marriages, and he does this through his instrument, the church. From the point of view of Christians, therefore, marriages effected as the Germanic peoples insisted upon effecting them were not really marriages at all; they were regarded as illicit unions. But from the point of view of the Germanic people, marriage—and divorce—had no possible involvement in Christian doctrine.

For a long time there was in most parts of Europe—especially the rural areas, which overwhelmingly predominated—a kind of standoff. Gradually, however, we can see Christianity winning out. And it was vital, from the point of view of Christian discipline, that Christianity should win out in this matter. For there is no union, no ceremony, more fundamental in most human lives than that of marriage; and had Christianity been made forever an outsider in this matter, a great deal of its spiritual influence would have been accordingly destroyed. The time came when, with much pressure and, we may be sure, proffered rewards in the forms of blessing, the reluctant Germanic families were persuaded at least to hold their own private ceremony on the church steps, or at the entry to the chapel. Priests and others would be mere onlookers. From this it was but a short step really, though one requiring varying amounts of time depending on the part of Europe and the tenacity of Germanic custom, to taking the marriage ceremony into the church, all the way down to the altar. The final step was an obvious one: the priest would himself, speaking in God's name, effect the union, with the families now the onlookers.

There were, it should be stressed, many other ways in which the conflict of Christianity with the kinship community could be seen not only during the Middle Ages but even on into the modern world. What is today still called "common-law marriage" was no more than cohabitation by man and woman without either clerical or civil blessing that could be proved by witnesses to have lasted for some years. Such marriage was regarded as valid almost everywhere, in the United States as well as in Europe, until fairly recently. The point to be emphasized here is simply that common-law marriage was only a persistence of the Germanic claim of autonomy in matters of marriage. And throughout medieval and modern history, the Christian religion has steadfastly opposed such unions on the ground that not man but God makes marriages. Likewise, Christianity opposed other aspects of the traditional kinship community, such as the "oaths of compurgation," through which vows of loyalty to kinsmen were made superior to vows taken to God and church.

None of this is to suggest that conflict between the religious community and the kinship community is invariably fundamental. There have been, surely, far more instances of complementarity between the two than of discord or conflict. We can no more deduce firm and unyielding conflicts from social structure than we can harmonies. History alone will inform us in these matters. And, keeping the history of the West well before us, we can hardly overlook the instances of conflict between Christianity and the kinship system. Jesus' words "He who loves father and mother more than me is not worthy of me" could have been as easily addressed to other than kinship roles in surrounding society. And in due time, following the initial period of primitive Christianity, sentiments of like character, also drawn from Jesus' words in the New Testament, were indeed addressed to other roles: those of soldier, businessman, political ruler, all in society whose organizations or communities could now and then threaten that fundamental loyalty to Christ that the Christian community demanded.

Conflict between Christianity and external society is to be seen in one shape or another in whatever period we turn to during the nineteen hundred years which separate our age from the organizational beginnings of Christianity. If I have centered this section around the single conflict of religion and kinship, it is only because this type of conflict involving the history of religion is much less well known than others—for example, that between Christianity and the political states. The first century A.D. was not far along before Christian successes in proselyting were such as to stir profound concern in the minds of imperial officials and, no doubt, large numbers of more or less conservative Roman citizens no more eager to see established ways of thought challenged by new doctrines than are a great many people in our own age.

Whether in conflict with the traditional Roman *patria potestas*, with the Roman state and military legions, or later, during the period of the Reformation, with the national state, conflict with other institutions has been a persistent aspect of the history of Christianity. And the reason for this lies, as I have suggested, in a communal ethic in Christianity, which included, or sought to include, the total life of the individual. Such an ethic could not help, cannot help even today, but bring Christianity into direct confrontation with other institutions, among them those of the state, the economy, and war, each of which also seeks a larger share of individual allegiance.

Saint Augustine and the City of God

Nowhere in the long history of Christian thought and literature is there more testimony to what I have just said about the inherent conflict between the religious community and the surrounding world than in the writings of Saint Augustine (354–430). Here we shall have particular reference to the most famous and undoubtedly the greatest of his works, *The City of God*. Written in the early fifth century, it is addressed not to any visible community on earth, not even to the community of Christians within which Augustine lived the greater part of his own life, so much as it is to the *invisible* community that Augustine saw as formed by all genuine believers, all true children of God, from Adam onward. In its extraordinary command of the philosophy, science, and literature of the ancient world, in its virtual intoxication with God and the evidence of his presence in the universe, *The City of God* was regarded even in its own time as second only to the Gospels themselves in the authenticity of its Christian message. And it has been regarded very nearly so ever since. Not only Roman Catholics through all ensuing centuries, but even the Protestants of the sixteenth and seventeenth centuries who revolted against the Church of Rome have drawn immeasurable vision from its pages.

Crisis is at the very heart of the book. There was, first and most evident, the crisis of the Roman Empire, which by the late fourth and early fifth centuries lay virtually beleaguered by barbarian Germanic military forces. Even the Sacred City itself was in mortal danger. In the year 410 it was invaded and sacked by the soldiers of Alaric. In the minds of countless Romans, Christian as well as pagan, the awful question raised itself: Was the conquest of Rome, along with prior enfeeblement of Roman character and strength, the result of ancient pagan gods' displeasure with the Romans over their government's acceptance of Christianity as the official religion? All the overtones of crisis attended this question; and it was to this question, as we shall see, that Augustine replied with *The City of God.*

But behind the book lies another crisis, a personal one: the crisis of faith that had been induced in Augustine by his momentous conversion from the pagan religion of Manichaeism to the Christian faith and creed. It must be seen as one of the profoundest, most agonizing conversions in religious history. It is in Augustine's *Confessions* that we are enabled to see in full intensity this personal crisis, which was no less fruitful for his ideas and works than that of the Roman Empire. The *Confessions* stands alongside *The City of God* as among the most profoundly conceived religious works in all history.

During his lifetime (354–430) Augustine wrote on a wide range of subjects: religious, political, historical, and philosophical. We shall confine our attention to but two of his many books, the two I have already mentioned; from them we shall gain sufficient insight into the Augustinian conception of the religious community.

The Confessions

Let us begin with the personal crisis of faith, so eloquently described at length in the *Confessions.* From it we learn that although he was first brought up by his mother in the Christian faith, he left it after he went off to school, becoming a convert to Manichaeism, a religion of which the central idea is the remorseless and endless struggle between the powers of Good and Evil, of Light and Darkness. For some time following his schooling, Augustine lived in the city of Rome, teaching and studying philosophy, active with the Manichaeans, who quickly recognized his intellectual powers. At their behest he went in 384 to Milan, there to continue his teaching and studies.

There, shortly after he arrived, he underwent a conversion to Christianity that, in the light of subsequent Western history, proved nearly as momentous as the earlier one of Saul on the road to Damascus. Augustine tells us in his *Confessions* that even before departing Rome for Milan he had been deeply troubled by certain doubts regarding Manichaeism. It was in Milan, however, that these doubts came to the surface; and there, after two years of profound spiritual agitation, incessant study, and deep soul searching, he was converted to the gospel of Christ. He was baptized a Christian at the age of thirty-three, on Easter Sunday, 387. There followed an impressive career of renown within the church, which bore fruit not only in his matchless religious writings, along with his philosophical, historical, and political treatises, but also in a notable succession of church offices culminating in 395 in his appointment as bishop of Hippo, a city in North Africa a few miles from where he was born. He lived in this city until his death in 430.

I have briefly sketched Augustine's biography because, unlike the case of most of those that concern us in this book, the events of his life compete strongly with the ideas of his books for our close attention. In few minds has the deep disquietude of a personal life become so sensitively translated into the varied problems and themes of distinguished works in philosophy and theology.

We see this most luminously in the *Confessions*, which is at once autobiography and religious mysticism at the highest level. In it we have an opportunity to see the degree to which a mind, troubled, agitated, and driven by forces external and internal, can find in the repose of religious dogma a sense of certainty and a feeling of community, of oneness with past, present, and future, that has never ceased to fascinate its readers down to the present day. Augustine's has been called a God-intoxicated mind. There is no exaggeration in the words. The opening words of the *Confessions* are: "Great art thou, O Lord, and greatly to be praised; great is Thy power, and of Thy wisdom there is no end. And man, being a part of Thy creation, desires to praise Thee. . . ." And praise God Augustine does, through several hundred pages, by making the events of his own troubled life but steps in God's final demonstration to him of the sacred community that is the Church of Christ. There is, of course, a great deal in the book about Augustine—his deep respect for his pagan father, his adoration of his Christian mother, his schooling, the sexual temptations to which he succumbed, the mistresses he loved, his adventures in politics and in the Manichaean religion and with cherished friends, and, finally, the details of his conversion and subsequent service to the church; but it is a mark of the book's genuineness that all of these facts are set up, not so much as milestones in Augustine's personal life, as tributes to God. The *Confessions* is basically an apologia with a mystical structure, in other words, an explanation of how Augustine found his way to God.

It also shows clearly his adoration of his mother. Psychoanalysts have sometimes made this relation of Augustine to his mother the key factor in his whole life, seeing in his conversion to Christianity, and in his inexhaustible and almost caressing love of God, a sublimation of his unquenchable adoration of his mother. There is undoubtedly something in this, though the springs of motivation run deep and in confused channels. One need but read the impassioned and sensual account midway in the *Confessions* of a long visit with his mother not long before her death, when she was fifty-six and he thirty-three, only shortly after his baptism in Christ, to see the full basis of psychoanalytic interpretation. Rarely has love of either God or mother been more beautifully and movingly expressed, or more closely joined and more intimately with sensual as well as spiritual delights.

But the major point of the *Confessions* is, as I have said, its detailed account of a personal quest for belief, a quest that reached its final resting place in the community of Christ. The following passage reveals clearly enough the soul of lover, of poet, of seeker of intimacy beyond all known intimacies, of mystic, in Augustine:

> The angels fell, the soul of man fell, and they have thus indicated the abyss in that dark deep, ready for the whole spiritual creation, unless Thou hadst said from the beginning, "Let there be light," and there had been light, and every obedient intelligence of Thy celestial City had cleaved to Thee, and rested in Thy Spirit, which unchangeably is "borne over" everything changeable. Otherwise even the heaven of heavens itself would have been a darksome deep, whereas now it is light in the Lord. For even in that wretched restlessness of the spirits who fell away, and, when unclothed of the garments of Thy light, discovered their own darkness, dost Thou sufficiently disclose how noble Thou hast made the rational creature; to which nought which is inferior to Thee will suffice to yield a happy rest, and so not even herself. For Thou, O our God, shalt enlighten our darkness; from Thee are derived our garments of light, and then shall our darkness be as the noon-day. Give Thyself unto me, O my God, restore Thyself unto me; behold, I love Thee, and if it be too little, let me love Thee more strongly. I cannot measure my love so that I may come to know how much there is yet wanting in me, ere my life run into Thy embracements, and not be turned away until it be hidden in the secret place of Thy Presence. This only I know, that woe is me except in Thee—not only without, but even also within myself; and all plenty which is not my God is poverty to me.[8]

It would be hard to find in the entire literature of lyric love, let alone the literature of religious mysticism, more ardent, more sensuous, more opulent words than those. If, as I have said, Augustine's was a God-intoxicated mind, it was also a love-intoxicated one. And in his case the fusion was a mighty one, issuing in lines of poetic loveliness as well as in lines of magisterial philosophic profundity.

And underlying his whole life was the desperate search for, and then veneration, cherishment of, intellectual peace. The final lines of

[8] *The Confessions of St. Augustine*, trans. J. G. Pilkington (New York: Heritage Press, 1963), p. 259.

the *Confessions* show the extent to which Augustine had found this peace, this community of mind, heart, and soul, in his God:

> . . . But Thou, being the Good, needing no good, art ever at rest, because Thou Thyself art Thy rest. And what man will teach man to understand this? Or what angel, an angel? Or what angel, a man? Let it be asked of Thee, sought in Thee, knocked for at Thee; so, even so shall it be received, so shall it be found, shall it be opened. Amen.[9]

The City of God

But we must now turn to *The City of God*, which of all Augustine's works is the one most closely concerned with matters related to the nature of man, society, culture, and history. He wrote this work during the years 413–426, when his own by-now-unassailable faith in Christ and his knowledge of Christian writ, as well as of pagan philosophy, were all at their height, as were his own personal powers. Gone in these years are the kinds of issues with which he had wrestled so strenuously earlier, amply described in the *Confessions* some two decades before. What we now find, however, are problems, issues, torments which sprang, not from personal life and nature, but from the age in which he lived. This was the age in which the once-invincible power of the great and renowned Roman Empire had proved itself unequal to the invasion of the Germanic barbarians.

It would be hard to find a proper analogue today to the symbolic significance of the sack of Rome by Alaric and his Visigoths in the year 410. The road leading to this event had been, of course, a long one, measured in number of square miles that had fallen to barbarians, number of areas in the entire known civilized world from which Roman governors and legionaries had been forced to retreat, no longer protected by the once-mighty lifelines of Roman power and and wealth. The third century, as we know from many texts and inscriptions, had been a hard one in Rome itself, abounding in famine, plague, as well as military hardships and political dislocations. All of this the Roman people had been able to assimilate in their minds if only because adversity had been gradual and cumulative. Now, however, they were confronted with what for a thousand years had been deemed impossible: the fall of the "eternal" city, before the fierce soldiers of Alaric. This dread event in 410 understandably had the effect of summoning up for Romans bitter and melancholy remembrance of all past defeats and convulsions in society. It was not difficult for the pagan Romans to match these with successes that had attended Christianity ever

---

9 Ibid., p. 285.

since its acceptance by the government in the fourth century. Why, a growing number of people found themselves asking, should not Rome's decline and now disaster be attributed to the Romans' own true gods' punishment for the betrayal of faith involved in Rome's official acceptance of Christianity?

This was, in a very real sense, Augustine's point of departure. His *City of God* is made the powerful and lasting religious work it is by the fact that it is simultaneously theology and philosophy of history. Both aspects of the book are direct responses to what appeared to Augustine himself as well as to countless non-Christian minds in the ancient world as the crisis of empire, the crisis of the celebrated Pax Romana. Rome had fallen, tragically and desolatingly, in the popular mind. How was this fall to be explained? And, by no means incidentally, what was Christianity's—and the Christian God's—role in the fall of Rome?

Augustine's answer was a powerful one—powerful, we know, in the estimation of his own day and powerful also during the next fifteen hundred years in the effect which it and its philosophical method were to manifest on nearly all writers, whether religious or secular, who dealt with the origin, development, and fate of mankind. For Augustine was the very first philosopher in Western history to conceive mankind as a single, unified entity, possessed of a history of its own in precisely the sense that any single people or nation is so possessed. We call this the *ecumenical idea*. All previous philosophers and historians had conceived of and dealt with only single peoples, such as the Greeks, Persians, Egyptians, Romans—in occasional interaction with one another, yes, but nevertheless distinct and separate, in no way mere elements or phases of some larger total entity known as mankind. For Augustine, however, all such individual peoples were indeed but elements or phases of the larger, temporally continuous entity which he designated as "the human race" or "mankind." All racial, ethnic, political, and national differences became muted in Augustine's mind, only ephemeral and superficial. What is alone fundamental and lasting through human history is mankind as a whole, product of God's creative will and enjoying existence throughout its history only in God's contemplation.

It was this envisagement of a unified, total, organismic mankind that allowed Augustine to deal with each specific people known to him—Hebrews, Babylonians, Egyptians, Greeks, Romans, and others—as manifestations of "stages" of development in the life of mankind. The epitome of the Augustinian view of human history is to be found in the following brief passage, one that would prove to be perhaps the single most quoted, or at least used, analogy in the next fifteen hundred years of Western writing on the philosophy of history:

> The education of the human race, represented by the people of God, has advanced, like that of an individual, through certain

epochs, or, as it were, ages, so that it might gradually rise from earthly to heavenly things, and from the visible to the invisible.[10]

How could such a rendering of human history—in which Augustine with vast historical detail drawn from all records known to him and other scholars sets forth at length the history of mankind—be a solution to the problem of the crisis of empire that was, as I noted, the point of departure for *The City of God?* The answer is clear: by showing that contemporary troubles, in Rome and in the world at large, are manifestations of the "old age" of mankind—of the "individual" to which Augustine likens mankind, its history and its "education" in time. The world as a whole, declares Augustine, is now in its very old and hence feeble and declining age. When decay has reached a certain further point, "then shall the figure of this world pass away in a conflagration of universal fire, as once before the world was flooded with a deluge of universal water." [11]

This, then, is the perspective in which Augustine sets the time of troubles that was Rome's in his own fifth century. It is a historical perspective, or, more accurately, a developmental one, through which the hardships of the present are made to seem the consequences of inexorable trends and forces that have been operating from the very beginning. It is obviously a contextual view and also an evolutionary (in the social-religious sense) view that Augustine gives us.

Mankind began in one man, Adam, and all that has happened to it since—all its nobility and its baseness, its achievements and its failures, its glories and its ignominies—has proceeded from potentialities that God placed in Adam and then Eve. Not for Augustine any notion of multiple origins for mankind, with ineradicable racial or other differences in the various branches of the human race. Mankind is a single entity. *All* men are the descendants of Adam. All history, through the successive ages and epochs represented by the peoples known to us, is but the unfolding of potentiality, the manifestation of the divinely created latency.

The organismic view is strong in Augustine's work. The history or development of the human race in all time is, he tells us, analogous to the growth of a single individual. Thus we have in Augustine the conception of genetic continuity of stages in time, one emerging from the other. We have the conceptions of "youth," "maturity," and "old age" applied to society and culture—with the senescence of a single people, and eventually of mankind as a whole, built just as organically into its development as are the two earlier stages. It was absolutely inevitable, Augustine writes, that Roman civilization should someday decline and then suffer extinction; the same fate had befallen other peoples, he points out. It has

---

[10] Augustine, *The City of God*, trans. Marcus Dods (New York: Random House, Modern Library, 1950), bk. 10, sect. 14.

[11] Ibid., bk. 20, sect. 16.

befallen them, as it is now befalling Rome, because growth and decay are the law of all things, world and mankind included.

The Greeks and Romans had believed in the principle of growth and decay; but for such philosophers as Plato, Aristotle, Lucretius, and Seneca, reality consisted of an endless series of cycles of growth and decay. There was no view of mankind as a single organism made up of interdependent parts undergoing this cycle and being foredestined to universal destruction in time through decay. Augustine, however, saw but one process of history; one that involved mankind as a whole, one that had a single origin, one that would someday have a single ending in total catastrophe. Then, with human history completed for all time, the *transhistorical* would begin, and the City of God would be realized for eternity. We shall come back to this in a moment.

The process Augustine describes for us is a *necessary* one, that is, structurally and genetically necessary. Nothing in the development of the human race has been the result of chance or accident. God laid out a plan of development when he created the first human being, and not even his omnipotence has ever been used, Augustine argues, to deflect mankind from the course of development set for it. It was *necessary* that there be the Fall, with Adam and Eve thus sent out into the world and with the human race their issue. It was *necessary* that Cain kill Abel. It was *necessary* that the Hebrews emancipate themselves from the Babylonian captivity. For all that the books of the Old Testament give us is part of the chain of events leading inexorably up to the appearance of Christ. It was *necessary* that Christ die for the sins of mankind. And, concludes Augustine, in detail and at length, it is *necessary* that not only Rome but all mankind should at this time be in irreversible decline, with the total and eternal ending of human history but a short time away. Everything that has happened, is happening now, and will happen in the short time remaining is necessary, for the reason that it is all drawn directly from the human constitution, from the nature of mankind as God created this nature and then allowed it to grow and develop.

Thus we are given, in matchless detail of argument, the Augustinian epic of man. It was one that served admirably, for Christians at any rate, to explain why Rome was undergoing its convulsive, empire-shattering dislocations. It put these dislocations in a philosophy of history, in a pattern of human development, that went all the way back to the beginning of man. The entire epic of man arose, for Augustine, from man's own divided nature, containing both good and evil elements that are constantly at war with one another.

Actually, we can see in *The City of God* two epics, though they are closely joined to each other. In one, the best known, we have the epic of the Fall. In the beginning life was good, a reflection of the goodness of the God that created life. But through egoism, lust, and selfishness, reflected in Adam's sin, came about the momentous fall from grace, when Adam and Eve were expelled from the Garden of Eden. From this unfolds a picture of an incessant cumulation of evil in the world, making necessary the eventual destruction of mankind and the world, a destruction that was already beginning, Augustine believed, in the Roman Empire of his time.

But we should not be blind to the other epic that is clearly set forth in *The City of God*: that of progress in knowledge, culture, and the arts. Despite a widespread view that Augustine was concerned only with the decline and degradation of mankind, he gives us a superb picture of man's progress through the ages in book 22 of *The City of God*. In an almost odelike way, suggestive of ancient Greek and nineteenth-century philosophers of progress, Augustine recounts the wonders of achievement that man has made possible through his own efforts:

> What wonderful—one might say stupefying—advances has human industry made in the arts of weaving and building, of agriculture and navigation! With what endless variety are designs in pottery, painting, and sculpture produced, and with what skill executed! What wonderful spectacles are exhibited in the theatres, which those who have not seen them cannot credit! . . . To express and gain entrance for thoughts, what a multitude and variety of signs there are, among which speaking and writing hold first place! What ornaments has eloquence at command to delight the mind! What wealth of sound is there to captivate the ear! . . . What skill has been attained in measures and numbers! With what sagacity have the movements and connections of the stars been discovered! . . .[12]

There is thus in *The City of God*, at one and the same time, the epic of man's intellectual, artistic, and technological advance and also the epic of his spiritual and moral fall. And it is the genius of Augustine to fuse these, to make them interdependent. For he shows us that from the beginning, with the very first biblical man, in whom there was a combination of good and evil, all that has intensified man's intellectual advance has intensified his moral decline as well. Augustine was not the first to put together the notions of good and evil in this fashion: far back in Greek thought can be found the idea that knowledge can corrupt morality. And, as we know, this idea remains powerful even in our own day. In the writings of such prophets of our own age as A. J. Toynbee, Albert Schweitzer, and Reinhold Niebuhr, is to be found the view that the psychological qualities which go into the making of technology,

12 Ibid., bk. 22, sect. 24.

science, and the arts—such qualities as ambition and desire for status, fame, and power—can also corrupt the character of individuals and lead to a weakening of the social bond.

And this conflict is at the very heart of what Augustine calls the two cities: the City of God and the City of Man. He tells us in the final paragraph of book 14 that these two cities have been formed by two loves: "the earthly by the love of self, even to the contempt of God; the heavenly by the love of God, even to the contempt of self. The former, in a word, glorifies the self; the latter God." [13]

It is in the running commentary throughout Augustine's book on the two cities that we are best able to see the very luminous vision of community in Augustine's mind. Each of the two cities is in its way a mode of community. That which he calls the City of Man is community built upon the web of men's social, economic, and political interests. It can produce good things, and often has, as we have just seen in Augustine's ode to human progress. But it remains nonetheless a precarious community, for it is founded alone upon love of man and of the interests that are inseparable from man. If it is rooted in love, this is still *profane* love, not the immortal *sacred* love, in which self is forgotten, that is found only in the community of God.

From the time of the Fall, there has been relentless conflict between the two cities, or communities. I mentioned above Augustine's early religious devotion to Manichaeism, with its conception of constant and abiding warfare between the community of Light and the community of Darkness, between absolute Good and absolute Evil. Although Augustine became a Christian, he retained this obsessive interest in conflict. And conflict is the very essence of the relation in his work between the two communities.

The human race, he tells us, is distributed "into two parts, the one consisting of those who live according to man, the other of those who live according to God. And these we mystically call the two cities, or the two communities of men, of which the one is predestined to reign eternally with God, and the other to suffer eternal punishment with the devil. . . ." [14]

Augustine does not categorically repudiate the City of Man. All of us, in at least a part of our lives, must live in this city; for it is our economy and polity. Good things, reckoned in earthly terms, spring from it. At its highest and best, Augustine declares, the Roman Empire was a splendid manifestation of the City of Man. Augustine plainly gloried in being a Roman. But it is the fate of this city that it must in time die, to be succeeded by the city that is built upon sacred love, love of God.

This city has always been available to man, even before Christ's

---

[13] Ibid., bk. 14, sect. 28.   [14] Ibid., bk. 15, sect. 1.

appearance on earth, and if the community of sacred love has been an invisible one, with members known to one another through their hearts rather than senses, it has been nonetheless real. In no way does Augustine restrict eternal bliss in the next world to those formally identifiable as Christians. There were noble and pious men who lived before Christ revealed himself on earth, and there have been very wicked men since, among them those professing themselves to be Christians. The elect— those who by inward grace are foredestined to Heaven—began with Abel; the evil and accursed ones, those foredestined to Hell, began with Cain.

Again it must be stressed that the cornerstone of each of the two types of community is a kind of love. The love that unites members of the City of God is selfless, transcending ego as well as body. But the love on which the City of Man is founded is rooted in ego; it is the very opposite of selfless and disinterested love. When, finally, the earthly realm is no more, destroyed by the ultimate holocaust Augustine confidently expected in the not-distant future, and the wicked—those who knew the good but chose evil instead—have been consigned to an eternity of Hell, then and then only will the community of God, the City of God, emerge in all its everlasting beauty and bliss.

In the very last section of *The City of God* Augustine describes this final, blessed community:

> How great will be that felicity, which shall be tainted with no evil, which shall lack no good, and which shall afford leisure for the praises of God, who shall be all in all. . . . All the members and organs of the incorruptible body, which now we see to be suited to various necessary uses, shall contribute to the praises of God; for in that life necessity shall have no place, but full, certain, secure, everlasting felicity. . . . True peace shall there be, where no one shall suffer opposition either from himself or any other. . . . And in that blessed city there shall be this great blessing, that no inferior shall envy a superior, as now the archangels are not envied by the angels, because no one will wish to be what he has not received, though bound in strictest concord with him who has received; as in the body the finger does not seek to be the eye, though both members are harmoniously included in the complete structure of the body. And thus, along with his gift, greater or less, each shall receive this further gift of contentment to desire no more than he has.[15]

In that passage, especially the final two sentences, is to be found the essence of what was to become the major social philosophy of the Middle

---

[15] Ibid., bk. 22, sect. 30.

Ages. There is a certain irony in the fact that an ideal—the functionalist-organic ideal of human relationships—which Augustine had located in the hereafter, in the eternal community of the elect, was to become, above all in the writings of Thomas Aquinas, the greatest philosopher of the Middle Ages, the ideal for society in this world. Human society, Aquinas repeatedly stressed, is to be seen as after the model of the human organism, with the same functional coordination of parts, the same kind of hierarchy of functions and members ranging from the simplest all the way up through the divinely created mind and soul to God, and the same subordination of each single part to the organic whole.

And for all the manifest exceptions, angularities, vices, and floutings of the Augustinian-Thomist ideal, the society of the European Middle Ages is the best example we have, in the West certainly, of an entire social order constructed substantially, rationalized entirely, in terms of a prophetic-religious ideal. This ideal, transferred from the heavenly to the earthly realm, was Augustine's. And a great deal in the medieval social order resembled, for good or ill, the kind of articulation of elements Augustine had in mind in the passage above. Ideas of individual equality, freedom, and rights were scarce during the Middle Ages; what abounded were corporate communities, commencing with the church itself, to which men owed duties and services. The essence of the medieval order was hierarchy, in which each man gave and received what his functional place in the social order demanded. Communality and membership were central in the medieval scheme of things. The whole order was conceived as a kind of *communitas communitatum,* a community of communities; and whether it happened to be monastery, guild, university, knighthood, manor, fief, or patriarchal family, it was the individual's duty to serve his community. Society was conceived by medieval philosophers as a great chain of being ranging from the simplest organism at the bottom all the way up to God at the top, and each link, however humble, was deemed vital in the divine chain. This, too, was a profoundly Augustinian conception.

Nothing escaped, in theory at least, the contemplation of the church. The undisputed function of the arts—architecture, music, painting, sculpture, and literature—was sacred: the celebration of God and the Christian epic. One would be hard put to find any example of art in the twelfth and thirteenth centuries, even in the two centuries following, that did not direct itself to religion and its central elements of drama. Precisely the same was true of philosophy: no matter how far afield the philosophers might range, seeking learning and inspiration from Aristotle and many others in the ancient world, even from the Moslem world to the south, the unifying objective of all learning and contemplation was religious. Nor was the matter any different in medieval science. The Middle Ages must be accounted one of the world's great periods of scientific investigation, despite the common myth to the contrary; and one can today only marvel at the works of a Robert Grosseteste or a Roger Bacon in such fields as physics, optics, color, chemistry, astronomy, and even psychology. But in science as in philosophy and art, the ultimate and unifying purpose was held to be the greater understanding of God and God's works.

The Decline of Religious Community: Erasmus and Montaigne

Even before the Middle Ages had ended, there were abundant signs of forces which would weaken substantially the ideal of religious community conceived by Augustine and rationalized by medieval philosophers in a wealth of scholastic detail. Some of these forces we have already noted in the two preceding chapters: military and political centralization that could only work against any form of internal community in the larger social order, and also the atomizing consequences of the revived study of Roman law and of philosophical nominalism. Clearly, not even the structure of the Christian community would long resist such forces as these.

There are, however, two other forces with which we must deal, both of them manifest in high degree during the period of the Renaissance. The first is *secularism,* which for present purposes we may define as the turning of creative and scholarly attention from the sacred to the material, the worldly, the human—in short, to the secular realm. The second, an intensified version of the individualism we have seen to be associated with the study of Roman law and with nominalism during the Middle Ages, I would call *subjectivism,* an increased attention to the internal, reflexive, and purely personal qualities of human behavior and consciousness. To a great degree these are the two forces which compose the Renaissance, especially in its fifteenth-century beginnings in Italy.

Secularization could not help but lead to a relaxation of the ties of community. For community, where it is strong, is always founded upon some kind of dogma—be it the dogma of procreation, war, revolution or religion. The medieval community had been one of faith in the Christian epic: everything—art, philosophy, science, life itself—was deemed significant only to the degree that it either reflected or led to the search for God. This, as we have seen, was the heritage of Augustine. Now, however, commencing in the late fourteenth and early fifteenth centuries, we become aware of new and different criteria of excellence, drawn from life on this earth; from humanity, from literatures other than the Christian, and from sheer individuality.

I do not mean that there is any clear evidence of men loving God less, of being worse Christians in, say, the fifteenth century than in the thirteenth. It is always difficult to compare intensities of faith from age to age, from culture to culture—that is, with respect to individuals. I mean only that the power of the *visible community* of God was plainly beginning by the fifteenth century to lose its evocative force. And what was in effect taken away from the external community, represented by Christian dogma, was given, so to speak, to the individual; to his imagination, his reason, his aspiration, and eventually to his claimed innate virtue. It is in this respect that the second of the two forces, subjectivism, becomes paramount in the Renaissance.

In one of the most famous passages in his *Civilization of the Renaissance in Italy,* Jacob Burckhardt writes:

> In the Middle Ages both sides of human consciousness—that which was turned within as that which was turned without—lay dreaming or half awake beneath a common veil. The veil was woven of faith, illusion, and childish prepossession, through which the world and history were seen clad in strange hues. Man was conscious of himself only as member of a race, people, party, family, or corporation—only through some general category. In Italy this veil first melted into air; an *objective* treatment and consideration of the State and of all the things of this world became possible. The *subjective* side at the same time asserted itself with corresponding emphasis; man became a spiritual *individual,* and recognized himself as such.[16]

As Burckhardt—and by our day, many another historian of modern culture—points out, the Italian humanists were the first to give vivid evidence of this profound change of temper. They were learned in the classics of Greece and Rome. So, however, had been the great philosophers and scholars of the thirteenth century; but where a Thomas Aquinas had made his scholarship a monument to the community of God, the scholarship of the humanists was more nearly a monument to man himself, his emotions and feelings. Such writers as Petrarch, Salutati, Valla, and Boccaccio—the last-named famous to this day for his *Decameron,* a collection of bawdy, often irreverent and anticlerical, always charming tales of men and women, their innermost feelings, passions, and emotions, as well as their appetites for all aspects of the sensuous life—may indeed have had faith in God and have wished to serve him in their fashion, but they obviously had little if any wish to serve what they could see of the external trappings of the Christian church.

What the humanists did wish to serve, as their lives and writings

---

[16] Jacob Burckhardt, *The Civilization of the Renaissance in Italy,* 2 vols. (New York: Harper & Row, Torchbooks, 1958), 1: 143.

make plain enough, were the power and wealth of the princes around them and a conception of religion that is highly subjective and individualistic. The individualism that is to be seen in the flamboyance, cultivated eccentricity, bravado, and diverse color of the Italian Renaissance can be seen in different but related form in the preoccupation with self and the innumerable states of consciousness of self. Rarely in history has there been an age comparable to the Renaissance—not only in Italy but in France and other parts of the West—in its dedication to the individual and the most individualistic types of thought and conduct. And as such modern scholars of the Renaissance as Charles Trinkaus have shown in great detail, following Burckhardt, along with this individualism went a growing preoccupation with man as subjective being. This subjectivism bears such fruit as the works of Erasmus and of Montaigne—though we should not be blind to the secular qualities of their works either, so evident in the astonishing range of subjects, drawn from all ages of history and all parts of the world, in Montaigne's *Essays*.

We must not overlook what is central here: the erosion of the sense of religious community. It does not matter that the Renaissance may be associated in our minds with some of the most vital and creative qualities of mankind, not to mention literary and artistic works of boundless importance. We are concerned with the fate of the Christian community during this early-modern period. And we can hardly escape the conclusion that everything serving the interests of the secular and the subjective, no matter how brilliant and lasting in the history of Western culture, was bound to militate against that communal and corporate conception of Christianity born of Augustine which became the very cornerstone of medieval civilization.

Nowhere is this fact more evident than in the writings of Erasmus at the very beginning of the sixteenth century and of Montaigne toward the end of that century.

Erasmus

That Erasmus was Christian in belief and motivation stands without question here. He was surely as devoted to furthering the interest of religion as was his friend Sir Thomas More—who, as we know, lost his life on the block for his refusal to go along with the king of England in a policy that involved, from More's point of view, base subordination of church to royal centralization. Both Erasmus and More were deeply Christian in their convictions. Nevertheless, it is impossible, as one reads Erasmus, to miss the greater devotion to the individual, his nobility as well as his folly, his emotions as well as his mind. And, hovering over this Erasmian preoccupation with individuality and the things of this world is the whole spirit of rejection of a Christianity become, in the very visibility of all the marks of ecclesiastical dominance, too corporate, too communal, too repressive of individual faith and reason.

How far Western thought had come from the medieval ideal of the corporate Christian community when Erasmus wrote at the end of the fifteenth century may be inferred from the following passage, to be found in his *Education of a Christian Prince*:

> Do not think that the profession of a Christian is a matter to be passed over lightly, entailing no responsibilities unless, of course, you think the sacrament which you accepted along with everything else at baptism is nothing. And do not think you renounce just for the once the delights of Satan which bring pain to Christ. He is displeased with all that is foreign to the teachings of the Gospel. . . .
>
> But on the other hand, do not think that Christ is found in ceremonies, in doctrines kept after a fashion, and in constitutions of the church. Who is truly Christian? Not he who is baptized or anointed, or who attends church. It is rather the man who has embraced Christ in the innermost feelings of his heart, and who emulates Him by his pious deeds.[17]

Some of the words in the second paragraph are as Protestant in religious character as any that Luther or Calvin would write. There is a difference, however; and it lies in the fact that whereas Luther and Calvin carried their criticism of the corporate church to the point of outright rebellion, calculated and systematic, against Rome, Erasmus did not. And the reason he did not is worth emphasis: not because he lacked personal courage, but, rather, because he felt that no religious matter should be regarded as vital enough to be carried to the point of revolt. A pious, genuine Christian, Erasmus yet saw religion as something personal, internal, even vital, but not something that should be made coterminous with all thought and life. This is why, although Erasmus was suspected of heresies by Rome and known to be a good deal less than reverential in his attitude toward the popes and the ecclesiastical hierarchy generally, he was actually hated by some of the Protestant reformers—hated because the very humanism of his mind would not let religious dissent, any more than religious orthodoxy, be carried to the point of fanatical militance, an attitude he detested as much as did his contemporary Sir Thomas More, and as some decades later, did Montaigne, who so eloquently expressed the fact in his majestic *Essays*.

How unlike any medieval mind Erasmus's was can perhaps best be seen in his most famous work, *Praise of Folly*. Its title in Latin, the lan-

---

[17] Erasmus, *The Education of a Christian Prince*, trans. Lester K. Born (New York: Columbia University Press, 1936), p. 153.

guage in which Erasmus wrote the book, is *Moriae Encomium, moria* meaning "folly" but also having a clear relation to the name of Erasmus's beloved friend, Sir Thomas More. Indeed the book is dedicated in effect to Sir Thomas. *Praise of Folly* is a work of genius: subtle, graceful, tranquil, but with a meaning that could be lost on no mind: nothing less than the bankruptcy—in Erasmus's view—of the once-great Christian civilization, which had become by the end of the fifteenth century a thing of empty forms, ceremonies, dogmas, and rituals, its life having disappeared. Folly, for purposes of the book, is a goddess, or more accurately, a personification of all the humility, humor, wit, and insight Erasmus had drawn from the greatest of the Greek and Roman philosophers and the most imaginative of the classical poets—with Lucian undoubtedly in the forefront of these influences on Erasmus's mind. Erasmus's praise of Folly is for her reactions, the very essence of which is wit, irony, and satire, to what civilization had become in the West in Erasmus's time.

What Folly clearly loves is the pure, classically based, free, and inquiring individual mind. What Folly detests, or at least is boundlessly amused by or disparaging of, is cant, pretense, pomposity, idle spinning of logic, empty argumentation, and, above all, mere ritual and ceremony. And a very great deal of all this Erasmus found, of course, in the very institutionalized, ceremony-ridden Christian church. Not a little of the book is concerned with the church and with Folly's barbs at priests, monks, bishops, and logic-chopping theologians. Here is a passage, referring to monks, that leaves us in no doubt at all of Erasmus's views on these persons:

> . . . I do not see how anything could be more dismal than these monks if I did not succor them in many ways. For though people as a whole so detest this race of men that meeting one by accident is supposed to be bad luck, yet they flatter themselves to the queen's taste. For one thing they reckon it is the highest degree of piety to have no contact with literature, and hence they see to it that they do not know how to read. For another, when, with asinine voices, they bray out in church those psalms they have learned, by rote rather than heart, they are convinced that they are anointing God's ears with the blandest of oil. . . .
>
> The greater number of them work so hard at their ceremonies and at maintaining the minutiae of tradition that they deem one heaven hardly a suitable reward for their labors; never recalling that the time will come when, with all these things held of no account, Christ will demand a reckoning of that which He has prescribed, namely charity. One friar will then show a paunch which has been padded out with every kind of fish; another will

spill out a hundred bushels of hymns. Another will count off so many myriads of fasts, and will lay the blame for his almost bursting belly upon his having always broken his fasts by a single dinner. Another will point to a pile of ceremonies so big that seven ships could scarcely carry it. Another will boast that for sixty years he never touched money, except when his fingers were protected by two pairs of gloves. . . .[18]

To like caricature and satire Erasmus subjects many another late-medieval religious and social type. He is no less devastating on lawyers, a great many professors and scholars, civil servants, and other esteemed worthies of the day than he is on monks, priests, and bishops. His mordant thesis is that apart from an instinct for folly, for being able to see the humor in what surrounds them, people would undoubtedly put an end once and for all to a great many of the leading lights of society.

The same astringent wit is applied by Erasmus to some of the most cherished and sacred relationships of the social order. Here, for instance, is Folly on marriage:

> . . . Good Lord, what divorces, or worse things, would not happen all over the place, were not the domestic association of man and woman propped up and fostered by flattery, by jesting, by pliableness, ignorance, dissimulation—satellites of mine, remember. Mercy me, how few marriages would come off, if the husband prudently inquired what tricks his seemingly modest little lady had played long before the wedding. And still fewer, though entered upon, would last, did not most of the wife's doings escape her husband's knowledge, through his negligence or stupidity. But these blessings are owed to Folly. She brings it about that the wife pleases the husband, the husband pleases the wife, the household is tranquil, the alliance holds. A husband is laughed at, called cuckoo, cuckold, or what not, when he kisses away the tears of his whorish wife; but how much happier thus to be deceived than to harass himself by unresting jealousy and to spoil everything with distressing brawls.[19]

If ever the lethal quality of wit and humor, caricature and satire, has been demonstrated irrefutably in the history of Western writing, it has been by Erasmus. What the poet Lucian did in the ancient world of classical decadence, Erasmus did in the fading period of the once-great and buoyant medieval civilization. Each attacked, not from hatred,

---

[18] Erasmus, *Praise of Folly*, trans. Hoyt Hopewell Hudson (Princeton: Princeton University Press, 1941), pp. 85–87 passim.

[19] Ibid., pp. 27–28.

malice, or bitter cynicism, but from sheer love of life, of individuality, of the natural, as opposed to the stilted and pompous in the world. It would be hard to find a mind more instantly engaging, a spirit more whole-heartedly genuine and gracious, than that of Erasmus. And his learning was the equal, if not the superior, of any other's of his day. Erasmus was honored wherever he went in Europe by the greatest of scholars, poets, philosophers, and statesmen—by all indeed save the hypocrites and poseurs.

But we must make no mistake about the impact of such a mind as Erasmus's on the corporate character of the Christian community. Like all lasting communities, it was supported in very large part by elements of hierarchy, authority, ritual, dogma, sacrament, and habitual allegiance. And these, in their more flagrant forms at least, were precisely the qualities at which Erasmus leveled his devastating learning and wit. All that Erasmus, and the other humanists of his day, gave to the individual, to reason, to feelings and emotions, they were taking away, either deliberately or in effect, from the religious community that had flourished in the West for so many centuries.

If it be wondered at this point what, precisely, was the contribution of an Erasmus, and of the other humanists before him, to the study of society, to social philosophy proper, the answer is simply this: By their diminution of the power of the sacred, by their attack upon the very citadel of society in the medieval world—that is, the church—the humanists could not help but bring society and human behavior into a more finite compass that would in time suggest the possibility of an outright philosophy of society, even a science of society. To deal, as Erasmus did, with the church as a purely human institution—at least so far as clerical manifestations were concerned—was to make not only religious but all other behavior seem amenable to rationalistic modes of inquiry. To settle upon the individual, with his passions, his emotions, his follies, as well as his habits and reason, was to give a concreteness to social philosophy that could not have been possible in an age when all things were seen in terms of their relation to God.

Montaigne

Apart only from Shakespeare, it is impossible to think of any writer of the sixteenth century whom we continue to read as avidly as we do Montaigne. He is generally regarded as the founder of the essay form of literature; and it is possible through Montaigne's writings to see the distinct affinity between this form and the kind of subjectivism, of concern with self and with the innermost selves of others, we have found to be a cardinal aspect of the Renaissance. Despite the immense variety of experience covered by Montaigne, ranging, as we noted earlier, over the whole world and all ages, despite, in short, his ostensible concern with the external, whether close at hand or at great distance, always we find this experience brought close to Montaigne himself, to his own reason, emotions, feelings, and other reactions. Montaigne is no less secular of mind than Erasmus, no less concerned with the relativity of externalities in the world; and he carries Erasmus's fascination with individuality to heights of subjective assessment that we find nowhere else in Western literature except in Shakespeare—who was, as we know, strongly influenced by Montaigne's writings. In one respect, at least, Montaigne went considerably beyond Erasmus; his notable and profound skepticism. "Que sais-je?" "What do I know?" This is the famous question that Montaigne asked in one of his essays. By it he meant, "What among the many forms of revealed knowledge can best be taken as assured, as absolute and certain?" His answer was, in effect: "None of them." Only the knowledge that one gains through personal experience, through inquiring of one's self, through understanding of one's self, can be accounted reasonably certain. To place reliance upon external testimony, upon the bodies of knowledge that are proclaimed as certain throughout the world, is always treacherous, for there one finds almost infinite disagreement.

Montaigne was himself a Catholic, and he managed to remain on good terms indeed with the papacy. This was in part the result of a certain tact Montaigne exercised in dealing with clearly Christian subjects, and in part of a growing acceptance by Rome of the works of the Renaissance. The Protestant Reformation was in full force during Montaigne's lifetime, and with it the bloody wars of religion between Catholics and Protestants. Nothing horrified Montaigne more than the kind of war, cruelty, and devastation that grew out of impassioned religious conviction. If the Church of Rome was more tolerant of the skepticisms and secularisms of the Renaissance tradition than it had been a century or so earlier, this can be explained in considerable part by the urgent need of the late-sixteenth-century papacy to concentrate its powers on the fast-growing Reformation, a movement related to the Renaissance in roots but very different in the character of its thrust. We shall come to the Reformation and its revolt against Catholicism in the next section of this chapter. It will suffice here to emphasize that whatever may have been Montaigne's many reservations about Catholic Christianity, they were relatively mild alongside his distrust of the spirit of impassioned revolt, the bitter sectarianism, and the seeming fanaticism of the burgeoning Protestant movements.

But the essential point to grasp about Montaigne is his aloofness from all the religious doctrine of his century. For that matter, we cannot but be struck by his extraordinary objectivity about everything in his time and culture. Nothing less than the world, as he had been able to know the world through his own travels and experiences and, most important, through his astonishingly wide reading, was the real subject of Montaigne's *Essays*. A good deal of that liberation from European ethnocentrism which would mark the rise of the social sciences in Europe a century or two later can be traced directly back to the cosmopolitan nature of Montaigne's writings, which became popular and widely read from the moment of their publication in 1580. The spirit of skepticism that transfuses everything he wrote, his willingness to consider the morals of the most remote and primitive people as worthy of his respect, his capacity to deal with human nature in all its variability, and not judge nor condemn it except when wanton cruelty was involved; all of this stamps Montaigne's as one of the most civilized minds in history. His influence was immediate, ranging from direct impact upon Shakespeare to providing the foundation for Descartes's momentous rationalism in the next century, a rationalism that began, as had Montaigne in his *Essays*, with the spirit of skepticism.

Even today we can only marvel at the sheer diversity of Montaigne's interest in man and his works throughout the known world. His essays deal with quite literally every subject that can be found today in the social sciences: the nature of culture, the many types of social organization, the effects of emotions on the mind and on behavior, the consequences of varying types of government, the problems of wealth and of poverty, the different roles of birth, marriage, and death in human societies, and so on.

His famous essay "Of Cannibals" must be regarded as very close to the beginning of modern anthropology—not only in its subject, primitive peoples, but in the dispassionate and tolerant spirit with which Montaigne approaches primitive customs. He sees these peoples and customs indeed as being closer to nature than our own:

> The laws of nature still govern them, very little corrupted by ours; even in such pureness that it sometimes grieves me that the knowledge of this did not come earlier, in the days when there were men who would have known better than we how to judge it. I am sorry that Lycurgus and Plato had not this knowledge; for it seems to me that what we see in intercourse with those nations surpasses not only all the paintings wherewith poetry has embellished the golden age, and all its conceptions in representing a happy condition of mankind, but also the idea and aspiration, even, of philosophy.[20]

Not that Montaigne is succumbing in this essay to the mannered exoticism that would lead in the eighteenth century to the cult of the noble savage; not at all. He is frank in his description of the bloody wars and the cruel-

---

[20] *The Essays of Michel de Montaigne*, trans. George B. Ives, 3 vols. (New York: Heritage Press, 1946), 1: 276.

ties among the cannibal peoples, and of his own distaste for the practice of cannibalism. But he is equally frank in his description of the spirit of kindness, gentleness, and morality that prevails in each of the cannibal peoples in their relations among themselves. And most important, Montaigne is saying to us, given our own barbarities and wanton cruelties, our religious wars that would be bound to horrify the cannibals, we have no right to judge these primitive peoples as being morally worse than we are.

Montaigne devotes individual essays to such subjects as these: "By Divers Means a Like End Is Attained," "Sadness," "Of Idleness," "Of Fear," "Of the Power of Imagination," "Of Custom and the Inadvisability of Changing an Established Law," "Of the Custom of Wearing Clothes," "Of the Vanity of Words," "Of Drunkenness," "Business Tomorrow," "Of the Affection of Fathers for Their Children," and "Of Cruelty." There is indeed very little that is human, that relates in any way to human society and to human mind and emotion, that Montaigne cannot be found to deal with in the *Essays*. And there is never a subject treated that is not suffused by Montaigne's own ready imagination, on the one hand, and his immense learning in the ways of other peoples, ancient, exotic, and modern, on the other.

What Montaigne cherished above all else was ordinary, unaffected individual decency, in whatever walk of life it is to be found. He detested pomp, ceremony, and ostentation as he did pretentiousness of mind or excessive concern with status in individuals. One of his most revealing essays, called "Of Pedantry," mocks learning merely for its own sake, making it evident that we indeed but rarely encounter genuine wisdom among those for whom mere number of books read is the touchstone of distinction.

> What does it avail us to have a stomach full of food, if it does not digest, if it does not become transformed within us, if it does not increase our size and strength? . . . If our minds do not go a livelier pace, if we have not sounder judgment, I would as lief that the student had passed his time playing tennis; at least, his body would be the better for it.[21]

Clearly, Montaigne is directing his words against the universities of his time and also the extramural humanists who had by then become frequently arrogant and pompous in their vaunted learning.

No matter what Montaigne writes about, whether a cultural trait, an institution, or an emotion, always he takes us far into the literatures of other peoples—chiefly, it is true, those of the Greeks and Romans, especially the latter, but with frequent references nonetheless to others he had become aware of in some degree. He did all this not to parade his

21 Ibid., pp. 183–84.

learning, a practice for which he had nothing but distaste, but to provide a unique means of making people understand the immense variety that can attend the good, the true, and the beautiful. His essays are a powerful testament in behalf of tolerance, of creative skepticism, and of the goodness that can dwell within the individual, irrespective of nationality or class.

But laud Montaigne though we will and must for his brilliance, his learning, and his moral goodness, we cannot be blind to the impact his ideas had, and were bound to have, upon the dogma and the structure of the medieval religious community. Montaigne's work, irresistible though it may be, is a far cry from the uses to which an Augustine, a Thomas Aquinas, even a Petrarch, had put their learning, their comparable mastery of the classics of the ancient world. For these, especially Augustine and Aquinas, the uses of learning were, above all else, to the greater glory of God and the community of Christ. Man was important, vital indeed, but only as he was cast in the image and likeness of God. Very different is the spirit we find in Erasmus and Montaigne. For all its intrinsic nobility, it cannot be seen as other than a powerful manifestation of the Renaissance erosion of the religious community which had come into being with Augustine's *City of God*.

The Revolt against Religious Community: Luther and Calvin

Decline or erosion of community through secularization, individualism, and skepticism is one thing; a very different one is calculated revolt against community. The most expressive way of dealing with the great Protestant Reformation of the sixteenth century, at least from the point of view of the history of social philosophy, is explicitly in terms of a revolt against the corporate, visible, Catholic community that had come into full being by the thirteenth century and that began, as we have seen, to suffer the erosive, individualizing changes of the Renaissance.

That important differences of purely doctrinal character between Protestantism and Roman Catholicism existed in Luther's and Calvin's age is not to be doubted. But these differences seem minor alongside the much more profound and far-reaching differences between the Catholic church and the newly emerging Protestant sects and cults in their ways of regarding the nature of the religious community and, not least, the believer's relation to community and its works.

Luther

From the time in 1517 when Luther nailed on the church door at Wittenberg his famous theses of religious belief, in effect proclaiming the directness of relation between God and man without necessity of intermediation by the church and its innumerable agencies in society, Protestantism may be said to have been in process of revolt against visible community. This revolt against community is the very essence of the Reformation and the immediate basis of the individualism that has ever since been the hallmark of Protestantism as compared with Catholicism.

What aroused the ire of Luther, and of more than a few other scholars and theologians in his day—most of them in one or other of the universities of the time—was the manifest corruption of the church in both economic and moral matters. Luther himself was a member of the Catholic church, specifically an Augustinian friar. I noted above that in many ways the Protestant reformers traced their theological lineage back to Augustine. Much of what Augustine had repudiated in the paganism of his own day seemed to a succession of church reformers—Hus, Zwingli, Melanchthon, Luther—to have become by their time a hateful excrescence on the body of the Christian Catholic church itself. High among these seeming excrescences the reformers listed the so-called indulgences. These were, at their worst, hardly more than nakedly exploitative documentations of forgiveness in advance sold by representatives of the church to all who would buy them, with the money going back to the papacy in Rome.

To princes as well as peasants in early sixteenth-century Germany, the church seemed increasingly corrupt and exploitative, more and more concerned with extracting financial tribute to support the notorious luxury and immorality widely believed to have become the very substance of the papacy in Rome. How far such charges against the church were in fact valid and how far they were moralistic cover for the German laity's desire to hold more tightly to their wealth, to be free to seek it in ways forbidden by the church, and to have greater autonomy generally in their economic, moral, and intellectual lives, is not a matter we need explore here. The truth surely lies somewhere in between: we shall leave it at that.

Our important concern here is not the substantive validity of charges of profligacy and corruption and immorality in the Roman Catholic church, but the fact that these charges were powerful weapons in the revolt that had been germinating for a long time in Europe, especially northern Europe, against the papacy and against the whole communal conception of Christianity and that Luther and Calvin brought to sucessful fruition. And, as I have noted, revolt against the visible community of the church—together with the hierarchy, discipline, statuses and roles which made up this visible community, as they must any visible, corporate community—is the very heart of the Protestant Reformation.

We may readily grant that a great many of the Protestant sects, and in due time the churches which sprang from sects, themselves became much more tightly woven communities of faith than the Roman Catholic church had been for many centuries. In short, Protestantism has a communal side of its own: it is far from being all individualism and the sanctity of individual faith and conscience. Nevertheless, it was in the name of individual faith and conscience, and in direct challenge to the legitimacy of the church's right to dominate this individual faith and conscience through its priesthood and its ordinances and sacraments, that Luther began the first major revolution in European history. That it was a spiritual one, concerned with matters of faith and morals rather than with politics (at least overtly—politics had its full share of impact on Luther and Calvin!) does not affect its designation here as a revolution. As we shall see in the next chapter, all major revolutions are, or shortly become, spiritual-moral, or they fail before they are well under way. The line from the Lutheran revolt to later, secular-political revolutions such as the great French Revolution is clear, continuous, and vital.

All successful revolutions are combinations of nihilism and affirmation. We shall see this again and again in the next chapter; it is equally relevant here with respect to Protestantism. The *nihilistic* element in Luther lies in his onslaught against the corporate church, its sacraments— the majority of them, at any rate—its hierarchy, and the authority it claimed in matters of the external social, economic, and political behavior of individuals. From beginning to end, we find Luther in direct, acknowledged, and militant revolt against the church's concern with anything but individual faith and conscience.

The *affirmative* element—equally vital in any revolution—is to be found precisely in that last point: individual faith and conscience. From the time Luther first threw down the gauntlet to Rome with the theses he nailed to the church door at Wittenberg, through almost every one of his major works, to his final triumphant challenge to the papacy, his unvarying emphasis was on the individual's own faith and conscience—not, be it noted, his reason or his right to freedom in all moral and social respects, but to his faith alone. "Faith alone"; this, above any other single phrase, summed up Luther's revolt against not merely Rome but any conception of religion as inseparable from visible community with the hierarchy and authority it inevitably imposed upon the individual.

With this revolutionary insistence upon the divine right of individual faith went an equally revolutionary insistence upon the equality of all possessed of genuine faith. This meant, first of all, a denial that any priesthood could intervene between man and God:

> Therefore everyone who knows that he is a Christian should
> be fully assured that all of us alike are priests, and that we all

have the same authority in regard to the word and the sacraments, although no one has the right to administer them without the consent of the members of his church, or by the call of the majority (because, when something is common to all, no single person is empowered to arrogate it to himself, but should await the call of the church).[22]

And in his "Appeal to the Ruling Class" Luther wrote along the same revolutionary lines:

> To call popes, bishops, priests, monks, and nuns, the religious class, but princes, lords, artisans, and farm-workers the secular class, is but a specious device invented by certain time-servers; but no one ought to be frightened by it, and for good reason. For all Christians whatsoever really and truly belong to the religious class, and there is no difference among them except insofar as they do different work.[23]

And in Luther's "The Freedom of a Christian" he writes:

> In addition, we are all priests, and thus greater than mere kings, the reason being that priesthood makes us worthy to stand before God, and to pray for others. For to stand before God's face is the prerogative of none except priests. Christ redeemed us that we might be able spiritually to act and pray on behalf of one another just as, in fact, a priest acts and prays on behalf of the people.[24]

Is it not apparent in these three brief passages how close is the link between Luther—at least at this point in his career—and the whole revolutionary mentality, which comes into political prominence only in the late eighteenth century? If it be true that religion is one of the oldest authorities in history, it nevertheless has to be confessed that religion can enjoin revolt. In this sense, Luther is far from being the first Protestant in postmedieval Western history. That honor might well go to Joan of Arc, who "heard voices" that were not those of the church or of the feudal lords. The price she had to pay was, as we know, the stake; nor was she the last to be burned alive for obeying the private voices that she heard and urging others to heed them also. There is, indeed, a succession of

[22] Martin Luther, "The Pagan Servitude of the Church" (usually referred to as "The Babylonian Captivity of the Church") in *Reformation Writings of Martin Luther*, trans. and ed. Bertram Lee Woolf, 2 vols. (London: Lutterworth Press, 1952), 1: 318.

[23] Martin Luther, "An Appeal to the Ruling Class," in Woolf, op. cit., 1: 113.

[24] Martin Luther, "The Freedom of a Christian," in Woolf, op. cit., 1: 366.

minds leading straight from the high Middle Ages to Martin Luther who also defended their beliefs on the ground of ineluctable faith and conscience. Overwhelmingly they were declared heretics and dealt with accordingly; only successful flight could save them in many instances. But in Luther's time—and place: northern Europe, well away from the papacy and its techniques of spiritual coercion—matters were very different. By the sixteenth century the political and economic development of the whole of northern Europe was such as to provide safe support for Luther and his doctrines; and, as the record makes clear, he never lacked for listeners and readers. Unquestionably one of the most powerful and creative thinkers in the history of the human race—and also, at times, one of the most ruthless, even brutal—not even his strength, boldness, and brilliance could have saved him from dire punishment had the political and economic situation not been propitious.

He could be harsh, even vilifying, to supporters of the Roman Catholic church—many of them gentle and learned minds:

> Come forward, then, all ye fair-speaking toadies of the pope; make ready, and rid yourselves of impiety, tyranny, treason against the Gospel, and the crime of slandering your brothers. You proclaim them to be heretics if they do not agree with the very fabrications of your own brains, or if they do not think them inherently right and proper even where contrary to Scripture—as is both patent and potent. If any are to be called heretics and schismatics, it is . . . you Romanists [who] are heretics and impious to plain passages in divine Scripture. Get rid of these things, my friends.[25]

Luther did not hesitate to condemn all corporate aspects of the church, declaring them, one and all, to be manifestations of the very paganism the Christian church had in its early years combated. He denounced monasteries and their accumulated learning, art works, libraries, and innumerable acres of reclaimed, tilled, and fertile fields. He condemned the use of paintings, sculptures, and other forms of ornamentation in churches and chapels, though he did not go as far in this respect as did Calvin and the Puritans a little later. He denied the jurisdiction of the ecclesiastical courts. He repudiated all the sacraments but baptism and the last rites, declaring, as we have seen, every man's right to perform these acceptable ones. Marriage, far from being a religious sacrament, was in fact, according to Luther's preaching, a civil rite to be performed by the state. Finally, he denied the efficacy of the good works of one's life to earn one grace, to guarantee one's salvation. We find

[25] Luther, "The Pagan Servitude of the Church," in Woolf, op. cit., 1: 221.

Luther repeatedly attacking as pagan and corrupt the church's historic emphasis on good works, including charity, as a road to heaven. All the good works and deeds in the world will not merit one salvation, Luther declared, unless at the same time one's individual faith is pure. Faith alone is sufficient, however, without good works, for grace and community with God.

"As the soul needs the word alone for life and justification, so it is justified by faith alone, and not by any works. . . . Therefore the first care of every Christian ought to be to lay aside all reliance on works, and to strengthen his faith alone more and more." These often-quoted words of Luther come close to epitomizing the Protestant Reformation.

Side by side, however, with Luther's effort to fragment the visible Christian community, to liberate, as he might have said, its indwelling Christian individuals, went a strong belief in stern, hard *civil* rule. When, largely as a result of Luther's own preachings, the oppressed peasants revolted against their masters, Luther did not hesitate to urge that they be put down as ruthlessly and bloodily as might be required.

From the very beginning, in fact, Luther made clear his profound belief in the mission of the political state—the secular, autonomous state, the state freed from any obligation whatever to Rome or to any aspect of organized Christianity. His *Address to the Nobility of the German Nation* is not only, as it is most often characterized, a plea for cultural as well as political nationalism—which Luther himself furthered through his momentous translation of the Bible into the common German tongue. This important work is also a virtual ode to the intrinsic goodness of the political state and the freedom of political authority from all moral or social checks. Luther must thus be seen, together with Calvinism, as among the strongest forces in modern Western history for popularizing the political state and the political habit of mind.

From Luther's doctrines comes the fateful emphasis upon the "divine right of kings"; the right of the political ruler to seek, on his own, direct sanction from God in support of his rule. In the same way that Luther enjoined the individual communicant to live by faith and conscience alone, to be his own priest, and to be suspicious always of the externalizations of religion, so he enjoined the civil ruler, the king or prince, to be assured of his direct sanctification by God. Any thought of a possible intermediation by church or religion between ruler and God was as repugnant to Luther as any thought of intermediation by priest between individual and God.

For all his hatred of the authority of the church, along with such other manifestations of medieval association as monasteries and guilds, Luther did not hate the idea of power. There is, indeed, an affinity between Protestantism and power—power of state and power of economy —that goes back to Luther and comes down to the contemporary world. Much that Luther took away from the church in the way of traditional authority, he promptly bestowed on the political state: "Those who sit in the office of magistrate sit in the place of God, and their judgment is as if God judged from heaven. . . . If the emperor calls me, God calls me." [26]

In a classic psychoanalytic study of Luther, *Young Man Luther*, Erik Erikson has suggested, with much learning and insight, that while a very young man, Martin Luther suffered a deep and obsessing crisis of personal identity. Erikson suggests further that a great deal of Luther's subsequent career, including not only his revolt against Rome and his espousement of individualism in faith and morals but also his endorsement of the absolute power of the state and of civil rule in all matters except pure religious faith, all springs substantially from psychological conflicts in his own being that attained almost convulsive quality. Luther's doctrines, his alliances with different religious and political groups, his whole massive effect on history, are all thus made to seem in some degree at least the outcome of a personal crisis of identity, the germination of which Erikson has no difficulty in seeing in Luther's adolescence.

It cannot be denied that a great deal in Luther's personal life—qualities of brilliance, boldness, and immense personal force and leadership, as well as an often disgustingly rank covetousness of power—can be shown to be related to something approximating a crisis of identity. More than a few of the world's great can be shown to be individuals deeply obsessed with their own identity, especially where wealth, status, and power are involved. We see this in a Luther; we also see it in a Napoleon or a Hitler. It cannot be denied that life for such individuals is a kind of continuing crisis, never really resolved, in which the search for personal identity becomes obsessive.

No doubt it is the conjoining of personal, psychological crisis with the kind of crisis existing externally in structures of wealth and power—the kind of crisis history so plainly shows to have existed in early-sixteenth-century Europe, particularly northern Europe—that most often produces those explosions of society of which the Reformation is a prime example. For our purposes, however, it will suffice merely to note that in Luther, as in Augustine a thousand years earlier, we see the manifest result of perceived crisis.

Calvin

Let us turn now to John Calvin. Here we can be briefer, for so much that has been said about Luther's impact on Western thought holds true

[26] Quoted by Roland Bainton in *Here I Stand: A Life of Martin Luther* (New York: Abingdon-Cokesbury Press, 1950), p. 238. To this may be added these other much-quoted words of Luther: "The civil sword shall and must be red and bloody."

also for Calvin. There is in Calvin a like repudiation of the corporate conception of Christianity; and a like emphasis upon the individual nature of the religious experience, with intraindividual qualities of faith and grace superseding those qualities which come from pope, priest, good works, liturgy, and the other externalities of the visible church. Calvin went even beyond Luther in his hatred of all these last, in his insistence upon the individual character of man's relation to God and of man's quest for salvation.

What had been gradually built up over the centuries in the way of canon, tradition, and corporate reinforcement by the church of the individual's search for grace and salvation is stripped away ruthlessly by Calvin. There is no salvation for man, Calvin tells us, save that which lies within his own individual powers. There are three steps in this salvation.

> First, we must begin with a sense of individual wretchedness, filling us with despondency as if we were spiritually dead. This effect is produced when the original and hereditary depravity of our nature is set before us as the source of all evil. . . .

The second step in salvation, also individual, is when man,

> animated by the knowledge of Christ, . . . again begins to breathe. For to one humbled in the manner in which we have described, no other course remains but to turn to Christ, that through his interposition he may be delivered from misery. *But the only man who thus seeks salvation in Christ is the man who is aware of the extent of his power*; that is, acknowledges him as the only Priest who reconciles us to the Father. . . .

The third and final stage in individual salvation is reached by man

> when instructed in the grace of Christ, and in the fruits of his death and resurrection, *he rests in him with firm and solid confidence, feeling assured that Christ is so completely his own, that he possesses in him righteousness and life.*[27]

Observe in these passages the heavy, almost awesome responsibility that Calvin reposes in the individual Christian. Whereas on the one hand the Roman Catholic church had made salvation possible only through the corporate community of the church and thus, by the very authority it

---

27 John Calvin, *Tracts and Treatises on the Reformation of the Church,* trans. Henry Beveridge, 3 vols. (Grand Rapids, Mich.: Wm. B. Eerdmans Publishing Co., 1958), 1: 133–34. Italics added.

imposed upon the individual relieved that individual of some of the burden of responsibility for his own salvation, on the other hand, Calvin, in liberating the individual from this corporate authority, isolates him also from the sense of participation in a visible community. What had been a shared responsibility of church and individual is now, in effect, made the responsibility of the individual alone. And note, too, in the passage above Calvin's final emphasis on "firm and solid confidence." The implication is clear: inasmuch as one achieves grace by his individual powers alone, fully manifesting his confidence in his capacity to achieve it, it follows that one will be disposed to *demonstrate* his candidacy for eventual salvation, by as many as possible of the outward signs of personal confidence and certainty, including those of personal well-being. We shall come back to this point in a moment, for it is pertinent to the historical relation between Calvinism and the rise of capitalism.

It is Calvin, among the sixteenth-century Protestant reformers, who is chiefly responsible for a resuscitation and an adaptation of the primitive Christian faith in being among the "elect," those predestined by inward grace to eternal salvation. How, asks Calvin, "can anyone begin truly to fear God unless he is persuaded that God is propitious to him? And whence this persuasion but from confidence in acquittal?" Granted that it is complex, and may even be dangerous, to dig too deeply into the matter, the "Predestination which Paul recommends" is the very rock of Christian faith.

> For he wishes the Ephesians to know and be assured that they have been made partakers of heavenly grace in Christ, as they had been chosen in him before the foundation of the world. Thus therefore it becomes all believers to be assured of their election, that they may learn to behold it in Christ as in a mirror.[28]

Is it any wonder that the followers of Calvin—the Huguenots in France, the Puritans in England, and others—became known not merely for the stringency of their faith, the severity of their individual self-discipline but also for a proclaimed personal righteousness that could often range from sternness to chill arrogance? Not since the early Christians in Rome, who had also demonstrated by manner as well as word—as Pliny tells us in one of his letters to the emperor Trajan on the Christians —their superiority, rooted in absolute confidence in their predestined salvation, to the non-Christians around them, had Christians in western Europe exhibited the kind of faith united with militance and overwhelming confidence to be found among the Calvinists. Their hatred of Roman

---

[28] John Calvin, "Antidote to the Canons," in Beveridge, op. cit., 3: 155.

Catholicism became boundless, as did their antagonism to all works—moral, social, economic, aesthetic, and literary—in any way associated with the Roman church. In the individual alone lay grace; in individual faith alone lay godliness; and in the invisible community of the elect alone lay salvation.

Effects of Calvinism

The impact of Calvinism upon the social order was immediate and drastic. In Geneva, whose citizens invited the French-born Calvin to put his religion into effect there, changes were profound. Everything in any way suggestive of corporate Christianity was destroyed or removed. Valuable works of art, libraries, tapestries, even the stained-glass windows in chapels and cathedrals, all were uprooted, pulled down, done away with in the name of a religious reformation that would brook no impediments of any kind to the direct relation of man and God, the immediacy of pure faith. To this day one may see in Geneva the effects left upon the once richly ornate, magnificently designed cathedral, which had been built under Catholic auspices long before Calvin took over the government of the city in 1536. Everything was removed, torn down, reshaped or rebuilt that could possibly be, and the very shape of the cathedral was altered—all this in conformity with the Calvinist declaration of the sufficiency of faith alone, the individual's and not the community's, and of the potentially corrupting influence upon faith of all that in any way served other ends, whether moral, aesthetic, social, or whatever.

In England, following the capture of power there in the mid-seventeenth-century Civil War by Cromwell and the Puritans, changes of social and cultural nature were as great as those in political structure. In many parts of England fanatic Puritans destroyed or damaged priceless works of art in the churches on the ground that until these had been extirpated, it would be impossible to remove the spiritual effects of the hated Catholic (whether Roman or Anglican did not matter) liturgy. All religious holidays in England were banned; even Christmas was declared by the Puritans a proper workday. The Sabbath alone was to be given to God, and on this day no one was to interrupt in any way his direct devotion to God. An abundance of holidays could only encourage individuals to deviate from proper habits of work, to indulge in sloth, possibly even drunkenness and other immoralities. The theaters were closed down, as were many other places of public entertainment, on the belief that immorality flourished in these places and also that no public assemblies should be held save those committed to God's worship.

It is in such acts—to be seen wherever Calvinist Protestants lived and had the power to invoke them, in Geneva, in Commonwealth England, in New England, and elsewhere—that we can descry the affinity between Calvinism and capitalism. This aspect of Calvinism, and of Puritanism, was given its most detailed and influential statement in Max Weber's famous essay on the Puritan ethic and the rise of capitalism, written in the early twentieth century, one of the seminal works in the modern sociology of religion. We shall come back to Weber's work in the final section of this chapter, when we deal with what I call the "rediscovery of the religious community" in the nineteenth century. But well before Weber wrote on the subject—as early as the seventeenth century—the strong affinity between Calvinists and the economic motivation to trade and commerce had been noted by European observers.

There was, in the first place, Calvin's strong belief in the existence in society of a class of the spiritually elect, those predestined to salvation. Clearly, mere dedication to trade and economic gain could not make one a member of the elect. But, as we noted above, "firm and solid confidence" is the mark of the individual who has reached the third and final stage of grace, testifying to his inner knowledge of being predestined to heaven; and by what better means than visibly affluent success, or at least incessant devotion to trade, can one make evident to others in society the confidence he reposes in his own assured salvation?

Second, there is no question but that Calvin himself and also from the beginning many of his most eloquent followers saw in hard work, in economic achievement, a mode of "calling" that was in its own way fully as sanctifying as any of the numberless callings within the Roman Catholic church. Calvinism condemned everything in Christianity, that is, historical Christianity, that could not be linked directly with God, Christ, Scripture, and individual faith. There is the same loathing of good works among Calvinists as among early Lutherans. And a great deal of what all Protestants took away from the doer of good works, including the mendicant friars, they vested in the individual who resolutely looks to his own welfare. This, essentially, is what is meant by the so-called Protestant ethic.

Third, and in many respects most crucially, the sheer social effect of Calvinism upon traditional, Catholic-engendered structures of society was enough to open the way to trade and manufacture. After all, few things are more limiting to the capitalist spirit than the whole assortment of work-dismissing, leisure-providing feast days that come with such frequency wherever Catholic culture is ascendant. The Catholic community of religion that had reached its height in medieval Europe encompassed, as we have seen, quite literally every aspect of life: economic as well as cultural, aesthetic, and social. Inevitably the economy would, if not actually be made to suffer, at least be inhibited by a large variety of observances in the social order that, in effect, made economic pursuits difficult, or at any rate seem less worthy. When the Puritans, after gaining political power in England, banned feast days and work-stopping ceremonies of all kinds, they may have had only religious austerity in mind. But inasmuch as the overwhelming majority of Puritans were themselves members of the middle class, engaged in day-to-day work, their economic efficiency would naturally be improved. And it is clear enough that economic productivity is bound to be enhanced by a religion and polity in which even Christmas Day is declared to be a day of work. Likewise, the innumerable motivations, incentives, and habits associated with work, with profit and affluence, are bound to be enhanced.

Calvinism also had a strong impact upon politics, or rather, upon the relation between religion and politics. In the first place, Calvinists felt repugnance for the Catholic church and from this followed equal repugnance for all forms of political government that either were based upon Catholicism, as in France and many other parts of the Continent, or had once been based upon Roman Catholicism, as in England—which even now still manifested strongly Catholic character even though its ties with Rome had been broken by Henry VIII. And, feeling repugnance, the Calvinists chose to do something about it. They were a profoundly activist group, ready to turn to war and repression if necessary in order to achieve that degree of autonomy for themselves that their religious faith demanded.

This is, of course, the crux of Calvinism's relation to the struggle for political freedom in Europe, the basis on which John Milton could write, in his celebrated *Areopagitica*, published in 1644, one of the greatest of all testaments to freedom of the mind. Milton was himself a Puritan, a hater of all forms of Catholic ritualism, whether Roman or Anglican, and equally a hater of all forms of interference with the Puritans' freedom to worship, think, and act as they deemed proper and necessary. Milton and other Puritans were astute enough to realize that the surest guarantee of this freedom for Puritans lay in a commonwealth that granted freedom of thought to everyone—or almost everyone: Milton was very hostile to popish writings, of course, and he did not believe that atheists, among others, should be allowed to write their beliefs for public consumption.

Struggle for freedom of belief and thought is not, however, the whole story of the relation of Calvinism—and Protestantism generally—to the state and political power. Like Luther, Calvin believed that political rule was legitimated directly by God, and required no mediation, no diversification or division, by any corporate church. Resistance was urged against Catholic rulers, true, but such resistance was justified in the name of revolt against Catholicism. The ruler who seeks his own communion with God, who knows that no church may intercede, rules by a divine right. It would be hard to find anywhere in history a government more rigorous, more despotic in matters of culture, belief, and action, than the Puritan government of Cromwell in England. Moreover, Calvinist opposition to the whole great expanse of associations and institutions that had arisen in the Middle Ages and were hence stamped in substantial measure with

Catholic influence—not only monasteries and ecclesiastical courts but guilds and a great many charitable bodies, for example—could not help but be of immense assistance to those centralizing monarchs of the age who, for largely economic and administrative reasons, also sought the extermination of these associations and institutions. As we saw above in our consideration of Luther and also in the preceding chapter on the political community, a large measure of responsibility falls on Protestantism for the rise of the modern centralized political state.

Nevertheless, the pristine Protestant, and especially Calvinist, emphasis on the individual cannot be denied. It would be inaccurate as well as ungenerous to imply that the purpose of Protestantism was political. It aimed squarely at the individual and his liberation from that whole complex of traps and corruptions Protestants saw not merely in the Roman Catholic church itself, along with all its diverse agencies, but in the whole culture surrounding the church from the twelfth century on. To Protestants of militant determination, everything associated with Catholic medieval society—literature, art, architecture, philosophy, and scholarship, as well as outright Catholic theology—was suspect.

This, then, is the clear and lasting contribution of Protestantism to political, economic, and social modernity: its overriding emphasis on the individual, at the expense of all the external ties, bonds, symbols, and works that are the attributes of community—that is, *visible* community. For, as we have seen, there was a profound conviction in the minds of Luther, Calvin, and all the major Protestant reformers, that to externalize religion is to run the high risk of degrading or corrupting it. And anyhow, no one from Jesus onward had ever denied that the ultimate place of religion is in the human spirit, in the individual mind and faith. In many respects the Protestant Reformation may be seen as an effort to recover for Christianity the singleness of purpose that had characterized it when the Gospels were written. How, in all logic and evidence, could one possibly deduce from these Gospels the complicated culture, the vast and diversified community serving so many social, cultural, and religious purposes, that Catholic Christianity had become by the late Middle Ages?

The greatest single piece of imaginative literature produced by the Protestant Reformation was John Bunyan's *Pilgrim's Progress*. The full title of this work, read by so many millions of persons from when it was published in 1678 down to the present, is *The Pilgrim's Progress from This World to That Which Is to Come*. Everything essential to Protestantism is to be found in this extraordinary book. Cast in the form of allegory, it recounts the adventures of its hero, Christian, in his journey from the City of Destruction to the Celestial City. Every possible trap and temptation is laid before Christian as he passes through the Slough of Despond and escapes from Doubting Castle and Vanity Fair. Every possible argument against individual faith is met by Christian in his encounters with Mr. Worldly Wiseman, Faithful, Hopeful, and others. Everything is, however overcome by Christian; his solitary pilgrimage is successful. What the literary historian Edward Dowden has written about *Pilgrim's Progress* is instructive:

> All that is best and most characteristic in Bunyan proceeds from that inward drama in which the actors are three—God, Satan, and the solitary human soul. If external influences came from events, or men affected his spirit, they came as nuncios or messengers from God or the Evil One. Institutions, churches, ordinances, rites, ceremonies, could help him little or not at all. The journey from the City of Destruction to the Celestial City must be undertaken on a special summons by each man for himself alone; if a companion join him on the way, it lightens the trials of the road; but, of the companions, each one is an individual pilgrim, who has started on a great personal adventure, and who, as he enters the dark river, must undergo his particular experiences of hope and fear.[29]

In that passage, written, to be sure, only with John Bunyan's *Pilgrim's Progress* in mind, we can see easily enough the central elements of the Protestant movement in the sixteenth and seventeenth centuries: the isolated, self-sufficient individual, the strict individuality of faith, devotion, piety, and grace—and also of guilt, fear, apprehension, and redemption. Not in the structure or authority of community, but in the recesses of the solitary individual spirit, is religion set by the great Protestants of the Reformation. Granted that, like Augustine, whom they revered as much as did any Catholic of the time, they could think in terms of an invisible community of the elect; such community was nonetheless invisible, without substance save as it emerged from the perpetuality of individual assent, of which it was constantly obliged to reassure itself, without any of the customary trappings of community.

R. H. Tawney has written;

> The difference between loving men as the result of first loving God and learning to love God through a growing love of men may not at first sight seem profound. To Luther it seemed an abyss, and Luther was right. For, carried, as it was not carried by Luther, to its logical result, the argument made not only good works, but the sacraments and the Church itself unnecessary.[30]

29 Edward Dowden, *Puritan and Anglican* (London: K. Paul, Trench; Trübner, 1901), p. 234

30 R. H. Tawney, *Religion and the Rise of Capitalism* (New York: Harcourt, Brace, 1926), p. 97.

The Enlightenment

While Luther and the other Protestant reformers of the sixteenth and seventeenth centuries were not willing to carry the Lutheran emphasis upon absolute individualism to its logical conclusion, others, especially in the eighteenth century, were more than willing. From the point of view of the history of social thought, the eighteenth century, notably in France during the Enlightenment, was virtually buoyed up by hatred of and attack upon the church, together with all its corporate, ecclesiastical, and cultural attributes.

The emphasis upon the individual and his *faith* that we find in Luther and Calvin becomes increasingly, through the seventeenth and eighteenth centuries, an emphasis upon the individual and his *reason*. Rationalism was, so far as its attitude toward Christianity was concerned, the true successor in these centuries to the Protestant revolt. More and more we find an insistence upon the foundations of religion—true religion—in reason and its own mode of logic. Revelation would not do. Reason was, however, a double-edged weapon, as events proved. For it was not a very long step from the position that reason justifies religion to the position, admittedly a dangerous one, that what reason does not justify does not belong in religion.

The whole philosophy, or theology, of *deism* came into existence and flourished in the eighteenth century. God was allowed the privilege of existence by the deists; but any thought of an interfering God, a God whose character was either protecting or punishing, was repugnant to reason. God, the deists said in effect, had created the cosmos at some remote time in the past and had then retired from the scene, leaving the world's inhabitants to exist in terms of the natural laws he had originally enacted. It was widely believed by deists that man carried in his own nature all the essential requirements for both order and progress.

There was also the testimony of the scientific revolution. No single physical philosopher or scientist was more admired in the late seventeenth and the eighteenth centuries than Isaac Newton, whose great work on the physical world had laid bare, so it was believed, all the secrets of physical nature. Alexander Pope spoke for many a mind in his day when he wrote:

> Nature and Nature's laws lay hid in night:
> God said, Let Newton be! and all was light.

That Newton himself to the end of his life remained religious, and also deeply interested in theological problems, was of far less interest to the secular-minded and to rationalists generally than the fact that the laws Newton had discovered could be set up in place of a personal God.

The eighteenth century in France was one of relentless attack upon

Christianity by the rationalist philosophers. Basically, attack upon the social and corporate nature of Christianity was what the Enlightenment in France was all about. Despite the persistence of the belief that the philosophes were unfailingly dedicated to the principles of free thought and speech, with Voltaire supposedly defending to his death the right of a man to say anything, however offensive to Voltaire's own reason, there is very little in the actual history of the period to support it.

The historian Robert R. Palmer has written tellingly on this point:

> In theory, the Church had to be intolerant, for it was responsible to God for bringing the true faith to mankind. In theory, the philosophers stood for toleration of all beliefs and the free expression of all ideas. In fact, however, the situation was less simple. The philosophers were by no means willing to allow liberty to their opponents, not even to those who were far from representing the formidable power of the Church. Their method was not often the mild persuasion favored by liberals. They talked much of reason, but their sharpest instruments were ridicule and vilification, which enabled them to throw off a man's arguments by defaming his character or belittling his intelligence. . . . Freron, a Catholic journalist and conservative, was called by Voltaire, in a single work, a scribbler, scoundrel, toad, lizard, snake, spider, viper's tongue, crooked mind, heart of filth, doer of evil, rascal, impudent person, cowardly knave, spy, and hound. He found his journal gagged, his income halved, and his career ruined by the concerted attacks of the philosophers. To silence him, at least two of these philosophers, Marmontel and d'Alembert, appealed to the censors whose very existence the enlightened thinkers are supposed to have abhorred. . . .[31]

Nor must we forget the profoundly *political* orientation of most of the rationalist philosophers in eighteenth-century France. In the preceding chapter we had occasion to observe Rousseau's hatred of Christianity for the very reason that it insisted upon autonomy from the political state. It is preposterous, declared Rousseau as Hobbes had declared a century earlier, to think of separating "the two heads of the eagle," that is, the church and the state. In Rousseau's political community, as we saw, there would bē a strictly political religion—the civil religion, so called—based only upon the citizen's love of his country. The

---

[31] Robert R. Palmer, *Catholics and Unbelievers in Eighteenth Century France* (Princeton: Princeton University Press, 1970), pp. 6–7. This splendid work of scholarship, first published in 1939, unsettles a good many conventional notions about the liberality and tolerance of the philosophes.

philosophes in this respect, too, were but carrying to its logical conclusion a position first stated by the Protestant reformers. Luther, Calvin, and others earlier and later had argued that everything possible, including the responsibilities contained in certain of the sacraments, should be transferred from church to state. The philosophes virtually adored the state, seeing in it a possible instrument of power—an instrument more easily made subject to reason, they thought, than any other institution in society—with which to work toward reconstruction of society, including the abolition of Christianity, in its present form, at least.

There was also a distinct affinity between the Protestant revolt and that all-out revolt against the Christian church we find at the high point of the French Revolution. I shall reserve for the following chapter on the revolutionary community a detailed treatment of the Jacobins and their consecration of reason and revolution. It is enough to point out here that destruction of the church in France, along with confiscation of its property, abolition of its perpetual vows, and general atomization of its corporate nature, was by 1792 perhaps the major objective of the Revolution. This destruction was accomplished, of course, in the name of individual freedom, equality, and political fraternity. My chief point here, however, is not the destruction of Christianity in France during the period of the Revolution, but rather the lineal relationship of that destruction to the Protestant revolt two centuries earlier. Here again we may turn to a clarifying comment by Professor Palmer:

> There was much in the Revolution recalling the Protestant revolution of the time of Luther and Calvin. Couthon cried out for a religion of God, not priests. Extremists smashed images in the churches. Jacobins generally thought well of Jesus, but considered most of Christianity since the first century a corruption of simple truths. Like early Protestants, they held religion to be internal, but the doctrine of man's natural goodness relieved them of much wrestling with the soul.[32]

Without question, the French Revolution is the most vivid and dramatic instance in history of the destruction—temporary though it proved to be—of a universal religion within a single area. All the unalterable animosity against the Roman Catholic church that had begun even before Luther and Calvin, that had had expression in the rise of Protestantism and, later, of such dilutions of Christianity as were to be found in deism, came to a head in 1793–94 in France. We shall have much more to observe about this in the next chapter; for the moment we can content ourselves with Tocqueville's words on the subject:

[32] Robert R. Palmer, *Twelve Who Ruled* (Princeton: Princeton University Press, 1941), pp. 322–24.

> For something was taking place in France that the world had not seen before. In earlier ages established religions had been violently attacked, but this had always been due to the rise of a new type of religion and the fanaticism of its adherents. . . . In France, however, though Christianity was attacked with almost frenzied violence, there was no question of replacing it with another religion. Passionate and persistent efforts were made to wean men away from the faith of their fathers, but once they had lost it, nothing was supplied to fill the void within.[33]

In Western thought since the French Enlightenment and Revolution, nothing fundamental has been added in the way of attack upon organized religion. No matter where we look in subsequent movements—positivism, Marxism, utilitarianism, or the doctrines of Sigmund Freud—we find little that adds in any significant degree to what had been powerfully said by such philosophers of the Enlightenment as Diderot, d'Alembert, and Voltaire and by the leaders of the Jacobins during the Revolution. What Luther and Calvin had begun in their Bible- and God-based attack upon the Roman church with its whole vast corporate system, was continued by philosophers and revolutionaries who did not let even the Bible and the idea of God intervene between their attacks and the total annihilation of institutional religion. For them, all religion, whether belief, sacrament, text, or liturgy, was no more than an "illusion," to use the term Freud was later to direct at religion.

No member of the Enlightenment would have disagreed with Freud's proposition that religion everywhere is but the manifestation of an infantile dependence upon authority and that the proper answer to religion is emotional and intellectual maturity. It may be said that Freud's prescription for this maturity of mind was more fundamental than that of the philosophes, in that he was concerned with the subconscious, they with the conscious mind only, as it could be reached by rational philosophy and science. Perhaps this is so: who can be sure of such things? The important point, in any event, is that both the eighteenth-century rationalist philosophers and Freud saw religion as but a superstructure of belief, not needed by the rational, knowledgeable mind.

To this observation one more is worth adding. In exactly the same way that the rationalism of the philosophes became, in the hands of the Jacobins, itself a form of religion—complete, as we have seen, with liturgy, public prayer, and a representation in sculpture of the goddess Reason—so has Freud's psychoanalysis. Few detached observers would deny that whatever the analytic function of psychoanalysis in the clinic,

---

[33] Alexis de Tocqueville, *The Old Regime and the French Revolution* (New York: Doubleday & Co., Anchor Books, 1955), p. 149. This study was originally published in France in 1856.

that body of text, creed, and conclusion that is the published work of Freud has become fully as dogmatic and as sacred for believers as anything to be found in religion proper. As we shall see in our consideration of Durkheim at the end of this chapter, there is a solid reason for this, which lies, as Durkheim emphasized, in the capacity of literally any belief, no matter what its object, to achieve the status of the sacred.

The Rediscovery of Religious Community

There is irony but also fertile instruction in the fact that the nineteenth century—coming, as it does, hard on the heels of the Protestant Reformation, the Age of Reason, the Enlightenment, and the Revolution—should be one of the richest of all centuries in philosophical and literary expressions of religious community. The irony is obvious. For nearly three centuries the major tendencies of Western social thought had been in the direction of secularization of thought—and, even where thought remained religious, of substantial reduction of the communal and symbolic elements of religion. The Revolution, through its dechristianization decrees and its virtual consecration of individual rationalism, must have seemed to many minds at the end of the eighteenth century the final chapter in the history of Christianity. There were many then, and many throughout the nineteenth century, for that matter, who declared that the day of Christianity, as the age of religion generally, was over. Science, positivism, secular democracy, and technology: these, it was said by many, had already succeeded religion in the minds of the literate and educated. All that was necessary for final victory over religion was merely to make all persons educated.

Despite such secular confidence, the nineteenth century must be seen nevertheless as one of the major creative ages in religious thought. And the crowning irony is that those very communal, corporate, social, and aesthetic qualities of religion that had been most under attack during the three preceding centuries, became in the nineteenth century the ones most celebrated and studied. It would be hard to exaggerate the importance to social thought of this nineteenth-century religious revival, evidences of which we can see in many areas; philosophy, sociology, literature, as well as formal theology itself.

It would be absurd to suggest that this recrudescence of religious community affected all thinkers. Some of the greatest and most influential remained as impervious as had any philosophe in the century before to the call of traditional morality and religion. There was, for example, Jeremy Bentham in England, in every sense an intellectual child of the Age of Reason. Bentham detested religion in all its forms, particularly its Christian, corporate one. Removal from society of the influence of the church was a sovereign need, Bentham thought. Through reason and science would men live with one another and govern themselves. No one either in the nineteenth or in any other century outdid Karl Marx in denouncing religion. For Marx, religion is rooted in social oppression; it is, he declared, at best a kind of narcotic, through which the social and economic distress of the masses is rendered less poignant:

> Religious distress is at the same time the expression of real distress and the protest against real distress. Religion is the sigh of the oppressed creature, the heart of a heartless world, just as it is the spirit of an unspiritual situation. It is the opium of the people.[34]

So Marx wrote in his *Toward the Critique of Hegel's Philosophy of Right*. But observe in those words, hostile though they be, a certain understanding, nevertheless, of the functional role of religion. It is an understanding, even a lurking sympathy, that we do not find among any of the philosophes, a group that Marx rather despised for all the radicalism they and he had in common. Marx sees that religion can have a dual function that sets it higher than mere superstition; it can help men bear earthly distress *but also stimulate them to seek the end of distress.* Furthermore, Marx and Engels were both fascinated by the history and the sociology of religion. For all Marx's belief in the expendability of religion, once the ending of capitalism had done away with man's alienation on earth and, thus, his need for religion, he was yet deeply interested, as a scholar, in the history of Christianity. Engels, in his *On the History of Early Christianity*, went so far as to liken nineteenth-century communism to first-century Christianity. Both, he argued, can be seen to appeal predominantly to, and be most deeply rooted in, the oppressed and downtrodden classes, the proletariats of the two civilizations.

Marx's and Engels's interest in religion presaged, it is fair to say, the increasingly religious, or at very least prophetic, role that Marxism was to play in both Europe and Asia during the twentieth century. It is in no way to overlook Marx's repudiation of religion so called, or to detract from his philosophical powers of analyzing religion in its relation to society, to observe that it is, as prophet, armed with a millennialist message uniting past, present, and future, that he assumes his major significance to the contemporary world. Not perhaps since Christianity was founded in the first century has there appeared in the West a doctrine combining as much proffered hope with as much militance and zeal as we find in the message offered the downtrodden, the oppressed,

---

[34] Karl Marx, *Toward the Critique of Hegel's Philosophy of Right*, in *Marx and Engels: Basic Writings*, ed. Lewis S. Feuer (New York: Doubleday & Co., Anchor Books, 1959), p. 263.

and the disinherited by Marx and his followers. With good reason has A. J. Toynbee referred to Marx as falling in the line of Western prophets that began in ancient Israel. With equally good reason did Bertrand Russell compare the position of Marx with that of religious leaders such as Jesus or Mohammed, the Marxian division of society between the proletariat and the bourgeoisie with the Christian division between the elect and the damned, the historical dialectic with God, and the Marxian idea of final, fulfilling revolution with the Christian idea of the Second Coming. It would not be at all surprising if, a century hence, historians regularly placed Marx once and for all among the religious prophets of history. The increasingly sanctified place occupied by the writings of Marx, Engels, and Lenin in many parts of the world and their favorable comparison with the Bible in sheer mass of readership would suggest that they are far from least among the prophetic or religious writings of the nineteenth century.

Nevertheless, for the real rediscovery of the religious community in nineteenth-century social and moral thought, we are obliged to look elsewhere. Taking religion in the strict and conventional sense, we are confronted by the establishment, differentiation, and diffusion of more sects and faiths within Christianity in that century than perhaps in any other, certainly after the Reformation. Almost as though in explicit reaction to the formalism and rationalism of eighteenth-century Christianity, there arose, in England and the United States especially, a veritable tidal wave of religious enthusiasm, revivalism, and fundamentalism that gave Christianity an emotionality as well as mass appeal that had rarely before been seen in like intensity. And almost as though in like reaction to the Enlightenment's repudiation of religion, with its writ, liturgy, and ritual, we see at the intellectual and scholarly level a genuine renascence not merely of theology in the strict sense but of interest in the nature of religion, in religious communality, in religious history, and in the relationship religion should have to society. That last is important. For the true role of the religious community in nineteenth-century writing is as much to be inferred from its fundamental place in a discipline such as sociology as from its position in formal theology.

In what follows I shall be concerned with six remarkable thinkers of the century, all of whom reveal the appeal of religious community, regardless of how it is defined, both to eminent intellectuals and to wide sections of the reading public. The first three—Chateaubriand, Newman, and Kierkegaard—are sufficiently indicative, I think, of the restored passion, and also of the restored sense of Christianity as being first and foremost a community, that is to be seen in Christian writing. The other three—Comte, Weber, and Durkheim—are of course social philosophers, none of them professedly Christian or even religious in the ordinary sense of the word—Durkheim being, indeed, a declared atheist. They are responsible, nevertheless, for some of the profoundest insights into the communal character of religion and the functional relation of religious commitment to the social order.

Chateaubriand

François René de Chateaubriand (1768–1848), although born and baptized a Roman Catholic, spent most of his youth and young manhood as a free thinker, more nearly of the church-hating philosophes' persuasion than of anything that could in effect be called Christian. Prior to the Revolution he spent much of his time in the company of the secular-minded, antitraditionalist intellectuals who filled the salons of Paris. It was the Revolution itself that seems to have been the watershed of his intellectual career. His *Historical, Political, and Moral Essay on Revolutions*, written during a stay in England and published in 1797, took the form of a comparative examination of twelve significant revolutions in history. Applying a good deal of ingenuity and much learning, Chateaubriand reached the conclusion that all revolutions, including the one going on in France in his time, are futile, and that, whatever may be the apparent benefits they achieve at first, they inevitably reach a condition scarcely different from that existing when they started. Despite a promising framework of analysis and occasional insights which remind one of Burke's great treatment of the Revolution in 1790 and of Tocqueville's a half-century later, Chateaubriand's book is not a very good one. The author himself apparently realized this, for we find him condemning, even seeking to suppress, his own book a few years later. The reason for this lies undoubtedly in the fact that although he had been critical of the Revolution, he had been critical also of Christianity. And it was only shortly after its publication that he underwent a momentous conversion back to Roman Catholic Christianity.

This was signalized in the book for which Chateaubriand remains famous, and which is fairly widely read even today, *The Genius of Christianity*. In his own day, it was without any question the most widely read and influential book on Christianity to be found in Europe or America. It was published on April 14, 1802, four days after Napoleon's announcement of the final signing of the Concordat, the treaty that restored the church to a good deal, though not all, of its pre-Revolutionary status in France. Chateaubriand himself had become converted to Catholicism in 1799; and *The Genius of Christianity* is nothing so much as a celebration of his conversion, giving an account of, on the one hand, his own inner ecstasy and, on the other, those aspects of Christianity which seemed to him the vital and triumphant ones.

In point of fact, *The Genius of Christianity* is not, at bottom, either a very good book or among the better books celebrating Catholic Christianity during the first quarter of the nineteenth century. Many have pinpointed faults in the book's theology and in its evocation of the history of Christianity, and some have even questioned its entire sincerity. There were people in Chateaubriand's day who sneered that while Napoleon had made Christianity once again legal, Chateaubriand had made it fashionable. Nevertheless, allowing for whatever truth there may be in these criticisms and charges, *The Genius of Christianity* proved to be an event. Without any question it was itself responsible for a large number of the conversions to Catholicism that took place in Europe and America during the first half of the century; and no one can take from it the sheer force of style, the brilliance of word and phrase, and the almost magnetic effect its succession of paragraphs can have.

But beyond even this stylistic allure is the way in which Chateaubriand presents to us Catholic Christianity—all religion, for that matter. This way is aesthetic and sociological, even psychological, as much as it is doctrinal or an account of Christ's teachings or the laws of the church. For more than any other book in the century, *The Genius of Christianity* deals with religion as *a form of community*—aesthetic, psychological, social, and moral community—a refuge for those unable or unwilling to tolerate the monotony of life or the torments and alienations of ordinary existence.

Chateaubriand argues that religion is indispensable to society: as a mechanism of stability, as an integrating force, and as a body of symbols of allegiance to the social bond. He anticipates Durkheim in his analysis of the cultural elements and forces of the word *sacred*. For, like Durkheim, Chateaubriand is saying that, irrespective of the name we give it or of our specific faith, some experience of the sacred is inevitable in life. No social system can survive, he tells us, that is based entirely on the ordinary passions and instincts—much less one founded on reason alone, which had been celebrated by the philosophes. From the beginning, Christianity has been essentially a community of the sacred, Chateaubriand argues. It is in this light, first and foremost, that he presents religion; hence the unwonted attention he gives in *The Genius of Christianity* to such matters as hierarchy, structure, ritual, and ceremony. Not even when Christianity had been under severest attack, in the middle of the eighteenth century, had any of its supporters ever thought to defend it in these terms. If they had, they would no doubt have been demolished by the philosophes, whose attack on Christianity was but a part of a larger, wider attack upon authority and hierarchy in general in society.

There is much in the book about the "mysteries" of Christianity, those wells of meaning and emotional experience which transcend anything reason alone can create or sustain. It is in his elaboration of these that Chateaubriand's writing becomes most bell-like and sonorous, even poetic in intensity. For very good reason the book is widely regarded by historians of literature as a major beginning point of romanticism—or, rather, the specific type of romanticism that became a vogue in the early nineteenth century. Like or dislike the book, no one can take from it its richness of imagery, its sensuous quality, which one is more accustomed to find in the writings of the romantic poets and novelists of the day than in works on religion.

We must consider also the mood of the book: one of melancholy, of reflective, resigned sorrow for man's condition which is bred in him from the beginning and which he can never escape. The book is of course the very opposite of those works on religion which seek to promise happiness, joy, and mental elevation as the reward for conversion. Just as the so-called gothic novels of the day took pleasure, so to speak, and gave pleasure in their way, through incessant concern with the morbid, the dark, and the somber, so does Chateaubriand's book. Religion is community of the sacred; it is also community of tragedy. Tragedy is man's fate; religion is but recognition of this.

Nor can we overlook Chateaubriand's stress upon the beauties, the aesthetic values, of Christianity. This, too, takes us a long way in our understanding of the appeal of religion. At its highest, religion is a work of art. Chateaubriand goes into some detail in dealing with the historical relation between Christianity and the production of the great works of art in European culture. It is at least partly in these terms that he is most critical of Protestant Christianity. The Protestants, in their single-minded desire to achieve absolute purity of faith, had driven from religion the feelings, the symbols, the communalities, and the aesthetic rewards that have ever been vital elements of the religious arm of society. Secularism, Chateaubriand tells us, with its total abnegation of religion, had been preceded by Protestantism, with its partial but nonetheless crucial abnegation of all those aspects of Christianity that connote community, structure, and authority, as well as those aesthetic and symbolic elements the Puritans had so harshly expunged.

There is also Chateaubriand's idea of the role of religion in thought: here, although in no degree dispassionate, much less scientific, Chateaubriand may be seen as a kind of precursor to Durkheim. A full century later, in his *Elementary Forms of the Religious Life*, Durkheim would demonstrate the religious roots of man's basic categories of thought. Chateaubriand is concerned with these roots, though, as I have suggested, in the spirit of missionary, of devout partisan. He is more interested in attacking the idea of secular reason than in seeking to expose the developmental origins of reason and thought; but the fact remains that in his attack on secularism he reminds his readers that there are pre-rational bases for the authority of reason and that reason unsupported by religious faith is weak and tenuous for most persons amid the pressures and torments of social existence.

Finally, we should note the effect *The Genius of Christianity* had in restoring the medieval period to some of the favor in Western thought it had begun to lose in the late Renaissance and had come close to losing altogether in the Enlightenment Chateaubriand's book makes us see the beauties of medieval architecture, in its cathedrals and chapels, of the works of art directly inspired by medieval states of mind, and of the eminently ritualized forms of worship which had come to full development in the Middle Ages. A great deal of the nineteenth century's aesthetic, social, and moral interest in medievalism—reflected by much of its historical scholarship as well as by its novels and poems and essays— takes its departure from Chateaubriand's attitude, admittedly an often adoring one, toward the Middle Ages and its highly communal character. In sum, whatever the book's deficiencies, it must be accounted a major point of departure for the enormous interest in religion, its roots, contexts, and consequences, revealed by the nineteenth century.

Newman

The conversion of John Henry Newman (1801–90) to Roman Catholicism at the midpoint in his life was, like the much earlier one of Augustine, rich in doctrinal and historical consequence. Newman's *Apologia pro Vita Sua*, a spiritual autobiography, is perhaps the greatest work of its kind in Christian literature excepting only Augustine's *Confessions*. His *Grammar of Assent* is by all odds the most learned and brilliant argument to be found in modern literature for the indispensability of dogma to belief and assent of any kind. It is also one of the most powerful nineteenth-century arguments against intellectual modernism. Newman's *Idea of a University Defined* virtually canonized the liberal arts as the real foundation of any university worthy of the name; and the structure he saw in the university remains to this moment the most widely accepted one in the educational philosophy of America as well as many other parts of the world. His idea of the university was based solidly on the Oxford which he loved so deeply and from which comes his communal sense of learning and its relation to society and culture.

There are two works that I want to stress in this treatment of Newman. The first is his *Essay on the Development of Christian Doctrine*. Published in 1845, just prior to his conversion to Roman Catholicism, it is impressive on two counts. First it must be regarded as a highly sophisticated statement of the whole theory of developmentalism, applied, of course, to Christian uses. In the section above on Augustine I emphasized the fact that he had a perfectly coherent theory of developmental progress, resting, not on God's continuous intervention, but on what Augustine himself referred to as "man's own efforts." There is, in short, a clearly distinguishable strand of religious developmentalism in

Western thought, which Augustine had the key role in bringing into existence and which John Henry Newman perfected as a methodology.

Newman saw Christianity, its thought and structure alike, as a kind of social system, built around a single and essential idea: man's salvation through Christ. But far from Christianity's being, or ever having been, an unchanging thing, it has been from the start, Newman argues, in a continuous process of development. To those who in Newman's day taunted the church with the distance between its complexity, richness, diversification, and immensity and the simple, homogeneous apostolic Christianity of the Gospels, Newman's book was a powerful reply. For he seized upon the secular idea of developmentalism to demonstrate that the difference between the two Christianities was only a difference of developmental stage. One does not expect the mature human being to resemble in physiognomy the infant from whom he is sprung. No more, Newman said, should one expect the mature Christian community, nearly two millennia old, to resemble in appearance the tiny Christian church of the first century.

Developmentalism is, then, Newman's method; and this is, as I have said, one of its two highly impressive attributes. The other, flowing directly from the first, is the overriding conclusion that the Christian community, along with its underlying dogma, is in constant state of development, and that this is its health and vitality. The question arises immediately, however: Are there not false or deleterious processes of development? Newman, thinking above all of the Protestant Reformation and what it had sought to do to the Christian community, answered in the affirmative. How, then, do we distinguish the false and pathological from the true modes of development? His answer is a triumph of the use of the organic analogy, the same analogy that underlay the secular theory of developmentalism in the emerging social sciences:

> The most ready test is suggested by the analogy of physical growth, which is such that the parts and proportions of the developed form correspond to those which belong to its rudiments. . . . That development, then, is to be considered a corruption which *obscures or prejudices its essential idea,* or which *disturbs the laws of development* which constitute its organization, or which *reverses its course of development*; that is *not* a corruption which is *both a chronic and active state,* or which is *capable of holding together* the component parts of the system.[35]

In that single passage, as is perhaps obvious, are to be seen, first, the vital idea that the Christian community is a system, that its parts

---

[35] John Henry Cardinal Newman, *An Essay on the Development of Christian Doctrine* (London: James Tovey, 1845), pp. 58, 63–64.

are articulated by relation to common function, that the test of corruption is whether a change or growth prejudices this function or idea, and that the ultimate test of salutary or healthy development of the religious community is the degree to which the development shows itself "capable of holding together the component parts of the system"; and, second but not less important, the clear implication that anything, whether from outside the community or from within, which serves either to individualize or atomize the community, or to dislodge its intrinsic function and authority with respect to its own members, is baneful in itself and a mark of false or corrupt development.

The same profound sense of religious communalism is carried over into Newman's *Idea of a University*. Nowhere has the corporate conception of the university had more eloquent expression. For Newman the university is far more than a place of research only, of teaching only, or of study only. Its essence is intellectual fellowship; only through such fellowship, at all levels, and with fruitful communication among all these levels, can there be a university. I know of no finer passage anywhere in the vast literature of higher education than this one in which Newman makes plain what he means by the enlargement of the mind that is, he has just said, the prime purpose of the university's distinctive form of education:

> . . . The enlargement consists, not merely in the passive reception into the mind of a number of ideas hitherto unknown to it, but in the mind's energetic and simultaneous action upon and towards and among those new ideas, which are rushing in upon it. It is the action of a formative power, reducing to order and meaning the matter of our acquirements; it is a making the objects of our knowledge subjectively our own, or, to use a familiar word, it is a digestion of what we receive, into the substance of our previous state of thought; and without this no enlargement is said to follow. There is no enlargement, unless there be a comparison of ideas one with another, as they come before the mind, and a systematizing of them. We feel our minds to be growing and expanding *then*, when not only we learn, but refer what we learn to what we know already. It is not the mere addition to our knowledge that is the illumination; but the locomotion, the movement onwards, of that mental centre, to which both what we know, and what we are learning, the accumulating mass of our acquirements, gravitates. And therefore a truly great intellect . . . is one which takes a connected view of old and new, past and present, far and near, and which has an insight into the influence of all these one on another; without which there is no whole, and no centre. It possesses the

knowledge, not only of things, but also of their mutual and true relations; knowledge not merely considered as an acquirement, but as philosophy.[36]

The idea of a true university is, then, for Newman inseparable from the community of thought, knowledge, and human fellowship within which alone can knowledge be other than static, sterile, and deadening to the mind. Just as he declares religion, in the true sense, to be inseparable from the community of piety that is in his view the church, so is higher education but an extension of the religious community—concerned, however, not with piety as its essence, but knowledge rather—in the degree to which it unites a function with a visible community.

So vital for Newman is the communal character of the university that he even gives the facts of human interaction and communication made possible by residence there a status superior to the mere existence of great libraries and learned faculties. The following passage makes that preference very clear and also reveals a quality of modernity regarding the university that may be found extremely attractive at the present time:

> I protest to you, Gentlemen, that if I had to choose between a so-called University, which dispensed with residence and tutorial superintendence, and gave its degrees to any person who passed an examination in a wide range of subjects, and a University which had no professors or examinations at all, but merely brought a number of young men together for three or four years, and then sent them away, as the University of Oxford is said to have done some sixty years since, if I were asked which of these two methods was the better discipline of the intellect . . . , which of the two courses was the more successful in training, moulding, enlarging the mind, which sent out men more fitted for their secular duties, which produced better public men, men of the world, men whose names would descend to posterity, I have no hesitation in giving the preference to that University which did nothing, over that which exacted of its members an acquaintance with every science under the sun.[37]

Such is the degree of Newman's conviction of the inherently communal nature of the true university. For the massive diploma mills of

[36] John Henry Cardinal Newman, *The Idea of a University Defined* (London: Longmans, Green & Co., 1923), p. 134

[37] Ibid., p. 145.

our own day, seeking to substitute atomistic courses, units, and grades for the experience of intellectual community, Newman could have only emotions ranging from despair to contempt. He was himself one of the most learned men of his day, a distinguished teacher, we may believe, as well as thinker and writer. But for Newman, either education was rooted in community or it was rooted in nothing. Precisely the same vision illuminated his sense of Christianity. He left the Anglican church of his birth for the Roman Catholic church because after years of agonized reflection he could not dismiss his growing conviction that Rome was the very center of that Christian community of which Augustine had written fifteen hundred years earlier. Nothing communal—not university, not family, not church—was alien to Christianity, Newman believed, and he could no more imagine a true university without some degree of commitment to religious ends than he could imagine a Christian commonwealth without universities. If, in his brilliant *Genius of Christianity,* Chateaubriand had pointed to the rediscovered aesthetic and liturgical values of the Christian community, Newman, perhaps above any other mind of the century, pointed to the even more fundamental intellectual and moral values of this community.

Kierkegaard

From the Catholic Newman we move now to a philosopher of religion who recognized no church of his day as being the true one. Danish and Protestant by birth, Søren Kierkegaard (1813–55) lived in an almost agonized state of crisis: personal crisis springing from his deep-rooted sense of guilt, anxiety, and aloneness in the spiritual universe; social crisis springing from his sense of the consequences to the civilized world of the loss of authority.

As Walter Kaufmann has written, Kierkegaard was haunted by the necessity of authority. Profoundly individualistic though he was, in his incessant preoccupation with inner states and with the solitary individual's crushing responsibility in the world, for him all that was wrong in the world, in the church, and with man came directly from loss of authority, from man's unwillingness or inability to live within the structure of authority.

> Kierkegaard insists, for example, that Christianity was from the start essentially authoritarian—not just that the Catholic Church was, or that Calvin was, or Luther, or, regrettably, most of the Christian churches, but that Christ was—and is. Indeed, though Kierkegaard was, and wished to be, an individual, and even said that on his tombstone he would like no other epitaph

than "That Individual," his protest against his age was centered in his lament over the loss of authority.[38]

Professor Kaufmann has not only reached into the essence of Kierkegaard in the passage above but also done much to relate Kierkegaard to the mainstream of nineteenth-century social life and thought in western Europe. For it is in this century that we see most vividly the reaction to the individualistic rationalism and the fragmentation of community embodied in the thought of the two preceding centuries. We look in vain for a systematic philosophy or theology of community in Kierkegaard. Not for him the welcoming arms of the Roman church; nor did even any of the Protestant sects or churches possess appeal. One and all, they seemed to Kierkegaard to have compromised that fundamental and utterly vital authoritarianism that must always, he believed, be the soul of religion.

And authority is, of course, one of the oldest and most visible of the manifestations of community. There can be no genuine community without an internal authority, one that binds the individual to itself and that provides him sanctuary from the alienation and atomization of an age of crisis, and a buffer from the external powers that always in such an age threaten to tyrannize. In such a time of crisis Kierkegaard believed that he lived. His continuing influence upon the generations of theologians and philosophers since has rested, indeed, upon this intimacy of his with crisis, for the very elements that Kierkegaard saw as fundamental to the crisis have remained fundamental in the minds of all those who, in our own day, have found themselves turning to the community of religion in one or other of its forms.

It is fascinating to discover that Kierkegaard regarded the year 1848 as being "beyond all comparison the richest and most fruitful year I have experienced as an author." For this was the very year that marked the great transition in the life of Karl Marx. It was also a vital year in the life of Alexis de Tocqueville, whom we shall come to in a later chapter. The year 1848 was one of revolution all over western Europe. Out of this year, more than from any other single one in the century, came those ideologies of radicalism, conservatism, and liberalism which have guided Western social thought ever since. But whereas Marx derived from the developments of the year 1848 the radicalism that would buoy up his thought thereafter, and Tocqueville the special and humane form of conservatism that would go into his study of the sociology of revolution in France, and whereas others like Mill would derive an ever-stouter faith in liberalism, we find none of these in the religion-

---

[38] Walter Kaufmann, Introduction to Søren Kierkegaard, *The Present Age*, trans. and ed. Alexander Dru (New York: Harper & Row, Torchbooks, 1962), pp. 27–28.

intoxicated Kierkegaard. What Kierkegaard wrote in 1848 was his powerful and still deeply moving *Christian Discourses*. Cast in the form of a series of sermons, this book is at one and the same time an attack on the society around him, an eloquent testament to anxiety in man, and a presentation of the authority of the community of God that is open to those able to see and understand.

In his journal, in the entry for March 27, 1848, Kierkegaard wrote:

> So here I sit. Outside everything is in movement, nationalism surges high in all, everyone talks of sacrificing life and blood, is perhaps also ready to do it, but supported by the omnipotence of public opinion. And I sit in a quiet room (doubtless I soon will be in bad repute for indifference to the national cause); I recognize only one danger: the religious danger. . . .[39]

By "the religious danger" Kierkegaard meant, of course, the danger to ourselves that comes from failing to live within the strict and absolute authority of Christ and taking refuge instead in one or other of the spurious manifestations of security which fill modern society. He employs in this book the device of addressing himself to "the heathen," by which he means not only those outside the fold of Christianity but those within the fold. With this device Kierkegaard uses another, through which he pretends to draw from the wisdom and understanding of the birds and the lilies of the field, holding these and their intrinsic piety up to the heathen who suffer the torments of anxiety. Each chapter is devoted to a different manifestation of anxiety: the Anxiety of Poverty, the Anxiety of Abundance, the Anxiety of Lowliness, the Anxiety of Highness, the Anxiety of Presumption, the Anxiety of Self-Torment, and, finally, the Anxiety of Irresolution, Fickleness, Disconsolateness.

It would be difficult to find a more searching and, from the religious point of view, radical examination of the ills of modernism than that given us in this extraordinary, parablelike work. Each of the essays, or sermons, begins, following a statement of the particular form of anxiety with which Kierkegaard is concerned, with the words "This anxiety the bird has not." Thus is established the principle, the dogma, that from God's world of creatures, untouched and unspoiled by the vanities of culture, anxiety is absent. But within a few paragraphs come the equally important words "The Christian has not this anxiety." Only among the heathen—among whom, as I have said, Kierkegaard places the overwhelming majority of professing Christians—are the anxieties of man's consciousness to be found. The *Christian Discourses* ends with the

---

[39] Søren Kierkegaard, *Christian Discourses*, trans. with an Introduction by Walter Lowrie (New York: Oxford University Press, 1961), p. 6.

following pregnant paragraph, as good as any to be found in all Kierkegaard's voluminous writings for the purpose of epitomizing his thoughts
on authority and obedience:

> Let us in conclusion think of the birds, which had their
> place in the Gospel and should have their place in the discourse.
> The bird so obeys God that this is the same thing as being wilful;
> the Christian so denies himself that this is the same thing as
> obeying God; the heathen is so wilful that it is eternally apparent
> that he does not obey God. The bird has no self-will to give up;
> the Christian gives up his own will; the heathen gives up God.
> The bird neither won nor lost God; the Christian won God and
> accounted it as everything; the heathen lost God and accounted
> it as nothing. . . . The obedience of the bird serves to the honour
> of God, the Christian's more perfect obedience still more so; the
> disobedience of the heathen refuses to honour God, he serves
> for nothing but to be cast out as salt which has lost its savour.[40]

It is not, let us emphasize, obedience to any existing church that
Kierkegaard stresses. He is radically Protestant in his dislike, his repudiation, of the visible church. He would not even take the sacraments
from a minister or priest, demanding that they be administered him by
a layman at his death; this denied him, he refused the sacraments. Even
so, authority is Kierkegaard's obsession. Only in the demanding authority
of religion, in total obedience to Christ and in equally total repudiation of the pleasures and aspirations of the world, would human beings
find respite from the kinds of torment he described so eloquently in the
Christian Discourses.

Only Alexis de Tocqueville among nineteenth-century thinkers
speaks to us today as eloquently and pertinently in moral and spiritual
matters as does Kierkegaard. When we turn to such a work as *The
Present Age,* one of the briefest of Kierkegaard's voluminous writings,
it is hard to think he is not writing directly to us in the latter part of
the twentieth century. The following paragraphs make this fact vivid
and incontestable:

> Our age is essentially one of understanding and reflection,
> without passion, momentarily bursting into enthusiasm, and
> shrewdly relapsing into repose.
> If we had statistical tables of the consumption of intelligence
> from generation to generation as we have for spirits, we should
> be astounded at the enormous amount of scruple and delibera-

---

[40] Ibid., pp. 92–93.

tion consumed by small, well-to-do families living quietly, and at the amount which the young, even children, use. For just as the children's crusade may be said to typify the Middle Ages, precocious children are typical of the present age. . . .

Nowadays not even a suicide kills himself in desperation. Before taking the step he deliberates so long and so carefully that he literally chokes with thought. It is even questionable whether he ought to be called a suicide, since it is really thought which takes his life. He does not die *with* deliberation but *from* deliberation. . . .

A revolutionary age is an age of action; ours is the age of advertisement and publicity. Nothing ever happens but there is immediate publicity everywhere. In the present age a rebellion is, of all things, the most unthinkable. Such an expression of strength would seem ridiculous to the calculating intelligence of our times. On the other hand a political virtuoso might bring off a feat almost as remarkable. He might write a manifesto suggesting a general assembly at which people should decide upon a rebellion, and it would be so carefully worded that even the censor would let it pass. At the meeting itself he would be able to create the impression that his audience had rebelled, after which they would all go quietly home—having spent a very pleasant evening. Among the young men of today a profound and prodigious learning is almost unthinkable; they would find it ridiculous. On the other hand a scientific virtuoso might draw up a subscription form outlining an all-embracing system which he purposed to write and, what is more, in such a way that the reader would feel he had already read the system; for the age of encyclopedists, when men wrote gigantic folios with unremitting pains, is gone. Now is the turn of those light-weight encyclopedists who, *en passant*, deal with all the sciences and the whole of existence. Equally unthinkable among the young men of today is a truly religious renunciation of the world, adhered to with daily self-denial. On the other hand almost any theological student is capable of something far more wonderful. He could found a society with the sole object of saving all those who are lost. The age of great and good actions is past, the present is the age of anticipation when even recognition is received in advance.[41]

It is, clearly, an age of blandness, of superficiality, of submerged vigor, and of atomized thought that Kierkegaard describes with biting

41 Kierkegaard, *The Present Age*, pp. 33, 35–36.

irony in the passages just quoted. And such intellectual blandness can only result in alienation of the spirit, along with a spreading inability to act positively in the name of God or conscience. Not long before Kierkegaard wrote the words above, Tocqueville, in his *Democracy in America*, had also described the contemporary scene—in Europe as well as America—as one in which capacity for revolutions of thought had virtually disappeared, in which a kind of monotony of the spirit had descended upon human beings, creating apathy and indifference. This, Tocqueville thought, was the result of the cultural homogeneity that democratic leveling had produced in the modern West. It could well have been Tocqueville rather than Kierkegaard who wrote the words that follow:

> Throughout many changes the tendency in modern times has remained a levelling one. . . . In order that everything should be reduced to the same level, it is first of all necessary to procure a phantom, its spirit a monstrous abstraction, an all-embracing something which is nothing, a mirage—and that phantom is *the public*. It is only in an age which is without passion, yet reflective, that such a phantom can develop itself with the help of the Press which itself becomes an abstraction. . . . The public is, in fact, the real Levelling-Master rather than the actual leveller, for whenever levelling is only approximately accomplished it is done by something, but the public is a monstrous nothing.[42]

Tocqueville had written of the public and of public opinion in modern democracy that it exerted a power greater even than that of the Spanish Inquisition over human creativity; for, whereas the Inquisition had only threatened originality, modern public opinion dissolves it. Kierkegaard, plainly, is of like mind. And just as Tocqueville had seen in modern democracy a force capable of eventually destroying individuality, with great individuals becoming constantly fewer, so Kierkegaard sees individual impotence where once individual power and initiative had flourished.

> No single individual (I mean no outstanding individual—in the sense of leadership and conceived according to the dialectical category "fate") will be able to arrest the abstract process of levelling, for it is negatively something higher, and the age of chivalry is gone. No society or association can arrest that abstract power, simply because association is itself in the service of the levelling process. . . . The abstract levelling process,

[42] Ibid., pp. 59–60.

that self-combustion of the human race, produced by the friction which arises when the individual ceases to exist as singled out by religion, is bound to continue, like a trade wind, and consume everything.[43]

Only through the authority—and, simultaneously, the freedom—of religion, Kierkegaard declares, can the individual hope to achieve the measure of greatness and heroism that is denied him in an age of mass leveling and extinction of the social and cultural sources of greatness. What Rousseau and the French Revolution have created is a setting in which any possibility of secular redemption is destroyed. All efforts along that line can lead only to greater leveling and tyranny of the phantom public. Religion alone can provide the supporting pillars necessary for reasserting, at one and the same time, individuality and community.

Because Kierkegaard's obsession with the role of the individual in universe and society, with his loneliness, which the assistance of none of the visible forms of community could remedy, has been considered perhaps the real source of modern existentialism, his abiding interest in community has often been overlooked. We find writers even suggesting that Kierkegaard *should* have been concerned with community. But such observations do not help us; they lack true insight. Kierkegaard saw man (and this is his relation to existentialism) as a being in dread, despair, and anxiety—not wanting to be, of course, but destined to be, so long as the only refuges offered him were those built upon intellectual commitment, organization, and the manipulations of democratic, industrial mass society. Only through subjective commitment of the individual, through a mode of consciousness and of communication extending beyond purely intellectual-manipulative types of relationship, was community possible. This community, for Kierkegaard, would be first and last the *I-Thou* relation of man to God, but from this would spring an *I-Thou* relation of man to man also.

This, then, is Kierkegaard's link to the contemporary age, with its profound quest for community. If we are looking for the terminology of community that we find in so many other religious minds of the nineteenth and twentieth centuries, we shall not find it. Not for him the visible, historic church that Newman was committed to—nor, for that matter, any other existing form of Christian church. We do not, in fact, find in Kierkegaard abundant reference to community of any kind. What we do find, however, is, first, a deep, crisis-bred, agonized sense of the individual's anxiety, despair, and alienation—the product, Kierkegaard felt, of man's estrangement from the true, binding, and absolute

43 Ibid., pp. 55–56.

authority of Christ; and, second, a poignant sense of man's relation to God, the *I-Thou*, man-God tie going well beyond anything Luther or Calvin ever had in mind, the full realization of which *is* community: the deepest form of community possible, on which alone could other, social and visible, forms of community be built. Only through authority, though, the absolute authority of Christ, could man's existential aloneness be terminated.

Comte

How powerful and sweeping a current was religion in nineteenth-century thought, despite the efforts of philosophes, revolutionaries, and others in the rationalist tradition to banish it from the Western mind, can be well illustrated by the rise of the new science of sociology. From its beginnings in the writings of Auguste Comte (1798–1857) down through the seminal works of Max Weber and Émile Durkheim, a concern with religion, its roots, social nature, and values, has been one of the two or three most fundamental areas of modern sociology. It is irrelevant that few if any of the central figures in the sociological study of religion were themselves believers to any notable degree. What is important is that sociology alone among the social sciences, particularly in the writing of Comte, Weber, and Durkheim, reinforced the view that, right or wrong, religion is a universal and ineradicable aspect of the human condition.

We do not ordinarily think of Comte—whose name is inseparable from the origins of systematic sociology, who coined the word *sociology*, and who was long famous for his philosophy of science—as a part of what I have called here the religious community. He was, however; and before he died, he made sociology synonymous with religion; specifically, what he called the Religion of Humanity, with society the "Grand Being." During his very last years Comte even came to regard himself as a messiah, as the pope of the new Religion of Humanity, with Paris the seat of the new papacy in the same way that Rome had been for the Christianity that Comte believed had now become obsolete. And, with Comte's full approval, there were even groups that met in religious assembly, in a number of cities in Europe and America, to worship and perform rites in the name of the Grand Being, society.

It is easy enough to dismiss this phase of Comte's life as that of a mind deranged, messianically obsessed. And we know Comte had suffered a severe mental breakdown in earlier years. Certainly, all who have dealt with Comte as rationalist and positivist—which he was—have either ignored his religious obsessions or else considered them as aberrations of later life. It is well to remember, however, that in his earliest writings Comte, who was born a Roman Catholic but left this religion while a student, never to return to it, argued the necessity of a "spiritual power" that would be, along with family, city, and political government, an essential element of society. Even in the period when Comte was primarily concerned with science, with positivism, as he called the scientific spirit, he made clear his distaste for the antireligious views of the Enlightenment. No society, he thought even then, could possibly survive without a commitment to spiritual principle that would be equivalent to religion. In these early essays Comte emphasized his opposition not only to the Enlightenment's secularism but also its individualism, theory of popular sovereignty, and philosophy of rights. Comte regarded all of these as not merely unscientific but also inherently destructive of the social bond.

Even so, it would be possible to conclude from Comte's first major work, for which he is even today most famous, *The Positive Philosophy* (1830–42) that he was basically hostile to religion. For there, to account for the intellectual development of mankind, he introduces his Law of Three Stages, according to which mankind everywhere must pass through the stages of *religion, metaphysics,* and *science.* The religious stage of human evolution is declared to be the most primitive and, further, the absolute opposite of the scientific stage, which Comte termed the most recent in mankind's development. The great objective of the day, Comte argued—and in a way that pleased rationalists throughout the world, for he was a notable figure in the judgment of many—was to prepare men's minds for the inevitable onset of the scientific or positive age. And this could only be done by freeing them from all lingering traces of the religious view of life. The larger work of banishing religion from the civilized world had already been done, Comte said, by the "metaphysical" stage of European development, the stage marked by the Age of Reason and by the philosophers of the French Enlightenment, who had, he thought, negated the fundamental propositions of religion. In any event, the future belonged to science, to technology, and to industry: so Comte argued with an eloquence that made him one of the most admired figures in European rationalist circles.

But when Comte's next major work, *The Positive Polity* (1851–54), was written, a major change of orientation was evident. Now the scientific is subordinated to the religious; or rather, the scientific is made into the religious. This vast utopian work, which Comte specifically subtitled *A Treatise on Sociology,* was written as an example of what both the new science of sociology and, at the same time, the new sociology-governed society of the future would be like. In it we find that reigning scientists have become priests in name and fact, that science or positivism is the Religion of Humanity, that it will be to the people exactly what Christianity was during the Middle Ages, that it will have its due ceremonies and rites (which Comte recounts in a degree of detail that is often amusing to any contemporary reader), and that the Grand Being, society, will forever replace in mankind's consciousness all earlier and false deities.

Here again, it is tempting to regard such ideas as aspects of a deluded mind, as many readers have done. But it would be unfortunate to overlook in Comte's celebration of his Religion of Humanity some extraordinarily sharp insights into the nature of religion and the relation of religion to language, culture, and human values.[44] Religiously obsessed Comte may have become in his later years, but in no degree did he lose the faculty of dissecting and analyzing, and also of generalizing; and, allowing only for the evangelical cast of so much of *The Positive Polity,* we find this faculty vividly and fruitfully in evidence in his treatment of religion as an essential part of society.

Without going into detail here, it is possible to find clearly set forth in Comte's treatment of religion several perspectives which have been part of sociology from Comte's day to our own. First, religion is held to be inextricably a part of the social bond. If Comte went well beyond ordinary sociological analysis in his reference to society as the Grand Being, deserving of worship, he nonetheless made clear that, whatever else we might think religion to be, it is manifest in social roles, statuses, and primary modes of social interaction. Second, Comte made religion a fundamental element of the whole process of socialization. As Durkheim was to emphasize a generation later, Comte stressed the intimate relation between sacred values and the set of prejudgments which underlie all communication, all language, all socialization in the largest sense of the word. Third, Comte presented religion as a vital integrative mechanism for society and for culture, the framework of all the smaller integrative mechanisms one finds in family, neighborhood, local community, and the other associations in the social order. Fourth—a mark of the age in which Comte lived and wrote, an age, as I have said, that rediscovered the social, cultural, and aesthetic aspects of religion—he gave lasting emphasis to the ritual character of religion, to the rites and ceremonies, as distinct from doctrines and beliefs, which form its structure, no matter what beliefs a specific religion may be founded upon in strictly intellectual terms. Fifth, religion is to be seen in Comte's presentation as the aboriginal source of man's most fundamental ideas and values. Weber and Durkheim would carry this aspect much farther, and in much more objective fashion, than Comte did; but we must not be blind to its existence in Comte's works. Sixth and finally, Comte gives primacy to the whole spiritual-religious realm in understanding social evolution and social change. All change, he argues, is basically change of mind and of values—sacred values. Well before Weber's masterpiece

---

[44] Comte's treatment of religion is to be found in the second of the four volumes which form his *Positive Polity*. See my *Sociological Tradition* (New York: Basic Books, 1966), especially chap. 6.

on the Protestant ethic, Comte had set forth in detail the impact of Protestantism (a religion he disliked intensely because of its individualism and its general depreciation of the external ties of religious community) upon European culture.

Objectionable as the thought may be to the more secular-minded contemporary social scientists, the origins of systematic sociology are deep in a cast of mind, to be seen in Comte and others of like interest in his day, that is religious to the core. In every relevant respect, the rise of sociology is a part of the nineteenth-century rediscovery of the religious community.

Weber

The relation between sociology and religion is nowhere better illustrated than by the monumental works of Max Weber (1864–1920), the man who, along with Émile Durkheim, is generally regarded as one of the two dominating thinkers in contemporary sociological theory. Weber's interest in religion was profound and encompassing. His theory of charismatic leadership or authority is, of course, religious in its essence. The charismatic leader is possessed of powers believed by his followers to be divine in source—at the very least, sacred. The charisma that marks the special type of authority to be found in such figures as Buddha, Jesus, and Mohammed, in time becomes "routinized," that is, transferred from the charismatic figure to tradition, ceremony, dogma, and association. Charismatic authority is, Weber argued, among the most vital of all causes of social change.

Weber is famous, too, for the breadth, depth, and intensity of his comparative studies of world religions. No scholar to this day has equaled the sweep of Weber's sociological inquiries into religions of the past and present. For Weber, religion was an inextinguishable element of the human community; and conversely, community, together with the roles, statuses, norms, and types of interaction which are the microcosmic constituents of community, is an inextinguishable element of religion, irrespective of creed. Weber's studies of the relation between religion and social structure remain to this moment the finest yet done in comparative-historical terms by either social scientists or historians.

It is impossible to do more than refer in briefest terms to the scope and detail of Weber's studies of the religious community. What is best emphasized here is the single work in this field for which Weber even now is most famous: his *Protestant Ethic and the Spirit of Capitalism.* Quite apart from the intrinsic interest of the book, much of its classic importance in history and the social sciences comes from its implicit powerful criticism of Marxism and the economic interpretation of historical change. The Marxist theory of history rested on the claimed primacy of the economic factor. It was, Marx had declared, changes in the economic relations of men which had in turn led to changes in other spheres of society and culture, thus producing modern capitalism and its surrounding society. Throughout history, Marx wrote, property, economic relationships, and the class struggles emanating from these relationships had been dominant in mankind's development and must be regarded as analytically prior to any understanding of social change. Marx, in short, did not take kindly to any view of social change and development in which religious or other spiritual factors were basic.

It would be false to suggest that Weber was primarily motivated by desire to refute Marx. Weber was deeply informed in Marxist scholarship, however, and we know that there was much about this scholarship and its implicit theory of society and history that offended his scholarly sensibilities. The essential point in any event is not motivation but effect. And the effect of Weber's *Protestant Ethic* was to throw a good deal of doubt both upon the Marxist-materialist explanation of the rise of capitalism and upon the materialist envisagement of history as a whole.

Weber was by no means the first to note the high correlation between the rise of capitalism and the appearance beforehand of Protestantism in the crucial areas of western Europe. Certain Catholic historians and philosophers, among others, had called attention to that correlation or coincidence, but Weber supplied a generally convincing explanation of the phenomenon, cast in terms of a theory of values and social actions. He noted the correspondence of Protestant mentality in Puritan England, and in Puritan America also, and a general attitude toward life that discouraged indolence, leisure, and other interferences with vigorous activity in this world. We have noted in an earlier section of this chapter the Protestant condemnation of those types of ritual and ceremony and holiday that could be seen as barriers to full economic life. In his capacity as historian, Weber was aware of all this.

He went further, however. He set himself to the intensive reading of Puritan sermons and other writings of the late sixteenth and the seventeenth centuries. He began to sense a relation between Protestant, especially Calvinist, emphasis upon the solitary character of individual salvation and a certain form of spiritual anxiety in Puritans which could best be allayed through incessant demonstration to themselves and others that they were among the elect, destined to salvation, with their own composure and material welfare in this world the infallible signs of such predestination. Even though many, though by no means all, Puritan divines were antipathetic to worldliness in any form, including the gain of riches, Weber was able to show that a spirit inclining toward dedicated, rationalist, disciplined cultivation of material gain—the spirit of capitalism—was an unintended but real outcome of Calvinist doctrines.

The point to emphasize here is that Weber took the matter of capitalism's origins out of the economic or technological area and located them, at least in substantial degree, in the utterly noneconomic area of religious thought and commitment. Considered as a piece of historical analysis, *The Protestant Ethic* is original and noteworthy. Considered as a refutation of the Marxist or materialist theory of history, Weber's book is impressive. But its largest significance for present purposes is its triumphant demonstration of the important place occupied by the study of religion, as an area of motivation and of other incentives to social action, in the whole understanding of society, social behavior, and history. That Weber's book has occasional flaws, and that it has been substantially corrected by later scholarship, is true enough. And we should emphasize at this point that, contrary to the belief of many, Weber at no point ever declared religion the sole causal factor in the rise of Protestantism. The fact remains that *The Protestant Ethic,* written by a deeply scholarly, almost wholly nonreligious mind, stands as one further testament to the rediscovery of the religious community in the nineteenth and early twentieth centuries.

How deep a hold religion had upon Weber's mind as an area of investigation and scholarship may be seen by mere random examination of the vast range of his work that followed *The Protestant Ethic.* Here we find exhaustive studies of Judaism, Hinduism, Confucianism, and other major religions of mankind. His announced intention was to compare the non-Christian religions in order to see, by contrast, what lay in Christianity that made for its fusion with not simply capitalism but the whole modernist temper—rationality, bureaucracy, technology, individualism, and the like. And much of his work does indeed concern itself with this question. But the studies take us a great deal farther: they give us perspectives on the relation of different kinds of social classes and castes with various kinds of religion; and they light up the relation between religion—religious tradition, rite, routine, and community—and charisma, between types of religion and varying intensity of desire to create monastic and other forms of communal structure, and, finally, between types of religion and types of world view, culture, and social system.

How religious Weber was in his own beliefs and feelings, we do not know with any degree of certainty. Clearly he was not an active, committed member of any church or sect. Very probably he was skeptical in religious matters so far as his personal belief went. No one, however, has exceeded Weber in his respect for the importance of religion as an integrative force in society or for the crucial character of religious belief in matters of social change. There is a vast gulf between the kind of contempt for religion and the repudiation of it as a serious force in the future of Western society that is evident in the writings of the utilitarians and rationalists of the mainstream in Weber's day and the conception of the function, role, and lasting normative significance of religion we find in Weber's works.

Finally, it should be emphasized that a great deal of the alienation, the general mood of disenchantment, the spiritual leveling, and the bureaucratization of mind and culture Weber saw around him in the West sprang, in his judgment, out of the spreading detachment of human life from the kinds of consensus and commitment fundamental to religion. One of Weber's most famous passages gives witness to this view of things. It is to be found at the very end of *The Protestant Ethic*, where Weber is reflecting on the dominance of the material in modern Western society and the seeming decline of motivation toward economic growth and advancement.

> Since asceticism undertook to remodel the world and to work out its ideals in the world, material goods have gained an increasing and finally an inexorable power over the lives of men as at no previous period in history. Today the spirit of religious asceticism—whether finally, who knows?—has escaped from the cage. But victorious capitalism, since it rests on mechanical foundations, needs its support no longer. The rosy blush of its laughing heir, the Enlightenment, also seems to be irretrievably fading, and the idea of duty in one's calling prowls about in our lives like the ghost of dead religious beliefs. . . .
>
> No one knows who will live in this cage in the future, or whether at the end of this tremendous development entirely new prophets will arise, or there will be a great rebirth of old ideas and ideals or, if neither, mechanized petrification embellished with a sort of convulsive self-importance. For of the last stage of this cultural development, it might well be truly said: "Specialists without spirit, sensualists without heart; this nullity imagines that it has obtained a level of civilization never before achieved." [45]

Durkheim

Only Émile Durkheim (1858–1917) rivals Weber in profundity and reach of his sociological understanding of religion. Durkheim considered himself an atheist; but no one, in the judgment of qualified observers, religious or nonreligious, has written more penetratingly than he on the functional relationship of religion to society. Quite as much as Comte

[45] Max Weber, *The Protestant Ethic and the Spirit of Capitalism*, trans. Talcott Parsons (New York: Charles Scribner's Sons, 1958), p. 181.

and Weber, Durkheim was opposed to the conventional rationalist explanation (or dismissal) of religion and its states of mind. "The theorists who have undertaken to explain religion in rational terms have generally seen it before all else a system of ideas, corresponding to some predetermined object." But, Durkheim says, if we turn to the appraisals and experiences of those are themselves committed to religion, we find that the least important aspect of a religion is what it says about things. By all odds the most important quality of a religion is what is does to make action possible, to make life durable:

> The believer who has communicated with his god is not merely a man who sees new truths of which the unbeliever is ignorant; he is a man who is stronger. He feels within him more force, either to endure the trials of existence, or to conquer them.[46]

This sense of the life-giving, life-reinforcing nature of religion springs in the first instance, Durkheim tells us, from the sacred community of believers, from the indispensable feeling of collective oneness in worship and faith. To suppose, as Protestants and secularists alike have supposed, that religion is a basically individual experience "misunderstands the fundamental conditions of religious life."

It is the *cult* that is primary, taking this word to mean the community of whatever size within which rites and beliefs are to be found. Hence comes the vital importance of *rites*, the specialized ceremonies through which one is enabled, first, to become a member of the sacred community; second, to remain in kinship with whatever it is the cult worships or venerates, whether this be god or totem; third, to be able to ward off the evil influences that beset man; and, fourth, to leave this world in death under the most benign auspices. Far more important than any belief or doctrine, Durkheim argues, is the rite, for it is the rite that unifies the cult and establishes the communicant in the cult forever.

How vital Durkheim thought the religious community to have been in mankind's history is tellingly illustrated by his theory of the origins of thought, more specifically, the fundamental categories of thought. The only way thinking of any kind is possible, Durkheim observes, is through a kind of framework composed of basic ideas or categories which in a sense precede the individual's empirical experience. Examples of these basic categories of thought are *causality, force, time, space,* and so on. We do not inherit these through the germ plasm, despite the argument along this line by the so-called intuitionists or apriorists. Neither, how-

[46] Émile Durkheim, *The Elementary Forms of Religious Life*, trans. Joseph Ward Swain (Glencoe, Ill.: Free Press, 1947), p. 416.

ever, do we acquire the categories through simple additive, cumulative individual experience, as the associationists and radical empiricists have argued. How do we acquire them? From the culture around us, Durkheim declares. But how did such categories of thought become implanted in human culture in the first place, to be transmitted thereafter by being absorbed through processes of individual acculturation by countless generations of individuals? Durkheim's answer is surely among the most extreme arguments ever given for the functional indispensability of religion to society and mind. Not even Augustine could have more directly argued the primacy of religion in society.

> At the roots of all our judgments there are a certain number of essential ideas which dominate all our intellectual life; they are what the philosophers since Aristotle have called the categories of the understanding: ideas of time, space, class, number, cause, substance, personality, etc. They correspond to the most universal properties of things. They are like the solid frame which encloses all thought; . . . They are like the framework of intelligence. Now when primitive religious beliefs are systematically analyzed, the principal categories are naturally found. They are born in religion and of religion; they are a product of religious thought.[48]

From the prior notion of some supernatural being—god, spirit, or whatever—capable of doing all things, comes the original notion of cause. And, correctly enough, Durkheim notes the tendency of most thinking about causation, even in relatively recent times, to cast itself in what are essentially religious terms. For Durkheim, who found the origin of religion in consecration of the community and its power, it was this unlimited power vested in the community, in society, over the individual whch gave rise to the notion of causative force that was not itself effect of some prior cause. And from the vital necessity in primitive life of correctly marking the number of days and nights in between occasions appropriate for homage to the supernatural came the sense, duly transcribed in such cultural ways as calendars, of the passing of time—the rhythmic periodicity of time or the flow of time, as the case may be. Even human conceptions of space, Durkheim argued, can be shown to be drawn directly from the arrangements of things around them in immediate space—be it physical or social.

There is no need to multiply examples; nor is there room here to go more deeply into Durkheim's analysis of the matter. Suffice it to say that few sociologists or philosophers concerned with the origins of

48 Ibid., p. 9.

thought have been in any marked degree satisfied with Durkheim's treatment. Very probably the question of ultimate origins of thought and its processes and categories is unanswerable save in the most general evolutionary terms. But what emerges satisfyingly and lastingly in Durkheim is, first, his demonstration that, leaving aside absolute origins, the nature of a specific culture does indeed strongly affect individuals' specific ways of thinking about even the most abstract, ethereal, or supernatural matters. And, second, it is impossible to find significant fault with the larger point of Durkheim's treatment: the powerful role that religion, the sacred, and the sacred community have played in human thought and life from the beginning down to the present. Nor can religion be relegated, as the rationalists and secularists have sought to relegate it, to the past, or to those areas of the present still dominated by survivals of the past. If Durkheim's book has one overriding conclusion, it is that religion—at least as he defines and describes it, conceived as the consecration of the community or as the community of the sacred—is eternal in the human experience:

> Thus there is something eternal in religion which is destined to survive all the particular symbols in which religious thought has successively enveloped itself. There can be no society which does not feel the need of upholding and reaffirming at regular intervals the collective sentiments and the collective ideas which make its unity and its personality. Now this moral remaking cannot be achieved except by the means of reunions, assemblies, and meetings where the individuals, being closely united to one another, reaffirm in common their common sentiments; hence come ceremonies which do not differ from regular religious ceremonies, either in their object, the results which they produce, or the processes employed to attain these results. What essential difference is there between an assembly of Christians celebrating the principal dates in the life of Christ, or of Jews remembering the exodus from Egypt or the promulgation of the decalogue, and a reunion of citizens commemorating the promulgation of a new moral or legal system or some great event in the national life? [49]

49 Ibid., p. 427.

4 The Revolutionary Community

Revolution and Western Society

Beginning with this chapter, we turn to three quite different types of community in Western social thought. Thus far we have been concerned with continuities of ideas that have not only paralleled but in substantial degree reflected major institutions in Western social life: the military, the political state, and Christianity. Now we shall turn to three patterns of community which, far from paralleling or reflecting established institutions, are best to be seen in outright confrontation with them: sometimes in revolutionary challenge to such institutions, sometimes in repudiation and withdrawal from them, and sometimes in major efforts to transform centralization of authority into the values of diversity and pluralism. We shall be concerned in what follows with, first, the revolutionary community in the West and then, in the two succeeding chapters, with the ecological and pluralist communities.

249

The revolutionary tradition, as we understand it today, is relatively recent, hardly going back before the seventeenth-century Puritan revolt in England and not acquiring its full modern flavor until the French Revolution at the end of the eighteenth century. Assuredly, as will be noted, there have been revolts, uprisings, and insurrections of one kind or another, doubtless since the beginnings of human history. But revolution, as we use the word today (and omitting the derivative usages that go with substantial scientific or technological changes), is something quite distinct from these. It is, in the first place, fundamentally political in character: concerned with the calculated overthrow of some existing political order, using as much force and terror as are deemed necessary to effect radical changes in men's moral, economic, social, and intellectual lives. Only since about the eighteenth century, actually (with the exception as noted of the Puritan revolt in the preceding century in England), has the political state—that is to say, political power—been vested by philosophers and others with the kind of potentiality for social or moral reconstruction characteristically sought by revolutions. The modern revolutionary mentality has required, above all else, conviction of the sanctified nature of political power when directed to chosen moral and social ends. Revolution, as we use this term in Western history, is first and last *political* revolution, its ends and means alike conceived as political in the first instance, whatever may be its ultimate vision of human society.

But while the political mentality is crucial to the revolutionary community, it is not possible to understand the distinctive character of that community in the West since the eighteenth century through politics alone. Two other types of mentality are very characteristic of revolution, even if they are not, like the political, a part of its essence: they are the *religious* and the *military*. The modern revolutionary community, from the time of the French Revolution—which has been ever since a kind of archetype of revolutionary thinking in the West and other parts of the world as well—down to Mao Tse-tung and Fidel Castro, is an amalgam of political, religious, and military values. We cannot hope to understand this preeminently modern type of mentality except in light of that fact.

Politics provides the ends of revolution, but the zeal and sense of mission without which no revolution can hope to succeed are clearly of religious substance. Tocqueville was the first to point out the profoundly religious quality of the French Revolution's temper of mind, its view of man and man's relation to society and history. Without a basically religious sense of dedication, the revolutionary-radical mentality does not emerge from the peculiar preoccupation with power that is at the core of politics.

Likewise there are aspects of the revolutionary tradition that are more nearly military than anything else. The resemblance between the words militant and military is more than verbal: most of the world's militant organizations, past and present, have modeled themselves in some degree upon the military community. Even the church can take over the symbols, titles, and techniques of warfare—as is suggested by the example of the Jesuit order in Catholic Christianity, at least when it was brought into existence by Ignatius Loyola, himself a retired soldier.

If the zeal of political revolution suggests religion, the organization and techniques of revolution suggest the army—more accurately, for the most part, guerrilla forces. The greater revolutionary figures of modern times, including Lenin, Stalin, Hitler, Mao, and Castro, have all had profound elements of military leadership in their makeups. Beyond this, in our age, there is an ever closer liaison between revolution and war, with the symbols of the one easily serving the other on frequent occasion.

The Elements of the Revolutionary Community

Despite a still widespread belief, revolution as we have known it in the West since the eighteenth century is no spontaneous welling up of the masses, no inexorable, deterministic response of large aggregates to conditions of poverty, political deprivation, or social injustice. Such conditions may, and usually do, obtain to some degree; and for revolutions to be successful, as they have been in France, Russia, China, and other areas in modern times, significant numbers of people, though rarely if ever majorities, must early become involved, for short periods at least, in order to furnish necessary contexts of revolutionary action. But the heart of every revolution, successful or unsuccessful, lies in small minorities—elites, as they are known in modern social theory—composed of dedicated, often professionally trained individuals, conscious of themselves as communities, and working with technical knowledge as well as moral zeal toward the overthrow of a political order by whatever means are necessary. Such elites or communities are crucially involved in every revolution in history: the Puritan revolution of seventeenth-century England, the American and French revolutions of the eighteenth century, the sporadic and essentially small-scale European revolutions in the nineteenth century, and, not least, the great, world-transforming twentieth-century revolutions in Russia, China, and many other places.

None of this is to imply that appropriate social, economic, and political conditions are not necessary or that privations, oppressions, and intolerable inequities in the surrounding scene may not exist to give urgency as well as success to revolutionary aims. I am only emphasizing that while all such conditions may indeed be present, what is crucial and indispensable in revolution is the presence of the revolutionary community. We must turn now to some of the vital elements of this type of community, be it community in the practical sense of those such as Jacobins or Bolsheviks who have brought down governments, or in the more philosophical sense with which we are concerned in this book.

Myth

The first and utterly indispensable element of any genuine revolutionary community or elite is belief in some form of goodness lying in human nature or in society, requiring only the liberative action of revolutionary violence to become manifest and dominant. Belief in this goodness as an ineradicable part of humanity's true nature must be so absolute that all existing institutions, values, and authorities which dominate men may be considered evil, corrupt, and waiting to be exterminated. Such myth or dogma may have heavenly overtones, as was the case with certain terroristic, religion-intoxicated groups in the late Middle Ages who believed that the Second Coming could be effected, and eternal bliss commenced, only through radical extermination of all persons and property. There was, as we have already seen, a profoundly revolutionary character to primitive Christianity, which arose directly from its own dogmatic belief both in the imminent millennium, heralded by the Messiah, Christ, and in the total corruption of pagan society. The tie between professed religion and revolutionary behavior has been close throughout history, for it is the kind of blinding vision of the total good, or of total redemption, springing largely from religion that is most likely to make everything around one seem unworthy at best, hatefully corrupt and degenerate at worst.

But such vision of good, of the millennium, of salvation, such myth and dogma need not be religious in the overt sense of this word. As Tocqueville pointed out, the most important attribute of the leaders of the French Revolution was their commitment to an absolute form of good—civic purity and morality—that may have been conceived in terms of this world and without appeal to God but that was nonetheless religious in spirit and intensity. Marxism, as we have also noted in another connection, has a profoundly religious character for those who live by its tenets. Belief in the total evil of this world and in the inexorable coming of the good, just, and classless society where all men will be equal is certainly a secularization of deep Judaic and Christian beliefs. Myth, in the strict sense in which I use it here, is as essential to the revolutionary movement as it is to religion.

The Necessity of Violence

No genuinely revolutionary movement is to be found that does not declare violence and force, even all-out war and terror, to be necessary.

Marx had nothing but contempt for those who thought powerful governments could be overthrown through means other than violent ones—given the predictable efforts by such governments to defend themselves. It was over the issue of violence and use of war that Lenin broke sharply with other early-twentieth-century European socialist leaders. Lenin thought he could see signs of a developing pacifism, of an anarchist-oriented renunciation of violence, in the writings of these individuals, several of whom were powerful in the European socialist movement. All violence is good, Lenin declared, that helps the workers' revolution, even the violence of imperialist wars. The objective, he wrote, is to turn the imperialist war into a workers' war, not to abjure war as such. Sorel, Fanon, Castro, Mao—there is no major exception at all to the point here being stressed: true social change requires revolution; revolution is unthinkable without violence; hence violence is necessary.

The Holiness of Sin

Violence is also *good*. It is impossible to miss in the revolutionary tradition, from the Jacobins' solemnly announced policy of public terror, through some of the writings of Marx, Engels, Lenin, and Sorel, all the way down to the revolutions in Russia and China in the present century, the belief that violence, force, and repression are good—so long, that is, as they serve the ends of the revolution. Acts such as murder, kidnapping, treason, torture, mutilation, vandalism, and arson, which are ordinarily deemed to be sinful, at very least immoral and illegal, take on a quality nothing short of holy when committed in the name of the revolution. It is not merely that these acts are regarded as allowable, as tactical necessities of the revolution against established order. The important point is that they are regarded as good, indeed as holy,[1] the committers of the acts being sanctified through blood, devastation, and whatever else the toll of the revolution may be. Acts from which members of the revolutionary community might have shrunk in horror in their individual, prerevolutionary identities become saturated with a special and redeeming form of piety.

Terror

Hence arises the necessity of terror. The Jacobins, at midpoint in the French Revolution, were the first to give rhetorical and systematic promulgation to the strategy of terror. Terror is, however, one of the oldest means of military domination of an area or a people. Ancient armies,

---

[1] I have taken the brilliant phrase "the holiness of sin" from the title and theme of an article by Gershom Scholem. First written in Hebrew in the 1930s, it was reprinted in English in *Commentary*, Jan. 1971, pp. 41–70.

following, surely, the timeless example of primitive bands of predators, used the strategy of terror: total devastation of lands, killing of all the inhabitants of a given village, town, or small province, publicly flaunted torture or agonizing execution of selected individuals, as in the Roman practice of crucifixion, and so on. All of these are acts of terror, the purpose of which is much less what they do to the actual victims than what their example does to other members of the social order. The evidence is as clear today as it must have been thousands of years ago that terror mounted on a large-enough scale can induce almost robotlike behavior among the masses for indefinite periods of time. This is as true of revolution as of warfare. There is no instance of successful revolution since 1789 that has not made use of terror, with victims numbering many millions as in the Soviet Union under Stalin and China under Mao; and all revolutionary philosophers and tractarians have been aware of the necessity of terror.

Beyond this, however, is the conviction in the minds of those who employ the tactics of terror that it can act as a kind of cauterizing agent against the accumulated poisons and corruptions virtually all revolutionary thinkers see in the order they desire to destroy. Just as a white-hot steel bar was once used against gangrene, thus saving the individual's life at whatever cost in immediate pain, so, revolutionists often believe, terror instituted against the members of a corrupt society can be a means of protecting them from further effects of the evils within that society. The spiritual properties of terror were constantly proclaimed by the Committee on Public Safety during the months in which dozens, sometimes hundreds, died daily in the public square under the guillotine's blade and many more persons were put to the torment of secret imprisonment, of torture, or advertised suspicion.

Totalism

The claim of the revolutionary community upon its members, of revolutionary belief upon its devotees, is total. In this respect, as in others, it resembles certain types of religious sects, including those of the early Christians. No other allegiance, whether to family, nation, or religion, is recognized as warranting the slightest withholding of loyalties to the revolutionary dogma by those sworn to its support. Indeed members of the revolutionary community prove themselves through their willingness to cast off, to renounce publicly, or even to betray relatives, friends, and fellow citizens. The totalitarian states of the twentieth century, communist and fascist alike, were presaged by the efforts of the Jacobins in 1793 to secure the total commitment of all French citizens to the ideals of the Revolution. And it is impossible to understand the development of the ideology of totalitarianism, which had its first major manifestation in Russia in 1917 following the triumph there of the Bolsheviks, apart from the writings of Marx and Engels, among others.

Elites

No revolutionary community or revolutionary philosophy is without a sense of being or espousing an elite. The Jacobins were such an elite for a time during the French Revolution. Marx and Engels saw the Communist party as the elite vanguard of the working class; and their heirs, from Lenin and Trotsky down to contemporary heads of the revolutionary states of the world, see it in precisely the same way. There has never been expressed, in the writing of any major revolutionary philosopher, the belief that revolutions are the spontaneous outpourings of militance from the masses. Conditions among the masses may be crucial for the operation of elites, but apart from this operation, there can be no revolution. Marx, for all his emphasis on the necessity of historical context, of requisite historical development, was never in any doubt of the absolute necessity of leadership, the kind he saw emanating from those who alone understood history and its laws.

Revolutionary philosophers have been as determined as religious prophets to have followers or disciples, whose understanding of the truth and whose commitment to it are the signs of their membership in the community founded by a particular revolutionist. There is the same kind of doctrinaire factionalism, the same kind of insistence upon absolute adherence to creed, among revolutionists in modern western history that there is and has been for many centuries among the deeply religious. Marx's own insistence upon discipleship, upon total agreement, from others is a matter of well-attested record, but we find the same insistence in the writings or actions of all other declared revolutionists. And such marks of devotion and fidelity are marks, too, of membership in the elite.

Revolutionary elites, like most elites in the world, make access or membership extremely difficult to achieve. High qualifications are demanded; long, intense preparations are required; screening is formidable; and a whole battery of criteria are employed through which neophytes may prove their dedication, strength, and loyalty. In such respects the revolutionary community is one with the religious sect and the military community alike. In revolutionary organizations such care derives in part from the need to be sure that the enemy through his secret police does not manage admission to the community and, thus, the revolution's destruction. In larger part, however, such trials, tests, and proofs are reflections of the revolutionary community's sense of its elite, even aristocratic, character in society.

Centralization

What Simmel wrote on the secret society is utterly pertinent to revolutionary groups, which are themselves, prior to victory at least, secret societies:

> Corresponding to the outstanding degree of cohesion within the secret society is the thoroughness of its centralization. The secret society offers examples of unconditional and blind obedience to leaders who—although, naturally, they may also be found elsewhere—are yet particularly remarkable in view of the frequent anarchic character of the secret society that negates all other law. The more criminal its purposes, the more unlimited, usually, is the power of the leaders and the cruelty of its exercise. . . .[2]

Simmel notes that it is the very stringency of discipline within the secret society that enhances the members' sense of freedom from the toils and iniquities of the larger society:

> The interrelation between the needs for freedom and for a bond operates here; it appears in the rigor of ritual, which combines the extremes of both: for the sake of a balanced life-feeling, the excess of freedom from all otherwise valid norms must be brought into equilibrium by a similarly excessive submission and renunciation of the will . . . .
>
> Secret societies which, for whatever reason, fail to develop a tightly solidifying authority are, therefore, exposed typically to very grave dangers. . . .[3]

It is this inherent, structurally vital centralization of power within the revolutionary community that explains the almost invariable tendency of societies that are brought into being through revolution to be themselves highly centralized in authority and function. For the new society is but the revolutionary community writ large—that is, at least in intent. Hence comes the profound emphasis—to be seen in the final pages of Marx's *Communist Manifesto,* dealing with centralization of the means of communication as well as of heavy industries and other parts of society—upon the same kind of obedience and total commitment from members of the new revolutionary state that had existed in the small revolutionary community.

[2] *The Sociology of Georg Simmel,* trans. and ed. Kurt Wolff (New York: Free Press, 1950), p. 370.

[3] Ibid., p. 371.

But as Simmel tells us, all efforts to carry revolutionary zeal and unity beyond a certain point are destined to failure. The degree of commitment that may be demanded of the small elite cannot feasibly be demanded of a population of a hundred million people or more. Secret societies, revolutionary communities, elites, and aristocracies: all of these, Simmel noted penetratingly, are small. Efforts to diffuse their values into large-scale populations are invariably futile. What results when such diffusion fails, assuming it is ever tried, is, as we have seen, the instituting of terror. If the larger population cannot be persuaded or converted, it can at least be terrorized into the obedience called for by centralization of power.

Premodern Rebellion

It may help us further in understanding the revolutionary community if we look at a few instances of prerevolutionary thought and behavior in Western history. I have said that the revolutionary community does not much predate the eighteenth century. It was then, most strikingly in the French Revolution, that the idea of violent capture of political power *for political ends* first manifested itself in Western history as the calculated prelude to a widespread reformation of society. It was the French Revolution that set the pattern, that became the model, for the succession of political revolutions which flared up all over nineteenth-century Europe and also for the revolutions of the twentieth century, foremost among them the Bolshevik Revolution in Russia in 1917.

But while it is true that political revolutions did not exist prior to the eighteenth century, there is no historical dearth of rebels and movements of rebellion that could not fail to affect profoundly the systems of authority around them in their respective times and places. The rebel is, surely, one of the oldest of social types or roles in history. Adam's rebellion against God is at very least an allegory of the horror in which rebellion has been held by most of the religious minds of the world. As the Old Testament also records, Cain was, as well as a fratricide, a rebel, not directly against God, but against the kinship bond. Without much doubt, the most ancient of all forms of rebellion was that of son against father. Sigmund Freud made this kind of rebellion, which he conceived to have taken place at the very beginning of the history of the human family, the archetype of man's revolt against culture. Who can doubt that rebels—against patriarchalism, against the war chief, against the priest—have existed from earliest times? Who can doubt, either, that a great deal of human culture is the response, often deadly, to acts of rebellion. From earliest records we get a clear view of the horror, fear, and hatred in which the rebel was held by the community, whose cohesion, whose orthodoxy, was the surest strength against the forces of nature.

The rebel may or may not be inclined toward overt acts of violence. Jesus was a rebel. Although he did not hesitate to drive the money changers from the temple and to declare his opposition to certain elements in the Judaea of his time, violence, even systematic subversion of religion and social order, was alien to his ends. Jesus was nevertheless a rebel, for his whole aim was that of withdrawing people from their traditional practices and relationship and attracting them to himself and to the God for whom he believed he alone spoke. The crucifixion on Golgotha was the punishment accorded a rebel.

Three quarters of a century before Jesus was born, Roman society, in Italy proper, knew what fear of a rebel and rebellion could be, fear that struck deep in the Roman government and citizenry. Spartacus, a slave and gladiator in a small town near Naples called Capua, unable longer to endure the cruelties to which Roman slaves were exposed at that time, led them in a revolt. No one has reconstructed the revolt of Spartacus more fascinatingly, and with closer regard for historical actuality, than Arthur Koestler. His novel *Spartacus* gives us brilliant insight into background, events, and probable motives of the revolt. Fleeing to Mount Vesuvius, Spartacus was joined by an ever-growing number of other slaves who had also escaped their status. Within a few weeks there were thousands of them, under the tight and, we may judge, brilliant command of Spartacus. They commenced their march to the tip of Italy, where Spartacus planned that they would commandeer boats and cross the Mediterranean. Beyond doubt they would have succeeded in this escape had many of Spartacus's slave troops not chosen to remain in Italy longer for purposes of plunder. Rome's own apprehension shortly became near terror, and Roman legions were mobilized hastily under the great Pompey to put down the rebellion and end the plunder. For a time it was not even certain that the professional legions would be able to put down Spartacus and his troops, such was the skill of his command and the bravery and ferocity with which they fought. They were finally defeated, however, by Pompey's legions. Although Spartacus himself had always treated Roman prisoners humanely, six thousand of Spartacus's slave troops, after their capture by the Romans, suffered crucifixion, the most agonizing form of death known at that time, their bodies hanging from crosses up and down the Capua-Rome highway. Spartacus himself was saved from this execution by dying in battle.

But, though Spartacus and his fellow slaves were in clear revolt, it cannot be said that they waged a revolution. For revolution implies capture, or desire to capture, the government, and there is not the slightest evidence for concluding that either Spartacus or his men had any interest beyond liberation from slavery, loot and plunder, and final escape from Italy.

Nor can we term as revolutions those messianically inspired, apocalyptically motivated uprisings in various parts of late medieval and early modern Europe that could at times lead to pillage, burning, looting, and human slaughter. Norman Cohn, in his *Pursuit of the Millennium*, has described in rich detail many of these terroristic outbreaks. He shows us how the medieval tradition of prophecy inherited from the early Christians and also from the Jews became transmuted into forms of behavior that neither could ever possibly have intended. Such was the exaltation occasionally produced in the popular mind during the Middle Ages and after by imagined visions of the impending millennium that groups found themselves following prophet-leaders into ordinarily unimaginable modes of behavior.

Religious though these revolts were in inspiration, economic and social conditions provided contexts that were crucial for them. As Professor Cohn shows in his book, the majority of individuals who joined the rebellions were drawn from the rural proletariat, a class that was not merely economically poor but in process of being dislocated from accustomed status. Beset by insecurity, tormented by loss of status and role, made into marginal men by being uprooted from the community through plague, war, and enclosure of the traditional commons, these individuals were prototypes of the twentieth-century masses. It is, indeed, one of the objectives of Cohn's book to show the affinity between these religious-millennialist groups and the political-millennialist groups that have created the totalitarian societies of our century.

But while social and economic and psychological conditions clearly lay behind much of the rebellion at any given time, the objectives were uniformly and overwhelmingly religious—millennialist and apocalytic in the strict sense of these words. As Professor Cohn writes:

> For what the *propheta* offered to his followers was not simply a chance to improve their lot and to escape from pressing anxieties—it was also, and above all, the prospect of carrying out a divinely ordained mission of stupendous, unique importance. This phantasy quickly came to enthrall them in their turn. . . .
>
> A boundless, millennial promise made with boundless prophet-like conviction to a number of rootless and desperate men in the midst of a society where traditional norms and relationships are disintegrating—here, it would seem, lay the source of that peculiar subterranean fanaticism which subsisted as a perpetual menace to the structure of medieval society. It may be suggested that here, too, lies the source of the giant fanaticisms which in our day have convulsed the world.[4]

---

[4] Norman Cohn, *The Pursuit of the Millennium* (New York: Harper & Row, Torchbooks, 1961), pp. 318–19

It is difficult for our own highly politicized age to believe easily that motives other than political reform and transformation can generate systematic rebellion of groups against their social order, for purposes of rescuing human lives from poverty and oppression. But down until the late eighteenth century in the West, the motivations for revolt came from religion alone. Such revolt, as I have noted, could take the form of overthrow of a township or small fief, butchering of all who opposed the revolt—and often even of individuals who did not seek to oppose the revolt at all—and raising of Christ's victorious standard. It could involve, in short, the force, the violence, the terror, and the cruelties that go into all revolutions. But the objectives of the millennialists were invariably those of religious character, almost always springing from a belief that since the Second Coming would manifest itself in some kind of world holocaust, the best way of hastening this catastrophe and hence the Coming was through devastation and slaughter. The number of lives taken, and of homes and towns burned through these religious-inspired revolts was small by comparison with the effects of feudal and national wars. But the power of impassioned, fanatic belief in an ideal, whether religious, economic, or political, united with the techniques and stratagems of force and violence was to prove itself in later centuries. The quasi-religious intensity of modern political revolutions and totalitarian governments is, as Professor Cohn demonstrates, lineally descended from the religious revolts of the late Middle Ages.

Nor can we overlook the Reformation in Western history. We have already seen the intensity with which Luther and Calvin fought the Church of Rome in the sixteenth century. That their war with Rome was essentially religious, that is, doctrinally concerned with the teachings of Christ, cannot detract from the fact that rebellion against authority—ecclesiastical authority—is of this same revolutionary essence. And inasmuch as there were political states in Europe whose rulers were themselves Roman Catholic, sworn to support of the Roman Catholic church, the Protestant revolt against Rome was bound, on occasion, to have decided political implications. The Peasants' Revolt in Germany during Luther's time was touched off in substantial degree by Luther's sermons and pronouncements on religion; but that revolt had, all the same, a strongly political cast, which resulted in the sacking and burning of many a noble's or landlord's estate. Luther himself, as we have seen, felt obliged, in the interest of supporting the political order around him, to denounce the leaders of the Peasants' Revolt, and indeed to call for its swift and bloody repression. What Luther, and also Calvin, wanted was not political revolution, not social revolution, but reform of the church. If this required secession from Rome, all well and good, but the idea of political revolution as such is foreign to both Luther and Calvin.

Much closer to modern revolutionary temper is the seventeenth-century English Civil War. In many ways this war between Puritan militants and the defenders of the Catholic Stuart monarchy is the very closest we come to genuinely political revolution prior to the eighteenth century. For, while religion may have been the core of the Puritan rebellion, it was not easy then, nor is it easy today, to separate distinctly religious and political objectives. They were closely intertwined. How, after all, were Puritan militants—the self-styled saints—to revolt against the hated popishness of the English monarchy except by revolting against the monarchy itself? It is not mere coincidence that the principal breeding grounds of Puritan rebellion against the Stuart monarchy and the Roman church were, first, politics-ridden London and, second, the so-called New Model Army. And no one can gainsay the fact that the single most dramatic act of the Civil War was the public execution of Charles I: Not until the politically motivated French Revolution a century and a half later would another European monarch be decapitated. In short, the seventeenth-century Puritan uprising in England was, of a certainty, strongly charged with political issues. And the rise and spread of the Levellers during and after the Civil War gave the whole rebellion the clear mark of social, that is, equalitarian, objective. The Levellers movement drew its recruits largely from the lower orders of England's towns, chiefly those of London, whose first religious exhilaration had acquired social tinges. These were, for the most part, small shopkeepers, journeymen, and even young apprentices. Their inspiration may have been the true gospel of Christ, but the Levellers' immediate enemies proved often to be landlords, merchants, and capitalists.

But this said, we cannot overlook the fact that throughout the English Civil War the fundamental issue, the driving motivation, of the rebels was as religious as had been the case in any of the medieval and postmedieval rebellions we have just been considering. Granted that the Puritan uprising had unmistakably political and social consequences—how could it not have?—what made Cromwell's armies fight with almost limitless ferocity was the belief that they were fighting God's battle. If an approximation of democracy and of social egalitarianism appeared now and then, these were, as they were clearly regarded at the time, by-products of the greater struggle that was profoundly and uniquely religious. What the Puritan true believers desired was the rule of the saints, a rule that would be the first step toward the kingdom and dominion of God. However important politics and economics were, they were rarely more than derivative or incidental aspects of the Puritan movement, as in earlier centuries, religious millennialist values dominated utterly.

Still another type of premodern rebellion deserves mention. This is what the English historian Eric J. Hobsbawm has referred to in his arresting book *Primitive Rebels* as the "social bandit." We are best acquainted with this type through the legend of Robin Hood, who, with such notable fellow archers as Little John and Friar Tuck, led his men in attacks upon the wealthy and exploitative. Robbers or bandits they were in substance, but, as we know, what made their enterprise romantic and idealistic was the fact that they confined their depredations to the property and purses of the rich and seized upon opportunities to aid and succor the poor.

The line between the bandit who identifies with and gives aid to the poor on the one hand, and the revolutionary who, in his support of social objectives, does not hesitate to rob, on the other, is clearly a very thin one. Most revolutionaries have, at one time or another, committed crimes against property; often they have felt obliged to take life. And even if the overwhelming majority of thieves, robbers, and bandits in history have had little sense of social mission, the relatively few who have are worthy of note.

Hobsbawm—whose book deals with other types of "primitive rebel" as well—defines the social bandit in the following terms.

1. He must be assisted by the population around him at least to the extent that they will do nothing to aid the legal and police authorities in his capture; often households will give him actual help, even secret sanctuary.

2. The social bandit attains his folk role through having committed an offense that is not regarded as immoral or evil by the people in his locale but is made into a "crime" by definition of the distant authority of political government. "The State shows an interest in a peasant because of some minor infraction of the law, and the man takes to the hills because how does he know what a system which does not know or understand peasants, and which peasants do not understand, will do to him?" [5]

3. It is important that the social bandit be widely regarded as honorable and, above all, committed to the poorest and lowest in status of the population. "Admittedly almost anyone who joins issue with the oppressors and the State is likely to be regarded as a victim, a hero or both. Once a man is on the run, therefore, he is naturally protected by the peasants and by the weight of local conventions which stands for 'our' law—custom, blood feud or whatever it might be—against 'theirs,' and 'our justice' against that of the rich." [6]

4. Normally the social bandit tends to be young and unattached, save possibly to a handful of others like himself, "if only because it is much harder for a man to revolt against the apparatus of power once he has family responsibilities." [7]

---

[5] Eric J. Hobsbawm, *Primitive Rebels* (New York: Frederick A. Praeger, 1963), p. 16. Reprinted by permission of Praeger Publishers.

[6] Ibid., p. 15.   [7] Ibid., p. 17.

5. He is endowed by folk belief with a sense of moral superiority to the trappings of social position and to wealth as such, the latter being important only insofar as it aids the poor and works against the rich.

It is the merit of Hobsbawm's book that he shows the extent to which social bandits have figured in the actual lives of rural peoples in many parts of southern and southeastern Europe. Why there have not been more social bandits, either in fact or legend, in city populations, we do not know for sure. But as Hobsbawm makes clear, ruralism is a fundamental historical context of this type of rebel. The following passage is noteworthy:

> The fundamental pattern of banditry, as I have tried to sketch it here, is almost universally found in certain conditions. It is rural, not urban. The peasant societies in which it occurs know rich and poor, powerful and weak, rulers and ruled, but remain profoundly and tenaciously traditional and pre-capitalist in structure. An agricultural society such as that of East Anglia or Normandy or Denmark is not the place to look for social banditry. (This is no doubt the reason why England, which has given the world Robin Hood, the archetype of the social bandit, has produced no notable example of the species since the 16th century. Such idealization of criminals as has become part of the popular tradition, has seized upon urban figures like Dick Turpin and Macheath, while the miserable village laborers have risen to little more than modest admiration for exceptionally daring poachers.) Moreover even in backward and traditional bandit societies, the social brigand appears only before the poor have reached political consciousness or acquired more effective methods of social agitation. The bandit is a pre-political phenomenon, and his strength is in inverse proportion to that of organized agrarian revolutionism and Socialism or Communism. . . .
>
> In such societies banditry is endemic. But it seems that Robin-Hoodism is most likely to become a major phenomenon when their traditional equilibrium is upset: during and after periods of abnormal hardship, such as famines and wars, or at the moments when the jaws of the dynamic modern world seize the static communities in order to destroy and transform them. Since these moments occurred, in the history of most peasant societies, in the 19th and 20th centuries, our age is in some respect the classical age of the social bandit. We observe his upsurge—at least in the minds of the people—in Southern Italy and the Rhineland during the Revolutionary transformations and wars at the end of the 18th century; in Southern Italy after

Unification, fanned by the introduction of capitalist law and economic policy. In Calabria and Sardinia the major epoch of brigandage began in the 1890s, when the modern economy (and agricultural depression and emigration) made their impact. In the remote Carpathian mountains banditry flared up in the aftermath of the First World War, for social reasons. . . .

But this very fact expressed the tragedy of the social bandit. The peasant society creates him and calls upon him when it feels the need for a champion and protector—but precisely then he is incapable of helping it. For social banditry, though a protest, is a modest and unrevolutionary protest. It protests not against the fact that peasants are poor and oppressed, but against the fact that they are sometimes poor and oppressed. Bandit-heroes are not expected to make a world of equality. . . .[8]

In short, the social bandit's function is terminated when rural, chiefly peasant, traditionalism is terminated by the advancing forces of political and economic modernism—including reform and revolutionary movements. The social bandit becomes, in his way, as helpless against the tides of modernity as does the peasant or the handicraftsman. He is made obsolete by changes, often welcomed, that are taking place in the very people for whom he has become a folk hero.

It is not easy to separate the wheat from the chaff amid all the accounts of social bandits in folk literature. Such is the urge on the part of many people to invest banditry with the romance which surrounds a Robin Hood that oftentimes individuals are cast in roles that ill befit them—that would, in fact, have surprised no one as much as the individuals themselves had they chanced to hear of the legends. In the nineteenth-century American West, there were a good many bandits, robbers, rustlers, and so on, of whom a few such as Jesse James and his brothers have occasionally been cast by popular ballad or Tin Pan Alley imagination into Robin-Hoodish roles. But inasmuch as the United States has never had, in any significant degree, a genuinely rural-traditional culture, much less a highly traditional peasantry, it would be rather astonishing if many Robin Hoods were to be found in our past. From the beginning, America has been capitalistically oriented; economic protest in this country has taken the forms of organized reform or revolutionary movements.

It is interesting to note in passing that the most recent efforts in America to endow a social movement with Robin Hood overtones have been with respect to the Black Panthers. To the extent that individual Black Panthers have broken property laws through robbery, it could be

8 Ibid., pp. 23–24.

said—and has been said by a few, including the Panthers themselves—
that they were utilizing robbery in the claimed cause of idealistic uplift
of impoverished blacks. As we know, the Black Panthers have in some
cities done very positive, humanitarian things indeed for the black poor
—such as providing breakfasts for needy black children and superintend-
ing recreation halls for children and indigents alike. And, as this is being
written, there is a strong effort to make the black prisoner in American
penitentiaries appear to be the victim of political-racist ideology and
hence, a potential revolutionary, as well as one guilty of a particular
crime against the laws of society. In addition, black culture in the United
States, by virtue of the blacks' historic position—first slavery, then servitude of an ethnic-traditional type not unlike that of the peasantry in
preindustrial Europe—qualifies at least in some degree as the kind that
according to Hobsbawm produces Robin Hoods.

There are, however, two major arguments against any such characterization of Black Panthers. In the first place, there is no consistent
pattern among them of liaison with crime, nothing that stamps crime as
a way of life with them—as is true, for instance, of the Mafia (also occasionally idealized as "social" criminals). And in the second place, there
is little premodern about the specific kind of revolutionary behavior
that the Black Panthers represent; it is as modern as that of Communists.
As we shall see in the final section of this chapter, race has come close to
succeeding capitalism and nationalism as the primary motivation for
modern revolution.

The French Revolution
and the Jacobins

The first distinctively modern political revolution is that which began
in France in 1789. In a score of ways this revolution was to provide a
lasting model for subsequent revolutions and innumerable revolutionary
efforts, and for the whole philosophy of revolution that has burned
so brightly in the nineteenth and twentieth centuries. Whatever may
have been the role of the merely accidental or casual in its outbreak,
whatever may be the disparate historical causes of this event, the French
Revolution had acquired by 1790, as Edmund Burke was the first to see,
a momentum of its own, based upon limitless faith in goals, absoluteness
of moral power, and a profound sense of the contrast between total good
and total evil. For comparable spiritual intensity we would have to
go back to one or another of the millennialist-terrorist religious groups
referred to above. And for comparable militance—manifest in crowd
and army alike—we would have to go back to the Crusades or the Wars
of Religion. But what separates the French Revolution from any other
event in all history before 1789 is that this spiritual intensity, this mil-

itance, and the whole totalitarian morality that accompanied them were united, not to religious or moral goals as such, but to the uses of political power for the purpose of completely transforming society.

The French Revolution is very different from the American Revolution that had taken place a few years earlier—undoubtedly one of the sources of motivation for revolutionary unrest in France. In the strict sense of the word, it was not a revolution that had taken place in the American colonies, but a war of liberation from the mother country and nothing else. One finds no evidence in the speeches and writings of even the most ardent of the Americans engaged in war with England of a desire for any substantial modification of social, economic, and moral authorities. There was no determination to transform family, religion, property, language, education, or anything else the colonists had inherited from their European forefathers. And resolute though the Continental Congress and its army under George Washington proved to be, we find an utter absence of the kind of revolutionary moralism and spiritual fanaticism that had become, by 1791, major aspects of the French Revolution. Only in the most limited and conventional sense can the war between the American colonies and England be termed a revolution —though it would be a mistake, of course, to discount American appeal to some of the same "natural rights" that the makers of the French Declaration of the Rights of Man were to appeal to, just as it would be a mistake to dismiss the effects of American colonial success on revolutionary aspirations elsewhere in the world.

The single greatest difference between the American and the French revolutions is that whereas the former was limited in objective—limited to liberation from the British government—the latter was, almost from the beginning, unlimited. By late 1790, when the Jacobins were in effective control of the Revolution, its announced purposes had long since ceased to be simply those of liberation from a corrupt monarchy or of government reform. They had become, as first Burke and then, a generation later, Tocqueville perceived, boundless in scope, with their object all mankind, not just the French people, and boundless in other respects: in determination, not simply to reform, but totally to reconstitute society and morality. It is to the Jacobins that we must turn now. They are the first unmistakably modern revolutionary community in the West, and, in a variety of ways, their legacy is to be found today in all parts of the world.

Their beginnings were simple and undramatic enough. The first Jacobins were a few radical Bretons attending the States General in Paris as deputies in 1789. Their name came from their first meeting in a room in a Jacobin monastery in Paris—*Jacobin* being then the Parisian word for *Dominican*. From Paris the Jacobin movement spread. Overwhelmingly middle-class though Jacobins were throughout France, as the movement made its way throughout France in the form of clubs, by one of history's ironies it was to self-declared working- and lower-class movements that the principles of Jacobinism were to spread during the next century or two. And, for all the largely middle-class composition of the Jacobins in France generally, the Paris club, which by its location was dominant in matters of national policy, was ever more strongly working-class in membership. It was the Paris commune that proved, throughout the Revolution, to be the key commune in all France. Paris was a predominantly working-class city, and it was inevitable that the increasingly radical Jacobins would draw heavily upon working-class inspiration and energy for the more drastic measures, such as the Terror, that were to be invoked after about 1792.

The Jacobins began as a lobbying group, which at first worked through very sophisticated pressure techniques. Their use of propaganda was efficient; they created newspapers through which their versions of events could be distributed over all France, even other parts of Europe. A complicated but effective network of agents from town to town was devised through which pressure, threat, and, in time, terror could be brought to bear upon strategically important officials and assemblies. In the National Convention itself, Jacobin influence was markedly successful from the outset, although full Jacobin authority in France had to wait until late 1792 and early 1793. From 1790 on, the most radical pieces of legislation passed by the Assembly or the Convention invariably had Jacobin influence behind them. Even in the beginning, the clear marks of Jacobin ideology were a radical, people-based democracy, along with a strong interest in political centralization, which would be able to effect reform more easily in France, and in authoritarianism, from which speed of action could more easily flow. Once the Jacobins attained supremacy, in 1793, these ideological principles were sovereign. The Terror was no more than the effort, through whatever means were required, including torture, imprisonment, and death through a substantial number of public beheadings over a period of months, to make Jacobin political principles prevail throughout France. Even after the official downfall of Jacobinism in France, even indeed after the rise of Napoleon as emperor, the effects of Jacobinism remained profound. Not only were the essential principles of centralized administration rooted in the popular mass basically taken over from the Jacobins, but a great many influential Jacobins became key figures in the Napoleonic government. Among them was the hated Fouché, who had been head of the Jacobin secret police in 1794 and who became Napoleon's indispensable minister of police.

The acknowledged hero of most Jacobins was the philosopher Rousseau, whom we have considered earlier in this book. Rousseau had died eleven years before the outbreak of the Revolution, but largely through Jacobin influence his writings became virtually biblical in inspiration to many revolutionary legislators and administrators. It is easy enough to see why his influence should have prevailed. Rousseau's doctrine of the general will lent itself admirably to ideas and techniques of centralization, radicalization, even of permanent revolution and of terror. Rousseau had seen traditional society as scarcely more than a network of tyrannies over the individual, from the patriarchal family through the local community, the church, the guild, and the educational system, to the monarchy itself. He had also regarded this assemblage of institutions as by nature corrupt and ineffective. What was required, declared Rousseau, was to institute through the general will the untrammeled power of the people; and he did not shrink—in the famous chapter of his *Social Contract* called "The Legislator"—from recognizing the need for absolute and centralized power in effecting this power of the people. Rousseau's own hatred of all the intermediate groups of society, like family, guild, community, and church, which interposed themselves between the mass of individuals and the government, could be, and was, easily translated by the revolutionary government into a series of implementing laws.

Thus we find in the Revolution as early as 1790 the clear declaration that legitimate power exists in the people alone; that freedom means, not the autonomy of traditional associations and institutions in society, but the total liberation of the individual from these entities, that all must be destroyed or sharply subordinated which militates against either the collective power of the people or the liberty of the individual. Between 1790 and 1794 a striking and, so far as all future revolutionists were concerned, never-to-be-forgotten series of drastic laws was passed. The patriarchal family was abolished and the small conjugal family, regarded as the only legal one, instituted in its place. The guilds were abolished at a single stroke, and all new forms of private, partial economic and social association made illegal if membership in any one of them exceeded a couple of dozen individuals. The church, first sharply limited in authority, was in effect destroyed by 1794 when the dechristianization decrees were issued (which we considered in the chapter on the religious community), its property expropriated, and the termination of its clerical and monastic vows declared. Property was individualized, as were all contracts. These and other laws—especially those affecting education, which under revolutionary decree was made the monopoly of the state—had the effect, on the one hand, of atomizing traditional society and, on the other, of politicizing French society and culture to a degree hardly known before in human history, save possibly in the final centuries of the Roman Empire. And in all of this, the ideas of Rousseau were without any doubt the generating influences. It was no wonder that the Jacobins regarded him as very nearly a saint.

This virtual canonization of Rousseau by the Jacobins suggests what is perhaps the single most vital aspect of the whole Jacobin revolutionary movement: the conscious, systematic, and far-reaching *conversion of politics into religion*. We must remember that on this point Rousseau had been as emphatic as on any in his powerful writings. He had declared the necessity of what he called a civil religion if the people were to achieve total power and if the general will was to replace all traditional authorities in their lives. The Jacobins were not slow in following Rousseau's prescription.

We find that, very early in the life of the movement, ritual became common at meetings of the clubs. Hymns were composed, modes of prayer created both for individual and collective use, and the fundamental ideas of the movement given an increasingly sacred and dogmatic cast. Civic processes, festivals, and feasts of religious love became common by 1791. The historian Crane Brinton has described in great detail many of these religious manifestations of Jacobin democracy:

> As early as 1790 the Jacobins of Paris were told that they had achieved the "apostolate of liberty." The word apostle was subsequently on everyone's lips. The town clubs sent "apostles" or "missionaries" out into the country districts, still in unphilosophic darkness. . . . Many an apostle became in some degree a martyr, a word much in favor among the Jacobins. . . .
>
> Odd phrases of purely religious connotation keep recurring and Jacobin language, in its higher flights, is extremely theological. At Luneville, separate benches were preserved for proselytes; the poet laureate of this same club refers to the Marseillaise as a *cantique*. The second register of the club of Bergerac is inscribed *registre sacré*. At Ais, only "pure, true, and just men" will be admitted to the *Sanctuary of the Revolution*. The hall of the club of Montauban is the *sanctuary of the temple of liberty*. The adjective holy was used freely, *notre sainte constitution*, for example. . . . A constitutional priest addressing the society of Bordeaux saw fit to phrase his adhesion to the revolutionary cause thus: "I believe in the all-powerful National Assembly, creator of good and liberty." And the president of the society at Bergerac hailed "the election of our new [constitutional] bishop, which will cause to flow through our souls the precious balm of a constitution founded on the unshakeable base of a holy faith!" [9]

Bear in mind that all of this sprang from a group that was political to the core, concerned above all else with the political transformation of France from the monarchical, aristocratic, and tradition-bound society it had been for centuries into a revolutionary republic. Bear in mind,

[9] Crane Brinton, *The Jacobins* (New York: Russell and Russell, 1961), pp. 192, 194–95.

too, that the first objects of the Jacobins' reforming zeal when they achieved power anywhere were representatives of the church: bishops, priests, monks, nuns, and others. The celebrated dechristianization decrees of 1793–94 had as their declared aim the extermination from France of Christianity in all its aspects. Earlier the revolutionary government had expropriated the church's property, had taken over responsibility for direct payment of wages and other support to those priests who were willing to swear an oath of loyalty to the new French state— with imprisonment or death the penalty for those who would not swear this oath; had separated all schools and colleges from the church; had declared null and void all the perpetual vows within the church; and had made matters concerning rites of baptism, marriage, and death the first responsibility of the state, not the church. In short, all social, visible aspects of the church had been either destroyed or politicized. Now, in the dechristianization decrees, the Jacobins were declaring even belief in the Christian god to be impious and punishable.

It is in light of the religious vacuum created by all these laws and decrees against the church that we can best see the rise of the new politically based, politically oriented religion. How deeply religious, how sacred a thing the Revolution became in the minds of some of its leaders may be inferred from the following passages from a speech given by Robespierre on May 7, 1794:

> The French people appear to have outstripped the rest of the human race by two thousand years; one might even be tempted to regard them as a distinct species among the rest. Europe is kneeling to the shadows of the tyrants whom we are punishing. . . .
>
> Yes, this delightful land which we inhabit, which Nature favors with her caresses, is made to be the domain of liberty and happiness; this proud and sensitive people is truly born for glory and virtue. O my country, had fate caused me to be born in a foreign and distant land, I should have addressed to heaven my constant prayers for thy prosperity; I should have shed tears of emotion at the story of thy combats and thy virtues; my eager soul would have followed with ardent anxiety every movement of thy glorious Revolution; I should have envied the lot of thy citizens, I should have envied that of thy representatives. . . .
>
> Fanatics, hope for nothing from us. To recall men to the pure cult of the Supreme Being is to strike a death-blow at fanaticism. All fictions disappear before the truth, and all follies collapse before Reason. Without compulsion, without persecution, all sects must mingle spontaneously in the universal religion of Nature. . . .

Robespierre now proposes the following decree:

> Article I. The French people recognizes the existence of the Supreme Being, and the immortality of the soul.
>
> Article II. It recognizes that the best way of worshipping the Supreme Being is to do one's duties as a man.
>
> Article III. It considers that the most important of these duties are: to detest bad faith and despotism, to punish tyrants and traitors, to assist the unfortunate, to respect the weak, to defend the oppressed, to do all the good one can to one's neighbor, and to behave with justice towards all men.
>
> Article IV. Festivals shall be instituted to remind men of the Deity, and of the dignity of their state.
>
> Article V. These festivals shall be named after the glorious events of our Revolution, the virtues which are most dear to men, and most useful, and the chief blessings of Nature.
>
> Article VI. The French Republic shall celebrate every year the anniversaries of July 4, 1789, August 10, 1792, January 21, 1793, and May 31, 1793.[10]
>
> Article VII. It shall celebrate, on successive *décadis*, the following festivals: the Supreme Being, and Nature; the human race; the French people; the benefactors of mankind; the martyrs of freedom; . . .
>
> Article XII. Any meeting of aristocrats, or any that contravenes public order shall be suppressed.
>
> Article XIII. In the event of troubles caused by or arising out of any form of public worship, all those who excited them by fanatical preaching or counter-revolutionary suggestions, and all those who provoked them by unjust or uncalled-for acts of violence, shall be equally punished with all the rigour of the law. . . .[11]

There is no need to add to the evidence for the religious flavor of the Jacobin movement contained in the paragraphs above. I am not suggesting that a new religion was the most important element of Jacobinism, for nothing should be allowed to detract from the profoundly political character of the Jacobins' aims for France. But these political aims could never have achieved the intensity they had by 1791 had they not taken root in a Jacobin psychology that was religious to the core. Indeed, it was the Revolution's religious fervor that allowed the slogan "Liberté,

---

[10] These dates commemorate respectively the fall of the Bastille, the fall of the monarchy, the execution of Louis XVI, and the expulsion of the Girondist deputies.

[11] Quoted in George Rudé, ed., *Robespierre* (Englewood Cliffs, N.J.: Prentice-Hall, 1967), pp. 69–73 passim.

egalité, fraternité" to become worldwide in its impact before the eighteenth century had ended. Wherever the troops went, after revolutionary France became engaged in war that was to spread, all the way to Russia, there went also the new French national flag, the tricolor, and the slogan, which could not help but have at least potentially revolutionary significance in every area they reached.

It was the religious-moral element in the Jacobin movement that, above anything else, led to the character of the Reign of Terror in France during 1793 and 1794. Granted that it was the need for national mobilization caused by France's war with the rest of Europe which was the ostensible, and no doubt precipitating, reason for the Terror. But there have been national wars before and since that did not give rise to the relentless ferocity within a country toward many of its own citizens which we find in France at the height of the Revolution. Even the *levée en masse*—national conscription, the first in the history of Europe—could have been effected without the Terror. So, in all probability, could the measures taken by the government to consolidate and centralize industry, to raise taxes to unprecedented heights, to conscript property and wealth, and to do all else that the war required. What, however, could not be accomplished without the Terror was that total remaking of the nation's moral and spiritual nature that the Jacobins so passionately desired.

It is no wonder that as the Revolution progressed beyond its early, relatively limited goals, the place of Rousseau became ever more exalted. Whereas his *Social Contract* had been one of his least-read books prior to the Revolution, passages from it were read at street-corner gatherings in Paris and other French cities after 1790. Why not? No revolution has ever succeeded, or presumably will ever succeed, without virtually incessant nourishment from the kind of revolutionary dogmas we find in Rousseau, Marx, Lenin, and others. As Robert R. Palmer has written of Rousseau:

> He became the great revolutionary of a revolutionary age. Among contemporaries who boldly rewrote human history, arraigned kings, and exploded religion, among humane and ingenious authors who proposed this or that change in government, or the economy, or education, or the law, Rousseau alone went straight to the absolute foundation. . . . He was the revolutionary *par excellence* because it was a moral revolution that he called for, a revolution in the personality and in the inclination of the will.[12]

12 Robert R. Palmer, *The Age of Democratic Revolution: The Challenge* (Princeton: Princeton University Press, 1959), p. 114.

In his *Discourse on Political Economy* Rousseau had written:

> If it is good to know how to deal with men as they are, it is much better to make them what there is need that they should be. The most absolute authority is that which penetrates into a man's inmost being, and concerns itself no less with his will than with his actions. It is certain that all peoples become in the long run what the government makes them: warriors, citizens, men, when it so pleases; or merely populace and rabble, when it chooses to make them so.[13]

Hence the extraordinary amount of detail we find in Jacobin plans for the remaking of France first, and then the rest of humanity. "The transition of an oppressed nation to democracy," declared the Committee of Public Safety, "is like the effort by which nature arose from nothingness to existence. You must entirely refashion a people whom you wish to make free, destroy its prejudices, alter its habits, limit its necessities, root up its vices, purify its desires." [14]

As Professor Palmer has written: "In 1792 the Revolution became a thing in itself, an uncontrollable force that might eventually spend itself but which no one could direct and guide. The governments set up in Paris in the following years—the Convention, the Committee of Public Safety, the Thermidorians, the Directory, however they might differ, whether 'Jacobin' or 'anti-Jacobin' in their composition—all alike faced the problem of holding together against forces more revolutionary than themselves." Robespierre is quoted by Palmer as declaring: "If the basis of popular government in time of peace is virtue, the basis of popular government in time of revolution is virtue and terror: virtue without which terror is murderous, terror without which virtue is powerless." [15]

This, then, is the essence of terrorism, which is so vital to all revolutions worthy of the name: the systematic, relentless uprooting of all old ways of thinking, living, believing, and even remembering. As George Orwell has told us in his great novel *1984*, the revolution is able to reach full fruition, and then maintain itself, only through massive rearrangements of the human mind. The so-called Newspeak in Orwell's grim utopia consisted of revolutionary leaders' not only making old words

[13] Jean Jacques Rousseau, *Discourse on Political Economy*, in *The Social Contract and the Discourses*, trans. G. D. H. Cole (New York: E. P. Dutton, Everyman's Library, 1950), pp. 297–98.

[14] Quoted in John Morley, *Rousseau*, 2 vols. (London: Macmillan & Co., 1905), 2: 132.

[15] Robert R. Palmer, *The Age of Democratic Revolution: The Struggle* (Princeton: Princeton University Press, 1964), p. 35; idem, *Twelve Who Ruled* (Princeton: Princeton University Press, 1941), p. 276.

serve new meanings and making new words official but, more important, altering prejudgments, destroying ancient associations of symbol and belief, and creating, so to speak, memories and traditions where none had existed.

In a very real and powerful sense, this is what the Jacobin revolutionaries and some of their even more revolutionary offshoots—such as the Babouvists, followers of Babeuf and Buonarroti, whose fanatical, terroristic, and millennialist visions went even beyond those of a Saint-Just or a Robespierre—sought to accomplish: the wiping out of a complete culture and mentality and the creation of an utterly new one. And the leaders of the Revolution were extraordinarily skillful in doing all of this.

The immediate reason for the creation of the all-powerful Committee on Public Safety (the last word should in fact be translated "Salvation") on April 6, 1793, was simply to reinforce the reforms that had already been effected by the Revolution. But the Committee went far beyond this, as revolutionary tribunals invariably do, and it commenced the Terror. Not only were those languishing in jails brought forth for public execution on the guillotine on grounds of being "enemies of the people," but new "enemies of the people" were systematically and ruthlessly found. For many weeks, the guillotine worked every day without stopping, with crowds numbering in the thousands encouraged by the Committee to come and applaud the executions and hurl curses at the literally thousands who were to be beheaded. And all who were to be executed were carried by government order in tumbrils that passed through the most crowded streets of Paris. Only thus could the fear of death be made to sink deeply in the popular mind; only thus could fear lead to that transformation of morality and belief in the popular mind which would be capable of making even the most far-reaching government acts immediately acceptable, even praiseworthy. The capacity of fear of death, mutilation, and torture—abject, mind-seizing, soul-transforming fear—to produce public order, and then, on that base of passivity, gradual adoration of that very government which executes, tortures, and exiles, is very great indeed. One may note parenthetically that to this day in Soviet Russia, such is the dread aroused by the memory of the Stalinist mass executions during the 1930s that only the rarest and bravest—and internationally lauded—Russian scientists or artists dare to do so much as write a letter of protest about government acts. And sober, highly informed, perceptive students of Hungary have declared that such is the dread still associated with the Russian invasion of 1956, followed by the tortures and ruthless executions of tens of thousands of Hungarian citizens, that any other uprising in Hungary is unthinkable for at least the remainder of this century.

The Committee on Public Safety in Paris lasted only two years, the influence of the Jacobins hardly longer. In the very nature of things, the Rousseauean-Jacobin work of transforming French culture and society could not go beyond a certain, time-given limit. But one must be impressed by what *was* accomplished in this respect—accomplished permanently not merely in France but in other parts of the Western world that found themselves obliged to follow French revolutionary example. Let us glance at a few of the direct consequences of the Reign of Terror under the Jacobin revolutionaries, working from their small, tightly contained, deeply fanatical cells or clubs through the machinery of government that they managed to dominate.

A system of official, regularized, nationwide police, including secret police, was brought into existence for protecting the aims of the Revolution from possible counterrevolutionaries. Universal manhood suffrage was inaugurated and, virtually at the same time, universal military conscription as well. The first national conscription or draft in history was the work of the Jacobins, who sought to oppose the rest of Europe and at the same time to carry the message of the Revolution as far into the rest of the world as possible. A new calendar was established, which was shrewdly designed to wipe out traditional associations in the public mind of the days, weeks, and months and, through renaming these, to create fresh associations that would be bound to reinforce the Revolution and to aid in creating a new popular "memory" of the past. (This new calendar did not survive the height of the Revolution, and no revolutionary government since has dared to try so drastic an act of cultural-psychological surgery on a populace. But the idea behind it has proved to be powerfully attractive to others with similar intent; and there are other ways than calendar manipulation by which the time symbols of human memory may be affected.)

Out of the Jacobin rage to centralize and make things uniform and homogeneous in France came abolition of the traditional French provinces and communes, dating back to the early Middle Ages. In their place were set up, with geometric precision and scrupulous measurement, *départements, cantons, arrondissements,* all designed at one and the same time to win Frenchmen over from their devotion to their old haunts and surroundings and to remind them of the supremacy of Paris and the national government that would govern as directly as possible through these new political subdivisions. A new system of weights and measures and of coinage was also devised, which also proceeded with mathematical rigor from the rationalists' adored decimal system. In this manner, too, was effected a substantial wrenching of the French mind from accustomed associations. Nor should we omit mention of public education, which was, declared Danton, the most pressing necessity, after bread for the masses, in the work of refashioning the French mind, morality, and culture. All private schools, colleges, and universities were either abolished or else transformed into publicly owned and operated institutions. Educational centralization prevailed. From the ministry of education in Paris radiated outward lines of policy and curriculum, appointment of teachers, admission of pupils and students, design of buildings, finance, and so on, which encompassed the totality of France down to the smallest hamlet. Education was declared compulsory for all, but its content and character were to be set solely by the government of France, and in a strictly uniform fashion.

These measures, all originated by the Jacobins and all taken in the name of advancing the Revolution, are but a few of the drastic changes which were effected, or attempted, by the revolutionists. There is no need here to mention again the revolutionary laws I referred to in earlier chapters regarding family, religion, and industry in France—equally drastic, equally far-reaching, equally "impossible" under ordinary circumstances—given human resistance to change above levels of minor modification. They, too, were aspects of the Jacobin aim of achieving virtue and reason through terror. Only through terror, indeed, could any of these major revolutionary changes ever have been achieved. We may perhaps declare them, or many of them, rational and desirable; but on the evidence of history, rationality and general desirability are rarely enough to bring about major changes in society. It is inconceivable that changes of the magnitude of those I have mentioned, and many others, could ever have been implemented without the use of terror—and this on a constantly widening, deepening, intensifying scale.

It does not matter, really, for purposes of revolutionary terror how many persons are actually executed, publicly or secretly, so long as the *fear* of execution—or of torture or imprisonment or expropriation of property—becomes sufficiently widespread. It has been estimated that only about ten thousand persons lost their lives through execution on the guillotine in the public squares of Paris and a few other cities in France during the Terror. But when one adds to this number the hundreds of thousands, the millions, who were made aware of these executions through one means or other, and also of the existence of the Jacobin secret police, paid informers, and clandestine agents operating either for money or from revolutionary passion, the real effects of terror can be more adequately assessed.

Even to *seem* an enemy of the Revolution could be fatal. For, as Hannah Arendt has emphasized, well before the French Revolution had come to its end, the worst of all crimes was hypocrisy:

> The momentous role that hypocrisy and the passion for its unmasking came to play in the later stages of the French Revolution, though it may never cease to astound the historian, is a matter of historical record. The revolution, before it proceeded

to devour its own children, had unmasked them, and French historiography in more than a hundred and fifty years, has reproduced and documented all these exposures until no one is left among the chief actors who does not stand accused, or at least suspected, of corruption, duplicity, and mendacity. . . .

It was the war upon hypocrisy that transformed Robespierre's dictatorship into the Reign of Terror, and the outstanding characteristic of this period was the self-purging of the rulers.[16]

In the Jacobin effort to exterminate all hypocrisy, we have, as is evident enough, one more instance of the profoundly religious element that lies in all genuinely revolutionary behavior. Only those who conceive themselves as pure in faith, and for whom purity of faith and life is the sovereign virtue, can fully understand the hatred and fear which are aroused by hypocrisy, on the one hand, and heresy, on the other. Every revolution spawns its heresies: beliefs which are stimulated by revolutionary-religious intensity but which in one way or other are judged by those in power to represent a perversion or betrayal of the faith. Persecutions of the religious are always fiercest and bloodiest when they come from the religious. Likewise, punishments of revolutionaries are generally most drastic when they come from the revolutionaries who happen to hold power and make the effective judgments of what is truly revolutionary and what is counterrevolutionary or subversive to the revolution—what, in short, is declared by those in power to be hypocritical or heretical.

In his fascinating book *Terror and Resistance,* E. V. Walter has isolated five key qualities in terror successfully applied by governments or groups. Professor Walter's points apply specifically to the primitive societies, notably West African chiefdoms, in which he has found the technique of terror used; but they are, as he himself concludes, applicable to revolutionary movements such as those modern European ones in France and Russia.[17]

First, there must be a shared ideology:

In West Africa, religious ideas about the authority of ancestral spirits licensed the destructive acts of the secret orders. In terroristic despotism, the collective fantasy about the omnipotence of the great destroyer-provider legitimated his violence;

[16] Hannah Arendt, *On Revolution* (New York: Viking Press, 1963), pp. 94–95. Rousseau, in the *Social Contract,* had written in support of the death penalty for those citizens who behave as though they do believe in the "dogmas" which underlie the good society.

[17] E. V. Walter, *Terror and Resistance* (New York: Oxford University Press, 1969), pp. 340–43 passim. The quoted passages that follow are all from this source.

victims were dismissed as evildoers. . . . The French Revolutionaries described the Terror as the tyranny of the people against the tyranny of kings; victims were defined as aristocrats or as enemies of the Revolution. Nazi ideology justified the violence of the master race against its foes. Soviet terror was officially defined as the weapon of the proletariat against the class enemy.

Second, the victims of the process of terror must be expendable. Rarely if ever are the victims of terror those whose technical value to the regime in power is substantial. "If the violence liquidates persons who are needed for essential tasks, or if replacements cannot be found for their roles, the system of co-operation breaks down."

Third, a system of dissociation comes almost immediately into play. The actual executioners and torturers are themselves kept as insulated as possible from the general population. Even more important, the victims' identities are effaced as fully and quickly as possible. They are consciously made into nonpersons, outsiders beyond the pale.

Fourth, terror is balanced by

working incentives that induce co-operation. Hannah Arendt has argued that ideology provides the motor in totalitarian systems to overcome the paralysis of terror. . . . Terror works against the refusal to co-operate, but it is not a substitute for co-operation itself.

Fifth, positive, integrative relationships which are vital to the regime must survive the terror:

Perpetual fear, suspicion, and unpredictable behavior can rupture the traditional bonds of kinsmen, friends, and fellow workers. If the impact of terror destroys the network of relationships that supports collective activities and political interactions, the entire co-operative system will break down. The terror can destroy itself by tearing apart the social organization necessary to maintain it.

This, essentially, was what happened to the Jacobin influence on the Revolution in 1794 at the time of the so-called Thermidorean reaction, when the fall of Robespierre signaled the end of the extreme form of the Terror and the more dramatic phase of the Revolution. No matter what the personal details or the day-by-day sequence of actions and events, the overriding and governing circumstance was the ever-more-destructive impact of the Terror on the social structure of France.

Up to a certain point the effect of the Terror had been beneficial to the radical objectives of the Jacobin leaders of the Revolution. Beyond that point, as it appeared to a steadily growing number of eminent revolutionaries, there lay, not the success of France, but its inexorable destruction through the Terror's ravaging forces and the almost certain invasion of France by other European countries. Hence, came the end of the Jacobin revolutionary community.

But 1794 saw the end only of official Jacobinism; the really fundamental principles of this revolutionary movement lived on in France and in Europe as a whole. From that day to this, the Jacobin image of revolution and of the revolutionary transformation of a social order, an image itself formed, as we have seen, of Rousseauean elements, has continued to be the dominant one in all major revolutionary circles. There would be later revolutionaries, like the Bakuninist anarchists, who would disparage the Jacobins, and with them Rousseau, as instruments of a despotism greater even than that flowing from monarchies and aristocracies. But the Bakuninist, anarchist vision of revolution was nonetheless founded on the memory—enhanced by time and romantic yearning—of what the Jacobins had managed to accomplish in the short period 1790–94. Marx and all of the Communists who took their official origin in Marxian principles professed to regard the Jacobins as members of the bourgeoisie, incapable of establishing a genuine revolution, or capable at best of what might be called protorevolution. But nothing can be found—whether in Marx, in Engels, or in Lenin—in Marxian anticipations of the actual character of revolution that is not directly descended from the glittering spectacle of the Jacobin effort to re-create, through absolute reason, virtue, precept, and law, with terror as their instrument, an entire social order.

The Jacobins translated religious millennialism into political revolution, that is, *permanent* revolution. The emphasis is important; for all the major Jacobin leaders, and most notably for the greatest of them, Robespierre and Saint-Just, the work of revolution in the social order was deemed to be unending. It was not enough that the rule of virtue be attended merely by the toppling of monarchs and aristocrats. Such, the Jacobins ardently believed, is the heritage left by earlier ages of ignorance, superstition, evil, and downright resistance to the good that long periods of time are required for the work of reform and redemption. The work of the revolution must be seen, therefore, as continuing into ever-higher levels of mind and morality, into ever-more-intimate spheres of the individual's life, and into the most private recesses of institutions and personalities. Only thus is it possible to envisage the arrival on earth in the remote future, for the first time in human history, of the absolutely virtuous society. Again we are obliged to refer to Rousseau, who said, "He who dares to undertake the making of a people's institutions ought to feel himself capable . . . of changing human nature, of transforming each individual . . . of altering man's constitution for the purpose of strengthening it . . ." and who also said, "If you would have the general will accomplished, bring all the particular wills into conformity with it; in other words, as virtue is nothing more than this conformity of the particular wills with the general will, establish the reign of virtue." [18]

These are the injunctions which underlay so much of the hard, concrete legislative work of the successive revolutionary governments and which supplied so much of the fervor that alone made tolerable to men such as Danton, Robespierre, and Saint-Just the often gruesome work of the Terror. In one form or another, such injunctions give spirit to just about all the other political revolutions which have occupied so much nineteenth- and twentieth-century history.

Never before in history had strictly political objectives been served by men of so millennialist a turn of mind, with such boundless willingness to sacrifice all, with such zeal in prosecuting objectives of purely social, economic, and political character, with such depths of fanatical belief in the rightness of their mission.

All that the Jacobins lacked for a complete theory of revolution, which would make the dream of revolution a message of salvation as universal as the supernatural one of the early Christians, was a powerful, historically rooted sense of cosmic purpose—more specifically, a sense of history as a single process of movement toward an end or objective, a sense of society as driven by some dialectic or law through which revolution and reconstruction would be, not simply desirable products of hope and chance, but made *necessary* by laws of history every bit as inexorable in their operation as those of the physical world. This lack was repaired by Karl Marx and the whole system of ideas, insights, and prescriptions we call Marxism, the single greatest revolutionary movement in human history.

Marx and the Communist Revolution

I do not mean that Marxism was the sole legatee of Jacobinism and its dream of secular salvation. There were many radical and revolutionary movements in nineteenth-century western Europe and other parts of the world, all of which took inspiration in some measure from the unforgettable spectacle of the Jacobins' wielding of revolutionary power that threatened for a time to become total. It was one of the most radical of French revolutionists, Gracchus Babeuf, who wrote, "The French

---

[18] Jean Jacques Rousseau, *Social Contract*, in Cole, trans., op. cit., pp. 38, 298.

Revolution is only the forerunner of a much bigger, much more solemn revolution, which will be the final one." Babeuf's words came very shortly after the French Revolution. There were many who echoed his conviction that there would be in time another revolution, vast, encompassing, and *final*. Again, it is worth commenting on the likeness between the religious and revolutionary views of society and history, each with its distinctive form of eschatology.

Among the revolutionary movements spawned by the example of the French Revolution and the consequences of the two great transformations of Western society that we call the democratic revolution and the industrial revolution, each of which had a dramatic impact in the first part of the nineteenth century, was that of the anarchists, among them such notable names as William Godwin, Pierre Joseph Proudhon, and Peter Kropotkin. The anarchists have every right to be included in any treatment of modern revolutionary movements, and this holds true down to the present moment. Even so, however, we shall defer treatment of this philosophy until the next chapter, on the ecological community. Revolutionary in most respects the anarchists were; but their transcending significance seems to me to lie, not so much in a stress upon revolution—with its implications of violence, centralization of power, myth in the form of philosophy of history, and the other elements we have located in the revolutionary community—as in *renewal*. I mean the kind of renewal of human life proclaimed in anarchist doctrines of mutualism, nonviolence, cooperation, free association, and the close relation of man to nature and in the whole spirit of voluntarism that characterizes the great majority of anarchist writings.

There is also the fact that, however much the ideas of anarchism may be admired and however deep their hold on a few nineteenth- and twentieth-century minds, there is no doubt whatever that Marxism was the ascendant philosophy and movement before the end of the nineteenth century. The major revolutions of the twentieth century have been Marxist in inspiration. Revolutionary writing that followed in time the essential works of Marx nearly all tended, with the conspicuous exception of the anarchists', to draw from or to build on Marxism. In terms of the results they effected, the major revolutionaries of the late nineteenth and the twentieth centuries have been Lenin, Trotsky, Stalin, and Mao Tse-tung. They, and many others too numerous to mention here, all drew inspiration from Marx alone. Even Mussolini, who founded the Fascist movement in Italy, had spent his life, virtually up to the moment of the famous March on Rome, as a Marxian revolutionary. And, leaving aside those who actually led revolutions, we cannot miss the fact that the principal philosophers and theorists of revolution, and of the doctrines of socialism and communism, have been, with the rarest of exceptions, Marxist in orientation. The anarchists are, indeed, the only radical group of any significance at all that has not followed Marx. From the time that Marx and Proudhon fell out, there has been nothing but complete antagonism, hostility reaching the intensity of hatred, between anarchists and all those who have been inspired by Marx.

There are many reasons for the triumph of Marxism over all other radical movements which were flourishing during the first three quarters of the nineteenth century. Three reasons seem to me outstanding, however, all of which are aspects of the very essence of Marxism.

First is the unmistakably, profoundly, and undeviatingly revolutionary character of Marx's own mind. There have been occasional interpretations of Marxism—among them those of Eduard Bernstein in Germany and some of the Fabians and other English socialists—that have emphasized the *evolutionary* character of Marxism. Such an evolutionary character exists in Marx's portrayal of the long historical succession of fundamental types of society: slavery, feudalism, capitalism, and eventually socialism. But nothing detracts from the fiercely, eschatologically, passionately *revolutionary* nature of Marx's mind and character. Not one of the elements of the revolutionary community I described at the beginning of this chapter is missing from Marx or from Marxism, taking its tactical as well as philosophical nature into account, or from the actual processes of the Marxist-inspired revolutions.

Second, despite the fundamentally revolutionary nature of Marxism, it accepted a large part of the existing scene as not merely a real, a necessary condition of socialism, but also as desirable. Unlike some radical movements of the nineteenth century, anarchism included, Marx and Engels hailed industrialism (minus private property and private profit), technology, urbanism, mass democracy, and even the factory system as such as the necessary structure for production. In short, Marx worked with history.

This leads to the third essential element of Marxism: its philosophy of history. Marx offered a dynamic of history that could make revolution seem the inevitable emergent of historical development, rather than simply the product of human volition at a given time irrespective of historical circumstances. Nowhere is this view of revolution more vividly and powerfully expressed than in the famous *Communist Manifesto,* written by Marx in collaboration with Friedrich Engels and first published in 1848. Of all Marxist writings, this brief work has had the greatest influence during the past century in Europe and in the world at large on the theory and inception of revolutions. It has been read by literally millions and been the basis of thought and discussion for literally hundreds of millions of persons, down to the present moment.

Behind the writing of the *Manifesto*—in which Marx's hand is clearly the dominant one—lies a Jacobin-derived passion for revolution, evidence of which we can find in Marx from the time of his student days at the University of Jena. It was there Marx acquired his love of philosophy, his veneration particularly for the great Hegel, and his close identification with quasi-revolutionary student movements, many of which founded themselves on left-wing applications of Hegel's philosophy. Marx's student radicalism and his fast-forming dedication to the goal of revolutionary socialism made an academic career impossible for him in Germany; he thus turned for a period of time to journalism as a livelihood. It was indeed in his capacity as journalist that he wrote some of the articles on war and the military which we have already had occasion to consider in the chapter on the military community. Eventually Marx made his way to Paris, where he spent most of the decade of the 1840s, in almost constant association with others of revolutionary views and also in writing the philosophical and political essays which first set forth the distinctively Marxian view of society and history.

One of these essays—or, rather, a few fragments from it—will serve adequately to show how deeply implanted in Marx's mind a *historical* view of revolution had become during these years. The essay is Marx's famous "Critique of Hegel's Philosophy of Right." He writes:

> Revolutions need a *passive* element, a *material* basis. Theory is realized in a people so far as it fulfills the needs of the people. Will there correspond to the monstrous discrepancy between the demands of German thought and the answers of German reality a similar discrepancy between civil society and the state, and within civil society itself? Will theoretical needs be directly practical needs? It is not enough that thought should seek to realize itself; reality must also strive towards thought.[19]

It would be hard to find any passage in Marx's writings, early or late in his life, that more succinctly expresses the essence of the Marxian view of revolution. To be sure, revolution must have the kind of zeal and dedication that Jacobins and others richly manifested; but zeal is not enough. With it, or underlying it, rather, there must be an objective, material condition of society, arising from historical development, that can alone make zeal and bloodshed worthwhile. Unless the historical condition is right, governments in power cannot be captured, their force seized by revolutionaries to be used in behalf of the revolution.

Marx went further. Until there has been brought into existence a social class that is conscious of itself as a social class and conscious, too, of a revolutionary mission, there can be no adequate base for revolutionary effort. Even while still a student at Jena, Marx, deeply impressed

---

[19] Karl Marx, *Early Writings*, trans. and ed. T. B. Bottomore (New York: McGraw-Hill Book Co., 1964), pp. 53–54.

by the great industrial changes taking place in Europe and the emergence there of an industrial working class, had come to see in the industrial workers the best possible basis of future revolution. He thus wrote, in the same essay from which I have just quoted, the following prescient words:

> No class in civil society can play this part unless it can arouse, in itself and in the masses, a moment of enthusiasm in which it associates and mingles with society at large, identifies with it, and is felt and recognized as the general representative of this society. Its aims and interests must be the aims and interests of society itself, of which it becomes in reality the social head and heart. . . .
>
> Where is there, then, a real possibility of emancipation in Germany?
>
> *This is our reply.* A class must be formed which has radical chains, a class in civil society which is not a class of civil society, a class which is the dissolution of all classes, a sphere of society which has a universal character because its sufferings are universal, and which does not claim a *particular redress* because the wrong which is done to it is not a *particular wrong* but *wrong in general.* . . . This dissolution of society, as a particular class, is the *proletariat.*
>
> The proletariat is only beginning to form itself in Germany, as a result of the industrial movement. For what constitutes the proletariat is not naturally existing poverty, but poverty artificially produced, is not the mass of people mechanically oppressed by the weight of society, but the mass resulting from the disintegration of society and above all from the disintegration of the middle class. . . .[20]

There we have, vividly expressed, the essential source of the Marxian theory of revolution, a theory in which history is obviously crucial. One must desire revolution—there can be no substitute for the participant's revolutionary zeal and directness of action—but revolution at the right time, that is, the time made "right" by historical conditions. If there is one overall perspective separating Marx from all other revolutionists before, during, and after his time, it is the intimate linkage we find in his mind between the action and its setting.

From his early years Marx settled on *capitalism*, as he called it, as the prime source of the ills of his own day and as the prime target of both historical analysis and revolutionary action. Others in Marx's day, as revolutionary in thrust as he, might make religion or the state the principal tyranny over man, and hence the major objective in revolutionary efforts to achieve man's liberation. But Marx declared capitalism to be the fundamental, shaping, and determining factor in contemporary society, as economic relations in one form or another—master-slave or feudal, for instance—had always been throughout history.

Capitalism is also the source, Marx declared in his early writings, of *human alienation*. This is a concept Marx derived from Hegel—who had used *alienation*, however, to refer to a timeless condition of man's mind, one that followed from its capacity to be both actor and thing: a *subject* that seeks to dominate its fate and an *object* of others' domination. The result, Hegel implied, was a built-in feeling in the human mind of estrangement from self, of reflexive alienation. Others, however—mostly Hegel's students, especially those known as the "left Hegelians"—looked for other sources of alienation. Some, like Feuerbach, found it to rise from religion. All institutional religion, wrote Feuerbach, is a reflection of the individual's loss of self to some externalization, some projection of self, he calls "god." The removal of institutional religion is necessary to man's recovery of self and hence to the termination of his alienated state of being.

But Marx, who had studied Hegel devotedly and was himself, in the beginning, one of the "left Hegelians," saw the matter very differently. There is indeed alienation, Marx wrote, to be found in the individual's loss of control, of personal wholeness; but this alienation is basically *economic*. It is not a timeless ontological condition, as Hegel had implied; not the result of religious subjection, as Feuerbach had argued; not, primarily, the result of political power, as some of the anarchists claimed. Alienation is economic, and it is inseparable from capitalism, that is, private property.

> In what does alienation consist? First that the work is *external* to the worker, that it is not a part of his nature, that consequently he does not fulfill himself in his work but denies himself. . . . His work is not voluntary but imposed, *forced labor*. It is not the satisfaction of a need, but only a *means* for satisfying other needs.
>
> The object produced by labor, its product, now stands opposed to it as an *alien being*, as a *power independent* of the producer. . . . The performance of work is at the same time its objectification. This performance appears, in the sphere of political economy, as a *vitiation* of the worker, objectification as a *loss* and as *servitude to the object*, and appropriation as alienation.[21]

21 Karl Marx, *Selected Writings in Sociology and Social Philosophy*, ed. T. B. Bottomore and Maximilian Rubel (New York: McGraw-Hill Book Co., 1956), pp. 169–71.

For Marx the only way in which man's alienation can be ended on earth is through eradication of private property, the profit system—in a word, capitalism, with its associated institutions:

> Religion, the family, the State, law, morality, science, art, etc. are only particular forms of production and come under its general law. The positive abolition of private property, as the appropriation of human life, is thus the positive abolition of all alienation, and thus the return of man from religion, the family, the State, etc. to his human, that is, social life.[22]

Although alienation as a concept disappeared from Marx's writings after publication of his and Engels's *Communist Manifesto* in 1848, the idea never disappeared from Marx's mind of the individual's victimization by capitalism, of the tyranny of work under a system of private property, and of the fetish of commodities (a phrase Marx used much later, in *Capital*, which has some relation at least to alienation) to be found under the hated capitalist system.

It was a short step from the writings quoted thus far, all from his young manhood, to the famous and, as history proved, electrifying *Communist Manifesto*. This work, small in size but vast in effect, had been commissioned from Marx and Engels by the Communist League, a secret revolutionary society to which Marx belonged which held a clandestine meeting in London in 1848. The manuscript was sent to the printer in London just a few weeks before the Revolution of 1848 broke out in France.

Everyone knows the exhilarating words with which the *Manifesto* begins: "A specter is haunting Europe—the specter of Communism." [23] From this opening line we move quickly into what is at one and the same time an interpretation of human history, an assessment of capitalism and its two great classes, bourgeoisie and proletariat, and, not least, a prescription for the beginning of the proletarian-Communist revolution when a country has reached the proper stage of development.

"The history of all hitherto existing society is the history of class struggles." [24] So opens the historical section. It was the genius of Marx and Engels thus to set their own time—or, rather, their political-revolutionary desires for their own time—in a historical context that reached back all the way to the beginning of society. Marx had earlier come to the conclusion that only through the struggle of the industrial proletariat against the capitalist class could successful revolution be effected. Now he adds to this the conclusion that history has from the beginning been

22 Ibid., p. 244.

23 Karl Marx, *Communist Manifesto* (Chicago: Charles H. Kerr, 1940), p. 11.

24 Ibid., p. 12.

characterized by class struggles—between freeman and slave in the ancient world, lord and serf in the medieval world—and that the present struggle between bourgeoisie and proletariat is in lineal descent from the others. In all earlier situations it was the oppressed class that eventually became dominant, but only through major changes in social structure by which the previously dominant class had been rendered obsolete, so to speak.

Today, Marx writes, the bourgeoisie is dominant in every country in the world that is not still in a feudal or lower stage of development. The bourgeoisie has risen from its medieval subjection to guild masters, lords, and bishops to present supremacy in matters economic, political, social, and intellectual. The breakup of medievalism meant the emergence of this class which Marx and Engels do not hesitate to laud as the greatest, in terms of sheer technical accomplishment, of any known thus far in history. Moreover, it is the bourgeoisie that has created the technological setting within which socialism and then communism will eventually flourish. There is nothing of the utopian or idyllic socialist in Marx. Each great age of history develops within the womb of the preceding age, and new forces and structures do not emerge until old ones have been made obsolete by the workings of history.

Capitalism is only now just beginning to show the same kind of internal stresses that have been the fate of all preceding historical ages —stresses which are invariably the consequence of class struggles. In due time, Marx and Engels assure us, capitalism will undergo the same disintegration that befell feudalism earlier in western Europe; but this will happen only when the working class expands vastly and also becomes conscious of itself as the vanguard of progressive development. Even now, workers revolt and are occasionally victorious,

> . . . but only for a time. The real fruit of their battles lies, not in the immediate result, but in the ever expanding union of the workers. . . .
>
> This organization of the proletarians into a class, and consequently into a political party, is continually being upset again by the competition between the workers themselves. But it ever rises up again, stronger, firmer, mightier.[25]

Through capitalism's own inability to contain the conflicts it engenders through private property, through profits, and through its incessant creation of propertyless masses, the time must shortly come in the most advanced capitalist countries when the objective situation is right for the Communist-led, proletarian-manned revolution. By virtue of the ever-weakening condition of the bourgeoisie combined with the

25 Ibid., p. 24.

sheer mass of the proletariat and, above all, its leadership—which must come from Communists, who understand the course of history and the material conditions necessary for revolution—the proletariat will supplant the bourgeoisie, and the advent of socialism will be at hand.

I have said that the major difference between Jacobin and Marxist revolutionary conceptions lies in the latter's envisagement of history, which I have just briefly described. But the similarity between these two conceptions is overwhelming when we look at the political nature of the socialist revolution and the actual steps it follows, as these are to be found in the *Manifesto*. No Jacobin would have been astonished by the *Manifesto* or felt a stranger to its detailed program of the probable changes immediately necessary once the proletariat and the vanguard of Communists have attained command of a social order. Such proposed changes or actions included abolition of corporate property in land; adoption of a heavy progressive income tax; abolition of all right of inheritance; confiscation of the property of all emigrants and rebels; centralization of credit in the state; centralization of means of communication and transport in the state; extension of factories owned by the state; establishment of industrial armies, especially for agriculture; combination of agriculture with manufacturing industries; gradual abolition of distinction between town and country; free education for all children in state-operated schools; combination of education with industrial production; and so on.

All of these, with the possible exception of one or two, are directly in line with actions that had been taken by the Jacobins in 1791–94 during their brief hegemony in France; and it may be assumed that Marx would have endorsed other such Jacobin changes in social order as those we have already seen to apply to family, local community, aristocracy, and church. The essential point is that Jacobin centralization, rationalization, and nationalization, Jacobin use of absolute political power, and Jacobin effort to abolish the distinction between the political order and the social order are all contained explicitly or implicitly in the Marxian preview of the nature of the Communist revolution.

True, Marx and Engels declare their faith in the eventual disappearance of "political power" once the work of the revolution has been accomplished and all traces of the traditional social order have been removed. But so did the Jacobins declare that all manifestations of the Terror, all overt uses of political power and legal force, all evidences of militarization of society would vanish once the people had become virtuous through and through and the inherited effects of predemocratic superstition and evil had been eradicated. In the *Manifesto* it is not "virtue" as such that is heralded by the revolution—only classless society, society without private property. It was—and still is—the Marxist argument that all political power is but evidence of the supremacy of one social class over another.

> Political power, properly so-called, is merely the organized power of one class for oppressing another. If the proletariat . . . makes itself the ruling class, and, as such, sweeps away by force the old conditions of production, then it will, along with these conditions, have swept away the conditions for the existence of class antagonisms, and of classes generally, and will thereby have abolished its own supremacy as a class.
>
> In place of the old bourgeois society, with its classes and class antagonisms, we shall have an association, in which the free development of each is the condition for the free development of all.[26]

Clearly, given the mountain of corruption, tyranny, superstition, oppression, and evil that must have piled up in any society, from the Marxist point of view, as the consequence of many millennia of class-ridden history, nothing short of permanent revolution extended over a very long period of time could possibly be equal to the task of removing the mountain. So it had appeared to the Jacobins and so it has, on the evidence, appeared to the descendants of Marx in those parts of the world where Marxian Communists have triumphed through revolution —as in Soviet Russia, China, Albania, and others.

Again it must be stressed that revolution in the sense established by the Jacobins and continued by the Marxist Communists, among others, is a transfiguration of religion, a continuation of religious purposes by other means. How can either virtue or total equality, as the end and objective of revolutionary action, ever be achieved in life—that is, to the complete satisfaction of all, or of all who managed to hold the seats of power?

The Marxist conception of revolution is eminently religious—using the word in its prime senses of purification, redemption, and relation of ends to cosmic or social purposes. In the *Manifesto* and then in a series of writings by Marx and Engels to come during the full generation following the *Manifesto*'s publication, including such notable works of Marxian genius as *The German Ideology*, *Capital* (especially the Preface to the second edition), *The Eighteenth Brumaire of Louis Napoleon*, and *The Civil War in France*, a remarkably coherent picture unfolds of the nature and necessity of the revolutionary community and its eventual triumph. It is as coherent and passionately stated as anything we might find in Augustine or in any of the utterances of those millennialist religious leaders of the apocalyptic-terrorist movements at the end of the Middle Ages we considered earlier in this chapter.

For Marx, revolution—and the eventual achievement of the com-

[26] Ibid., p. 42.

munist order—was absolutely *necessary*: that is, made inevitable by the dialectical forces of conflict and the embedded tendency toward human progress that he believed he had irrefutably discovered in the pages of history. *All* history, he wrote, is a history of class struggle. Each resolution of a class struggle lifts the human mission in history to a higher place. Class struggle and its resulting dialectical resolution will always exist everywhere so long as private property exists, forming the base for class society. Class struggle or conflict is the necessary dynamic in history. Such struggle revolves around the contradictions within a social order that are the inevitable results of property and class. These contradictions, when they have accumulated to a sufficient point, result in the inevitable destruction of a particular social order, with the new and succeeding order bound to emerge from the "womb" of the preceding one. "No social order ever disappears before all the productive forces for which there is room in it have been developed, and new, higher relations of production never appear before the material conditions of their existence have matured in the womb of the old society." [27] The historic importance of capitalism, Marx declared, is that under it class conflict, between bourgeoisie and proletariat, is brought to its greatest intensity. This conflict, he believed, can be terminated only by the triumph of the proletariat and, with this, the final, absolute extinction of private property and thus of class conflict. In sum, socialism or communism is not—as other socialists of the time seem to be arguing—merely desirable, merely an objective for social action. It is, above all, *historically inevitable,* made so by the forces of the social order, by the dialectic of history. Social action, including force, violence, war, and bloodshed, is necessary, or probably necessary, given the effort of the old order to maintain itself; but these, however passionately mobilized and supported by the courage and arms of the workers, are destined to utter failure unless the historical moment is a propitious one. Unless history has itself reached the objective point when revolutionary violence can serve as "midwife," as it were, only futility can attend revolutionary actions. This was the sovereign message of Marx to the world. In it is religious certitude, boundless moral confidence, and a sense of millennialist fulfillment one ordinarily finds only among the dedicatedly religious.

One finds in Marx and Engels the same mixture of what might be called the "objective" good and the "subjective" good that we find in the eschatological religions, Christianity being a splendid example. Subjectively, the evils of capitalism are foremost in the consciousness of a Marxist, just as the evils of paganism in the late Roman Empire were foremost in subjective Christian thought. Objectively, however, it is possible to see these evils as necessary, and therefore historically good,

[27] Karl Marx's Preface to *A Contribution to the Critique of Political Economy,* in *Karl Marx and Friedrich Engels: Basic Writings on Politics and Philosophy,* ed. Lewis Feuer (New York: Doubleday & Co., Anchor Books, 1959), p. 44.

steps toward the ultimate redemption of man and society. How firmly Marx believed in this distinction may be inferred from a piece that he wrote on the British exploitation of India. Granted, Marx said, that the motives of the British are odious and their techniques often stupid, and granted, too, that there is superficial charm in the traditional Indian family, village, and caste, each with its protection of the individual. In point of fact, though, considered historically—that is, as a necessary stage in the evolution of society toward socialism—it is *good* that Britain should be engaged in her rape of traditional Indian society, for this inevitably takes India that much nearer the termination of feudalism, the achievement of capitalism, and thus eventually the attainment of the final, classless stage of socialism.

One looks in vain in Marx for a clear picture of the socialist society of the future, just as one looks in vain for a clear picture of social class, the fundamental elements of political power, and the fate of dialectically driven progress when all contradictions in the social order have been abolished. Marx could write in the *Anti-Dühring* of socialist life in a way that suggests the pastoral simplicity of primitive communism; Engels, in reply to some anarchist tract, could declare that the factory system, with its iron discipline engendered by the machine, would be just as basic to socialism as to capitalism; each could suggest on occasion that political power was no more than an appurtenance of the dominant social class; and each could write of the dialectic as though it would miraculously continue to drive mankind to ever-higher levels even in spite of the divisions and contradictions which had, throughout all preceding history, been the necessary bases of that dialectic.

But never mind! Ambiguities, lacunae, and rhetorical inconsistencies notwithstanding, what Marx's work all adds up to is, on the one hand, a system of economics and sociology that has inspired a very large number of intellectuals during the past century and, on the other, a secular eschatology that has been the stuff of hope for many millions.

During the century that has passed since Marx completed his major writings, beyond all other social, economic, and political ideas his have clearly had the paramount influence upon the course of world history. We may adapt the opening words of the *Manifesto* to say that "a specter is haunting the world—the specter of Marxism." Not since Christianity so profoundly and widely affected first the Roman world, then in time all the rest, through incessant expansion of its own spirit of nihilism and affirmation, has any single body of ideas come even close to dominating the lives of peoples and nations everywhere. Merely to glance at a map of the world at the present time and to note the number of major nations, foremost among them Soviet Russia and China, where the principles of Marxism have been made a very way of life, is to get at least an approximate idea of the influence of the Marxian doctrine of revolution.

But such assessment is hardly enough. For even the nations in which

Marxism is not the official philosophy or creed have been, at one time or other, strongly affected by the "specter" of Marxism. Excepting only the United States among major nations, strong Marxist-oriented workers' parties appeared almost everywhere in the late nineteenth and early twentieth century. And even in the United States, where no such parties arose in significant or lasting form, no one could be blind to the impact on thought and culture of both the associations and the ideas that sprang from Marx's works. Small though socialist and communist parties have been in the United States, their oftentimes strenuous prosecution of their ends has had demonstrable effect upon the history of organized labor, not to mention other institutions in American life.

Far above even these overt, practical manifestations of Marx's impact on the twentieth century has been his lasting effect on thought—on the social sciences, philosophy, even literature. Granted that in western Europe at this time such intellectual influence may be substantially less than it was a generation or two ago, the fact remains that Marx must be accounted one of the two or three minds that have had the most decisive effect in shaping modern thought. Freud's is undoubtedly the nearest to a rival influence in this respect. No matter that the informed historian of ideas can find, easily enough, obvious forerunners to Marx, from whom he derived many of his own ideas; no matter that even in the area where Marx thought himself most original, social dynamics, we have no difficulty in showing his lack of originality. The overriding fact is that Marx's peculiar fusion of the ideas of his forerunners and contemporaries has proved to have, without any question, the most powerful influence on Western thought of any distinguishable set of ideas and doctrines we can find in history since the advent of Christianity.

But for purposes of this chapter on the revolutionary community, it is Marx's seminal role as revolutionist that must be emphasized. His own ideas were born in the context of passionate belief in revolution; they developed through some four decades in the continuing context of revolutionary dedication; and they have been transmitted to others of equal revolutionary dedication right down to the present moment. Except as manifesting the spirit of Marxism, it is simply impossible to understand the motive forces associated in our time with the names of such individuals as Stalin, Mao, Castro, and many others whose domination of sections of the earth, large or small, has proved so decisive.

Lenin and World Revolutionism

It was Vladimir I. Lenin, lifelong apostle of revolution and devoted, almost reverential student of Marx and Engels, above any other single figure, who transformed the principles of his revered Marx into the essential style of revolutionary action during the past century. Interestingly, the upper-class Russian Lenin came from a nation that, on a strict reading of Marxist texts, should have been among the last in Europe to undergo a "workers' revolution." For, as we have seen, the theory of Marxism argued that the revolution of the proletariat would occur where capitalism had become sufficiently developed to have reached its inevitable point of structural degeneration, thus making the organized efforts of the revolutionary workers more likely to succeed. Russia had begun to industrialize itself by the end of the nineteenth century, but it was over-whelmingly rural and agricultural, even feudal in the Marxist sense of the term.

Nevertheless, there had been strongly revolutionary cliques and secret societies in Russia throughout much of the nineteenth century; and by the end of the century, when the prestige of Marxian socialism had become great in other parts of Europe, we find the character of Russian revolutionism changing markedly under the effects of Marxian principle. Lenin was by no means alone in the work of giving Marxist structure, or rationalization, to preexisting revolutionary tactics and politics; but on the evidence of results attained, he is certainly the greatest in that work. Marx himself, before his death in 1883, had become interested in Russian revolutionary movements; and although he was fully aware that conditions in Russia did not represent his own essential principles regarding the development and decay of capitalism, nevertheless he thought Russia might well be the setting for a major revolutionary outburst. Reformism and gradualism, which had become far stronger in Western workers' movements than suited Marx's revolutionary proclivities, were relatively absent from Russian worker-peasant revolutionary groups; and it was precisely on this basis that Marx could see possibilities of that direct, revolutionary action which was beginning to look less and less likely in Germany, France, and England—all countries which by virtue of relatively advanced industrialism might be expected, on strict reading of Marx's major works, to have first experienced the kind of revolution Marxism's development and analytical theories prophesied.

But we are obliged to turn to the principal works of Lenin for the strategic adaptation of the principles of Marxism to the realities of revolutionary action. Lenin was not in the same class with such students of Marx as Karl Kautsky and Rosa Luxemburg so far as sheer learning and philosophic grasp both of history and of the actual tenets of Marxism were concerned. But few individuals in history have ever shown as much capacity for opportunistic utilization of principle as did Lenin, once the situation in Russia attained revolutionary possibilities, early in the twentieth century.

Lenin's *What Is to Be Done?*, published in 1902, is probably his major work from any point of view, certainly from that of the adaptation and reorientation of Marxism to which I have just referred. What we find in this book is an almost passionate insistence upon the *revolutionary* character of Marxism, in response to what Lenin felt was a destructive reliance by more and more Marxian socialists in western Europe on what might be called Marxism's developmental or evolutionary aspects. It will be remembered that Marx was indeed an evolutionist in his approach to society, seeing capitalism as the evolutionary emergent of preceding stages of society, the whole process governed by what he thought of as the iron laws of history. And it was from this clear evolutionary emphasis that such early-twentieth-century socialists as Eduard Bernstein in Germany and the Fabians in England declared their belief in the possibility of peaceful attainment of socialism—that is, through continued working out of the processes Marx had found in capitalism, which would, on their own, lead in time to the end of capitalism and its replacement by socialism.

But, as the careful reader of Marx knows, his work also clearly contains, as in *The Eighteenth Brumaire* and *The Civil War in France,* elements that indicate an unambiguous recognition of, indeed a welcoming of, direct action, as violent and warlike as is called for by circumstances. And this is the side that Lenin chose to give full emphasis to in his bitter opposition to the more evolutionary or gradualist socialists of his day, who claimed to speak authoritatively for Marx and Engels.

What Is to Be Done? is the embodiment of this emphasis by Lenin, written some fifteen years prior to the outbreak of the 1917 revolution through which he and his followers destroyed the semisocialist, peace-oriented Kerensky government and created the world's first communist society. It is in this book that Lenin sets forth the theory of the necessary militance of the working class, which alone, he argued, following Marx, can lead peasants and other classes into socialism. And it is in this book also that Lenin sets forth the principle of the dedicated revolutionary community; that is, the Communist party, which, however small it may be in numbers, must in turn, he argued, give necessary leadership to the working class, using any and all techniques of force, power, war, bloodshed, and conspiracy that may prove necessary.

> In order to be fully prepared for his task, the working class revolutionary must also become a professional revolutionary. . . . A workingman agitator who is at all talented and "promising" must not be left to work eleven hours a day in a factory. We must arrange that he be maintained by the Party, that he may in due time go underground, that he change the place of his activity. . . . When we have detachments of specially trained working class revolutionaries who have gone through long years of preparation (and, of course, revolutionaries of "all arms"), no political police in the world will be able to contend against them, for these de-

tachments of men absolutely devoted and loyal to the revolution will themselves enjoy the absolute confidence and devotion of the broad masses of the workers. . . .

Only a gross failure to understand Marxism . . . could prompt the opinion that the rise of a mass, spontaneous labour movement relieves us of the duty of creating as good an organisation of revolutionaries as *Zemla i Volya* had in its time [Lenin is referring to an earlier revolutionary group in Russia the militance of which he admired], and even an incomparably better one. On the contrary, this movement *imposes* this duty upon us, because the spontaneous struggle of the proletariat will not become a genuine "class struggle" until it is led by a strong organisation of revolutionaries.[28]

Lenin, in short, believed that neither the end of capitalism nor the rise of socialism would ever come from internal, structural processes alone, that the only way the working class could be made into a genuinely revolutionary movement was through incessant domination of this movement by such "educated representatives of the propertied classes" as himself—that is, by individuals dedicated to Marxism, permanent revolution, and absolute destruction of capitalism and imperialism.

In a certain sense, Lenin is the Saint Paul of Marxism. It is entirely possible that, attractive though it was to revolutionary elites in Europe by the end of the nineteenth century, as well as to many intellectuals generally, Marxism would have become no more than just another social doctrine in the history of ideas. Lenin made sure this would not be the case through his translation of the economics of Marxism into a revolutionary tactics of power—that is, into a *politics* of Marxism with no holds barred. And because Lenin removed Marxism from the study, kept it from being largely a philosophy of the decline and fall of capitalism, and adapted it to the purposes of revolutionary movements everywhere— peasant or worker, European or non-European—he must be accounted the single follower of Marxism who did the most to universalize it, just as Paul had universalized and had brought into the world marketplace the tiny sect that was primitive Christianity.

In one important sense, though, Lenin did not so much universalize as localize Marxism. From Marx's stirring emphasis on "workers of the world" and from the harsh words in various parts of the Marxian corpus on nationalism and the obsolescence of nations, it was possible to conclude that in terms of strict Marxism the great revolution of the future had to be worldwide in scope, not limited to any one nation. Lenin's

28 V. I. Lenin, *What Is to be Done?* in *Selected Works*, 12 vols. (New York: International Publishers, 1929–43), 2: 146–49.

belief was different—and, surely, more practical. The revolution must obtain a secure foothold in one country; then, and only then, could the work of spreading revolutionary symbol be effectively carried out. Achieved socialism in one country could then be an exemplar to the workers of other parts of the world.

One other major idea in the strategy of revolution is Lenin's, though one can find ample source for it in certain final passages of the *Communist Manifesto*, to which I referred above. Lenin's famous phrase "the dictatorship of the proletariat" must certainly be regarded as a milestone in the development of twentieth-century revolutionary programs. It is true that to read Marx's emphasis on "centralization" and on the proletariat's eradication of all other classes and groups in the eventual workers' revolution is to find quickly enough the source of Lenin's thinking here. Marx was no liberal, no believer in individualism; he had a very clear conception of the kind of ruthless use of power and terror that would be required by the revolution. Even so, we cannot take from Lenin his credit for fashioning the phrase that has become one of the half-dozen master phrases of contemporary revolutionary thought.

The seeds of the phrase, and of the whole totalitarian form of government that was to spring from its implications, are to be found in Lenin's earliest reflections upon the needs of revolution. True, they can also be found, as we observed above, in the final passages of the *Communist Manifesto*, which called for a high degree of militant centralization of government. Lenin, however, carries the Marxist argument much further:

> To speak of pure democracy, of democracy in general, of equality, of liberty, and of the people, while the workers and all the toilers are starving and in rags, are ruined and tortured, not only by capitalist wage-slavery, but also by four years of predatory war, while the capitalists and the profiteers continue to own their ill-gotten "property" and their "ready-made" apparatus of state power means mocking at the toilers and the exploited. . . . there is no way of emancipating labour from the yoke of capital except by substituting the *dictatorship of the proletariat* for the dictatorship of the bourgeoisie. The dictatorship of the proletariat is alone able to liberate mankind from the yoke of capital, from the lies, the sham and the hypocrisy of bourgeois democracy, which is democracy *for the rich*; it alone is able to establish democracy *for the poor*. . . .[29]

From the idea of dictatorship of the proletariat it was, of course, but a short step to that of the dictatorship of the Communist party, which

[29] The State and Revolution," in *Selected Works*, 7: 219–20.

was, by Leninist definition, the essence, the spokesman, of the proletariat. And from this idea of dictatorship it was an even shorter step to that of the kind of dictatorship of a small group, eventually of one man, so well illustrated by the postrevolutionary history of Soviet Russia.

The centralization we observed above among the several vital elements native to the revolutionary community has the closest affinity, obviously, with the centralization of command we find in the military community. As we saw in the chapter on the military community, it was the signal achievement of Marx, Engels, Lenin, and Trotsky to unite revolutionary and military principles, recommending utilization of military techniques, especially those of guerrilla warfare, for revolutionary objectives. And once revolutionary victory is assured, all Communist states, as their histories make clear enough, make increasing use of the symbols of war and militarism—combined, to be sure, with the symbols and dogmas of revolutionary world crusade—to achieve and maintain order.

It is impossible to overstress this union of military and revolutionary elements in the twentieth-century Communist states. Without significant exception these states have come into existence in time of war and, more important, have been brought into being by revolution in countries that have first suffered defeat by a foreign military power. As will be remembered from the discussion of Lenin in the chapter above on the military, not least among his contributions to the strategy of revolution was what he called the turning of imperialist wars into civil wars. There is not the slightest ground for supposing that the Bolshevik Revolution in 1917 could ever have gotten off the ground, indeed could even have been begun at all, had it not been for the Russian defeat by Germany in World War I, one of the most devastating, shattering, bloody, and politically humiliating defeats ever suffered by one national power at the hands of another.

In his *State and Revolution* Lenin argued that the state "in the proper sense of the word" exists, and can exist, only in a form of society where one class dominates and exploits another. Once the revolution has become successful, the apparatus of the state will become progressively more unnecessary, and its administrative bureaucracy will gradually disappear.

> The dictatorship of the proletariat, the period of transition to communism, will, for the first time, create democracy for the people, for the majority, in addition to the necessary suppression of the minority—the exploiters. Communism alone is capable of giving really complete democracy, and the more complete it is the more quickly will it become unnecessary and wither away of itself. . . .

Finally, only communism makes the state absolutely unnecessary, for there is *no one* to be suppressed—"no one" in the sense of a *class*, in the sense of a systematic struggle against a definite section of the population. We are not utopians, and we do not in the least deny the possibility and inevitability of excesses on the part of *individual* persons, or the need to suppress *such* excesses. But in the first place, no special machine, no special apparatus of repression is needed for this: this will be done by the armed people itself, as simply and as readily as any crowd of civilised people, even in modern society, parts two people who are fighting, or interferes to prevent a woman being assaulted. And secondly, we know that the fundamental social cause of excesses, which consist in violating the rules of social life, is the exploitation of the masses, their want and their poverty. With the removal of this chief cause, excesses will inevitably begin to *"wither away."* We do not know how quickly and in what order, but we know that they will wither away. With their withering away, the state will also *wither away*.[30]

No reader of this book, surely, will need to be reminded that Soviet Russia, now more than fifty years away in time from the success of the Bolshevik Revolution, is very probably the most centralized, bureaucratized, and collectivized political state in history. We cannot be sure to what extent Lenin himself realized that once brought into being, power of the intensity and scope demanded by a large-scale revolution is rarely if ever dislodged, and that to argue as he did in the foregoing passage is hardly more than a terminological trick for tactical purposes. Lenin may have actually believed that the period of dictatorship of the proletariat, and of the Communist party, would be a brief one; that the remains of pre-socialist society would be quickly eradicated; and that the social and economic conditions which would then exist would require no state, no bureaucracy, no force, no police system—only the people organized with that minimum of bureaucratic apparatus dreamed of by all nineteenth- and early-twentieth-century socialists and anarchists.

What is important here, however, is the fact that Lenin is the true author of the twentieth-century revolutionary-military-political state. He is the true successor of the Jacobins. Marx and Engels supplied the philosophy, dogma, myth, rationalization, and vision; Lenin translated these into actual military-revolutionary tactics. He proved that by sufficiently astute domination of a scene created by history, by the boundless use of force and terror, and by relentless tightening of political power over all social groups, the dogma and the dream of revolution could be translated

[30] *Selected Works,* 7: 82–83.

into first the capture, then the total management, of the modern masses.

It was also Lenin who showed the way to the twentieth-century totalitarian state, which in its Soviet Russian, Fascist Italian, Nazi German, and Chinese forms can best be described as the political institutionalizing of permanent revolution. The totalitarian state everywhere comes into existence on the basis of revolution and terror. Without these the degree of power represented by this form of state cannot possibly be achieved. And it is only through continuation of revolution—against each successively higher level of resistance, real or imagined, that traditional society offers—and of terror that the otherwise precarious structure of the total state can be held together. War, or preparation for war, is the prime necessity for the total state in its relation to outside states, if its own power is to remain formidable. Terror, or constant threat of terror, is the prime necessity within the total state if its roots are to be sunk deep in popular consciousness. Lenin, by converting the Marxian theory of revolution into a strategy and tactics, proved to be, as he himself realized, the true successor of the Jacobins.

Sorel and the Ethics of Violence

The sheer, persisting power of the Jacobin legacy of revolutionism in France is attested by the fact that, with almost minimal exceptions, the greatest revolutionary theorists of the modern world have either been French themselves, like Proudhon and Sorel, or done their seminal work in France, as did Marx in the 1840s, or written in the French language, as did the twentieth-century Frantz Fanon. We shall reserve treatment of Proudhon for a later chapter. Despite his clear relevance to the revolutionary community, his lasting significance lies, I think, in his theories of federalism and what he called mutualism, both more appropriate to chapters that follow. Fanon will be considered in the final section of this chapter. We must now turn, however, to the ideas of Georges Sorel, no less than the others an intellectual descendant of Jacobinism and without question one of the most original minds of his day.

It is interesting to note that Sorel began as an engineer, working for the French government until 1892 in this capacity. Further, he began his career as a strong conservative in political matters. He early acquired a deep dislike of liberalism in any of its forms, and this dislike never left him to the end of his life. It was entirely from the viewpoint of a philosophical conservative, steeped in the ideas of Tocqueville, Taine, Le Play, and other conservatives, that his earliest criticisms of liberalism and democracy were written, beginning with his tract on the Bible in 1889, his striking defense of the execution of Socrates in the same year, and his more ambitious *Decline of the Ancient World*, published in 1894. In all of these we find a fascination with the phenomena of decay and disintegration of the lives of nations. We find also a conviction, which he never lost even after he had become an avowed radical, revolutionist, and advocate of systematic violence, that the histories of nations and other social organizations show the chief causes of their decline and decay to lie in the intellectual dogmas of liberalism, secularism, and individualistic democracy. In the beginning, such antagonisms produced in Sorel a kind of Burkean conservatism. Later, after he had discovered Marxism, the same antagonisms intensified his radicalism, reinforcing his view that only through total revolution could the scene be cleared for a new society that would be freed of the bourgeois dogmas he so thoroughly detested.

To say that Sorel "discovered" Marxism is not enough. For we see in him in the very act of discovering Marx's writings also a kind of revolt against certain influential elements of Marxian thought. I refer to its "evolutionary" elements, in which the final act of revolution is virtually made into a kind of birth pang of the natural, developmental emergence of a new social order. In Sorel's time, many Marxists—the so-called gradualist or revisionist school—were so convinced that capitalism was destroying itself through the iron laws of contradiction Marx had discovered that they saw little reason to prepare for or organize the revolution which Marx himself never ceased to have as a conscious object.

In his *Decomposition of Marxism,* Sorel made evident enough his utter scorn for this whole tendency of liberal, progressive, gradualist Marxism. Marx himself Sorel regarded as one of the great minds of all history, and he declared Marx to be, in effect, his own preceptor. But, despite his veneration for Marx, his pivotal theory of property and its determinative effect upon human behavior, his theory of class struggle, and his envisagement of bourgeois society as corrupt, Sorel could not for a moment agree that there was anything self-destructive in the structure of capitalism. The evidence, Sorel declared, is that capitalism is becoming ever stronger through its spreading of wealth to the lower classes and its capacity to weld the working classes into its own system of capital, profits, and wages. How, he asked, could revolution be expected through normal processes of capitalist operation, when these processes were spreading wealth throughout society to a degree never before known in history? Evolutionary or gradualist socialism was, therefore, a contradiction in terms. There would never be an end to capitalism and a creation of a just and heroic new society until a new post-Marxian vision appeared that would mobilize the workers in the same way that Christianity had succeeded in mobilizing its believers against the Roman imperial government in the first and second centuries.

In a brilliant work, *The Illusions of Progress,* written in the early years of this century, Sorel expressed, with wit as well as venom, his contempt for the idea of progress—an idea that, as we have seen, had had immense influence upon Marx, among a great many others, in the nineteenth century. The modern theory of progress, Sorel declared, is essentially a "trick" played by intellectuals (whom he detested in the aggregate), in which imagined improvement from one generation to another in a few insignificant realms is made into a huge, encompassing dogma embracing the whole of culture and civilization. Far from being able to observe any steady cumulative progress in history, wrote Sorel, we see instead long vistas of sterility, desuetude, and actual stagnation interrupted occasionally by the rising of a few great ideas, themes, or individuals who alone manage to lift human society into occasionally better, nobler periods—which, in turn, are usually short in duration. The idea of progress is a sop to consciousness, a clear product of bourgeois duplicity. So declared Sorel in one of the most original books of the age. Between his *Decomposition of Marxism* and his *Illusions of Progress* there is the closest possible intellectual affinity.

It is this contempt for all bourgeois-liberal ideas that underlies his single most famous work, *Reflections on Violence*. This may not be his most brilliant or original piece of writing, but it is nevertheless the only really distinctive major expression of the theory of revolution to appear during the half-century following Marx's death. That it did not succeed, as did Marx's *Communist Manifesto,* in becoming the tractarian base of a mass revolutionary movement in the world, and that it is far too learned, too subtle in its analyses, and often too erratic in its judgments of others ever to serve this function of mobilizing masses of people as well as galvanizing intellectual elites, should not prevent us from understanding its true importance in the history of the modern revolutionary community.

Let us begin with the key word in both book and title: *violence*:

> There are so many legal precautions against violence, and our upbringing is directed towards so weakening our tendencies toward violence, that we are instinctively inclined to think that any act of violence is a manifestation of a return to barbarism. Peace has always been considered the greatest of blessings and the essential condition of all material progress, and it is for this reason that industrial societies have so often been contrasted favourably with the military ones.[31]

Now, Sorel was no sadist, no intellectual brute seeking violence and destruction for their own ends. He lashed out often at the executions perpetrated by the Jacobins during the Terror in the French Revolution, regarding them as both inhuman and stupid. Sorel was not, in short, a lover of violence for its own sake. But it was a cardinal part of his social philosophy that in the long run the greatest danger any society has to

[31] Georges Sorel, *Reflections on Violence*, trans. T. E. Hulme and J. Roth (London: Collier-Macmillan, 1961), p. 180.

face is, not violence, but *decadence*. Many of the moral and legal discouragements of violence, he thought, are, in the first place, masks for the blandness and inertia of the society in which these discouragements are found and, in the second place, they are cover-ups for that form of violence contained in legal force.

Sorel, who had become an ardent socialist, who hated what he regarded as the corrupt and decadent bourgeois society around him, believed that so long as social thought, morality, and law discouraged violence in all its forms, just so long would bourgeois society continue and become ever more decadent. Great ages of history, Sorel tells us, have been ages not only of turmoil and dislocation but also, on frequent occasion, of violence. Change is never gradual, uniform, and easy. Genuine change involves a severe wrench from old ties and roots. Change is itself a form of violence—to the human spirit and to social relationships. If the change from bourgeois capitalist society to socialism is ever to be effected, it will have to be a sharp and convulsive one. All simple schemes of meliorism, of gradual reformism, are deceptive: they imply that major changes can occur without convulsion, without dislocation—without violence.

Sorel even seeks to show that violence is common in the vital beginnings of all major forms of association. He draws from the history of workers' movements, of the factory system, and even of religious societies like Christianity to show that in their periods of growth and welding of structures, violence is far more common than it is in our decadent society today. Violence, like conflict, is a means of generating loyalties and the hatreds necessary when one group or class is seeking to destroy a social order it believes to be evil or corrupt. Above all, only accepting the necessity of violence can insure the onset and the success of the revolution.

> Proletarian violence not only makes the future revolution certain, but it seems also to be the only means by which the European nations—at present stupefied by humanitarianism—can recover their former energy. This kind of violence compels capitalism to restrict its attentions solely to its material role and tends to restore to it the warlike qualities which it formerly possessed. A growing and solidly organised working class can compel the capitalist class to remain firm in the industrial war; if a united and revolutionary proletariat confronts a rich middle class, eager for conquest, capitalist society will have reached its historical perfection.[32]

32 Ibid., p. 92.

And capitalism, having reached its historical perfection, is then ripe for the revolution that will spell its death. Even allowing for the major intent of the foregoing paragraph, it is hard to miss the sense of the *heroic* in Sorel. We know from some of his earlier works, even those written during the period of his conservative beginning concern with social matters, that Sorel had a profound interest in heroes—in the Bible, in Homeric times, and in the early Middle Ages. It is hard for heroism to exist in circumstances that are bland, soft, and too well organized. And it is hard, too, for heroism to exist except in the context of violence, or at least the constant possibility of violence.

Clearly, though, the overriding reason for Sorel's projection of violence into his own day was as a means of separating the faint of heart in the socialist movement from those who might be depended upon to carry it through to successful conclusion. Violence, in other words, becomes a means of establishing authenticity. Again we come back to that word which we found central in Jacobinism during the Terror: if hypocrisy is the greatest of sins, then it is vital that one establish his own authenticity. Those willing to engage in violence, irrespective of its consequences, are manifestly more heroic, more trustworthy, more dedicated than those who profess commitment to goals but shrink from the means necessary to achieve them: so argues Sorel in his ethics of violence.

But violence for its own sake is not enough: This he repeatedly makes clear. It must serve a cause that strikes deep in the workers' hearts —deeper than reason itself, far, far deeper than mere perception of pragmatic utility would make possible. This means, for Sorel, *myth*: "a body of images which, *by intuition alone*, and before any considered analyses are made, is capable of evoking as an undivided whole the mass of sentiments which corresponds to the different manifestations of the war undertaken by Socialism against modern society." [33]

In the same way exactly that the spirits of early Christians were buoyed up by the "myth" of salvation and eternal bliss to be their lot in the next world, thus making worthwhile, even vitally necessary, all sacrifices in this world, so must the spirits of workers be buoyed up by an equivalent myth. This was what Sorel and the syndicalists of his time called the "general strike":

> Every time that we attempt to obtain an exact conception of the ideas behind proletarian violence we are forced to go back to the notion of the general strike; and this same conception may render many other services, and throw an unexpected light on all the obscure parts of Socialism.[34]

[33] Ibid, pp. 122–23. [34] Ibid., p. 119.

Quite simply, the general strike is a strike of *all* workers at the same time. Its setting may be a single community or province; or it may be the nation; or, by the highest stretch of imagination, it may be world-wide. But on whatever scale, the general strike will be a simultaneous walking off the job by a substantial number of workers—by *all* the workers in a given place. Sorel compares the general strike to Napoleon's theory of the battle, which declared that the battle is successful only if it crushes the adversary; so with the general strike. It alone among the various types of workers' strike is calculated to crush the adversary—in this instance the capitalists, the hated bourgeoisie.

The idea of the general strike, on whatever geographic scale, was far from being original with Sorel. Others earlier, impressed by the idea of military mass as this had been presented to the world by the armies of the French Revolution and Napoleon, had conceived of *worker mass*, with its implication of total destruction both of capitalists and of the system that contained workers and capitalists. The syndicalists were foremost among radical revolutionaries in advocating the goal of the general strike. What Sorel did, however, was lift the idea from attacks by socialist critics. These critics, thinking of the sociological and psychological difficulties of ever getting all the workers in a nation or the world at large to unite on so drastic an objective, and also of the heavy force with which governments would seek to put down all such worker actions and declare them conspiratorial, had denounced the idea of the general strike. To them Sorel replied:

> The possibility of the actual realisation of the general strike has been much discussed; it has been stated that the Socialist war could not be decided in one single battle. To the people who think themselves cautious, practical, and scientific the difficulty of setting great masses of the proletariat in motion at the same moment seems prodigious. . . . It is the opinion of the Socialist-sociologists, as also of the politicians, that the general strike is a popular dream. . . .
>
> And yet without leaving the present, without reasoning about the future, which seems forever condemned to escape our reason, we should be unable to act at all. Experience shows that the *framing of a future, in some indeterminate time,* may, when it is done in a certain way, be very effective, and have few inconveniences; this happens when the anticipations of the future take the form of those myths, which enclose with them all the strongest inclinations which recur to the mind with the insistence of instincts in all circumstances of life; and which give an aspect of complete reality to the hopes of immediate action by which,

more easily than by any other method, men can reform their desires, passions, and mental activity. We know, moreover, that these social myths in no way prevent a man profiting by the observations which he makes in the course of his life, and form no obstacle to the pursuit of his normal occupations.[35]

As Sorel then goes on to emphasize, the great mass religious movements of history have been based upon myth in this sense of the word. The earliest Christians expected the early return of Christ and, with his return, eternal bliss. This did not come about, of course, "but Christian thought profited so greatly from the apocalyptic myth that certain contemporary scholars maintain that the whole preaching of Christ referred solely to this one point." [36] So has it always been, Sorel argues, when it comes to large numbers of human beings engaged in activities that are dangerous, that call for supreme courage and willingness to sacrifice. There must be myth. The revolutionary and Napoleonic armies carried wherever they went the myth of the people's state founded on the principles of liberty, equality, and fraternity. Admittedly, the French state of the time did not come very close to reflecting these principles in fact; but this did not matter. The great ideal, however unrealizable it might be on this earth, was sufficient to convert many Frenchmen into passionate fighters for France.

So with the workers' revolution. Sorel would have granted instantly that the worldwide general strike his vision encompassed might never come to pass. In fact, Sorel would surely have said that it *probably* would never come to pass. But the sheer effect of there being such an ideal among workers' groups around the world, of living to the utmost in support of this idea, of believing in it as deeply as early Christians believed in the second coming of Christ, would be to strengthen the cause among revolutionary workers and hasten the revolution in such form as it might actually take.

In sum, what Sorel contributed to the theory of revolution was a degree of emphasis on action, even violent action, and on the role of belief, ideal, or myth that had tended—especially among a growing number of Marx's followers—to be subordinated to, even discouraged and dismissed by, Marx's own heavy emphasis on the material factors of history and his belief in the progressive development inherent in the historical process objectively considered. What Sorel said to all concerned was that the rhetoric of progress and developmentalism and of gradualism must never be allowed to hide the fact that revolution is, and must always be, a destructive act of violence.

---

[35] Ibid., pp. 123–25 passim.   [36] Ibid., p. 125.

Fanon and the Revolution
of Race

Our final example of the philosophy of revolution and of the persisting legacy of Jacobinism is the French black Frantz Fanon. Quite apart from the intrinsic interest of his writings, he is made relevant, of course, by the fact that the greatest single eruption of revolutionary consciousness in the mid-twentieth century is that associated with the black people: those in Africa and those in the United States, whose civil rights movement commencing in the 1950s is undoubtedly the closest thing to revolutionary stress this country has experienced since the Civil War. In our day, color has come close to replacing nationality and economic class as the major setting for revolutionary thrust, strategy, tactics, and also philosophy.

Not that revolt in the name of race is completely novel to the twentieth century. By all odds the most historic of black revolts, and the most far reaching in political terms, was that of the celebrated Toussaint L'Ouverture (1744–1803). A self-educated Haitian slave, of black ancestry on both sides, who was freed shortly before the uprising in Haiti in 1791—one of the by-products of the Jacobin message to the world—he shortly became not only the leader of the blacks in Haiti but, as evidenced by his successful campaigns against both the Spanish and the British, a military strategist of signal ability. In 1801 Toussaint and his black troops captured Santo Domingo and overthrew the government there. He governed the island until 1802, showing impressive knowledge of political administration, when he was captured by French forces sent by Napoleon. He died in a French prison a year later.

It was not, however, until the present century that revolts of black peoples became the stuff of really widespread revolutionary consciousness. And not until this century did there begin to appear a genuine literature of black revolution comparable to the kind of writing earlier generated by nationalist and economic class currents. For a long time, predictably, political nationalists and Marxist revolutionaries sought to submerge the facts of racial unrest and revolt in the already existing theories of political and economic revolution. Thus, Marxist writing has, on the whole, endeavored to persuade blacks and other races historically under white domination that they fall into the more general category of the proletariat. If there is a single fact, however, that stands out in all this, it is that racial revolution as an aspiration is becoming increasingly separate from other philosophies or strategies of revolution.

Of all those in this century who have seen the unalterably racial character of revolutionary action in different parts of the world, Frantz Fanon is almost certainly the one most likely to survive longest as a philosopher of revolution. Born in French-dominated Martinique in 1925, he studied in France, became a psychiatrist following graduation from medical school, and went to work first in a French hospital in Algeria during the 1950s at the very height of the revolutionary efforts of the Algerian National Liberation Front (FLN) to separate Algeria from France. He became dedicated to these revolutionary strivings and resigned from the hospital and from government service. First an editor of the FLN's newspaper, later an ambassador to Ghana from the newly formed Algerian Republic and also an envoy to the Congo, he spent the remainder of his very brief life (he died of leukemia in the United States in 1961) in the cause of racial, chiefly black, revolution. Products of an educated, very gifted, indeed brilliant mind, his few works, short as they are, are likely to become classics in the whole sphere of the Third World, that world of previously colonial people throwing off first the political and military ties binding them to Western society and then, more slowly but powerfully, the cultural, social, and psychological ties.

As a psychiatrist, Fanon knew how deeply these last were rooted in the minds and spirits of the colonial peoples throughout Africa, Asia, Oceania, and other parts of the world, such as the United States, where large aggregates of a particular race or ethnic strain had for long periods of time lived under the domination of other races. Not only as a political revolutionist deeply devoted to the cause of colonial uprising but as a psychologist, he made the phenomenon of race central in his thinking.

Moreover, he saw race as the central fact of history, most especially that of modern times, when the entire rest of the world opened up, through exploration, imperialism, and war, to Western-white consciousness. All efforts to submerge racial differences in the nonracial perspectives emphasized by Western whites, such as Marx himself, are doomed to failure. For Fanon blacks and whites constitute, and must always constitute, two hostile camps:

> This world divided into compartments, this world cut in two is inhabited by two different species. The originality of the colonial context is that economic reality, inequality, and the immense difference of ways of life never come to mask the human realities. When you examine at close quarters the colonial context, it is evident that what parcels out the world is to begin with the fact of belonging to or not belonging to a given race, a given specie. In the colonies the economic substructure is also a superstructure. The cause is the consequence; you are rich because you are white and you are white because you are rich. This is why Marxist analysis should always be slightly stretched every time we have to do with the colonial problem.[37]

[37] Frantz Fanon, *The Wretched of the Earth*, trans. Constance Farrington (New York: Grove Press, 1968), pp. 39–40. This work, Fanon's major one, was first published in 1961, the year of his death.

Fanon did not lack respect for Marx; nor has any protagonist in the uprisings and revolutions of the colonial peoples who has ever read Marx. In those parts of the revolutionary writings of Fanon and others directed solely to capitalism, we find little that is not clearly Marxist in inspiration and perspective. But the major point here is that such parts tend to be small in scope and implication. Overshadowing these are the parts of Fanon's writings directed to the phenomena of *race* and *color*. Marx's work was limited exclusively to the economic-social roles of human beings, as he himself emphasized at length in the Preface of his *Capital*. The importance of blackness and whiteness interested Marx no more than did, for example, the status of human beings as Jews, Gentiles, Catholics, and Protestants.

The distinguishing feature of twentieth-century revolutionary behavior and thought has proved to be, however, precisely its racial character. The signal revolts of the past half century, the major insurrections and mass liberations, have been precisely those buoyed up by appeal to race and color. The greatest single twentieth-century revolutionary movement has been that of the blacks, revolting against not capitalists primarily, but *whites*—in Africa and, to a modified degree, in the United States and other Western countries.

And ethnic revolt—whether black, Oriental, Chicano, or whatever —has commonly carried with it hostility to all manifestations of Western-white culture, not merely those identifiable as capitalist. In Marxism there is hostility only toward private property and capitalism—not, certainly, toward technology, the factory system, rationalism, and other key elements of Western modernity. But the distinctive flavor of such a writer as Fanon, and nearly all other philosophers of ethnic or racial revolution, is hostility toward the whole of Western culture, including its celebration of rationalism, technology, and even its definition of democracy and socialism. What Fanon desired above all other things was the assumption of identity by blacks for the first time since they were subjugated by whites—including, as he made plain, such whites as missionaries, progressive humanitarians, socialists, and others who believed themselves deliverers of the blacks.

What does the black man want?

At the risk of arousing the resentment of my colored brothers, I will say that the black is not a man.

There is a zone of nonbeing, an extraordinarily sterile and arid region, an utterly naked declivity where an authentic upheaval can be born. In most cases, the black man lacks the advantage of being able to accomplish this descent into a real hell.

Man is not merely a possibility of recapture or of negation. If it is true that consciousness is a process of transcendence, we have to see that this transcendence is haunted by the problems of love and understanding. Man is a *yes* that vibrates to cosmic harmonies. Uprooted, pursued, baffled, doomed to watch the dissolution of the truths that he has worked out for himself one after another, he has to give up projecting onto the world an antinomy that coexists with him.

The black is a black man; that is, as the result of a series of aberrations of affect, he is rooted at the core of a universe from which he must be extricated.

The problem is important. I propose nothing short of the liberation of the man of color from himself. We shall go very slowly, for there are two camps, the white and the black. . . .

We shall have no mercy for the former governors, the former missionaries. To us, the man who adores the Negro is as sick as the man who abominates him.

Conversely, the black man who wants to turn his race white is as miserable as he who preaches hatred for the whites.[38]

Those words are among the very earliest Frantz Fanon ever wrote, in a work first published in France in 1952, when he was but twenty-seven years old. He had not yet declared himself, as he was to do shortly, a lifetime servant of the revolutionary struggles of blacks and other racial colonials, had not yet thought out the philosophy of revolution that would appear in such writings as *The Wretched of the Earth*. But it is impossible to read the staccato sentences of the passage just quoted without realizing that the seeds of revolutionary mission had early been planted in Fanon's heart and that the mission would carry him well beyond anything to be found in organizations like the Communist party.

Escape white capitalism, yes, and also its colonialism. This would be as far as the Marxist could go with the revolutionary philosophers of the Third World. But the Fanons of the world clearly have no intention of confining their work to erasing white capitalism and white colonialism. Their aim is the total eradication of the sense of blackness that has grown from centuries of commingling with the whites:

For not only must the black man be black; he must be black in relation to the white man. Some critics will take it on themselves to remind us that this proposition has a converse. I say that this is false. The black man has no ontological resistance in the eyes of the white man. Overnight the Negro has been given two frames of reference within which he has had to place himself. His metaphysics or, less pretentiously, his customs and the sources

[38] Frantz Fanon, *Black Skin, White Masks*, trans. Charles Lam Markmann (New York: Grove Press, 1967), pp. 10–11.

on which they were based, were wiped out because they were in conflict with a civilization that he did not know and that imposed itself on him.[39]

Fanon makes plain that it was not the fact of colonialism as such which had the most destructive effects upon black cultures in Africa; nor, in America, was it necessarily the harsher aspects of slavery, and then postslavery subjection, which proved to have the most disintegrative effects upon the blacks. On the contrary, it was often the ostensible avenues of assimilation and integration which have led to such destruction or disintegration of black identity. Nor does it avail the oppressed race, Fanon emphasizes, to accept in every possible detail the culture of the oppressor:

> Yet the necessity that the oppressor encounters at a given point to dissimulate the forms of exploitation does not lead to the disappearance of this exploitation. The more elaborate, less crude economic relations require a daily coating, but the alienation at this level remains frightful.
>
> Having judged, condemned, abandoned his cultural forms, his language, his food habits, his sexual behavior, his way of sitting down, of resting, of laughing, of enjoying himself, the oppressed *flings himself* upon the imposed culture with the desperation of a drowning man.[40]

Here we come to Fanon's doctrine of violence and of its function in the oppressed race's purging itself of the consequences of colonialism. Violence is made necessary, Fanon argues, by the very cultural and psychological depths of what the black man has absorbed, through one or another form of colonialism, from the white. "For the native, this violence represents the absolute line of action." [41] Violence becomes, in Fanon's thought, very much what terror had become in the minds of the Jacobins in France 1793 and of the Bolsheviks in Russia prior to the revolution there: a mode of establishing authenticity. "Where have you worked? With whom? What have you accomplished? . . . You could be sure of the new recruit when he could no longer go back into the colonial system." [42] He could no longer go back, that is, to the security of servile status as a black because through an act of violence he had become an outlaw. Thereafter, only in the revolutionary community, itself founded upon the dogma of the necessity of violence and terror, would the indi-

---

[39] Ibid., p. 110.

[40] Frantz Fanon, *Toward the African Revolution*, trans. Haakon Chevalier (New York and London: Monthly Review Press, 1967), p. 39.

[41] Ibid.   [42] Ibid.

vidual outlaw black be able to find the security his nature demanded, the refuge from that alienation which had been his lot from the beginning, even though he may never have recognized it until his forced retreat from white society.

> This assumed responsibility for violence allows both strayed and outlawed members of the group to come back again and to find their place once more, to become integrated. Violence is thus seen as comparable to a royal pardon.[43]

Violence is necessary also to the emotional or affective formation of not merely the revolutionary community but the new state that is designed to follow.

> The mobilization of the masses, when it arises out of the war of liberation, introduces into each man's consciousness the ideas of a common cause, of a national destiny, and of a collective history. In the same way the second phase, that of the building up of the nation, is helped on by the existence of this cement which has been mixed with blood and anger. . . .
> At the level of individuals, violence is a cleansing force. It frees the native from his inferiority complex and from his despair and inaction; it makes him fearless and restores his self-respect. . . . When the people have taken violent part in the national liberation, they will allow no one to set themselves up as "liberators." They show themselves to be jealous of the results of their action and take good care not to place their future, their destiny, or the fate of their country in the hands of a living god. Yesterday they were completely irresponsible; today they mean to understand everything and make all decisions. Illuminated by violence, the consciousness of the people rebels against any pacifications.[44]

One of the most penetrating and sociologically informed of all Fanon's discussions of revolution and its consequences among the native peoples of the Third World is to be found in a brilliant section of his *Wretched of the Earth* entitled "Spontaneity: Its Strength and Weakness." Here we find Fanon coming to grips with the kind of tensions that must exist among the blacks themselves, or other natives long subject to white rule, the direct outcome of their uneven, incomplete assimilation of Western ideas. Thus he observes the strong opposition existing almost everywhere between the elite groups of natives, on the one hand, them-

---

43 Fanon, *The Wretched of the Earth,* pp. 85–86.
44 Ibid., pp. 93–94.

selves schooled in Western ideas of nationalism, administrative centraliza-tion, and the whole rationalized view of government, and the rural masses, on the other hand, who tend to take self-protective refuge in actually intensified native ways, many of which are tribal, kinship- or village-rooted, and to be proudly illiterate in Western languages and often dedicated to religious and magical ways of behavior which seem only superstitious and obsolete to the urban-based, nationalist, more or less Westernized native elites.

As Fanon notes, the latter, the native elites of the towns, are them-selves preoccupied with the problem of identity and authenticity. The whole purpose of their revolutionary being is the renewal of racial and cultural identity that has been emasculated by Western white culture. They are made uneasy in certain respects by possessing a literacy, a sophistication, and a set of norms they have managed to acquire, generally through the universities, from the very West they are dedicated to expunging. From one point of view at least, the greatest amount of "authenticity" or, as Fanon occasionally calls it, "spontaneity" lies pre-cisely in the rural-tribal masses of the hinterland. Fusion of the two elements is, however, difficult. The rural peasantry is likely to distrust the urban native elites almost as much as it distrusts and fears the white culture by which it has for so long been exploited. The rural masses tend still to live under tribal chiefs, shamans, and codes of authority in which personal-kinship ties are primary. The urban native elites have, of course, long since abandoned these. They cannot help, in short, seek-ing revolutionary renewal through political techniques as Western as any to be found in modern Europe or America.

This condition of deep division in the people persists well into the society of the new nation that is established following their liberation from the Western country by whom they have previously been dominated. Whereas in the cities the labor union has become the most effective tactical weapon to combat colonialism and its masters, the natives of the rural areas know nothing of labor unionism, and when efforts are made to organize the peasantry into rural labor unions, they commonly fail. The rural masses have their own trusted forms of association.

> The Westernized elements experience feelings with regard to the bulk of the peasantry which are reminiscent of those found among the town workers of industrialized countries. The history of middle class and working class revolutions has shown that the bulk of the peasants often constitute a brake on the revolution. Generally in industrialized countries the peasantry as a whole are the least aware, the worst organized, and at the same time the most anarchical element. They show a whole range of charac-teristics—individualism, lack of discipline, liking for money, and

propensities toward waves of uncontrollable rage and deep discouragement which define a line of behavior that is objectively reactionary.[45]

This is, of course, precisely the set of characteristics Marx railed against in his fulminations against the peasantry and what he called the idiocy of rural life. Before Marx the Jacobins had held identical views of the recalcitrant, objectively reactionary peasantry; and after Marx the Bolsheviks in Russia and then the government of Soviet Russia expressed the same views, Stalin's prime objective being the virtual destruction of the rural masses. In the native rural areas, revolutionary behavior tends, as Fanon sees clearly, to take the form premodern revolutionism has taken everywhere: the kind of revolutionism we considered earlier in this chapter under the headings of religious-popular millennialist revolt and what Hobsbawm calls social banditry. But for this kind of insurrectionary behavior the sophisticated, educated native leaders of the cities, along with the labor unions they have helped organize, have nothing but contempt and often hatred.

It is plain, however, that unlike the Jacobins and Bolsheviks, Fanon haš a deep feeling of attachment to and a revolutionary faith in the rural-peasant, or tribal-native, forms of action. Like Sorel, Fanon has a profound distrust of the militance that is urban-based: it tends, he declares, to become as corrupt as the society that dominates. Urban native elites tend too easily to become merely reformist in mentality, the thrust of revolution spent, the galvanizing effect of violence lost. It is, Fanon believes, in the more rooted and authentic culture of the rural masses—tribes, chiefs, magicians, and all—that one is more likely to find that degree of consecrated action, unremitting struggle, and dedicated violence which can alone maintain both negritude and the spirit of revolutionary struggle. Above all, in Fanon's view, violence—incessant, unremitting violence—is required for the revolution. Only thus, he declares in the very words of Sorel, can the authenticity and dedication of the revolution be guaranteed; only thus can the revolutionary community be prevented from dissolving.

To the Western-educated, sophisticated political elites of the Third World cities Fanon writes:

> The nationalist militant who has fled from the town in disgust at the demagogic and reformist maneuvers of the leaders there, disappointed by political life, discovers in real action a new form of political activity which in no way resembles the old. These politics are the politics of the leaders and organizers living inside history who take the lead with their brains and their

[45] Ibid., p. 111.

muscles in the fight for freedom. . . . Violence alone, violence committed by the people, violence organized and educated by its leaders, makes it possible for the masses to understand social truths and gives the key to them. Without that struggle, without that knowledge of the practice of action, there's nothing but a fancy-dress parade and the blare of trumpets. There's nothing save a minimum of readaptation, a few reforms at the top, a flag waving; and down there at the bottom an undivided mass, still living in the middle ages, endlessly marking time.[46]

So might a Jacobin have phrased the matter in 1790, a Babouvist a few years later, an anarchist or communist in the late nineteenth century, a Bolshevik in 1917, a dedicated Nazi in 1933, or a Maoist in our own day. Only through violence can the mission of the revolution be carried to the consciousness of the masses; only through terror can the dream of revolutionary redemption be preserved; and only through incessant, relentless direction by the holy elite that acts as the vanguard of the revolution can authenticity be saved from corruption by the values, ideas, and institutions the revolution is pledged to exterminate. This is Fanon's message, just as it has been the message of every revolutionary in history. It does not matter from the point of view of the dynamics of revolution, whether the basic dogma pertain to the people or the proletariat, the black race, or some other segment of the population believed to contain within itself some absolute form of goodness that only awaits liberation. The essence of the revolutionary community, irrespective of precise dogma, lies in its belief that violence alone can achieve fundamental change in society and that violence or terror remains, whether in practice or posed threat, the sole means of maintaining the authenticity of the revolution against forces which are always seeking to corrupt this authenticity.

Revolution and Modern Man

In many ways the most remarkable of all forms of community in modern thought and life is that with which we have been concerned in this chapter: revolution. For revolution is basically nothing less than overthrow of constituted authority in society. As one reflects on the matter even briefly, he is astonished, all things considered, that the revolutionary mode of thought, even if it is still opposed in specific situations, is among the most honored in modern times. Prior to about the seventeenth century, nothing was regarded with greater horror than calculated revolt against kings, princes, and other rulers. The worst tortures and executions

46 Ibid., p. 147.

were reserved for the convicted enemy of public order. For several centuries there was a profound vein of Western thought in which political rule, more especially rule by kings, was deemed to be divine in origin, and thus revolt against it to be iniquitous and deeply impious as well as a violation of law and convention.

> *The heavens themselves, the planets and this center,*
> *Observe degree, priority, and place,*
> *Insisture, course, proportion, season, form,*
> *Office, and custom, in all line of order.*

So wrote Shakespeare in *Troilus and Cressida* (act 1, scene 3), and, a few lines following, these celebrated words:

> *Take but degree away, untune that string,*
> *And hark, what discord follows. Each thing meets*
> *In mere oppugnancy.*

I do not suggest that philosophers had been unmoved by tyrannical power. Throughout the Middle Ages the necessity of moral limits upon power was stressed, a view that John Locke reached, largely through the writings of the Elizabethan theologian Richard Hooker, at the end of the seventeenth century to become the basis of his defense of the change of monarchs in England in 1688. But nowhere do we find an abstract, general theory of revolution in politics. The very word *revolution* was limited in its meaning to astronomical phenomena, to the turning of heavenly bodies on their axes or the orbiting of one body around another.

The eighteenth century changed all that, when the idea began to be first current, then followed with outright devotion, that it may be in the highest interests of morality, of goodness and virtue, to overthrow a political order declared, in the name of natural or social rights, to be illegitimate. It was Rousseau, as we have seen, who, more than anyone else in the century, made revolution not merely the privilege but the duty of the politically righteous. Across the Atlantic was the glittering spectacle of the American colonists in military-revolutionary opposition to the constituted authority of the British. And then, at the very end of the eighteenth century, came that culmination of all the revolutionary thought of the period, and that prototype of all subsequent revolutions in the world, the French Revolution, led preeminently by the consecrated Jacobins, the first group in history that may properly be considered a revolutionary community in the full, modern sense of the word. In thought, word, and act, the Jacobins were the essential and complete revolutionists.

Since the eighteenth century the word revolution has occupied a steadily rising place in Western social thought. Political to the core in the eighteenth century, its referent came to widen, as we have seen, to economic, social, and, in our own century, racial spheres, all the while, however, retaining its prior connotation of *political* power; that is, the legitimacy, the sanctity, of using political power to accomplish social and moral ends. So popular, indeed, has the word *revolution* become that today we use it widely for all manner of changes—major changes, at any rate—in science, technology, the arts, and even legislation. To refer to a modification of thought or life as "revolutionary" today is to accord it the highest accolade.

And consider the number of twentieth-century societies whose roots are revolutionary: America, France, Russia, and China are perhaps the most spectacular, but there are literally dozens that would declare their origins to be revolutionary, and with sound historical reason. To honor the revolution that is the historical origin of one's government is at the present time as sacred an obligation as once was the commandment to honor one's father or god. It was revolution in the eighteenth century that really produced in subsequent Western life the whole vein of what we call radicalism—in many ways the most cherished, even if frequently and massively opposed, of modern man's ways of thinking, whether in political, social, economic, or sexual matters. The three great Western ideologies since the eighteenth century, which have spread from the West to all other parts of the world, are what we call "conservative," "liberal," and radical." All have been given their distinctive shapes in our contemporary culture by the phenomenon of revolution—whether in support or in opposition. Those who first fought the idea of revolution in the West did so chiefly on the ground that if it were to become accepted in one sphere of life—the strictly political, say—it was bound to spread inexorably and relentlessly to all other areas, thus, it was argued, making any kind of social life impossible. We may of course differ with that final conclusion, but no one surveying the history of the world since about 1800 will doubt that the first part of the prediction did indeed become fulfilled.

It is impossible to find in Western thought before about two centuries ago any philosophers more than faintly touched by the theme and the mystique of revolution. During the past two centuries, however, it is not only difficult but impossible to deal with social thought except by giving a very large place to the philosophers of and participants in the revolutionary community. The philosophes, especially Rousseau, Paine, Jefferson, Robespierre, Saint-Just, Babeuf, Cobbett, Marx, Engels, Proudhon, Sorel, Lenin, Toussaint L'Ouverture, Fanon: these are but a handful of the names which fill the recent past with dedication to the revolutionary community. Without number are those in the present who are similarly dedicated.

The revolutionary community, in the strict sense of the term, is the most recent, the most distinctively modern, of all forms of community in Western thought. Few would deny that it has become one of the most honored in the ranks of intellectuals. Allied, as it has increasingly become in our century, with the military community, it may yet prove to be the triumphant community in the modern world.

5 The Ecological Community

Withdrawal and Renewal

Periodically in the history of the West since the fall of the Roman Empire, we find groups turning their backs upon the established social order and withdrawing to more or less remote places in order to seek renewal of what they believe to be man's natural tendency toward genuine community and morality. Paralleling this social tradition, often indeed embedded in it, is an intellectual tradition based upon the same fundamental values of withdrawal and renewal.

It would be a mistake, I believe, to refer to this pattern of the search for community as revolutionary, though in some of its manifestations, as among the nineteenth-century anarchists, it has assuredly verged on the revolutionary. And there can be no question of the inherent radicalism of this type of community. Even so, revolution is not its essential character; for whereas the overriding objective of revolutionary action is the overthrow and capture of an existing social order, with immediate, forced adaptation of human behavior to revolutionary power and design, the objectives of the action and thought with which this chapter is concerned are, with the rarest of exceptions, peaceful, not concerned with capture and forced adaptation, noncoercive, and seeking fulfillment through example or vision rather than through revolutionary force and centralization of power. The uncovering of those autonomous and free interdependences among human beings which are believed to be natural to man and his morality: this—not the violent capture of government, army, and police—is the most fundamental aim of the tradition of community in Western social thought I call ecological.

I have chosen the word *ecological* to describe this mode of community. This word, in its Greek root *oikos*, refers directly to the household and, by clear implication, to the natural and harmonious interdependences of the household economy. This is the sense in which Aristotle uses *oikos*. In modern post-Darwinian usage, *ecology* has reference to the natural interdependences found among organisms, including human beings, and between organisms and their environment. In our day the word has come to take on an added dimension of meaning, one that is moral, concerned with preserving or restoring environment in such a way that now-threatened interdependences among human beings and other organisms, and the myriad physical and biological contexts of these interdependences, may be protected, or else the ground laid for their renewal.

All three of these meanings are to be found in the communal tradition that is the subject of this chapter: the close, cohesive interdependences symbolized by the small household economy; the interdependences among organisms and between organisms and environment which are natural, in contrast to those which are contrived or artificial; and the profound sense of a web of life existing between man and the rest of nature that man endangers only at his own peril.

The first expression of the ecological community in the West after the downfall of Rome is the monastic order that began in the sixth century with the remarkable Saint Benedict of Nursia. I shall give a good deal of attention to monasticism, most especially to the little book *The Rule*, which contains Benedict's prescription for the desired relationships of the monastic community and the community's relationship to its physical environment and to other parts of human society. Without any question, it seems to me, the monastery, especially as it was conceived by Benedict, is the true source of most of our Western ideas of community achieved through the processes of withdrawal and renewal.

Second is the whole utopian tradition in Western literature. Beginning with Sir Thomas More's extraordinary *Utopia*, which remains to our day the single most readable and inspiring account of the ideal-imaginative community, this powerful theme of interest in community is reflected in some of the most notable books produced by the Western mind. Not since More's book was written at the beginning of the sixteenth century in England, has there been a single period in which major, widely read, often profoundly evocative works in this genre have not been written. When one thinks of the number of actual "utopian" communities that have been the product, in some degree, of this vein of imaginative literature, he has some notion of the extent to which art can influence life.

This suggests still another—though, as noted, closely related—type or manifestation of the ecological community in Western civilization: the immense number of ideal communities—I mean communities formed in light of some ideal—that came into existence in western Europe and the United States during the nineteenth century. The Oneida community, Brook Farm, and New Harmony are but three of the best known of these. The actual number is very large, including many communities, such as that of the Latter-Day Saints in Utah—Deseret, as it was first called— which were no less ideal and utopian in character for having been generated by deeply religious precepts. The spread of these utopian communities in the nineteenth century is one of the great chapters in social history. In such communities, whether religious or secular in inspiration, can be seen basically the same kind of response to social problems as were the monasteries of the sixth and succeeding centuries.

Next, and closely related to many of these nineteenth-century utopian communities, is the whole philosophy of anarchism. This is the philosophy associated with the names of such notable European minds as William Godwin in England, Pierre Joseph Proudhon in France, and Peter Kropotkin first in Russia, then in various parts of the West. Nor were declared anarchists lacking in the United States, Josiah Warren and Benjamin Tucker being but two of the better known. Anarchism falls, as we have already had occasion to note, somewhat within the revolutionary tradition as well as that with which we are here concerned. There is no doubt of many anarchists' desire to see the whole of society reconstructed and, with this, such evil institutions as the political state and private property abandoned permanently by man. Proudhon made much of revolution; and Bakunin, for a time at least, even declared the necessity of violence, though such declaration was temporary in his own writing and altogether uncharacteristic of anarchism generally. Even so, for all the revolutionary element in anarchism, it belongs in largest part, I believe, with the tradition we shall consider here. For, beginning with Godwin and coming down to the twentieth-century writings of Peter Kropotkin, what we find overwhelmingly in anarchist philosophy is an emphasis on renewal through discovery rather than revolution, a reassertion of what is believed to be essential in man's nature rather than a demand for the forceful creation of a new nature for him, and reliance upon simple, untrammeled cooperation and love among human beings rather than coercion in any of its manifestations.

These are the four major types of ecological community in Western thought, and the ones we shall be concerned with for the most part in this chapter. The reader will note, however, as we proceed that the fundamental concept of ecological relationship in the physical and social worlds is connected historically with other major Western intellectual movements as well, among them the rise of economics in the eighteenth century and the momentous philosophy of Darwinism in the nineteenth.

The Elements of the Ecological Community

The Idea of Nature

Fundamental among the elements of the ecological community is the strong sense of its being natural, as a form of human interdependence, and hence in strong contrast to the artificiality of the surrounding society. I use the word *nature* here in its pristine sense of the Greek *physis*, which includes a great deal more than is denoted today by our word—conventionally used to describe the physical and the biological. When the Greeks referred to the nature of an entity, they meant its normal, inherent constitution or manner of growth in time. When they referred to change, they distinguished between the change that is natural to an entity—which they likened to growth—in contrast to the kinds of change that are artificial, springing from chance or alien impact. Similarly, when they referred to the natural structure of something, they were thinking of how it would be if nothing had ever interfered with its structure, thus causing it to lose the nature with which it had been endowed, or at least to be sharply modified, or to have its true nature obscured by mere appearance.

From the Greeks down to our own time, there has been a persistent interest in the "natural" versus the "conventional" or "artificial." On the one hand, this interest has underlain the development of science; for the Greeks defined science as the search for the nature of things, which would be conducted through reason, observation, comparison, even experiment. On the other hand, however, interest in nature produced the desire to find, uncover, or else create forms of relationship among human beings that would be more in accord with how they had been originally, before accident or human evil had altered them, and thus—so it was believed—purer in quality and truer to the actual nature of man.

It is this second application of the idea of nature that interests us here. We shall find that from the form of monasticism that began with Saint Benedict in the sixth century, through the whole literature of utopianism, down to the philosophy of anarchism, there has been a powerful conviction that the larger society suffers from forces which have corrupted its true character, its nature, and that it is important for human beings to renew nature by forming communities free from the corruptions and degenerations of the larger society. These communities would be, in their structures, processes, and the demands they made upon individual members, in accord with what had once been, what ought to be, and what could be. Sometimes we find the word *nature* used as a synonym for the divine. So it was by Benedict and his monks. So it was by Sir Thomas More in his *Utopia*, so it is today in a good many of the communes established during recent years in America. But it need not be. It assuredly was not so used by the great majority of anarchists of the nineteenth and early twentieth centuries, nor by a good many others in history for whom the word *nature* has been the talisman, so to speak, of the good, the true, and the beautiful.

I do not imply in this section that the concept of nature has influenced only those relatively few who form what I call the tradition of the ecological community in Western thought: that would be far from the case. At very least from the time of Aristotle, to go to the "nature" of a thing has been the overriding objective of all philosophers and scientists. Rare is the social philosopher down to the present who has not made use of the idea of nature—the state of nature, the condition of nature, the natural order, and so forth—in justifying a particular process of development or a distinctive pattern of association. Adam Smith sought to reconstruct an entire European economic order in terms of the concept, in the "natural system" he believed to underlie the conventionalities, traditions, and laws that mere history had left as its deposit. The idea of nature has been one of the master ideas of Western thought. But its paramount and distinctive significance has been among the philosophers of the ecological community.

The Web of Life

The "web of life" is, of course, the essential meaning of the word *ecology* as it is used today in both scientific and lay thought. It was Charles Darwin, above any other thinker, who made the idea of the web of life a widespread one, though examples are certainly not lacking from the time of pre-Socratic philosophers, most notably Empedocles and Heraclitus, and, perhaps most vividly, several centuries later, in Lucretius's *On the Nature of Things*. Aristotle, who was a very good naturalist, all things considered, was impressed by not merely what he called the hierarchy or scale of the natural order but also the functional relationships to be found among the different divisions of this natural order. It is impossible to believe that Aristotle would have been surprised by very much of what is associated with the name of Darwin twenty-five hundred years after his own time: by the idea of the emergence of the species from one another in time, but not by much else. Throughout Western history, from the sixth century B.C. at any rate, there have always been minds keenly alive to the continuity of things in the world, to what was called the "great chain of being"; and this carried with it the clear sense of man's relatedness to other spheres of the physical and natural order.

This sense is a profound one in the communal tradition I call the ecological community. From the Benedictines and then nearly all of the other medieval monastic orders, through the utopian writings of Sir Thomas More and his many successors, down to the nineteenth- and twentieth-century anarchists, there has been a deep and vitalizing awareness of man's relationship with other beings in the kingdom of life and of the necessity of maintaining this relationship, indeed of heightening it, through close contact with the land and all that grows on the land. There is an unmistakable respect for the soil, its resources and the forms of life that live on it, to be found in the Rule of Saint Benedict; and, as we know, the very genius of monasticism lay in its insistence upon harmonious balance between thought and culture, on the one hand, and labor in field and forest, on the other. This respect becomes virtual adoration in More's *Utopia,* where town and country are cardinal elements of each of the subdivisions of society More describes and where, as in the monastery, each citizen is expected to partake of the nourishment provided by nature as well as by thought, learning, and the arts. And, in such a work as Kropotkin's *Fields, Factories, and Workshops,* published in 1898, we find an identical insistence upon such interpenetration of nature and culture. Nor could any Benedictine or any inhabitant of More's Utopia have outdone Proudhon in reverence for what he called "the communion that exists between man and nature."

What biologists were to call the "web of life," following the works of such nineteenth-century naturalists as Darwin, would have been perfectly intelligible to Benedict and no doubt even more to the incomparable Saint Francis of Assisi, whose paeans to nature, sermons to birds and animals in the wilderness, and odes to the sun and moon were anything but the eccentricities of idle romanticism they are so often, and ignorantly, declared to be. They were, in fact, lyric expressions of a conviction that life is one and that God exists as truly in plant and beast and fowl as he does in man's own being. From beginning to end, the ecological tradition of community is rooted deeply in the conception of the web of life. Whether religious or secular in premise, this conception carries with it a strong conviction of the inviolability of nature and of the evil desecrations and bootless exploitations of nature.

Cooperation

Cooperation was the essence of the monastery's economy—in the beginning, certainly, of each of the major orders, and throughout the history of monastic ideals in the West—as it has been of all other forms of the ecological community. We find it stressed in a variety of connections in More's *Utopia*. There is not a single one of the numerous nineteenth-century utopian communities that failed to reflect hostility toward the competitive, profit-oriented, individualist order of industrial capitalism and to emphasize those assertedly natural modes of cooperation to be found among human beings wherever they have not been corrupted by the rust of exploitation in society. And cooperation is, as we know, the very heart of the anarchist prescription for society. Here, too, we find a reflection of the other elements—the idea of nature and the concept of the web of life. For cannot nature be shown to be cooperative in the union of things that produce life? And is not cooperation, in some degree at least, the essence of the web of life? The relation between the ferns that conserve moisture for the roots of a tree and the tree that gives the ferns their needed shade is nothing if not cooperative. What Kropotkin was to call "mutual aid" in the title of his greatest book is no more than cooperation. It is to be found, admittedly, in all other forms of community, whether political, revolutionary, or religious, but it is the very essence, and the highest ideal, of the ecological community.

Autonomous Association

By the term *autonomous association* I refer to groups, associations, and communities which are, as nearly as is humanly possible, free of arbitrary authority or coercion. This insistence can at times take on very naïve form in the ecological—and especially the anarchist—tradition. We occasionally find passages suggesting that even the gentlest, love-inspired authority of one person over another, as, for example, parent over child, is wrong. Art and music which do not emerge spontaneously, which require the slightest preparatory discipline for their understanding or enjoyment, can once in a while be found to be condemned in this tradition of the free mind and autonomous association.

Such expressions are, however, exceptional. There is discipline to be found in the Benedictine Rule, though its setting is the Rule itself, not the will of any human being or group. Discipline is enforced, though only through simultaneous explanation, by the magistrates in More's Utopia. And Proudhon, for all his insistence upon autonomous association and individual freedom, yet declares a strong family system, even a patriarchal one, to be indispensable to the formation of personal character in the anarchist community.

The important point, though, is the overwhelming stress of the ecological community upon association that is as spontaneous and free, as far from coercion and repressive law, as possible. It is not correct to say that anarchists condemn order and authority. What one must say instead that anarchism takes a very dim view of any form of order and authority that does not spring as far as is possible from man's own assent to it. Even the discipline of the Benedictine Rule, and of all subsequent forms of monasticism, is conditional upon the member's desire to remain within the community. We shall find Benedict extremely loath to see discipline inflicted upon an errant member; and when it has to be, it must be, Benedict tells us, in successive degrees, to allow the errant member ample time to reconsider, with expulsion only a final resort. The spontaneity and autonomy of relationships among human beings are deeply prized in the ecological tradition.

"Multiply your associations and be free," Proudhon wrote. There is in the ecological community, for the most part, the same veneration of diversity and decentralization that we shall find in what I call the plural community, to be treated in the next chapter. More than anything else, it was the Marxist emphasis upon centralization of power during and after the revolution in Russia in 1917 that led to the final, irreparable break between the Communists and anarchists of the world. Dislike of centralization is an essential feature of the entire ecological tradition.

Simplicity

Finally, throughout the ecological tradition of community we find a condemnation of hyperorganization, of undue complexity of culture, of idle multiplication of rules. From Benedict to Kropotkin there is a profound conviction that the highest possibility of true morality and love is to be found in the life that is as liberated as possible from complexity and overrefinement of function. In the mainstream of the ecological tradition this has never meant stark austerity or abstinence. One of the greatnesses of Benedict's Rule is its insistence upon as normal a life as possible, with ample sleep, rest, good food, and the best of wine, with continuous development of man's mental as well as his spiritual nature. There is a total absence in Benedict of any kind of self-mortification, of bizarre and cultivated forms of flagellation of either body or mind. There is, nevertheless, a clear and unwavering emphasis upon simplicity. Precisely the same is true of More's *Utopia* and of the prescriptions and often detailed suggestions we get in anarchist visions of the good life. There is no morbid denial of natural appetites, nor a precious eschewal of the technology that makes a civilized existence possible: none of this. But always, from monk to anarchist, there is an insistence that simplicity should reign in all things: simplicity of mating between the sexes; of child rearing; of economic production, distribution, and consumption; of schooling; and so on. Nature, it is said, is simple for those who understand; society should be also.

Western Monasticism: Benedict of Nursia

The monastery, with its familiar associations of celibacy and individual retreat, may not at first seem an apt example of the ecological community.

If we were to confine our attention to some of the recurrent forms of monasticism—those found chiefly in Egypt, Christian and pre-Christian, which stressed individual renunciation of all fellowship, mortification, even flagellation, of the flesh, and abstinence from food and drink to a degree that barely maintained the flicker of life—we should have every reason to reject monasticism as a form of the ecological community. There is little if anything in common between the pathological behavior of a Saint Simeon Stylites and the kind of life commonly found in the ecological community, whether it be religious or secular in inspiration.

But if we consider instead, as we shall in this section, the Western strain of monasticism that began largely through the efforts of Benedict of Nursia in the sixth century, we find ourselves at the very heart of what is distinctive in the ecological community. In it we can see vividly the idea of nature, of the two societies, of communal cooperation, and of simplicity, the emphasis on the web of life, and, giving it lasting strength, the spiritual ideal. And what Benedict founded at Monte Cassino became, within a very few centuries, one of the greatest social and cultural movements in the history of Western society.

Western monasticism is based on withdrawal from society, but rarely if ever does one see that abjuration of life, that frenzied mortification of body, mind, and spirit, and that contempt for everything human and social, which have become the very hallmarks of Eastern monasticism— symbolized for most of us by the religious manias of a Saint Anthony or a Saint Simeon Stylites, each choosing to live alone, save for vermin, insects, and snakes, in total filth and abasement of person—the better, it was believed, to achieve oneness with God.

Examples are not lacking in the West of this form of monasticism; but they are, and have been since the Benedictines came into being in the sixth century, exceedingly rare and utterly unrepresentative of Western monasticism, in which, far from a hatred of nature, natural impulses, and natural forms of interdependence, there has been instead an acceptance of these. But the acceptance has been *disciplined*. One does not find anywhere in the mainstream of Western monasticism the view that nature—fields, forests, lakes, streams, the mountaintops, plains, and valleys—is something to be ignored, overwhelmed by, or exploited. On the contrary, had it not been for the succession of monastic movements of the Middle Ages, it is highly unlikely that the reclamation of marshes, waterless areas, and impassable forests would ever have been begun—that is, in nonexploitative fashion.

These Western monastic movements really begin with the famous Benedictine order at Monte Cassino in Italy, founded by Benedict of Nursia. His origins are obscure; we are not certain in what year he was born, and his death is placed somewhat uncertainly in 547. We know that as a young man Benedict went to Rome to study philosophy and theology. He then departed Rome for Subiaco, where he lived in solitary meditation, achieving within a very few years a wide reputation for both piety and learning. There, so far as we can tell, he first conceived the idea of a monastic order that would serve God and mankind but that would diverge utterly from the bizarre and, as Benedict clearly felt, degrading forms of monasticism that were notorious in Egypt and elsewhere. There, too, he must have conceived the Rule, a body of prohibitions and injunctions set in the form of a prologue and some seventy-three brief chapters, which was to guide not only the Benedictine order but, in due time, many other monastic communities. The final words of the prologue suggest the essence of what Benedict had in mind:

> Therefore must we establish a school of the Lord's service; in founding which we hope to ordain nothing that is harsh or burdensome. But if, for good reason, for the amendment of evil habit or the preservation of charity, there be some strictness of discipline, do not be at once dismayed and run away from the way of salvation, of which the entrance must be narrow. But, as we progress in our monastic life and in faith, our hearts shall be enlarged, and we shall run with unspeakable sweetness of love in the way of God's commandments; so that, never abandoning his rule but persevering in his teaching in the monastery until death, we shall share by patience in the sufferings of Christ, that we may deserve to be partakers also of his kingdom. Amen.[1]

When Benedict left Subiaco, it was with a small number of monks, followers of his who had pledged their devotion to the monastic ideal as described in the Rule. The group finally settled at Monte Cassino, a mountain immemorially known as a holy place, going far back indeed into pagan religion. Thus began the famous Benedictine monastic community, which was itself to multiply and, even more impressively, to become the model of a large number of other monastic orders all over the world. Even today one finds himself deeply impressed by the combination of gentleness, compassion, piety, and wisdom in the successive chapters of the Rule. All aspects of the monastic day are covered, though briefly and unobtrusively, for the very essence of the order was its communality and, within this, the absolute equality of duties and rights.

Above all else, the monastery was pledged to work—manual and intellectual alike: "Idleness is the enemy of the soul. The brethren, therefore, should be occupied at stated hours in manual labour, and again at other hours in sacred reading." [2] There follows a precise ordering of the amount and time of each kind of work, set forth with due allowance for

---

[1] *The Rule of Saint Benedict,* in Latin and English, ed. and trans. Abbot Justin McCann (Westminster, Md.: Newman Press, 1952), p. 13.

[2] Ibid., p. 111.

the changing seasons and the amount of sunlight. Benedict was mindful of the existence of individual skills, not shared by everyone, but he was careful to enjoin that such skills must be kept in their place:

> If there be craftsmen in the monastery, let them practise their crafts with all humility, provided the abbot give permission. But if one of them be puffed up because of skill in his craft, supposing that he is conferring a benefit on the monastery, let him be removed from his work and not return to it, unless he have humbled himself and the abbot entrust it to him again. If any of the work of the craftsmen is to be sold, let those who have to manage the business take care that they be not guilty of dishonesty. . . . And, as regards price, let not the sin of avarice creep in; but let the goods always be sold a little cheaper than they are sold by the people of the world, *that in all things God may be glorified.*[3]

It is interesting to observe that Benedict does not allow age alone to be the basis of status within the monastic community. The abbot is enjoined to select monks for special responsibilities solely in terms of his judgment of their ability, irrespective of anything else: "And on no occasion whatever should age distinguish the brethren and decide their order; for Samuel and Daniel, though young, judged the elders."[4] Apart only from function itself—and all functions within the community are judged equal in worth, however much they may vary in skill, strength, or complexity—the sole means of judging status shall be by time of entry into the monastery.

It is a striking commentary on the essential *healthiness* of Benedict's mind that the monastery, though properly secluded, is never cut off from human society. Nor are mind and body dealt with at any time other than with respect. He was careful to see to it that the monks should have ample rest, even adjusting this to the time of the monastic year: nine hours' sleep in the winter, when nights are long, five in the summer. Manual work is not actually enjoined, but it is strongly recommended, in alternation with the mental activity that goes into either prayer or scholarship or the business affairs of the monastery. Food and wine, far from being made to seem unworthy of Christian dedication, are expressly recommended in proper moderation. Deliberate starvation of body and mental faculties seemed as impious to Benedict as did wanton gluttony at the opposite extreme. Such indeed became the fame of Benedictine food and drink as centuries passed that more and more visitors found their way to the monasteries kept by Benedictines. For visitors, though lodged separately from the monks and kept from all ordinary communication

---

[3] Ibid., p. 129.   [4] Ibid., p. 143.

with them, were always welcome, and special visitors' quarters were to be found in all Benedictine abbeys.

As all students of the Benedictine Rule have noted, one of its most remarkable qualities—considering that it is for a monastic organization—is that it is composed of injunctions and prohibitions which elevate, rather than degrade, the human body and its functions. As Jean Decarreaux has written:

> The Easterners treated their bodies like enemies that had to be exhausted by fasting, vigils, hairshirts, chains, or stones, throwing themselves into amazing feats of asceticism. But Benedict's view was that the body should receive sufficiently humane treatment so as to be at all times the good servant of the soul. He did not think of the soul dwelling within the body as a prison, but as part of a whole of which each component should be treated so that the entire system developed harmoniously.[5]

Discipline was, of course, evident. No form of society, however small and consensual, can long survive without a structure of authority involving at least a few injunctions, demands, taboos, and forms of punishment. What impresses the reader of the Rule, however, is its extraordinary absence of coercion, compulsion, or any kind of force. Benedict clearly believed that a proper mental framework was desirable above all things: not mere overt obedience, least of all mechanical imitation or conformity, but, rather, the development in the individual of a deep desire to do what was functionally and morally required by monastic existence. There is, thus, not a word in the Rule expressly enjoining chastity. It was assumed as a precondition of the original decision of an individual male to become a member; it was assumed as a vital part of his service to God and to the community; but—and this is the essence of the whole spirit of the Benedictine order—it is not decreed in actual words. The same, precisely, is the case with monastic silence: rather than demanding absolute silence from the brothers, Benedict asks instead for the spirit of silence, thus to encourage the inward observation and the meditation necessary for the purification of one's self. It is not poverty that Benedict demands, only a spirit of economy, of discipline of one's appetite. In fact, as we have seen, the Rule insisted upon good, full, balanced fare, even granting the monks their right to wine in moderation.

There is humanity, in the ordinary sense of this word, in the Rule. Thus in Chapter 36, "Of Sick Brethren," Benedict writes:

> Before all things and above all things care must be taken of the sick, so that they may be served in very deed as Christ him-

---

[5] Jean Decarreaux, *Monks and Civilization*, trans. Charlotte Haldane (London: George Allen & Unwin, 1964), p. 224.

self; for he said: *I was sick and ye visited me*; and *what ye did to one of these least ones, ye did unto me.* But let the sick on their part consider that they are being served for the honour of God, and not provoke their brethren who are serving them by their unreasonable demands. Yet they should be patiently borne with, because from such as these is gained a more abundant reward. Therefore let the abbot take the greatest care that they suffer no neglect.[6]

And from the brief but powerful chapter "Of Old Men and Children" comes the following:

> Although human nature itself is drawn to pity towards these times of life, that is, towards old men and children, yet let them be provided for also by the authority of the Rule. Let there be constant consideration for their weakness, and on no account let the rigour of the Rule in regard to food be applied to them. Let them, on the contrary, receive compassionate consideration and take their meals before the regular hours.[7]

In that one short paragraph alone, the extraordinary Benedictine fusion of benevolence and natural discipline is to be seen in a way that epitomizes the entire work. Charity and kindness are to be shown toward the old and the still helpless young, yes, but without diminishing the sense of social authority, of social structure, that every study ever made of the subject has clearly shown is, as much as anything else, the sign of one's being a part of a community, rather than merely its ward or appendage.

Benedict was a strong believer in diversity of work among his brethren. As we have before seen, he declares idleness "the enemy of the soul." It did not matter much in his judgment what kind of work was being done, mental or physical, so long as it served a distinct purpose. The larger purpose of doing anything was, of course, commitment to God's will. But there was also purpose to be seen within the secular or lay order of the day: the purpose behind the seeding, tilling, and harvesting of the fields; the purpose behind the kind of work that is inseparable from reading and study; the purpose behind prayer. The following paragraph is eloquent in these regards:

> . . . From Easter until September the 14th, the brethren shall start work in the morning and from the first hour until about the fourth do the tasks that have to be done. From the fourth hour until about the sixth let them apply themselves to

---

[6] *The Rule of Saint Benedict,* p. 91.
[7] Ibid., p. 93.

reading. After the sixth hour, having left the table, let them rest on their beds in perfect silence; or if anyone wishes to read by himself, let him read so as not to disturb the others. Let None be said early, at the middle of the eighth hour; and let them again do what work has to be done until Vespers. But if the circumstances of the place or their poverty require them to gather the harvest themselves, let them not be discontented; for they are truly monks when they live by the labour of their hands, like our fathers and the apostles. Yet let all things be done in moderation on account of the faint-hearted.[8]

The last sentence in that passage is evidence enough of not only Benedict's deep charity and compassion but also his penetrating insight into the competitive impulses which can operate even when the setting is communal. What he is saying is that even the most virtuous of objectives must be pursued in moderation, without the kind of single-mindedness, the fanatic intensity, that has so often in history transformed even the good into the despotic and corrupting.

It should not be imagined that Benedict was unmindful of the temptation that lies in all flesh to evade rules, to be slothful, even outrightly at times delinquent. Profoundly disposed though he was to let spirit and consensus govern the community, he yet knew that on occasion authority would have to be asserted; otherwise the values supporting consensus would gradually erode away. But no one can read the sections on discipline in the Rule without marveling at Benedict's singular lack of any love of power, that is, power for its own sake. If assertion of authority is required to restrain some wayward or shirking member, well and good, but authority must not become its own excuse for being:

If any brother shall be found contumacious, or disobedient, or proud, or a murmurer, or in any way despising and contravening the holy Rule and the orders of his superiors: let such a one, according to our Lord's commandment, *be admonished secretly by his superiors for a first and a second time.* If he do not amend, let him be rebuked publicly before all. But if even then he do not correct his life, let him suffer excommunication, provided that he understands the gravity of the penalty. If, however, he be perverse, let him undergo corporal punishment.[9]

The whole intent of punishment is, quite clearly, cure, not the utilization of authority, much less of force, as a good in and for itself. Only as a last resort, be it noted, is the individual to be actually excommunicated from the monastery or, if he resists this, given corporal punishment. In the system of authority, as in the fulfillment of the various duties

8 Ibid., p. 111.   9 Ibid., p. 73. Italics added.

of the monastery and also in the ranking of individuals and in recognition of their appetites for food, drink, rest, and sleep, we cannot help but be struck by the obvious effort to achieve what is most natural, most healthy —in the mental and moral as well as physical senses of this word—and best for all concerned. Respect for nature was, for Benedict and his followers, no more than a form of worshiping God. To work in the fields; to harvest crops; to tend gardens, to look out for the condition of the soil and of the streams and forests and fields around the countryside; all of this was, along with the reading of texts, the study of philosophy and theology, and prayer, a proper expression of man's gratitude to God.

Bear in mind that the time when the monastery at Monte Cassino first came into being was a very dark and troubled one indeed in the West. Italy was overrun by warring soldiers. Government, in any traditional sense of the word, was reduced to impotence and anarchy. Rome itself was filled with peasants who had been driven by war and starvation from other parts of Italy. The once proud learning and culture and technology of the Romans were scarcely more than a shambles. Truly, a crisis of the spirit, as well as of government and society, existed. And it is precisely as a response to this crisis of the spirit that we must see the whole Western monastic movement, which is, as I have suggested, the first manifestation of the modern ecological community.

> The trunk of Monte Cassino spread out over Christianity its branches through which ran the Benedictine sap: missionaries throughout the Western world, masters of small schools, choristers of the services, men of learning who applied the working rule to research, pioneers and cultivators of large agricultural enterprises, all of them honourably, rightfully, and faithfully, claimed to be the sons of their Patriarch. Benedict was not only the Patriarch of the Western monks but also, as Pius XII said, the father of Western civilization.[10]

The late medievalist James Westfall Thompson has written as follows on the contribution of monasticism to Western civilizations:

> In the redemption of the wilderness monasticism was more influential than any other force in the Middle Ages. Voluntarily seeking isolation, the monks penetrated into the depths of the forest, which gradually were cleared and converted into tilled fields; sought the fastnesses of the mountains and constructed roads over saddles and through passes; drained swamps; built dikes.[11]

[10] J. Decarreaux, op. cit., pp. 231–32.

[11] James Westfall Thompson, *An Economic and Social History of the Middle Ages* (New York: Century Co., 1928), p. 146.

And, concluding a long chapter on monasticism, Professor Thompson writes:

> Judged by a modern standard, the root of monasticism was a selfish one, for the primary aim of the monk was to save his own soul, to keep it uncontaminated from the world by isolation, to purge his soul by ascetic practices. Yet the monasteries distributed relief, fed the hungry, clothed the naked, befriended the friendless, protected the widow and the orphan, maintained hospices and schools. Is one to think that all these things were done as "good works" in order that the bestower might get credit in heaven? Or was there genuine charity, real humanitarianism, in the doing of them? Whatever the fundamental motives of monasticism, there are few who will deny the substantial worth of the monks' services to society during the Dark Ages.[12]

Nor were the Benedictines alone in their dedication to communality, to nature, and to that spontaneous relation between man and man and between man and God, representing the whole world of nature, that we have seen was the mark—the ecological mark!—of the Benedictine pioneers. We should not omit mention of the Irish monasteries, derived as much from the great Irish Celtic clans as from Christianity. Perhaps above any single force in the West, Irish monasticism was responsible between about 600 and 900 for keeping the best of Western culture alive. Ireland was uniquely celebrated during this period for its learning and for its hospitality to scholars. The Irish monasteries were scarcely less noted for their fascination with nature and, most especially, with wild life. Strange as it may seem today, the Irish monks were famous for their feats of taming the wildest of animals around them and making them parts of the monastic community. Not only deer, marmots, and birds of all kinds were tamed and fitted into communal life but even wild bears. Dancing bears were common, and it is entirely possible that the origin of this form of domestication lies in the Irish monastery.

Saint Francis

The closeness of monasticism to nature was to continue, with rarest exceptions, throughout the history of the medieval monastic movement. Of all the luminaries of the Middle Ages, Saint Francis of Assisi, founder of the Franciscans, friars and scholars devoted both to the poor and to philosophical learning, is perhaps most renowned for his relationships with all forms of natural life. His long sojourns in the wilderness, where he seems to have lived quite literally in companionship with birds and

---

[12] Ibid., pp. 153–54.

animals, are famous. Among the most celebrated of his feats is that of the taming of the fierce, man-eating wolf of Gubbio. Granted that the story, as we find it in the religious volume that celebrates his life,[13] is much embroidered in the details; there is, nevertheless, substantial evidence that Saint Francis did in fact go by himself to seek out the wolf that had terrified the entire population of the little town of Gubbio, that he did in fact tame this beast and then bring it back to Gubbio with instructions to the citizens to feed it and otherwise care for it until its natural death. His sermon to the larks is one of the best known of all Christian celebrations of the divine wisdom inhering in nature, and it may be fairly conjectured that when Kierkegaard in the nineteenth century wrote his sermons on the birds, with which we have already dealt, he was consciously following in the tradition of Saint Francis. There is simply no question that this extraordinary figure was the supreme author of the philosophy of love in Western thought. Himself a military veteran who had known all the harshness and privations of war, even suffering a period of imprisonment as a captive, he made love no thing of weakness and retreat from life's actualities, but, rather, a powerful force in behalf of the whole of society and also of nature. Wherever the Franciscan friars went in the thirteenth and later centuries, they took with them the philosophy of making love, not fear and hate, central in human life.

There is unquestionably a profound pantheism in the thought of Saint Francis; some might say even animism. For him more even than for earlier great monks, nature and all its aspects were holy, animate, and an inseparable part of the very divinity of man. The following chapter titles from *The Mirror of Perfection* attest this aspect of Saint Francis's existence: "And, firstly, of the love which he especially had for the birds which are called larks"; "How he wished to persuade the emperor to make a law that men should make a good provision for birds, and oxen, and asses, and the poor at Christmastime"; "Of his love for water and stones and wood and flowers"; "That he would not quench the fire that had burnt his hose." Between Saint Francis and Brother Fire, as he was wont to call it, there was a bond that reached all the way to the sun itself. One of the most famous of Saint Francis's songs is his "Cantico del Sole," or "Hymn to the Sun." It is almost pagan in its adoration of the sun:

> In the morning when the sun rises, every man ought to praise God, Who created it for our use, because through it our eyes are enlightened by day. Then in the evening when it becomes night, every man ought to give praise on account of Brother Fire, by which our eyes are enlightened at night; for we be all as it were

---

[13] See *The Little Flowers of St. Francis*, ed. Father Damian J. Blaher (New York: E. P. Dutton, 1951), chap. 21. This excellent edition also contains *The Mirror of Perfection* and the famous *Life of St. Francis* by Saint Bonaventure.

blind, and the Lord by these two, our brothers doth enlighten our eyes. . . . And because He deemed and said that the sun is fairer than other created things, and is more often likened to our Lord, and that in the Scripture the Lord Himself is called "the sun of Righteousness," therefore giving that name to those praises which he had made of the creatures of the Lord, what time the Lord did certify him of His kingdom, he called them "The Song of the Brother Sun." [14]

It would be absurd to imply that the monastic movement, Benedictine, Franciscan, or other, did not suffer the organizational diseases which are ever the lot of even the most dedicatedly communal and natural of associations. The very successes of the monastic orders generally proved to be the seeds of their ultimate vices. The Benedictines, who, as we have seen, began with not only a superb sense of authority and organization but also a civilized liking for good food and wine in moderation, together with rest in proper alternation with work, fell victim before very long to abuses of all of these virtues. Hence came the succession of reform movements: within the Benedictine order itself and also in the form of new monastic orders striving to return to the basic principles Benedict himself had set down. During the centuries following that in which the Benedictines came into existence, a succession of monastic organizations were founded: the Cistercians, Cluniacs, Franciscans, Dominicans, Jesuits, and others. Not all of them sought to follow in detail the principles to be found in Benedict's Rule. Some prized withdrawal for its own sake; others strove to fuse withdrawal with revolutionary zeal to generate the motive forces of a new and more Christian society; still others, like the Franciscans, were concerned with urban problems and willing to remain as an enclave within the cities in seeking to solve them; still others, such as the Jesuits following the Reformation, conceived themselves as soldiers of Christ, dedicated to the furtherance of Catholic Christianity against its enemies, using whatever means might from time to time suggest themselves. In sum, despite the exemplary character of the Benedictine model, corruptions, various forms of hyperorganization and centralization and bureaucratization, not to mention modes of precapitalist behavior, were to be found in even the best of the monastic movements.

There were abundant individual problems, too. The lax, lazy, lecherous, often barely literate, and sometimes predatory monk has his place in the literature of the late medieval and early modern West, and no doubt for good reason. No community or association known to man thus far has proved successful in binding all its members to strict probity and honor. Punish the backsliding monk though the monasteries might, he was yet a vivid type to many who either suffered under him or regarded

14 Ibid., p. 387.

him with emotions ranging from amusement to contempt. There was reason enough, surely, for the less than laudatory terms in which the great Rabelais described the monk as a social and religious type. And we may take for granted at least some substance behind the often hilarious, erotic picture which Boccaccio gave of him—and also the female of the type—in his famous *Tales*. Moving from one monastery or abbey to another through the centuries following Saint Benedict's establishment of the Western type of monastic community, the careful student will have little difficulty in amassing a collection of peccadilloes equal to any that could be found in other parts of society.

All of this is true enough. But its truth tends to pale into relative insignificance alongside the far greater and more lasting truth of the extraordinary accomplishments that were the consequences of Saint Benedict's noble Rule and of his brilliant organizational genius. He may not have been, strictly speaking, the first of the monastic entrepreneurs in the West, but he was beyond any doubt the greatest of the early ones, the one whose model of communal asceticism and communal achievement proved to be the most powerful and persuasive.

Not often, if at all, have histories of social thought dealt with Saint Benedict. We should not ordinarily think of the starkly stated, simple, and unpretentious regulations which form his Rule as "social theory" or "social philosophy." And yet they were. His Rule was as much a response to crisis—the crisis of the church, already by the sixth century showing distinct signs of rigid bureaucracy and misused affluence—as any customary text in the history of social thought. All the elements of social thought are to be found in Benedict's work: personality, values, association, function, and, above all, community. And there are few treatises in social thought that have proved to have the enormous practical effect of Benedict's writing. Quite apart from monastic movement after monastic movement, through the Middle Ages and early modern era, that sprang from his vision of religious community, there are more than a few examples in our own time of people, mostly young, whose communal abodes in what is left today of wilderness have at least some relation in both inspiration and design to that which we find in Saint Benedict's writing.

What Benedictine precept and example prove conclusively is the lasting power of the communal ethic even in a religion that has become as vast and far-flung, as wealthy and complexly organized, as the Christian, either as a whole or in any one of its major institutional expressions. For without ever declaring itself in any way a revolutionary movement, dedicated to destruction of a social environment that could not have helped but seem evil at times to members of the monastic-communal orders, the monastic movement has nevertheless, right down to the present moment, had enormous influence in changing the ways of Western society: sometimes culturally, sometimes socially, sometimes even technologically.

Violence, attack, and destruction were utterly alien to this movement from the very beginning. It was not even concerned, as we have observed, to seek conscious reform of Christendom's ecclesiastical structure. All the same, we should find it very difficult to account for the fertility of Christianity in producing its great complex of reform and even revolutionary movements apart from the ethic of brotherhood, community, and service to the social order that sprang in the first instance from the Rule through which the great Benedict sought to show and preserve what he regarded as the very essence of the Christian community.

Sir Thomas More's *Utopia*

Let us turn now to a notable example of still another form of ecological community, this time, however, an imaginary form, one that never became actual, that existed only in the fertile mind of its distinguished author, but that has been the inspiration of many a community since, whether actual or imaginary. More's *Utopia* is, apart from Plato's *Republic*, which is a very different kind of work in dominant theme, unquestionably the most famous presentation of the utopian community in the history of the West.

The book was written in the very early sixteenth century, first published in Latin in 1516, and then translated into English in 1551. Like all major works in social philosophy, this one can be seen as a response to conditions in which More lived: economic, social, and political conditions which very clearly troubled his humane mind. Merely by carefully reading *Utopia*, with its detailed descriptions of the lives, customs, and social organization of More's imaginary people living off in some vague part of the then New World across the ocean, we can infer easily enough what troubled More specifically about the England of his own time. The contrasts are vivid enough; and, lest there be any misunderstanding, More employs in his story the device of a narrator, named Raphael Hythloday, who is intimately acquainted with the sixteenth-century English scene and uses his knowledge to pinpoint contrasts between this actual scene and the remarkable society he claims to have visited once while sailing the distant seas. The device is a clever one, and also powerful, for More is thus enabled to criticize as much as he likes (no small feat in the repressive age he lived in) merely by putting into the mouth of his protagonist well-chosen praise of the ways of the Utopians.

Sir Thomas More (1478–1534) lived during an age of increasing centralization of political power in England under the bold and ruthless Henry VIII, whom More served with high honor for a considerable period. Nowhere did Henry's policy fall with more devastating effect than upon the Roman Catholic church, prior to his rule the only recognized church in England. First, through his divorce from Catherine of

Aragon, without the pope's ratification, in order to marry Anne Boleyn; second, through the Act of Supremacy, stemming from the divorce but much greater in implication, whereby he made the king sovereign of the English church; and third, through his notorious expropriation of all the monasteries in England, much of their wealth being turned over to his own favorites and some of the greatest collections of books and manuscripts in the West being destroyed: these were the ways in which Henry made the political power ascendant to a degree unknown in western Europe since the days of the Roman Empire.

Nor were the depredations of church and monastery the entire story. It was during the reign of Henry VIII that the momentous enclosures took place in rural England—done by act of Parliament but, as we know, with Henry's full support and encouragement—by which many thousands of Englishmen and their families were forced off the lands they and their forebears in the village communities had worked for many centuries so that countless sheep could be grazed there, to take advantage of the high price of wool in the world market. If any single event can be said to have established the poor as a permanent class in England, it was this. We know that few things done during the age shocked Sir Thomas More as much as this; there are several references to the enclosure acts in the *Utopia*.

Two things should be stressed about the age of Henry VIII. In the first place, it was an age of enormous increase in aggregate wealth for England and of the production of large numbers of newly wealthy families, the majority giving allegiance to Henry. Affluence and ostentation became rife in England—side by side with the increasing number of the disestablished and impoverished—and this alone, as we know from reading the *Utopia*, shocked Sir Thomas More's humane sensibilities sufficiently to have led to the book. In the second place, and paralleling the explosion of affluence, was the enormous increase in the politicization of English society. The Act of Supremacy, through which the autonomy of the church was forever ended, had its fitting consequences in the other decrees and laws through which the power of the political government was both intensified and widened. In England, as elsewhere in Europe, the medieval immunities so long enjoyed by guild, monastery, village community, and other associations were coming to an end, the result of the state's increasingly fundamental inroads into the lives of the people.[15] Sixteenth-century England was, in short, an age of profound political centralization, dislocation of numerous social autonomies, and a huge increase in wealth, in many instances based upon the impoverishment of sections of the population.

[15] See my *Quest for Community* (New York: Oxford University Press, 1953), especially chap. 2, "The State as Revolution."

These were the conditions surrounding More's life and the ones to which so much of his *Utopia* was in fact addressed. It required courage to write *Utopia*, for criticism such as this was not something Henry VIII relished from anyone, not even from so lustrous a mind as More's. But Sir Thomas More's life, almost beyond anyone else's in English history, is a tale of infinite courage indeed, for he paid with his life for his devotion to intellectual and religious principle. He was, in addition to being one of the most admired scholars of Europe—close friend and associate of the great Erasmus—a magistrate and advocate in matters of law and diplomacy that early earned him title and the boundless admiration and trust of Henry VIII. Had Sir Thomas More chosen to abandon principle, it is certain that he would have been richly rewarded in all possible ways. But he did not so choose. From the time of his earliest service to the king he was troubled by what he knew to be the inclinations of royal power. He opposed the divorce of Catherine of Aragon; he refused to break silence with respect to the Act of Supremacy; and although the expropriation of the monasteries did not begin to occur until the year of his death, it may be safely concluded that these designs of Henry and his compliant minister Thomas Cromwell were well known to him.

In any event, despite his nearly universal esteem in both England and Europe—esteem based as much upon moral integrity and personal gentleness as upon his scholarship and illustrious service to his nation— Sir Thomas More paid with his life for his refusal to countenance Henry's despotism. He was executed on the Tower block, following two years of imprisonment. A later chancellor, Lord Campbell, one of More's successors, declared the execution to be "the blackest crime that has ever been perpetrated in England under the form of law." The scholars and other humanists of Europe were, we are told, filled with horror by Henry's act. And Emperor Charles V said that he would rather have lost an entire city than one such counselor as Sir Thomas More.

So much for the author and the environmental conditions of More's great *Utopia*. The book is in substance the account of an imaginary people living in a social system that was in many respects the very opposite of that of the England of Henry VIII in which More lived. But its imaginary basis notwithstanding, it is hard to read this account of the people of Utopia without a sense of verisimilitude that is at least equal to most accounts of actual peoples.

The first point to make about More's Utopia is in accord with the dominant theme of this chapter: that is, its ecological quality. I have said that the hallmark of the ecological community, real or imaginary, is its construction along lines of what is held to be *natural* to human beings; to arise from their intrinsic natures rather than from artificial law and custom. Repeatedly in More's *Utopia* we find the author stressing this quality of the society he portrays.

Thus, describing the mythical Utopians, More writes:

For they define virtue to be a life ordered according to nature; and that we be hereunto ordained of God; and that he doth follow the course of nature, which in desiring and refusing things is ruled by reason. . . . Then if it be a point of humanity for man to bring health and comfort to man, and specially (which is a virtue most peculiarly belonging to man) to mitigate and assuage the grief of others, and by taking from them the sorrow and heaviness of life, to restore them to joy, that is to say to pleasure; why may it not then be said that nature doth provoke every man to do the same to himself? . . . For when nature biddeth thee to be good and gentle to others, she commandeth thee not to be cruel and ungentle to thyself. Therefore even very nature, say they, prescribeth to us a joyful life, that is to say, pleasure as the end of all our operations. And they define virtue to be life ordered according to the prescript of nature.[16]

How very different, how utterly opposite indeed, does Sir Thomas find the England of his day from a society based upon man's true nature. We shall come to the details of Utopian society in a moment. It might first be useful to get a sense of how More reacted to the England of the early sixteenth century, an England, as I have said, that was in the full tide of commercial affluence and political consolidation. In the early part of the book, Raphael Hythloday, the narrator of the long account of the Utopians, is asked if perchance he has ever visited England. His answer is affirmative and emphatic: he has indeed; and what he has seen in England, he does not like. He refers to the barbarous institutions of people that will, through calculated act, force large numbers into poverty and then punish them by execution if they steal: "For great and horrible punishments be appointed for thieves, whereas much rather provision should have been made that there were some means whereby they might get their living, so that no man should be driven to this extreme necessity, first to steal and then to die." [17] No punishment, however extreme or horrible, will dissuade men from stealing when they are nearing death through starvation.

Other evils in England are related by More. There is, for example, the wanton idleness of the very rich. This class of gentlemen

do not only live in idleness themselves but also carry about with them at their tails a great flock or train of idle and loitering serving-men, which never learned any craft whereby to get their

16 *The Utopia of Sir Thomas More*, ed. William Dallam Armes (New York: Macmillan Co., 1912), pp. 135–36.

17 Ibid., p. 33.

livings. These men, as soon as their master is dead, or they be sick themselves, be incontinent thrust out of doors. For gentlemen had rather keep idle persons than sick men. . . . Then in the mean season they that be thus destitute of service either starve for hunger or manfully play the thieves.[18]

Nothing seems to have distressed the gentle Sir Thomas more than the enclosure acts, which, as earlier noted, had driven so many of the peasant farmers from their land and turned once rich arable into pasture land for tens of thousands of sheep. Here are the bitter words More puts in the mouth of his character, Hythloday:

"Forsooth," quoth I, "your sheep, that were wont to be so meek and tame and so small eaters, now, as I hear say, be become so great devourers and so wild that they eat up and swallow down the very men themselves. They consume, destroy, and devour whole fields, houses, and cities. For look in what parts of the realm doth grow the finest and therefore dearest wool, there noblemen and gentlemen, yea, and certain abbots, holy men, God wot, not contenting themselves with the yearly revenues and profits that were wont to grow to their forefathers and predecessors of their lands, nor being content that they live in rest and pleasure, nothing profiting, yea, much noying the weal public, leave no ground for tillage; they enclose all in pastures; they throw down houses; they pluck down towns; and leave nothing standing but only the church, to make of it a sheep-house. And, as though you lost no small quantity of ground by forests, chases, lawns, and parks, those good holy men turn all dwelling-places and all glebe land into desolation and wilderness. . . . By one means, therefore, or by other, either by hook or crook, they must needs depart away, poor, silly, wretched souls; men, women, husbands, wives, fatherless children, widows, woeful mothers with young babes, and their whole household, small in substance and much in number, as husbandry requireth many hands. All their household stuff, which is very little worth, though it might well abide the sale, yet being suddenly thrust out, they be constrained to sell it for a thing of naught. And when they have, wandering about, soon spent that, what can they else do but steal, and then justly, God wot, be hanged, or else go about a-begging? . . .

"Thus the unreasonable covetousness of a few hath turned that thing to the utter undoing of your island, in the which thing the chief felicity of your realm did consist." [19]

18 Ibid., p. 34.   19 Ibid., pp. 38–39, 40, 41.

Add to the above More's scathing criticism of the weakening of the whole family system in England, through destruction of the economic base on which alone the strong family can rest; the presence in England of more and more wayfarers, wanderers without roots or hope of secure context, always the raw material of the kind of riot and mob action that so frequently invited the answering response of king, army, and sheriff, as the case might be; the ostentatious luxury of the rich side by side with the rags and hovels of the poor; the idle pomp and expense (as it seemed to More) of a large standing army; the increasing pollution of towns and countryside by human beings who had lost any sense of identification with their society; add all of this, and we have a very bitter indictment indeed by More of the England of his day. It is hardly a matter for wonder that he wrote the book in Latin and published it abroad.

Of the radical character of the indictment there can be little question. Sir Thomas was, by any available standard, a radical with respect to the conditions of English economy and society. But it must be emphasized that, like so many radical minds prior to the eighteenth century, he was also, and very deeply, a traditionalist. We might well call him a reactionary in the literal sense of the word. For the model of society that he uses as the basis of his indictment of the commercialism, profiteering, social atomism, and political centralization of sixteenth-century England is a model drawn, not from the imaginary future, but from the remembered past. Allowing always for the exceptions and the details which an imagination as fertile as his could conjure up easily enough, the society of the Utopians that he draws for us is, in very large part, an evocation—a romanticization, if we like—of England's medieval past.

I noted above that among the influences working on Sir Thomas's mind was the monastic tradition: not the kind that, all too often, he saw corrupted in his own day by the same commercial practices that were to be found in the nobility, but, rather, the kind that had first been brought into existence by Benedict of Nursia. Without question, Plato's *Republic* was an influence upon More. But there are several vital constitutive elements of the *Utopia* that were clearly suggested, not by Plato, in whose work these do not exist, but by the Christian primitivism and naturalism of the monasteries at their best.

The first of these I have already stressed: the depiction of Utopia as a form of community arising directly from what is natural to man—that is, what accords with his true nature, in contrast to artificial habits and wants, products of a social order that has become unnatural and irrational. Repeatedly, as I have said, More emphasizes this quality of all the relationships to be found among the Utopians in their relationship to their environment. Beyond this, More is careful to make plain that all the Utopians engage in farming; in the working and the tilling of the soil and in the harvesting of the crops:

> Husbandry is a science common to them all in general, both
> men and women, wherein they be all expert and cunning. In this
> they be all instruct even from their youth; partly in schools with
> traditions and precepts, and partly in the country nigh the city,
> brought up as it were in playing, not only beholding the use of
> it but by occasion of exercising their bodies practising it also.[20]

Besides the agricultural arts which bind the Utopians to the nourish-
ing soil, all members of the community are expected to learn one or more
handicrafts such as cloth working, masonry, blacksmithing, and carpentry.
Each family makes its own clothing, simple but capable of long wear
and subjection to every kind of weather. Such clothing is more or less
identical among the Utopians, allowing only for differences between that
worn by women and by men and by the married and by the unmarried.
For the most part, boys and girls learn their crafts from their parents,
but if a child, usually a boy, should demonstrate some unusual aptitude
for a craft other than his father's, he may be adopted by a family in which
that craft is to be found. Nor should anyone be obliged to stay with but
one craft:

> If any person, when he hath learned one craft, be desirous
> to learn also another, he is likewise suffered and permitted. When
> he hath learned both, he occupieth whether he will; unless the
> city have more need of the one than of the other.[21]

All of this bespeaks, not any Platonic confinement of husbandry and
handicraft to lesser strata in the population, but, rather, the monastic—
and, by our contemporary standards, the ecological—ideal of such activities' being spread among all the people, at least those who are physically
qualified. Nor is there any of the celebration of leisure that we find in
Plato and so many of the classical philosophers. Plainly, as the following
passage suggests, More feared the baneful effects of idleness as much as
had Saint Benedict and Saint Francis. For all who fall clearly in the
ecological tradition, idleness is a form of "rust of the soul."

> The chief and almost the only office of the syphogrants [over-
> seers] is to see and take heed that no man sit idle, but that every-
> one apply his own craft with earnest diligence; and yet for all
> that not to be wearied from early in the morning to late in the
> evening with continual work, like laboring and toiling beasts. For
> this is worse than the miserable and wretched condition of bond-
> men; which, nevertheless is almost everywhere the life of work-
> men and artificers, saving in Utopia. For they, dividing the day

[20] Ibid., p. 99.   [21] Ibid., p. 100.

and the night into twenty-four just hours, appoint and assign only six of those hours to work; three before noon, upon the which they go straight to dinner; and after dinner, when they have rested two hours, then they work three; and upon that they go to supper. About eight of the clock in the evening, counting one of the clock as the first hour after noon, they go to bed. Eight hours they give to sleep. All the void time, that is between the hours of work, sleep, and meat, that they be suffered to bestow, every man as he liketh best himself: not to the intent that they should misspend this time in riot or slothfulness; but, being then licensed from the labor of their own occupations, to bestow the time well and thriftfully upon some other good science, as shall please them. For it is a solemn custom there to have lectures daily early in the morning, where to be present they only be constrained that be namely chosen and appointed to learning. Howbeit a great multitude of every sort of people, both men and women, go to hear lectures; some one and some another, as every man's nature is inclined. Yet this notwithstanding, if any man had rather bestow this time upon his own occupation, as it chanceth in many, whose minds rise not in the contemplation of any science liberal, he is not letted nor prohibited; but is also praised and commended as profitable to the commonwealth.[22]

Granted that there is an almost lyrical quality to this description of the lives of the Utopians; it would nevertheless be shortsighted not to see that in Sir Thomas's praise of manual work in the fields and at the craftsman's table, as well as his celebration of learning and art—imparted to all those interested and able through lectures and writing—and also his division of the Utopian day into periods of different kinds of work, of rest and sleep, and of play ("after supper they bestow one hour in play"), we have before us something extremely close to the monastic ideal to be found in Benedict's Rule.

One major difference between the monastic movement and More's Utopia is, of course, the presence in the latter of the family. (This also constitutes a significant difference between More and Plato; for although Plato allowed family ties to exist among the common people in his Republic, these ties were explicitly banned among the all-important guardians—whose fidelity to their duties in command of the state might suffer, he thought, if marital relationships and parental love were allowed to exist.) More was himself a happily married man, and the love he enjoyed from his children endured, as we know, to the day of his execution. He was, by all accounts, an affectionate father, one who from the

22 Ibid., pp. 101–2.

beginning took rare pleasure in the company of his children, but, at the same time, one who believed in proper discipline.

So strongly does Sir Thomas believe in the joys and virtues of the marital tie for his Utopians that he has them rigorously forbidding sexual relations among their young prior to marriage. Violations of chastity are indeed to be punished by prohibition of the guilty from ever marrying, unless perchance the ruler should give them pardon.

> That offence [violation of premarital chastity] is so sharply punished because they perceive that unless they be diligently kept from the liberty of this vice, few will join together in the love of marriage; wherein all the life must be led with one, and also all the griefs and displeasures that come therewith must patiently be taken and borne.[23]

The proper and widely accepted age for marriage is eighteen for the woman and twenty-two for the man. One Utopian marriage custom deserves note: that whereby the intended partners to the marriage must show themselves naked to each other prior to the marriage ceremony. The Utopians, on being informed of the absence of this custom among other nations, point out the absurdity through which people in these other nations, who would never dream of purchasing a horse without having saddle and blankets fully removed, "yet in choosing a wife, which be either pleasure or displeasure to them all their life after, they be so reckless that all the residue of the woman's body being covered with clothes, they esteem her scarcely by one handbreadth (for they can see no more but her face)." [24]

Nor was Sir Thomas opposed to divorce under proper circumstances. Marriage in Utopia is supposed to, and almost universally does, last until death of the man or wife. But if, in the opinion of the council, one partner to the marriage has been guilty of adultery or of some continuously intolerable form of behavior to the other, then the marriage may be broken. However, only the innocent partner may remarry; the other must, for his or her sins, remain forever unmarried. There is still another form of divorce, which suggests the most recent and humane divorce legislation of modern times. If a Utopian man and woman, however long married, find they can no longer live harmoniously together and either or both wish separation and then remarriage, this can be arranged, provided only that in the judgment of the ruling council a fair effort has been made to make the marriage work. Shrewdly, however, More has the council "loath to consent to" such divorce, "because they know this to be the next way to break love between man and wife, to be in easy hope of new marriage." [25]

---

[23] Ibid., p. 158.   [24] Ibid.   [25] Ibid., p. 160.

There is a strong atmosphere of pluralism and of decentralization in More's *Utopia*. The family is the most fundamental unit, and its authority over its own members is deemed inviolable by outside authority unless the family manifests some degree of cruelty or neglect—offences which Utopians dislike intensely. From the family one moves on to the kindred —that is, the extended family—which, like the ancient clan, is also a unit of social organization and authority. Government of the larger society rests in the hands of a body of phylarchs, each chosen by election to represent thirty families. Representing every ten phylarchs is an archphylarch. All the phylarchs, two hundred in number, of Utopia, choose a prince from a list of four candidates presented to them—the prince to serve for life, unless from his office he should come to aspire to undue power in which case he is removed by the phylarchs. The phylarchs themselves are chosen for but a single year, though we learn that these individuals are commonly reelected. In a shrewd measure designed to prevent any ruler from ever conspiring against the people, all major matters are sent for approval to the two hundred phylarchs, who themselves commonly consult with the families that belong to their respective divisions of government.

Inasmuch as every family is itself a unit of government—economic, social, and political, more or less sovereign within its own sphere—it will be seen that what Sir Thomas has in mind for the larger society is a kind of functional democracy, or republic; that is, no artificial division is made between "political," "economic," and "social" matters. All, without exception, are deemed the responsibility of a society that has the family for its irreducible unit and a government that, quite literally, represents the families.

As he loved the family in its sphere of production and consumption, so did Sir Thomas plainly love the city as a proper unit of social life. Utopia, as More describes it briefly, is about two hundred miles broad. It is given geographical protection by a nearly impassable desert on one side and by the sea on the other, with a natural and easily defended harbor offering access for such commerce as the Utopians care to conduct. There are fifty-four cities, no two of them any closer together than twenty-four miles, thus making possible the preservation of the open country-side around each city and, most important, that degree of husbandry that More so prizes for each family as its economic foundation. Each city governs itself in all strictly internal matters, with only those functions common to two or more cities being exercised by higher agencies in Utopian government. Always, as is evident, the principles of local auton-omy and decentralization are observed; for nothing seemed to More so injurious to a society as centralization of power, with bureaucracy its inescapable result.

Just as More hated political centralization, so he hated the kind of society that springs from unbridled private property, profit, and, above all, use of money. It would not perhaps be correct to refer to More's Utopian society as a rigorously egalitarian communism. He was shrewd enough to know that absolute egalitarianism is incompatible with the degree of individuality every creative society must reinforce and that any effort to undergird an absolute communism must be followed by political despotism. Even so, having made these qualifications, one is deeply impressed by More's dedication to equality and to communality. He himself lived in an England that was fast losing what simple equality it had once possessed and also what small communality had once lain in the village community, the guild, the monastery, and other medieval institutions. What we find in More's *Utopia*, therefore, is an overriding emphasis upon the two virtues of equality and communality:

> Every city is divided into four equal parts. In the midst of every quarter there is a market-place of all manner of things; thither the works of every family be brought into certain houses and every kind of thing is laid up several in barns or store-houses. From hence the father of every family or every householder fetcheth whatsoever he and his have need of and carrieth it away with him without money, without exchange, without any gage or pledge. For why should anything be denied unto him, seeing there is abundance of all things and that it is not to be feared lest any man will ask more than he needeth? For why should it be thought that man would ask more than enough which is sure never to lack. Certainly, in all kinds of living creatures, either fear of lack doth cause covetousness and ravin, or, in many, only pride; which counteth it a glorious thing to pass and excel other in the superfluous and vain ostentation of things; the which kind of vice among the Utopians can have no place.[26]

Elsewhere in More's *Utopia* one will find a kind of qualification of the view of human nature contained in the passage just quoted, which takes into consideration the fact that under the best and most affluent of common circumstances, there may well be some lazier or more covetous than others, with whom the community must deal properly and strictly. But for all More's common sense regarding extremes, his overall conclusion is a direct and simple one: what More, like Benedict before him, detests is money relationships, individual greed and ostentation, and a society based exclusively upon competition for gain. And what he likes above all, also like Benedict, is a society in which the principle of communality pervades all things, a communality rooted in the family. Thus

[26] Ibid., p. 111.

the fairest and most accurate statement to make about *Utopia* is that, while economic communism is not made an isolated fetish there, as it has so often tended to be in the secular socialist, especially Marxist, tradition of the nineteenth and twentieth centuries, it does indeed exist in More's cherished commonwealth: the inexorable consequence of the ecological principle of community that underlies all aspects of the commonwealth.

It is another mark of the eminent humanity of More's mind that complete freedom of religion exists in Utopia—though he was himself a devout Catholic.

> There be divers kinds of religion, not only in sundry parts of the island, but also in divers places in every city. Some worship for God the sun, some the moon, some some other of the planets. . . . But the most and wisest part, rejecting all these, believe that there is a certain godly power unknown, everlasting, incomprehensible, inexplicable, far above the capacity and reach of man's wit, dispersed throughout all the world, not in bigness, but in virtue and power. Him they call the father of all.[27]

The essence of Utopian religion is, thus, the essence of each of the other major spheres of life in that society: *nature.* In the late seventeenth and the eighteenth centuries, the principles of what was portentously called "natural religion" were to be set forth in many a book and essay; but none was much more than an elaboration of the simple description contained in the passage quoted above from *Utopia.*

There is no better, certainly no more amusing, expression of More's contempt for all the unnatural excrescences of civilization, the idle luxuries and avarice-producing refinements of wealth, than his discussion of the place of gold and silver in Utopia. Each, he has his Utopian spokesman say, must be kept in its proper place—which is well below that of such clearly useful metals as, say, iron and copper. Gold among the Utopians is used for but one purpose: making chamber pots!

Romantic, or reactionary, Sir Thomas More may well have been: he has been called this often enough during the past century. And, as we have seen, the imagined European past, particularly the monastic past, was a powerful model for More in constructing his Utopia. All of what I have called the elements of the ecological community, most especially the principle of nature and respect for nature, are to be found as readily in *Utopia* as in the Benedictine Rule written nearly a thousand years before. So much is true. But it would be a great error to overlook the immense influence More's work—traditionalist, romantic, nostalgic,

[27] Ibid., p. 169.

or what we will—had in shaping the European radical mind during the four centuries that have passed since his death.

He was one of the very first, if not the first, to call attention to economic, social, and political evils for what they were in fact. He did not, wittingly or unwittingly, dismiss these as being merely inevitable manifestations of the human condition or as marks of God's displeasure with his creation. Granted that Sir Thomas did not seek through either revolution or reform the remaking of the English nation: efforts of that kind in the cause of humanitarianism would not be made for two or three centuries. What he did do, however, and with luminous and lasting effect, was to hold up a *secular* and, with only a slight exercise of the imagination, *realizable* alternative to the dismal conditions he saw forming in his own England. That he chose to set this superb alternative in a distant place was no more than tribute to the impact being registered by accounts of voyages and explorations in the New World of the Americas and tales of the exotic peoples there. Much of the allure of the "natural," and much of the repugnance felt by humane minds for what Europeans were doing to their own natural areas through business, war, and tech-mouth, of peoples in the Americas and elsewhere whose lives were lived nology, sprang from the fast-spreading accounts, printed and word-of-close to nature, simply, cooperatively, communally, with full respect to the needs, desires, and affections which spring directly from human nature. Not without shrewd reason, therefore, did Sir Thomas, writing only two or three decades after the discovery of America, utilize the name of Amerigo Vespucci early in his book as being the captain under whom his fictional Hythloday, narrator of the description of Utopia, had earlier sailed. The device was bound to enhance credibility, to warm the reader's sense of verisimilitude.

To ask whether *Utopia* is a "socialist" or "communist" book is, at bottom, irrelevant. Each of these words today takes on meanings acquired in the late nineteenth and early twentieth century, and is likely to create in one's mind visions of the actualities of existing nations ranging, from, say, England as it has been since World War II all the way to Soviet Russia or Maoist China. The point is that between More's Utopia and any actual socialist or communist nation in the contemporary world there is as much solid difference as there is between his ideal society and any manifestation of capitalism. Utopia, as described in More's vivid pages, is the very opposite of the huge, nationalist, collectivist, centralized, and bureaucratized societies of the twentieth century, whether these be labeled "socialist," "communist," or "capitalist." In short, it cannot be said that More's remarkable book has exerted any influence upon the course of actual political, economic, and social history in the Western world.

Nor would it appear to have influenced significantly any of the great mass movements of reform and revolution which have taken place since the French Revolution. I said above that the book has clearly had effect upon the Western mind; of this there can be no question. But if we look at the kinds of organized social and political movement—nineteenth-century populism in the United States, and socialism in Europe, and those vaster, more powerful ones of communism and fascism in the twentieth century—which have actually affected the characters of governments and economies, it would be hard to trace any line of relationship back to More's *Utopia*.

Where the book would appear to have maintained its greatest influence—or, certainly, relevance—is in those fewer and smaller contexts, off the main line of history, in which the utopian ideal has remained vivid right down to the present moment. It was Sir Thomas More who gave the English language the words *utopia* and *utopian*. From his book two lines of succession may easily be traced. The first and most obvious is that of the many literary-philosophical utopias that have been written and widely read throughout the past four hundred years. Scarcely a century had passed when Sir Francis Bacon wrote his *New Atlantis* and Campanella his *City of the Sun*. Neither of these has the charm and readability, much less the wisdom and humanity, of More's book. There have been waves, so to speak, of utopian books, popular and learned, during the centuries since More's death, each tending to become structured around the dominant interests and imaginative hopes of its age. Science, for example, was emphasized in Bacon's *New Atlantis*. The utopias of a century later in France, most of which were projected imaginatively into the distant future, expressed themes of popular egalitarianism and of humane, enlightened political power. Nineteenth-century literary utopias stressed, for the most part though not universally, industrialism and technology, seeking to show how these seemingly destructive forces in civilization might be given creative effect if they were but set in cooperative commonwealths. Edward Bellamy's *Looking Backward*, published in America in 1887, was an effort, clearly modeled on More's *Utopia*, to describe the cooperative regime in which Americans would be living in the year 2000. His book sold more than a million copies through successive editions. Many were the utopias conceived and written in the nineteenth and early twentieth centuries, all of them examples of man's capacity for holding the glass up, even as Sir Thomas More did, to existing evils and miseries by showing what might prevail, what could be realized, were men's spirits equal to the task. That the historical determinists, the so-called realists, such as Marx and his followers, had nothing but contempt for this utopian tradition, whether in literature or in those actual manifestations we shall deal briefly with next in this chapter, does not offset the deep fascination that written utopias, beginning with More's great work, have had down to the present.

Ecology as Laissez-Faire:
The Physiocrats and Adam Smith

It is interesting to note that modern economics as a discipline came into being in the eighteenth century on the basis largely of the desire to bring about the same kind of ecological harmonies in society at large that we have just seen in More's *Utopia*. The phrase *laissez-faire*, meaning "let alone," is from the writings of one of the Physiocrats, a group of French philosophers concerned foremost with the establishment of an economic regime that would operate through its own intrinsic harmonies and balances rather than through the kind of dense legislative and bureaucratic controls then much in evidence not only in France but in other parts of Europe as well. Across the English Channel, about the same time, appeared the work of the Scottish moral philosopher Adam Smith, whose *Wealth of Nations*, published in 1776, is generally regarded as the founding work of modern economics.

Both the Physiocrats and Smith were profoundly interested in what they regarded as the *natural order*, the order of human relationships most in accord with man's actual nature, which—so it was argued—would be in existence were it not for the kinds of interference with man's nature emanating from the political state, the church, and other well-meaning but disruptive influences in the economy. Despite a belief fairly widespread in our own day, Adam Smith was by no means the uncritical worshiper of business interests and finance that he might seem to be, judging from the particular pattern so-called laissez-faire economics was to take in the nineteenth century in Europe and America. Careful readers of his *Wealth of Nations* and also of his earlier work, *The Theory of Moral Sentiments*, will find a mind keenly tuned to the needs of all classes in Europe, especially the poorer ones. For it was Smith's belief that much hardship and misery sprang directly from governmental alliance with some of the more powerful economic interests, thus degrading the economy as a whole and risking the impoverishment of many of the smaller farming and business entrepreneurs.

There is, both Smith and the Physiocrats argued, a natural and spontaneous economic order, one that will manifest itself through its own powers if only, as a first step, all present institutionalized controls are removed, especially the centralizing, constricting political kind which are rooted in a false conception of the role of government. In each human being, Smith tells us, lie a mind and nature sufficient to that individual's own economic and moral interest if they are but trusted. Enlightened self-interest, Smith thought, is a far better mainspring for economic life than the misplaced and wholly inadequate meddling that comes from external institutions. If all human beings are allowed to pursue their economic interest in competition with one another, the results will be beneficial to all, and for society as a whole, Smith wrote, it will be as though an "invisible hand" were regulating the operation.

Further, we learn from both Smith and the Physiocrats (whose very name indicates belief in a natural order that should be allowed to govern) that a harmonious balance is possible between agriculture and business, as well as within each great sphere, if it is permitted to come into being through cessation of special subventions and taxes which now prevent its existence. Their study of economic phenomena led the Physiocrats to compare the economy, in its natural, untrammeled form, to a human body, with the several natural channels of wealth and production like the veins and arteries of the body. The entire confusing and inhibiting structure of existing taxation, with its innumerable levels and sources, could be abolished, the Physiocrats argued, and replaced with a single tax—on the initial phase of production, which lay in agriculture according to the Physiocrats—if only a wise and powerful government would for the first time in history obliterate the present artificial and corrupt social order and then allow the natural order to come into being of its own power.

There are many differences between Adam Smith and the Physiocrats, and Smith was much abler and more constructive. But they had in common a strong belief in the existence of a natural economic order, arising from the innate character of man, that would come into existence if only present repressive and interfering institutions were removed. They also had in common a belief in the proper balance between agriculture and industry, one that was a part of the same natural order. And, finally, we find in the writings of both Smith and the Physiocrats—and then throughout most of the so-called classical tradition in nineteenth-century economics—a deep belief in the autonomy and simplicity of economic and social behavior. This whole tradition of thought has come to be labeled laissez-faire simply because of its fundamental conviction that if human beings were but left alone to their own intelligences and interests, a harmonious, balanced, simple, and autonomous system of economic activity would result, one that would be true to nature.

Is it not fascinating that the same qualities which Benedict had made so basic to his Rule and to the monastic system he founded, and which Sir Thomas More had declared to be the constitutive elements of his cherished imaginary community of Utopians, should in the eighteenth century have come to be regarded by some of Europe's most distinguished philosophers as the qualities best fitted for the whole society—as, indeed, the very elements of the whole society—if only nature were allowed to take command?

Alas, what actually came into existence in the nineteenth century— and often under the spur of Adam Smith's imagined message, so largely distorted and misapplied—was a system in which increasingly centralized political power and ever-widening governmental bureaucracy were united with large-scale industry. Adam Smith and the Physiocrats would have been horrified had they chanced to visit the economic scene of, say, England and the United States in the late nineteenth century and see the new kinds of power that had come into being. For such structures of political and economic power were the very opposite of what they had had in mind. Who knows, perhaps they would have become members of the utopian-anarchist movement to which we turn now.

The Milieu of Modern Anarchism

Our concern in the rest of this chapter will be the philosophy of the anarchist community that came into being in the nineteenth century and that flourishes to this day as one of the major types of the ecological community. We shall be principally interested in the works of Pierre Joseph Proudhon and of Peter Kropotkin, each a mind of authentic stature in the history of Western social philosophy and together the indispensable sources of modern anarchism. As will be apparent enough when we look in detail at their ideas, both men must be seen as lineal successors to Saint Benedict and Sir Thomas More, strange as it may seem to link the revolutionary philosophy of anarchism, overwhelmingly secular and generally hostile to the Christian church, to a tradition that began in the Christian monastery during the age following the downfall of Rome.

But, as we have repeatedly seen, major ideas are never reducible to mere lineal emanations of other ideas. Great ideas are responses to the challenges of the milieu in which they arise, however constituted they may be of premises, insights, and perspectives of earlier thinkers. If we are to understand the impact in the nineteenth century, and also in our own day, of the ethic of anarchism, we must turn to certain contextual conditions of the early nineteenth century in the West.

The French Revolution

There is, first, the influence of the French Revolution, which had both a positive and a negative aspect. Without question the French Revolution was the immediate source of inspiration for anarchism, as it was of so many other nineteenth-century ideas and social movements. The spectacle of a group of men, the Jacobins, effecting a monumental change in an entire social order, annihilating ways of behavior and belief many centuries old, and bringing into existence new ways, the products of idealism, reason, and power; this acted, as we have seen, like a magnet for all minds eager to do something about the conditions—so often of tyranny, travail, and torment—that had been created by history. The revolutionary emphasis on freedom—on the liberation of large numbers of individuals from the fetters of tradition, from the dead hand of the past—could not fail to be intoxicating to a great many rationalists, reformers, and revolutionists. Equally intoxicating was the clear evidence of what could be done in the way of systematic reconstruction, or novel organization, and of planning based on reason and idealism. The anarchists were no more immune than were divers other reformers and revolutionists of the age following the Revolution to the temptations presented by this great spectacle.

But the Revolution, as we have also seen, had another side as well: it revealed a face of absolute power, ruthless use of terror, and repression of individual freedom. In order to accomplish the objectives of individual freedom and national unity based upon the will of the people, it was necessary, as the revolutionists saw it, to destroy all that lay between individual and the state: tradition, convention, corporation, association, and community. This side of the Revolution was no less imposing to many minds in Europe than the other side, that of freedom and fraternity. The French revolutionary government not only abolished such associations as guild, local community, and patriarchal family—or enacted laws that would have abolished them had the Revolution continued many more years—but in the so-called Loi Chapelier of 1791, it forbade the creation of any new associations capable by their position intermediate to individual and state, of detracting from that unity of consciousness which Rousseau had called the general will and which was the dream of every Jacobin. There was, in short, a monolithic, collectivist, centralized, and inevitably bureaucratized side to the Revolution that was no less vivid in many eyes than that of liberation, secularization, and rationalism.

The anarchists were among the very first to see this, the dark side of the Revolution. Along with such western European conservatives as Burke, Bonald, and Hegel, and such liberals as Lamennais and Tocqueville (all of whom we shall deal with in the next chapter), the anarchists, representing the radical left, found this side of the Revolution wholly repugnant. They did not like the centralization of power they saw in the Revolution, the unitary collectivism the Revolution represented, and the stringent laws prohibiting free association of the people in cooperatives, communes, and labor unions; and they did not like the overwhelmingly bourgeois cast of the Revolution, reflected in its general acceptance of capitalist industry, the factory, and, above all, private property.

This is why we shall find throughout the history of nineteenth-century anarchism an extremely critical view of the Revolution in general and of the Jacobins in particular. The anarchists did not accept, as did Marx and the main line of radicalism in the West, the necessity of violence and of terror; they did not see history as a unilinear, inexorable, and irreversible process, as did the Marxists; they opposed utterly the centralized collectivism that the Revolution ushered in and that Marxism, from the *Manifesto* right through to Lenin and Stalin, took virtually for granted. Without exception, the major anarchist philosophers, beginning with William Godwin in England—an individualist-anarchist rather than a communal-anarchist—through Bakunin, Proudhon, and Kropotkin, down to Alexander Berkman and Emma Goldman, rejected this legacy of the French Revolution: the legacy of centralization and unitary collectivism. And with their rejection of this went also a rejection of nationalism in any of its forms, socialist as well as capitalist. They saw, and see to this day, the national state as an enemy of social progress and of creative freedom even greater than capitalism itself. For, as the anarchists early perceived, with its centralization and collectivism, its indoctrination of belief in itself and its culture, the national state achieves a degree of absolute power that no other form of relationship, not even the great economic corporation, can possess. Democracy—that is, the national democracy of the Revolution and the nineteenth and twentieth centuries—is only the absolute state carried to its *nth* power: so, at one point in his life, declared Proudhon.

Hence derives the characteristic and persistent anarchist insistence on freedom and autonomy of association and on free cooperation among individuals, rather than regimentation; hence the emphasis on diversity of culture and variegation of social attachments, and on the spontaneous types of local, regional, and functional association—rural as well as urban. It is no wonder that anarchists and Marxists so early became sworn enemies.

Industrialism

The second major element in the milieu of anarchism, and as great a stimulus to anarchist reaction as to that of any other nineteenth-century reform or revolutionary movement, was the new industrialism. The anarchists and Marxists were one in their animosity to private property and private profit. Private property is theft, Proudhon declared, and his words were accepted by all subsequent anarchists as a true statement of reality. Property originates in land and in the resources contained in the land, in the anarchists' view, and this gift of nature is not to be exploited, not to be made the basis of a class system that divides the few who own from the vast mass of those who, unlucky enough to be deprived of ownership, are obliged to live in virtual slavery to them. There is not an iota of difference between anarchist and Marxist attitudes toward property and profit. Like the Marxists, the anarchists saw the fruits of industrialism to be poverty, dislocation, and misery for the great majority of persons in society. For the anarchists the factory was no more than a conversion to private economic use of the system of rigid military discipline they saw also in the state.

The last point suggests one major area of disagreement between anarchists and Marxists: whereas Marxists tended to accept all the structural characteristics of capitalist production, including the factory system, technology, and the dominance of city over rural areas, anarchists foresaw the ending of the factory system, the complete decentralization of technology, and a general restoration of rural patterns of life. We can see how sharp the differences between Marxists and anarchists were—and remain to this day—in a caustic essay, clearly directed against the anarchist left, that Engels wrote in 1874 and published in Italy, in which he declared to be nonsense all implications that with the termination of private property there could be any termination of the rigorous authority the factory system enjoined upon workers by virtue of its technology. The future, Engels insisted, even under socialism and communism, lies in the large, centralized, mechanized factory, not in any creation of small units of production that can be managed cooperatively. "Wanting to abolish authority in large scale industry is tantamount to wanting to abolish industry itself, to destroy the power loom in order to return to the spinning wheel." [28] The Marxists were content, in most respects, to maintain the physical structure of capitalism, transforming only the system of property and ownership underlying it. The anarchists, however, with their hatred of bigness, centralization, and monolithic collectivism, declared the mere abolition of private property to be no real answer if the major structural forms of capitalism, such as the factory system, were to be left largely untouched.

Utopianism

The third element of the age that clearly affected the nature of anarchist philosophy, and that also became one of the points of profound difference between the anarchists and Marxists, was the vast profusion of nineteenth-century socialist or communist utopian communities. Despite widespread belief that the most characteristic feature of the nineteenth century in western Europe and America was its individualistic capitalism, more careful investigation suggests that its real distinction was in the wave of voluntary association that rolled then across the Western landscape. This was the century in which labor unionism really came into existence, the first significant associations of craftsmen since the medieval guilds had been destroyed by nationalism and capitalism. It was the century, too, in which a considerable number of professions came into

28 Friedrich Engels, "On Authority," in Karl Marx and Friedrich Engels, *Basic Writings on Politics and Philosophy*, ed. Lewis S. Feuer (New York: Doubleday & Co., Anchor Books, 1959), p. 483.

formal existence, such as the fields of medicine, engineering, and law, with tight associations to match the self-consciousness of their practitioners.

But far more interesting, and of vital significance to anarchist thought, was the cooperative and communal movement, manifest in many hundreds, even thousands, of ventures ranging from consumer cooperatives such as the famous Rochdale Society, founded in 1844 in England, to the intensely communal associations into which thousands of men and women threw themselves, along with their money, property, and children, forming utopian societies dedicated in one degree or another to the anarchist ideal of renunciation of formal government. Despite the understandable tendency today to think of the nineteenth century exclusively in terms of its economic individualism, capitalism, and burgeoning national states, the fact is that no other period in all history vies with it in the number of books and articles, missionaries, and other spokesmen, and actual examples dedicated to furthering the ideals of practical socialism in the form of utopian communities.

Much of this was strictly religious in inspiration: for example, Hutterite, Shaker, Perfectionist, and even, to a degree at least, Mormon. What we have already seen to be the intensity of the religious community in matters of mind and belief was very easily extended to matters of property and government. To this day there are religious associations, successful by communal norms, which live as far as possible from the larger society and which practice a high degree of communality in all matters excepting, for the most part, only family practices. Although religious communality in this sense was a product of the Reformation, to be seen among some of the millennialist Protestant sects spawned by the sixteenth-century revolt against Roman Catholicism, it was not until the late eighteenth and early nineteenth centuries that such religious communities really flourished. The great amount of open, generally free land in the United States and adjacent territories made this country a natural gathering point for many such groups.

By no means all the century's utopian-communal groups were of religious origin. A great many individuals were inspired by such secular philosophers as Charles Fourier (1772–1837). Fourier's writings stressed the existence in all individuals of certain natural passions or instincts which had but to be released and channeled properly for a genuine social harmony to be brought into being, a harmony that would make law and government in the formal sense unnecessary. The doctrines of philosophical anarchism, which varied a good deal in what they actually proposed, were uniform in rejecting both private property and, at the same time, formal, coercive government. Proudhon, whom we shall reserve for treatment later in this chapter, was perhaps best known for his principles of decentralization and pluralism; but his doctrine of "mutualism" was very close to the ideas of Fourier and also of the later Kropotkin.

Hundreds, perhaps thousands, of villages and towns in the United States were founded in the first instance by small groups of families determined to escape the tyranny, as they saw it, of private property, on the one hand, and coercive political government, on the other. Some of these tried valiantly to disseminate their beliefs by means of lecturers, missionaries, and the printing of tracts for free distribution in the United States and Europe. In the territory, later the state, of California alone dozens of such communities came into existence.[29] In a few instances religious conceptions underlay the communalism, but in many others the secular philosophies of Fourier, Comte, Proudhon, and Marx were operative.

Probably the leading nonreligious efforts of utopian cooperative communalism in the United States were those constructed in terms of the ideas of the brilliant Englishman Robert Owen (1771–1858), who, following his wholly successful experiment with the cooperative-communal principle in New Lanark, Scotland, sought to disseminate his ideas to other parts of Europe and the United States. Best known of his efforts in America was the ill-fated New Harmony project in Indiana. Strains within and pressures from without led to its demise, but Owenite principles remained nonetheless vivid to a great many others with utopian-communal objectives. Between 1820 and 1828, approximately a dozen Owenite communities sprang up in the states of Indiana, New York, and Ohio. Fourierist principles of natural social harmony also had their spokesmen in America—among them Albert Brisbane and Horace Greeley. Apostles of Fourier's philosophy sprang up throughout urban America in the early nineteenth century: within a decade of its arrival in this country, not less than thirty-three "phalanxes," each seeking the 1,620 members prescribed by Fourier—all of whom were to live in attempted communal association, without private property or profit and as remote as possible from the values of the larger American society— had come into being in the Middle West and the Middle Atlantic areas. The longest to survive were the Wisconsin Phalanx and the North American Phalanx, the latter in New Jersey—each numbering, however, only about a hundred members.

The famous Brook Farm in New England, the subject of one of Nathaniel Hawthorne's books, was a community of intellectuals who were seeking the simple, natural life, away from city and industry, emancipated from the strains and tensions of commerce and politics. It, too, went through a Fourierist phase (it had been tinged with transcendentalism when it was founded), and in 1844 the farm was renamed a phalanx. One of the best known and also longest-lived of all of the century's utopian ventures was that of Étienne Cabet (1788–1856), a Frenchman who, inspired by Robert Owen's ideas, first wrote of a celebrated

---

[29] See the interesting account of some of these in Robert V. Hine, *California's Utopian Colonies* (San Marino, Calif.: Huntington Library, 1953).

imaginary utopia in *Voyage en Icarie* (1840) and then, leading a group of his disciples from France, set up a community on the Red River in Texas. Here they quickly went bankrupt, and then they moved to Nauvoo, Illinois, only recently vacated by the quasi-communal Mormons on their way to Utah. There were repeated secessions, caused largely, apparently, by Cabet's own messianic-dictatorial temperament; and a dozen or so new Icarian communities were founded in different parts of the Middle West, some of which survived in more or less communal form until the end of the century.[30]

Darwinism

The fourth and final element in the milieu of anarchism is, strange as it may seem, the philosophy of Darwinism—or at least a signal element of Darwinian thought. For most of us, Darwinism suggests anything but communality and cooperativeness in nature. What, after all, is Darwinian natural selection but competition to the death within the species for limited food supply? The image of "nature red in tooth and claw" emerges easily from our reading of the *Origin of Species*, and what has come to be called "social Darwinism" is scarcely more than a celebration of the necessity of competition and conflict in the social sphere.

But there is another side to Darwin's work and to biology generally, one concerned with ecological interdependences among plants and animals. As we shall shortly see, Kropotkin made the vivid passages on ecological harmonies in nature in Darwin's *Origin of Species* and other works his own point of departure for what is even today the best of all modern studies of the ecological community, *Mutual Aid: A Factor in Evolution*. Most of that book is concerned in considerable detail with manifestations of mutual aid in human society, but it begins with some striking examples of mutual aid in the biological world generally, some of them the products of Kropotkin's own observations and researches, some of them drawn from Darwin's many works.

Darwin's great work *On the Origin of Species by Means of Natural Selection* was not published until 1859. The philosophy of anarchism was already well formed by that time, and it would be wrong to imply that it either arose from or was dependent upon the philosophy of biological evolution. There is no doubt, however, that the immense prestige of Darwin's name in western Europe from the 1860s on, and the great influence of the idea of evolution generally, supplied very important reinforcement to the theme of ecological interdependence, of natural harmonies of relationship among all biological beings, that we find among

[30] For an excellent short article on nineteenth-century communal experiments, see Dorothy W. Douglas and Katherine Du Pre Lumpkin, "Communistic Settlements," in *Encyclopedia of the Social Sciences*. A very useful bibliography is attached.

late-nineteenth- and early-twentieth-century anarchists. After all, if co-operation could be shown to be, not merely a utopian ideal, not merely something desirable on ethical grounds, but a fundamental principle of nature, then the cause of the anarchists and others who espoused the ideals of cooperation and communalism would be markedly helped.

In any event, biological confirmation of the ideal of cooperation did not have to wait for the appearance of Darwin's great work in 1859. As I indicated at the beginning of this chapter, the fascination with nature and its relationships that we find throughout the ecological tradition, not excluding the monastic communities of the Middle Ages, carries with it the clear implication that a bond exists between man and nature, between human relationships and the relationships of plants and animals. The respect, the reverence for the natural world and all its inhabitants that we find in the works of Saint Benedict, Saint Francis, and many other spokesmen of monasticism was based in large part upon the awareness of likenesses and also harmonies throughout the natural sphere.

Beyond this is the fact that from the time when the study of biology came into existence among the ancient Greeks, it clearly recognized patterns of interdependence and cooperation. There are ample indications of this in the writings of Aristotle, who was as fine a naturalist as he was philosopher. And the Roman Lucretius, in his *On the Nature of Things*, made much use of the symbolism of sex and love in his descriptions of the close relationships among, not merely plants and animals, but even the physical atoms in space from whose primordial collocations and patterns, according to this remarkable philosopher-scientist, everything began. Throughout the long period of Christian thought, the idea of the great chain of being, reaching from the smallest, simplest being at the bottom all the way up to God, was fully capable of assimilating in philosophical and theological terms the kinds of relationships in nature that the Benedictines and other monastic orders regarded directly and empirically.

The eighteenth century was an age of extraordinary, profoundly creative work in biology. There was Goethe in Germany, as proud of his botanical studies as of his great poetry and drama; there were Bonnet and Maupertuis, among many others, in France. The great taxonomic work that had been done by Linnaeus, showing the classificatory relationships among the species, genera, and orders throughout the biological realm, inevitably led to more specialized works on ecological relationships in nature, however these might be termed. The unity of nature, the continuity of man's nature with that of the rest of the biological world: all of this was well known and written about widely. And in England there was the remarkable Erasmus Darwin, grandfather of Charles.

A few words on Erasmus Darwin are in order here, not only because he was the grandfather of both Charles Darwin and also the great geneticist

Francis Galton, but because he was in his own right one of the most original thinkers ever to have concerned himself with the world of nature. He is best known for his biological-philosophical work *Zoonomia*, published in 1794. He had earlier, however, written two studies, *Botanic Garden* and *Loves of Plants*, which clearly reveal a mind as sensitive to the empirical aspects of biology as to those which took form in his semi-philosophical theory of evolution. In his *Temple of Nature*, published in 1802 just after his death, Erasmus Darwin set forth in verse a view of the ecological order in nature and of the mechanisms of evolution that differs only slightly from that of his more famous grandson Charles. Those today who believe mistakenly that the theory of evolution—even, for that matter, the supporting theory of natural selection—dates back no earlier than from Charles Darwin's *Origin of Species*, published in 1859, need only read the writings of his grandfather.

Nevertheless, it is impossible to take from Charles Darwin either his individual status as scientist or his historic relation to the diffusion of the evolutionary idea throughout modern thought. And throughout his life Charles Darwin was fascinated by the interdependences, the forms of "cooperation," to be found in the natural world. Undoubtedly the best known of all his accounts of these ecological relationships is the one referring to cats, field mice, bumble bees, and red clover: the more house cats, the fewer field mice, and hence the more bees to fertilize and spread the red clover. Reduce the number of cats and the number of mice must shortly grow with consequent destruction of the nests and combs of the bees and, in turn, a diminished supply of red clover, for want of the all-important fertilization supplied by the bees.

> Hence it is quite credible that the presence of a feline animal in large numbers in a district might determine, through the intervention of first mice and then of bees, the frequency of certain flowers in that district! [31]

A later student of the subject, fresh from reading Darwin and knowing the penchant of old maids for cats, carried the ecological equation one step further and made the amount of red clover a function of the number of old maids in a given district.

In a less-known passage, however, Darwin gives us an even more instructive, and for our purposes more relevant, account of the ecological web. It is worth quoting in detail:

> . . . In Staffordshire, on the estate of a relation, where I had ample means of investigation, there was a large and extremely

[31] Charles Darwin, *Origin of Species and The Descent of Man* (New York: Random House, Modern Library, n.d.), p. 59.

barren heath, which had never been touched by the hand of man; but several hundred acres of exactly the same nature had been enclosed twenty-five years previously and planted with Scotch fir. The change in the native vegetation of the planted part of the heath was most remarkable, more than is generally seen in passing from one quite different soil to another: not only the proportional numbers of the heath-plants were wholly changed, but twelve species of plants (not counting grasses and carices) flourished in the plantations, which could not be found on the heath. The effect on the insects must have been still greater, for six insectivorous birds were very common in the plantations, which were not to be seen on the heath; and the heath was frequented by two or three distinct insectivorous birds. *Here we see how potent has been the effect of the introduction of a single tree, nothing else whatever having been done, with the exception of the land having been enclosed, so that cattle could not enter.*[32]

I have stressed Darwin's final sentence because, by making proper analogy, it tells us something else that is very important about the ecological community as it appears in Western history from the time of the founding of the Benedictine monasteries in the sixth century right down to contemporary hippie communes in Oregon or New Mexico. There is not only a profound sense of man's continuous relatedness to other forms of life on earth but also a distinctive sense of hope and promise that arises out of the formation of a mere one or two, or at most a few, such communities in a given area.

Precisely as the introduction of a single kind of tree, in the example given by Darwin, could so vitally affect the character of an entire area, adding in time to the area a large number of plants and insects which could never have originally been anticipated, so, it has been thought by many of eminence in the history of the ecological community, can the introduction of but one or two communities founded in accord with the principles of nature in due time powerfully affect an entire social order. It is in this strictly ecological sense that this form of community indeed has revolutionary possibilities—as revolutionary as was, in its way and for its area, Darwin's Scotch fir.

What Darwinian biology—and ecology generally—contributed to the nineteenth-century theory and practice of the ecological community was, however, nothing as direct as the preceding paragraph might imply. Their contribution was an ever-widening sense of the interdependence of all orders of life on the planet and also—though this is rarely realized with respect to Darwin—a keener appreciation of cooperation and mutual aid

32 Ibid., pp. 57–58. Italics added.

among even the lower forms. There is an interesting section to be found in Darwin's *Descent of Man*, published in 1871, twelve years after his most famous work, in which he describes in some naturalist detail the "social" or "mutual service" proclivities of wild animals and birds:

> The most common mutual service in the higher animals is to warn one another of danger by means of the united senses of all. . . . The leader of a troop of monkeys acts as the sentinel, and utters cries expressive both of danger and of safety. Social animals perform many little services for each other: horses nibble, and cows lick each other, on any spot which itches. . . . Animals also render more important services to one another: thus wolves and some other beasts of prey hunt in packs, and aid one another in attacking their victims. . . . Social animals mutually defend each other. Bull bisons in North America, when there is danger, drive the cows and calves into the middle of the herd, whilst they defend the outside.[33]

What is so often to be found among animals is, Darwin stresses, utterly universal among human beings. Were it not for the "social nature" of man, Darwin argues, which has from the beginning prompted him to live in tightly knit communities, with the individual's communal impulse often higher indeed than his purely self-preservative instinct, the evolution of man, as we know it, would never have taken place.

> As man is a social animal, it is almost certain that he would inherit a tendency to be faithful to his comrades, and obedient to the leader of his tribe; for these qualities are common to most social animals. He would consequently possess some capacity for self-command. He would from an inherited tendency be willing to defend in concert with others his fellow-men; and would be ready to aid them in any way which did not too greatly interfere with his own welfare or his own strong desires.[34]

Such words make evident enough that, however great a stress Darwin did in fact give to competition and conflict among members of the same species as the mechanism of the principle of natural selection, this was by no means the only emphasis in his thinking. All too often lost on the so-called social Darwinists, with the unvarying emphasis in their writings upon the positive and creative effects of struggle and strife, are the clear passages in all of Darwin's major works that stress the indispensability of "mutual service."

---

[33] Ibid., p. 474.   [34] Ibid., pp. 480–81.

Proudhon and Mutualism

Godwin

Strictly speaking, the philosophy of anarchism begins in the nineteenth century not with Proudhon but with the Englishman William Godwin. Godwin's *Enquiry Concerning Political Justice* was published in 1793, when the French Revolution was at its very height. What I have said above about the double and contradictory influences of the Revolution upon anarchism is amply illustrated in Godwin's life and thought. Thrilled though he plainly was by the outbreak of the Revolution in France, he hated the millennialist intensity and the terrorism of the Jacobins, and there was nothing in the extreme political centralization of the Revolution that he could find acceptable. The fundamental argument in the *Enquiry* is that there can be no justice in any form of society that does not conduce to universal happiness. And for Godwin such happiness was inextricably bound up in the virtually absolute freedom of the individual. In Godwin's view, man is naturally good, naturally pacific, and naturally compassionate. Anything that acts as a check upon man's nature must be regarded as potentially tyrannous and contrary to the principle of justice.

Of the anarchist drift in Godwin's thinking there can be no doubt. His dislike of the political state and of private property was boundless. Man's nature requires no external, coercive authority for its beneficent fulfillment: only utter freedom from restraint of any kind. And property, far from being legitimately an individual or even family possession, must be seen as open to all human beings, and the monopoly of none. Centralization, collectivism, bureaucracy in any form—all these are repugnant to Godwin.

But Godwin's anarchism is rooted in the individual alone. It is not the anarchism of the community, the cooperative relationship, which, above all else, this philosophy had become by the time of Proudhon, as it has continued to be down to the present day. There is little if any hint in Godwin of what I call the ecological community, of interdependences among men that are no less interdependences for being rooted in nature. Godwin finds even simple cooperation among a few individuals dangerous in implication, to be avoided as far as possible:

> From these principles it appears that everything that is usually understood by the term "cooperation" is in some degree an evil. A man in solitude is obliged to sacrifice or postpone the execution of his best thoughts to his own convenience. How many admirable designs have perished in the conception by means of this circumstance? The true remedy is for men to reduce their wants to the fewest possible, and as much as possible to simplify the mode of supplying them. It is still worse when a man is also

obliged to consult the convenience of others. If I be expected to eat or to work in conjunction with my neighbour, it must either be at a time most convenient to me, or to him, or to neither of us. We cannot be reduced to a clockwork uniformity.

Hence it follows that all supererogatory cooperation is carefully to be avoided, common labour and common meals. But what shall we say to cooperation that seems to be dictated by the nature of the work to be performed? It ought to be diminished. . . . Hereafter it is by no means clear that the most extensive operations will not be within the reach of one man; or, to make use of a familiar instance, that a plough may not be turned into a field and perform its office without the need of superintendence. It was in this sense that the celebrated Franklin conjectured that "mind would one day become omnipotent over matter." [35]

Whatever Godwin's brilliance of mind, however intense his hatred of coercion, especially political, and of private property, and however great his faith in the freedom that arises from untrammeled human behavior, such a passage as the one above clearly indicates that, anarchist though he may indeed have been, Godwin has only a tangential relation to the ecological community. Ideas of cooperation, communalism, mutual aid, and interdependence are all clearly alien to his thinking. It would be impossible to find a more individualistically oriented mind anywhere in the history of Western thought than that of William Godwin. He was indeed an anarchist in the root sense of the word, but by no stretch of imagination can he properly be brought within the philosophy of the anarchist *community* that first flourished in the writings of Proudhon and that has ever since been the hallmark of the mainstream of anarchism.

Proudhon

Pierre Joseph Proudhon (1809–65) is largely the unfortunate victim of the ascendancy Marx and his followers ruthlessly achieved after about 1870 in western Europe, an ascendancy that permitted nothing but contempt for Proudhon and his ideas within the official circle of socialism. At first drawn together, in the 1840s in Paris, by their common dislike of capitalism and bureaucracy, Marx and Proudhon became bitter enemies. Proudhon was increasingly repelled by Marx's egoism and impatience with any ideas save his own. Marx, in turn, became more and more distrustful of Proudhon's aversion to any kind of revolutionary action that contained the potentialities for centralization of power, terror, and repression. Marx saw his opportunity to demolish Proudhon once and for all when the latter wrote his *Philosophy*

---

[35] William Godwin, *An Enquiry Concerning Political Justice,* ed. Raymond A. Preston, 2 vols. (New York: Alfred A. Knopf, 1926), 2: 267–68.

of Poverty, a book that, though naïve in many respects, has suffered a neglect by subsequent generations out of all proportion to its no doubt substantial faults. Marx, in bitter and satiric reply, wrote his famous *Poverty of Philosophy*, an attack that presaged the hatred Marxists would ever after bear Proudhon and the anarchists.

For all the obloquy that was his fate when radical ascendancy passed to Marx and to German socialists generally, Proudhon must be regarded as one of the most brilliant thinkers of the nineteenth century, far more imaginative than Marx and, very clearly, far more devoted to freedom—both individual and associative.

There can be no question of Proudhon's radicalism. He detested above all things private property and the centralized political state. In 1840 he published his *What Is Property?* His answer rang through the radical circles of Europe: "Property is theft." Proudhon's reputation was made among the militant elements of the then-forming working-class movements, especially in France and, in time, Italy and Spain—countries where anarchism was to remain strong in both principle and action down into the twentieth century. In 1853 appeared Proudhon's great *On Justice*, and then, just after his death, *On the Political Capacity of the Working Classes*, the work that probably exerted the greatest single influence on the European working-class left. In both of these works we have powerful statements of not only Proudhon's hatred of private property and profit, which he saw as the twin pillars of capitalism, but also his hatred of the centralized, bureaucratic state.

Proudhon advanced two major principles of reform and positive revolution—both of which were to take deep root in the anarchist movement everywhere and, by late in the century, to influence Kropotkin strongly. The first was what Proudhon called mutualism; the second was federalism. We shall see the second principle again briefly in the next chapter, on the plural community: federalism is, and has always been, a vital element of the pluralist view of legitimate authority. But it is also a vital element of anarchist doctrine, nowhere more resplendently expressed than in Kropotkin's works, which we shall come to shortly.

By *mutualism* Proudhon meant, in the first instance, an economic system that would, he hoped, replace capitalism. It would be based upon common ownership of property and upon a system of free credit and equitable exchange arising directly from the communal associations in which workers and all other members of society would for the most part live. But mutualism was for Proudhon more than a mere economic principle: he saw it as an expression of the *naturally* mutual ties that could be seen in all parts of human society not yet corrupted by either the private-property system of capitalism or the centralization of the state. Proudhon, unlike Marx and his followers, had profound faith in the family, specifically the patriarchal family. This group, the oldest and most basic representation of mutual aid and of the unforced social bond, would be the key community of the anarchist social order. From it would arise, however, a federal structure of organization and authority: through local community, industrial and agricultural working association, province, all the way up to the central government. Government would not, however, rule the lives of individuals directly. This, Proudhon believed, would lead only to the kind of bureaucratic centralization he hated in the existing state, which he declared to be the product of Rousseau's despotic general will, of Jacobinism, and of the collectivist nationalism everywhere coming into existence. The only true and genuine alternative to existing oppression, Proudhon declared in a definition that has remained classic, is *anarchy*.

> By the word I wanted to indicate the extreme limit of political progress. *Anarchy* is, if I may be permitted to put it this way, a form of government or constitution in which public and private consciousness, formed through the development of science and law, is alone sufficient to maintain order and guarantee all liberties. In it, as a consequence, the institutions of the police, preventive and repressive methods, officialdom, taxation, etc. are reduced to a minimum. In it, more especially, the forms of monarchy and intensive centralization disappear, to be replaced by federal institutions and a pattern of life based on the commune.[36]

Proudhon, unlike Marx (who in his *Manifesto* referred to "the idiocy of rural life") believed deeply not only in agriculture as a way of social life but in the land and physical nature as such. It is this aspect of his thought that places him here in this chapter on the ecological community more fittingly, I believe, than in the chapter on the revolutionary community—even though Proudhon believed with almost religious zeal in the necessity of revolution. In land and in what grows from the soil Proudhon could find, just as had others before him starting with Benedict, all the essential principles of mutuality, of ecological interdependence. To become divorced from the land is to court an alienation of spirit not curable by any of the techniques or luxuries of civilization. Much of the malaise to be found in modern civilization is the consequence, Proudhon believed, of people's no longer being attached directly to the soil:

> People are no longer attached to the land as they used to be. . . . People are attached to the land as they are attached to a tool,

---

[36] *Selected Writings of P. J. Proudhon*, ed. Stewart Edwards, trans. Elizabeth Fraser (New York: Doubleday & Co., Anchor Books, 1969), pp. 91–92. No other single volume in English gives as fine a picture of Proudhon's thought as does this excellent selection.

or even less than that, to something which enables them to levy a certain revenue each year. Gone is the deep feeling for nature, the love of the soil, that only country life can give. In its place is the conventional sensibility peculiar to blasé societies who know nature only as it appears in the novel, the salon or the theatre. . . .

We have lost our feeling for nature. Our generation loves the fields and the woods as the magpie loves the gold it steals. We want them only for their investment value, so that we can indulge our rustic fantasies and build country nursing homes, or so that we can experience pride of possession and be able to say "this is mine." We no longer feel the powerful attraction and sense of communion that exists between man and nature. . . .

Nevertheless, man loves nature more deeply than anything else. I will not try to explain this love—indeed who can explain love—but it is genuine love, and like all real sentiments it has its own mythology.[37]

Proudhon did not believe a reconstruction of the social order could come about without revolution—without, that is, a radical break with tradition and convention: "A revolution is, in the moral sphere, an act of sovereign justice that results from the force of circumstances." [38] Elsewhere he declared, "Revolutions are the successive manifestations of Justice operating in human life. This is why the starting point of each revolution is a preceding revolution." [39] Even so, despite Proudhon's almost odelike appeal to revolution, it is hard to avoid the conclusion that for him the real, true revolution to be worked for is more nearly a built-in process, something akin to what he calls "permanent revolution," than the type of violence-begotten, terror-maintained thing we have seen it to be in the ideals of Jacobins, Marxists, and the followers of Sorel.

A revolution is a force against which no power, divine or human, can prevail; whose nature it is to be strengthened and to grow by the very resistance it encounters. A revolution may be directed, moderated, delayed: I have just said that the wisest policy lay in yielding to it, foot by foot, that the perpetual evolution of Humanity may be accomplished insensibly and silently, instead of by mighty strides. A revolution cannot be crushed, cannot be deceived, cannot be perverted, all the more, cannot be conquered.[40]

37 Ibid., pp. 261–62.   38 Ibid., p. 161.   39 Ibid., p. 158.

40 P. J. Proudhon, *General Idea of the Revolution in the Nineteenth Century*, trans. John Beverley Robinson (London: Freedom Press, 1923), p. 15.

But revolution is for Proudhon a decidedly different thing from what it is for Marx—and also for the Jacobins. It is impossible not to conclude that *revolution*, in Proudhon's thinking, is but a word for any major, decisive, and irreversible change in society. He declares businessmen to be revolutionaries for profoundly altering the economic systems of Europe, Alexander the Great a revolutionary for reuniting Greece, Julius Caesar a revolutionary for founding the Roman Empire, Saint Louis a revolutionary for organizing the guilds in the early Middle Ages.

Proudhon also has a strong sense of revolutions which, though so styled, turn out to be meretricious. The great French Revolution was, Proudhon argues, only half a revolution. While it succeeded in overthrowing the holders of power in *l'ancien régime*, it did not succeed in transforming the system of power itself. What happened, Proudhon tells us, was that power became even greater, more centralized, more oppressive under the Jacobins than it had been under the monarchs:

> The principle of centralization, widely applied by the Committee of Public Safety, passed into a dogma with the Jacobins, who transmitted it to the Empire, and to the governments that followed it. . . . To sum up, the society which the Revolution of '89 should have created, does not yet exist. That which for sixty years we have had, is but a superficial, factitious order, hardly concealing the most frightful chaos and demoralization.[41]

Is the time ripe, Proudhon asks, for another of the genuine revolutions that are only occasionally to be seen in history? His answer is an emphatic yes. The century's political and industrial scene, he declares, is clearly ready for a drastic change:

> All minds, being bewitched with politics, society turns in a circle of mistakes, driving capital to a still more crushing agglomeration, the State to an extension of its prerogatives that is more and more tyrannical, the laboring class to an irreparable decline, physically, morally, and intellectually . . . .
>
> In place of this governmental, feudal, and military rule, imitated from that of the former kings, the new edifice of industrial institutions must be built; in place of this materialist centralization which absorbs all the political power, we must create the intellectual and liberal centralization of economic forces. Labor, commerce, credit, education, property, public morals, philosophy, art, everything in fact requires it of us.

[41] Ibid., pp. 44–45.

I conclude:

There is sufficient cause for a revolution in the nineteenth century.[42]

There are abundant contradictions in Proudhon's thought, as well as lapses of judgment on occasion, the consequences of allowing principle to be carried to any length, however absurd the result; and it would be silly to pretend otherwise. Proudhon was a brilliant thinker, quick in reacting to situations, deeply imaginative, often proceeding by intuition alone. There is nothing in him like the systematic quality we find in Marx's *Capital* or the superbly logical, even scientific, always empirical progression of argument we see in Proudhon's great successor Peter Kropotkin.

What is chiefly notable in Proudhon is the vision of reconstruction yielded by his imagining of a postrevolutionary scene. Far from being a necessitarian, deterministic emanation of the present—as was so much of Marxism's philosophy of history and society—it gives us a genuinely different picture of things, a picture standing in marked opposition to all of the fateful trends of collectivism, uniformity, and centralization that liberals and radicals alike were beginning to worship under the illusion of historical determinism.

To the growing bigness of things economic and political, Proudhon opposed the necessity of a society based upon small groups and communities. These would be only loosely connected in a commune, which would be the next-highest level of organization. Each group—whether a family or a local or work association—would be sovereign over all matters affecting it alone. There would be no masses of individuals each directly related by a potentially tyrannous conception of citizenship to the all-powerful central state. Federalism and mutualism would be the keys to the good society. From mutualism would proceed the groups and communities made desirable by human nature and social function, with a maximum of autonomy in each. From federalism would proceed the necessary political structure of that autonomy to be found in each form of group and association. Thus would be achieved, not direct rule through centralized bureaucracy, but indirect rule, with a high premium placed upon decentralization and division of powers.

We have already seen Proudhon's passion for nature and for rural areas—in such marked contrasts to Marx's denunciation of "the idiocy of rural life"—and his insistence that only through a renewed communion with nature can man realize his true spiritual and moral possibilities. Austerity is a pervading theme of Proudhon's writing. He believed, just as had Saint Benedict more than a thousand years earlier, that the freest and purest life is that lived amid a minimum of luxuries. Nature—the

[42] Ibid., p. 74.

nature of man and the nature reflected by the fields, streams, and trees—
is for Proudhon, as for Benedict and Sir Thomas More, the key to everything. All groups must be natural ones.

> Every time that men with their wives and children assemble
> in one place, live and till the soil side by side, develop in their
> midst different industries, create neighbourly relations among
> themselves and, whether they like it or not, impose on themselves
> a state of solidarity, they form what I call a natural group, which
> soon sets itself up as a political organism, affirming its identity in
> its unity, its independence, its life, its own movement (*autokine-
> sis*) and its autonomy.[43]

Proudhon is the first—many would say the greatest—anarchist. As I
noted above, Godwin's claim to the label of anarchist is supported only by
his repugnance to government and coercion in any form and his faith
in the goodness of man's nature. It is vitiated, however, by his inability,
or refusal, to accept even those forms of relationship among men that are
cooperative and communal in character. Proudhon undoubtedly learned
much from Godwin, or at least from the tradition that Godwin began; but
Proudhon went beyond Godwin in his realization that the individual
man is helpless until he joins with others in some pattern of association,
some form of community, to rescue himself from the aloneness that too
often breeds despair, morbidity, and helplessness. It was the philosophy of
mutualism, of mutual aid and love, founded by Saint Benedict above all
others and given lasting expression by the gentle but resolute Sir Thomas
More in his *Utopia*, that Proudhon presented as a radical way going beyond Godwin's noble but inherently fallacious individualism. With this
profoundly communal ethic of mutualism went federalism: the necessary
counterpart of the mutual-aid community, for all the occasional Proudhonian idiosyncrasies that could carry it to pragmatic absurdities. As we
shall see in the next chapter on the plural community, there is a powerful
bond between the conservatism of an Edmund Burke or an Alexis de
Tocqueville and the radicalism of a Proudhon or a Kropotkin, to whom
we turn now, the essence of which is their common conviction of the
affinity between the ecological community and a system of authority in
the larger society predicated upon decentralization and federalism.

Kropotkin and Mutual Aid

Of all the anarchists, however, it is Peter Kropotkin who deserves our
greatest attention. He was, by all accounts, an admirable human being,

---

[43] P. J. Proudhon, *On Justice*, quoted in James Joll, *The Anarchists* (Boston:
Little, Brown and Co., 1964), p. 77. This study of anarchism cannot be praised too
highly for its lucidity and its scholarly detachment, combined with an overall sympathy
and respect for its subject.

with an excellence of character like that of Saint Benedict and Sir Thomas More. Anarchist by principle, adored by Europe's working classes, he nevertheless never, so far as we have record, incurred the enmity of governments either in the capitalist West or, after the Bolshevik Revolution of 1917, in Soviet Russia, whose system of government he opposed just as profoundly as he did capitalism.

Born in Moscow in 1842, the son of a wealthy and powerful noble family, with the title of prince, he almost immediately attracted attention for both intellectual and moral reasons. He was actually a page in the czar's household for a time, and later rose to high position in government office. All the while he was serving his government, however, he was at one and the same time adding to his knowledge of both the physical and the social worlds. His quest for the first took him all over Siberia and much of Asia, as well as Russia; that for the second took him into spheres of society, especially the peasantry and working class, that he would normally, as a high-born Russian, never have seen.

It was his interest in the peasantry and their culture, which he acquired fairly early in his life, that was to prove decisive for his own career. Not only a student of the peasantry, he was also, with rising intensity, their advocate, and it was not long before his political work in their behalf led to imprisonment in 1873. He managed to escape after two years, fleeing to France, and all of his property was confiscated by the Russian imperial government. His political beliefs, by this time anarchist in character, cost him imprisonment in France; but such was the personal esteem in which he was held that he was pardoned, never again to be imprisoned though he did not at any time relinquish or even moderate his deep commitment to the principles of anarchism. He spent most of his remaining years in England, though for a considerable period of time he lived in the United States—where, despite the fact that anarchism was at that time feared almost as much as religious heresies had been in the Middle Ages, he seems to have aroused no hostility. He was invited to contribute articles to some of the major journals and papers of the day, and not infrequently attended meetings of scientific and scholarly societies. He gave many lectures in the United States, in some of the greatest academic institutions. In Europe, especially in France and the Latin countries of Italy and Spain, he had an almost godlike significance for members of working-class movements, who revered him as much for his personal integrity—everywhere known as incorruptible—as for his social and political principles in their behalf.

Following the triumph there of the Bolsheviks, Kropotkin returned to his beloved Russia. There he found the same acceptance and was held in the same esteem as in Europe and America, though he never concealed his deep opposition to the tenets and practices of Bolshevism—and, for that matter, much of Marxism, in whatever manifestation. When he died in 1921, the Communist government offered a full state funeral, declined by Kropotkin's family in accord with his own simple anarchist wishes in these matters, and made his birthplace a museum containing his books and manuscripts, as well as the substantial collection of artifacts he had gathered through a long and rich lifetime together with the many honors heaped upon him by peoples throughout the world.

Although Kropotkin's philosophy, like Proudhon's, was revolutionary in essence and implication, there is little about revolution in his writings. This may well be invariably the case with those who are the true revolutionaries in man's history, those whose ideas contain the most radical changes.

Indeed, anarchism as a philosophy and way of life is singularly free of revolutionary utterance, in the sense of *revolution* used by Marx and his inheritors. As we have just seen, Proudhon's use of the word was almost identical with "developmental tendency in society" or "historical interruption of continuity." Even where revolutionary aspiration has gone beyond this, it has been largely through expressed ideal and through example, rather than through advocacy of force and violence. The nearest thing to an exception lies in a brief period in the life of Bakunin, another major nineteenth-century anarchist figure, imposing in presence and utterance but with a mind far from the stature of either Proudhon's (and before him Godwin's) or Kropotkin's. Russian-born, of an impulsive and generally uncritical nature though not without an occasional touch of inspired genius, Bakunin came for a short time under the influence of another Russian, the baleful but superficially attractive terrorist Nechaev. This man is described by James Joll as a "self-made revolutionary, a dark, lonely tortuous man, part *poseur*, part fanatic, part idealist, part criminal." [44]

It was under Nechaev's influence, brief and uncharacteristic though it was among the major influences on his life, that Bakunin for a time turned to the advocacy of violence and terror. In collaboration with Nechaev, Bakunin wrote a work called *Revolutionary Catechism* and another called *Principles of Revolution*, as well as several briefer tracts, all proclaiming the necessity and holiness of revolutionary terror. In one of these occur the following words:

> The revolutionary despises and hates present-day social morality in all its forms . . . he regards everything as moral which helps the triumph of revolution. . . . All soft and enervating feelings of friendship, relationship, love, gratitude, even honour, must be stifled in him by a cold passion for the revolutionary cause. . . . Day and night he must have one thought, one aim—merciless destruction.

[44] Joll, op. cit., p. 94. Joll is absolutely correct in his reference to Bakunin and to Nechaev's influence on him as an interregnum in the history of anarchism.

> We must recognize no other activity but the work of exter-
> mination, but we admit that the forms in which this activity will
> show itself will be extremely varied—poison, the knife, the rope,
> etc. In this struggle, revolution sanctifies everything alike.[45]

The mannered, romantic, and almost fatuously stylized character of
the preceding words will be recognized by almost everyone. Nechaev himself proved shortly after these lines were written to be nothing at all
of a revolutionary in any genuine spiritual and social sense of the word:
only a barely sane, pathological type, driven by his own inner compulsions
to mindless actions culminating eventually in the senseless, motiveless
murder of a Russian student. The consequences of this he was able to
escape for a time by fleeing Russia; then he made an effort to seduce the
great Herzen's daughter for her money, his life finally ending in sordid
imprisonment in Russia. There is not the slightest indication that
Nechaev's life was even remotely inspired by any interest in or love of
people. But of his dark fascination to others there is, unhappily, not the
least question.

Bakunin himself emerged from his Nechaev-induced spell of intoxication with the uses of violence and returned to the espousal of nonviolence
that is the hallmark of the main tradition of anarchism. Unfortunately,
what he wrote during his association with Nechaev remained in print, to
inspire several individuals, among them the assassins of President McKin-
ley in the United States in 1901 and of the Archduke Ferdinand in Serbia
in 1914, to acts of violence that had ugly effects upon the anarchist movement for a fairly long period of time.

But, except in the sense we have seen revolution to have in Proudhon's work—evolutionary, in fact—any ideas of forced and violent change
have been utterly alien to the anarchist tradition. And it is for this reason
that a man of Kropotkin's great stature, for all his uncompromising profession of the anarchist creed, could enjoy the respect of so many whose
social and economic views were diametrically opposed.

Kropotkin's greatest work, without question, is his *Mutual Aid: A
Factor in Evolution*. As I suggested in the preceding section, this book,
the most learned of all anarchist works, took its immediate departure from
his awareness of how seriously misunderstood Darwinian biology was in
his own time. Kropotkin was himself a geographer and naturalist, and
he knew very well the many manifestations of the ecological principle in
nature—just as, being also a learned social scientist, he was aware of the
kinds of ecological relationship in human society to which Adam Smith
and the economists had pointed. For Kropotkin—unlike the millennialist-
and revolution-inspired socialists of his day—the prime objective was not
the total extermination of any order, capitalist or other, but rather the
removal through peaceful, nonviolent means—including the kinds of

---

[45] Ibid., p. 95.

utopian communalism we have seen—of all those forces presently in the social order that repress, defeat, or hide the *very substantial manifestations of mutual aid already existing.* The prime goal of reconstruction, Kropotkin thought, was, first, to forget the catchwords *capitalism, revolution,* and *socialism,* each conceived as an absolute, and then to work in any one of scores of ways for the ascendancy in society of the principle of mutual aid, building on such examples of it, like the guilds, village communities, co-operatives, communal experiments, and so on, as are already present, though in too small number.

What we find in *Mutual Aid* is a brilliant and learned exposition of the ecological principle of cooperation among orders of life throughout nature and society. Its very chapter headings indicate this: "Mutual Aid among Animals," "Mutual Aid among Savages," "Mutual Aid among Barbarians," "Mutual Aid in the Medieval City," "Mutual Aid amongst Ourselves." The point of Kropotkin's book is to demonstrate conclusively that the major constitutive processes in human history—the hallmarks of what is distinctively human, what has been most universal and, indeed, has survived the longest—far from being individualism, competition, and struggle, have in fact been the very opposite of these: community, co-operation, and mutuality.

> After having discussed the importance of mutual aid in various classes of animals, I was evidently bound to discuss the importance of the same factor in the evolution of Man. This was the more necessary as there are a number of evolutionists who may not refuse to admit the importance of mutual aid among animals, but who, like Herbert Spencer, will refuse to admit it for Man. For primitive Man—they maintain—war of each against all was *the* law of life. . . .[46]

Kropotkin gives us a massively illustrated and documented account of the long succession of patterns of mutual aid in human society. He does not, like so many writers—alas, even still today—on primitive society, on early historical society, and above all on medieval society, make the invidious distinction between "traditional" and "modern," with the almost invariable implication that what is not "modern" must be utterly irrelevant at best, superstitious and obsolete at worst. For Kropotkin there is as much to be learned and admired in the communal structures of the so-called primitive peoples or the Germanic barbarians or the peoples of the Middle Ages as in those of our own time. Evolutionist though Kropotkin was, he still did not deem bad or obsolete everything past, or good or inevitable everything present. It was a major article of his philosophical

---

[46] Peter Kropotkin, Preface to *Mutual Aid: A Factor of Evolution* (London: William Heineman, 1908), pp. xiv–xv.

principles that we can learn from the past as well as the present, from the simpler peoples as well as the complex ones.

Hence occur the superb discussions in the book of not merely the clans of primitive peoples but also their often remarkably complex non-kinship systems of mutual aid and cooperation; hence his expert and sympathetic treatment of the medieval institutions of guild, monastery, and village community—the latter a form of agriculture still strong in his native Russia but fast going out of existence in western Europe, even in the remotest corners, as the result of enclosure acts and the substitution of practices of individualism, competition, and private profit; and hence, finally, his exhaustive description of the patterns of mutual aid still found among us in the present: age-old neighborhood structures, communal effort even in towns, extended families, and—even more interesting and important, Kropotkin thought—new forms of mutual aid such as great consumer and producer cooperatives, labor unions, insurance companies, and the like.

The overriding argument that Kropotkin sought always to make in his major writings was that the task of reform, even of revolution in the nonviolent sense of the word, was to uncover existing patterns of mutuality, identify them, and reinforce them; in short, to regard them as good and to be used as building blocks for the future—rather than, as did the Bolsheviks so momentously after they took power in Russia, to declare *everything* in a social order corrupt or degenerate or obsolete, and to obliterate even those Russian cooperatives and village communities where the socialist ideal, albeit in primitive form, had so long flourished. Even industry, Kropotkin pointed out, had flourished on the basis of impulses and structures that were cooperative rather than competitive:

> To attribute, therefore, the industrial progress of our century to the war of each against all which it has proclaimed, is to reason like the man who, knowing not the causes of rain, attributes it to the victim he has immolated before his clay idol. For industrial progress, as for each other conquest over nature, mutual aid and close intercourse certainly are, as they have been, much more advantageous than mutual struggle.[47]

It was Kropotkin's goal to found ethics on the principle of mutual aid. To this end he went back to the evolutionary origins of things:

> That mutual aid is the real foundation of our ethical conceptions seems evident enough. But whatever the opinions as to the first origin of the mutual-aid feeling or instinct may be—whether a biological or supernatural cause is ascribed to it—we

[47] Ibid., p. 298.

must trace its existence as far back as to the lowest stages of the animal world; and from these stages we can follow its uninterrupted evolution, in opposition to a number of contrary agencies, through all degrees of human development, up to the present times. . . .[48]

Although Kropotkin was an anarchist, deeply devoted to the expressions of mutual aid that were connected with the utopian movement of his century and, as we have seen, profoundly antagonistic to the ethos of both capitalist and nationalist systems, he was yet able to recognize the possibilities of reform within both these systems. He did not, in other words, make the mistake, self-defeating in the long run, of assuming that because *some* or even *many* aspects of the society around him were bad, therefore *all* aspects were bad, contaminated like apples in a barrel from the existence of a single rotten one. This, he thought, was one of the cardinal errors and evils of Bolshevist philosophy. It was both possible and constructive, Kropotkin believed, to work with what materials one had and within whatever part of the system one found oneself living.

That is why his *Fields, Factories, and Workshops*, published in 1898, is such a momentous and, when correctly understood, still highly relevant work. It falls in not only the ecological but the pluralist-decentralist traditions of thought on community. Anything that could be done within the present system, Kropotkin believed, to encourage the ecological principle of balance between industry and agriculture, between mental and manual work, could not fail to help in building the better society he saw as the successor to the present one. This book belongs to the level of social-science studies that had really begun with Frederick Le Play in France, and was to include in due time the seminal works of Patrick Geddes and Victor Branford in England, of Gusti in Rumania, and of Lewis Mumford in the United States: studies of the social order that were almost impeccably objective, uniting analysis and observation on the one hand with near searchlight vision on the other. Much of what we today call regional or city planning commenced with these studies. Idealistic in theme, they were yet founded on the realities of means and ends. They did not make means sovereign over ends; and they did not, in arriving at ends, convert human society into an assemblage of angels.

What Kropotkin dares to point out in this book—and his boldness is more impressive when set against the socialist rather than the capitalist gospel of the time—is that the best contributions of even the accepted industrial-capitalist order are to be found in the witting or unwitting preservation of the balance between industry and agriculture and between intellectual and manual labor. Throughout the book, as is equally true of *Mutual Aid*, is a realization of the necessity of this balance if society is

48 Ibid.

not to become so one-sided in its development as to court both corruption and eventual breakdown. That same reverence for the ecological principle of balance we have seen to exist in Benedict, and then in Sir Thomas More and also—though differently oriented—in Charles Darwin, we find in Kropotkin.

But whereas Adam Smith had seen in division of labor a principle of social harmony, Kropotkin, much more in the spirit of Alexis de Tocqueville, saw in it, when exaggerated and exploited, the possibility of the degradation of the human being:

> Skilled artisanship is being swept away as a survival of a past condemned to disappear. The artist who formerly found esthetic enjoyment in the work of his hands is substituted by the human slave of an iron slave. Nay, even the agricultural labourer, who formerly used to find a relief from the hardships of his life in the home of his ancestors—the future home of his children—in his love of the field and in a keen intercourse with nature, even he has been doomed to disappear for the sake of division of labour. He is an anachronism, we are told; he must be substituted, in a Bonanza farm, by an occasional servant hired for the summer, and discharged as the autumn comes: a tramp who will never again see the field he has harvested once in his life.[49]

Kropotkin was no hater of machines, no categorical dismisser of technology—quite the contrary. There is, he says, "hardly one single branch of industry into which machinery work could not be introduced with great advantage, at least at some of the stages of manufacture." [50]
The point is, not that machinery be repudiated but that it be assimilated into social contexts within which not only machinery but human personality and human relationships prosper. It is, above all things, the "industrial village" that Kropotkin sees as the sole hope of any humane, life-giving assimilation of technology and industry:

> Why should not the cottons, the woolen cloth, and the silks, now woven by hand in the villages, be woven by machinery in the same villages, without ceasing to remain connected with work in the fields? Why should not hundreds of domestic industries, now carried on entirely by hand, resort to labour-saving machines, as they already do in the knitting trade and many others? There

---

[49] Peter Kropotkin, *Fields, Factories, and Workshops: Or, Industry Combined with Agriculture and Brain Work with Manual Work* (London: Thomas Nelson and Sons, 1898), p. 19.

[50] Ibid., p. 350.

is no reason why the small motor should not be of a much more general use than it is now, wherever there is no need to have a factory, wherever factory work is preferable, as we already see it in certain villages in France.[51]

Kropotkin was wise enough to see that the essential, lasting problem of technology and industry could never be solved merely by the ordinary socialist response of having "government" or "the people" take them over, that is, collectivizing them. The only answer, Kropotkin felt, was a massive decentralization of modern industry—and also of the whole political structure—and the preservation of the village, to him the prime hope of industry, as it had been for many thousands of years of agriculture. Granted that there are a few types of industry which by their nature must have a different context: "oceanic steamers cannot be built in villages." Well and good; but why, Kropotkin asks, must all industry, the five-sixths, even nine-tenths, including that which does not demand special sites and clusterings of workers, be patterned after the tiny part, such as coal mines and steel mills, that do? Why deprive human beings of opportunities for the open fields, for part-time participation in agriculture, for the feel of nature which, on all evidence, they so largely seek, when by abandoning the present inherited system of centralized industry and government, it would be possible for workers in industry to be at one and the same time workers in the fields?

> The moral and physical advantages which man would derive from dividing his work between the field and the workshop are self-evident. But the difficulty, we are told, is in the necessary centralization of the modern industries. In industry as well as in politics centralisation has so many admirers! But in both spheres the ideal of the centralisers badly needs revision.[52]

Kropotkin was no romantic lover of agriculture and manual work for their own sakes. He gives us instances of agricultural communities seriously disadvantaged in all respects by their distance from both the machinery and the mechanical skills that could render such a labor-saving boon to agricultural workers. In itself, industry, like manual work of any kind, is just as great a boon, a virtue, as living in and working in the fields. There is nothing in Kropotkin of the cult of nature, the kind of thing that so filled the late eighteenth century, with people of the upper classes sighing over the beauties of nature but hesitating to leave their drawing rooms and not hesitating to exploit the farm workers grievously. Kropotkin sees many hardships in the agricultural village that could be and

[51] Ibid., p. 351.   [52] Ibid., p. 352.

should be relieved by technology and by seasonal opportunity for farm workers to work in industry. "Agriculture cannot develop without the aid of machinery, and the use of a perfect machinery cannot be generalised without industrial surroundings: without mechanical workshops, easily accessible to the cultivator of the soil, the use of agricultural machinery is not possible." [53]

What, in sum, is required—and for Kropotkin it does not seem important whether the overall system is called socialism or capitalism or whatever—is a balance everywhere between industry and agriculture, and also between intellectual work and manual:

> Have the factory and the workshop at the gates of your fields and gardens, and work in them. Not those large establishments, of course, in which huge masses of metals have to be dealt with and which are better placed at certain spots indicated by Nature, but the countless variety of workshops and factories which are required to satisfy the infinite diversity of tastes among civilised men . . . factories and workshops into which men, women and children will not be driven by hunger, but will be attracted by the desire of finding an activity suited to their tastes, and where, aided by the motor and the machine, they will choose the branch of activity which best suits their inclinations. . . . Very soon you will yourselves feel interested in that work, and you will have occasion to admire in your children their eager desire to become acquainted with Nature and its forces, their inquisitive inquiries as to the powers of machinery, and their rapidly developing inventive genius.[54]

Such is Kropotkin's adaptation and development of the ideal of the ecological community that, as we have seen, came into existence during the final days of the Roman Empire, when, in Benedict's view of the situation, the hope of mankind lay in starting afresh, seeking once again that balance of nature, that equilibrium between intellectual and manual labor, between field and workshop, between activity and creative leisure, demanded by the human mind and character for their highest expression. Allowing for all the differences between Kropotkin's age and Benedict's, and between that of either and Sir Thomas More's, we cannot but be struck by the similar nature of the crises all three minds saw in the

---

53 Ibid., p. 358.

54 Ibid., pp. 417–18. We know that the great Mohandas Gandhi in India was deeply influenced by Kropotkin's ideas. Gandhi made preservation of the Indian village community and a balance between agriculture and manufactures crucial in his movement. The anarchist movement has also generally made these objectives paramount in its philosophy.

societies around them, and the similar nature, too, of their responses. For Peter Kropotkin, as for Saint Benedict and Sir Thomas More, the problem of community, that is, genuine and lasting community, resolved itself into a rediscovery of nature: not merely the protection and proper development of nature in the external, physical and biological, sense, but also in the sense of seeking to build community—and in the long run, society as a whole—on the most natural of interdependences among men, such as the village, autonomous association, and region, and, finally, on the natural division of man's intellectual and manual abilities.

6 The Plural Community

History and Pluralism

It has been the fate of pluralism in Western thought to take a rather poor second place to philosophies which make their point of departure the premise of, not the diversity and plurality of things, but, rather, some underlying unity and symmetry, needing only to be uncovered by pure reason to be then deemed the "real," the "true," and the "lasting." William James, the great American philosopher and psychologist, once divided all human minds into the tender minded and the tough minded. The former, James wrote, include those who, beginning with Plato, have declared unity and system to govern all things. The latter are those who, distrusting all unitary systems, find reality to lie in the concrete and the particular, in multiplicity and plurality rather than in unity.

It is not strange, if one reflects on the matter a moment, that most of us should prefer unity to plurality—whether in life or in our intellectual efforts to explain life and the universe. Human thought, abstract thought at any rate, begins with religion. As Durkheim argued, though admittedly not with complete proof, even the basic categories of our thinking stem from what were once religious categories. And the very essence of religion is belief in some pervading spirit or god or being that is at once sacred and unifying. Foremost in each of the great world religions from the time they arose was the idea of a single omnipresent, omnipotent god.

With the rise of rationalism in ancient Greece, the ideal of unity remained as vivid as in the preceding age of reliance upon gods and goddesses for explanation. That it reduce complexity to simplicity is, of course, one of the common criteria of explanation—artistic, philosophical, or scientific. When one can point to a dozen different things and prove that they are no more than appearance and that reality lies in some single substance of which the dozen things are but unreal manifestations, he has, by the lights of most of us, effected a major illumination of reality. There were Greek philosophers, among them the Pythagoreans, who declared reality to be one, all that appears plural being illusions of our senses. And from the time of the Greek rationalists down to the present day, there has been an almost irresistible allure in the writings of those philosophers and social scientists concerned with the nature of social behavior who have found, or thought they have found, a unitary system, pattern, and organization.

It is no different with community and its philosophers. The monistic spirit of Plato has been overwhelmingly dominant in Western thinking on the subject of political organization. The idea of sovereignty, which clearly implies but one absolute power lying in the social order, with all relationships, all individuals indeed, ultimately subject to it, has been the characteristic approach to the political community, as we have seen, since the time of Cleisthenes.

Even so, there have been some momentous exceptions to this political monism in the West—not many, to be sure, and not honored in nearly so extravagant a fashion as the monistic systems, but present nonetheless in the Western tradition. I call these exceptions *pluralism*, and our concern in this chapter will be with those thinkers who have resisted the appeal of the One, the unitary and the monistic, and have found not merely reality but freedom and justice and equity to lie in plurality.

There have been several scenes in history notable for their expression of pluralism in social thought. In one of the earliest, Aristotle was able to observe some of the consequences of the kind of absolute unity of community written about by his teacher, Plato, and effected by his own one-time pupil, Alexander the Great, in the great, centralized, sprawling Alexandrian empire. Living in such a setting, Aristotle found himself responding in praise of diversity, plurality, and differences of both cultural and intellectual kind. He was also to feel compelled to praise the virtues of decentralized authority in society and the proliferation of as many distinct forms of associative life as are reconcilable with the demands of stability and liberty.

Or the scene may be like that in which Althusius found himself at the beginning of the seventeenth century in western Europe: one characterized by the strivings of nationalist monarchs to impose political centralization upon the still predominantly feudal society of the West, and by the emerging concern of such thinkers as Hobbes, and before him Bodin and Machiavelli, with removing as much traditional diversity as possible and, especially in Hobbes's case, making the legal-political community not merely absolute but allowing the existence within itself of no other significant kind of community. It was against such emerging ideas that Althusius wrote his great work on pluralism—nearly a half century, actually, before Hobbes's *Leviathan* appeared—giving Western society the momentous concept, revived from medieval law, of *communitas communitatum*, that is, a community of communities, rather than the kind of monolithic aggregate based upon centralization and atomization that Althusius saw reflected in the works of those who took as their model the modern national state, sprung from the Renaissance. And with this vision of the diverse, plural community, Althusius presented also the vital principles of decentralization of political power and intermediation of membership in the state—principles to which we shall return in several of the contexts that follow.

Or, to come down closer to our own day, there is the scene presented by nineteenth-century Europe, a scene compounded of the elements of nationalism, bureaucracy, and military centralization. The first to respond in memorable fashion to this scene was Edmund Burke, whose remarkable *Reflections on the Revolution in France*, published in 1790, was not only, as events proved, the most accurate forecast of the course that revolution would take but a signal prophecy of other revolutionary trends in the nineteenth and twentieth centuries. And after Burke came Tocqueville, Burckhardt, Weber, and Durkheim, different in their individual thrusts of mind and spirit but alike in their perceptions of the harm being done western European society by the twin forces of political centralization and economic atomization, and alike too in their vision of an alternative pluralist, decentralized society, as we can see clearly enough in their writings.

Admitting the fact that the pluralist envisagement of community has never had the sheer appeal, the capacity to generate movements in its behalf, of the political, religious, and revolutionary communities, we cannot be blind, nevertheless, to the persisting effect some of the intellectual elements of this form of community have had on Western thought.

The Elements of the Plural Community

Plurality

The first of the conceptual elements of the plural community is precisely that suggested by the word *plural* itself: that is, plurality. The good community is not founded upon a single objective or pursuit—whether kinship, religion, or politics—but upon a plurality of communities, each holding its proper and due place in the larger social order. Hence, as noted above, derives the all-important idea of *communitas communitatum,* community of communities. The nature of man cannot be confined by any single value, expressed by any single kind of relationship. The potential diversity of the human mind must be matched by a diversity of types of community within the social order, each as autonomous as possible within its own sphere of function, each with a measure of authority of its own based upon its unique function and no more disposed to transgress upon the function and authority of any other community than to have its own function and authority invaded. The plural community is not only characterized socially by plurality of membership in groups, association, and a wide range of communities but also culturally by diversity of belief and idea and style of living. Such diversity is no more indeed than the cultural accompaniment of social plurality.

Autonomy

What characterizes the pluralist view of autonomy can best be epitomized in the word *functional*: each group or community within the larger community should be endowed with the greatest possible autonomy consistent with performance of its function *and* with performance by other groups and communities of the functions embedded in them by tradition or plan. The family, the church, the labor union, the university: each of these is an association built around a very distinctive function. The success of each will be dependent, therefore, upon the degree of autonomy it possesses in the performance of its distinctive function—and, too, in its sense of freedom from unnecessary encroachments by other associations in society such as the larger, encompassing political government.

Decentralization

Authority in society—the larger system of authority and structure of authority within each of the component communities and associations—should be as far as possible from centralization in one single body or individual. How, indeed, can centralization of power avoid dislocating, even atomizing, those associations in society that seek to maintain their functions but see their authority diminished through transfer of powers to some central agency? Whether in political government, church, labor union, corporation, or university, there is, as abundant evidence suggests, a degree of centralization beyond which lies only progressive atrophy of smaller units within. Hence comes the stress, from Aristotle to the nineteenth-century anarchists—and also, interestingly enough, as we shall see, the nineteenth-century European conservatives—upon decentralization, upon delegation of authority to the associations and communities composing the social order.

Hierarchy

There is no form of community, whether kinship, military, or revolutionary, without some system of stratification of function and responsibility. Wherever two or more people associate more or less regularly, there is bound to be some form of stratification or hierarchy, no matter how fleeting and minor. In the plural community, however, hierarchy of function and authority is made a prized, built-in attribute. Hierarchy is not merely unavoidable; it is good in itself, and should be recognized as such. The plural community is, from the viewpoint of its philosophers, a kind of chain of being, which rises from the smallest possible communal link at the bottom to the most important—in the cultural as well as political sense—at the top. The units of hierarchy in the plural community are like the vertebrae of the backbone. They are as indispensable to structure as are any of the nonhierarchical, "horizontal" segments of society. As there is a stratification of values and goals in any civilized community, so is there bound to be a stratification of the groups and communities reflecting these values and goals. All efforts to pretend otherwise can but lead to the leveling and atomization that produce the mass society.

Tradition

Defined strictly and according to etymology, tradition means only the handing down, the transferring, of ideals and practices. There is a strong element of the customary and the habitual in tradition. Commonly we contrast law and tradition, though obviously law may itself become a tradition, and tradition—usually, however, only when there are alarming signs of the scuttling of tradition by minorities—may become the basis of law. The philosophers of the plural community, however, almost unfailingly treat tradition as something emerging from community, from consensus, from a stable base of social interaction that makes law in the formal and prescriptive sense unnecessary. The plural community, as we find it for the most part in Western thought, and especially in the writings of Althusius, Burke, and Tocqueville, is characterized overwhelmingly by tradition in contrast to law, that is, formal, calculated, and prescriptive regulations. As the good society is regarded by the philosophers of the plural school as a hierarchy of communities, so is it regarded as a hierarchy of traditions.

Localism

Last is the element of localism. The emphasis on the family, neighborhood, small community, and local association is strong in the philosophy of the plural community. In many ways, the greatest single cause of the antipathy toward modern society that we find among the nineteenth- and twentieth-century philosophers of pluralism is the fact that, in Disraeli's words, "modern society acknowledges no neighbors." A half century before Disraeli wrote those words, the great Edmund Burke, writing in opposition to the centralization and nationalization wrought by the leaders of the French Revolution, declared:

> No man was ever attached by a sense of pride, partiality, or real affection to a description of square measurement. . . . We begin our public affections in our families. . . . We pass on to our neighborhoods, and our habitual provincial connections.[1]

The sense of place, of locality, is a profound one, as we shall see, in the philosophy of the plural community. Most alienation, it is thought, by whatever name it is called—estrangement, rootlessness, anomie—is the consequence of human beings' having been uprooted from place, from accustomed habitat, separated from what Burke called the "inns and resting-places" of the human spirit.

Aristotle: The Revolt against Platonism

The plural community really begins in the West with Aristotle's *Politics*. More concretely, it may be said to begin with Aristotle's systematic and relentless, if dry, criticism of his teacher, Plato, and of Plato's inspired portrait of the political community, which we have already considered in this book. Where Plato had expressed his craving for and adoration of unity, Aristotle, in less brilliant but no less profound fashion, called for plurality, diversity, and division in the good community and saw in the search for unity carried too far the danger of not only tyranny and suffocation of spirit but even subversion of the political community itself.

Two thinkers more unlike than Plato and Aristotle it would be hard to conceive, and there is some humor, therefore, in the fact that the latter should have been Plato's student for nearly twenty years. Plato's mind excelled in the qualities of the prophet and the artist. As we saw in the account of his political community, there was not merely religious

---

[1] Edmund Burke, *Reflections on the Revolution in France* (New York: Holt, Rinehart & Winston, 1965), p. 243. This classic testament of conservatism and criticism of revolution was first published in 1790.

but also lyrical, poetical insight in his treatment of politics. For sheer intuitive, prophetic, lasting brilliance, it is doubtful that Plato has been surpassed, or perhaps even equaled, in all Western history. For all his understanding of the nature of politics and the appeal of the political community, Plato's mind was that of the religious poet. Aristotle, in sharp contrast, was the scholar, the researcher, the empiricist. This is not to imply that he was lacking in qualities of intellectual brilliance and profundity, only that he regarded brilliance and profundity with suspicion unless these qualities were supported by study, analysis, and observation of all relevant data. We see precisely the same distinction between Plato and Aristotle as we shall see between such eighteenth-century philosophes as Diderot, Condorcet, and Rousseau and such late-eighteenth- and nineteenth-century pluralists as Burke and Tocqueville. We find Plato, like the philosophes, rich in appeal to pure reason, in intuitive boldness, and in revolutionary impulse, desiring unity and centralization above all; whereas we find Aristotle, like the pluralists, rich in the opposite of these qualities, appealing to observation, experience, tradition, and study, rather than pure insight.[2]

Aristotle, born in 384 B.C., was the son of a successful physician in Thrace, which undoubtedly accounts for, first, his lifelong interest in biology and, second, his concern with natural classifications, which was to extend in time to the constitutions of the Greek states. He went to Plato's school in Athens simply because it was the best to be found, and he stayed there for twenty years until Plato's death in 347. Aristotle then spent the next twelve years in various activities, apparently involving much traveling, and it was undoubtedly during this period that he commenced his writing. For a while he was tutor to the young Alexander of Macedon, destined to become the greatest warrior-emperor of the ancient Hellenistic world before Rome's final ascendancy, and we may assume that Aristotle followed his illustrious pupil's subsequent career with much interest. In the year 335 Aristotle opened his own school in Athens, and most of the works by which he is known today were written during the dozen years that followed. He died in 322, just one year after the death of Alexander the Great.

Despite the historic association of Alexander and Aristotle, and Aristotle's undoubted interest in the campaigns and political achievements of his former pupil, there is little if any direct evidence of the impact of the Alexandrian empire, or of the momentous fusion of peoples that took place as the consequence of Alexander's victories in the Near Eastern world stretching all the way to India, on Aristotle's work. The

---

2 It would be as wrong to imply that the first-named tendency of mind has been lacking in knowledge and experience as that the second has been lacking in brilliance and prophetic insight. We are concerned only with overriding emphasis, with general thrust.

sociologist in Aristotle might have been expected to show more interest in the demographic, social, and cultural results of the mixing of Hellenes with the many peoples to the east. But the fact is, no such interest is to be found.

Yet, even so, there are solid grounds for assuming that a good many of the differences to be found between Plato's approach and Aristotle's are the result of the latter's living in the world of Alexander rather than that rather dismal, melancholy, profoundly defeated world that had been Plato's—the world of the beloved polis, the Athenian city-state, *in extremis.* It was, as we saw, Plato's obsession with the crisis of the polis which, more than anything else, led to his preoccupation with an ideal community, political to the core, possessing all the unity, order, and measured symmetry he felt had been lost as the result of not merely Athens's defeat by Sparta but endemic diseases of polity.

Aristotle was farther away in time from the traumatic experience of the fall of Athens. But in his world existed the phenomenon of Alexandrian empire, with techniques of rule and aspects of government and power that Plato could not have guessed at. I am inclined to think that, notwithstanding Aristotle's preoccupation with what he saw as Plato's errors, it was as much as anything the spectacle of the Alexandrian empire—its triumphs, yes, but also its fatal flaws, the result of imperial centralization, bureaucratization, and loss of consensus—that inspired him to turn from his beloved biological world to the problems of politics.

In any event, we get in Aristotle's *Politics* a very different view of the legitimate political community from that which Plato had provided. Enchantment may be lacking in Aristotle's pages; as I have said, no one could claim for a moment that Aristotle on politics is nearly as fascinating, or even as interesting, as Plato. But if one will give himself to the reading of the *Politics,* overlooking the somewhat disorganized sequences of argument and seemingly random insertion of empirical data in passages where they do not always seem to be very pertinent, he will find some of the wisest, most astute, and learned observations on the nature of community to be found anywhere in Western history. Aristotle was without any question the most erudite, most widely and deeply learned mind for his period that the West has known. Quite apart from the investigations he and his students at Athens conducted in the realms of astronomy, physics, chemistry, meteorology, climatology, and all aspects of biology, we know that there were numerous and extensive projects of research as well in the social and political sciences; for example, the famous examination of the histories and natures of the political constitutions of more than a hundred and fifty Greek cities. Only one of these, that on the city of Athens, has survived; and a good deal of what we know about the history of Athens is owing to this piece of Aristotelian scholarship.

Our concern here is not with the whole or any substantial part of

Aristotle's political philosophy, but one subject alone: the quality of pluralism that Aristotle believed fundamental in the good community. Inevitably he addresses himself to Plato's earlier words; for—as may easily be taken for granted—Plato was still, well after his death, a powerful intellectual eminence in Greek life and thought. And it was Plato who was regarded, surely, as the preeminent advocate of the unified, monolithic, total political community—even as he continues to be today. Inevitably, then, the following quotation from Aristotle will be seen to be directed toward Plato, through his notable protagonist, Socrates. The passage gets us off splendidly:

> The error of Socrates must be attributed to the false notion of unity from which he starts. Unity there should be, both of the family and of the state, *but in some respects only.* For there is a point at which a state may attain such a degree of unity as to be no longer a state, or at which, without actually ceasing to exist, it will become an inferior state, *like harmony passing into unison, or rhythm which has been reduced to a single foot.*[3]

Aristotle's objective in his *Politics*, most especially in the notable second chapter of the work, is to consider "what form of political community is best of all for those who are most able to realize their ideal of life": in short, not the ultimate, abstract, or timeless *idea* of the political community that Plato, virtually in shock from the aftermath of the Peloponnesian War, had written of in *The Republic*, but instead the political community most likely to be realized by human beings as they are constituted and within circumstances that are most probable. Haunted by confusion and seeming breakdown, Plato had declared for absolute unity, as we observed in the chapter on the political community. For Plato, "the greater the unity of the state the better." But this superficially attractive judgment of Plato is rejected utterly by Aristotle. He writes:

> Is it not obvious, that a state may at length attain such a degree of unity as to be no longer a state?—since the nature of a state is to be a plurality, and intending to greater unity, from being a state, it becomes a family, and from being a family, an individual; for the family may be said to be more one than the state, and the individual than the family. So that we ought not to attain this greatest unity even if we could, for it would be the destruction of the state.[4]

---

3 Aristotle, *Politics*, trans. Benjamin Jowett (Oxford: Clarendon Press, 1923), chap. 2, sect. 5, 13–15. Italics added.

4 Ibid., sect. 2, 2–3.

A state, Aristotle goes on, is made up of different kinds of human beings: "Similars do not constitute a state." A state is not like a military organization the effectiveness of which depends upon total unity and a blurring of the differences among those who form the organization. In the good state it is important that the dissimilarities among people and their customs be both recognized and protected, so far as is possible. Failure to do this, and the effort to achieve in the state a form of community as close as that of family, cannot fail, he emphasizes, to result in a monolithic unity: a celebration of the one, rather than the many, and hence a totalitarian type of society.

Aristotle dislikes communism, whether of property or of wives and children, for precisely the same reason he dislikes the kind of extreme unity that Plato had set up as his ideal. Plato, as we must recall here, had not made communism of property and wives a requisite for his political community as a whole: only for that part of it represented by his cherished guardian class, the philosophers who would rule it. But it is this very concentration of communism that bespeaks Plato's admiration of it and his dislike of both private property and the family—as well as of other forms of autonomous or independent association.

Aristotle sees many problems arising from such economic and sexual communism in practice. Even supposing, he tells us, that the highest achievement of the political community is its absolute unity, in what way are we justified in concluding that common ownership of property and wives and children—that is, collective ownership—is preferable to a condition in which each man has property, wife, and children with the consequence that all men have these but not in corporate or collective fashion? Could not, Aristotle asks, as much of the unity necessary to the state arise from the latter condition as from the former? And would not the latter condition be more easily and realistically manageable for the government?

> For that which is common to the greatest number has the least care bestowed upon it. Everyone thinks chiefly of his own, hardly at all of the common interest; and only when he is himself concerned as an individual. For besides other considerations, everybody is more inclined to neglect the duty which he expects another to fulfill; as in families many attendants are often less useful than a few.[5]

Each citizen will under the canon of communism have a thousand sons, but he will have none his individually and hence demanding his protection. "Anybody will be equally the son of anybody, and will therefore be neglected by all alike."[6]

---

5 Ibid., sect. 3, 4–5.   6 Ibid.

Loss of the kinship principle will only lead, Aristotle argues, to loss of one of the most useful forms of social constraint in society: the kind that arises from love, intimacy, and close community. And what is lost in the way of social constraint will not easily be compensated for through political laws against the kinds of offenses which arise among human beings when there is no sense of closeness, of brotherhood, of kinship. Likewise, an individual's relation to property vital in his development of mind and character. The aim should be, not to abolish this relation, but to multiply it throughout the community so that every man will know it and, in this respect at least, be like his fellow citizens. But communism of property, Aristotle writes, will only succeed in blurring the sense of relationship and dissolving the protective relation between a man and his property. Property that is the possession of all is nobody's, hence nobody's responsibility.

Another effect of political unity in the Platonic sense would be to weaken, even to destroy friendship. No one has ever exceeded Aristotle in his praise of friendship for the inestimable good it confers upon the larger social order. In his *Ethics* he gives us two long, profoundly conceived, and fascinating chapters on the nature of friendship, its duties and privileges, its relation to love, and its role in both the social order and the formation of personality. In friendship, as in love, Aristotle concedes the importance of communality. "Friends' goods are common property," he tells us, quoting an old saying of the Greeks. The good commonwealth is one in which there are many such communalities of friendship and love. But the effect of *political* communism, and of the unification and centralization which would accompany it, could only be to dissolve or to loosen the friendships and other intimate communities within the social order.

Clearly, from Aristotle's point of view the danger inherent in Plato's or any other form of communism lies in its capacity to tyrannize in the small things as well as the large. We shall find this theme an almost constant one in the writings of the pluralists, from Aristotle down to Burke and Tocqueville. Intimacy, unity, and even communality are virtues in a small group such as the family, monastery, small village community, or, for that matter, any small community that is built around an ideal or a moral virtue. To transfer to the state or other large-scale association the kind of communality that fits the small group, is, from Aristotle's point of view and from that of the entire pluralist-decentralist-localist tradition in Western thought, to invite regimentation, sterile uniformity, and repressive collectivism.

We do not find in Aristotle any perspicuous outline of an ideal state. There is no stated preference for, say, a monarchy in contrast to a republic, a republic in contrast to a democracy. In part this is the result of what I have called the analytic-empirical cast of Aristotle's thought in politics: he was more interested in the description, classification, and analysis of states than in setting forth, as Plato had, the outline of the ideal. Aristotle, as we have had occasion to note, was the first real social scientist, in his attitude toward human behavior in society.

But there is another, possibly stronger, reason for Aristotle's aversion toward limning the ideal political government: he did not have an ideal of government so much as he had an ideal of *the relation between government and the social order.* What was important was, not whether government was monarchy, oligarchy, or democracy, but whether the family, private property, legitimate associations, and social classes were able to maintain themselves free of incessant political invasion or domination irrespective of what form of government existed. From Aristotle's viewpoint—and this would be the basic viewpoint of Burke, Tocqueville, and other nineteenth-century pluralists—almost any form of political government was good *if* it preserved the all-important spheres of autonomy to which each of the major groups and institutions was entitled within the social order.

Here we have the heart of the difference between Plato and Aristotle. Plato had believed so deeply in the political community that he had desired to see it become all in all; not a community of communities, but instead a community of individuals emancipated from all other communal or associational ties—in short, a monolithic, unitary, absolute community. Aristotle, recognizing the importance, even desirability, of the political community, saw it as destined inevitably to totalitarianism unless its power over human beings was checked and balanced by the powers of other communities within the political order, such as kinship, religion, locality, and others of social or cultural type. And in this difference between Plato and Aristotle we have the essence of the difference, which has survived throughout Western thought down to the present moment, between political monism and political pluralism.

Althusius and the Rise of Modern Pluralism

Despite Aristotle's influence, it is not until we come down to the late sixteenth and early seventeenth centuries that we find a full-fledged and systematic vision of the plural community. The kernel of this type of community is assuredly to be found in Aristotle's reaction to Plato, but it is only that: a kernel, important though it be. Nor is there any other classical thinker, Greek or Roman, in whom we can find a more extended treatment. There were those, like Cicero during the late Roman Republic, who celebrated freedom and moral virtue in politics and prescribed limits to the power of the political arm of society. But, apart from the kind of emphasis we have seen in Aristotle on the necessity of protecting certain spheres of life, such as kinship and property, from political assimilation, and on the dangers inherent in all types of unitary, monistic community, we get little else. Even Aristotle's brief treatment of the necessity in large states of some degree of delegation and decentralization is predicated upon pragmatic expediency rather than a clear, firm view of the inherent desirability of decentralization.

What was required for the beginning of the modern view of the plural community was the kind of conflict of values that existed in western Europe at the end of the Middle Ages, a conflict that can be epitomized for the moment simply as one between the values of medievalism, on the one hand, and those of the emerging centralized, national state, on the other. In order to provide a setting for Althusius's philosophy of pluralism, it will be useful to refer again to medievalism and its traditions, for these strongly influenced his major ideas.

The period of the Middle Ages, whatever else one may wish to say of it, offers a notable example of a society organized along pluralist lines. Without exception the elements we have already seen to be the vital ones of the plural community were abundantly manifest in western European society from the period just following the fall of the Roman Empire down until approximately the sixteenth century. This was close to a thousand years, a very long time during which it was possible for certain structural principles to become very powerful indeed. No single person or group of persons ever had any prior plan or vision of these principles. They were nonetheless real, nonetheless implicative of human lives, and were to be seen in the countless customs and traditions of localities and regions and in the diverse network of functions, authorities, and allegiances that existed in the absence of any central political authority worthy of the name.

True, from the time of Charlemagne there was the so-called Holy Roman Empire; but, in the words of wit that have served all students of the subject, this structure was in fact neither holy, Roman, nor an empire. Loose in conception, and impossible to implement, given the lack of either means of communication or pragmatic principles of administration—much less the kind of *technology* always necessary for large-scale centralization of government—the Holy Roman Empire was little more than a phrase.

Even had there been some organizing genius equipped with the necessary principles of administration and technology, he would have found it exceedingly difficult, certainly by the tenth and eleventh centuries, to make substantial impact upon localisms, regionalisms, and varied forms of feudal organization, each of which tended to be jealous of any outside interference. And by the twelfth and thirteenth centuries towns were springing up all over western Europe, each as jealous as any feudal principality of its autonomy and corporate freedom. And within the towns were the guilds of crafts and trades, along with other urban associations, which insisted upon their proper due of autonomy. At the base of the social structure was, of course, the strong family system: the clan, kindred, and household. There were also, as we have seen, the monasteries coming into existence by the hundreds during the high Middle Ages, all of them concerned with their freedom as much from ecclesiastical authority as from that of any feudal prince. And, finally, there was the vast and powerful Christian church, which at that time no secular authority would have dared challenge seriously or for long.

The pluralism of the Middle Ages was, in short, a pluralism of functions, authorities, and allegiances. There were many of each; and although there was almost incessant conflict—if we may believe later historians—there is no contradiction between the facts of pluralism and conflict. The necessity, even value, of conflict—in moderate degree, at least—is recognized by all exponents of pluralism.

There was also in the philosophy and theology of the Middle Ages a high regard for the legal and philosophical reality of each form of association. "Realism" is the name we give to this doctrine in medieval philosophy. Almost from the time that philosophical realism was being taught in the universities (which were still another form of vital communal association to spring up in medieval society), it was being challenged by doctrines we call "nominalist," which declared that the unity of the group is only in its name (*nomina*) and that reality is to be found in the atomistic individuals who compose it. But it cannot be denied that in systems of social philosophy and law, down until rather late in the Middle Ages, it was the realist view of society that dominated.

The nineteenth-century historian Otto von Gierke has admirably summarized the medieval social system under the heading of the principle of federalism. He writes:

> The properly medieval system of thought started from the idea of the whole and the unity, but to every lesser unit down to and including the individual, it ascribed an inherent life, a purpose of its own, and an intrinsic value within the harmoniously articulated organism of the world-whole filled with the Divine Spirit. Thus in accordance with the medieval scheme of things it attained a construction of the social whole which in effect was federalistic through and through. . . . Between the highest Universality or "All-Community" and the essential unity of the individual there is a series of intermediate unities, in each of which lesser and lower units are comprised and combined. The political theories endeavor to set up a definite scheme descriptive of this articulation of mankind; for the church they follow the existing hierarchical system, and for secular societies they set up a parallel system by enlarging the Aristotelian gradation of communities.[7]

[7] Otto von Gierke, *The Development of Political Theory*, trans. Bernard Freyd (New York: Howard Fertig, 1966), pp. 257–58. Von Gierke's work was first published, in German, in 1880.

In kinship, religion, social class, local community, region, guild, monastery, university, and various other types of community lay, then, the medieval system of federalism, one that can be truly described as a *communitas communitatum*. We must not idly glorify this system in the act of merely describing it. It has too often been romanticized. Beneath its federal structure, despite—or even because of—its functional autonomies and corporate liberties, there could be, as we know, cruelty, deprivation, exploitation, and by modern standards a very low level of life and literacy. Nevertheless it is precisely this medieval pattern of social and political life that furnishes the background, the context, and, most important, the actual themes of what we call the plural community in modern Western social thought. Without exception, from Althusius through Burke and Tocqueville to Max Weber, it is the general medieval set of social and political principles that supplies the substance of pluralist reactions to the modern centralized, bureaucratized, and collectivist state.

It was, indeed, in fundamental repudiation of medieval principles of authority that the modern state arose in the sixteenth and seventeenth centuries. There is no need to repeat here what we considered in this connection in the chapter on the political community. Suffice it only to recall that first Bodin, Hobbes, Locke, and Rousseau, then the legislators of the French Revolution and, following that great event, the philosophical radicals in England, who took their point of departure from Jeremy Bentham: all, without exception, saw the elements of medievalism as their hated enemy and in the centralized political state the context of lasting liberation from these medieval elements.

But at the very time when the theory of the modern political state was being formed by such men as Bodin and Hobbes, there was at least one remarkable mind that saw the hope of freedom to lie in some judicious balancing of the medieval elements with the theory of political sovereignty. This was Johannes Althusius (1557-1638), one of the authentically great minds in the history of social theory and the true founder of the philosophy of the plural community. He was a devout Calvinist, on the one hand, and a professor of law, on the other. Like his revered forerunner John Calvin, he was, in other words, a man of both the church and the civil law. But unlike Calvin, Althusius saw less than moral perfection in a theocracy. Any monopoly of authority by any single institution—church, state, or any other—he regarded as dangerous to freedom. And it was precisely this same belief that resulted in his notable repudiation of the unitary, sovereign political state, the theory of which had been set forth by Machiavelli more than a century earlier and, most profoundly, by Jean Bodin only a short time before Althusius commenced his own writing.

It is to Bodin especially that Althusius addresses himself in his greatest work, the *Politics*, published in 1603, just twenty-seven years after Bodin wrote his *Commonweal*, the work in which the unitary theory of political sovereignty was first presented. Bodin had declared absolute, perpetual, and total sovereignty to be the attribute of the political state alone, an attribute that can never be surrendered by the sovereign—which Bodin saw as the person of the king, or, rather, as the institution of the monarchy. As we saw in earlier chapters, Bodin, for all his espousal of unitary political power, yet had a deep appreciation of the variety and the corporate character of medieval society. And, as will also be remembered, he gave to the family, the household, absolute immunity from invasion even by the supposedly omnipotent sovereign. Nonetheless, as a response to the problem of civil order and what seemed to him the manifest incapacity of the church or any other single medieval institution to meet it, Bodin endowed the political ruler with a sovereignty that was theoretically absolute and imprescriptible.

Althusius found this conception of sovereignty untenable on grounds of natural and moral law. Sovereignty, he declared, belongs to the people, and they can never rightfully surrender it; they can only delegate their ultimate, residual power to kings or to other forms of government. When this delegated sovereignty is abused in the performance, it may, Althusius insisted, be taken back by the people in popular assembly. The important point is that, for Althusius, sovereignty can never be permanently alienated from the people.

Nearly two centuries later, this basic tenet of popular sovereignty would be taken up by Rousseau and made the basis of his revolutionary *Social Contract*. But, as we observed in our consideration of Rousseau and the political community, he saw goodness in popular will only to the extent that it had become liberated from all possible influences of traditional society. For Rousseau, the general will could exist, and could be invariably right in its judgments, only when its wielders, the people, had become purged of all social and cultural influences stemming from family, local community, guild, church, or other social elements. It was indeed this aspect of the matter that rendered Rousseau's doctrine of the general will the single most revolutionary doctrine in the history of political thought. Popular sovereignty was, as we observed, for Rousseau a means of permanent revolution in the social order.

Althusius, however, saw the matter in very different terms. For him the people was no abstract or atomized entity, divorced from social and cultural identity bestowed through the various groups, communities, and associations which in fact make up a population. On the contrary, for Althusius popular sovereignty lay in the people considered only in terms of their actual, historically developed, traditional communities and groups. These groups and communities—ranging from family through neighborhood, parish, guild, or corporate association of any form, to church—would be the true units of the political commonwealth. The political sovereign, which is to say, the people corporately organized, would govern through a visible instrument of state—monarchy or whatever—but such government would express itself through, would indeed depend upon, the traditional communities, rather than the artificially atomized population that Bodin had to some degree created in his theory and that would appear in full in the theories of Hobbes and Rousseau after Althusius.

We thus have what Althusius is most famous for: a principle of federalism, of which the nineteenth-century anarchists as well as political pluralists and guild socialists would avail themselves in their prescriptions for the good society. For Althusius, as for the later pluralists, federalism is a means of governmental decentralization based upon natural or traditional communities, each of which, along with the formal organs of political government, will participate in the governmental process.

> Politics is the art of associating men for the purpose of establishing, cultivating, and conserving social life among them. Whence it is called "symbiotics." The subject matter of politics is therefore association, in which the symbiotes pledge themselves each to the other, by explicit or tacit agreement, to mutual communication of whatever is useful and necessary for the harmonious exercise of social life.[8]

Observe in Althusius's definition the emphasis on *association*. It is an emphasis that will remain, down through the nineteenth and into the twentieth centuries, the very core of the pluralist tradition. Association is deemed to be man's natural existence—not merely one type, but a diversity of association, corresponding to the diversity of man's own mind and character. Association is regarded as indispensable to the development of man's personality, his normal refuge from the uncertainties and insecurities of existence, also as his only possible bulwark against the invasion of external authority or power. As we shall see, Burke, Tocqueville, Proudhon, and others find in multiplicity of association the best guarantee against the atomization of society and culture to which a single unchecked, undivided system of power inevitably leads.

For Althusius, who was one of the very first in modern Western thought to see the dangers inherent in the emerging national state and its centralized government, it was normal to describe associative variety in the terms he knew best: that is, those supplied, as it were, by the whole medieval structure, which was beginning in his day to show the

---

8 *The Politics of Johannes Althusius* (abridged from *Politica Methodice Digesta, atque Exemplis Sacris et Profanis Illustrata*, 3d ed.), ed. and trans. Frederick S. Carney (Boston: Beacon Press, 1964), p. 12.

effects of strains and stresses generated by the rise of nationalism and of industry and commerce greater than anything known before. We have seen how Sir Thomas More reacted to these stresses in his vision of Utopia. It is no utopia that Althusius has in mind, no far-off, imaginary society, but, rather, a society he thought perfectly possible in western Europe itself.

The strong element of medievalism in Althusius may be gathered from the following passage, in which he seeks to show how diversity may yield what he calls "the concord of order and subjection":

> Just as from lyres of diverse tones, if properly tuned, a sweet sound and pleasant harmony arise when low, medium, and high notes are united, so also the social unity of rulers and subjects in the state produces a sweet and pleasant harmony out of the rich, the poor, the workers, the farmers, and other kinds of persons. If agreement is thus achieved in society, a praiseworthy, happy, most durable, and almost divine concord is produced.[9]

The passage is actually quoted by Althusius from a contemporary, Peter Gregory, but it may be taken as fully reflective of Althusius's own views. We noted above that Aristotle also used a musical metaphor to describe the unity in plurality that was, he thought, the highest type of unity, the only type that does not sink into mere uniformity or regimentation in the social order, as harmony into mere unison in music. The metaphor of musical harmony is a common one among pluralist writings; and one finds it used often by theologians during the Middle Ages to give added expression to the kind of society they favored, hierarchical and diverse in social composition yet at the same time unified.

There are, Althusius writes, two broadly distinguishable types of association: the natural and the civil. Society as a whole is a tissue of these two types and their concrete representations. The preeminent example of natural association, Althusius tells us, is the family, highly symbiotic in character.

> The private and natural symbiotic association is one in which married persons, blood relatives, and in-laws, in response to a natural affection and necessity, agree to a definite communication among themselves. Whence this individual, natural, necessary, economic, and domestic society is said to be contracted permanently among these symbiotic allies of life, with the same boundaries of life itself. Therefore it is rightly called the most intense society, friendship, relationship, and union, the seedbed

9 Ibid., p. 21.

of every other symbiotic association. Whence these symbiotic allies are called relatives, kinsmen, and friends.[10]

Two points must be stressed in Althusius's treatment of the family. First, although he has called it a natural form of association, he means nothing that could be termed biological, that is, the emanation of instinct alone. Althusius has in mind the larger kinship group, the kindred and clan as well as the small conjugal union; and he is well aware that such groups are, as he puts it, "covenanted," planned, deliberately formed in society, in the same way as nonkinship groups. The family is, in short, a *social* unity in every sense of the word. Second, Althusius regards study of the family as being just as much a part of the discipline of politics as is that of any other form of association, including political government itself: "Certain writers eliminate, wrongly in my judgment, the doctrine of the conjugal and kinship private association from the field of politics and assign it to economics." [11] As we saw in the earlier chapter on the political community, all the major philosophers of political sovereignty—Hobbes and Rousseau among them—were to do precisely this: take the family essentially out of the study of politics altogether, just as they removed it, except in the most limited, conjugal sense, from their ideal commonwealths. For Althusius, however, the kinship community is the fundamental circle of association in his desired state, the source of and model for all others.

Next in order of importance among component associations in the pluralist society is what Althusius calls the *collegium*. The very word suggests a medieval influence. The world of the Middle Ages, after towns and cities had begun to develop and spread, was full of collegia, groups, associations, sodalities, and other types of systematic gathering which had one or another of the social and cultural interests of the age as their reason for being. A collegium could be a craft guild, a merchant guild, a monastery, a college or university, a mutual-aid brotherhood, a court, a regular friendship group; in other words, any kind of association that had some more or less definite function. It did not matter whether this function was economic, religious, military, or educational.

> The types of *collegia* vary according to the circumstances of persons, crafts and functions. Today there are *collegia* of bakers, tailors, builders, merchants, coiners of money, as well as philosophers, theologians, government officials, and others that every city needs for the proper functioning of its social life. Some of these *collegia* are ecclesiastical and sacred, instituted for the sake of divine things; others are secular and profane, instituted for

---

10 Ibid., p. 23.   11 Ibid., p. 24.

the sake of human things. The first are *collegia* of theologians and philosophers. The second are *collegia* of magistrates and judges, and of various craftsmen, merchants, and rural folk.[12]

Next in order in the hierarchy of associations is the city, which is, in Althusius's classification, the first and most important of public, in contrast to private, associations.

> The public association exists when many private associations are linked together for the purpose of establishing an inclusive political order. It can be called a community, an associated body, or the preeminent political association.[13]

The elements of the urban community are, not individuals as such, but, rather, the small, private associations and families we have just described. There is a governor or "superior" for each city, and the government provided by the city extends to all matters common to families and other private groups within the city. Such government does not, however, extend *within* each of these private groups, for that would be, in Althusius's terms, an unwarranted invasion of the autonomy, the associative freedom, to which each is entitled by its nature.

Urban communities are either rural or industrial, Althusius tells us, depending upon the preponderant type of economic activities. But irrespective of economic base, all cities will have substantially the same kind of government. This will be by an elected council, members of which will be called senators, and which will be presided over by the superior, prefect, administrator, or whatever he may be called. The council and prefect will have only such direct powers, *no others*, as may be delegated by wish of the community's citizens—the heads of families and others who are entitled to vote. Fundamental to the urban community is the network of economic functions, social affiliations, and cultural and intellectual attachments, as well as kinship lines, that alone can provide the base for the kind of communication Althusius prizes. Plainly, Althusius has a high regard, almost a reverence, for the city. And this too stamps him as medieval in inclination; for, from the twelfth century on, the towns and cities in western Europe were the centers of association most prized by men of intellect and learning, by artists and artisans in all fields.

Next and largest of the associations that compose the commonwealth is the province. Territorial in base, also called, as Althusius tells us, a region, district, diocese, or even community, it is an aggregate of cities, suburbs, villages, and other smaller territorial entities. To the province

12 Ibid., pp. 32–33.　　13 Ibid., p. 34.

are assigned the functions and responsibilities too large or too general to be met by one or another of the cities or towns that make it up. Its purpose is to deal with matters common to these, just as the purpose of the city is to handle matters common to the private groups which compose it. The province, it must be emphasized, is either secular or religious; for Althusius, strongly influenced in all matters by the medieval pattern, sees the whole of society as divided between the sacred and the profane, with the church's sphere equal in importance to the state's. This suggests, again, the inherent pluralism of Althusius's philosophy of the state; others, starting especially with Hobbes, who wrote shortly after Althusius, insisted that social order was impossible unless church was rigorously subordinated to state.

There is, finally, the state itself, the commonwealth, the largest of political organizations, the one within which, indeed, all of the above fall, and the government of which is the visible manifestation of the sovereignty belonging, for Althusius, inalienably to the people as a whole. We shall not venture here into a detailed study of the structure of this government. Following the federalism that is the constitutive principle of his whole system of thought, Althusius sees this government as confined in its operations solely to those matters that cannot easily be dealt with by smaller units. Nor is the power of this government ever more than a grant from the people. Althusius agrees with his predecessor Bodin that sovereignty is indivisible; but whereas Bodin had located sovereignty in the apparatus of government, Althusius places it in the people, from whom it arose in the first instance through covenant or contract. And, in Althusian theory at least, the people are morally free, even obliged, to withdraw this power from government whenever in their opinion the covenant has been violated.

But the distinctive, original genius of Althusius is not in his theory of contract or even of popular sovereignty, impressive though his statement of each is for his day. It lies in his conception of the principle of federation, whereby all power, all authority in any form—religious or lay, governmental, provincial, city, collegial, or whatever—would manifest itself through intermediate associations, through layers of function, authority, and allegiance that would act, at one and the same time, as buffers for the individual against the remote, centralized, and collectivist power of the state and as means of diversifying the social bond.

Other seventeenth- and eighteenth-century theorists of the political order, especially Hobbes and Rousseau, diminished the importance to man of these forms of association, terming them, in effect, obsolete at best and inimical to public order at worst. For the vast majority of political philosophers, sovereignty resided in the state alone, composed of individuals united solely by political ties of citizenship; all other social bonds could be dispensed with. But this was not the view of Althusius.

For it cannot be denied that provinces are constituted from villages and cities, and commonwealths and realms from provinces. Therefore, just as the cause by its nature precedes the effect and is more perceptible, and just as the simple or primary precedes in order what has been composed or derived from it, so also villages, cities, and provinces precede realms and are prior to them. For this is the order and progression of nature, that the conjugal relationship, or the domestic association of man and wife, is called the beginning and foundation of human society. From it are then produced the associations of various blood relations and in-laws. From them in turn come the sodalities and collegia, out of the union of which arises the composite body that we call a village, town, or city. *And these symbiotic associations as the first to develop can subsist by themselves even without a province or realm.* However, as long as they are not united in the associated and symbiotic and universal body of a province, commonwealth, or realm, they are deprived of many of the advantages and necessary supports of life. *It is necessary, therefore, that the doctrine of the symbiotic life of families, kinship associations, collegia, cities, and provinces precede the doctrine of the realm or universal symbiotic association that arises from the former associations and is composed of them.*[14]

Unfortunately, the ideas of Althusius had little if any effect in the seventeenth and eighteenth centuries. If they had had a significant effect, western Europe might have been spared the age of the absolute, centralized, and omnicompetent state, built upon atomized individuals and upon the wreckage of the social groups and associations Althusius cherished. Such was the counterattraction of such ideas as Hobbes's, Rousseau's, and Bentham's all without exception, as we have seen in the chapter on the political community, involving centralization and collectivization of power in the state, that the ideas of Althusius were lost completely from sight. Not until the late nineteenth century, and then among but a handful of scholars, did Althusius come in for attention again.

His reward, or vindication, lies in the fact that although his name remains even today relatively obscure, the fundamental principles he espoused have proved steadily more attractive as the basis of attack upon the centralized, omnicompetent state. To more and more of those who seek the philosophical foundations of a free society, it has become apparent that the solitary individual is a precarious and insecure foundation for freedom and rights. Only in the autonomous group, association, and community is it possible to maintain a realistic base of resistance

[14] Ibid., pp. 201–2. Italics added.

against the ever-centralizing, ever-aggrandizing tendencies of the modern Hobbesean, Rousseauean political state. In short, Althusian pluralism and federalism remain to this day immensely viable, at least potentially, even if Althusius himself continues to suffer widespread neglect among social scientists and philosophers who have been reared in the traditions of Hobbes and Rousseau.

Conservative Pluralism: Burke, Bonald, Hegel

It was the French Revolution at the end of the eighteenth century that produced, in strong reaction to its centralization and collectivization of power, the third wave of pluralist-federalist ideas in Western thought, which was to have diverse expression indeed in the nineteenth and twentieth centuries, ranging from conservative to radical.

Interestingly, though hardly astonishingly, the attack commenced in the writings of those whom today we regard as conservatives, even reactionaries. After all, it was traditional society—the forms of association and community in eighteenth-century France, and western Europe as a whole—that, as we know, bore the brunt of the French Revolution's onslaught. What the revolutionists detested, as had the philosophes before them, was the whole system of religion, class, and culture identified with Christianity, feudalism, and all that went with these two great persisting medieval forces. Appropriately enough, it is from eighteenth- and early-nineteenth-century defenders of this traditional-medieval social structure that the earliest response comes against the French Revolution and its works. In destroying, or seeking to destroy, such entities as church, monastery, local community, guild, patriarchal family, and aristocracy, the leaders of the Revolution almost inevitably evoked powerful counteraction.

Burke

The reaction begins in England, with Edmund Burke (1729–97). Himself a Whig, throughout one of the most admired careers in the history of Parliament Burke was preoccupied by some five different revolutions in all, to four of which he gave stout and unyielding support: the English revolution of 1688, four decades before his birth, the American Revolution, the revolt of the Bengalese in India against the British East India Company, and the sporadic insurrections of Irish Roman Catholics against English forces in Ireland. What Burke hated was, in his words, "arbitrary power." He detested it in the form in which the British exercised it against the Americans—thus driving the colonists, as Burke saw the matter, to justified revolt against the British crown—or in the form it so quickly took after 1789 in France in the hands of revolutionary assemblies and conventions.

Precisely the same hatred of arbitrary power can be seen as the cornerstone of Burke's famous speech before Parliament in 1788 against Warren Hastings for his administration of the East India Company in India. From Burke's point of view, this administration had been responsible not merely for numberless brutalities and oppressions of the Indian people but for a calculated and systematic destruction of the very character of Indian society: its kinship system, its village communities, its castes, and other manifestations. It was, declared Burke, Hastings's corrupt and arbitrary power that lay behind this whole ugly episode of British history. A few quotations from Burke's speech will serve to make evident enough a point of view that was to carry forward to his famous attack on the French Revolution:

> I must do justice to the East. I asssert that their morality is equal to ours, in whatever regards the duties of governors, fathers, and superiors; and I challenge the world to show in any modern European book more true morality and wisdom than is to be found in the writings of Asiatic men in high trust and who have been counsellors to princes. . . .
> That the people of Asia have no laws, rights, or liberty, is a doctrine that wickedly is to be disseminated through this country. I again assert, every Mohammedan government is, by its principles, a government of law. . . .
> The principles upon which Mr. Hastings governed his conduct in India, and upon which he grounds his defence . . . may all be reduced to one short word—*arbitrary power*.
> Law and arbitrary power are in eternal enmity. Name me a magistrate, and I will name property; name me power, and I will name protection. It is a contradiction in terms, it is blasphemy in religion, it is wickedness in politics, to say that any man can have arbitrary power.[15]

These few lines from Burke's celebrated indictment of Warren Hastings in Parliament are sufficient to give the powerful and characteristic flavor of Burke's animosity to centralized, arbitrary power wherever it might be found: in the British East India Company against the people of India, in the aggressive acts of the British government against the American colonists, in the Protestant-motivated English exploitation of Catholic Ireland, or, finally, as Burke saw the matter, in the hands of French revolutionaries, the Jacobins principally, who applied analogous techniques of centralized and despotic power against their own society in the name of the rights of mankind, of rationalism,

[15] *Edmund Burke: Selected Writings and Speeches*, ed. Peter J. Stanlis (New York: Doubleday & Co., Anchor Books), pp. 399, 400, 398.

and of absolute virtue. We may agree or disagree with Burke in his indictment of the French Revolution. There is no doubt that he is occasionally guilty of flights of rhetoric and extravagances of sentimentality with respect to tradition. But there is nevertheless a clear consistency in Burke's view of power that stretches from his almost religious veneration of the English revolution of 1688 through his impassioned defense of the American colonists, the Indians, and the Catholic Irish against his own beloved England.

Burke was indeed a traditionalist. He had a profound belief in the rights, liberties, and equities that, in his view, derive basically from natural law but are shaped by history and given setting in traditions, conventions, and habits. It was precisely in defense of traditional rights and liberties developed historically in each and every society that Burke opposed "arbitrary power," no matter what its source or justification. Burke believed such power wrong when he saw it extended abroad to the American colonies and to the people of India from his own beloved Britain; and he believed it to be equally wrong when, from across the Channel, he saw what he felt to be the same kind of power directed at the traditional social order of France by a new, violence-engendered, self-appointed body of men in the name of revolutionary government. Despite the fact that substantial numbers of his fellow Whigs—in many instances men who had joined with him in his defense of the Americans and in his attack on the East India Company—tended, at least through 1790, to endorse the Revolution in France, Burke did not hesitate a moment in attacking it.

Within a year of the Revolution's outbreak, Burke had written and published his *Reflections on the Revolution in France*. Quite apart from its almost instantaneous electric effect at the time, generating both agreement and dissent, often passionate, this book has proved to be, for its eloquently expressed principles, one of the greatest of all works in the history of Western political and social philosophy. It is also the very fountain of modern philosophical conservatism. To describe the book in these terms is not to imply that it is always free of error or partisanship. What major book in social thought ever is? And it was Burke's unqualified repudiation of the principles of the French Revolution that led him to break with his beloved Whig party in England, that caused him to resign his seat in Parliament, and that, in light of the agonizing emotional turmoil that accompanied these actions, undoubtedly hastened him to his death a few years later.

There were many who declared Burke a traitor to his own Whig principles when he launched his attack on the French Revolution in 1790. Had he not defended the American Revolution a few years before? Had he not defended India from the depredations of the British crown through the East India Company? And the Catholic Irish? Why, then, did he turn on the liberal-democratic revolution in France—as it seemed to be to so many liberal-progressive minds in England—in obvious repudiation of his own earlier views?

The answer is that Burke, whatever his biases, prejudices, and occasional errors, did not turn on his earlier views. His attack on the French Revolution sprang from precisely those principles that had underlain his defense of the American colonists and of the people of India. These principles were rooted in Burke's profound belief in the superiority of traditional society and its component groups and associations, as well as what he regarded as its inherent organic processes of change, over centralized political power: the kind that he had first seen wielded by the British crown against the American colonists, then by the East India Company against the villages, families, and castes of India, and now, in 1789–90, by the new French revolutionary government against church, family, village community, province, guild, and other elements of French society. Whig or no, Burke's basic principles can be seen to have stemmed from the very beginning from a deep love of traditional society in western Europe and elsewhere and, above all, a desire to protect that traditional society from the techniques of power he saw in modern political government. And it is this very love of tradition and its autonomy from centralized and rationalized organization that has proved to be the rock on which modern conservatism has been built in the West—in England and America and on the Continent. Burke is, we are justified in saying, after Aristotle the preeminent conservative in the entire history of Western thought.

It is not Burke's conservatism as such, however, that interests us here, but the ingrained pluralism of his attack on political centralization. He would doubtless not have accepted this characterization, and even from our vantage point his main thrust would not at first sight seem pluralist. He does not make that sharp distinction between the political state and the rest of society that we saw to be vital in Althusius and that is the hallmark of most recent pluralist writing. For Burke, state and society are virtually the same, and when he refers, as he so often does, to "civil society," he is referring to an organic union of government with all spheres of the social order.

Nevertheless, the clear identity of these last, and their own autonomous, moral right to existence and to protection from the depredations of political government, is a fundamental element of Burke's thought. No matter how deeply grounded government may be, or may appear to be, in popular will, in claimed popular interest, it does not, in Burke's view, have the right wantonly to invade the religious, kinship, professional, and other areas of the social order. To those who declare society a contract, and who claim the consequent right of a group acting in the popular interest to break this contract, Burke writes with passionate emphasis:

> Society is indeed a contract. Subordinate contracts for objects of mere occasional interest may be dissolved at pleasure—but the state ought not to be considered nothing better than a partnership agreement in a trade of pepper and coffee, calico or tobacco, or some other such low concern, to be taken up for a little temporary interest, and to be dissolved by the fancy of the parties. . . . It is a partnership in all science; a partnership in all art; a partnership in every virtue, and in all perfection. As the ends of such a partnership cannot be obtained in many generations, it becomes a partnership not only of those who are living, but between those who are living, those who are dead, and those who are to be born.[16]

Each particular society, Burke goes on, is a particular contract that is itself but a clause in "the great primeval contract of eternal society," and no one group in any one society has any reasonable right to violate the social bond. Governments are "not morally at liberty at their pleasure, and on their speculations of a contingent improvement, wholly to separate and tear asunder the bands of their subordinate community, and to dissolve it into an unsocial, uncivil, unconnected chaos of elementary principles." [17] Burke has scant use for any view of man's nature that sees the basis of order, freedom, or even individuality in the highest sense of the term, to lie in man as a biologically created being. The basis of all these is inseparable from civil society, from the fabric of community. Nor does Burke have any higher regard for so-called natural rights, those which are declared anterior to social rights. There are no rights, Burke insists, that are not grounded in the social order.

He does not proscribe any and all change in society: "A state without the means of some change is without the means of its conservation." He calls to witness England's decisive change during the Restoration and the revolution of 1688:

> At both those periods the nation had lost the bond of union in their ancient edifice; they did not, however, dissolve the whole fabric. . . . They acted by the ancient organized states in the shape of their old organization, and not by the organic *moleculae* of a disbanded people.[18]

It must be borne in mind that the social order Burke revered above all others was the one he could still see ascendant in his beloved England, which had sprung in the first instance from the Middle Ages, which covered the whole of Europe at its height, and which he could see now

---

[16] Burke, *Reflections on the Revolution in France*, p. 117.

[17] Ibid. [18] Ibid., pp. 23–24.

suffering destruction in France. This social order was founded on kinship, neighborhood, religion, social class, and territorial units such as provinces that reflect historical tradition, rather than caprice or the pretended intellect of a single group or generation. It must accordingly be dealt with respectfully and cautiously when change is being considered.

> The science of constructing a commonwealth, or renovating it, or reforming it, is, like every other experimental science, not to be taught *a priori*. Nor is it a short experience that can instruct us in that practical science; because the real effects of moral causes are not always immediate. . . .[19]

Nothing is more abhorrent to Burke than philosophies of society that make atomistic individuals the units of the social order. Society cannot be understood except in terms of itself: that is, customs, conventions, groups, and communities. The nature of society is too complex ever to be brought within the sphere of some single, unitary pattern of authority or organization. So, too, Burke argues, is the nature of man:

> The nature of man is intricate; the objects of society are of the greatest possible complexity; and therefore no simple disposition or direction of power can be suitable either to man's nature, or to the quality of his affairs. When I hear the simplicity of contrivance aimed at and boasted of in any new political constitutions, I am at no loss to decide that the artificers are grossly ignorant of their trade, or totally negligent of their duty. The simple governments are fundamentally defective, to say no worse of them.[20]

It was this aspect of the French Revolution that Burke despised and feared above all others: the resounding effort, in the name of the claimed simplicity of nature, to impose rationalist simplicity upon all the plurality, diversity, and multiplicity of the social order as it is given us in experience. The leaders of the Revolution sought to clear away the confusion, as they saw it, of traditional society in France, which fell in their category of the hated "feudal," and to replace the whole of this by a politically planned and regulated social order that would be constructed through abstract reason alone. This was the kind of reason that Descartes had proposed to all thinkers, in sharp contrast to the knowledge that is based upon tradition or learning. It had become the very staple of the eighteenth-century *philosophes* in their attacks on French traditional society; and it was now the lever, resting on the fulcrum of

19 Ibid., p. 72. 20 Ibid., p. 73.

sheer power, through which the revolutionary legislators intended to dislodge the hated institutions of the old order. Through reason alone, operating in terms of newly created units of territory and population, would the future society in France be governed. Here are Burke's words on the matter:

> The French builders, clearing away as mere rubbish whatever they found, and, like their ornamental gardeners, forming everything into an exact level, propose to rest the whole . . . on three bases of three different kinds: one geometrical, one arithmetical, and the third financial; the first of which they call the *basis of territory*; the second the *basis of population*; and the third the *basis of contribution*.[21]

Burke is referring to revolutionary erasure, through specific laws, of the ancient communes, guilds, corporations, estates, provinces, and ecclesiastical districts in France, since the Middle Ages the basic units not merely of French society but of political representation, each an amalgam of custom, function, and habitual allegiance. In their place would now be instituted totally new units ranging from geometrically exact pieces of territory, to be called *départements*, *cantons*, and so on, through numerically equal aggregates of the population, to sectors of the population chosen for taxation purposes. It was the aim of the revolutionary legislators to abolish all traditional allegiances, to found new ones that would be from the start in harmony with revolutionary purpose, and to make the city of Paris the focal point of the entire centralized, rationalized system.

Burke, however, saw the remaking of French society in a light very different from that in which the French legislators, and likewise many liberals in his own country, saw it:

> To a person who takes a view of the whole, the strength of Paris thus formed, will appear a system of general weakness. It is boasted that the geometrical policy has been adopted, that all local ideas should be sunk, and that the people should no longer be Gascons, Picards, Bretons, Normans, but Frenchmen, with one country, one heart and one assembly. But instead of being all Frenchmen, the greater likelihood is, that the inhabitants of that region will shortly have no country. No man was ever attached by a sense of pride, partiality, or real affection to a description of square measurement. He never will glory in belonging to the Checquer, No. 71, or to any other badge ticket.

[21] Ibid., p. 213.

We begin our public affections in our families. No cold relation is a zealous citizen. We pass on to our neighborhoods, and our habitual provincial connections. These are inns and resting-places. Such divisions of our country as have been formed by habit, and not by a sudden jerk of authority, were so many little images of the great country in which the heart found something which it could fill. *The love to the whole is not extinguished by this subordinate partiality.*[22]

In that final sentence, quite apart from the very eloquent passage that contains it, can be seen the vital difference between the pluralist-decentralist view of the state and the view we observed in the works of Plato, Hobbes, Rousseau, and other exponents of the monolithic political community. For the latter, the existence of the smaller allegiances in society can only militate against the larger. To the pluralists, however —and this applies whether we are dealing with conservatives, liberals, or radicals—the small, partial, or local centers of authority and allegiance are vital not only to human personality and freedom but to any genuine sense of the large community of which they are organically component parts.

Burke was the first of the modern conservatives to launch an attack on the revolutionary-democratic state for what he felt to be its invasions of the legitimate spheres of authority and function in other parts of the larger social order. In part because of his own signal influence, in larger part because the crisis of mind precipitated by the Revolution was bound to evoke like expressions from others similarly affected, a kind of renascence of conservative pluralism followed by a very few years Burke's great *Reflections*. In England there were Southey and Coleridge, both deeply influenced by Burke; in Spain Balmes and Donoso y Cortes; in Switzerland Karl Ludwig von Haller; in France Bonald, Maistre, Chateaubriand, and Lamennais; and in Germany Adam Müller, Justus Möser, and the great Hegel. For present purposes it will suffice to describe briefly the pluralist ideas of two of these thinkers, Bonald and Hegel. Each exerted immense influence during and after his life.

Bonald

The greatest work of Vicomte Louis de Bonald (1754–1840) was his *Theory of Political and Religious Authority*, published in 1796, just six years after Burke's *Reflections* had appeared in England. The influence of Burke is plain enough in Bonald's conception of the nature of society and of legitimate authority. So, too, is the influence of the Middle Ages.

22 Ibid., pp. 243–44. Italics added.

It is to medieval society that Bonald, even more than Burke, looks for the model of an alternative to the industrial and democratic societies he could see forming around him. Very clearly, Bonald prefers the cultural diversity, the social autonomies, and above all the sheer traditionalism of the Middle Ages to the kind of society in which he was living. His pluralism is, like Burke's, one of traditional authorities left alone by the political arm of society.

Legitimate society is not composed of socially detached individuals equipped with politically given rights and freedoms, but of groups and communities, each authoritative in its own sphere: so argues Bonald. In much the manner of Althusius, Bonald sees legitimate society as a hierarchy ranging from the family at the bottom, the very molecule of society, through professions, guilds, rural communities, and similar groups, all the way to the political government and the church (Bonald was a devout Roman Catholic).

Each of these communities or associations possesses its own intrinsic authority, its *pouvoir*. The pluralism of Bonald is rooted deeply in the concept of authority; but it is multiple authority. The social bond reduces itself, in Bonald's eyes, to a plurality of bonds: to be seen in the family, the guild, the class, the church, as well as the political state. "Each of these," writes Bonald, "is a definitive authority in its own sphere, and the more definitive if the authority is common; if these authorities were not able to exact obedience, all domestic and political society, even all association of interests, would be impossible." [23]

Political representation should not be along lines of mere territorial units and arithmetically based segments of population. Bonald has the same dislike of territorial-populational representation we have just seen in Burke, hence his preference for a functional system of political representation. The real units of the state should be the units of society: community, guild, profession, corporation, and so on. The government, he declares, "should rule the individual only through the medium of the corporation." [24] (Bonald uses corporation here to refer to any of several collective or communal units in society.)

By virtue of the same orientation toward the component groups of society, Bonald espouses a pronounced theory of federalism in government. His preference for monarchy rests largely on his belief that under monarchy the social relationships of human beings are better respected. Democracy, on the other hand, tends to level social strata and at the same time to atomize social relationships. Equality, he suggests, tends to lead toward ever-greater national collectivism, likewise the result of the democratic theory of sovereignty, according to which residual power

[23] *Œuvres Complètes de M. De Bonald*, 3 vols. (Paris: 1864), 1: 56–57. My translation.

[24] Ibid., p. 262.

is taken from the people considered as an undiversified collectivity, thus bringing about increasing centralization. Not the least of Bonald's objections to democracy is the mass militarism it creates; he had seen the democracy of the French Revolution produce the first universal conscription in modern European history, the *levée en masse*.

No government can be a legitimate one, Bonald tells us, if it does not respect other sectors of association in society. Religion, for example, is entitled to its own form of government. For Bonald the only true religion was Roman Catholicism, and he proposed what came to be called ultramontane Catholicism: that is, a Roman Catholic church responsive only to Rome, never to any of the national powers that since the seventeenth century, and particularly since the French Revolution, had sought to nationalize Catholicism, much as had Henry VIII in England. Not only religion but also family, guild, local community, occupational association, and province: each of these must have its natural authority respected, and each must to some degree be a channel for the authority of the political government in its relationships with individuals. "If in the machinery of the state, the operation fixes itself at the center, the extremities will perish."

Hegel

In Germany the effects of the French Revolution on social thought were no less striking. If the national collectivism of the French Revolution created aspirations along the same line for a united Germany, to be freed of its feudal heritage for once and all, it also produced countereffects analogous to those we have just seen in Burke and Bonald. Burke's reaffirmation of the legitimacy of tradition and the right of historically formed social groups and communities to be spared the incursions of political power, even when such power was supposedly rooted in the people as a whole, was widely admired in Germany at the beginning of the nineteenth century. A whole school of historical conservatism arose there, just as in England and France and other parts of Europe. Of a sudden, institutions such as social class, church, local community, and guild took on an importance among many scholars in Germany that they had not possessed during the Enlightenment a half century earlier. And with this rediscovery of traditional society came also in the minds of a substantial number a spreading awareness of the virtues of at least some degree of pluralism and federalism in government.

It will serve our purposes if we confine our attention solely and briefly here to Georg Wilhelm Friedrich Hegel (1770–1831), recognized even during his lifetime as the greatest German philosopher of his day. Hegel was himself an ardent believer in the political state as the highest form of human institution. Moreover, in his youth he had been deeply impressed by the ideas of the Enlightenment, and he greeted the French

Revolution with enthusiasm. By middle age, however, his social philosophy had changed a great deal, unquestionably as the result of intellectual influences beginning with Edmund Burke. If he never relaxed his devotion to the state as such and its sovereignty, he nevertheless came to see the state as but one of a number of institutions vital to man, with its effective power over individuals accordingly limited, or at least channeled through other institutions. His *Philosophy of Right*, published in 1821, is an almost perfect expression of the ideas Hegel came to hold on the subject of state, society, and overall system of authority.

In his work we can see that Hegel viewed society as plural, possessed of not one but several natural centers of authority. He deals with the family, with social class, with occupational associations and professions, with local community, town and church, all at length and in detail. Over all these towers the government of the political state: Hegel leaves us in no doubt of that. But this state must not be one that rules individuals directly, as had been proposed by Hobbes and Rousseau, the French revolutionary state being the prime exemplar. Rule must be mediated: "The constitution is essentially a system of mediation. In despotisms where there are only rulers and people, the people is effective, if at all, only as a mass destructive of the organization of the state."[25]

Like Burke and Bonald, Hegel sees the vital importance of institutions and communities existing between the individual and the power of political government, to serve as buffers, hence his strong advocacy of church, local community, profession, and especially occupational associations:

> It is true that these associations won too great a measure of self-subsistence in the Middle Ages, when they were states within states . . . but we may nonetheless affirm that the proper strength of state lies in these associations. . . . It is of the utmost importance that people should be organized because only thus do they become mighty and powerful. Otherwise, they are nothing but a heap, an aggregate of atomic units. Only when the particular associations are organized members of the state are they possessed of legitimate power.[26]

Hegel is, in short, as apprehensive as Burke, Bonald, or any of the other conservative pluralists of the creation, through political centralization and other forces such as industrialization and commerce, of mass society, society devoid of relationships other than those of political power. Hence derives his preference for monarchy—but monarchy elected—over

---

[25] Georg Wilhelm Friedrich Hegel, *The Philosophy of Right*, ed. T. M. Knox (Oxford: Clarendon Press, 1942), p. 292.

[26] Ibid., pp. 290–91.

democracy: democracy, he believed, would lead far more readily than would monarchy to atomization of society and to centralization of political power. In this Hegel was one with Bonald and Burke. Government is to be federal. It must confine itself to those matters that cannot be dealt with by other social, local, and functional associations in society; and when it operates, it must govern, so far as possible, through these associations. Even in his conception of a legislature, Hegel followed the pluralist-federalist principle: Associations such as university and church would elect representatives, as of course would occupational associations generally, along with purely territorial units.

Liberal Pluralism: Lamennais and Tocqueville

By the 1820s, chiefly in France, pluralism was well on its way to becoming a liberal, even radical doctrine. The same perspective that could lead a Burke or a Bonald to see the power of the state, whether grounded in individual or popular sovereignty, as potentially destructive of the natural authority of society and its internal communities, could lead others to see that all individual liberties would be destroyed as well by the state's destruction of these traditional communities, unless these associations were replaced by new forms which would also serve as buffers between man and the state.

It is well to remember that prior to the rise of liberal pluralism in nineteenth-century Western thought, the basis of freedom for the individual was commonly found—by Locke, Rousseau, and most others concerned with the problem—in liberation of the individual from all forms of social constraint, especially traditional forms. Only through man's emancipation from his historic social affiliations of family, guild, church, and other unities, and through his total membership in the general will—the will of the single association of the people-based political state—could he enjoy the fruits of freedom. So argued Rousseau, and so argued a great many who saw the advance of democratic power as necessarily carrying with it the advance of individuality, of individual freedom.

But just as the conservative pluralists had seen in the advance of unchecked, undivided political power, irrespective of its foundation, a kind of juggernaut that would weaken the social order and leave the individual in a social and moral vacuum, there were now those who saw this same power, this same advancing democratic sovereignty, as the means of stifling individual freedom. The pluralist emphasis on social and cultural diversity, upon a multiplicity of authorities in society, becomes almost overnight a new kind of emphasis on the foundations of freedom.

Lamennais

We see this pluralist liberalism at its greatest in the writings of Alexis de Tocqueville, to which we shall come shortly. But it would be unjust to omit reference to another Frenchman who must be accounted a predecessor of Tocqueville and whose own personal transition from conservatism to liberalism is among the more fascinating episodes of the nineteenth century: Félicité Robert de Lamennais (1782–1854).

Lamennais began as a devout Roman Catholic, deeply conservative in his religious and political values, in the beginning concerned above all else with the autonomy of the church in European society and with the religious freedom of the individual, as he saw the matter, from the secularism and political domination of the state. Such was the brilliance and power with which Lamennais argued the case of the church against the forces of modernism that by 1820 he had become widely regarded as the preeminent spokesman of the church outside the Vatican. His *Essay on Indifference* was a powerful plea for traditionalism in morals, monarchy in politics, and recovery of all possible intellectual and social authorities from what he regarded as their imprisonment by secular state and economy. We are told that such was the esteem in which Lamennais was held by the pope that the rank of cardinal was offered him sometime in the early 1820s. Yet scarcely a decade later, Lamennais had been excommunicated, and his writings placed on the list of those banned by the church; and, far from being recognized as a conservative, Lamennais was in the forefront of liberal, even radical social causes.

It is not possible to go into the details of this dramatic transformation; they are, in any case, obscure. A personal rebelliousness, doubtless part of his temperament from the start, a kind of non-Protestant protestantism, an individualism, an intensity he could not control, very probably entered into his fast-increasing difficulties with the Vatican in the years just preceding his break with the church. Our interest here is in his ideas; and in these we may see a continuity despite his radical break with the church to which he had given his love and sworn his devotion for so many years. In effect, what led to his loss of confidence in the church, and then his expulsion from it, was hardly more than his carrying to other spheres of society the principles he had limited in the beginning to the church alone. From a position in which he argued for the complete autonomy of the church in society, he had, by 1830, reached the point of arguing for the autonomy of *all* associations in society, including those new kinds that conservatives tended to distrust: labor unions, cooperatives, and liberal political parties. He and several of his followers founded a newspaper, *L'Avenir*, that made freedom of association, local liberties, and decentralization of government its highest principles. From a strictly intellectual point of view, in other words, it was the very logic of Lamennais's early position that resulted eventually in his break with the church. He was but extending to new forms of association in society the same rights of autonomy, of communal status in the law, that he had at first sought only for the church.

At the base of Lamennais's political philosophy is a distrust of individualism, on the one hand, and of the power of the state, including the democratic state, on the other. Individualism, he insisted, cannot by its nature save men from the incursions of political power. On the contrary, individualism leads toward isolation, estrangement, and alienation, conditions which can only cause men to welcome the power of the state as a form of relief.

> From equality is born independence, and from independence isolation. As each man is circumscribed, so to speak, in his individual life, he no longer has more than his individual strength for defending himself if he is attacked; and no individual strength can offer sufficient guarantee of security against the incomparably greater force which is called sovereignty and from which arises the necessity of a new liberty, the liberty of association.[27]

Only within the contexts of close, voluntary, autonomous association, in short, can the individual receive the reinforcement necessary to both his own security of mind and status and his freedom from the threats of external power. These contexts of association in turn demand, as Lamennais saw, the even wider contexts of diversification in culture, multiplicity in social authority, and, perhaps above all, decentralization in government. Though a government may claim to be, may in fact be, rooted in the political will of the people, periodically expressed through mass vote, this in itself cannot possibly offset the danger that always lies in political power. This danger can be offset or sharply reduced only through a federalization of government, a decentralization of administration, a constitutional respect for the liberties of local communities, regions, and all forms of legitimate association. "Centralization," wrote Lamennais, "induces apoplexy at the center and anemia at the extremities."

Tocqueville

Alexis de Tocqueville (1805–59) is generally regarded as the profoundest and most penetrating student of egalitarianism, and the first in the nineteenth century to appreciate fully the impact upon traditional society of

27 Félicité Robert de Lamennais, *L'Avenir*, in *Œuvres Complètes*, 3 vols. (Brussels: 1839), 2: 440. My translation.

modern democracy. Born of a French noble family, several members of which had been guillotined or imprisoned during the Revolution, and exposed from boyhood to all the ideological currents which swirled in the wake of the Revolution, he made the study of revolution and democratic egalitarianism quite literally his life's work. For more than a decade, culminating in the Revolution of 1848, Tocqueville was one of the preeminent political figures in France. He was a member of the Constitutional Commission during that revolution and was appointed foreign minister in 1849. When, shortly after, he retired from politics, it was because of ill health and a desire to begin writing a history of the French Revolution. For years he had been at work in the archives on this enterprise. From his labors came *The Old Regime and the French Revolution*, regarded to this day as very probably the most brilliant analysis of the French Revolution ever written.

What Tocqueville is most famous for, however, is his earlier *Democracy in America*, based on a visit of less than a year that he had made to the United States while still in his twenties, the first volume of which appeared in 1835, the second in 1840. This book established him immediately as one of the foremost minds of Europe. On both sides of the Atlantic, *Democracy in America* was hailed as an impressive study of a new nation as well as a profound work in political philosophy. To this moment *Democracy in America* is regarded as the best study ever made of the American people, its institutions, culture, values, and social psychology. Few are the Americans today who, reading its pages—especially those of the second volume, which is overwhelmingly sociological in character—cannot say: "This is how we are."

Yet, for all its detailed and illuminating insights on America, the book is more nearly a work in political philosophy, concerned with the general foundations of liberty irrespective of exact locale, than a study of American culture as such. Tocqueville indeed alerts us to this fact in his Preface, when he acknowledges that he came to America to see not so much the Americans themselves and their concrete culture, but rather "the image of democracy itself, with its inclinations, its character, its prejudices, and its passions in order to learn what we have to fear or to hope from its progress." [28]

For Tocqueville—as for Bonald, Hegel, and Lamennais, among many others in Europe—the greatest of modern events in its impact upon human culture had been not the American Revolution, but the French Revolution. Its centralization, rationalization, and popularization of

---

[28] Alexis de Tocqueville, *Democracy in America*, trans. Phillips Bradley, 2 vols. (New York: Alfred A. Knopf, 1945), 1: 14. The first volume of this work, originally published in France in 1835, is primarily concerned with the political structure of democracy, the second volume, which appeared five years later, with the effects of democracy on society and culture.

political power, the image of which it went on to spread, and the sheer impact of its ideas and principles on the rest of the world, made it to Tocqueville the greatest single event in the history of Europe. Moreover, he saw the Revolution and the tidal wave of its democratic consequences as the culmination of a slow development of political power that had begun in western Europe in the late Middle Ages. Indeed, Tocqueville's overall philosophy of history rests on this vision. He saw democracy, in other words, as a chapter in, not the history of freedom, but, rather, the history of power. Democratic power, he thought, precisely because of its mass base, would doubtless prove to be more formidable, a greater threat to local, associational, and individual liberties, than any preceding form of political power, even the so-called absolute monarchies of the seventeenth and eighteenth centuries.

Unlike the conservatives of his day, Tocqueville does not seek to condemn, much less retard, the growth of democracy. He regards the spread of democracy through the world as inevitable, beyond the powers of any group or class to resist. Tocqueville does concern himself however with the relation of democracy to freedom, to the possibility of preserving the contexts within which individuality and freedom can alone thrive:

> It appears to me beyond a doubt that, sooner or later, we shall arrive, like the Americans, at an almost complete equality of condition. But I do not conclude from this that we shall ever be necessarily led to draw the same political consequences which the Americans have derived from a similar social organization. I am far from supposing that they have chosen the only form of government which a democracy may adopt; but as the generating cause of laws and manners in the two countries is the same, it is of immense interest for us to know what it has produced in each of them.[29]

It is possible to view Tocqueville's book from two very different but related perspectives: first, the actual, observable—or else, from his point of view, clearly foreseeable—effects of political democracy and its preeminent ethic, egalitarianism, upon other spheres of society; and second, what, if anything, can be or is being done, through differentiable processes, to offset this effect.

The first effect of democracy is sterilization of all social differences —class, regional, local, and associative—in the population. This is the outcome, of course, of the ethic of equality, of leveling those ranks in society that during the Middle Ages and the centuries following had been the prime means of social diversity. Tocqueville tells us that the

---

29 Ibid.

process of leveling can be seen operating for hundreds of years, down to the French Revolution, its high-water mark. The second effect, closely related to the first, is the centralization of power. For all that dissolves the social barriers of the population tends at the same time to make a homogeneous mass of the civil population; and the only means this un-differentiated mass has of expressing its wishes—all traditional social authorities having been weakened or dissolved—is through the central government. Thus arises the affinity between centralization of power and egalitarianism of social condition:

> The foremost or indeed the sole condition required in order to succeed in centralizing the supreme power in a democratic community is to love equality, or to get men to believe you love it. Thus, the science of despotism, which was once so complex, is simplified, and reduced, as it were, to a single principle.[30]

Already, Tocqueville believes, in America the effect of this combined centralization and egalitarianism has been to lower the quality of letters and the arts, the result of the creation of a public opinion that fears excellence and superiority and that makes a fetish of only what all men may be seen to have in common. Beyond this, the combination of power and equality has succeeded, he argues, in causing more and more people to feel insecure in their status; to manifest symptoms of alien-ation from self and society; to become obsessed by the marks of status; to covet wealth beyond anything known before in history—inasmuch as in a socially egalitarian society the possession of wealth is the only means of displaying what one may regard as his natural talents; to re-place honor by ambition alone; to turn to ever-more-labyrinthine bureaucratic structures in central government; to fear change; to abhor revolution in any form; to become ever more addicted to war; and ever more frequently to see absolute political power as the only form of seal-ing, protective community.

Such power, he tells us in one of the most celebrated chapters of *Democracy in America,* may come in time to seem to most people, not power, but freedom. The democratic multitudes, separated from hier-archy, isolated from traditional communities, confined to the recesses of their individual minds, may come to regard the sole remaining power of the state as, not tyranny, but a form of higher, more benevolent freedom-in-community:

> Above this race of men stands an immense and tutelary power, which takes upon itself alone to secure their gratifica-tions and to watch over their fate. That power is absolute,

---

30 Ibid., 2: 302.

minute, regular, provident, and mild. It would be like the authority of a parent if, like that authority, its object was to prepare men for manhood; but it seeks, on the contrary, to keep them in perpetual childhood. . . . After having thus taken each member of the community in its powerful grasp and fashioned him at will, the supreme power then extends its arm over the whole community. It covers the surface of society with a network of small complicated rules, minute and uniform, through which the more original minds and the most energetic characters cannot penetrate, to rise above the crowd. . . . Such power does not destroy, but it prevents existence; it does not tyrannize, but it compresses, enervates, extinguishes, and stupefies a people, till each nation is reduced to nothing better than a flock of timid and industrious animals, of which the government is the shepherd.

I have always thought that servitude of the regular, quiet, and gentle kind which I have just described might be combined more easily than is commonly believed with some of the outward forms of freedom, and that it might even establish itself under the wing of the sovereignty of the people.[31]

Such is Tocqueville's famous preview of the kind of totalitarianism that might arise from the very essence of democracy. Such, too, is his epitomization of the impact of democracy and egalitarianism upon culture, society, and the springs of individuality. It is anything but an optimistic forecast. Readers today may see in it, as in so much else that Tocqueville wrote, a grim warning of the worst, that is, the totalitarianism, that has in fact come into existence in the twentieth century: It is, all too obviously, the kind of passage that has made Tocqueville's name one with successful prevision of the future.

Tocqueville was one of the very first nineteenth-century social thinkers to become seriously interested in the problem of bureaucracy: that is, the problem created for free societies by the constant expansion of political administrations, with formalized, paid, permanent bureaucracies performing duties that had previously been performed by one or another of the social groups composing society. Later there would appear his superb study of the background of the French Revolution, *The Old Regime and the Revolution* (1856), in which he emphasized the fact that among the conditions creating the specific character of the French Revolution was the almost continuous centralizing of political administration that had been taking place in that country from the late Middle Ages on. The Revolution, he argued, in its own dramatic centralization of power was but the culmination of a history of centralization that had begun under the monarchy.

31 Ibid., pp. 318–19.

But there is much in the earlier work, *Democracy in America*, about the process of bureaucratization and its relation to democracy and to equality. There he emphasizes that the same historical processes that have led to democracy's replacing monarchy and aristocracy have led also to an increase in the size and strength of formal, paid, official administration. Tocqueville noted clearly the same fundamental relationship between mass democracy and bureaucracy that Weber was to see and indeed to make the very basis of his notable theory of authority and power. In the history of western Europe, the substitution of paid for unpaid functionaries is of itself enough to constitute a real revolution; and when monarchical governments begin to remunerate such officers as had hitherto been unpaid, "it is a sure sign that it is approaching a despotic or republican form of government." [32] The following passage is indication enough of the importance Tocqueville saw in the spread and intensification of bureaucracy in the modern era:

> All the governments of Europe have, in our time, singularly improved the science of administration: they do more things, and they do everything with more order, more celerity, and at less expense; they seem constantly enriched by all the experience of which they have stripped private persons. From day to day, the princes of Europe hold their subordinate officers under stricter control and invent new methods for guiding them more closely and inspecting them with less trouble. Not content with managing everything by their agents, they undertake to manage the conduct of their agents in everything; so that the public administration not only depends upon one and the same power, but it is more and more confined to one spot and concentrated in the same hands. The government centralizes its agency while it increases its prerogative.[33]

In Europe the Revolution at the end of the eighteenth century, even if it did not actually inaugurate bureaucracy, had vastly increased its sway. Wherever revolution breaks out, Tocqueville observes, centralization of power in the state is intensified. Everywhere it has "increased in a thousand different ways. Wars, revolutions, conquests, have served to promote it; all men have labored to increase it." [34] Thus there are two very different but functionally related tendencies in the modern world. On the one hand, we see "people escaping by violence from the sway of their laws, abolishing or limiting the authority of their rulers and princes. . . ." [35] On the other, in the selfsame countries we also see

---

[32] Ibid., 1: 208. [33] Ibid., 2: 307. [34] Ibid., p. 313. [35] Ibid.

the incessant increase of the prerogative of the supreme government, becoming more centralized, more adventurous, more absolute, more extensive, the people perpetually falling under the control of the public administration, led insensibly to surrender to it some further portion of their individual independence, till the very men who from time to time upset a throne and trample under a race of kings bend more and more obsequiously to the slightest dictate of a clerk. Thus in our days two contrary revolutions appear to be going on, the one continually weakening the supreme power, the other as continually strengthening it; at no other period in our history has it appeared so weak or so strong.[36]

Even war appears to Tocqueville to be greatly expanded in its scope, much more likely to leave its stamp of regimentation and despotism upon society under democracies than other types of government. Whereas in Europe before the Revolution, war had been relatively limited in size of armies, types of objective, and overall intensity, the rise of the revolutionary mass armies changed all that. Side by side with univeral manhood suffrage in revolutionary France went universal military conscription of men. Although democracies may be slower to engage in war than are dynastic monarchies, they are more likely, once war is under way, to extend its duration as well as its social, moral, economic, and political scope. The effect of democracy is to give a mass basis to war and also to moralize it—that is, to endow it with spiritual and moral objectives which serve to hide underlying material conditions. Moreover, the centralization of government to which democracies normally tend in their processes of administration is greatly enhanced by war. For success in war depends to a large degree upon the means by which all the nation's resources are transferred to a single point: "Hence it is chiefly in war that nations desire, and frequently need, to increase the powers of the central government." [37]

Here, then, is the dark side of democracy that Tocqueville, writing in the 1830s, sees in Europe and America, based in part on a projection of his fears into the future. There is, however, another perspective regarding democracy and its relation to freedom that we may draw from Tocqueville. And this second perspective gives us, not an intimation of a necessarily despotic future for democracy, but instead a highly empirical statement of the kinds of conditions which can coexist with democracy and which offer assurance of the protection of freedom. Here we are exposed to the federalist, decentralist, and pluralist Tocqueville. Here, also, we are treated to some of Tocqueville's most discerning observations

[36] Ibid.   [37] Ibid., p. 300.

on American political society. For in America Tocqueville could see at least the possibilities of a continued degree of freedom within democracy that were much more difficult for him to find in his own France, or in Europe generally.

Fundamental among the causes of continued freedom in American democracy, Tocqueville shows us, is the American principle of division of authority in society. Whereas in Europe, he says, the approach to freedom is through an actual weakening of the structure of authority, thus enhancing individual rights, in America the same gain to individual rights and freedom is obtained through diversification of authority, through the principle of one type of authority being held in check by another. "The authority thus divided is, indeed, rendered less irresistible and less perilous, but it is not destroyed." [38] This principle underlies, Tocqueville observes, not merely the overall structure of authority in America but also each of the several major institutions in American life, including religion, economy, and political government itself.

A second source of freedom in America, in Tocqueville's judgment, is the great appeal of local institutions to all Americans and the opposition that is mustered to any outside threat to these institutions. Such localism is important, Tocqueville believes, to all forms of government, but nowhere is it more necessary than in a democratic people.

> How can a populace unaccustomed to freedom in small concerns learn to use it temperately in great affairs? What resistance can be offered tyranny in a country where each individual is weak and where the citizens are not united by a common interest? [39]

A third element in American freedom is the federal system of political government, which prevents the central government, especially either the executive or Congress, from ever attaining the kind of power over human lives that Tocqueville sees as the principal danger to freedom in the European nations. In the first place there is the division of political authority among executive, legislature, and judiciary in the American national government. But even more important in the federal system is the division of authority between the national government and the governments of the component states. The inviolability of the states against actions of the central government not specifically permitted by the Constitution means that the states will always serve, Tocqueville argues, as limits, as buffers, to the power of the national government. Similarly, as he notes, within each of the states much the same kind of federal system is operative all the way down to the smallest of local communities.

[38] Ibid., 1: 70.   [39] Ibid., p. 95.

Fourth among conditions for freedom in American democracy is the independence of the press:

> The more I consider the independence of the press in its principal consequences, the more I am convinced that in the modern world it is the chief and, so to speak, the constitutive element of liberty. A nation that is determined to remain free is therefore right in demanding, at any price, the exercise of this independence.[40]

Fifth, and from Tocqueville's point of view perhaps the most vital of all, among the contexts of freedom is freedom of association. As we have seen, the essence of the problem of freedom lies for him in the exposure of individuals ever more directly to the power of the state. The modern history of the West has been marked by the erosion of the traditional social contexts of existence, foremost among them social class contexts. The idea of the theoretically free individual, his freedom guaranteed solely by a political constitution, seems to Tocqueville a weak idea in practice, as against the sovereignty of the state. This weakness can only be offset, Tocqueville argues, by unlimited freedom of association:

> At the present time the liberty of association has become a necessary guarantee against the tyranny of the majority. . . . There are no countries in which associations are more needed to prevent the despotism of faction or the arbitrary power of a prince than those which are democratically constituted. In countries where such associations do not exist, if private individuals cannot create an artificial and temporary substitute for them, I can see no permanent protection against the most galling tyranny; and a great people may be oppressed with impunity by a small faction or by a single individual.[41]

In the passage above, Tocqueville is referring to what he calls *political* associations, such as free parties and other forms of political action whereby political ends may be achieved. Later in his book he writes, however, with the same appreciation of *civil* associations, those concerned, not primarily with political objectives, but with intellectual, cultural, and social pursuits, all of which serve further to diversify the social bond, to multiply the sources of social identification for individuals, and to make even more difficult the rise of the political mass, so easily captured and exploited both by faction and by central government.

---

40 Ibid., p. 193.   41 Ibid., pp. 194–95.

What Tocqueville admires almost above any other single feature of American society is the profusion of both political and civil associations he found there on his visit in 1831–32. Tocqueville is writing about the United States in the following passage:

> There is only one country on the face of the earth where the citizens enjoy unlimited freedom of association for political purposes. This same country is the only one in the world where the continual exercise of the right of association has been introduced into civil life and where all the advantages which civilization can confer are procured by means of it.[42]

In both types of association Tocqueville saw powerful means of achieving for citizens the strata of intermediate association and allegiance that would arrest both the tendencies toward social atomization resulting from the impact of democratization and industrialization on traditional society and, at the same time, the tendencies toward the monopolization of economic and social function in the central government invariably preceding or accompanying monopolization of power, as his observations in Europe had taught him.

In sum, at the base of Tocqueville's pluralism lies his rigorous distinction between social authority—the kind of plural social authority that is to be found in the very fabric of the diversity of social associations and communities—and the sovereign power, in political government alone, that so easily becomes transmuted into despotism unless it is incessantly checked by counterauthorities. This is precisely the distinction we have seen in Aristotle, though hardly more than adumbrated in his political writings, in Althusius, and in Burke and the early-nineteenth-century conservatives. It was first Lamennais and then—profoundly and systematically—Tocqueville who translated the distinction between authority and power into the basis of liberal social philosophy.

A Note on Radical Pluralism

By radical pluralism I mean primarily the anarchist and syndicalist and guild-socialist ideas which began to flower in the latter part of the nineteenth century and which remain viable even at the present time, in one form or another, in Western and also non-Western thought. If I deal only very briefly with these ideas here, it is chiefly because we had an opportunity in the preceding chapter to see much of their import in the philosophies of the ecological community based on the ideas of Proudhon and Kropotkin.

42 Ibid., 2: 115.

There is, as must be wholly apparent by this time, a very close relation between the ecological community, in its major philosophical expressions, and the plural community.[43] The same impulses that led Proudhon or Kropotkin—and, in some degree at least, Sir Thomas More and Saint Benedict before them—to focus on the natural, autonomous community, which would draw equally from the forces of physical nature and civilization, led them also to espouse a philosophy of authority luminous with decentralization and pluralism. For how could the ecological community exist in its multiple forms unless it were granted the kind of autonomy and basis for diversity of type and function that go only with larger structures of authority characterized above all by federalism and decentralization?

Whereas *conservative* pluralism saw its mission essentially as the recovery or reinforcement of historic and traditional groups and communities, and whereas *liberal* pluralism was concerned chiefly with relationships between the democratic state and a structure of social authority that would promise the highest degree of individual freedom, what we find in radical pluralism is a vision of a totally new society, which would be built on the ruins of capitalism and nationalism. But from our point of view here, the chief distinction of the radical vision of the future is that it is in its way fully as pluralist, localist, and dencentralist as anything to be found among the liberals and conservatives who looked to Tocqueville and Burke for inspiration.

We cannot appreciate the full significance of radical pluralism, the kind found in the works of the anarchists, syndicalists, and guild socialists, if we do not keep in mind the fact that the main tradition of European radicalism—that is, after about 1870—was Marxist in inspiration. Marx won out, basically, in the First International with the expulsion from that short-lived organization of the Proudhonian anarchists. With the formation of the Second International and the very strong Marxist–German Socialist influence, the triumph of Marx and his doctrines was virtually assured. And when Lenin and the Bolsheviks won out in the Russian Revolution of 1917, the structure of radicalism throughout the world became overwhelmingly Marxist.

There is little if any pluralism to be found either in the ideas of Marx and Engels or in the Marx-inspired world socialist and communist movement. The stated ideal of both Marx and Engels, repeated by Lenin, was, as we observed in the chapter on the revolutionary community, the eventual withering away of the state. But from the time when Marx and Engels wrote the *Manifesto*, indicating in detail the specific measures of revolutionary political centralization of power and

---

43 For this reason I forgo quotation or detailed analysis here. The passages in the preceding chapter from Proudhon and Kropotkin amply reflect their pluralism respecting authority as well as the ecological nature of the communities they espoused.

function that, they argued, must follow revolutionary success, the emphasis was almost entirely on political centralization, political nationalization (of industries and property), and political rationalization. Marx himself had little to say about the specific character of the socialist, classless society to which he looked forward. He referred contemptuously to the "kitchen recipes" of those utopians who gave detailed thought to the nature of postcapitalist society. History, Marx declared, resolves all major problems of organization. Further, a great deal of the *technical* structure of capitalism—cities and a generally urban dominance, technology, factories, and so on—would, Marx and Engels thought, continue, becoming the substructure of the socialist society of the future. Both Marx and Engels were almost savage in their denunciation of anarchists and syndicalists; and so, basically, have been all subsequent Marxists.

In any event, we find little or nothing in Marxist writing and in the mainstream of socialist and communist pronouncements, about the kind of matters that profoundly interested such anarchists as Proudhon and Kropotkin and such guild socialists as those who came to intellectual prominence in England especially at the turn of the century: nothing of any significance about the balance between physical nature and social life, the indispensability of localism, the necessity of pluralism in function and allegiance, the values of decentralization, or the crucial importance to man and state alike of diversity in association and the intermediary functions of association. Marx's hatred and contempt for anything smacking of utopianism, diverting attention from the class struggle as the sole arbiter of history and new forms of social organization, led him to neglect almost completely most of the aspects of radicalism that figure so prominently in the writings of the pluralists—anarchists included.

Nevertheless, despite the immense power of Marxist thought in radical circles during the past century, the pluralist-ecological ideas of the nineteenth-century anarchists and syndicalists would appear to be steadily rising in interest and appeal. In utter contrast to Marx, Proudhon felt it vitally important to deal with the nature of power, the distinction between authority and power, the necessity—for freedom, at any rate—of autonomous associations, of decentralization of economy, society, and state alike, and of federalism as a constitutive principle in all institutions. Only by the diversification of society, Proudhon declared, can freedom be assured. "Multiply your associations and be free," Proudhon told workers and all others. Unlike the Marxists, who thought only in terms of a single, centrally led proletariat and, for the distant future, a "classless society" conceived, so far as we can determine, much in the fashion of Rousseau's democracy of the general will, both Proudhon and Kropotkin stressed the need for diversification of all society and also the importance of building the good society, with or without revolution (Kropotkin, for one, did not at all like or even anticipate revolution), based on the natural communities that may already be seen forming even under capitalism. Whereas Marx and his followers tended to depreciate the family tie, many of them declaring for what was once called "free love" and the elimination of kinship values of any kind, both Proudhon and Kropotkin, and all anarchists since with few exceptions, lauded the family relationship, seeing in the varied forms of love and attachment that it represents the key elements of the whole social system.

From the beginning, the anarchists expressed much historically grounded dislike of Soviet Russia. Kropotkin, as we have seen, was profoundly critical of Russian communism, staying away from Russia until shortly before his death, going back indeed only to die where he was born. Nor have any other anarchists in the twentieth century found anything but a monolithic political despotism in either Russian or any other form of national-collectivist socialism—all, without exception, strongly structured by militarism. The radical pluralism that began with the anti-Marxist anarchists and syndicalists of the nineteenth century remains to the present moment the strongest and the most consistent attack from the left upon modern nationalism and political centralization. Joined as it is with one variant or another of the utopian-ecological community, there is nothing surprising in the fact that such pluralism, whatever its faults, is the closest thing we have to a genuine ideological alternative to Western society as it is presently constituted.

Sociological Pluralism: Durkheim and Weber

The discipline of sociology largely arose in the nineteenth century among the very circumstances in which we have found the beginnings of modern pluralism. August Comte, whom we have already discussed briefly in light of his Religion of Humanity and who actually founded sociology as a systematic discipline, regarded the French Revolution very much as did liberal pluralists like Lamennais and Tocqueville. He, too, found revolutionary centralization oppressive and the banning of free association in the Revolution and in the following Napoleonic period inimical to freedom and justice. In his utopian *Positive Polity*, Comte made the values of federalism, functional representation, regionalism, and localism vital to the success of the new positive society that he hoped would shortly replace the nationalist collectivisms rising all over Europe in the aftermath of the French Revolution.

Likewise Frederick Le Play, perhaps the outstanding empirical sociologist of the nineteenth century, made these pluralist ideals basic in his philosophy. His influential book *Social Reform in France* (1864), based upon his earlier researches in comparative social and political organization, made decentralization of power the foremost objective of a new France. Closely related to this objective were his recommendations for a greatly vitalized kinship system, for maximum use of social and cultural voluntary associations, for revival of the traditional importance of the local community, and for planning that would be regional rather than nationalist in emphasis. Unlike the positivist Comte, Le Play was a devout Catholic and politically an avowed royalist. But the two men had a great deal in common in their envisagement of the good society.

Precisely the same basic values are to be found, though in modified form, in the writings of the two nineteenth-century men who remain to this moment the most creative forces in contemporary sociological theory: Émile Durkheim and Max Weber. They are well enough known for their contributions to the central areas of present-day sociology. They are not so well known for their hostility to many of the same forces that had occupied the minds of conservative, liberal, and radical pluralists alike for their espousal of generally pluralist values.

Durkheim

Émile Durkheim was brought to an appreciation of the social group by awareness of the same forces that had captured Tocqueville's and Proudhon's attention in France. These were, as we have seen, social dislocation, political centralization, and the seeming spread of the contexts of alienation and anomie. Durkheim, writing at the very end of the nineteenth century, was, moreover, as keenly struck by the continuing effects of the French Revolution in Europe as had been Lamennais or Tocqueville. It was, Durkheim declared, the erosion of the traditional social authorities in society that presented the essential outlines of the social problem. And, as he recognized, this erosion had been generated in the first place by the consequences of the French Revolution. The major problem of social reform, Durkheim thought, was to find new forms of social membership and authority which would give individuals the same sense of being vital parts of the social order that they had received from the older and now defunct forms.

Although there are hints of sociological pluralism in Durkheim's first major work, *The Division of Labor,* published in 1893, it is when we come to his *Suicide,* published in 1897, that the hints become clear statements. In the final section of that work, where Durkheim is considering the social means that might reduce the incidence of suicide in modern society, we are given a proposal that might easily have come from Tocqueville (who had also, it might be noted, indicated awareness of the rising incidence of suicide in modern life, one of the consequences, as he thought, of the democratic revolution).

Suicide, Durkheim observed in what is by now a classic phrasing of the matter, has the highest rate among those sectors of the European population where group ties have become weakest, or where the normative structure that is commonly an aspect of social groups has become lacking in capacity to give meaning to individual behavior. Hence Durkheim's classification of types of suicide into "egoistic" and "anomic," the first reflecting a degree of individualism that leads to a pathological separation from the group, the second reflecting a degree of separation from clear-cut norms or values that leaves the individual with feelings of rootlessness in moral matters. (There is a third type of suicide, which he termed "altruistic," that is the consequence of too strong an attachment of the individual to the group; but this, Durkheim observed, occurs only very rarely outside either primitive or else highly traditionalist societies.)

How is the incidence of suicide to be reduced in modern Western society? Only, Durkheim declared, through a reduction in the degree of social individualism, of social atomization, brought about by democracy and industrialism since the French Revolution. How is this reduction to be accomplished? Not, Durkheim argued in terms suggestive of Tocqueville or Proudhon, through intensification of the political tie, through political law or political reconstruction alone; for since the French Revolution the state has been among the chief causes of social atomization. Its administrative centralization has had the effect of removing from traditional influence other, nonpolitical, associations; the great intermediate ones such as the extended family, the church, social class, and the guilds. Such centralization and weakening of traditional authority have created, in short, a kind of social vacuum. And, Durkheim suggested, it is precisely among those aggregates of the population where modernism is most plainly to be seen—the secular, the industrialized, the single, the urban, the professional, and the educated—that we tend to find the highest rates of suicide. Among the rural peasantry, among religiously orthodox Catholics and Jews, and among other remaining traditional social elements, suicide rates are relatively low.

Neither the state, through its own inherently atomizing political power, nor the by-now-small family system, nor education by itself, nor religion as such, Durkheim concluded, can be expected to reduce either suicide or any of the other manifestations of pathological individualism in modern society. None of these elements is sociologically relevant. What is alone relevant is the establishment in society of significant intermediate associations that will take the place of the presently eroded, diminished, traditional associations. We live in an irreversibly industrial society, Durkheim wrote, and the new forms of association must therefore be fundamentally economic in nature. They must be addressed first and foremost to the needs of industrial workers, professional people, shopkeepers, and the many others who now lead lives surpassingly estranged from the social order.

Durkheim's proposal—stated only briefly in *Suicide*—was, therefore, the creation of new industrial *syndicats,* occupational and professional associations which would be intermediate between the individual and the otherwise impersonal economic and political orders. Though basically economic, each of these associations would become, through taking on other functions, cultural, social, and psychological associations as well, centered in, not one, but several spheres of individual existence. Since the underlying problem is one of social antinomy, of the individual's sense of conflict with the social order, the means of meeting it must also be social.

> The only way to resolve this antinomy is to set up a cluster of collective forces outside the state, though subject to its action, whose regulative influence can be exerted with greater variety. Not only will our reconstituted corporations satisfy this condition, but it is hard to see what other groups could do so. For they are close enough to the facts, directly and constantly enough in contact with them, to detect all their nuances, and they should be sufficiently autonomous to be able to respect their diversity.[44]

These new occupational associations would be in many ways like the great guilds of the Middle Ages, organizations that had survived in France until they were swept away by the Revolution at the end of the eighteenth century. Admittedly, these guilds had become too strong; they reflected a kind of corporate egoism. But the Revolution substituted, Durkheim tells us, an individualistic egoism, the inevitable consequence of its wholesale leveling of the population:

> The great change brought about by the French Revolution was precisely to carry this leveling to a point hitherto unknown. Not that it improvised this change; the latter had long since been prepared by the progressive centralization to which the old regime had advanced. . . . Since then, the development of means of communication, by massing the populations, has almost eliminated the last traces of the old dispensation. And since what remained of occupational organizations was violently destroyed at the same time, all secondary organizations of social life were done away with.[45]

Durkheim sees these new intermediate associations as possessed of considerable political and legal authority over their members. Purely economic associations would be necessarily inadequate to the social problem; for its essence is the re-creation of viable centers of social

44 Émile Durkheim, *Suicide: A Study in Sociology,* trans. John A. Spaulding and George Simpson, ed. George Simpson (Glencoe, Ill.: Free Press, 1951), p. 380.

45 Ibid., p. 388.

authority, of community, of perceived membership. Our historical development, Durkheim writes in a passage the intensity of which is reminiscent of Tocqueville or Proudhon, has swept away all older forms of intermediate social organization. "One after another, they have disappeared either through the slow erosion of time or through great disturbances, but without being replaced." [46] Clan, kindred, parish, ancient guild, church no longer suffice, their functional position having been eroded away; and therefore we are obliged to create new associations which will perform in individual lives essentially the same social, economic, political, and psychological functions once performed by the older associations.

Durkheim's fundamental pluralism began with his reflections on suicide and the contexts necessary to its reduction in modern society. But it did not end there. Through the rest of his life we find him engrossed in the problem of authority—that is, social authority—and its relation to state, economy, and other major spheres. It is not extreme to say that Durkheim was obsessed by authority. His entire approach to the understanding of religion, of morality, of reason itself, stems from his profound sense of the role of social authority in human lives. Each of these is, in its most imposing form, itself a type of authority; each emanates from that larger authority which is the social bond.

But while Durkheim was obsessed by the problem of authority he was concerned no less with the kinds of authority that could coexist with human freedom and social progress. Anything resembling a political despotism was repugnant to him; he detested the centralization and nationalization involved. The modern state, he writes, in words almost like Proudhon's,

> is as intrusive as it is impotent. It makes a sickly effort to extend itself over all sorts of things which do not belong to it, or which it grasps only by doing them violence. . . . While the state becomes inflated and hypertrophied in order to obtain a firm enough grip upon individuals, but without succeeding, the latter, without durable social relationships, tumble over one another like so many liquid molecules, receiving no larger energy to retain, fix, and give them structure.[47]

Authority there must be. But authority must be as diversified as are the major interests in society. There must be the authority of kinship, of religion, of local group, of province, above all of the socioeconomic occupational or professional association. This is Durkheim's major theme, first stated, as noted above, in the final pages of *Suicide* in 1896, powerfully

[46] Ibid.   [47] Ibid., p. 389.

restated in the long Preface to the second edition of *Division of Labor* in 1902, and to be seen in one form or another in such other works as *Moral Education* and *Professional Ethics and Civic Morals*, both published posthumously from lectures and writings of the years before his death.

What Durkheim did was to take the same overall perspective of community we have seen in the writings of the conservative, liberal, and radical pluralists, and, without relinquishing any of the premises of these ideologies, convert the perspective into the theoretical structure of a system of sociology. There is very little difference indeed between the vision of the good society that we can infer from Durkheim's writings on the nature of the social bond and the vision that is given us directly in the writings of Burke, Tocqueville, and Proudhon.

Weber

In Max Weber also are to be found strong elements of pluralism. However, he gives us nothing quite so forthright as Durkheim's proposal for intermediate professional associations. One is obliged, more than with Durkheim, to deduce the overall pluralism of Weber's moral imagination, of his ideally constituted society. But such deduction is not difficult. Weber, too, reacted strongly to the currents of power that had been created in the first instance by political centralization in the West: above all to bureaucratization. More than any other social philosopher or social scientist in the West, Weber is *par excellence* the student of bureaucratization, a process in modern (and also ancient) history that he could analyze in dispassionate detail and at the same time dislike intensely, especially in the forms it has taken in the modern Western state.

Weber's life work began, as we know, with reflections induced by his perception of the shift of Western society in his own youth from traditionalism—what Tönnies called *Gemeinschaft*—to modernism in politics, economy, education, and the other major spheres of the social order. His very first published work of any lasting significance was based on a study in eastern Germany in 1890 of the transition of agriculture from communal "status" to a condition characterized by increasing individualization, use of wages, and "contract"—both quoted words used in the sense in which Sir Henry Maine had used them in his epochal *Ancient Law*.

There were many in Germany during Weber's lifetime who were also deeply concerned with problems of freedom and the vitality of the social bond which had been created by nineteenth-century forces of political centralization, cultural nationalism, and rising bureaucracy. Otto von Gierke, jurist and historian, was the author of the monumental *German Law of Associations* and was primarily responsible for rediscovering the works of Althusius. The Swiss Jacob Burckhardt, writing and teaching in German, who was famous preeminently for his study of the Italian Renaissance, also took a dominantly pluralist-decentralist view of the needs of not merely German but all European society. As much as any historian in his day, Burckhardt perceived, in the same perspective that we have seen to flow from the works of Burke and Tocqueville, the twin dangers of political centralization and social atomization. He, too, conceived the most urgent goal to be arresting these tendencies through a revitalization of culture and society that would liberate human beings from the bureaucratic envelopment of their social existence. No wonder Weber, like Burckhardt, Tocqueville, and many others in Europe, was preoccupied by the historical shift of western Europe from traditional-communal society to ever-growing, centralized political aggregates.

This shift is in many ways the essence of Weber's sociology. He epitomized it in the transition from what he called *traditional* to *rationalized* structures of authority, a transition that he showed has occurred not once but many times in the history of civilization. Bureaucracy, for Weber, is but a signal manifestation of the larger current, rationalization. In whatever sphere we see rationalizaton taking place, according to Weber, its principal characteristic is the replacement of diversity in the social bond by increasing unification; of tradition by formal, calculated, positive law; of the spontaneous and autonomous by the ever more insistently planned, directed, and centrally governed.

It is as philosopher and scientist of authority that Weber is still, down to the present moment, most highly regarded. Whether in his studies of religion, economy, social stratification, or even the arts—notably music—Weber's concern is with the structures of authority which are one with the structures of organization in these areas. His classification of types of authority as "traditional," "rational," and "charismatic" is, as nearly as any one thing could possibly be in the works of so many-sided and vast a mind, the keystone of his massive scholarship.

As Weber himself was surely aware, and as other scholars have emphasized, all three of these types of authority were the products in his thought of the French Revolution. As much as Durkheim, Marx, Tocqueville, Kropotkin, and, before them, Burke and the conservatives, Weber was obsessed with the currents of change in society that went straight back to the French Revolution. Again, we are obliged to note in passing the extraordinary, the unique, influence upon thought of this great event at the end of the eighteenth century. What the French Revolution came almost immediately to signify to European minds was the sudden impact of men and events upon the *traditional* structure of authority in the West and the replacement of this structure, first, by one the revolutionists sought to derive from reason alone, which would be, to use their talismanic word, *rational,* and second by still another, this one *charismatic* in its intensity and appeal, coming directly from the magnetic presence of Napoleon. Not perhaps since Julius Caesar in Rome of the first century B.C. had there appeared in the West a political figure with the sheer luminosity of mind, character, and strength that Napoleon revealed to ever-increasing multitudes in France after his great military victories. Even after his eventual defeat at Waterloo, his exile, and his total loss of formal power, his name remained, and is to the present moment, sacred in France—as anyone is aware who has visited his tomb in Paris and seen the reverential expressions on the faces of so many Frenchmen, brought there, more than a century and a half after his death, by the adoration that persists from generation to generation.

These, the traditional, the rational, and the charismatic, are the central categories of Weber's sociology of authority, just as they were the central categories of the response to the Revolution everywhere in Western thought in the nineteenth and early twentieth centuries. What Weber did, as every sociologist and political scientist today knows, was to convert them into a typology enabling him to study systems of authority, in many sectors of the larger social order, throughout human history, non-Western and Western alike.

By traditional authority, Weber meant "a system of imperative co-ordination . . . believed in on the basis of the sanctity of the order and the attendant powers of control as they have been handed down from the past." [48] It is not force or coercion, nor inherent rationality, that is the motivating influence of traditional authority, but instead the belief by a significant number of persons that such authority is beyond either force or reason, that it is sacred, with a value and appeal arising from the sheer length of time it has existed or from the number of "sacred" persons who have been involved in its development. Legitimacy is here conferred, in short, by traditionality, by the belief that the authority in question has always existed. All genuine, lasting communities have a substantial degree of authority that is traditional, that arises, so to speak, from the very actions of the communicants, from those who are *in* the community.

Rational authority is best signified for Weber by bureaucracy. Here, he writes, we are dealing with a "system of rules that is applied judicially and administratively in accordance with ascertainable principles . . . valid for all members of the group."[49] The aim of rational authority, as the very term suggests, is to construct relationships in terms of the principles of reason and reasoned equity. The mere age of a relationship of authority can be no justification, nor can the greater or less degree of sacred-

48 Max Weber, *The Theory of Social and Economic Organization,* trans. A. M. Henderson and Talcott Parsons, ed. Talcott Parsons (New York: Oxford University Press, 1947), p. 341.

49 Ibid., p. 333.

ness of the founders of the relationship. The organization is itself supreme; and the statuses, roles, and norms of the organization are drawn —or are supposed to be drawn—from planning and calculation, under the sovereignty of reason. Obviously, as Weber realized, no perfectly rational or rationalized organization has ever existed. It is the nature of human beings to respond on occasions, no matter what organization they work or live in, to nonrational incentives, including those of tradition and of charisma in one form or other. It is, regarding this as well as the other two types, the ideal-type that Weber is interested in, the theoretical model.

Charismatic authority is the kind belonging to some individual who, whether from magical, religious, military, or other powers, comes to seem possessed of a genius or prophetic quality the rest of us lack. Moses, Jesus, Buddha, Caesar, and Napoleon are among the most renowned examples of charismatic authority, each the founder or the prototype of a system of belief and allegiance that may involve millions of people. We commonly think of this form of authority in connection with a religion, with the charisma of the founding figure transferring itself in time to all manner of objects, customs, and beliefs which become ritualized. But in the modern world, as Weber realized, charisma tends to be political as often as religious. Weber did not live to see the German society of Hitler, but there is much in his description of charisma in politics that would serve admirably for the special kind of relationship that existed for two decades between Hitler and a constantly growing number of persons. It was Napoleon's coup d'etat that fascinated so many nineteenth-century intellectuals, of the political left as well as right. The possibility of one man's possessing the kind of charismatic appeal that could reach the millions, through his seeming endowment with powers of compassion, insight, empathy, and, above all, strength well beyond those of the rest of us: this was what exhilarated the minds of a great many in the nineteenth century who were concerned with capturing political power. And this possibility has continued to exhilarate minds, as it doubtless will in the future. For there is no body of ideals, ideas, and objectives—at least where the organization or leadership of human beings is concerned— that charisma cannot vastly enhance.

Weber thought that most major changes in the history of human society have been the result of charismatic individuals. His theory of change in no way reduces itself to the "great man" hypothesis as this is commonly understood; Weber was too alert to contexts and historical conditions for that. But, more than most sociologists concerned with understanding social change, Weber stressed the importance of the individual endowed with charismatic powers, capable of swaying significant numbers of persons.

It is the fate of charisma, however, as Weber writes, to become routinized, to pass from the electric presence of the original, charismatic individual, into traditions or even into highly rationalized structures, such as the great modern churches and many other formal, large-scale organizations that came into existence originally through some superlatively equipped individual. Weber believed, as we are obliged to conclude from his writings just before his death, that charismatic authority, charismatic leadership, and charisma-generated change were all alike passing from the European scene. Such, he thought, was the rapidly growing stranglehold of bureaucracy in all sectors of Western society, that neither charisma nor tradition—in the historic sense of that word —would survive for long. All would, he reflected despondently, be replaced by bureaucracy.

> It is horrible to think that the world could one day be filled with nothing but those little cogs, little men clinging to little jobs and striving towards bigger ones—a state of affairs which is to be seen once more, as in the Egyptian records, playing an ever-increasing part in the spirit of our present administrative system, and especially of its offspring, the students. This passion for bureaucracy . . . is enough to drive one to despair. It is as if in politics . . . we were deliberately to become men who need "order" and nothing but order, become nervous and cowardly if for one moment this order wavers, and helpless if they are torn away from their total incorporation in it. That the world should know no men but these: it is in such an evolution that we are already caught up, and the great question is, therefore, not how we can promote and hasten it, but what can we oppose to this machinery in order to keep a portion of mankind free from this parceling-out of the soul, from this supreme mastery of the bureaucratic way of life.[50]

Clearly, there is much in common between that passage and the one quoted above from Tocqueville in which, in a mood of pessimism about what was to come for democracy and its bureaucracy, he foresaw a future of intense totalitarianism for Western man. Rationalization, including bureaucracy, need not be an iron cage, so far as Weber is concerned. As we read his long passages on bureaucracy and its modern development in the West, it is clear to us that Weber could see effects of a liberative nature in given places and times. If power is personal, capricious, and inequitable in its impact, then the instituting of a bureaucratized system of administration, in which office, not person, is crucial and in which clear and enforced norms of open achievement are present,

[50] Quoted in J. P. Mayer, *Max Weber and German Politics* (London: Faber and Faber, 1943), pp. 127–28.

can be, and has been, a positive aid in the development both of democracy and equality in a population. Weber was well aware of this, as had been Tocqueville who, it will be remembered, offered the development of bureaucracy, at certain stages of a people's history, as a clear index to the development also of democracy.

Nor can it be said that Weber was an unqualified admirer of either traditional or charismatic authority. His classification of authority into these types, along with the rational, was primarily for analytical purposes. But it is possible to see in Weber's mind an appreciation of the moral value of a mixture of all three types. A society governed by traditional authority alone would be static, undoubtedly inegalitarian, and without the resources of reason ready to be activated. Similarly, a society governed entirely by the personal charisma of some one individual or tiny group would surely verge on a condition that could range from despotism to fanaticism if long continued. A social order composed of charismatic individuals would be, of course, an impossible one. It is, in short, a society combining all three types of authority, and with these the social groups and strata which provide diversity and the possibility of change, that Weber clearly prefers. He was himself a man of profoundly liberal tendencies, but his preference for monarchy reveals that he could see many of the same possibilities of regimentation and monolithic collectivism in mass democracy that Tocqueville had seen.

Hovering over the Western world, Weber saw the specter of rationalization, of bureaucratization—not only in political government but in the economy, the educational system, religion, recreation, and all other areas of the social order—which would in time confine man, would stifle and immobilize him. Tradition and charisma alike would be reduced in authority, incapable of ever again being the basis of human behavior. That process of disenchantment of the world which Weber, following the German poet Schiller, saw in modern history, would be accompanied, in sum, by a process of destruction of social diversity, cultural variety, and political pluralism: the same process that Tocqueville had feared, that the anarchists Proudhon and Kropotkin had fought against, and that Burke, before the French Revolution was even well under way, foresaw as the principal legacy of unitary, rationalizing, regimenting mass democracy.

Epilogue

For more than two thousand years western European thought has been preoccupied by the problem of community: community lost and community found. Only in light of this preoccupation, it seems to me, are we able to grasp the distinctive character and the persisting urgency of social philosophy in the West. Whether in the wake of a dislodged kinship system in ancient Athens and Rome, or in the tension-charged atmosphere of the late Roman Empire, when intimations of fall were everywhere present to the Roman mind, or in the rise of the modern military-national state, with its devastating impact upon traditional society, or in the fateful conditions created at the end of the eighteenth century by the two revolutions, democratic and industrial, we have found the quest for community to be the other side of the coin of perceived crisis and conflict. Social thought in the West is a tapestry of longings, ideas, and aspirations, given unity by the search for community, and diversity by the many forms in which community has been made manifest.

There is, seemingly, no form of association that cannot become, given propitious circumstances, the basis of imagined, cherished, and proffered community. Family, race, locality, work, religion, education, war, power, even the perceived sense of kinship with nature—all these and others have served in one fashion or another to gratify man's desire for community and for that cherished legitimacy that community alone can give to authority, function, membership, and loyalty. In this book we have considered only a few of the patterns of community that Western man has in fact known. But they are the ones which have left the largest imprint on the pages of social philosophy in the West. They are the ones which have been, in their complex and ever-shifting relationships, at the very center of the biography of Western man.

Western social philosophy began, as we have seen, in the wake of a dislocation of man's very oldest form of community, kinship, and, with this, of almost equally old forms of association based on locality and ancestral worship. From this time on, in persistent parallel patterns, war, political power, religion, revolution, even nature, have become the substance of community in both the life and thought of the West. Different as are the writings and ideas of Plato, Aristotle, Augustine, More, Machiavelli, Hobbes, Rousseau, Marx, Tocqueville, and Kropotkin, all may be seen, from at least one great vantage point, as minds tormented by fear of the social void and in search of redeeming, fulfilling community.

Nor is the matter different in our own day. I have said almost nothing about the contemporary scene in this book. To have tried to do so would have been to make a long book impossibly long. But, as I wrote in some detail a quarter of a century ago in *The Quest for Community*, it is impossible to so much as scan the works of our foremost philosophers, theologians, sociologists, psychologists, and anthropologists, even of novelists, poets, and other imaginative writers, without immediately acquiring a sense of the urgent apprehensions of rootlessness, alienation, and estrangement in the twentieth-century mind, and also of the powerful appeal of community. But preoccupation with community is by no means limited to intellectuals. In various ways, ranging in America from the sometimes desperate efforts of uprooted, mobile members of the middle class to find community in suburb or political party all the way to youth's great rock festivals, the search for community is apparent, as scores of journalists and other writers are noting at the present time. Not a little of the heavy, perhaps damaging strain that is today placed upon the powers of government at all levels is the direct consequence of the sense of community denied in other spheres of social life. And in Europe, within living memory, we have seen the quest for community become involved in strange, often horrifying ways in totalitarian movements and states.

At no time in Western history have the themes of war, power, and revolution assumed such imposing and directive intensity in their proffer of community as they have in our century. Different though the great nationalist-collectivist political orders of our day may seem at first glance from the vision of the political community that reaches from Plato to Rousseau, they are nonetheless lineal products of this vision, and if political thought is at present in perhaps the greatest doldrums in several hundred years, it cannot be said that the fundamental philosophy of the political community is any less attractive to very large numbers of people. Nor will anyone be blind to the vast appeal of war and the military community in our century. What so many millions of Americans learned in the two world wars of this century—that war, for all its illth and horror, can be associated at times with a sense of national communal purpose that stands in vivid contrast to the loneliness, monotony, emptiness, and banality which for many people are the hallmarks of ordinary civil society. And, as is evident enough, the revolutionary community has come a long way indeed since the Jacobins thrilled or frightened Western society with their vision of a society formed in the image of absolute virtue through the utilization of absolute reason, power, and terror. One need only look at Soviet Russia, China, and Cuba, among other areas, to see how successful the revolutionary community can be, especially when it is united with the military and political communities.

But there is more in the twentieth-century Western search for community than war, revolution, and power. One would have to be singularly insensitive to what goes on around him if he did not observe the undiminished capacity of religion to inspire belief and a sense of community as well. Far from having been put to flight by the forces of modernity—rationalism, science, technology, and others—as secular-minded intellectuals once predicted would be the case by our time, religion shows every sign of spreading in intellectual, spiritual, and social power. One need but think of the names of Buber, Niebuhr, Tillich, and Barth to be reminded that our century is among the greater periods of theology in Western history. Nor should the momentous changes in the Roman Catholic church, amounting to a veritable twentieth-century Reformation, be forgotten. Whether in Christian, Judaic, or imported Eastern form, religion remains one of the evocative sources of belief and membership for human beings in our century.

Likewise, it would seem that kinship, not least in its extended family forms, is enjoying one of the periodic recrudescences this form of community has experienced ever since its fateful disruption by Cleisthenes twenty-five hundred years ago. Only a generation or two ago, imposing voices were declaring the bankruptcy of the family and its replacement by other, more individualistic and transitory ties. Events have proved these voices mistaken. The image of kinship is a powerful one at this moment, in art as well as life. Along with the rediscovery of ethnicity in contemporary American life, the rediscovery of family must be accounted one of the principal forces in culture and society. The manifestations of kinship as a symbol have become legion.

So, as I write, have those of the image of nature and ecology. I refer in part to Americans' unwonted attention at long last to relationships between mankind and a natural environment rapidly undergoing spoliation as the result of wanton use of industrial technology. A respect for nature and man's relationship to his fellow organisms and their common biosphere is certainly among the more impressive aspects of contemporary American, indeed Western, life. But I refer as well to the commune movement of our time. What else is the commune, rural or urban, but a contemporary manifestation of the same motivations we found in the life of Saint Benedict, in the writings of Sir Thomas More, and in their utopian-anarchist descendants in the nineteenth century? How many such communes there are today in the West—quite apart from the very large number of monasteries in the direct succession of medieval monastic movements—we do not know, nor do we know how long they will continue to exist. It is well to remember, however, that the ecological impulse toward community, the impulse toward the idea of nature and the ideals of simplicity, mutual assistance, and cooperation, is a seemingly ineradicable impulse in Western history.

There is, finally, the pluralist community. It would be absurd to claim, looking at the immense, centralized, nationalistic structures of power and economy which are the political orders of our age, that the philosophy of pluralism has had much if any effect. Even so, one of the clearest strains of thought to be found in our century—especially since World War II—is the greatly increased attention given by scholars and intellectuals to the ideas of decentralization, regionalism, localism, and voluntary autonomous association. Where, prior to World War II, the ideas of Burke, Tocqueville, and other pluralists were little noted in America, recently there has taken place nothing short of a renaissance of appreciation of these philosophers. The day would seem to be past in intellectual circles where centralization of power, collectivism, and bureaucratization of function are automatically accepted as not merely good but inevitable. It should be emphasized that the resurgence of philosophical conservatism in America after about 1945, based in large degree on Burke and Tocqueville, was followed by the rise of a New Left that took its initial philosophical position precisely in those values of decentralization and voluntary association, of localism and regionalism, that are counterposed to bureaucratic centralization whether in capitalist or socialist form.

What will be the future of community in the West? No one can be sure, of course, for the future is subject to speculation only, not scientific techniques of prediction. All we can do is consider alternatives and possibilities. As I write, it would seem exceedingly unlikely that the huge monoliths of military-political-revolutionary power we see abroad, all set deeply in the traditions of community we have examined in this book, will very soon cease to exist. One need only look at China, the largest single people on earth, and the extraordinary results it has achieved in the way of mass community through the symbols and techniques of revolution, war, and absolute power, to be reasonably sure that the age of the great monoliths is far from coming to an end. Nor does the probability seem great that societies such as our own in the West will become more deeply rooted in localism and regionalism, the values of decentralization and of voluntary association assuming ever greater authority in human lives. Quite apart from the presence abroad of potentially threatening military-revolutionary societies, we have learned that even in America there is by now a latent appeal in the centralized political community, certainly in times of economic crisis, and also in the kind of community that war and its sense of communal purpose can induce. Nor, finally, does religion—indestructible though its roots may be in the human mind—show any sign of becoming the base of an entire social order as Christianity did during the Middle Ages.

So much would appear to be true. But dogmatic conclusion in such matters, especially when the future is involved, is always hazardous and prediction downright foolish. Nothing must have seemed more imperishable to any intelligent and knowledgeable Roman of the Antonines Age—an age that Gibbon tells us in his *Decline and Fall of the Roman Empire* was one of the most prosperous and happy in human history—than the Pax Romana of which he was a part. That this immense and vital organization, stretching from the Middle East to Britain, from North Africa to the Danube, would within two or three centuries' time come to know defeat and disintegration without previous parallel in history, to be replaced, in the West at least, by a form of community resting largely upon the foundations of kinship and religion—such a prophecy would have seemed to any rational Roman of the second century sheer fantasy.

So we do not know. We are reduced to speculation. All we can be sure of is that we, too, live in an age like the age in which Saint Augustine wrote his *City of God*, one of great pessimism, melancholy, and rooted estrangement, not least in its literature and its social philosophy. The capacity for social as well as physical destruction in our time is vast, as we know, but whether amid circumstances of destruction—like those both Greece and Rome came to know well—or of the kind of relative political stability we currently enjoy, we can be reasonably certain that the threads of community we have seen persisting for two and a half millennia in the West will continue in one pattern or other.

Index